Into the Storm

by Meghan Brunner

This is a work of fiction. All the characters, locations, and events portrayed in this novel are either fictitious or are used fictitiously.

First published by AuthorHouse 05/14/04

ISBN: 1-4184-5559-8 (e-book)
ISBN: 1-4184-4656-4 (Paperback)
ISBN: 1-4184-4657-2 (Dust Jacket)

Library of Congress Control Number: 2004092339

This book is printed on acid free paper.

Printed in the United States of America
Bloomington, IN

All songs quoted herein are "traditional." This means they were written a few hundred years ago, before copyright laws, when no one paid attention to who came up with music… especially if the composer happened to be a peasant.

Faire-Folk on the World Wide Web:
http://www.faire-folk.com

======

This book is dedicated
to the rennies who come back
for more beatings, year after year...

...and to those whose memory-ghosts
haunt the hallowed grounds of Festival.

May we never forget the Magick you gifted us.

=======

ACKNOWLEDGEMENTS

There is much an author learns while trying to get his or her first book published—perseverance, faith, and patience are just the beginning. I knew there were folks who loved me, but to watch them go the extra mile—and keep running—was a humbling experience. Many went so far above and beyond the call of duty that I doubt they can still see it with a telescope. No book could be long enough to name you all and cry your praises, but every name and deed is scribed indelibly in my heart. Thank you, thank you. I hope every day to be the sort of person who deserves such a blessing.

I also owe a debt of gratitude to those who hashed over *Storm* to make it better than I could have dreamed: Mark, BJ, Lynn, John, Jean, Christopher, and Teri for red ink scrawled over endless drafts; Mark for geek skills extraordinaire; and Matt and Palidyn for the amazing artwork. Many thanks also to the folks at rec.arts.sf.composition, alt.fairs.renaissance, and the MRFfriends listserv for providing answers to random questions at two in the morning.

I would like also to pay homage to my blood family, who believe in me no matter what; my rennie family, who created a world too beautiful for any book to wholly capture; my teachers (in school and out) who gave me a love of the written word and encouraged me to share it; my muse and my characters, who share their lives with me; Natalie at GNS for the eleventh-hour laptop resuscitation; and last but not least, the fuzzies… Odie, whose spirit lights a path in my heart, and Tanuki, who contributed many lap-warmings, companionable naps, and a fierce vigilance against the dread computer cursor.

Now, a moment of silence please, for the ramen packets that gave their lives.

TABLE OF CONTENTS

~Prologue~
Pendragon Renaissance Faire
Friday Before Opening Weekend

"Somebody should get the shoe."

The olive-green eyes that peered down at Phoenix held a spark of irony in their depths. "I suppose by 'someone' you mean 'Ryna.'"

Phoenix giggled, but not hard. Her stomach still ached from their tickle fight. "You threw it."

"It's your shoe."

"Okay, fine. I'll get it." Phoe heaved herself to her feet and flipped her ebony braid over her shoulder. She pinned her love with a severe gaze. "But you have to explain why it went sailing through the door, Arbryna Tully."

The redhead reached up, toyed with one of the errant star-white tresses that framed Phoe's face. "Does it have to be the real reason?"

Phoenix rolled her eyes, but she couldn't help a smile. It felt good to be back at Pendragon—almost as if no time had passed since that gray and blustery day when the Gypsies had driven off into the sunrise. Some things stayed the same for every faire: vehicles rumbling past, the subtle excitement of a season about to begin, a dog barking, the music of a guitar not far distant. However, she'd missed the things that belonged to Pendragon alone: the smell of dewed red dirt, the low whistle and chugging of the train laboring by. And the knowledge that this year Phoenix ranked among the rennie veterans and Trailer Gods for true, not just as a guest.

A belovedly familiar face peeked around the dark blue lace curtain that covered the door, a battered loafer in one hand. "Lose something?"

Phoenix launched herself at her brother as he stepped up into the vardo. "Danny!"

He enfolded her in a very welcome embrace. "And how are you, Phoe-bea? Don't tell me Ryna's got you throwing shoes, now."

Phoenix grinned up at him, all chestnut hair and dark eyes and that lop-sided smile he saved just for her. "That was *not* my fault," she protested as he released her.

"We stopped by your tent earlier," Ryna told him, "but it didn't look like you'd made it in yet."

"Yeah, it's a little more faded and a little more patched than last year, but at least now I have it up on some pallets. Hopefully it won't be so prone to flooding."

"I'll be the last one to complain about your tent flooding." Ryna gave him a wink. "After all, it drove your sister into my vardo."

"Speaking of vardos," Dan trailed off, his expression grim. "Have either of you been up on site yet?"

The bottom dropped out of Phoe's stomach. "Um, no?"

"Well, to start with, I'm sure *Phuro* Basil told you that we have a new Artistic Director?"

Phoenix nodded. "He said he didn't like her, but he didn't say much else."

"Ah. Well. Richard Darnell, Pendragon's illustrious owner, replaced Eric with some ditz who's only ever managed community theatre. She's got some bug up her bra to make her mark on Pendragon by overhauling everything that's worked for years, and she does *not* like people disagreeing with her."

Ryna buried her face in the bedding and groaned. Apparently such a spectacularly stupid managerial decision had precedent. "I suppose that's why it took *Phuro* so long to get our contracts," she said, muffled from within the blankets.

"That would be why," Daniel said.

Phoenix recognized his clipped tone of voice... it had been common after parental lectures.

"I don't understand," she said. "I mean, Eric ran Academy, and he handed out awards and contracts and stuff, but how much damage could one person do?"

Daniel sighed. "Dickie cut the budget... again. I'm guessing Eric pitched a fit, so he hired Patty... and she has *no* judgment on what to cut and where. And that means—"

"Contracts," Ryna concluded, looking up. "Who'd we lose?"

"Too many. For starters, Peregrine Crest isn't coming back."

"But they said in Academy—" Phoenix started.

"The falcon show was one of the biggest draws, I know, second only to the Royals Revolting," Daniel agreed. "Academy, by the way, has been replaced with 'Rehearsals'—which is the same thing, but less helpful."

"Why get rid of Peregrine, though?" Phoenix asked. "It doesn't make sense."

"He wanted the stage fixed up; I guess the rotting wood back there had some sort of bacteria that was making the birds sick."

"And fixing up a stage takes money," Ryna continued his logic. "Who else?"

"A lot of street characters were offered half their usual pittance and walked. Patty also decided the stage crews would be better off entertaining people on street—as volunteers, of course, since they transferred areas. When the acts found out there wouldn't be anyone to help with hawking or hat pass, they left, too. Don't get me started on the horror stories I've heard about the Fantastical Feast. And the Queen's Tea is now commercial; they've put up a tent and everything. Christine is less than happy. It was her favorite part of the day."

"I think I played fiddle for them a couple times," Ryna put in. "It was fun—just the Court ladies and whomever happened by for entertainment."

"And then there's the 'Secret Garden' that got installed down the ravine behind Sherwood."

Ryna frowned. "I thought everything back there was DNR-protected wetlands."

Phoe started. "Really? How did the owner get a permit?"

He shrugged. "I'm pretty sure it is, and rumor says he didn't, though I don't know if that's accurate. And the vardo… the one behind Hollow Hill is gone. I fought for it—we all did—but our dear Artistic Destroyer decided that all you do is sit back there and wave to the crowd, and no one could convince her otherwise. She figured if she had it torn down, you'd all go play on street more."

A horrified silence descended over the vardo.

"Have you told the others yet?" Phoenix asked in a near-whisper, one comforting hand on her love's shoulder.

Daniel shook his head. "I wanted to talk to you two first."

Phoenix watched as Ryna wearily hauled herself to her feet and, with great effort, squared her shoulders. "The vardo survived a massive attack by the Shadow Fae. I suppose it was too much to ask for it to survive the latest Artistic Disaster. Gods, I hate it when this happens."

Liam stormed across Pendragon's grounds, the night in his eyes and darkness in his heart.

They were back.

He had seen them—providing, of course, that it had really been them and not another of the Shadow Fae's invented torments. It had seemed too… fleeting… for that, though—just a glimpse of the Gypsies' trailers as they bantered and set up camp. It had none of the carefully orchestrated feel of the Shadow's visions.

And it couldn't have been a glimpse of the past. His love was with them—with that redheaded bitch who had sent him to this hell for… ten months, it must be, if they were back, though he had long ago lost track of days. It was hard to keep count when sometimes the moon hung suspended for what seemed like months… and others, the sun raced for the west and appeared again in the east three times in what should have only been an hour.

But if they were back…

Ten months.

Ten months of wandering this deserted shadow of Pendragon, where landmarks flowed and shifted with the breeze. Ten months of enduring the Shadow Fae's torture. Ten months of visions designed to tear at his heart: visions of Phoenix with that bitch, visions of how it could have been had he won her instead.

Sometimes more than visions... sometimes he re-lived scenes from the year past, and a single word different would change their outcome, give him his love—

—or give him his revenge—

—or, sweeter, both.

And then in an instant it would be gone, triumph ripped from him as the Shadow Fae laughed at his curses.

Ten months of them gnawing at his soul, feeding on his energy, his vitality, even as he fed on smaller creatures such as the dog-sized lizard-thing he had claimed for his pet.

Ten months of fighting them, of learning scraps of how Magick worked here and using it to his advantage. Ten months of politics and intrigue. Even in a place like this—*especially* in a place like this—there existed a hierarchy, a network of knowledge... which creatures to cower to, which to kick.

He had not won—there was no winning here. But he had survived and even earned a modicum of safety, convinced and cowered and threatened the appropriate creatures until they either bored with him or learned to avoid him. Even the Three who had brought him here had not shown themselves for weeks.

A small victory, but not enough. He was still here, and his love was still with another.

It was all that bitch's fault.

And Liam would make her pay.

Pendragon Renaissance Faire

Weekend One: Fairy Nice To Sidhe You!

~*~

Treat yourself with a magical excursion to a new land, filled with wondrous surprises and now the fairies themselves! Our newest attraction highlights a weekend of enchantment as citizens of the realm are invited to visit the Secret Garden of the pixies, fairies, gnomes, and leprechauns. Enjoy the Realm's Fynest Repast while you wander through the town of the wee folk. Perhaps, if you look close enough, you'll even see one of them peeking back out at you! (Theme sponsored by Pots and Petals Nursery)

~*~

beep. beep. beep. beepbeepbeepbeepbeepbee—

"Off, you pile of griffin droppings! Turn *off!*" Ryna cried, smacking her alarm. She connected with the huge snooze button, halting the racket and causing clock's digital face to glow pleasantly blue.

7:00 AM, 8-12 SAT, 74° F it read.

"Stores should let you test these things before you buy them," Phoenix complained groggily. "That thing's worse than Danny's—at least his gave you more time before launching into hyper mode."

"*You're* coherent this morning," Ryna observed as she flopped back on her pillows, absorbing her bed's comfort a moment longer before crawling out to face the day.

Karma blinked at her person in protest, stretched in the most feline manner possible, and rolled on her back. Phoenix reached over to pay the proper homage of a tummy rub, and although this was not the person she had intended, Karma was not one to turn away adoration. She purred rapturously.

"Did you hear a weather report for today?" Ryna asked as she cleaned her love's glasses with a small spray bottle and a soft cloth, then handed them over. "I'm betting something really ugly, given that it's Opening Weekend."

"You bet right—thanks." Phoenix donned her spectacles and retrieved her hot weather garb: dirt-brown gauzy skirt, slate-gray gauze chemise, and dark blue bodice. Hip scarves and her copper-colored coin belt completed the ensemble.

Ryna pulled on gauze harem pants and a vest over her chemise, then started in on the scarves. "Are you dreading this season as much as I am?"

"I'm—trepidatious, but hopeful." Phoenix tied her bodice laces in a neat bow. "Anything in particular you want for breakfast?"

"Eh. Not hungry."

"Dry cereal and call it good enough?"

"Sure—whatever." She and Phoenix filled their leather mugs with honey nut O's before exiting into the cool clamminess of camp. Phoe grabbed her staff and battered straw hat on the way out.

Most of the Gypsy clan were already gathered, garbed and solemn, around the cold fire pit: *Phuro* Basil, his bushy white eyebrows knit; *Baba* Luna in pounds of jewelry that seemed to weigh heavy on her today; Tremayne, his lean height diminished by slumped shoulders; Tobaltio, gaudy flame-colored clothes out of keeping with the dismal atmosphere; Tanek, devil-may-care attitude vanished beyond recall—and poor Phoenix, looking out of her element for the first time in months. Ryna squeezed her hand in reassurance, earning a tiny, grateful smile.

They stood in awkward silence, waiting for the others: Esmerelda, with the dark beauty of her Mexican heritage; Niki, flighty yet sweet; Kaya, graceful and poised. Though they rarely attended Cast Call, they too stepped glumly from their vardos. It awoke a part of Ryna that longed to crawl up on her father's lap and have him make it all better with a few words and his hand rested on her head. She squelched the desire. She was too old for such nonsense now.

Baba Luna squared her shoulders. "All right, kids; let's get this over with."

With murmured agreement the others followed her through a blissfully normal campground. Privy doors banged, releasing bleary faire-folk in bathrobes—or less. A man in plaid boxers brushed his teeth by the door of his pop-up camper. A few people wandered from tent to tent delivering wake-up calls to friends, and many rennies straggled with the Gypsies up the steep Olympic Staircase. The impassioned cries of two people in the midst of an "in depth" anatomy lesson echoed across the campground.

"I guess that's one act that wasn't cancelled," Tremayne quipped.

Tanek stuffed his hands in his pockets. "Just like the Royals Revolting—every year, the same lines."

"You'd think they could start screaming something original," Kaya agreed. "It's not like they don't get enough practice."

Toby frowned in thought. "Wasn't their tent a little farther down last year? Sounds like it's echoing different."

"I hope so. If they picked the same spot every year, they'd eventually pound through and strike oil."

"*Baba* Luna!" Niki protested, flashing her pass to the preoccupied C-gate guard.

"You only wish you'd thought of it first," Ryna teased as they snaked through the entrance. A new yellow sign proclaimed it for "Servants of the King Only!" in black calligraphy… Ryna peevishly wondered why it couldn't read "subjects" instead.

A singed spot marred the thoroughly green area around Maypole—Ryna instinctively tossed up an energy shield between herself and it. She hadn't expected anything would grow where the Shadow Fae had claimed Liam… but still, she wished the fog that often graced Pendragon's mornings would cushion the sight.

No such luck. Today there was only harsh reality. The Blue-Legged Unicorn Eatery looked shabbier than she remembered, the Hay Roll and Jacob's Ladder signs more faded. Track's low yellow fence sported a fresh coat of paint, but Irish Cottage's thatch roof looked as if it had been raided for a bird's nest… the size of her vardo. Ryna kept her eyes on the ground as the Gypsies veered to the right around Cottage's empty sheep pen… and collided with Toby as he stopped cold.

"And may I ask where the hell this thing came from?" Esmerelda demanded of no one in particular.

Ryna barely restrained a whimper at the sight of the enormous vinyl tent that enveloped a good third of Shepherd's Green—and spanned nearly to the chess booth by Bedside Manor.

"Must be for the corporate parties and the new, commercial version of Queen's Tea that Daniel told us about," *Phuro* Basil observed acerbically.

"It's ugly. And it stinks like that damn bug bomb stuff." With a fastidious twitch of her skirts, Kaya continued on to Bakery Stage, giving the monstrosity a wide berth. The others followed. Ryna could almost feel the heavy chemical smell of the insecticide seeping into her soul.

A few tiles were missing from Bakery's roof, but otherwise the structure and its three-tiered stage had fared better than most buildings. The rennies assembled for Cast Call, however…

As always, they had arrived in various states of garb, coffee cups and breakfast plates in hand. More than the usual reluctance to be out of bed darkened the mood, though. Friends greeted one another not with "How've you been?" but with "How bad did they screw you?" Not even the Magistrate's Entourage and Royal Court had been spared; scowls and sharp movements marked the lacing of bodices and doublet sleeves. A few gave the Gypsies sympathetic glances.

Ryna smiled her thanks, though she found it hard to be strong under the force of their pity. And she had to be strong. Some of these people had watched her grow up, and in a way she knew she would always be proving to them that she was no longer a child.

Disgruntled energy rumbled around Ryna as she approached the stage to retrieve copies of Pendragon's newsletter *The Privy Councilor* and a few grids, which showed the remaining acts' schedules. Tension bunched her shoulders by the time she joined her family on their usual benches in the far right portion of the third and fourth rows.

"Good morning, everyone!" called a cheerful voice, and all eyes turned to the stage.

Ryna blinked. She'd expected hellfire and brimstone, or at least a whip… certainly not this cheerleader type with the clipboard and pen. She was all blond permed hair, blue eyeshadow, and a push-up bra.

"My name's Patty Kate—I'm the new Artistic Director, as I'm sure you all know—and I can't tell you how excited I am to be here," she bubbled.

"Mostly because she has to keep her words short and easy to understand," Toby muttered under his breath, and Ryna's mood lightened. At least this authority would be easy to mock.

"I know there have been changes made, and a lot of you peoples don't like change very much, but I'm sure in time you'll see what I've done is best for Pendragon. After all, what's really important is that our guests keep coming through the doors and having a good time!"

Some cheers went up, but many voices remained conspicuously silent.

"So no crabbies in front of the guests, all right? If you have any problems, please come talk to someone in management and we'll make sure your issues get taken care of."

"I have an issue with our vardo being destroyed. Suppose they'll build us a new one before Opening Cannon goes off?" Kaya asked.

"No, they'll fire your ass before you can cause trouble," *Baba* Luna observed acidly.

"Well, we've got lots of peoples with stuff to say before the day starts, so let's get on with it, shall we? I'd like to start the announcements by reminding everyone that the Secret Garden isn't quite open yet, so I'm depending on you all to encourage people to come back and see it next weekend in its full splendor!" The Artistic Director then stepped aside and motioned the first person in line forward.

Esmerelda rolled her eyes. "How in the world did she manage to screw so much up? Sheer ignorance and stupidity?"

"Don't let it fool you," *Phuro* warned. "She'll perky you into an early grave, but once she has an opinion, she won't give it up."

"And here I normally wouldn't mind having something that pretty screwing me," Tanek said with a dramatic sigh.

Niki leaned over and smacked him upside the head.

"Hi!" announced a fellow on stage. "I'm the new falconer—"

"What happened to Peregrine?" someone demanded from the benches.

Patty smoothly stepped in. "I'll be happy to explain things to you if you're really curious; come find me after Cast Call, okay? Next!"

"Can I kill her? Please?" Ryna begged as the falconer, confused, was herded off.

The remaining announcements were tellingly low-profile… reminders to drink water and where water could be found, pleas from the head of Front Gate not to go out the entrance doors, a request from the Lord Magistrate to come up with bits for

Closing Gate show, an announcement that all lost articles could be found at B-gate. Ryna noticed, however, that the Artistic Director spoke briefly with each person in line—and sent several away frowning.

All too soon, Perky Patty took the stage again. "Well, that looks like that's about it—oh, yeah, street performers need to check in with their liaison. Now, we're running a little short on time, so I'm going to have to ask you to find out which liaison is yours on your own—I'm sure that won't be a problem for you all. Okay? Okay! Now it's time for the—"

"ORT!" someone yelled.

"ORT?" A frown wrinkled her pretty brow. Lancelot whispered in her ear. "Oh! Official Renaissance Time. What a strange little phrase. The time is eight-twenty-five. And now, why don't you all come up to the stage and sing while I find a spot on a bench over there and direct! Oh, this is so much fun!" she cried, clapping her hands in delight.

More grumbling, though folks still lumbered up to the stage for the daily rendition of "Swing Low, Sweet Chariot."

Ryna turned her back and walked away with the other Gypsies.

They were not the only ones; other faces she recognized filtered away in disgust as the sweet, familiar notes filled the morning air.

* * *

A couple cracks, or maybe just the memory of That Night, had subtly transformed the Bear's fierce roar into an expression of startlement. It was a small change, though. There were no tents, no huge sponsorship signs.

Ryna could almost convince herself that everything was as it had always been.

The Traveler's Shoppe looked the same. The old picnic benches in the food courts looked the same. Woodland Stage, all balcony-like, had hardly faded. Sherwood Forest boasted a new sign done in hard-to-read green lettering.

Ryna's stomach dropped out on the road. She should be able to see the vardo behind Hollow Hill—but she could not. She sprinted the last bit to the grapevine gates. A rectangular patch of dirt glared at her from where the beautiful structure once stood. Six holes marked where the support posts had been. It was truly, truly gone.

"Home." Ryna leaned her head despondently against the gate's rough post. She remembered napping there when she could still count her age on one hand, curled in the nest of pillows, one curtain drawn down for shade, watching the dance show through the door on the vardo's short wall until the familiar sound of her father's fiddle and her mother's chiming coin belt lulled her to dreamland.

And now it was gone.

"So, what, she thinks taking away our vardo means we'll never take breaks?" Toby demanded rebelliously. "Fine. We'll take them in the campground or in the gazebo instead of in full view of the public. And if Ms. Artistic Asshat has something to say about it, she can—"

"We can build a new one," *Phuro* Basil said firmly. "It's just wood and nails and paint. They haven't taken away who or what we are. Besides, for all we know, we might be able to salvage materials from the old one."

Ryna remembered building it, the paintbrush in her young hand turning the wooden wheels (and her knees, and her shirt, and her fingers) green as her mother and father talked and laughed, painting the short wall's panels in vibrant colors while *Phuro* Basil hammered together the little stairway. Toby had cut lengths of pipe on which to hang the draperies, and Esmerelda and *Baba* Luna made thick tassels of yarn…

It had been so brightly warm that day, but not too hot, with the baked smell of hot dirt and dry grass in the air… the sort of day in which it seems that all of childhood exists. Before she had been a road rennie, there had been the vardo.

Had been.

Gone.

Her father's hand, comforting and familiar, rested on the crown of her head from behind. The younger fiddler choked back tears. She would *not* give Patty the power to make her cry.

"Oh, gods, I wonder if their insurance company knows about *that*," Tanek asked, pointing toward the tower near the Petting Zoo and the Children's Realm.

Ryna turned and gazed up at the huge yellow monstrosity. Pendragon's owner had wanted a giant slide—and as usual, had hired the lowest bidder without looking at a résumé or a blueprint. Only after the tower had been constructed did the engineers realize that the slide would have to end in the parking lot to keep the kids from becoming pint-sized missiles. Dicky Darnell had fired the engineers and abandoned the project, though he refused to destroy something for which he had paid. And so it had stood for years, a testament to the business sense behind Pendragon Renaissance Faire.

It appeared that now, however, management had decided to rectify the error. A gaudy sign declared it "Ye Olde Climbing Tower" and advertised a conveniently vague reward for anyone who reached the top. Another sign, equally ugly, advertised the health insurance company that had sponsored it.

"Ironic, isn't it?" asked a female voice behind them. "They even hired some bimbo to spend all day leaning out the top window calling for help. It's almost as stupid as that Secret Deathtrap they built down there."

Ryna turned to see her friend Alexis ruffling cropped, mahogany hair out of her eyes. She looked every inch a female Robyn Hood… complete with an air of mutiny.

"Hey!" Niki gave Alex a warm hug. "We didn't see you at Cast Call."

"I refuse to listen to a single thing our little Patty-Cakes has to say. She's nothing but a breakfast tart—all sugar and bad aftertaste—and I wouldn't eat either if my contract depended on it. Stupid two-bit small-time self-important callus-kneed cheerleader reject." The fuming Merry Maid assumed a tits-forward stance and pitched her voice higher. "Breathe in, breathe out. Let's have a little unity, here. If the people in the Royal Shakespeare Company can do this, so can we." Alex dropped the stance and snarled. "Fluffbunny. She *would* need a reminder to breathe in and out."

Ryna had the sudden urge to applaud. By the others' grins, they shared her opinion.

At least there was *one* good thing about this year: the Merry Maids were here—and in top form.

◇ ◇ ◇

Phoenix wandered, discouraged, down the line of food booths that comprised Upson Downs. The teenagers working them leaned, bored, on the worn wooden counters. Occasionally one let out a cry for the overpriced fare, but no one turned. Two Scotsmen trotted past with an empty cabriolet, in no apparent rush.

Everything and everyone seemed so half-hearted. Granted, the temperature was scaling the thermometer and humidity clogged the air, but still! It frustrated and angered Phoenix that no one fought harder against management's influence. She had spent the entire morning doggedly creating entertainment, but it was a one-woman show. The patrons wandering listlessly from shop to shop stared at her blankly when she spoke. Her fellow street actors looked like zombies, and if this was any indication of how few remained…

She pushed the thought away. Better to cling to the hope that the Gypsies' variety show, slightly over half an hour away, would go better.

"Phoenix!"

"Good day, Torin," she greeted her brother as he descended the staircase from Bedside Manor's upper level. "Or, at least, I hope it's been better for you than it has for the rest of Pendragon."

"Aye, if only," he said with an Irish lilt and an exasperated roll of his eyes. "Apparently we've been scheduled for a dance presentation beginnin' in five minutes, though we had to find out ourselves that our band from last year wasn't re-hired—and nearly every other band has been double-booked and is trying to sort themselves out. So we've dancers but no music. Da can play bodhran well enough, but one drum willna cut it, and I'm expected to dance."

"So a bodhran and one pennywhistle would work? Mine's in the vardo, but if I could borrow yours—"

A light dawned in his sea-colored eyes, though he tried to quell it. "I know how ye hate playin' before people—"

She shrugged it off. "Eh, I'm used to it now. Nowhere near as good as most, but I can plunk out a few songs."

"Along with me, then, bonnie lass." In his enthusiasm, he nearly dragged her past the end of Track, across Shepherd's Green, and through Cottage's front door, pausing briefly to bless the house and wipe his feet. Phoenix did likewise.

"Phoenix!" came a joyous shout, and a dark-haired lass of seventeen bounded over to give her a hug. "I have something for you!" With a look of intense concentration, she pried a ring off her sun-dark hand and offered it up.

"It's beautiful, Brigid," Phoe marveled, examining the little silver ring. The top was in the shape of a phoenix with little red mosaic bits lacquered to it. They looked for all the world like pimentos.

"I made it in shop class last year," she crowed.

"I shall wear it always," Phoenix promised, and paused a moment to take stock of Cottage's interior. The floorboard on which she stood sagged a bit, but otherwise the place was unravished. Same hearth at the right end of the room, same green hutch between the back and kitchen doors, same green burlap curtain that shielded the kitchen from prying patron eyes. Same thatch roof above and—as always—bits of thatch on the barnboard floor. Same whisk of the broom as Eryn swept.

The only problem was—

"What happened to your table?" Phoenix cried.

"Oh—I must've forgotten to mention that," Torin said sheepishly.

Eryn cast the standard-issue picnic table a dark look. "Somebody took it. They left our benches, but they took our pretty, carved table. And the lady who sings the 'Meadowlark' is gone, too. Patty wouldn't give her a contract. She said the Meadowlark-lady's act wasn't suitable for children."

Phoenix folded the youngest O'Malley in a comforting embrace. She'd grown—she came up to Phoe's chin now. "I'm sure she'll visit, duckling," the Gypsy said gently, then turned to the reason for her visit. "Torin tells me you Irish are in need of a musician for your dances."

"Musician? Did I hear someone say there's a musician in the house?" Phoenix looked up to see Aunt Molly hauling herself up to peer over the loft's railing. She looked blessedly the same as last year—same green and black outfit, same wildly curly red-brown hair. The tired hope in her eyes was new, though—and sad. Perhaps the luster *had* faded from Cottage—but at least the O'Malleys were fighting. This would be a place of comfort and home as long as one of them stood beneath its roof.

"I didna know ye played, herbmistress," Da said. He had a bit more of a paunch—and a stubborn set to his shoulders.

"Tin whistle. Amazing what a year with Gypsies will do to one's skills," Phoenix said with a wry smile.

"I'll bet," Ma agreed with a wink. Good old well-padded Ma, the essence of Irish hospitality. "I see ye've taken Cleavage Display 101."

The Gypsy gave herself mental kudos for not blushing, though she felt as if her tanned bosom had developed a magnetic attraction for eyeballs.

Aunt Molly trooped down the ladder from the loft. "Out, out, everyone find a partner and we'll see how much we've forgotten since last year."

Golden-haired Moiré levered up from the *seanchaí* chair and slouched out the door. Her corset seemed to be the only thing holding her up. Phoenix cast a questioning glance at the other O'Malleys, who shrugged. She had always been so prim and cheerful, before... now she was just another victim of the year. Hopefully the others would raise her spirits as the day went on.

Strange, though—she had the sparkle that Phoe associated with Magick and the Gypsies. And Phoenix was pretty sure she hadn't glowed like that last year.

Da retrieved his bodhran from a hook on the wall, and Phoe followed him outside. Flutters twitched her stomach at the prospect of playing during a show day, but trying to remember the steps to all those dances would be even worse.

Besides, the Irish swing wouldn't feel right without Ryna in her arms.

◇ ◇ ◇

With careful precision Liam made the symbol's final stroke in the dirt outside the bronze statue booth, then stepped back to survey his work.

It was nothing spectacular, really. The logo for the software company he and a couple friends had started in high school... apt, as the company's co-founders had been the ones to introduce him to Magick.

He'd always loved the marketing more than the developing, his compatriots had welcomed his charisma, and Liam had gained the ability to sidestep his father's fanatical interest in seeing him excel in sports after he'd brandished his first split of the profits. Liam smirked in memory. It hadn't even been *all* of his share.

Now it amused him to etch it in the ground outside this booth. The Bright Fae that called this place their home were so small that they couldn't understand the concept of a mortal—even a mortal as strange as he. And so every day he put it there—and every day they scurried about, franticly wondering where it had come from.

A small game—a petty game. But even such little bits of chaos planted might be useful eventually.

His pet cowered against his legs. Liam scowled at it, ready to give it a well-placed kick... and then he felt the cause for its distress, like a summer storm gathering on the horizon.

The signs were subtle at first, but Liam knew them well, even after months of their absence. The moment of disorientation… the straining sensation across his feet, as if his shadow wanted to tear free and flee.

And then the sudden, unreal calm, and the voice that assaulted Liam's ears with a sound like small shovelfuls of dirt poured over a stone coffin. "The Gypsies have returned…"

"And so has the one you claim for your love…" another added, its voice the crumbling of rotted paper.

"The one they call Phoenix…" the echo of the third voice shrieked through his head, raising Liam's hackles.

The Three.

His stomach clenched with fear, but he would not turn. He refused to give the creatures that satisfaction, although failing to acknowledge them in some manner only invited them to make their presence known in less pleasant ways.

"And?" Liam asked, feigning indifference.

They laughed, charred bones falling from rotten sinew. Even after all this time, it made Liam cringe.

"Poor, poor mortal…"

"We have come to grant your wish…"

"Your wish to return…"

He barked a laugh, unwise though it might be. They had grown sloppy—or stupid—if they thought anything so obvious would raise his hopes.

"He does not believe us…"

"He thinks we taunt him…"

"Even though aiding him furthers our cause…"

Their words gave him pause, as the Three had intended. Despite himself, curiosity tugged at Liam. He glanced over his shoulder. "And why should I believe that?"

"You have been here long…"

"You have learned the way of things…"

"The struggle for power between our kind and the mortal-kissers…"

Liam's mind raced. These things were cunning… but they had never approached him like this before. Either this was some new form of torture, or… "Go on."

"The mortals return to these grounds…"

"Our enemies gain strength from their happiness…"

"As we would gain strength from their fall…"

They were slick, but Liam couldn't help but wonder if desperation drove them… He had learned that if you showed weakness here, you paid for it. What better way to enlist his aid than to appear as if this was simply a tactical maneuver?

"Why me?" he asked. "Why not send one of your minions?"

"You are shriveled and dry…"

"A new use must be found for you..."

"You can serve us there..."

It was... feasible. Against better sense, Liam found his opinion swaying to their suggestions.

There had to be a catch. There always was with these creatures. "And what would be the price to return?"

"You claim the one they call Phoenix..."

"You destroy the Gypsies..."

"You pave the way for one of our superiors..."

That... was it? They must be desperate indeed... or hiding something.

But, really, what were his options—stay here for eternity? "Very well. If I am returned to my world *in physical form*, I will grant your request. W—"

"It is done..."

"Take this stone..."

"Use it to prepare..."

Then, their voices clashing in an unholy trio:

"You have until Darkmoon."

And they were gone.

Liam frowned at the marble-sized black sphere at his feet... its surface shifted and swirled almost imperceptibly as he gazed at it, though its hue never lightened. He bent gingerly to retrieve it—the touch numbed his fingers. The air he breathed felt thick, like cold steam.

It held power—that he could not deny. Maybe even enough power that it would return him home...

But what about the Bright Fae? If they had grown so strong that the Shadows had come to him for help, Liam could hardly escape their notice...

He shook his head firmly. It didn't matter. This was his chance at freedom. His chance at gaining his love. He would allow nothing to stop him.

Nothing.

"Somebody needs to tell those patrons that Spandex is a privilege, not a right," Ryna announced as Phoenix followed her into the shade of the oak near Bedside Manor, joining the mass of peasants waiting for Vilification Tennis to start.

Hayrold, face damp with sweat beneath his brown hood, gave her a wry grin as he leaned forward on his amethyst-topped staff. "It's that damn fairy costume contest they had outside Front Gate this morning—the winner got half off their ticket price."

"Cheap bastards," griped a fellow in a kilt sporting a tennis-ball-yellow stripe.

"Yeah. And the Secret Deathtrap's not even open yet," Bryn put in, her fingers tangled in the fellow's long, wheat-colored hair. "Oh, by the way—Phoenix, this is Marcus."

"A pleasure." Marcus grinned. "I like your hat. You didn't have that last year, did you?"

"Got it for Scheherazade in Arizona… you get sunburned so fast there," Phoe said. "You're one of the musicians, right? I think I saw you at Cottage a couple times, playing your… um…"

"Bouzouki—affectionately known as a mandolin with a glandular problem."

"So how bad are the musicians getting it this year?" Ryna asked, cutting into Phoe's musings.

Marcus rolled his eyes. "Don't get me started—you should see the grid. Patty rearranged everyone's spots… and most of the musicians are scheduled to be in two places at once."

"We're not doing much better," Phoe told him, "except for the two places at once thing."

"Oh? How so?" Bryn asked as a suave Gypsy in dark blue pants sauntered up to Hayrold. The gold thread adorning his battered yellow vest sparkled in the sun.

"Who're we up against?"

Phoenix blinked at the newcomer, startled. Hayrold had always been partnered with Piddle…

And then she looked closer, imagined the stranger's face streaked with dirt and his hair gathered in a topknot…

"*Piddle*??"

Hayrold grinned. "Cleans up good, doesn't he?"

"*That's* Piddle?!"

"The name is Chrysto—at your service," the former peasant declared with a gallant bow—and kissed her hand.

Phoe suppressed a giggle… and wondered what Tanek was going to think of his competition.

"It's his old character," Hayrold said, "back from before Eric outlawed any Gypsies who weren't part of your troupe."

"Why would he do that?" Phoe asked.

"We made it look like too much fun," Ryna supplied. "There was one year where it seemed like everyone went Gypsy, and Eric wanted diversity. So he banned everyone else… even if they'd had a Gypsy character for years."

"Not one of his more popular decisions," Chrysto observed. "But since we have new management, I thought I'd see if I could sneak it by."

"Is this where the Vilification folks meet up?"

All eyes turned to a barrel-chested fellow with a bench on one hip and garb slightly too nice for peasantry. "Planning to compete? The judge isn't here yet," Ryna said amiably.

"Actually… I *am* the judge."

A couple stunned exclamations—but mostly incredulous silence.

"Dare I ask why?" Hayrold inquired in a civil tone.

The fellow shifted his bench awkwardly, but an ironic smile quirked his lips. "She's twenty months pregnant and due to pop any day now. I'm just the poor schmuck who volunteered to step in for her."

Phoenix heard Pratt's distinctive guffaw and turned to flash the scruffy peasant a smile. A few other snickers went around as the tension eased.

"Well, at least that one's not management's fault," Bryn observed. "They might screw us over, but I've never heard of anyone getting pregnant from it."

"Listen, I don't know all the team names yet, but I brought some paper and pencils. I'll draw teams from my hat until I get a better feel for where everyone should go," the new judge said. "Anyone got the time? Are we about ready to start?"

"POT! Anyone got POT?" asked a peasant with light chin-length hair and bright eyes. Phoe thought she recognized him as one of Como Cottage's snake handlers.

"I don't think anyone established Peasant Official Time at Cast Call…" another Como Cottage peasant responded, this one a red-haired female in a patchwork chemise, tiered velvet skirt, and green leather bodice.

Hayrold made a *pffft* noise as he scribbled on his paper. "Yeah. I can imagine how *that* would've gone over."

"Well, the stage's clear—good enough for me. I'm going to go claim our space—one of you lovely ladies can bring up the hat when all the slips are in it." The judge hefted the bench onto his shoulder, turned for the crowd, and let out a bellow. "Coming THROUGH! Move it! Watch out! Clear the path!"

"Hey, anyone have a spare bodice and maybe a skirt?" Pratt asked.

The peasant collective turned to their fuzziest member as he leaned down to tug up one of his mismatched knee-high moccasins. Realization came quickly—and so did the giggles as the peasants scurried to action.

"Here, he can borrow my—"

"I have two skirts on; he can have the—"

"Gypsy, you have any spare scarves we can use to stuff—"

"—making them too even; no one will ever believe—"

"—a bit dangling out… like that, see?"

"Pratt *pretty*!"

Phoenix whipped around at the last exclamation to see a mop-haired peasant with a burlap muffin cap drooping over one eye. "Puddle!"

"Dead!" he declared gleefully, displaying a fox pelt puppet strapped to his right hand, its nose cleverly molded over his middle finger. And then, proudly indicating a small fox skull strapped to his shoulder, "Dead Too!"

"Goddess save us all," Phoenix said, trying not to giggle as she gave each of the Deads a welcoming pet on the head.

"I said, PLAYED OVER A NET OF PEASANTS!!!" bellowed the judge.

"That's our cue," Marcus said, and the peasants descended upon the Bear's raised stage in a great commotion that gradually resolved into a single-file line bisecting the performance space.

"That's better," the judge announced. "Our teams will be chosen at random out of a hat. Would one of the lovely ladies bring forth the hat?"

"Hat! Hat! Hat!" Puddle chanted.

"Hat! Hat! Hat! Hat!" the others joined in as Pratt swished onto the stage amidst laughter and cheers, apologizing daintily to all those he bumped on the way. Given the number of collisions, Phoe suspected his bumbling was intentional.

The judge claimed the hat from the fuzzy peasant and gave him a smart slap on the ass that made Pratt nearly leap into the net.

The audience roared with laughter.

"Our first round will be... Pog moe... how the bloody hell do you—"

"*Pog mó Thoin*!" Hayrold and Chrysto hollered as they marched onto stage.

"Uh... right. What they said, against... the Gypsies!"

A rush of adrenaline hit Phoenix as she followed Ryna over the boulders that ringed the stage and claimed their half of the grassy square.

"Couldn't you come up with a better name than that?" the judge chided.

Ryna shrugged. "Used to have a corner on the market."

Chrysto beamed charmingly.

"All right, all right, let's get this underway. Any coin I toss is going to get snatched up by you lot before it hits the ground—give me a peasant to flip!"

A lanky teenager in a baggy gray shirt and pants stood, pushing a clump of shaggy light brown hair out of his eyes before offering his hand to Phoenix.

Phoe grabbed his hand and gave him a subtle nod before making a show of hurling him across the stage. The boy threw himself at the ground with admirable abandon, tumbling the length of the stage as Chrysto cried, "Heads!"

"Penny on the ground!" Ryna tempted.

"Cleavage in the air!" Hayrold retaliated with a grin.

The peasant landed spread-eagled, staring with a blissful smile up at Ryna.

Phoenix faked giving him a good solid kick. He obligingly rolled to his stomach.

"See? Tails," Ryna offered winningly.

Chrysto conspicuously tossed the judge a heavy pouch—which the judge promptly tucked away. "Sorry, Gypsy—looks like heads to me. You plan to serve or receive, *Pog*?"

Hayrold leaned on his staff. "Well, it's been so long since these two have been serviced, I guess we'll bite the bullet."

"Very well—serv*ice*!"

Phoe took a deep breath, slowly let it out, calming the nerves that always hit when she stepped on stage, even after all this time. The game was beginning... but it was only a game. And the first match, at that. How hard could it be—even in front of all these people? She flexed her hands on her staff, trying to work off the adrenaline that made them shake.

Chrysto strode up to the net, pointing an accusing finger to Phoenix. "This woman is so ugly that at birth, they put tinted windows on her incubator!"

Phoenix graced him with a withering look, grabbed the first insult that came to mind. "After centuries of reincarnation... you're depressing the hell out of the Buddhists."

Only a small portion of the audience chuckled—Phoe winced. It had been a new insult—had it been to obscure?

"You're so ugly, you're goin' to Hell!" Hayrold declared. "God looked down on you and said 'DAMN!'"

That got a better reaction.

Theme, keep with the theme. Phoe turned to the audience. "In Biblical times, it was a miracle when an ass spoke. Things sure have changed..."

"This woman can't whistle," Hayrold scoffed. "She can't even blow air right!"

It must've been the delivery... Phoe'd heard the insult several times before, but this time it caught her flat-footed. She racked her suddenly empty brain, trying to come up with something, *anything*—

"The voices in this man's head never keep him awake," Ryna called, coming to Phoe's defense. "You can't transmit sound in a vacuum!"

"Speaking of vacuums," Chrysto parried, "I wasn't gonna sleep with your mom, but she was bent over and the vacuum sucked me right in!"

"Point!" the judge called over the smattered laughter. "Try to keep it down, guys. We've got a long way to go."

Hayrold stepped gamely to the net. "Your left eye must be fascinating... the right one keeps looking at it."

Phoenix made a face. "You're so disgusting, the plague caught *you*!"

Chrysto indicated Ryna for the audience's benefit. "This woman has a lot in common with a bowling ball... she gets picked up, fingered, thrown in the gutter, and she keeps comin' back for more!"

Hayrold gave him an incredulous look and a smack on the arm. "Don't piss off the redhead!"

Ryna put her hands on her hips and shot back: "I would've sent you a valentine, but I couldn't figure out how to wrap lace around a turd."

"Oh, crap, you pissed her off..." Hayrold bemoaned, shaking his head.

Chrysto seemed to be warming to his topic, though. "This woman has a lot in common with a moped—fun to ride until your friends see you on it!"

"This man boasts that he could marry any girl he pleases," Ryna retorted. "Except... he doesn't please *any* of them."

"Point!" The judge scowled at Ryna. "What did I tell you about keeping it down?"

"I didn't think it was *that* bad..." Ryna trailed off.

"Harpy!" Hayrold shot across the net.

It only took the fiddler back a moment. "Maggot!"

"Strumpet!"

"Privy licker!"

"Cankerblossom!"

"Patron fondler!"

"Fly-bitten buttmunch!"

"Bottom-trotting butt flea!"

"Daughter of a motherless goat!"

"Sperm-burping gutterslut!"

"Point!" the judge called, pointing to Ryna—but Hayrold didn't even pause. "Dankish, craven, rump-fed, bar-fowling, cum-gurgling guttersnipe!"

"POINT!"

"Misbegotten son of a penis-wrinkled whoremonger!"

"POINT!!!!!!!! Both of you go to your ROOMS!"

"Your mom eats cat poop!" Chrysto called into the sudden stillness—to the audience's delight.

"Point!" Then, to Hayrold and Ryna, "Do you two think you can play nice now?"

Hayrold looked chastened, but vigorously nodded.

"All right, then. Ser*vice*!"

The peasant stepped up to the net. "Ryna, why is it that any time anyone says *tallyho* you stand up and say, 'One!'"

Ryna gave him a scathing look. "Someone should rent you out to a near-sighted knife-thrower."

"This woman's so ugly that when she goes to the beach, cats try to bury her!" Chrysto returned. "And by cats, I mean bulldozers! And by bury, I mean use like there's no tomorrow!"

The judge shook his head in despair. "I refuse to give that one a point. It just encourages you." He turned to the Gypsies. "Go ahead and return."

Ryna stepped to the net. "I noticed they've put a new sign up by Globe Stage—maximum occupancy 860 patrons—or yo' momma!"

"Okay, *that* one I'll give a point. Ser*vice*!"

"Yo' momma's so fat, yo' daddy can't even *think* hard!" Hayrold accused.

"This man sent his picture to Lonely Hearts," Ryna told the audience. "Three days later he got a letter back—saying they weren't *that* lonely."

Hayrold leaned on his staff with a bemused expression. "Honey, you're gonna need bigger boobs if you're gonna be *that* stupid."

"It's nice to see you love nature despite what it did to you."

The peasant turned to Phoenix. "So, do you talk, or do I have to pull a string?"

Phoenix had been content to sit back and let Ryna work off some of her frustration… but an insult like that demanded action. She stormed to the net, words falling out of her mouth before she had even thought them. "You, sir, is what's left after rabid weasels finish mating!"

A stunned silence fell over the crowd—Phoenix, in reflex, started floundering. "You know, the fur… the foam… the schmutz…"

"Hold me!" Hayrold cried, burying his face in his partner's vest as the audience roared with laughter.

"That's GAME!" the judge blustered. "To *Pog*! There will be NO using the word SCHMUTZ—!"

Phoenix listened, wide-eyed, to the judge's rant as Ryna tugged her offstage. All this fuss over schmutz? The others had said far worse… hadn't they?

Schmutz was just… well, *schmutz*… wasn't it? Unless it didn't mean what she thought it, and…

Oh, gods. That had to be it. She'd said something horrible and not even known it. Phoe closed her eyes briefly. She only hoped she'd have a chance to make amends.

"Phoe, slow down!" Ryna cried, dodging patrons in her love's wake as the tossed peasant tumbled across the stage. Why on earth would anyone want to hurry with the sun glaring down?

"Heads!" a Vilifier called.

"I've got to find Hayrold," Phoe called back.

"He's not going to evaporate—I don't care *how* hot it is."

"I know, but I've got to—Hayrold, I am *so sorry*."

Ryna came even with the raven-haired Gypsy in time to see the peasant's befuddled expression.

"For what?"

"For what I said," Phoe got out in a rush. "I didn't really mean it, you know, and—I don't want you to think—"

Hayrold started giggling, making helpless gestures as he tried not to distract the patrons' attention from the budding insult match.

"Um, you're not offended, then?" Phoe ventured, cheeks reddening under her tan. She must've realized she should've known better. Ryna stifled her own smile; Phoenix really was awfully cute when she blushed.

"Offended!" It took another gale of laughter before Hayrold could put on a serious face, peasant character dropped. "My God, Phoe, your delivery was perfect! I had to bury my face in Chrysto's vest to keep from laughing!"

Phoe's lips twitched into a shy smile. "Then—it was a good thing?"

"It was a *great* thing. That insult rocked! Schmutz! Where do you come *up* with those?"

The smile turned to a full-fledged grin; Phoe hastily leaned her staff against the Bear and threw her arms around the peasant.

"With a reward like this, I should act offended more often!" he teased.

Ryna leaned back against the Bear's uneven surface, crossed her feet at the ankle, and watched as Hayrold gently returned Phoenix's hug—then gave her a little back scritch, emitted a giggle worthy of a cartoon character, and toddled off to get ready for tip collection. Ryna was glad to see Phoenix smiling too; the poor woman had been jumpy all day.

Phoe turned to retrieve her staff… and stopped, frowning.

The redhead looked over to where it had been—but was no longer. She frowned. It'd only been out of Phoe's hands a moment, and Ryna herself had been *right next* to it. She hopped up on one of the boulders surrounding the stage and scanned the crowd—it couldn't have gotten far.

Nothing.

"It's fine, really," Phoenix said before Ryna could get a word in. "Someone probably took it to Lost and Found. I'll check after VilTen's done."

Ryna raised an eyebrow, not inclined to believe her, but shrugged.

Let Phoe keep her innocence. It would be shattered soon enough.

Amazing how important a chunk of wood could become.

Although originally a prop for a Halloween costume, for the past year Phoe's staff had tromped all over the country with her, and despite what she'd told Ryna, its loss put her off balance. Her right hand felt empty without its familiar contours, and her character had no idea how to get from point A to point B without a staff to thump.

Already she'd visited Lost and Found three times, and it had only been an hour since VilTen ended. She'd talked to the rennies at Front Gate as well—no one would be able to sneak something so large off site. It was only a matter of time...

She sighed. At least she still had her dagger, which she suspected had followed her through *lifetimes*, and she still had her pouch. She fingered the tooled phoenix on its flap and smiled. She hadn't visited Catherine, the woman who'd given it to her, yet this year. Perhaps she still had the little play area with the leather dolls? She always welcomed Phoenix to interact with the children, and she could play dolls without her staff. Phoe veered toward the Narrows and Catherine's familiar shop...

... or, where Catherine's shop used to be.

The Gypsy frowned. The unassuming wood structure remained, though scarcely visible beneath the garish trappings of yet another souvenir booth. Although she doubted it would do any good, she approached the dark-haired teen hawking the shop's wares. *Figures. They get rid of the crews to advertise stage shows and stick them on T-shirt booths.*

"Come buy a medallion, m'lady! 'Twill go surpassing fair with thine costume."

Phoenix cocked her head at the lad. She gave him credit for a passable accent, though he should've used *thy*, not *thine*. She nudged her glasses up her nose. "Actually, I wondered if you could tell me what happened to the crafter whose shop used to be here."

The hawker stared slack-jawed at her, and for a moment Phoenix thought he would laugh in her face. "Wow," he said, dropping accent. "And here I thought that lady was just being weird. You're the sixth person to ask since I came on shift at noon."

Hope sparked in Phoe's heart. "You know, then?"

"Sure. She came by this morning while we were setting up and wanted us to pass the word that she's in a tent down by the boat."

Phoenix thanked him profusely and trotted back the way she'd come, turning left at Bedside Manor and heading toward *Lady Fortune* Stage.

"Angel!" Catherine greeted warmly when Phoenix finally found her tent—a tiny, ragged thing stuffed between three others.

Phoe gazed about, gave her friend a wan smile. "I see I'm not the only one who ran away with the Gypsies."

Catherine chuckled, though it had a dry sound. "The owner jacked up the rent on the booths in that section until one of us caved—and then stopped. If I'd known that was all it would take, I would've given in earlier, made things easier for the other crafters."

"And I suppose he generously offered to buy your booth at half its worth?"

"A quarter. Though he did let me have this little corner for half what I was paying for my old spot. I'm lucky I had this old tent from my early Rendezvous days or I would've had to rent one."

"Rendezvous?"

"You know—fur trade living history stuff. Same era as Fort Snelling down the road."

"Oh, right. I think I went there on a field trip in elementary school."

Catherine sighed. "Oh, Angel. I've been trying so hard to look on the bright side. I'm sure God has a reason for all this, but right now I just can't see it. Hardly anyone comes back here, and my tent's so hidden away. I don't even have room for a play area for the children."

Phoe leaned against one of the display tables. It shifted dangerously; she quickly straightened. "Is there any rule about not decorating your tent?"

The crafter considered. "Not—not that I know of."

"So, if you really wanted to, you could make bright banners and hang them around? Maybe even some pennants? You should come see what the Gypsies have done with…"

Realization of what she'd almost said hit Phoenix square in the gut.

There was no more vardo.

"With what?"

"Nothing." She sighed. "That is—the vardo we had up behind Hollow Hill was wonderfully decorated, but the Artistic Director tore it down."

Dismay shadowed Catherine's features. "Oh, Angel. That's awful!"

Phoe tried to shrug it off. "It is, but I'm mostly sad for the other Gypsies. I never really had a chance to get attached to it. Still—I'm sure you could come up with something on your own."

"Yeah." A slow smile turned the crafter's lips. "I'm a fairly good seamstress, and it wouldn't have to be fancy…"

"And I could pull out that doll you gave me, talk to it some while I'm on street, get the kids interested, then send them your way."

The look on Catherine's face was beyond grateful. "You do realize this is the second time you've rescued me, Angel."

"All in a day's work." Phoe gallantly tipped her straw hat on her way out, spirits unexpectedly lighter. Halfway to Cottage she realized that playing with her little doll might make up for the lack of her staff. She might get the hang of this yet.

Or… at least… until her staff returned.

◇ ◇ ◇

"Ryna! Ryna! Have you seen our table? Someone stole it!"

The young voice halted Liam's steps mere yards from the Information Booth near Bedside Manor. The two youngest Irish Cottage girls fuzzed into being amidst the babble of voices, the shout of a pickle vendor, the beating of a drum to a mandolin's spirited jig from the direction of Canopy Stage. He could see no other rennies, though.

The flame-haired girl held a stack of posters in both hands; the other, her dark hair in a long braid, was nailing one to the powder-blue wood of the booth's wall. They both glowed subtly—he'd never noticed it before, but they had the potential for using Magick…

Ryna appeared next to them, shining bright as the sun—Liam wished that inner fire would turn her to the useless ash she was. "Figures," she said with a disgusted look and a toss of her hair. "Someone took Phoe's staff too."

"Oh no! How? When?" the brunette cried, braid flying as she spun from her task. She'd blossomed over the past couple years—surely by now she must be old enough to be legally bedded…?

"At VilTen, right under our noses. Phoe leaned it up against the Bear for a moment, and when she turned back, it was gone. She's trying to pretend it doesn't bother her, but…"

"But it's her *staff*," Eryn filled in for her.

Liam's pet made a smug whuffling—he imagined it covered in broken glass. It yelped most satisfactorily just as the vision disappeared with an almost audible *snap*.

"Foolish mortal…"

"He wastes precious time…"

"He'll need this."

The words crawled through Liam's head an instant before a short, squat, four-eyed Shadow Fae was dumped unceremoniously at his feet.

And then, just as suddenly as the Three had come—they were gone.

Liam's pet sniffed cursorily at the newcomer, who bared a taloned hand at it. The pet recoiled—whether from threat or the thing's stench, Liam could not say. It reeked of things that should've been left buried. Three of the Fae's eyes blinked at him, lids sliding sideways and out of time with each other.

Liam crossed his arms, nonplussed. *Need* it? More likely that the Three needed it to herd him, keep watch… probably to report back.

But maybe, *maybe*… it could prove useful. And, at any rate, better the spy you know…

"I don't suppose you'll tell me anything helpful."

Something tickled the back of Liam's mind, the dark, feathery buzz like an undead mosquito. He frowned, shook his head to clear it.

The thing shot off a distinct impression of displeasure—and probably would have scowled had it possessed eyebrows. It pawed Liam's pockets.

Liam rounded on the creature, backhanding it into a heap three feet away. "Don't. Touch," he growled. "Understand?"

It raised its head slightly, but did not otherwise move. The buzz fluttered against Liam's consciousness again.

Must be the thing's primitive way of communicating, he thought. "What do you want?"

The thing gestured—something small, spherical. Ah. The marble.

Liam reached into his pocket, his fingers numbing as they brushed the little sphere. It shifted strangely against his skin, pulling at his soul…

The creature held out a tentative, taloned hand.

Liam looked it square in the eyes. "You make one move to run…"

It simply waited. Patient. Cowed.

It knew its master. Good. Liam held his hand out flat, the stone stark black against his pale palm.

In one liquid-swift motion the Fae folded Liam's fingers over the treasure and sent a surge of dark, suffocating Magick through hand and soul and stone.

Liam choked and gasped as he felt himself turning inside-out through the sphere, collapsing and sucking and expanding until the world exploded back into focus with a dizzying rush.

The sky looked… bluer. He could smell the turkey leg that the patron beside him clutched in one square fist. There were people… all around him, people. A little girl ran by, squealing with glee as the plastic ribbons of her wand trailed behind her. A pickle vendor nearby hollered a lewd comment; Liam could almost taste the brine from the bucket of his wares.

It was… real. No peek through the veil, no half-heard strain of music. It was *real.*

And then, with another twisting, stomach-wrenching inversion… it was gone.

The world stood silent and dead. He hunched on all fours, though he couldn't recall how he'd gotten there.

Slowly, deliberately, Liam pulled himself to full height, stared down at where his new minion had been.

But it was gone.

"Lililililililililililililili!" *Baba* Luna's shrill zaggarete halted the variety show. Heads swiveled to where she stood outside Hollow Hill's entrance; *Phuro* Basil hefted the serving platter of rice and curried chicken with an invitational waggle of his brows. It steamed fragrantly; a stack of flatbread and an enticing bowl of cool, glistening plums stood attendance on the low, round table.

Phoenix barely stopped herself from drooling.

"Ah! That would be dinner," Tobaltio declared with a broad grin

Esmerelda rolled her eyes. "That would be my brother, thinking always with his stomach… when he is not thinking with other things."

"I have been good!" he protested in wounded tones. "I have only seduced four—"

"Including the one with the gold bracelet?" prodded his sister.

"All right, five, but I got that bracelet for you—"

"And the one with the red hair?" Kaya ventured.

"Fine. Six. You see why I must keep up my strength by eating so much?" He put on his best innocent look. It made the crowd laugh, especially when he winked at a lady in the first row.

Phoenix casually baffed him on the back of the head as she advanced to center stage. "While Tobaltio is indulging his appetites, the rest of my Gypsy family will be distributing themselves among you and asking for donations so we can make a charm to cure him."

"Who said I wished to be cured!" Toby protested over the audience's raucous laughter as the Gypsies placed themselves in strategic tip-garnering locations.

Phoe watched with satisfaction as a surprising number of the crowd lined up to hand them money. Tips had been horrible for most of the day—but then, this had been an especially interactive audience. A little of the life was coming back to Pendragon.

Phoenix let herself through the new wooden gate and the round door to Hollow Hill; a wash of cool air and blessed quiet settled over her as she stepped into the concrete dome's sanctuary. Low light filtered through the two round windows screened against unwelcome bugs and prying eyes. Phoenix pulled dollar bills from her cleavage, placed them in the designated wooden chest, and indulged in a moment more of peace before ducking back into the sunshine.

Tremayne nodded greeting as he passed her on his way in.

"Here's a bowl," Ryna offered with a smile.

"Thanks." Phoenix scooped bits of everything into the container and took a spot beside Alaina Dale on a shady bench in the audience seating area.

"It always amazes me how good *Phuro* Basil's cooking looks, even on a miserably hot day," the Merry Maid commented as Phoe dug in with her fingers, glorying in the lack of silverware.

"Oh, *yum*," Niki enthused, plopping down one bench over, a plum in one hand and her bowl in the other. A pale bite-spot showed starkly against the fruit's dark skin. Niki licked the dripping juice off her wrist, and Phoenix watched several patrons trip over themselves at the casually sensual gesture.

"Would you stop giving the normals fantasy material?" Tobaltio griped good-naturedly as he and Kaya joined them.

"Dost thou protest?" Robyn questioned as she, too, sat down. "For, verily, I do not!"

Niki laughed and unrepentantly batted her eyes at Toby.

"Anyone know what happened to the Climbing Tower damsel?" asked Mutch, the youngest of the Maids. "I haven't heard her whiny voice in an hour."

"She quit," Lord Marion put in. "I talked to her on her lunch break; she said she was going insane yelling for help all day."

"And I talked to Patty about how it was distracting from our shows," Little Jen added. "She was amazingly sympathetic, especially when I added that it annoyed the 'guests' more than encouraged them. I don't think they'll hire a replacement."

"Was it?" Phoenix asked, hastily swallowing her rice. "Annoying the patrons?"

Jen shrugged. "Hell if I know. It was annoying me."

"Flicker stopped by earlier today," Tremayne spoke up.

Ryna perked. "Really? Did you talk to him about recording another CD?"

The elder fiddler nodded. "He would like us to be ready by next Monday. He was thinking—"

"Oh, Gypsies!" a frighteningly saccharine voice interrupted.

"Satyr dung," Ryna spat.

Phoenix guessed by the darted glances at Hollow Hill's door that she wasn't the only one with a sudden urge to run for cover.

Too late. The Artistic Director descended upon them, her Pepto-Bismol-pink satin court gown rustling with every step.

"Oh, I'm so glad everyone's here! Um, this *is* everyone, right?" Patty consulted her burlap-wrapped clipboard as she tapped a ballpoint pen against her chin. "I see ten on my notes, and I see ten here! My goodness there are a lot of you."

"What can I say?" Tanek asked, hands spread wide. A suggestive smile curved his lips; Phoenix could feel Charm Magick rolling off him in waves. "Gypsies, we spend much time multiplying, yes?"

Patty dusted off a bench before delicately perching on its edge. "Actually, that's why I came here," she said, suddenly earnest—and apparently immune to Tanek's wiles. She sniffed curiously at their steaming bowls of food. "My, that looks good. Do you mind?"

It would probably be a bad idea to point out that she's stealing food out of the mouths of the actors she's cheated, Phoenix thought as she demurely went to fill a bowl for the fluffbunny. A vivid mental flash from Ryna of "accidentally" spilling the food on Patty's obnoxious pink lap made Phoe suddenly glad she'd taken the chore upon herself. She delivered the bowl with a forced smile.

A frown creased Patty's powdered brow. "No spoon?"

"We Gypsies eat with our hands," Ryna commented tersely.

"Oh." She looked crestfallen, then turned a winning smile to Tanek. "Would you be a dear and go to the food booths right over there to fetch me a spoon? Not one of the ones from the jar out front that've been left out in the air—they're so... so..." She wrinkled her nose. "Have them get me a fresh one from the back. Thank you." She dismissed his presence and turned her attention to the rest of the Gypsy family, completely missing the vulgar gesture Tanek made behind her back.

The look on Ryna's face said she'd sent him a huge mental hug.

"As I was saying, I came here because I noticed you're not entertaining much on street," Patty scolded. "Now, I know it's the first day and all, and it's quite warm out, but that's no excuse."

The Gypsies gaped. Phoenix, noticing the other open mouths, closed her own.

"And I don't suppose our grid would be an excuse?" Tremayne asked with dangerous calm.

"Of course not!" She giggled as if it was the most ridiculous notion in the world. "Now that I've revamped it so that it's so much more orderly, everyone has lots of time off!"

Phuro Basil pulled a copy of the grid from his pouch and showed it to her. "I don't think you understand how our group does shows," he explained civilly. "The dance show requires nearly everyone to be present—either dancing or playing an instrument. The way we had it set up before, everyone had a chance for a break because *Baba* Luna and I had our own shows. Now you've taken them away and increased the number of variety shows, which the entire family must attend. The only show remaining that does *not* require everyone is the fire show, and Esmerelda and Tobaltio, who *do* the fire show, only get the Robyn Hood shows off."

"Exactly." Patty nodded decisively. "There are five shows daily where everyone should be out on street, and four others for everyone except your fire people."

"No offense," Kaya said bluntly, "but we need to rest. Eat. Go to the privies."

"And there is no reason you cannot be entertaining while you do so," Patty rebuked. "Remember, it's in your contracts that you be entertaining between the hours of nine and seven."

Tanek saved them having to answer by arriving, irked but trying to cover it. "They're very sorry, m'lady, but as it's so late in the day, the people at the soup booth aren't willing to open another package. I cleaned off one of the open ones for you, though."

Phoenix got the distinct impression that "cleaning" had involved spit and the seat of his pants.

"That's very sweet of you," Patty said, leaving the spoon on the bench as she stood. "Well, that's about it. I just came by so that we wouldn't have any misunderstandings. You're expected to do street theatre any time you are not on stage. Okay?" She favored them all with a dazzling smile before flouncing off in a swish of pink satin—the Gypsies' food-filled bowl still in hand.

Phoenix flinched. Rennies were creatures of tradition. They were also stubborn, prone to anarchy, and disinclined to do anything they were told... unless they had already decided they wanted to. Even then, they might change their minds on principle. Patty obviously didn't understand that coming in as an outsider, destroying everything they held dear, making demands, taking advantage of their hospitality, and stealing their possessions was the absolute *worst* plan.

Or maybe she didn't care.

"Bitch," Lord Marrion spat when Patty was out of earshot.

"I'll say," Toby chimed in. "Did you see how Tanek's Charm didn't even touch her?"

Tanek muttered something about evil incarnate and plopped down sullenly with his food.

"She reminds me of a junior counselor at the summer camp my parents sent me to every year," Niki mused. "She got fired when they found out that she was always late to breakfast because she spent her nights in the woods with a string of the male counselors."

Phuro Basil grimaced. "If only we could evict this one so easily."

"We could tie her up and dump her in the quarry," Ryna suggested hopefully.

Esmerelda shook her head. "Now, Ryna. You know better than that. Throw her in the swamp behind her precious Secret Garden. Folks will be less likely to find the body."

"Or toss her to the Shadow Fae," Tanek suggested. "No body at all."

Phoenix shuddered at the memory. The other Gypsies fell silent in dark recollection, too—or dark fantasies. Phoe knew she was still a rookie to this whole thing, but the thought that some of her fellow Gypsies might relish such a vision turned her stomach. "Or we could do something really creative and send her screaming into the night," she offered.

"There is always that," Tremayne said pensively. "There is always that."

His simple, contemplative statement frightened her more than the memory of Liam's last moments... Phoenix wondered why.

Here.

It was an impression, more than a word; Liam looked up sharply from concentrating on the marble. He'd gotten nothing but frustrated with it, no matter how hard he tried.

His new minion dropped a familiar staff on the ground three feet away.

Marble forgotten, Liam rose slowly from his seat on *Lady Fortune*'s stage, strode forward, and bent to claim the offering. His love's energy radiated from it, bright and true.

"Someone took Phoenix's staff, too," echoed Ryna's voice in his mind. *"She's trying to pretend it doesn't bother her, but..."*

Liam straightened, pinning the creature with a furious gaze. "Where did you get this?"

The thing blinked sideways at him, made what might have been a smile, and dashed off.

Liam took two steps to follow—

—felt the world shift dizzily around him—

—felt his foot meet nothing but air—

—and then he was curled on the ground with the vague impression that he'd landed hard, but no real memory of falling. Cautiously he rolled to his back, stared up at a dilapidated tree house that, from the stories he'd heard, hadn't existed for over a decade.

Something lurked inside its ramshackle boards. Liam had only enough time to realize that he should leave before it leapt from within its hut, its gray, hairless skin loose and flapping as it descended.

It spoke, its voice strange and crackling. Liam could not understand its words... but he did not need to. Its spindly fingers drove into his soul, paralyzing him as it fed from his vitality. Liam could only clutch the smooth, warm wood of his love's staff... and vow not to scream.

◇ ◇ ◇

"Door?" Ryna heard a voice beg; she opened the portal to see Phoenix, arms laden with precariously stacked plastic containers. Ryna rescued the top half so her love could pick her way up the steps without capsizing.

The raven-haired Gypsy gratefully placed her spoils on the counter. "I thought it was silly to bring so many containers, but now I wish we had more. Apparently no one else believes RFC food is the Realm's Fynest Cooking, either."

"It's first weekend. Not many people have figured out the leftover thing yet. I got a bunch from the ones I hit, too."

"There were a lot of cooked peppers, onions, and barbecued meat—it'll make a good stir-fry." Phoe folded onto the bed with casual elegance, one foot tucked beneath her and the other rested softly on the ground as she gave Karma the requested tummy rub.

Ryna's breath caught. Phoe played her character so well that sometimes Ryna forgot she wasn't as awkward as she pretended. Especially now, after a year with the Gypsies... the stumbling shyness had faded, leaving a quiet, shining confidence in its place.

"What?" Phoenix asked with the flash of a self-conscious smile and ducked her head, peering over the tops of her wire-rimmed glasses.

And then... there were those moments when she was, adorably, herself.

"You," Ryna said, kissing her fellow Gypsy's nose, "are entirely too dangerous when you smile at me like that."

"Like what?"

"Oh, sure, use your sorcerous ways to make me helpless."

Phoenix relented, giggling, and casually unlaced her bodice in a way Ryna was positive wasn't *intended* to be seductive...

Oh, admit it, she thought ruefully, turning to puzzle their foodstuffs into the fridge's limited space. *The way Phoe* sneezes *could turn you on.*

"We going up to the BLUE tonight?"

"Yup," Ryna agreed, trying hard not to listen to the enticing rustles emanating from the direction of The Bed. "Providing, of course, either one of us makes it out of this vardo."

"Oh, really? And why wouldn't we?"

Because I'd rather spend some predictably amazing time with you than risk discovering that the music jams are different, too, she thought, but told the other half of the truth: "Because you're over there undressing with more grace and Charm Magick than you'd ever admit to possessing."

A satisfied chuckle. "Serves you right."

"How so?" Ryna cried, and made the mistake of turning. *Oh, well,* she thought with a checked sigh. *It's nothing my imagination hadn't already come up with.*

"The first night I stayed here, you were over here stripping as if you were the only person for miles, and that music was on in the background, and you were the most stunning woman I'd ever seen—with or without clothes." She quirked an offhand smile as she fastened her bra and reached for her T-shirt with the pegasus on the front.

Ryna gaped.

Phoenix stepped over and slid her arms around Ryna, held her tight. "Ah, Artemis, will you never realize the effect you have on the rest of us lowly mortals?"

Ryna leaned into the embrace, safe and comforted in this love, protected from the turbulent changes of her world. "You, my Phoenix, are far from mortal."

A moment of silence, an extra-tight squeeze, and Phoenix released her. "Come on, Gyps-Fae. Let's go face the dragon together."

* * *

Music swooped in and surrounded Ryna like a warm cloak on a cold Arizona night as she stood in the doorway of the Blue-Legged Unicorn Eatery. Swift tears sprang to her eyes; in the dim light of candles, nothing looked changed at all. The floorboards were rough and worn, but no worse than they ever had been. The tables bore the scars and stains of many years. It even smelled like home: musky sweat and pungent wood smoke, the sweet-sharp scent of alcohol, the particular smell of Pendragon's dirt. The Gypsy bounded through the crowd to join the music jam playing an Irish rebel tune in the corner:

"Curse and swear, Lord Kildare
Feach will do as Feach will dare
Now FitzWilliam, have a care
Fallen is your star, low
Up with halberd, out with sword
On we go for by the Lord
Feach MacHugh has given his word
Follow me up to Carlow..."

Glory, glory, her soul sang as she sailed into the fray with a smooth run of notes, her world sweeping upward with the music. Cheers poured from the audience as the musicians fell into an instrumental bridge with enough energy to capture all but the least observant—or very drunk.

Ryna pounded her frustration into the music. For the space of a song, her soul joined with those of her comrades and all was right again in her world.

Here was music.

And family.

The fiddler's eyes met Phoenix's, dark brown and warm, as Phoe settled at a table nearby.

And love.

◇ ◇ ◇

beep beep bee—

Phoenix nailed the snooze button.

Ryna opened her eyes a crack, muttered a curse, rolled over, and firmly closed them again. Karma, thankful that her person had for once picked the sensible course of action and stayed in bed, purred her approval.

Phoe stumbled from bed, rummaged through the fridge, found some leftover stir-fry, plopped it in the microwave, and pulled on her garb.

Ryna did not stir.

"Artemis?" Phoenix called gently, resting a careful hand on her love's leg. "Breakfast's ready, and you're going to miss Cast Call if you don't get up."

The titan-haired Gypsy rolled onto her back, looked up at her vardo-mate, and said quite distinctly, "Fuck Cast Call."

It was not the language, but the vehemence that gave Phoenix pause. "Excuse me?"

"You heard me," Ryna grumbled as she burrowed beneath the covers.

Phoe stared at her, bewildered. "But last night..."

"Last night was wonderful. There was no Patty. But this morning, there will be Patty, and I'm not getting my ass out of bed at this hour to listen to the Psychotic Director be chipper. I'll be up for first show."

"Um, okay. I'll... tell the others, then," Phoenix said quietly and slipped out the vardo's door into the lukewarm humidity beyond. She wondered if Ryna would find the food in the microwave. She no longer had the stomach for it, herself.

The gravel of the dirt road crunched under her moccasined feet as she huddled towards the Olympic Staircase. A few other faire-folk emerged bleary-eyed from between trailers to join her migration, which encountered its last tributary from the denizens of Tent City.

"Abandon hope, all ye who enter here," a fellow rennie puffed as they ascended the staircase. His garb's bright colors and copious sleigh bells marked him a jester.

Phoenix gave him a wan smile. "I think Patty used the money she took from our contracts to install a set of hydraulics under this thing."

"That would explain why the stairs keep getting steeper." His bells jingled jarringly with every step. Phoenix gave thanks that she didn't have a hangover. If they were anywhere near as bad as people made them out to be, the noise would've been excruciating.

"Still," she said, "it's better than Highland Faire in Colorado. *Everything* is uphill there."

"Aptly named, then."

A largish fellow in a ratty black T-shirt lounged on C-gate's guard couch. He nodded vaguely as she whipped out her pass; Phoe gave him a smile and a wave before snaking through the entrance.

A light fog greeted her, as did the casual bustle of rennies preparing for Cannon. Workers in the Realm's Fynest Cooking booths yelled back and forth. Shopkeepers arranged their wares for the impending customers. Two women in chemises and bloomers meandered down the lane with collapsed hoopskirts slung over their shoulders as a fellow nearby plugged one ear, the better to make out the voice in his cellular phone. A man in a billowing shirt and neon blue biker shorts pleated his kilt on the runway-like jetty of Flying Buttress Stage as Phoenix passed between it and Track's yellow fence. The obnoxious white tent loomed ahead; Phoe skirted it with distaste.

"Where's Ryna?" Toby asked when she'd retrieved her grid and *Privy Councilor*.

"Um, I think she's boycotting Cast Call." Phoenix sat gingerly on a bench beside him. "She, ah, really wasn't in a very good mood."

Tremayne looked thoughtful for a moment, then shrugged. "She needs some space. Don't fret." He gave Phoenix the flash of a smile and a quick one-armed hug.

Phoe smiled back.

"Good morning!" called a nauseatingly chipper voice. "Um, peoples? If everyone could look up here, please?"

Baba Luna snorted. "Here we go again."

Phoenix heartily agreed.

Ryna's coin belt tinkled quietly as she clasped it around her waist. Her conscience pricked her for taking so long to make it on site, but she squashed it as she removed her fiddle from its nest under the bed and set out for Sherwood. *I don't care what that bitch says; I don't have to do anything except my shows.*

Faire site hummed with life. Patrons stared confusedly at maps while their children tugged their pant legs. RFC kids cried their overpriced food. A shirtless pickle boy in battered purple tights and a coin-edged scarf put on a one-man show; Ryna wondered if he would win the award for best entertainment by a non-entertainer. She hoped so. His eye-catching antics almost made up for the silence in Bardstone Hall, where the Three Rogues had played every morning since time out of mind.

Patches had broken the news last night, and even faced with this tangible absence Ryna could hardly believe it. Pendragon without the Rogues... without *Peter*... without his great, rolling laugh and intricate guitar picking... She was glad she had those pictures of her lugging him to Cast Call over her shoulder—though she wasn't sure which was the greater miracle: that she'd gotten his six-foot-something frame off the ground or that Peter had been up that early in the morning.

Another giant fallen.

The Maypole girls laughed as they untangled their ribbons for their first show of the day. She wondered if any of them realized what was happening to the world around them.

Probably not. Or, if they did, it was in that vague way people mourned the passing of a foreign leader or a bygone celebrity.

Ryna sighed and started down the Narrows. She felt old.

One of the tattered Royals Revolting belched loudly; Globe Stage's P.A. system made it echo.

The crowd laughed uproariously.

Ryna hurried along, repressing the urge to throw her shoe at them. *Gods. It's not fair. Their contracts probably pay twice as much as the rest of the cast combined.*

Up the hill, down the hill, right at the Bear, and down some more until Sherwood's shade enclosed her. Robyn and Jen exchanged quips over their lively bout of quarterstaves on the bridge, both sweating despite the early hour. A sizable audience peppered the benches; Ryna swung open the gate in the fence around Hollow Hill and let herself through the circular door in the brick-faced mound.

The concrete interior glowed with candlelight; half a dozen pins protruded from Esmerelda's mouth as she fussed over the bridal gown of the peaches-and-cream woman standing before her. Phoenix watched from a bench nearby.

"... pearls?" the lady asked.

"And little crystals," Phoenix added. "I know it would be a lot of work, Elda, but I could help. It would be worth it for my new sister-in-law."

Ah. Daniel's bride. Right, Ryna realized as the woman in question beamed at Phoe.

"Hello, Ryna," she greeted.

"Oh! Hi! Ryna, you remember Christine, right?" Phoenix looked surprised she hadn't noticed Ryna's entrance.

Ryna wasn't. She had herself heavily shielded to keep her family from suffering her rotten mood. It made her remember Alex's words, though: *"You Bright Ones. Sometimes I think you're all so used to relying on your talents that you forget to look for the stuff we normal people have to live by."*

For the first time, Ryna thought she might be right—not that it mattered. Why close your eyes in case someday you went blind?

"Hello, all." Ryna gave her love a quick kiss. "How was your morning, Phoe?"

"Well enough," she said with a broad smile. "Today is Cheer Up Ryna Day."

"Oh, really?" Ryna raised an eyebrow as she placed her fiddle case on the table.

"Really. After the variety show, we're going to play with the peasants. Apparently they have some extreme amusement planned."

"Not privy packs, I hope. I love you dearly, but stuffing myself in a plastic hut full of excrement and twelve unshowered peasants in this heat..."

"Not even the peasants are that crazy," Phoenix said, scrunching up her nose in the most adorable manner. "At least... I don't think so..."

Ryna's morning brightened considerably. "I can't wait. Elda? Show?"

"Mmm-hmm," she agreed around her mouthful of pins.

"Phoenix, see you at the variety show—you look beautiful, Christine; I can't wait to see it done," she added politely on her way out the door, though she thought wedding gowns were a lot of fuss for a few hours of wearing. Too many fripperies edged out the ceremony's meaning; thankfully she and Phoenix had been joined in their faire garb. Ryna smiled in memory as she ducked through the black curtain to Caravan Stage's left. The familiar campfire, the vardos circled 'round... *that* had been real.

"You missed the non-awardance of GEMs at Cast Call," Tanek greeted bitterly from his seat on the stage-vardo's side stairs.

Ryna halted with her fiddle halfway to her chin. She gazed down at him in disbelief as he picked at the latest hole in his heavily patched shirt. "Not a single Great Entertainment Moment?"

"Nope. Apparently our dear Artistic Dodo doesn't think we're entertaining. Or, at least, doesn't think we deserve recognition. I'd like to see *her* get her pink ass out here and do this all day."

"I for one would rather she kept her pink ass up in Bedside Manor's offices," the fiddler contradicted as she drew a quiet A from her instrument, then tweaked the peg a bit.

"If she was down here, she would see what we go through to make this place great."

"If she was down here, she'd spend more time pestering us." Ryna moved on to the E.

Tanek glared at her. "You don't get it, do you? Can't you see the Shadow Fae's hand in this?"

Ryna laughed outright. "In *Patty*?"

Tanek leapt to his feet, paced to the edge of the ravine, and stared down toward the gazebo. "Open your eyes, Ryna. There's darkness in everyone. *Everyone*." He turned, his expression caught between accusatory and lost. "And you treat it all like a game."

Here we go again with the inner darkness theory, Ryna thought with a mental roll of her eyes. "You're right. It's all an extremely deadly version of Chutes and Ladders. You found me out. So tell me what clued you in, my skipping merrily through hordes of Shadow Fae last fall when Phoenix and I hadn't even been handfasted a full day? Because I tell you, I was sure having fun then. Or wait, maybe it was when we were down south and—"

"You don't have to be sarcastic. *Some* of us take this seriously."

Be nice, Ryna. He's family, she reminded herself firmly, lowering her fiddle. "This is my home they're messing with, too, and you can bet your ass I'll be an anarchist about it. But there are still good bits left, and I'm not going to mope my way through the stuff that counts."

Tanek muttered a few rude words, plopped back down on the steps, and went back to picking at his shirt's hole and ignoring her.

Ryna shrugged and paid him the same courtesy—and moved on to the D string, cheered by her own words and eager for the adventure Phoenix had in store.

* * *

"Do you even know where the peasants are?" Ryna teased as she and Phoenix strode through the games area.

"Not a clue," Phoe answered cheerfully.

The shorter Gypsy grinned, caught in her love's infectious good mood. Her annoyance with Tanek had faded by the dance show's close, though he'd been chill towards her during the ensuing variety show.

Let him sulk—Ryna had better things on which to spend her energy.

A smattering of patrons milled in the privy area near the BLUE—a sure sign of peasant antics afoot, given that half the plastic huts' vacancy indicators showed green.

Sure enough, one of the Jiffs released the Leper—but in a clashing jester's outfit and a party hat.

"Trill!" Phoenix frowned at his staggering gait. "You look like you've got consumption."

"Oh, I've been consuming all right," he agreed heartily—the audience chuckled. "And it's great… C'mon, Pratt!" He lurched past as the peasant with mismatched boots and curling black hair stumbled out, party hat over one ear. By the time he reached the entrance to the privy area, Trill had gone and Puddle emerged from the plastic hut.

"Par-ty! Pud-dle! Blue!" he announced—and glared at the fox pelt puppet as it swayed woozily. "Dead! Bad!"

The pelt hung its nose, dejected.

More laughter from the patrons. A couple more straggled out of their privies and stayed to watch the show.

Next came Hayrold, dinging around with a noisemaker. "Whoo! Some party!" He grinned broadly at Phoenix and drunkenly draped an arm over each Gypsy's shoulder. "You wanna play?"

The herbwoman had her best severe on, but Ryna could tell she was biting the insides of her cheeks. Hard. They helped him stagger out of the privs, to the Drench a Wench booth, and through a secret door that led backstage.

"This way," the peasant said, sober now but still with his arms over their shoulders, veering left to the wall of privy backs.

A mob of peasants clustered around a Jiffy with the tank and rear panel removed.

"I don't believe it—you finished the trick priv!" Phoenix exclaimed, eyes shining.

Pratt of the mismatched boots grinned. "Well, we *did* have ten months."

"One more time through, then on to the next stop on the privy tour?" Piddle suggested.

Phoenix did a double-take. "What happened to your Chrysto outfit?"

"Patty caught me—said it wasn't in my contract." Piddle shrugged. "It was worth a try."

"I'll lock up and take the back way," offered an Irish-sounding lass.

"Sounds good," said Puddle, making a grand gesture to their new prop. "Gypsies first!"

Ryna laughed as Phoenix assumed a drunken stagger and dragged her through the gutted privy. She could only guess at what insanity might follow.

◇ ◇ ◇

A sheathed knife clattered on the wooden boards of Globe Stage.

Liam turned from the Royals Revolting's show and quirked an eyebrow at his lackey. It seemed frustrated. Liam's foul mood brightened marginally. "Problem?"

It wiped its taloned hands on its misshapen legs in a strangely human gesture of disgust.

Liam smiled grimly. "Well, now that I have you, you're going to tell me how to use this damn thing." He held out the marble. Discovering the reason behind the staff—and now the dagger—could wait.

It squatted on the ground, watching the show for a span of moments until at last it scratched something onto the stage with one of its claws, wisps of acrid smoke trailing up from the tortured wood.

Liam peered closely. The lines formed crude pictures.

The minion pointed at the person-shaped one, pointed to Liam.

Liam nodded impatiently.

It pointed at the other, a strange etching that looked like an upside-down four leaf clover with two stems—no, more like antennae. And then, forced upon him, the memory of the shifting, sucking inversion he'd experienced when the minion had used the marble on him… but this time he felt small, weightless, fragile.

Liam started, glared at the minion incredulously. "You can't be serious—I need to cross over, not—"

It interrupted him with an impatient gesture. *Practice.*

Again, more idea than word… but Liam had no doubt of its meaning. He bowed his head briefly. If he must start small and work his way up… if that was what it took to return to his world and escape the torments of unholy creatures that called this place their home...

With a resolute nod, Liam looked up again, a question about the dagger and staff cresting his tongue.

The minion was gone.

Question turned to a curse... but at least he had direction, now.

He picked up the dagger—and went to find a pawn.

"Bless this house and all within; keep them from the clutches of scary people in pink dresses."

"Phoenix! Ryna! Right in time for dancing lessons," Da greeted as the Gypsies wiped their feet and planted kissed hands on the green-painted doorframe.

"That we are," Phoenix agreed. "You need me to play again?"

"No need—we scrounged up a few folks at Cast Call this mornin'," Ma said. "Just dance, if ye'd like."

"And have an apple," Brigid added, handing one to each Gypsy on her way past.

Ryna grinned suggestively and held hers out. "Bite?"

"Temptress," Phoenix teased, taking a sample, crisp and tart.

"All right, you lovebirds, get out there," Auntie Molly shooed, and the Gypsies obligingly put their apples aside and lined up on the lawn.

Torin had captured a patron from somewhere; he escorted her to Ryna's side and took his place next to Phoenix. She had dark hair to her waist, a homespun robe, and startlingly gray eyes. Phoe would've taken her for a rennie if she hadn't been carrying a program.

"She's cute," Phoe commented quietly as her brother's partner and Ryna exchanged pleasantries.

"Yours too," Torin returned.

"You do realize I've forgotten most of the steps," Ryna cautioned.

Phoe gave her a mischievous grin. "We did well enough last time."

Ryna very nearly blushed. Phoenix caught a mental flash of them doing a very different sort of dancing—in the vardo. And then the fiddler wasn't the only one turning funny colors.

Eryn, beside her, gave her a quizzical look—Phoenix was spared providing an explanation by Aunt Molly's appearance, heralding the dance lesson's start.

Memory returned quickly—bounce forward, bounce back, turn by the corners. Soon a few musicians took up their instruments and hands began to clap the rhythm. Voices raised joyous hoots. One time through the forms put Phoe and Ryna at the set's top, bouncing playfully, flirtatiously closer before retreating, and again. Phoe skipped toward her brother's partner, right hand at shoulder-height, and made a quick turn with her in the set's center. Ryna took a turn next, Torin meeting hands with her with teasing gallantry. Then the process repeated with left hands.

Phoe grabbed her corner's hands and pulled her into a semi-adept Irish swing. Ryna and Torin fared better, though Ryna's instinctive reach wasn't quite high enough. It made a smile twitch across Phoe's lips as she bounced forward to link right arms with her love, and turn, and offer a left to the fatherly patron Eryn had chosen for a dance-mate. He looked a bit like Eryn—Phoe wondered if they shared blood ties. Then right to Ryna, and left, and right, and left, down the line until they met in the center for the final time.

Irish Swing. They slid into position without need of thought, a bright jolt of energy surging as right hands met hips and left hands clasped beneath—a circuit completed. Spinning, spinning back to the top, breaking free in unison, trajectory shooting them around the outsides of the lines, the other dancers falling in behind. They met again at the set's bottom, souls touching as they held their hands above their heads in a makeshift arch and everyone filed between with their partners.

Wait a beat, start again.

Meet and part, meet and part. Phoenix could see why dance had been a form of flirtation, once. It still was. Always skipping away, only to return. How long had they done this? Through how many eons had their souls danced? The eternity of it made Phoe's head spin. Perception warped around the edges; for brief seconds it was night, the air chill, and the patrons were in garb, too...

In a dizzying instant everything shifted back to rights. File through the arch. *This hasn't happened yet,* spoke an oddly clear voice in the back of her head. She wondered what it meant.

A last, long note, and olive-green eyes embraced her soul as Phoe bowed, solemnly, and Ryna swept an elegant curtsy.

When at last the musicians toddled off and she and Ryna were enjoying apples and much-needed water in the shade, Phoe spotted Hayrold shaking his amethyst-topped staff at the vinyl tent before continuing to edge around the Post-Parade crowd. He grinned as he toddled up the front walk. "I thought I'd find you here!"

"Peasants planning something?" Phoenix inquired.

"Not at the moment. I have something for you, though. "

"Would you want anything a peasant would give you?" Ryna bantered as he disappeared into Cottage, leaving Phoenix in acute curiosity. He emerged a moment later bearing a thick staff with a knobbly end. Phoe felt her eyes light as she rose.

"I've had it sitting around for a few years—it needed to belong to someone out here, but I hadn't found its person yet. It's not your old staff, but—"

"It's wonderful!" Phoe hefted her gift; it was heavy but well balanced, smooth though unpolished, and the top had an odd way of looking like a face from every angle. First those two indentations formed the eyes, and that little branch-off a nose—but then you turned it, the branch became an ear, and a new countenance melted into view. "What a lot of personality it has! Thank you."

"No problem," Hayrold said, giving her a little back-scritch. She could tell he was pleased. "Well, I'm off—run into you later?"

"You bet. C'mon, Ryna, let's see if we can find some groundscore to decorate my new stick."

*   *   *

Phoenix stared curiously down the haphazard trail to the Secret Garden. The trees held the mystery in their humid shadows; Phoe could discern nothing special about Pendragon's latest addition from her vantage point at the grapevine gate. What was down there that had so many rennies all in a tizzy? Would Ryna side with them?

Probably… in which case she gave thanks that management hadn't unveiled it yet. So far the Cheer Ryna Up day had been a success; her love had gone smiling to the dance show, and Phoe could tell from the feel of the music filling Sherwood that she was happy.

Perhaps it was selfish, but Phoenix didn't want anything wrecking her efforts.

"Well, honey, the map *says* the Secret Garden is here, but I don't see it."

The Gypsy turned to find a fair-haired four-year-old frowning intently up at a gentleman not much older than Phoenix herself.

"Then what's down *there*?" the girl demanded, pointing imperiously at the grapevine gates.

"Oh, you can't go down there now," Phoenix told her.

The little girl seemed surprised to have someone else address her. She stuck her finger in her mouth and cocked her head to one side, but did not hide behind her father's legs. "Why?"

Why indeed—think fast. "Because the brownies are still making things nice for people. They're perfectionists, you see. They don't want anyone down there until they're done."

It grabbed the child's attention, at least. "What's a per-fecs-yon-is?"

Phoenix squatted so she was more of a height with the girl and balanced herself with her staff. "That's a person who won't settle for things to be any less than exactly how they want it."

"Oh, like my brother. He always has to have things his way."

The father's sudden burst of laughter morphed into a discreet coughing fit.

Phoe grinned—as much at the child's escort as at the child. "Well, sort of like that. But it's more like someone who wants things to be the best they can be."

"Oh. Well, that's not my brother, then."

"Perhaps not," Phoenix agreed sagely. "Actually, brownies are little Faeries. Do you believe in Faeries?"

The child gave her a strange look. "Doesn't everyone?"

Phoenix mentally saluted the kid's parents. "If they don't, they should. For, you see, brownies are little Faeries who take care of people—but only when no one is looking. They do chores, like washing the dishes and baking bread. In return, people leave out something good for them to eat."

The girl considered that a moment, sucking on the end of one long pigtail. "So brownies will come and clean my room for me if I put some cookies on a plate? That's like Santa Claus, only better!"

The father's eyes widened with panic.

"Well, perhaps," Phoenix quickly amended, "but only if you already have brownies living in your house. Not everyone does."

"How do you know if you do?"

"Did your room ever clean itself overnight, or when you were out playing?"

The child looked crestfallen. "No. But Mommy does—is *she* a brownie?"

It took a great effort to not laugh. "Probably not; brownies are very small, shorter than a child, even. Don't worry about it too much. Ask your father to tell you about the Tooth Fairy."

She looked puzzled, but scampered off to a parent who shot Phoenix a grateful look before leading his daughter away. Phoe watched them go, the father already explaining the wonders of the first loose tooth.

Was any of it true? Phoenix had only met the Shining Ones, and then only once. True, there had been other creatures out that night, but her memory blurred when she tried too hard to remember. Mostly she recalled pain, and fear, and awe. Black things with claws, winged shadows with talons, brightness and light and wonder, but rarely form.

Did they not wish her to recall—or was the mortal mind simply incapable of retaining something so Other?

Perhaps someday she would have the chance to find out. Until then she could entertain children with the ideas of Faery that mortals had held for centuries... and maybe make a couple parents smile in the bargain.

Ryna glanced quickly around. Phoenix had gone to retrieve something from their vardo in the campground. Elda and Toby were in the middle of their fire show, poor souls, but thankfully fire drew attention. No one was watching her—and morbid curiosity had become too much to bear. The fiddler deftly slipped under the grapevine gate and scooted down the treacherously steep path to the Secret Garden.

She almost tripped twice before she reached the switchback's bottom, safely out of sight. The air's moisture still hung heavy, though at least she had escaped the blazing sun. Ryna wiped the sheen of sweat from her skin and moved further into the trees' welcome shade.

At first the Secret Garden wasn't so bad. The narrow, bumpy path would be impossible to get a wheelchair through—but that could be fixed, and likely explained why they hadn't opened it yet. It *was* pretty in its own way, and she could forgive its engineered-to-look-natural ambiance of bent sapling archways and artfully placed rocks… until she saw the houses.

She recognized them from a display in the Hall of Masters several years previous. They had been cute then, quaint cottages little more than half her height. She had respected their creator's attention to detail in that display setting… but here, nestled amongst trees and brightly colored blooms, they were nauseating.

She supposed they would be marketed as Faery houses, as if the Fae couldn't come up with something better than scaled-down replicas of human abodes. Egocentric, that was what it was. None of the Fae she'd met would even *fit* in one of those houses… not to mention the doors probably didn't work and they were doubtless empty inside. The Secret Garden's creators would be lucky if the Fae didn't take offense and prank them for seven generations.

Frequent signs advertised the greenhouse that had provided the flower gardens; apparently Dicky Darnell had found some poor sucker to donate them in return for their name painted on a few planks of plywood. Ryna snorted. It figured.

None too soon the travesties gave way to a narrow wooden beam over a corner of the marsh. Ropes tied to trees at either end provided crude handrails for the bridge; Ryna wondered if they would really keep someone from falling off.

Up a little path, around a corner, and a rustic bench sat in a sunny patch to the left. The Gypsy shook her head at it and moved on, down a little hill and around the final corner.

Someone had bricked over the side of the dirt embankment—leaving, of course, a couple fake windows and a fake door. She winced, sure its very cuteness had Tolkien rolling in his grave. To make it worse, three concrete ponds and a series of rocks formed the structure for a picturesque waterfall. A wooden bridge spanned the largest empty pool. Ryna quickly crossed it, hurried up the switchback trail (cringing at the blatant view of the crafters' trucks and cars and several booths' unadorned backsides) and snuck back into camp.

Let the others discover the horror for themselves. Ryna had no desire to be the bearer of such disgusting news.

* * *

"Amazing food as always," Ryna complimented *Phuro* Basil after her first bite of saffron fried rice. "You're the best cook in the world."

"Here here!" agreed the smattering of Merry Maids not engrossed in chewing.

The camp elder bowed gallantly from his seat, a twinkle of mischief in his clear blue eyes. "Ah, you only say that to flatter me, my dears."

"No," Toby disagreed as he took his turn in line. "They say it to get fed."

"Hey!" Ryna protested. "I'd come after you for that if I didn't have my hands full."

"That's why he said it, the big chicken," Tanek razzed.

"Oh, *now* who's the big chicken!" Toby teased back. "I'm sure you took note of the fact that my hands are full as well, my friend!"

Ryna grinned, cheered by the familiar banter. Things were returning to their normal swing—or trying very hard. If she didn't look over to Hollow Hill, didn't notice the huge empty spot where their vardo had been, she could almost imagine this was last year and they hadn't a care in the world.

"Yes, my child?"

The titan-haired fiddler turned to *Baba* Luna and the pale-haired wisp of a thing she was addressing. Even from where she sat a couple rows down, Ryna could see the dark circles under her eyes and the bone-weariness of her stance. In one arm she cradled a little bundle of joy—which probably accounted for her haggard appearance.

The young noble shifted the baby, shifted herself, and generally looked awkward.

"Here, let me hold—him? her?—for a moment," Tanek offered, setting down his bowl. "You look tired."

"Thank you," she said, succumbing easily to Tanek's Charm. "Her name's Morgan."

A lot of that going around on the circuit, Ryna thought.

"And what's *your* name?" Tanek asked.

"Emily."

Someone activated an anti-gravity chamber on Ryna's vital organs.

"She's beautiful," he murmured. "To what do we owe the honor of this visit? Is there something we can help either of you with? You can feed her in Hollow Hill if you need a quiet place to go."

"Uh—thank you. Thank you," she repeated, reminded again for some reason to be ill at ease, and finally blurted, "I didn't want to bother you all, but you're my last hope."

"If there's anything we can do for you, it will be done," Kaya assured her, rising. "Would you like some food? We have plenty."

"Thank you… the Bernatellis just stuffed me, though, and I don't think I could eat a bite more." She hesitated an instant. "I'm trying to find her father. His name is William Flynn. Some others called him Liam? Or Xander Thane?"

The anti-gravity chamber malfunctioned. Ryna's organs crashed to her knees. The other Gypsies stood frozen in horror; the Merry Maids prudently concentrated on their supper.

Morgan fussed.

"I'm told you don't have the best relations with him, but I asked the Village Militia and everyone else, and they all said to try you as a last resort, but that you might know. I think I conceived her Third Weekend last year, but I didn't find out until after Seventh, and when I tried to call him, no one answered. I thought maybe he'd gone on a trip, you know? For business or something? And he didn't come back, and he didn't come back, and early June came around, and I had Morgan, and I still couldn't find him, and I hoped at least someone here would know where he went, but he disappeared off the face of the planet and his phone line got disconnected a long time ago and this wasn't supposed to happen."

She looked as if she would have cried, if she'd had the energy. *There but for the grace of the goddess go I,* Ryna thought with genuine sympathy. If she'd been a little less insistent about the condom issue—if Phoenix… from what her lover had said, Phoe might never have even had the option, if she'd escaped from his spell a little later than she had…

"It was that first time, you know how it is? I hadn't known he was going to try for that… we were only fooling around… not that it wasn't nice, but he was just giving me a back massage, and before I knew it…" Suddenly she seemed to realize that the Gypsies were staring. "I'm sorry; I shouldn't—I'm sure you don't want to—If I've offended you, I'm sorry, I'll go, I'm just trying to find—"

Phoenix looked like she was going to be ill. Ryna put an arm around her love's shoulders.

"We understand," Niki said gently. "But I'm afraid there's nothing we can tell you that the others haven't. None of us have seen him since Pendragon ended last year."

A flickering light died in Emily's eyes. "Oh. Um, thank you. I'm sorry to have—I'll—I should—" She reached blindly for her child, which Tanek slipped into her arms. Ryna didn't miss the tears that had begun to spill down her cheeks—or the utter hopelessness she radiated. Even in her worst moments, Ryna had never felt that alone. She'd always had her family, her friends—

"Let us help you," Phoenix offered. "Even if it's just watching Morgan for a couple hours, or if you're so sick of changing diapers you could spit—"

Emily almost laughed at that. "You're so kind to me; you don't even—you don't have to—"

"You're a rennie," *Phuro* Basil said firmly. "We're all family, and anything we can do to help, Lady Emily, would be our honor."

"Thank you—thank you. I have to call my sister; she wanted to know..." With that, Emily wandered off.

Phoenix gazed down at her arms, seemed surprised not to find an infant there. Ryna knew exactly how she felt.

◇ ◇ ◇

"I want snuggled."

Ryna looked surprised at the request, but left her bodice half unlaced, sat down, and patted the bed beside her.

Phoenix gratefully curled up—garb, sweat, and all—in the brightly cold air-conditioning and rested her head on her love's lap. She closed her eyes, trying to shut out the memory of Emily's shadowed, tired expression. She looked so different from the cheerful, optimistic girl Phoe had known in Academy...

What if she and Ryna hadn't gone stargazing after the wolf run? Then there might never have been a battle, and Liam might have been there for Emily and his daughter...

"He started it," Ryna reminded softly.

"You keep saying you can't read minds."

"I can't. But I know you really well, and you try to take the guilt of the world on your shoulders. It doesn't belong there."

"She had my name—her name. Emily. I wonder if he thought she was who I used to be."

Ryna smoothed Phoe's hair with small fingers. "He never would've stayed with them, Phoenix."

"Morgan had his hair. Lots of hair. She's a pretty little thing, all sleeping and sucking her thumb and not knowing why all the adults are making such a fuss. Someday she'll miss him."

"Better that than knowing what he was really like. Maybe some gallant knight will come along and be the father she deserves. At least this way she has that chance."

It was bald truth as only Ryna could tell it. Phoenix felt a little better. "That could've been me. If I'd realized what he was doing a moment later, that would've been me. It sounded like he was in before she even knew it." She shuddered at the words—and the memories they evoked... the darkness of the Croft, the soft, seductive caresses disguised as a benevolent massage, the hazy feeling that she needn't move or speak out... It had been Magick, even then. It frightened her. "I might never have found you."

"*I* would've found *you*. And if you'd been preggers when I did—well, Tata raised *me* on the road. We would've figured something out. And we'll help this Emily out as much as we can. It'll be all right."

Phoenix nodded, heartened by her soulmate's confidence. "I suppose I should let you finish changing into your civvies."

"Only if you help."

Phoenix had the sneaking suspicion that Ryna was trying to distract her.

She didn't especially care.

"Gladly," she agreed with a promising tug on Ryna's bodice string.

* * *

"Aieeee! Getitgetitgetit!" Phoenix cried, launching through their vardo's lace curtain and into the deepening twilight.

"Phoenix! There are moths out there too!"

"I don't care!" she yelled back, heart thumping. "They're not bigger than the flyswatter!"

"Oh, for the love of—"

Phoe could tell Ryna was frustrated. She didn't particularly care. *I don't like things that flap at me,* she thought defensively. *And unlike a certain redhead I could name, I don't feel the need to be all butch when something makes my stomach flop.*

"What's up?" Tanek asked as he sauntered into camp looking rumpled and suave. He took a bite of apple, and had Phoenix been any other woman, her heart probably would've fluttered.

"There's a moth in the vardo. And if you laugh, I'll pound you."

The dancer did laugh, though not at her. "Ryna's rubbing off on you. And for the record, I hate spiders, so I don't have any rocks to throw."

Blink. "Spiders?" It was the last sort of confession she'd expected.

"They skitter—and some of 'em crunch in the tissue when you squish them."

"Should've heard him scream like a girl the first time one crawled up his arm," Toby ribbed from the porch of his vardo.

A fierce whacking from Ryna and Phoe's vardo. Then, "Got it!"

"I was six," Tanek said petulantly. "And Niki told you that story—you weren't even there."

"We were all playing Truth-or-Dare half drunk at our first cast party, if you will remember," Niki retorted primly from behind the lace curtain of her vardo. "Besides, you're the one who brought up my problems with the ladybug ride in second grade."

"She puked on my shoe," Tanek stage-whispered.

Phoenix giggled. If they were trying to distract her from the horror of the moth, it was working. "You puked on his shoe?"

"It might've been all the cotton candy," Tanek allowed as *Phuro* Basil loped into camp with an armload of wood. "Pink, if I remember. Everything she owned had to be pink—and she was convinced she was going to be a princess when she grew up."

"And Tanek was going to be Batman—or was it Robin?"

"At least you outgrew the pink thing—unlike Patty," Ryna commented, lounging against the doorframe in her green satin bathrobe, the moth balanced neatly on the end of her flyswatter. She flicked it toward the fire pit.

Phoenix shuddered.

"Just because you were the first one to see my new Underoos, Niki—"

"Shall we have a fire to celebrate surviving First Weekend?" *Phuro* Basil suggested, dumping the wood near the pit and dusting off his hands. "It's cooled down enough."

"Nice save," Niki joked, emerging in a casual-yet-sexy crop top and wrap skirt.

But then, she could make rags look like a fashion statement. *Must be in the way she wears them,* Phoenix thought. Goddess knew she'd worn some of the same stuff and not come off looking nearly so good.

"Purely selfish save," the camp elder contradicted, crouching to arrange the logs. "There are some things about Tanek's Underoos I'd rather not know."

Happiness swelled Phoe's heart, moth all but forgotten. *How blessed I am to be part of this,* she thought, settling down to build the fire.

◇ ◇ ◇

Liam cursed as his sight crashed back into his own eyes.

Two eyes—one vision... a dizzying relief after the moth's fractured perspective. If only he could stop feeling as if he'd gotten his mind caught in a blender...

The marble pulsed cold in his fist, pulling sickeningly at his soul. It made Liam want to heave into the bushes near the Throne in gamers' camp where he had found the moth.

Still, it had worked...

"You really should get past your hormones. Watching the object of your affections undress does not help your cause," a feathery voice mocked from the gloom.

Liam scowled furiously into the dead fire pit, trying to still the whirling agony in his head. The Shadow Fae were all around him, scuttling in the darker corners, weighing his every action—a pack of jackals waiting for a weak moment. They believed they knew him so well...

Let them think it. Far better that than admitting he'd found it impossible to decipher the world through the moth's eyes, had instinctively flown toward the light of his beloved...

Still, the sight-transfer had worked...

He grinned. Next time, he would be prepared.

◇ ◇ ◇

Phoenix paused sketching for a bite of ramen-and-veggie stir-fry, relishing the spice of *free* that seasoned the RFC food.

Nothing so base as leftovers had ever sullied her birth family's table; her mother only allowed painfully manicured dishes that leapt from the pages of highbrow cookbooks. Christine had teased Phoenix that eventually she would weary of eating endless variations of ramen and food booth scavenge and wish for fancy cooking again, but she had been wrong. In some strange way it had come to represent everything she loved about her new family—each simply themselves, unapologetically, and with a million properties to discover.

For example, Niki's habit of always dressing precisely, even when covered in muck and dirt from working the grounds crew. She rarely donned the jeans or T-shirt in which Ryna lived—it was always an interesting shirt paired with overalls or cargo pants or a skirt.

Phuro Basil's knack at fixing and crafting everything; *Baba* Luna's alchemical talent for transforming junk into art.

Tanek's complete inability to cook anything that didn't involve a tomato.

Esmerelda's patient, meticulous love of history's strange facts and explanations of how things came to be.

Toby's devotion to UFOs and conspiracy theories.

Tremayne, who saw so much and spoke so little.

Kaya's intuition for gifts... she'd given Phoenix magnetic poetry sets, somehow sensing that all her daughter-in-law lacked was the words to arrange. Phoe sometimes thought that she'd said more profound things in the past year with those little synthetic strips than she had in her entire life. She loved to watch Ryna pause by the fridge, checking for new creations.

Phoenix wanted to capture every bit of them, as if making a detailed catalog could somehow explain why they were such a part of her. Her journals from the past year brimmed with ink sketches and tiny handwriting in a quest for understanding—though all she had discovered was love.

Which was, in a way, its own revelation.

Her journals had followed her from her brother's house—they now resided in their own little cupboard. She'd also kept her sun crystal and a small supply of clothes. Her few other possessions were still in her room at Danny's, which he insisted on keeping as she'd left it. Living on the road meant traveling light, but Phoenix didn't mind. She had her words. They were all she'd ever needed.

Another bit of stir-fry, and this time Phoenix doodled a picture of Karma cleaning the pads of her left front paw like a child licking a lollypop half the size of its head.

Daniel had gifted her a set of art supplies and compartmentalized wooden boxes to protect them from the jostling of travel. These utensils were arrayed to her right. The sheaf of sketch paper that comprised her illustrated children's stories sat in a tidy stack to her left. They would be published separately, of course. They would be a raving success, of course.

She would have to find a publisher, of course, and that was the hardest part... especially since she had yet to muster the courage to submit them. Even with her family's support and boundless faith, she still cringed in anticipation of the rejection letters that would come before that one golden acceptance. The more she thought about the cruel, heartless industry of Publishers, Agents, and other Frightening Peoples, the harder it became to write anything at all...

...and the weather looked so nice outside, even if the thermometer *did* read ninety-three and it was probably humid and awful. Maybe Elda needed help sewing the pearls on Christine's dress...?

Sigh. No, no, must be a good bard. Must work. She could help Elda after dinner.

With steeled resignation, Phoenix settled down to her art.

Ryna cursed reflexively as she stuck her finger for the third time. She'd helped Esmerelda since she'd been old enough to sew buttons, but today she seemed better at poking herself than the cloth. She couldn't seem to get a good hold on the damn slippery little pearls, and there were a million of them. Elaborate bridal gowns might be pretty, but Ryna found them utterly annoying.

On the other hand, fripperies provided a blessing of profits for their crafters. Daniel's cheerful—and generous—investment in the gown kept Esmerelda from beading scarves that often took months to sell. Ryna sighed and stared out the window. Even from inside, the day looked sweltering and still.

"You're getting lazy in your old age," Elda quipped.

Ryna made a face. "Not on your life. It's disgusting out there."

"Resenting being shooed out of your own vardo?"

"A little. Phoe needs space to work... she gets so jumpy when anyone else is around. It's not like I ever spent much time there during the day anyhow, but..."

"The principle of the matter?"

Esmerelda could read her far too well. "It was only me for so long, and now having a roommate all the time, no matter how much I love her... Is that stupid?"

That earned a chuckle. "If it is, then so is half the world. Gods know Toby and I tear into it from time to time. He's so flighty—and I know he thinks I take things too seriously. Different reactions to the way we grew up, I suppose, and he can't help that he's an Air Element."

Ryna paused, wondering if her friend would say more. The most she had been able to get out of anyone about Elda and Toby's life before road was that they'd been "in a bad place." Esmerelda had dropped out of school and run off with her little brother after half a season at one of the California faires. She'd taken up hair braiding, face painting, and a score of other low-profile jobs until they could quit hiding; Toby had mostly hired himself out to crafters. Beyond that, no one ever said, and Ryna had been taught not to ask as soon as she'd been old enough to realize that her hodgepodge family had not always been together.

But, as always, Elda shrugged off the memories and smiled in a way that made her look older than her thirty-some years. "How hard is it to stay with someone when things are perfect? But if you love each other enough to stick together even when you get on each others' nerves... and sew ten million damn little pearls on her brother's fiancée's wedding dress..."

"Die, pearls, die!" Ryna cried, skewering another—and her finger. "Ow!"

Both women dissolved into giggles, the seriousness of the moment forgotten.

The elders' vardo looked as if Geppetto's cottage had been run over by a Mardi Gras parade. Carved images of the Gypsies adorned the cabinet doors. A patchwork quilt and throw pillows in clashing colors rested on the bed. An intricately constructed spice rack hung above the counter, filled with neatly labeled bottles. Outlandish magnets cluttered the refrigerator. Spare leatherworking tools and plastic jewelry fraternized on the table. Instead of feeling chaotic, the strangeness and color of *Baba* Luna's homey touches brought warmth to Basil's sedate craftsmanship—and his decorations lent the restful base that showcased her offbeat creativity. They were so different... and yet, they needed one another.

"Things will be all right with you and Ryna."

Phoenix tucked one of the errant tendrils of star-white hair behind her ear and gave *Baba* Luna a small smile. "You see that in the runes?"

She smiled. "I see it in your hearts. Is that what you asked?"

The younger Gypsy sighed, head propped on her hands, and gazed at the marked stones scattered across the silk scarf. "Well... I asked about Danny's wedding and dealing with my parents and all that, but..."

Luna eyed her shrewdly. "Then tell me their answer."

Another sigh, but this time Phoenix folded her arms on the table and focused on the task. She'd gotten better at reading rune stones over the past few months' instruction, but it was still a struggle to remember which symbol stood for what.

"Urus, Ansus, Perth—I'm standing at the edge of a rite of passage, and I have the strength for it, but I'm questioning everything... except that Perth is more about mysteries to be solved... I guess that could be me needing to figure out what to do about my parents. Isa—that's more of me feeling powerless and immobilized."

"And that you need to find out what's holding you there and why," Luna interjected. "Knowledge brings energy and empowerment."

"Gebo—partnership, that's me and Ryna," Phoe continued. "Sowelu, Mannas, Dagas—those are about finding your true self, right? Things won't be the same, but you have to trust yourself."

"And use your abilities. Keep going."

"Hagalas—those are the forces at work turning my world upside down, and Othila is dissolution, change, separation. Ingus is new beginnings and fertility, but it's way over there on the edge of the scarf, so I guess that means it's a long ways off... Odin is almost in the middle, and that's the leap-of-faith stone."

"Unknown Stone—but close enough. You've got the textbook meanings down. Now tell me what they *mean*."

"But—"

"Don't think," the elder Gypsy admonished, tapping the middle of Phoenix's brow. "Feel."

Phoenix closed her eyes and tried to obey, tried to let the stones speak to her. The more she concentrated, though, the harder it became to understand the tuggings at the edge of her consciousness. "It's... dark."

"Stop forcing it."

Phoenix huffed out a breath, frustrated. "I'm wasting your time."

"Nonsense. The runes are a tool—you just haven't gotten the hang of using them for anything except an answer. You'll get there. It might take a hundred more readings, but you'll get there. Now stop concentrating."

The door opened and closed; *Phuro* Basil tromped past the table. Dangerous currents swirled under the still pond of his energy.

"Um... things are going to be really unpleasant, but I'll survive?" Phoenix hazarded, and opened her eyes to see a fond smile creasing his grandfatherly face.

"Phoenix," he said, "you have described a large portion of life."

"Didn't go well?" Luna ventured.

He shook his head, exasperated. "I never actually *saw* Patty, although half the musicians at Pendragon must've been there to complain about their grids. I guess she had most of them scheduled multiple places at the same time—and rarely in their usual spots."

Phoenix nodded. "I think… Marcus was his name?… I think he mentioned something the first day about that, when we were waiting for VilTen to start. He's a musician."

"I heard the mimes are the only ones who got a break," *Baba* Luna said. "Apparently she's got a thing for guys in whiteface."

"And Lancelot the Lapdog," Basil put in. "He eventually came out and told me that her decision on the vardo is final… and that we have to show up for Rehearsals at Bedside Manor on Wednesday."

Baba Luna said a very unpleasant word.

"I should head over to help Elda with Christine's dress," Phoenix said as she gathered her runes. She didn't want to know what the stones would have to say about this latest development. Dealing with her birth family was bad enough… she didn't want to have to worry about her heart family, too.

*   *   *

Rehearsals… the mere thought of attending them tonight made Phoenix cringe. She'd avoided Ryna's tirades about them over the past couple days thanks to Christine's wedding gown, but now, staring up at the enormous sign at the Secret Garden's entrance, the horror of Patty came crashing back home.

A deep breath—Phoenix tried to push negativity from her heart, tried to see past the politics and disappointment, tried to have hope despite the painted pixies frolicking around flowery calligraphy. Tried to see with a rookie's eyes.

Another deep breath—cicadas whined in the soggy air. Phoenix pushed through the familiar grapevine gate and braced herself against the steep gravel trail and the latest attraction.

To her shock, it wasn't that bad. The trails were atrocious, but the woods had a cozy, timeless feel that pleased Phoe immensely. Rather than destroying the natural beauty with human accessibility, the landscapers had cleverly twisted it to their designs… a few bent saplings to form a tangled archway, a lichen-covered boulder for a resting place. It was so beautiful it looked engineered, so natural it seemed no human hand could have created it.

Except for the Faery cottages. They were quaint, meticulously constructed, and a little much, in Phoenix's opinion. And they were cordoned off by ropes that would keep adults out far more deftly than toddlers. Occasional signs advertised the garden center that made possible the hundreds of blooms. *Probably gave the owner a discount,* Phoenix thought. *That was nice of them; it must've cost an awful lot to get all those flowers.*

Another twist, another turn, and Phoenix stepped onto a wooden bridge with a close-up of the view she had admired from the gazebo. *Things* lived in that sun-drenched wetland—things not mortal, though certainly not threatening. The knowledge of them made her soul wiggle and purr.

Up a little more, around a little more, past a bench placed to give its occupants a pretty view, down a little, and a clearing opened before her. Brick faced the hillside to her left, punctuated by small round windows and a round door. A stream of water spilled over rocks on the far side, falling first to one pool, then another, and another. A wooden bridge spanned the third and largest pond, and little rock-lined plots of flowers and miniature vegetable gardens were scattered about like lilies on a pond.

"Now this is more like it," she whispered with a contented smile. A tuft of breeze kissed her cheek in agreement as Phoe found a comfy rock, pulled out her sketchpad and pens, and coaxed inspiration a little closer.

◇ ◇ ◇

Ryna put tingling-bright Magick behind an offhand gesture at her vardo door. It obligingly locked itself with a *snick*. "I can't believe we're doing this," she griped.

Kaya, *Phuro* Basil, and her father were the only ones who looked unperturbed. But then, Kaya and Basil were Water elements—nothing ruffled *them*. And her father… well, he was himself. The others were heartily annoyed, and Phoenix looked like she was trying very hard to be inconspicuous.

"We're trying to get our vardo back, folks," *Phuro* Basil reminded. "We don't want to make any waves. And that means playing along with Patty—for the moment."

The grumbles subsided, also for the moment.

Basil made a gallant, sweeping gesture, and they all trudged off through the heat, humidity, and dust.

A group of rennies swatting mosquitoes greeted the Gypsies on the green outside Bedside Manor. A couple people puffed pipes to keep the pests at bay, and Ryna gave silent thanks that she'd long ago learned how to repel the little bloodsuckers with Magick.

Too bad it didn't work on Patty.

"Wow! We have a *lot* of peoples here! This is *wonderful*!"

Tanek made covert gagging motions. Niki gave him an elbow to the ribs, though by the twist of her lips she agreed with him.

Patches gave Tanek a thumbs-up and sauntered over to join them. "Welcome to our little corner of Hell."

"It's pink," Phoenix blurted at the same time Ryna spotted Patty's frightening blouse-and-pleated-skirt combo.

"That's what makes it Hell," Patches explained.

"It's like a Catholic school uniform gone wrong," Tobaltio murmured in horror.

Phoenix shook her head. "I know all about those. That's worse."

"Really?" Tanek perked up. "Do you still have pictures?"

Ryna glared at the dancer before turning a considering eye to Phoe. Ryna knew her love had done the private school thing, but it had never occurred to her that she'd had to wear the outfit, too.

Phoenix blushed. "I am *not* showing you pictures. And as soon as I talk to him, I'm going to forbid *Danny* from showing you pictures, too. I know better than to give you people that kind of ammunition."

Tanek let out an aggrieved sigh.

Ryna made a mental note to get to her brother-in-law first.

The pink demon clapped her hands for attention, clipboard tucked under one arm, eyes sparkling like a cartoon character's. "Okay, peoples! Let's all stand in a big circle, okay? Big circle, come on, make room for everyone."

The assembled rennies shuffled into an amoeba-like ring. Patty frowned—but didn't push it. *Good girl,* Ryna thought with narrowed eyes and a thin smile.

"Wonderful! Great job, everyone! Remember, this is the *only* time you should *ever* be facing into a circle with your fellow performers. Anyone want to tell me why?"

"Because performer donuts are *bad*," called a mockingly innocent voice. "They leave out the *guests*!"

"Wonderful!" Patty exclaimed, making a note on her clipboard. "It's so nice to see you're learning from our little Rehearsals. Now—I want you to close your eyes—oh, I'm so anxious for this! The Royal Shakespeare Company does this exercise before every show; it develops communication skills and teaches you to trust your fellow actors and get in tune with the group dynamic." She took a deep, cleansing breath and beamed around the amoeba.

Ryna thought she might vomit.

"Okay, okay, okay now peoples, everybody close your eyes. Close 'em!" Patty waved her hands as if this would get the point across faster. It made her look like an agitated hummingbird. "Got them closed? Now we start at one and count up. People randomly call out a number. The goal is to get as high as we can—but if two people call out the same number, we have to start over."

"Doesn't it teach us to keep our mouths shut so we don't have to go back to square one?" queried a man's voice from a few people down.

"Of course not! It teaches… unity." She said it like a Holy Word, then followed it with another cleansing breath. "Unity. I'll start. One."

"Two," *Phuro* Basil offered from a little way down the line.

"Three," called a lady promptly.

A pause. Then a man voice: "Four."

"Five—"

"Six!" two people cried.

"Oops! Start over. One."

"Two."

"Three—"

"Four!" The same man. Now that she'd heard the voice a couple times, Ryna thought it might be one of the Bernatellis.

"Five," tried three voices.

"One.

"Two," leapt in a whole chorus.

"One."

"Two."

"Three."

"Four." The Bernatelli—Antonio. And two others.

A long pause. No one wanted to get caught. Two people got tired of waiting. "One."

"One."

"Two!"

"Thr—"

"Four!"

"Dammit, I want to do four!"

"Four's mine, I say, mine! Bwa-ha-ha!"

"Fiend!"

"Cad!"

"One!" yelled Patty. "Peoples, one! Let's have some unity here!"

"Two!" bellowed *Phuro* Basil.

The circle turned and stared at him in shock. Ryna couldn't believe her ears. Things had just been getting entertaining!

Basil smiled, cocked his head to Patty—her eyes still closed—and then pointed around the circle sequentially. Comprehension dawned across the other rennies' faces.

"Three," said the person next to him.

"Four," added the one next to her, and the numbers began to fly.

"Five!"

"Six!"

"Seven!"

Ryna peered through slitted eyes and smiled. Fine, they'd play her stupid game.

"Eight!"

But they'd play it by their own rules.

"Nine!"

And they'd win.
"Ten!"

*　　　　*　　　　*

"Well, that's it for today!"

Ryna almost had to hand it to Patty. Despite looking frayed around the edges, she had a grin plastered across her face. In pink lipstick, of course. Ryna wondered if everything that touched her turned pink.

"You can all go home now, and I'll see you bright and early on Saturday! Except for your people, Basil. If you could wait for me over by the stairs to Bedside Manor while I finish up one teensy-weensy bit of business…"

Phuro Basil gave her an admirably courtly nod and herded his family to the appointed place. Several rennies gazed at them in deep compassion.

"Wow, she's holding up really well," Kaya murmured.

"Yeah," Toby agreed. "It's going to make my job harder."

"Harder?" Phoenix echoed.

Toby shrugged. "Trying to figure out what it would take to make her go ballistic—preferably in public. Going to take more creativity than I thought."

"That's my little anarchist," *Baba* Luna said affectionately, and pulled him down to kiss the crown of his head.

"I think she serves the Greater Demon of Annoyance," Tanek muttered.

Elda shook her head. "Impossible. The others killed that one."

A smile twitched Tanek's lips. "Makes sense."

Ryna leaned against one of the lions flanking the stairs. Funny how tame it looked, staring blankly through molded eyes. No pools of endless black, no eldritch voices chanting grim songs. Hell, the thing didn't even have teeth.

Still, she had to work to banish the notion that she could feel sentience beneath the plaster and flaking grey-blue paint…

"Oh, thank you so much for waiting!"

Ryna turned from the once-living statue to something far more sinister.

"Who's in charge of your costuming?" she asked *Phuro* Basil. "Do you do your own?"

Esmerelda stepped to the fore. By her stiff stance and shuttered expression, Ryna could tell she was braced for battle. "I make most of them, though everyone designs their own from my historically accurate resources."

Preemptive justification? Yup. Definitely braced, Ryna thought with a wry smile.

"That's nice," Patty oozed condescendingly. "But I have to wonder if they're a little *too* historically accurate, don't you think, dear? People in America think of

Gypsies as showing a bit more skin—I'm sure you've heard this before from our guests."

"Patrons," Tanek and Toby muttered defiantly. If Patty heard them, she didn't let on.

"We want to give the people what they expect, and what they expect is a little more pizzazz. Sequins or something."

Ryna thought Kaya might choke. "*Sequins*?"

"You can do that for me, can't you?"

Elda's eyes bored directly into the Pink Pestilence's. "Let me get this straight, *dear*. You want me to entirely re-outfit ten people before next weekend?"

Patty smiled as if at a particularly bright child. "That won't be a problem, will it?"

"Yes, in fact, it will," Elda spat.

Ryna's eyes widened. Esmerelda was a Fire element—and had a temper to match. Thanks to a lesser talent in Earth she usually kept it under wraps, but angering her was still an enormously bad idea.

Phoenix looked like she wanted to hide. Ryna squeezed her love's hand, thankful they were both well out of the blast pattern.

"Well, I'm sure you'll figure something out. You rennies are a resourceful lot," Patty enthused, fluttering innocent "of course I'm not asking too much" eyes.

"But our bank accounts are not," Esmerelda countered harshly, unaffected by the display.

Phuro Basil tried to step in diplomatically. "We do this for a living, and as I'm sure you've noticed, it's not quite enough to support even—"

Esmerelda ran him right over. "Every one of us has to scrounge for jobs during the week days so that we can continue to show up and entertain your precious *guests*. My particular job is sewing clothes and costumes. For a living. Even *if* I could outfit ten people in two days—which, by the way, I cannot—it would take away from the money that's going to keep me from starving to death. Beyond which, if you haven't noticed, fabric costs money. So yes, it is a problem—unless, of course, you were planning to reimburse me for time and expense."

Patty sighed the sigh of one who is greatly put upon by irrational artist-types. "No, no, it's clearly written in your contracts that suitable clothing is the responsibility of each actor." She sighed again. Ryna wanted to choke the living daylights out of her. She doubted she was the only one. "I'll just write it in your contracts for next year that I must personally approve your outfits. In the meantime, you can go up to the Costume Shoppe after Cast Call on Saturday, and I'll make certain the Costume Director has something all set for you. Does that sound reasonable?"

Rage burned down Esmerelda's link like tumbling lava.

"Perfectly reasonable," *Phuro* Basil soothed, stepping between Elda and her target. Kaya surreptitiously laid a hand on Esmerelda's arm, soothing energy flowing like a river around her as the dancer gently pulled her back.

"Then it's all decided! It's always so wonderful to work with you peoples. I'll see your sunshining faces on Saturday!"

A tense moment reigned as Patty walked away. Ryna more than half expected Toby to Magickally put something large in her way so she'd trip over it... and felt a profound disappointment when he did not.

"I cannot be*lieve* that *bitch*!" Elda finally burst out when Patty was beyond earshot.

"Oh, yeah. Somebody needs to blow her balls out the cannon." *Baba* Luna seconded.

"Oh, is that why it didn't go off Sunday night?" Tanek asked. "Her balls gummed it up?"

"Let's put it behind us," *Phuro* said with a sigh. "We're safe for this year, at least, and I'm hoping she'll be gone by the time next year rolls around."

"Only six weeks to go," Tremayne reminded, and another little piece of Ryna's world curled up and died. If even her father was counting down to Final Weekend, what hope was there for any of them?

One of the statues?

Liam turned to his minion as his vision returned to his eyes. The transition still twisted his innards—but at least it lacked the pain he'd experienced with the moth. Inanimate objects lacked the mobility of living pawns—but they were also less likely to meet an untimely death at the business end of a flyswatter. "I wanted to see if it could be done."

It looked at him strangely. Images came to him again, this time of the Bear and the lions near Bedside Manor, their eyes sparkling with the unholy intelligence of the Three.

"They inhabited the statues," Liam corrected. "This is different."

Different. It paused, as if tasting different ways of phrasing its thoughts. *Mortals put strange cages on possibility.*

Liam bristled. "I notice it's been a few days since you brought me any presents. The Bright Ones too powerful for you?"

It blinked resentfully at him. The splat of emotion Liam received reminded him for all the world of a petulant child. *Like to see* you *try.*

"I have more important things on which to focus. If the Three wanted me to do it all myself, they wouldn't have sent you to step-and-fetch, would they?"

It subsided, though glowering.

PALIDYN 03

Liam turned back to the marble, still and cold against his palm—though even now its surface swirled and shifted improbably. He hadn't known the worn lion statues outside Bedside Manor would show him anything useful—he'd mostly been practicing for the sake of practice. The fates had been with him, though, and he'd learned a little more about the problems his enemy faced. Now he needed to devise a way to encourage their discontent. If the Bright Fae took strength from the return of the rennies, the Shadow Fae should gain strength from their unhappiness.

And that would bring him home.

In the meantime, he needed to find his pet. The damned thing had been absent for days, now.

And Liam was hungry.

The park looked pretty in a Victorian picnic way—lots of trees to shade the tables and benches from the blistering noonday sun—but otherwise utterly unremarkable. "Where are we?" Ryna asked as she climbed out of the truck.

"You'll find out when we get there." Phoenix took the redhead's hand and tugged her toward the tree line, where crumbling concrete stairs descended the embankment. The rubble—along with leaves and seed pods—littered the steps. Vast sections of the pipe that served as handrails were missing, and the limestone walls that anchored them were in only slightly better condition than the stairs.

Ryna liked it immediately.

"I used to pretend this was part of a lost civilization," Phoenix said as they started down.

"Ever find any ruins?"

"Only the creek."

"Pity." Ryna grabbed the rusty handrail—thankfully there was one, here—as her loafer slid on the debris.

"You all right?"

Ryna kissed the hand that shot out to prevent her fall. "All part of the adventure."

Phoenix grinned. Ryna loved it when she did that.

At the stairs' end (and boy, there were a lot of stairs!) a giant slab of limestone lay weathered and broken, as if the last steps had simply disintegrated. The scent of wet earth clung to Ryna's nose; the quiet swoosh of flowing water perked her ears. "Lead on."

Phoenix did, following a path hardly worth the name. It led them first forward, then to the left. The stream lapped over the trail in places, but Ryna trooped gamely on, enjoying the soft dirt beneath her shoes. The Fae lived here, wild and just out of sight. "You're sure there aren't any forgotten ruins back here?"

Phoenix laughed and dodged a low-hanging tree branch, her night-black braid swinging merrily against her back. The leaves of the undergrowth swayed in her passing, left a cool, green feel against Ryna's skin as she followed. Tiny red berries hung like miniature embers from the brush nearby.

The trail grew marshier until at length a brown plastic walkway replaced it, protecting feet too delicate to get wet. Ryna glowered at it. Trust humans to build such an obnoxious road through Faerie. They hadn't even shown the decency to use wood! That, at least, would've rotted away with time and the neglect that had been shown the rest of the valley.

Ryna sighed. At least there weren't any dumb little houses like in the Secret Garden.

After a time the walkway gave way to a wide, well-groomed path; a wooden bench nestled against the timberline across from an elegantly simple limestone bridge.

"You don't want to go on the other side," Phoenix warned. "The road's wide enough to drive a truck through."

As if on cue, the loud beeping of a construction vehicle rent the peaceful humidity. Ryna looked longingly back the way they'd come.

"You'll like what's at the end, trust me," Phoe coaxed.

Ryna did, though the signs of civilization increased. Retaining walls of limestone funneled the water where humans wished it to be, keeping safe their precious paths. To the left, massive limestone slabs tumbled broken against the slope as if some angry giant had hurled them from the opposite shore. Concrete blocks imitating a split-rail fence kept the embankment's earth from encroaching onto the path, now a dirt road. The rushing water became a roar as they reached another bridge, and this time Phoenix steered Ryna across it and up some stairs in considerably better repair than the ones they had descended.

"There," Phoe said, turning Ryna to the view-station's railing. "Minnehaha Falls."

Ryna looked. She had seen spectacular waterfalls in her time.

This wasn't one of them.

She had to admit it had a nice energy—the same way a panther in a zoo had a nice energy. Still, if she reached out, she could almost feel the place's memory for a time without pavement. She could tell by the distant cast to her love's eyes that Phoenix could feel it as well—probably stronger than she herself could. They stood in silence until a mother and her three boisterous children joined them. Phoenix simply smiled and led Ryna up the last of the steps.

The shorter Gypsy tried not to scrunch her nose. The park looked even more groomed here than it had at the wild end before they'd descended the stairs. Fake cobblestone paved the streets, although at least the low fence along the embankment was made of real river rocks. A cluster of people stood down the creek a ways. "What's over there?" Ryna asked.

Phoenix led her to a boulder affixed with a giant brass plaque. The plaque read:

Hiawatha and Minnehaha
By Jacob Fjelde
Erected in 1911 by means of funds
Raised through the efforts of
Mrs. L.P. Hunt of Mankato
And contributed principally
By the school children
Of Minnesota

Ryna stared at it, nonplussed, then looked around to see if it had a purpose.

The plaque's reason for being caught her off guard. Nestled among the trees on the opposite bank stood a statue of a Native American man with his lady in his arms, poised to chivalrously carry her across the water. The sun glinted off their dark copper hair; Ryna couldn't help the vague impression that in a moment he actually *would* take that next step… she glanced up to see her love pale and wide-eyed.

"It… shimmered," she whispered.

One copper-red eyebrow crept up. "Shimmered?"

"Like—I could actually see…" Phoenix tore her attention from the statue. "Never mind. I'm all right. Really. You want to grab some food before we start back? They've got the best peach ice cream, with chunks of real peaches—and hot dogs. Not in the ice cream, of course. There's something wonderfully processed about hot dogs, don't you think?"

The fiddler tried not to stare at her love as if she'd gone utterly mad. "Peach ice cream sounds great," she said as they started toward the visitors' center. Obviously Phoenix wasn't ready to talk about the shimmering yet, and Ryna knew better than to push it. "I read a book about this place once—*War for the Oaks*. A band of musicians got themselves entangled with a Faerie civil war. I guess I didn't really know this place was real."

"You believe in the Fae but not in a waterfall?" Phoenix laughed, sounding more herself. "I really love your world, Artemis. I'd rather disbelieve in waterfalls."

An eloquent shrug. "I'd never been here before. How was I supposed to know it was real? I've still got a copy, if you'd like to read it. Niki's had it for the past year and a half, but I'm sure she's done by now."

"Actually, Danny got me one for my birthday years ago, and I read it until it fell apart. I kept meaning to pick up a replacement."

"Must be fate—we don't need two sitting around."

A wry grin. "There's my practical Gypsy. Hey, you want to go visit my brother when we're done here? I'm sure he wouldn't complain if we hijacked his hot tub."

"As Toby would say, 'Twist my rubber arm.'"

◇ ◇ ◇

Phoenix stretched and sighed, reveling in the clouds of steam billowing around her as hot water pounded the top of her head, rinsing the conditioner from her hair. She wouldn't trade life on the road for anything… but there were those little luxuries she missed, like showers that didn't quit because your quarter ran out, and not having to wear flip-flops to keep from catching some strange fungus.

"Ready for some hot tubbing?"

Phoenix nearly jumped out of her skin. "Couldn't you make some noise when you're sneaking up on me?!"

"Sorry," Ryna apologized, and Phoenix suddenly found herself in the company of a cute, naked redhead.

"Ah—buh—" she sputtered, grasping for coherent thought.

The fiddler cast her a charming, over-the-shoulder smile. "You mind washing my hair for me?"

"Sure." Phoe leaned close for a kiss.

"Ah-ah." Ryna pressed fingers to her love's lips. "Save it for the hot tub."

"Hot tub. Right." Phoenix concentrated on dispensing shampoo into the palm of her hand—and trying to ignore the small, round, perfect person in the shower with her.

Ryna's hair was like—well, seaweed—when it was wet. Everyone's got like that. But Ryna's turned a comely shade of dark red, and there was a wonderful lot of it. Phoe lathered every inch, enjoying its thick weight against her hands, taking care to get the ends by the backs of Ryna's extraordinarily attractive knees. Then came a very thorough massage of the redhead's scalp, ignoring, of course, the quiet "mmm"s and the way Ryna's head tipped back slightly in pleasure.

"Rinse," Phoe ordered briskly, not trusting her self-control if this went on much longer.

Ryna looked entirely too pleased with herself as she turned and stepped back into the shower spray. "Sure you can make it through the next round?" she teased, caressing Phoe's cheek.

Phoenix's eyes fluttered closed, briefly. "No. And that's not helping," she scolded as Ryna sidled up just close enough to brush against her.

"I have to get out of the water so you can finish my hair," she protested, turning.

The conditioner went considerably faster, bringing Phoe to the most dangerous part...

The shower gel.

She nearly dropped the plastic mesh scrubbie-thing twice before she worked it into a lather. Ryna stood infuriatingly still, but Phoe could feel the tension radiating off her in waves as Phoe smoothed the scrubbie over rounded arms muscular from practice with fiddle and bow... over smooth, lightly curved back—suds rinsing down the channel of her spine... over delicate feet and perfectly-turned legs—

Dear gods there was a lot of her for someone so small! She could all too easily imagine that soft, wet skin full-length against hers, the soft *thump* as she pinned Ryna against the cool tile, small lips reaching for a kiss, and the dull squeak of tub floor beneath bare feet as she squirmed under Phoe's loving hands...

"I think that's good," Phoenix got out on a breath.

"You think so?" The redhead backed under the water, pale foam highlighting her every curve as it slid to the shower floor. She reached up and lightly brushed Phoe's ear; the raven-haired Gypsy closed her eyes at the touch...

And snapped them back open in surprise as the water ceased and the shower curtain rattled open. Ryna stepped onto the fluffy bath mat, surrounded in a cloud of fragrant steam. Phoe inhaled deeply, sure that the scent of lavender and lilac and apricot would always remind her of this moment.

Ryna cast a playful, seductive glance over her shoulder as she opened the bathroom door, letting in a frigid gust of air-conditioning. "So, how about that kiss?" she teased—and dashed down the hall.

After a moment of shock Phoenix scampered after her, leaving hair-drips and footprints of wet in her wake. By the time she reached the basement stairs she could hear the water running. Cold cement slapped her bare feet; the plush carpet in the hot tub room felt even more luxurious by comparison. Candlelight flickered over the North Woods mural painted across the walls, making wolves and Fae shift among the trees. Myrrh-scented smoke trailed upwards from a half-consumed incense stick; Ryna must have set things up here before joining her in the shower. No wonder she had been in such a hurry.

"It's deeper than I remember," Ryna complained from her perch on the dais surrounding the tub.

Phoe traced flickering shadows on the shorter woman's bare shoulder. "Nothing says we have to wait."

"Right, then."

Phoenix sighed in pleasure as she eased into the water's warm embrace. "I think I've dreamed forever about sharing this with someone I love."

Ryna stilled a moment, sensing the importance of the occasion. Then slowly, so slowly, she crossed the deepening water, rested one hand against the tub's edge, leaned close.

Phoenix looked up into her love's face, memorizing the elfin curve of cheekbone, the point of chin and ear. One finger reached hesitantly up to trace the familiar contours, to brush lightly over rounded lips. "I'm glad I get to share it with you," Phoe whispered.

Ryna nuzzled the palm of her hand. "I'm glad, too."

And then, gently, their lips met in a kiss full of dreams realized, and hope, and familiarity, and comfort, and love. The urgency of the shower melted away to this moment, this touch. They parted briefly, but Phoe drew her love back to the contact, and Ryna's hand began a slow caress down her side as Phoe reached for familiar curves.

They barely remembered to shut off the faucet.

* * *

"Ry?" Phoenix murmured blearily as Friday morning—well, early afternoon—intruded on her dreams. It took a few moments to realize she was back in the vardo, and alone.

Well, almost alone. A little foil-and-cellophane ball and a yellow scrap of paper rested on the shorter Gypsy's pillow. Phoenix pulled the paper up nearly to her nose to read its message:

Find all eight!
I love you!
(P.S.—Sorry I've been such a pain)

Phoenix grinned and carefully unwrapped the candy, a delicious-looking shade of dark brown. Curious, she bit it in half—the truffle melted into rich sweetness against her tongue. Dark chocolate, even. Phoe sighed in utter contentment and decided not to go looking for the others—it would be more fun to have them surprise her on the way.

◇ ◇ ◇

"What has my dear Ryna been up to?"

"Up to?" The redhead gave Toby her best innocent expression.

Unfortunately, he'd known her far too long—and gotten away with far too much himself—to buy it. He conveyed all this in one arched eyebrow, which Esmerelda echoed.

Ryna grinned sheepishly and relented. "Well, I realized I haven't been the easiest person to live with lately, so I hid a bunch of chocolate truffles in the vardo and left Phoe a note saying it was her job to find them."

Tobaltio gave her a broad hug. "That's my girl!"

Esmerelda sighed, shook her head, and went back to stitching the million little pearls on Christine's wedding dress. "The world could use a few more of you, Ryna."

Concern twitched across Ryna's features as she sat down beside the seamstress and threaded a needle. "Do I need to start looking for date material for you, lady? Celtic weekend isn't for another month yet, but there's never a shortage of kilts. I'm sure I could come up with someone."

She waved it off. "Too much hassle. Besides, three people would never fit in here on a long-term basis. I'd either have to get my own place or kick my darling brother out into the cold."

"Hey." Toby knelt beside his sister. "You know I'd work day and night to make you the vardo of your dreams if you found someone you wanted to share it with—or remodel this one for you and make my own at the same time. This was only meant to be temporary, and you know it."

"I know it." Elda ruffled her brother's hair and gave him an affectionate kiss on the brow, smoothed away the creases with a thumb. "And you're sweet. It's not that important. It always gets me a little when I have to deal with one of these things." She shook the mound of white in a halfhearted rustle. "Speaking of, you were out awful late last night, Ryna—I take it you and Phoe enjoyed yourselves?"

"Or each other," Toby muttered, earning a playful cuff from Ryna.

"Well, other than Phoenix being mortally embarrassed when our hot tub interlude was interrupted by Danny and Christine, who apparently were having the same ideas we were—it was great. All four of us ordered Chinese and ate out of the little white boxes and had a bit too much plum wine for any of us to be driving safely, so Phoe and I cuddled up in her old bedroom and slept it off, then rumbled back around dawn."

Two sets of eyebrows raised skeptically.

"Well, we *did* sleep. Some."

Elda laughed.

Ryna did, too, and wondered why no one had been smart enough to snap up her fellow Gypsy yet.

◇ ◇ ◇

"Mrow?"

Phoenix cringed at the muffled sound. She didn't want to look—but if she didn't, she knew from experience that Ryna's cat would just jump up on the bed with her prize. She steeled herself and looked down.

"Prow." Deposit one entrée—not even twitching.

"Oh, good kitty, Karma," Phoenix praised as effusively as she could. "Have you shown your little mousie to Mommy Ryna?"

Karma meowed proudly to indicate that the present had reached its intended destination. The mouse-thing had been spying on the Gypsies. Now not only was it no longer a threat, it could also be supper. How fortunate for her person's mate that she had joined the family of such a vigilant protector and talented huntress. Otherwise, she would be forced to subsist on those strange wavy crunchy bricks that came out of the crinkly wrappings and got all soggy in water. The little broken bits were fit for batting around the floor—but certainly not for eating.

"Mine? Oh, good kitty. Let me put this somewhere safe." Phoenix ripped off a few paper towels and tried not to think too hard about the day she'd found her mother's Persian on the Oriental rug, crouched over poor little Gerbildini. Her mother's shrieks hadn't been near enough payment for the loss of her beloved pet. And, of course, she'd gotten all the blame for not keeping a tighter cover on Gerbildini's cage… never mind the stupid cat.

Karma, satisfied that her contribution had been properly received, bounded through the lace curtain in search of more prey—and potential threats.

"Oh, look what you've got," Ryna exclaimed as she stepped up into the vardo.

"Lucky me."

"It means she loves you."

"So I keep telling myself. Excuse me while I go deposit this deceased hunk of 'love' in the underbrush." Phoenix tried not to sound peevish. She'd grown accustomed to the calico's very furry and very dead presents—but she still hated cleaning up after them.

"Thinking of heading up to the BLUE?" Ryna asked when Phoenix returned—sans mouse.

"That time already?" She checked the clock. "Yeah, I guess it's getting there. Still a little early, but that'll make it easier to get a table. Just let me clean up a few things first."

Ryna perched on the edge of the bed and very carefully avoided looking at the scattered art supplies. "Anything you don't mind me seeing?"

"Sure," Phoe agreed, mostly because Ryna was always so respectful of her privacy. She passed over a few sheets of sketch paper. "They're only roughs, but they're supposed to be your father."

"Nice. What sort of lighting are you going to use?"

"I thought maybe that slanty late afternoon sort, or maybe firelight. I suppose it depends on whether I want him in garb or in jeans. Jeans seem almost too mundane, but I don't want to be too dramatic." She sighed. "Do you musicians have any idea how hard it is to capture that ecstatic, glowy look you get when you're playing? Sometimes it makes the *dancers* seem easy to draw."

"Sorry," Ryna deadpanned, her gaze lingering on the sketch. "I'll try to be more banal."

"Don't you dare," Phoenix scolded, taking back the paper and kissing Ryna on the nose. "I like you glowy."

"Oh, good. I'd rather not give up Magick. I don't think I can do mundane."

"Lucky for you we'll never have to find out. Grab your fiddle—I'm almost done here."

◇ ◇ ◇

"Damn cat," Liam swore, detangling himself from the bushes where the creature had run for cover while separated from its body. It had taken days to successfully see through anything larger than an insect, and then Ryna's blasted familiar had pounced on his mouse before Liam even got it into Gypsy camp.

"It would pose you fewer problems if that were true…"

The voice caused another curse—though Liam had the sense to keep it silent. Had he known the Three would return so soon, he would have been more on his guard, would have braced for the effects of their presence. Just hearing the First speak made his brain feel as if it had spun in his skull, scraping against unforgiving bone the entire way.

"But you have problems greater than familiars and their meals…" rumbled the Second.

"Such as the ineptness of the spawnling you sent me?" Liam shot, too frustrated to temper his impertinence.

Thankfully, they ignored him. "There are arrangements to be made," shrieked the Third—and before the last echoes of its voice ceased assaulting his eardrums, Liam bristled.

"Arrangements? What arrangements? We made a bargain. I do as you request—breaking up the Gypsies and allowing passage to—"

Their words pounded straight through to his soul with the indisputable force of their unison, silencing him. "You must pick your sacrifice…"

It took Liam aback. "I assumed my freedom would be forfeit if I failed, as it was last time."

They laughed.

"He does not understand…"

"Foolish mortal…

"You must choose another to take your place…"

Take his place?

Dawning comprehension brought a smile to Liam's face. "Anyone at all?"

"One of the mortal-kissers' pets…"

"Choose wisely…"

"The sacrifice determines your success..."

"Very well," Liam said. Choose wisely—as if he needed to consider the matter.

As if he hadn't been considering it for months

"I choose Ryna."

◇ ◇ ◇

"Nugh." The curly-haired mandolin player from the Highwaymen plopped gracelessly on a spare seat. Night had finally enfolded Pendragon, and the BLUE was in full swing. "I am *so* not looking forward to this weekend."

"Oh, Nora, Nora, tell us how you really feel," teased Jug o' Punch's burly bodhranist. He swigged some Guinness almost as dark as his hair and beard. Phoenix had no idea how he could endure the stuff.

"Stuff it, Jerry," Nora warned. "Some goddamn patron swiped my mug off my belt on Sunday."

Everyone at the table winced. The leather mugs that nearly every rennie carried were *not* cheap, even for the plain ones—and Nora's sported complex Celtic knotwork.

"Ow. Did you tell Mac?" *Phuro* Basil asked. "You know he keeps a record of all the mugs, right?"

"I'm planning to tell him this weekend," she informed them. "I didn't notice until after Closing Cannon, and by then he'd already packed up and left. I needed to bring it in for a reseal anyhow, so maybe he'll catch it then."

"You know, I ran into Mother Goosed around noon yesterday—Sunday." Patches shook his head at the slip. "Yesterday by rennie time. Anyway, you know that pretty, carved-up staff of hers?"

"Oh, no," Kaya said, eyes wide. "Don't tell me they got that, too."

"She's had that since her rookie year," Tremayne said quietly, "and Ryna was barely starting to walk then."

Nora looked positively ill. "Suddenly I don't feel so bad about my mug."

"Or me about losing my staff," Phoenix seconded.

"You lost your staff?"

"Yeah," Phoe said with a sigh. "Somebody took it during VilTen. Hayrold gave me a new one, though, and I almost kinda like it better."

"Tanek's boot knife disappeared, too—I think it was Sunday morning," Niki put in.

"I guess that explains why he was so cranky." Ryna sighed. "I suppose we were about due for another one of those years... figures it would land right when we have enough other problems to worry about."

"Any progress on reconstructing the vardo?" Jerry asked.

Phuro Basil blew out a disgusted breath. "No. But not for want of trying. I sat in Patty's office for two days, and all I got was some cheerful bullshit from one of her flunkies that could best be summarized as 'when the Royals Revolting work for free.' And I got told that we have to go to Rehearsals."

"Going over her head next?" Nora asked.

The elder shrugged. "I'll try. Even odds says they back her up."

"All is not lost, though," Niki piped up. "Working on site crew does have some advantages. It turns out that they took special care to keep the parts as undamaged as possible. I know where they took them, and as soon as we have the go ahead, we can bring the stuff up and put it back together."

"Of course, that still requires getting the go-ahead. Gods, this is so depressing. Let's go play some music." Ryna stood. "Anyone with me?"

"All the way," Nora seconded, grabbing the beat-up case that housed her mandolin. "Jerry?"

He grinned broadly and tippered out a rapid succession of beats on his painted drum.

Phoenix leaned back and sipped at her cider. A sparkle crept into her soul as she watched her friends limber their babies. What a wonderful place the world was, when the worst of your troubles could be chased away with good friends and a song.

Pendragon Renaissance Faire

Weekend Two: Much Ado In Our Fair Hamlet

~*~

Thee charmes of the greate barde himself do nowe grayce a celebratione of thee highest calibre. Witnesse stage theatre and village performers, as the whimms of whimsie compelle them to honorre thee Masterr Shakespearre in storie and sonng. Ye Olde Calligraphers and Prynt shoppes doo extol the vyrtues of thee writtenne word. Seee lyfe throughe thee eyes of the six-teenth centyry peasant as you enjoy a fyne turkey legg. Huzzah! (Theme sponsored by Little Globe Theatre and Barde's Books)

~*~

beep. beep. be—

slap!

"Oh, no you don't," Ryna grumbled.

"Burrrr," Phoenix complained, hauling the alarm clock up to her nose. They'd gotten the one with the largest display in deference to her lousy eyesight, but the temperature reading still eluded her at distances greater than a foot. "It's not even sixty in here, Ryna."

Ryna nestled further under the covers. "Not that I'm complaining after last weekend, but I *really* don't think it's supposed to be this cold in August."

"I'm beginning to see the merit of skipping Cast Call."

"So don't go."

Phoenix sighed—and missed Ryna's motivating influence. With a supreme effort of will she dragged herself away from the nice warm bed with a nice warm Ryna in it and dug their electric space heater out of the closet. The little brown box, once plugged in, whirred industriously to life.

Karma purred rapturously, every calico hair vibrating, as she set about giving her right front paw a good nibbling. *Some* cats might be willing to sleep on the cold ground, but *she* for one preferred something a bit more civilized. That was one benefit of bonding with a person: they made certain you had a soft, warm place to nap—a more than fair trade for keeping them safe and sharing some spoils of the hunt.

Ryna, after cleaning her love's glasses so she could actually see out of them, kindly held Phoenix's clothes in front of the heater to toast while Phoe threw a couple sausages in the microwave, then scrambled into her garb with shivered thanks. Dressed and fed, Phoenix tucked her vardo-mate snugly under the blankets and kissed her—and Karma, who must not be forgotten—farewell.

The air outside hit her like a corpse's fist, clammy and chill. Phoenix walked briskly, wishing she had thought to unbury her cloak. Other rennies cussed under their breath (or at the top of their lungs) as they emerged from their sleeping quarters… though from the sounds of it, the folks in the loud sex tent were keeping each other quite warm. She thought she heard a yelp from one of the privies, too, and gave thanks that she had no need to visit Harvey, the privy monster.

Phoenix's boots remained dry for exactly as long as it took to get through C-gate. The dew on the grass happily transferred to passing feet, soaking both suede boots and socks by the time she reached Bakery Stage. The sparse crowd assembled for Cast Call munched gloomily on fruit from Styrofoam bowls. "Where'd the food come from?" Phoenix asked her fellow Gypsies.

Tremayne, Toby, and Tanek pointed with their forks to Bakery Stage. Phoe thanked them and joined the clump of rennies clustered around one corner of the stage. Jumbo-sized chunks of pineapple, cantaloupe, and watermelon filled plastic containers beside a stack of picnic forks and Styrofoam bowls. A brown, industrial-sized coffee dispenser hunched on the other side with its attendant tower of cups. Phoenix helped herself to everything except the coffee, then went after a copy of the *Privy Councilor* and the grid.

"Good morning, peoples!"

Grunts greeted the announcement. Phoenix darted a glance up to see a little crease in Patty's Barbie-perfect brow.

"Ooo, didn't like *that* much, did you sweetums?" Peyton muttered, checking the bench for stray objects and spills before sitting.

"Pey!" Phoenix greeted her lanky friend with a warm hug. "How've you been? We didn't see you last weekend."

"It took this long for me to get my contract, thanks to—"

"I *said*, good morning peoples!" Patty looked very near to stamping her foot.

"Good morning, Patty," a few rennies chorused with exaggerated cheeriness.

A perky smile bloomed across her face. "That's better! I hope you're all enjoying the fruit and coffee we arranged to have up here for you."

"If she thinks it's going to keep us from heckling, she's dead wrong," *Phuro* Basil commented between bites.

The other Gypsies and Peyton grinned at him—also between bites.

"Nice use of our contract money," an indeterminate voice called.

Patty seemed not to notice. "Well, let's start with announcements, shall we?" she enthused, then stepped back and motioned the first person up—a slightly portly fellow with a graying beard.

"Good morning!" he called, military sergeant style.

"Good morning!" the cast replied—much more enthusiastically than they had for the Artistic Director. Phoe wondered if Patty would fire him for that.

"I play the Sheriff of Nottingham out here. I know you vets know this, but just as a reminder to you all—and especially for the rookies—the cannon up on the hill is a piece of live artillery!"

"Not last Sunday it wasn't!" someone jeered from the audience a few chuckles went up.

Peyton quirked an inquisitive eyebrow.

"Cannon didn't go off last Sunday," Tremayne told him.

"Somebody tried to blow Patty's balls over the parking field," *Baba* Luna said, shaking her head ruefully. "Too big. They stuck."

Peyton almost nosed his food. His eyes teared as he choked and spluttered. "Pineapple. Ow."

The sheriff continued, unphased by the drama in the Gypsies' section. "We have to put real gunpowder in there, and we use real fire to make it go off. *Please* don't play around with it or put your garbage down the barrel. If you see someone messing with it, tell myself, one of the Militia, or one of the Bernatellis. This is a safety issue—please, take it to heart. Thank you." He stepped down the stairs at the stage's front to smattered applause.

"Top o' the mornin'!"

"Morning, Da!" several people called—many more let out cheers, Phoenix included.

"For anyone who doesn't know, Irish Cottage's table has gone missing!"

Astonishment and dismay rippled through the audience.

"B-gate!" someone yelled.

Da laughed. "Actually, you know, I think we've checked everywhere *but* B-gate. Anyway. We love our table. We miss our table. We *really* want our table back. If you or anyone you know even has an *idea* of where it's gone, *please* come talk to Ma or myself! Thank you!"

"Their *table*'s gone?" Peyton asked, dumbfounded, as Da stepped down. "Who would take Cottage's table?"

"It's not the only thing that's been stolen this year," Tanek said, "but I think it was the first. Didn't you say your brother found it missing when the O'Malleys went to clean out Cottage, Phoenix?"

"That's right," Phoe agreed. "They left the benches, but they took the table. The O'Malleys looked all over for it, too."

"Um, hello? Everyone? My name is Emily—"

"Hi Emily!" a chorus cried, and Phoenix's heart bled for her Academy-mate's obvious discomfort.

"—and this is my daughter Morgan."

"Awwwwwww..."

"What? Oh, she's ten weeks," she replied to an unheard question from up front. "Anyway, we're looking for her father. His name is Liam Flynn, and he played a member of the Village Militia named Xander Thane. He's not here this year, and the contact info he gave me is wrong. If you have any idea where he is or where he went, please, please—" She shook her head, swiped at her nose as she sniffled, and took a couple gulping breaths. "Please, I just—I need to find him."

"If we really were her last hope, she's in *major* denial," Esmerelda observed quietly as Mama Bernatelli stepped up, put a comforting arm around Emily's shoulders, and led her up through the door to Bakery's interior. Sympathy and outrage grumbled through the cast.

"Poor kid. Hey, where's half-pint Gypsy?" Peyton asked as somebody from Marketing stepped to the fore.

"Boycotting Cast Call on account of our Artistic Disaster," Phoenix told him. "I think she's developed an allergy to pink."

"Lucky her," *Phuro* Basil said. "I get to go deal with the Costume Nazi after this and see what wonderful little surprise our Artistic Deflator has left for our lovely dancers."

Phoe winced. She'd forgotten about that.

"Louder! We can't hear you!" someone shouted from the second row, unsurprisingly; Marketing personnel were known for their inability to project.

"They're holding a new Shakespeare-themed contest/game at Flying Buttress Stage, and they need contestants and crowd-wranglers. Talk to her if you're interested!" Lancelot bellowed on her behalf.

"Is there any compensation?" someone yelled from the crowd.

The marketing lady shook her head at Lancelot; he translated: "Marketing's undying gratitude."

"A pity they fired the stage crews," Tremayne observed.

"I hope no one shows up," *Phuro* Basil said. "It might teach them a lesson."

A few more announcements followed—notifications of an impending fencing tournament, costume contest, and bloomers competition; a reminder to drink water.

"And eat more fruit!" Patty chimed in cheerily.

A few of the more prominent "fruits" got up and did little boogies; Peyton climbed on a bench and called, "Oh, *stop*!" in his most flaming attitude.

Patty frowned. "All right, settle down, peoples. It's almost time to sing, and—"

"ORT! ORT!" the audience prompted.

"POT! POT!" cried the peasants.

Patty's eyes widened comically—Lancelot rushed up to whisper something in her ear. She frowned. "*Peasant* Official Time?"

"POT is eight-twenty-ish!" cried a voice Phoenix recognized as Hayrold.

"*Official time* is *eight-twenty-three*," she announced emphatically, looking like she wanted someone to chastise but unable to discern who'd spoken up. "And we've got a special guest conductor today, so everybody switch for the sing-along!"

The crowd's energy surged with hope, rennies shuffled up to the stage like horses anticipating dinner. A fellow of medium height and gray hair took the conductor's perch on the bench directly left of the aisle and four rows back. He stood with the almost vibrating attention of a terrier

"Swing low," he sang out crisply.

"Swing low," the rennies replied in joyous unison and (almost) perfect pitch. This conductor was one of them. For him, they would pour out their hearts. He took the musical gift, held it, shaped it—lengthening a word here, quieting the song there, throwing in an occasional staccato for emphasis until the first verse ended in a whisper.

"In the spirit of Shakespeare weekend, I say unto thee: Yay, verily, get thee down and boogeyeth!" he cried, giving his singers the reins for the romp-em, stomp-em second verse.

"I looked over Jordan, and what did I see-ee,
Comin' for to carry me home!
A band of angels COMIN' AFTER ME-EE
Comin' for to carry me home!
Swing low—"

"—Swing low—"

"—Sweet chariot!
Comin' for to carry me home!
Swi-ing low—"

"—Swing low, sweet—"

"—Chariot,
Comin' for to carry me home..."

Deftly he resumed the lead, gently gripping the control the rennies gave him, and drew forth the emotions they were all trying to express.

"How about for the finale, we have a great big 'take that'!" he suggested at the song's end, and let the cheers subside before releasing the singers for the last, glorious declaration:

"Ta-a-a-a-a-ake... THAAAAAAAT!"

◇ ◇ ◇

Ryna snapped awake, out of bed and tugging on her gauze harem pants before her panicked yelp had faded from the air. Why hadn't anyone roused her for Cast Call—or Cannon?! Hadn't Phoenix come in saying something about pineapple and their Artistic—

Memory caught up with her. Ryna uttered a big, ugly, pink swear word.

Karma stared at her, perturbed at having been so ingloriously unseated from her favorite napping place in the crook of her person's shoulder. Silly two-legged furless. Schedules were for the unevolved—unless the schedule involved food or a nap. She put her head down, closed her eyes, curled one paw over her nose, and returned to sleep in protest.

Ryna—being a considerate two-legged furless—went about dressing and eating in a civilized manner.

The frazzle of her waking stuck with her, though, and the choking humidity of the outside world did nothing to improve her mood. With a water-logged sigh, the fiddler trudged up to C-gate—and then had to take one of the secret entrances because she'd forgotten her pass and the gatekeeper stolidly refused to let her through without it.

Peachy, Ryna griped mentally, glancing around at the wilted patrons as she emerged from between two food booths. *Why don't you all go* home *so I can crawl back to my nice air-conditioning, too?*

"Um, excuse me?"

Ryna turned, forcing a smile for the timid patron clutching her program like a lifeline. "Lost?" she asked sympathetically. "That is one good thing about being a Gypsy. We are never lost—though we are very good at finding things."

The woman let out a hesitant little laugh, as if she couldn't decide whether it was polite or not. Or maybe she feared the humidity would drown her. "Um, no; that is, not precisely; I mean, do you know where I could find these people—the ones with the bells and the hankies?" She pointed to a picture in the program of a white-clad fellow with crossed green suspenders. He was mid-jump, a bright smile on his face. Either the picture had been taken when the weather was cooler or he was one hell of an actor. Or insane. Or all three.

"Ah, the Morris Dancers. You are looking to be with child?" The Gypsy could hear her love speak the teasing words in the back of her head; it was exactly the sort of thing Phoenix would've said. "The Morris Dancers, they are dancing for the fertility—you know this, yes?"

"Ah, um, no; that is, that's very interesting." The patron turned a flustered shade of crimson.

Ryna flipped through the limp program and pretended not to notice. "If you are wanting a baby, you should come to Gypsy camp, talk to *Baba* Luna. She could make you a charm—or perhaps sell a child to you. Much easier. None of that troublesome waddling around for nine months and sending your man for radishes and lizard's tongues."

The woman morphed from red to a vague shade of green. "Lizard's tongues?"

"Oh, yes. Phoenix, our herbwoman, highly recommends them. Strange—I am not seeing the Morris Men on the listing here. One moment." Ryna spotted a Scotsman in a kilt of Black Watch. She was intensely glad she didn't have to deal with nine yards of wool, though the updraft might have been nice. "You! Scotsman!"

He turned, smiled, approached. He was tall—well, everyone was tall to her—and lanky, with sandy hair, glasses, and a dust-green shirt. When he got closer, she recognized him as the leader of the Bagpipe Brigade. "Aye, lass, can I help ye with somethin'?"

"Do you know when the Morris Dancers will be out? They are not listed here."

His expression turned from cordial to solemn. "Nay, they willna be out this year. 'Tis the same trouble that has caused many fine acts to move on."

"Thank you," she said woodenly as he sidled up to the patron with a few charming words and an invitation to watch the Bagpipe Brigade.

Ryna hardly heard him. She had to find the other Gypsies. Now.

Of course, two cabriolets and the Royal Court *would* have to cross her path between C-gate and Sherwood.

Phuro Basil was shutting Hollow Hill's door behind himself and Niki when she skidded down the hill. He hurried to the fence where she leaned, trying to catch her breath. "Are you well?"

"Morris Dancers—gone."

He must have caught the weight of her gaze because when he spoke, there was a note of damning realization in his voice. "Everything was so stirred up, we didn't even notice—"

"I think the grounds did."

"This is sounding like weighty euphemism-in-front-of-the-mundanes talk," Niki observed, draping artfully over the fence.

Ryna tried not to feel sweaty, short, and peasantish in the presence of her feline grace. "The Morris Dancers didn't get a contract. They weren't here to bless the site."

"I guess that explains the light-fingered patrons." Her head dropped into her hands. "I don't suppose we could bless it ourselves?"

Phuro Basil shook his head. "I think it was partly tied to the fiddle—the fiddler made it of wood from the tree that became the Bear."

Niki frowned at Ryna in puzzlement. "I thought you and Tremayne had fiddles made from Bear wood."

"We do—there were three of them, but the Morris guy was the one who crafted them. That might make a difference."

"Blessing grounds is a Morris thing—has always been," *Phuro* Basil added. "The Ancient Ones might not take kindly to interlopers."

"I'd rather not take the chance of pissing them off," Ryna said, glad to be off the hook. She preferred to keep her fiddle's origins under wraps; the tree that had become the Bear had been ancient beyond kenning—and rumored to be sacred to the Fae. Ryna didn't know which annoyed her more—that her fiddle's composition made it a target for theft… or that some people thought it the source of her skill.

"So basically you're saying we're screwed."

"Pretty much," Ryna agreed. "Great way to start the morning, huh?"

Niki heaved a sigh. "And here I was feeling all hopeful after *Phuro* Basil got brushed off by the Costume Nazi."

Ryna did a double take. "What?"

He snorted. "Remember how last Wednesday Patty ordered me up to the Costume Shoppe after Cast Call? Well, apparently the Costume Director doesn't like her any more than we do. I waited in her office an hour before she finally said she had no time for me and sent me off."

"No sequins," Niki put in with dramatic disappointment. "Oh, *darn*."

"Great. And now Patty will turn this around until it's all our fault. I can hardly wait." With a disgusted growl, Ryna pushed herself off the fence and went to tune while the Merry Maids passed hat.

Hopefully the day would improve with the dance show. She really didn't want to deal with it getting any worse.

* * *

"It's-a truly that-a hideous."

Ryna turned from directing patrons to the fire show to see Papa Bernatelli staring up at the Secret Garden's peaches-and-cream sign. "It truly is," she agreed.

Phoe, beside her, shrugged uncomfortably. "I think the garden itself is actually kind of pretty."

"If you ignore the fact that it gives you a direct view of backstage," Ryna countered.

"You don't notice it so much," Phoe temporized, nudging her glasses up her nose. "Or, I didn't, anyway. I was too busy looking at the trees."

Papa smiled kindly at her. "Bless-a you for-a your innocence, Phoenix. Don't-a let this-a lot-a jaded vets take it-a from-a you." He cuffed Ryna lightly on the back of the head.

She mock-scowled at him, but a quiet part of her soul agreed. Far better for her love to always see the beauty in things. "So you came down only for assessing the real estate, yes?"

"Actually, I a came a down to offer you a Gypsies our kitchen for a the doing of-a your dishes." He nodded to where the vardo had once stood, with the Gypsies' modest kitchen behind it.

Ryna wrapped her arms around him in a fierce hug. "Thank you, Papa."

"Anytime," he said quietly, dropping character. "You give that lady of yours a chance. Let her show you *her* world for a change. It would do you good."

Nearby, a little girl in a butter-yellow dress tugged her father's hand. "What's it say, Daddy?"

"It says 'Secret Garden.'"

"Shhhh," Phoenix admonished. "It's a secret!"

The little girl giggled.

"I'll try, Papa," Ryna agreed humbly, watching as the child skipped through the grapevine gates, oblivious to the ghost of a little red-haired girl a couple decades before, hurrying through those same gates to share a piece of key lime pie with her beloved father in the now-absent vardo's shade.

She would try to enjoy what beauty remained.

But some things were too much to forgive.

◇ ◇ ◇

Liam scowled from his seat on Bedside Manor's steps as Ryna sauntered past, a giant basket of bread scraps on one hip. His pet cowered—Liam gave it a well-placed kick before rounding on his minion, marble brandished. "This thing. Can I use it to harm her?"

The Fae blinked sideways at him. *Can you?*

"I'm tired of your evasions," Liam snapped. "Either give me a straight answer or do the work yourself."

The Shadow Fae eyed him dubiously for a moment, then grabbed a length of dead wood from beside Liam and scurried to catch up with the redhead. As it came even with her it extended the tool—and for a moment both Fae and staff shimmered as Ryna's foot caught on the stick. Bread bits flew in every direction as she impacted the ground with a resounding *thump*.

A smile twitched the corner of Liam's mouth. He'd always thought the Three Stooges utterly moronic. He was beginning to revise his opinion.

The Fae limped back, leaning almost imperceptibly on the makeshift staff as an ugly twig of a woman with an enormous straw hat and a basket of fake eggs appeared beside the fallen Gypsy. "Oh, *my*, that was quite the spill!"

Liam could almost see the redhead grinding her teeth as she gathered her dignity and pushed herself off the ground. From the look on her face, she evidently thought the woman had something to do with her fall.

"Grace like that must be why the *other* Gypsies are the ones getting roses by the dozen."

Ryna cast her a scathing glance. "Why don't you go lick Patty's boots like a good little spaniel? I hear it's the only reason you got back into Pendragon."

"*I* heard that the only reason your bed isn't empty is because you use witchcraft to get people there… and when someone finally figured it out and dumped you last year, you stole the woman he replaced you with."

It was amazing—Liam could actually see the fury crackle around Ryna like flames. For a moment he thought she would hit the egg lady with her empty breadbasket.

"You know what your problem is?" Ryna demanded, voice rising with every word. "You couldn't get laid if you spent Funky Formal *naked* and *drunk* outside the Blue Barn with *VIRGIN* written in *honey* across your *NON-EXISTENT CHEST*!"

Liam choked back laughter. He'd forgotten how amusing the bitch could be when she got fired up. The object of her fury stood gape-mouthed.

"Mistress Eggs? Oh, *there* you are!"

The egg-lady turned toward the hail—and Ryna, scowling, stormed toward Sherwood.

And was obliged to genuflect as Royal Court promenaded past.

Liam enjoyed every one of her muttered curses.

◇ ◇ ◇

"Save me," Phoenix begged as she ducked into Irish Cottage's kitchen.

"You too?" Brigid asked, spooning drink mix into a battered tin cup. "I nearly landed on that stupid table when I was getting out of the rafters this morning—I'm going to have a bruise on my hip the size of the Royals Revolting's paycheck. And if one more patron asks if I'm Joan of Arc, I'm going to scream."

Phoe cocked her head. "I thought Joan was French."

"A fact wasted on a large portion of our guests," Moiré observed wearily as she filled pitchers from the yellow, barrel-shaped cooler.

"Who do *you* need saving from?" Brigid inquired.

"The other Gypsies. Everybody's snarling at each other. I'm amazed Ryna and Tanek haven't started dueling in the street."

Brigid winced. "Yikes."

Moiré glanced up at her sister. "How many scoops have you put in there?"

"Um, I dunno?"

Phoenix pulled the tin mug closer for inspection, jarring it slightly.

It stirred itself.

Three sets of eyes met over the cup of vividly orange liquid.

"You do know that the primary ingredient in that stuff is sugar," Moiré advised.

Brigid grinned. "After a day like today, I'm game." She took a swig. Her eyes widened. She giggled like a leprechaun. "Fwee!"

Curiosity got the better of Phoenix. "Let me try."

The tin cup felt cool against her hands; she stared into its bottomless orange depths for a moment before taking a deep breath—and a sip. It was sweet… oh, gods was it sweet. The buzz traveled through her teeth and went straight to her brain.

Moiré set the water pitchers down and motioned for the cup; Phoenix passed it over.

Her eyes nearly fell out of their sockets. "Oh my God—it's like being kicked in the face by a sugar cube."

"I know you call the normal water-with-powder Faery Drink," Phoe observed, "but—"

"Faery Glow!" Moiré cried. "Look at it! You could use it to—"

"Some lady tried to steal my shoes," Eryn declared as she tossed aside the green burlap curtain, her expression caught between flustered and irritated.

Brigid gave her an incredulous look. "Your shoes? Your smelly, stinky, beat-up shoes?"

"She just walked over with her kid and said, 'Here, honey, I bet these would fit you.' And they did, so the lady picked them up and walked off with them! I had to chase her down, and then she yelled at me because she wanted them for a souvenir!"

Phoenix couldn't help a giggle. "That poor child! Who would come to the faire and pick up a pair of old rennie shoes for their kid?"

"Probably the same lady who ran off with the sign from one of the pickle carts," Moiré said. "Safety Services was all over looking for her."

Faery Glow rocketed out Brigid's nose; Phoe winced in sympathetic pain as she sputtered and choked. "Somebody—?! How do you hide a three-foot-long plywood pickle?"

Even Eryn began to laugh. "I wish I'd been around when *that* call came over the radio!"

"Here—try this," Brigid offered.

The youngest O'Malley peered suspiciously into the cup. "What is it?"

"Faery Glow!" her sisters chorused.

Eryn seized the cup.

One drink, and she started vibrating. Brigid reclaimed the vessel before it could spill.

Aunt Molly appeared at Eryn's shoulder. "Oops! Beg pardon, Eryn. Need to get to the pitchers."

"You've got to try this." Brigid handed over the precious brew.

Aunt Molly sipped. A gleam entered her eyes. A conspiratorial giggle escaped her lips.

"MOLLY! BRIGID! ERYN!!!" Ma bellowed from the other side of the house. "WHAT ARE YOU DOING BACK THERE?!"

"Nothing!" the O'Malley women chorused.

"If 'tis so much fun as all that, bring me out some!" Da hollered.

Moiré grabbed the remainder of the drink mix and dumped the whole container in one of her freshly filled pitchers.

Phoenix grinned. Things were *definitely* about to get interesting.

◇ ◇ ◇

As if Ryna's day wasn't bad enough, Lady Dianne's cheesecake booth was gone.

Oh, you could still get cheesecake—on a stick, dipped in chocolate, and sold by the RFC kids. Ryna would be damned if she would support Dicky Darnell's faire-owned booths… and besides, what was the point? Nothing could compare to chocolate decadence—least of all RFC food.

It was only one little thing, she supposed, but *dammit*, she'd been *craving* chocolate decadence. Not getting it was sinking her already abysmal mood even further.

So, of course, it had to be then that she rounded the Chess Booth to find Patty lecturing an upset-looking Emily, who held Morgan protectively against her bosom. Ryna scowled—and made a beeline toward the distressed damsel.

"…and I think it would be a good idea for you to find someone to at least *pretend* to be the father."

"Would you *back off*?" Ryna burst out as she came even with Emily's shoulder. "You think there weren't any single mothers in the Renaissance?"

"We are trying to present good moral values at our show."

The Gypsy took a few tense moments to focus on not wrapping her hands around Patty's jewel-draped neck… "Then let her serve as a warning," she finally ground out.

Patty's eyes lit—she began scribbling away at her burlap-covered clipboard. "That's a *won*derful idea! Your job now will be to talk to *all* the teenage girls, so they won't wind up in the sinful state you've landed yourself in. You'll do that, won't you?"

"Ah—um—yes, yes of course," Emily stammered.

"Oh, you're such a dear! Why, you're becoming a valuable member of the cast already! I look forward to hearing all about your progress! Toodles!" she chirped—and flounced away.

Ryna made a rude gesture at her back. "I'm really sorry about that," she apologized to Emily when she'd calmed enough to speak. "Between Liam, and now Patty—I hope you realize that most rennies are decent people. Our old Entertainment Director would've gone out of his way to make things easier for you."

"Thank you," Emily said quietly. The poor woman had tears streaming down her face. "All I've ever wanted since I was a little girl was to be here, part of this community—and you just made it so I can stay. Thank you, thank you, thank you."

The Gypsy's face flushed with embarrassment and no little anger. She couldn't imagine having to show up, baby in tow, and deal with the gossip… and then have to defend her right to be somewhere she loved…

But her anger would not help Emily or Morgan right now. Ryna made her voice light. "Come have dinner with us tonight, if the Bernatellis or the O'Malleys haven't already snatched you up. And if Patty gives you any more grief, you can tell her I'm the father."

Emily laughed. It made the fiddler smile, though her heart ached with how absent the sound had been from Pendragon so far.

Maybe Phoenix was right; maybe a positive outlook and a little extra kindness could counteract Patty's influence. *If I have to bring the joy back to this place myself,* Ryna vowed, *then by the gods I'll do it.*

◇ ◇ ◇

"You know, I'm almost afraid to eat dinner given what happened both times we tried *last* weekend," Tanek said, glancing nervously about.

"Never fear, my friend; the chaos shields are firmly in place," Toby assured him, dishing a scoop of stir-fry into Emily's bowl and giving Tanek a hearty slap on the back.

Phoenix took the serving spoon and mentally debated whether he was goofing.

Ryna's delighted exclamation waylaid her musings. "You made banana slices!"

Kaya kissed her stepdaughter's head on the way through the gate. "Love you."

Niki raised one eyebrow. "Banana slices?"

Ryna held up one of the crock pickles as demonstration. "Kaya always used to cut my pickles the long way when I was little. She called them banana slices."

"It was a joke," *Baba* Luna explained, scooping up a triple fingerful of couscous. "She refused to eat bananas, silly child."

Ryna wrinkled her nose. "They're icky and squishy."

"Really." Phoenix took a seat beside Robyn. "Explains why you wound up with me."

Tremayne missed a step on his way to the benches.

Phoenix grinned sweetly at him.

"They call them pickle planks, now," Emily said as she picked a seat. "I saw them in the store the other day."

Ryna frowned, licking pickle juice off her fingers. "That's sad. A whole generation of children growing up without their mothers to cut banana slices for them."

One of those affectionate parent-looks warmed Kaya's eyes. "You're sweet, princess. But think, this way *everyone* gets to have banana slices, even if their moms don't know about them."

Phoenix leaned over to hug Kaya, a fist of gratitude squeezing her heart.

"Would you look at that," Mutch said, gesturing to the climbing tower.

Two masked men scaled the monstrosity as if out for a casual stroll, feet flat to the wall and bodies parallel with the ground, capes hanging straight down. The taller man wore a gray leotard, shockingly yellow utility belt, and a black ski cap with the bottom half cut away; the shorter had a red leotard and matching mask. They took their time, bantering and hurling curses at the round man in black and white leaning out the tower window.

"You were saying about chaos shields?" Elda queried, raising her eyebrows at her brother.

Tobaltio grinned. "I never said how big their area of effect was."

Phoenix sat back to watch the show. This was one kind of chaos they could definitely do with in greater amounts.

"Hafta-Harvey-hafta-Harvey-hafta-Harvey," Ryna chanted under her breath, bouncing on her toes as she ditched her basket of RFC leftovers on the vardo's counter and dashed back outside… and pulled up short on the other side of the road. Something felt out of keeping with the bright evening sunlight and the campground's cheerful conversation. Despite her bladder's urgency, Ryna hesitated as she reached for the privy door's handle.

The plastic vibrated against her tentative touch.

This is not good, she thought, taking a cautious step back.

A beat-up hatchback rumbled by, Mary Chapin Carpenter crooning through its stereo.

Ryna shook herself. *This is ridiculous. There are a billion people around, and I'm scared to go in the privy? What could* possibly *happen—not enough paper?* Dismissing her fears, Ryna pulled the door open.

Flies.

Hundreds—*thousands*—of flies, their shifting black bodies obscuring every inch of the interior's beige plastic. Ryna slammed the door and braced her back against it as her skin attempted to crawl off her body on dark, prickling centipede feet. She could feel the privy buzzing, feel the tapping of tiny feelers, tiny feet. Thousands and thousands of... She scrubbed her palms against her overskirt as she hurried away.

So much for the close, convenient privies, she griped mentally, trying to banish the slaughterhouse image with humor as she dashed down the road to the next-closest privy cluster.

A low, shivery hum greeted her before she so much as touched either door. She could feel the looming mass of flies inside, waiting, waiting...

Ryna wanted to scream. She felt like she was going to explode.

And then she realized why she was getting chills.

Shadow Magick.

Her eyes flashed with outrage as she threw open the door to a wall of insects... but this time there was order to it. Gradually, gradually, the swirling miasma of black took human form.

Her soul quailed in horror, briefly, before she regained her defiance. Ryna gathered Magick from the very air and used it to punch her words home: "Everyone. The. Hell. OUT!"

The flies broke at her command, turned and rushed past her in a wave. The Bright Magick filling her kept them at a three-inch distance, but still she wanted to bathe.

And then they were gone. The world stood still as Ryna simply breathed.

A cricket chirped plaintively as she stepped in and locked the door.

"Boy are you in the wrong neighborhood, kid," the Gypsy said as she layered the toilet seat with paper.

"You all right?" Toby asked as Ryna stalked into camp.

"The Shadow Fae are back."

"I hope people are in the mood for French fries tonight," Tanek said as he strolled into camp, arms laden with foil baking pans. "I've got a ton of them."

"Oh, goodie." Ryna stomped into her vardo and slammed the door behind herself. It failed to relieve her frustration.

The vardo enveloped her in delicious cold—and delicious solitude. No one attempting to mollify or cheer her. No one to maneuver around as she changed clothes. Ryna stripped off her garb and left the bits where they fell.

Karma flowed down from the bed to rub against Ryna's bare legs in hope of some scraps. Much as she loved a good, warm, furry mouse, variety was nice as well. Maybe her person would have some of that light-colored meat that came in strips.

Ryna put a couple bits of teriyaki chicken in Karma's bowl before turning to the task of storing the RFC plunder. An unfamiliar plastic container hulked between the water and juice pitchers; the exhausted rennie pulled it out and tossed the other food in the fridge. She nearly broke three fingernails before the lid yielded to her will, disclosing succulent pineapple.

Ryna grabbed a piece with her fingers. It was real pineapple, not the thin, sliced, too-yellow kind that came in cans. This was the way nature intended a chunk of fruit to be, irregular and perfect. The juice trickled into her hand, where she licked it before capturing the pineapple with her teeth.

Sweet. Cold.

Alone, with the last of the day's sweat drying against her skin, Ryna smiled. It was the best pineapple she had ever, ever eaten.

The music jam had not yet started. The BLUE felt strange to Phoenix without it—empty, loud, chaotic. She tried to ignore her unease, tried to remember if it had been this way last year. Surely then she'd only felt anticipation and wonder…

A fellow with pretty, pale eyes came over to the table she shared with Ryna. Phoe didn't know his name, but she thought Ryna had said once that they'd grown up at Pendragon together.

The fiddler gave him a welcoming smile. "Hey—I haven't seen you yet this year; I'm glad we didn't lose you."

"Oh, I've been around. Last weekend was pretty bad, though, with the grid all messed up."

Ryna rolled her eyes. "They rearranged ours, too. You get everything straightened out?"

"More or less. Everyone's started swapping with each other to get the spots we want."

"Won't the patrons' programs be off, then?" Phoe asked.

"Maybe." He shrugged. "But it might teach Patty to listen to our requests."

Phoenix had to admit a certain logic to that.

"Hey," Niki greeted as she joined the group. "I haven't seen *you* in forever! How's your year been?"

"Pretty good—until someone stole my hat today."

"Damn patrons," Ryna cursed. "That must be the twentieth thing that's disappeared in three days of faire."

"I'll keep an eye out for it," Niki promised.

"Thanks. I've got to go spread the word. I'm hoping it'll turn up."

Phoe chewed her underlip as he departed. "Have you noticed that the only things disappearing are really important to the owners but mostly have no resale value? I mean, Nora's mug you could, but a staff, or an old hat, or Cottage's table—"

Ryna paused, her mug half raised.

"Power items. Makes sense, kind of." A quirky smile flitted across Niki's lips. "It's too bad he's taken—I always thought he was awfully good-looking."

"He's the one who introduced me to aged Scotch... which, in my youthful naiveté, I figured I was tough enough to handle." Ryna grinned ruefully. "Only time I got so drunk I had to hang onto the world to keep from being thrown off."

Phoenix cocked her head, trying to imagine her love that thoroughly intoxicated—and failed. "I wish I'd known you then."

"I would've scared you silly—I was rebellious, and I didn't do subtle."

"How things have changed," Niki teased.

"Hey, I've gotten better!"

The dancer raised one elegant eyebrow.

"I have. A little."

The other joined it.

"Sort of."

Phoenix giggled. "You would've had me crawling out my window at two in the morning for some secret rendezvous. Patent leather shoes, pearls, foofy dress, and all."

A high, trilling laugh sliced through the crowd. "Oh, this is so *quaint*! Why didn't I come here *last* weekend?"

The Gypsies flinched.

Phoe held her breath, hoping it wouldn't ruin her love's evening; she was getting tired of having to coax Ryna out of her funks. *Be nice,* she scolded herself. *Just because you never had anywhere you got attached to...*

"It's the pink. It's got to be all the pink," Ryna said with a groan.

Peyton rolled his eyes as he flopped artfully into a seat. "Oh *God*, who invited *her*?"

"You think if we all pretend really hard she'll cease to exist?" Niki asked, uncharacteristically snippy.

"Worth a try, darling. Have you seen her *makeup*?" Pey asked with a conspiratorial snicker. "Someone needs to tell her that blue eye shadow went out over a decade ago. And that shade of lipstick..."

"Did I tell you I found her spawning grounds downstairs?" Ryna asked. "The privies were *thick* with flies."

"I know," Niki agreed. "I'm surprised they didn't lift off on their own."

"Really?" Pey looked puzzled. "I went down about ten minutes early to beat the shower lines, and I didn't notice it at all."

"*That's* Guinness? Yuck!" Patty exclaimed. "No, I like the clear stuff..."

"Oh, God, Patty-Cakes drinks cheerleader beer." Pey groaned. "I should've known."

"Just for that, I'm taking up Guinness. I don't care *how* much I can't stand it." Ryna made a face. "Come on, Phoe, maybe if we do dirty enough songs she'll get offended and leave. I see Karen up there, and Jerry, and—who in the world is that hanging all over him? She looks like she could be Patty's sister."

Phoenix pulled out her pennywhistle and hurried to join the musicians. Maybe the evening could be saved after all.

Liam gazed over the moon-bleached rows of Tent City. It had been pitifully easy to cast his vision through the little resin gargoyle someone had perched in a tree. It provided an excellent vantage point, and it could not be killed. Unfortunately, it couldn't move... and that meant waiting until Ryna's cat wandered past.

Did she even let the animal out during the weekend? He couldn't remember... and he had been waiting for so long...

There—there! The infernal creature *finally* meandered into his line of sight—and sat in the middle of the path to bathe its left hind leg.

"Here, kitty, kitty," Liam whispered with a twisted smile. It was a delicate thing, swapping vision with another creature. Creep up on them—softly, softly, so that they did not see the danger despite their awareness of forces most humans never acknowledged.

And then, at the last instant, a burst of power they would be too late to fight.

Liam had felt the tiny squeak of mouse, the last, terrified flutter of moth before he took over their bodies... but they had been simple creatures. This was a cat—and more than that, a familiar. It would recognize the threat sooner than the others. Had he been there in person, it would surely have felt him by now. He reached through the marble—carefully, carefully—could feel it shifting coldly against his palm.

The cat paused, stared blankly ahead for a moment—and moved on to grooming its bib, its leg still high in the air. A random rennie wandered past, stopped to give it a scratch behind the ears.

Now, while it was distracted. Liam flung his consciousness at the creature—

Moment of confusion as he met not resistance but acceptance—

Another of disorientation as his perspective shifted and he was suddenly staring at denim-covered knees—

And then pain, bright and sharp, as his soul was seized, twisted, torn, and hurled from his host.

Brief glimpse of furious, spectral feline eyes—
Stunned realization that the *cat* had been waiting for *him*—
And then the world flashed. And stopped.

◇ ◇ ◇

"I hope Jerry's new girl is good in the sack—because she's sure not much on her feet," Ryna commented acerbically as she locked the vardo door.

Phoenix looked like she was trying hard not to laugh. "It was nice of Niki to sit with her. She probably doesn't know anyone… I remember how lost I felt at the beginning of last year."

Ryna kicked her loafers off and snorted. She didn't know how Phoe and Niki tolerated fools so well, but she admired their patience. "Jerry always finds the fluffiest, youngest bit he can get without dipping into the jail-bait pool. I should've guessed his new one was a rookie."

"It's not that long ago *I* was a rookie!"

"Well, yeah, but you weren't like *that*." The fiddler waved the comment off testily and started shedding clothing.

"Well, I did think her obsession with her curling iron was a bit much," Phoenix relented, tucking a lightning-white lock of hair behind her ear. She bent to remove her socks.

Ryna tugged the second leg of her jeans off with a grunt. "I can't believe Niki offered that bimbo her vardo as a dressing room."

Phoe shrugged uncomfortably, focused on unbuttoning her shirt. "Maybe it's no big deal for her—she never makes it up for Cast Call anyhow. Maybe she felt like being nice?"

And I'm not. Ryna flinched. *Touché.*

Phoenix must have caught her expression. "I didn't mean it like—"

"Never mind." Ryna doffed her shirt, crawled into bed, and tried to pretend it hadn't hurt. "I deserved it. I'm sorry I've been such a bitch."

"No, I'm sorry. I shouldn't have—"

"I don't want to fight, and I don't want you feeling guilty, so don't worry about it, okay?"

Phoe turned off the light. "Okay."

Ryna's heart bled—her love's voice sounded so small in the darkness. "Phoe, I'm sorry. Please—come here."

Hesitantly her bedmate crawled under the light blanket, allowed herself to be cuddled.

Ryna closed her eyes, and lay with her love in her arms, and wondered why everything felt so wrong.

◇ ◇ ◇

"Gooooooooood morning!" Patty called to the assembled cast, her voice's pitch rising.

"Screeeeeeeeeew you!" Toby and Tanek mimicked—in unison—from Phoenix's right.

Phoe giggled.

The Artistic Director had on her bloomers, chemise, and corset—and her hair held back in a high ponytail with a brightly pink cloth binder. "Can you believe it's Sunday of Second Weekend already? This year is going so marvelously, and I'm just sure it'll only get better!"

"Marvelously. Big word. Suppose she knows what it means, or did she pick it because it sounds perky?" Peyton asked, leaning forward from his position one row back.

"Does she own anything that's *not* pink?" *Baba* Luna put in from Phoe's left.

"Someone has *got* to teach that girl to accessorize more," Peyton agreed.

"I wonder what would happen if we dressed her in black?" Toby suggested with an evil grin.

Tremayne, on Luna's other side, bit back laughter.

"She'd probably morph into her true Hell-spawn self," Tanek said darkly.

"Or implode like a little cartoon bubble," *Phuro* Basil said.

"It's supposed to be a little on the hot side today, so remember water, water, water! Our guests don't pay sixteen dollars and ninety-five cents to see you pass out from the heat, and we don't want to ruin the show for them, now, do we?" Patty beamed, blissfully unaware of the price on her head. "Shall we start out with morning announcements? Anyone?"

"Ticket price is up to seventeen dollars this year?" Tremayne asked.

Peyton nodded. "You'd think with all that they wouldn't have cut everyone's contracts."

"Cut *everyone*'s contract my ass." Tanek snorted. "The Royals Revolting have new boots this year—and the vendor they buy them from out here charges more than I paid for my car."

"Oh look, there's the Marketing Hangov—er—*Director*," Toby pointed out as a woman with sunglasses and far too much styling gel in her hair stepped to the fore.

"Louder!" someone from the back hollered before she had so much as said a word.

She looked pitifully back toward the production staff and various sundry others seated on Bakery's many tiers.

Lancelot stepped up. She handed him her notes. "There is yet another corporate party in the tent today," he bellowed. "This time for Wood Ease Unlimited."

Several ribald jokes flew though the air.

"Please come and entertain; you will win Marketing's undying love. Thank you."

The Marketing Director reclaimed her notes and fled to somewhere with less noise.

The usual motley crew of half-garbed rennies filed through: the Magistrate inviting people to come and play with his (bocce) balls, somebody looking for contact info for one of the rennies that hadn't made it back, an announcement that someone Phoenix didn't know had given birth to twins. The other Gypsies winced—evidently she wasn't much bigger than Ryna.

"And now," Patty chirped, reclaiming the stage, "I have an extra-special treat for you. Great Entertainment Moments are returning by popular demand—and now, in addition to a food book you get one of these neat pins! So get out there and be extra-special entertaining! We'll award the first batch of GEMs next Saturday!"

Peyton stared blankly at the stage. "Fruit and pins. That's why they couldn't pay us—they spent the money on fruit and pins."

"Don't fool yourself, lad," *Phuro* Basil told him. "I'm sure they got that stuff free."

"Not that I'd have time to earn one," Toby said sarcastically. "With the Agony Director's 'extra-special' grid, I hardly have time to hit the privies."

"Ah, but you should be hitting the privies *entertainingly*," Tanek mocked.

"*Phuro*, I was thinking," Phoenix said, "what if you, *Baba* Luna, and I took over the variety show? It'd give the others a little free time."

Phuro Basil looked pensive. "I think we could work something out before our first show. Of course, *Baba* still has to play for the dancers—"

"Pah." *Baba* Luna waved it off. "Give the other kids some time to wander."

"*Pee*-ples!" Patty shrilled, waving her clipboard. "I *said*, it's time to *sing*!"

"Suppose it'll tick her off?" Toby asked.

Tanek smirked. "We can always hope."

Ryna yawned and stretched. She'd planned to go back to sleep after Phoe's departure, but habit—damn it—had prevented her. So she'd curled up with her cat and her stepmother's most recently published romance novel.

Karma bathed her tail, ears cocked peevishly back. To think that *creature* her person had once mated with had shown the *audacity* to attempt controlling *her*! Why, she'd been forced to sit on the porch all night to keep her two-legged furlesses safe from him—and all she'd gotten was a few cursory scritches when her person's mate had opened the door. Lucky thing for them *both* that Karma was in a forgiving mood. Lick. Lick.

"Ryna?"

"C'mon in, Kaya."

The dancer sheepishly stepped through the lace curtain. "I don't suppose you have a pen I could borrow?"

Ryna raised an eyebrow. "What happened to your last pack?"

"Um, the usual?" Kaya's hopeful, purposefully innocent expression looked strange on a face that usually held only confidence.

The redhead sighed elaborately. "We *have* to get you some pencils. Pens don't last three days around you before they quit working."

Karma jumped down from the bed as Kaya opened the pen drawer. Perhaps this two-legged furless would find something good to eat in there. Or, at least, fun to play with.

"The last one lasted *almost* a week," Kaya protested. "And my favorite pen never gave out, but now I can't find it. The vardo sprites must've run off with it.

"You'd think a Water element would get along better with ink," the younger Gypsy grumped teasingly.

"I don't know. Maybe I suck all the juice out of it."

"Don't do it with this one, okay? I only have two more, and then where will you go?"

"To one of the other Gypsies, of course!" Kaya gave her an elfin grin and disappeared back outside.

Ryna quirked a smile at the space where the dancer had been, bent down to give the (slightly disappointed) Karma a couple scratches on the off-center copper splotch under her chin. Then she went about gathering her costume.

◇ ◇ ◇

"Bless this house and all within, and may they never run out of cod-liver oil." Kiss. Scuff scuff. Hand-plant.

"Ah, and if it isn't the lady of the hour!" Torin exclaimed grandly as he stepped up from the kitchen with an armload of wet dishes. The green burlap curtain settled into place behind him.

"And what hour would that be, Torin?" Phoenix inquired with a raised eyebrow.

"This one, apparently." He spared her a wink as Eryn unloaded the dishes onto the enormous, ugly, standard-issue table. They'd turned it since Phoenix's last visit; instead of pointing toward the hearth and jutting partway into the traffic flow between the front and back doors, it now spanned the space between the big green hutch and the window. It looked hard to maneuver around, though at least it made it more difficult for the patrons to get to the loft's ladder and the kitchen.

"I miss our old table," Eryn said, "but at least this one has more room for drying dishes."

"Aye," Torin agreed. "'Tis good for that. And for runnin' into. I'd rather have our old table back. I wager 'twas the dirty English stole it from us—not enough that they take our land, our freedom, and our religion—now they take our table!"

Da's face poked out from the kitchen. He motioned discretely for Phoenix to join him.

"Any word on the table yet?" she asked softly as she stepped into the kitchen's dim lighting. She could hear Eryn and Torin starting up a silly call-and-response song back in the house proper.

"Nothing but suggestions to talk to site crew—which we did last weekend and got the runaround. That's not why I asked you back here, though. Moiré went up in the loft about half an hour ago and she hasn't come down yet. I have a feeling she could use someone to talk to—someone female and her own age."

"Got it." Phoenix handed him her walking staff. "Keep this safe; I'll go see what I can do."

She found Moiré curled up on the mattress with her head pillowed on an old cloak, her bodice loosened, and tear tracks on her pale cheeks. Phoenix carefully shut the loft's trap door and sat beside her.

Moiré made a little sniffle-hiccup and met the brunette's eyes with a look of utter defeat. "I'm tired, my bodice doesn't fit right, my cleavage is killing me, I threw up in the bushes this morning, and I think I'm pregnant."

It took Phoenix a stunned moment to form words. "Are you sure?"

Moiré nodded miserably. "I'm late."

"How much?"

"A day."

"Only a day? Lots of women—"

"I think the puking part kind of gives it away. It's too early for Faire crud." She sniffed.

Phoenix wanted nothing more than to take her home, cuddle her, and make everything all better. "Have you told the father?"

A shake of her tousled blond head. It seemed so wrong to see her hair messy. "I can't. I don't know where to find him… I only saw him the once, and I thought maybe he was a rookie or someone's friend and I'd see him around this year, but…" she trailed off, tears pooling in her eyes again.

"Hey, hey, it's all right." Phoe stroked her arm reassuringly. This was not at all like Moiré, always so careful and precise. "You want to start at the beginning?"

The Irishwoman did the endearing little sniffle thing again, dried her eyes on the sleeve of her chemise, and sat up. "It happened the weekend before Opening," she said, her voice taking on the cadence she used for storytelling. "You know, when we have to get up in costume for the media—"

"You got pregnant at *Press Mess*?" Phoenix tried not to stare. The event was famous for the vast amounts of free beer served to the media.

"No, no—the night before." Moiré paused, collecting herself. "A group of us got together with our copies of *Midsummer Night's Dream* and candle lanterns and made a night of it, going from place to place on site, doing a scene here, a scene there... we'd reached that sprawling old oak behind Flying Buttress."

Phoenix nodded. It was a pretty spot.

"Everyone set their lanterns on the rocks for the scene between Titania and Oberon, and Puck was sitting up in the tree. I noticed this fellow hanging back from the rest... I'd never seen him before, but... oh, God. He was so perfect, Phoenix." Her voice wavered as her eyes went dreamy. "He had this beautiful, long, curling hair the color of sunshine, and his eyes were the most intense shade of... Isn't that silly? I spent all night staring into them, and I have no clue what color they were."

"Not silly at all," Phoenix murmured, though a sense of strangeness pricked the back of her mind. "Go on."

"Well, he sidled up next to me, and he nodded toward the fellow playing Puck, and he said, 'Not a bad likeness, though I think they should've cast *you* as Titania.' He was courtly, Phoe. Not play-acting like we do—it was like he'd really stepped out of the Renaissance. We spent the rest of the night together, and then... well..."

"You spent the rest of the night together," Phoe hazarded.

"It's all so hazy, but I know we used a condom—I even put it on him," Moiré said in a small, trembling voice. "Oh, God, Phoe, what am I going to do? I'm always so careful! I don't *do* one-night stands! When the rumor mill catches wind of this..."

Phoenix let out a breath. Time to be the voice of reason. "People will talk, but it's not the first time someone's gotten pregnant out of wedlock here, and I doubt it will be the last. I'll go ask Niki for one of her home pregnancy tests, and we'll see what there is to see, all right?"

Moiré nodded, pulling herself together.

"Will you be all right until I get back?"

Another nod.

Phoe cupped the blonde's cheek. "Even if it's as bad as you think, it won't be as bad as you think. You're a strong woman. You'll get through it, and we'll all be with you every step of the way."

Despite her brave words, Phoenix's mind whirled as she descended the loft's ladder, made a quick detour to reclaim her staff from Da, and headed for Sherwood. *The Fae... the father is Fae...* She felt crazy for thinking it; how could anyone mistake the Shining Ones for mortal? But then, there were all the old tales...

She would have to ask the Gypsies about it later.

The familiar sound of fiddles tuning drifted up the lane as Phoe neared the petting zoo. She put on a burst of speed and ducked behind the shingled vardo with the yellow trim and through the burlap-covered hole in the fence.

The first notes of the opening song rang through the air; Phoe banked right and dashed to the side stairs leading to Caravan Stage's vardo. "Um, Niki? Can I… can I ask you a favor?"

The dancer glanced at the ugly orange curtain that shielded the vardo's interior from patron eyes. Kaya stepped through it; there wasn't much time. She edged closer to Phoenix. "Sure, honey."

"Do you have any home pregnancy tests?"

"You want a—"

"For a friend! For a friend!"

"Yeah—sure." She retrieved a key from her bodice. "They're in my vardo next to the tampons."

"Thanks, Niki. I'll replace it next time I'm at the store," Phoenix promised, accepted the key, and dashed off.

When she returned from the campground, Phoe found Moiré seated in the shade of Tinker's Tree, trying not to look as if she was waiting for anyone. Eryn sprawled on the grass nearby, playing a game of Pope Joan with Ilya. Moiré rose smoothly, spoke a few words to Eryn, and glided towards the Gypsy.

"What did you tell her?" Phoenix asked.

"That I wanted to show you something I'd seen in one of the shops," she replied, eyes fixed straight ahead.

"Do you want to go downstairs?"

Moiré shook her head. "Too many rennies. You mind using the handicapped Jiff in the privies behind Cottage?"

"Sure."

Muggy, ripe air smothered Phoenix as she stepped inside the extra-large plastic hut. She handed Moiré the little kit and politely faced the other direction as her friend rustled clothing and got herself arranged. To relieve the tension (and distract herself from the heat and the smell) she read Moiré a limerick penned in blue ink on the beige wall:

"There once was a woman from Rolding
Who had a great Cleavage of Holding.
She stuffed down a claymore,
And said, 'Oh, there's way more
Will fit in by cleverly folding!'"

Moiré laughed. "Ah, Dungeons and Dragons strikes again." A pause, then, "I'm, um, done now."

Phoenix turned as Moiré finished settling her clothes. “Three minutes?”

“Three minutes.”

Phoenix could feel the stench seeping into her garb as they watched, silent, dripping sweat, trying not to breathe as the little strip faded into pink.

Moiré closed her eyes briefly and let out what might have been a sigh. She held the little strip over the receptacle for a moment, then let it flutter down to the blue that waited below. An odd, ironic smile quirked her lips. She squared her shoulders and strode to the door.

A flood of sunlight, fresh air, and the “Hallelujah Chorus” greeted them.

Phoenix stood like a trout, boggling at the odds that the peasants would choose *this* privy and *right now* for a serenade. The song wavered at the sight of the two of them together. The Gypsy nearly had a witty explanation formulated when Moiré spoke.

“I’m pregnant.”

The words fell like bowling balls into the stillness. The peasants glanced among themselves awkwardly, knowing they needed to say *something…*

“Congratulations?”

“I’m sorry—I mean, congratulations—”

“Congratulations, I think…”

“I’m not saying anything.”

“Is there—ah—anything we can do?” inquired Pratt.

“Anything you need? You know we’ll do whatever we can to help.” Puddle added, uncharacteristically verbose.

“Watermelon?” Hayrold suggested. “Pickles? Chocolate-covered cheesecake? All three at once?”

Moiré laughed a little at that. “No weird cravings yet, but you’re the first one I’ll tell.”

Bryn coughed. “Do you want us to… you know… keep this quiet?”

The mother-to-be shrugged. “Everyone will find out eventually. Just—give me a day. I want to tell the other O’Malleys myself.”

Nods, general consent, and well-wishings. Phoenix was still having trouble getting her eyes back in her head. Actual speech didn’t happen until they’d exited the privy area.

“I thought you were worried about the rumor mill?”

The Irishwoman sighed. “At least this way they can get it out of their systems now and my child can start here with everyone looking forward to meeting it instead of amidst gossip and speculation.” A sidelong smile twitched across her face. “Besides, I always wanted to be a mother, even if I hadn’t planned on it this soon. Now, would you like to help me pick out a pretty something to commemorate this day?”

“It would be my honor.”

◇ ◇ ◇

"Ryna? Is that you?"

The Gypsy froze six steps away from the dispersing Dance Jam crowd. Surely that couldn't be… surely, surely… She turned, slowly.

It was.

"Joshua," she said woodenly. "What are you doing here?"

"My firm transferred me here last winter—and let me tell you, winter is *hell* in this state."

"It is," she agreed distantly, sizing him up. He looked well… his already-dark skin was tanned a little more than she recalled, setting off his dazzlingly white smile. His eyes were still full of laughter, his garb endearingly rumpled. He still had that damned Charm that had gotten her in trouble so long ago.

"The other Gypsies said you'd moved here to live with your mother—I ran into them while I was on circuit for a few years after we met. Never made it up here, though. Other places were paying better. Nice site."

"It is," she said again, and felt like a complete lack-wit. She mustered some brainpower. "You must've gotten off road about the time I got back on—I only lived here while I was in high school."

"Yeah, I suppose that was about right. I started college, got a business degree. You'll probably say it's mundane, but it pays well. I must say—the years have been kind. You look exactly how I remember you—that was part of my shock. I couldn't believe you'd changed so little."

"I get that a lot," Ryna said, and a corner of her soul wanted to cry. How could he be so casual when he had been her first love—her first *lover*—and well he knew it. She had wept such bitter tears over him—and more when she had grown up enough to realize he had only been stringing her along with his promises of eternal love… as soon as he broke up with his fiancée.

Part of Ryna smoldered with anger. Part of her laughed. She had fallen for much the same line with Liam. *At least this one isn't allied with unspeakable evil—that I know of.*

"So—you dating?"

"Handfasted," Ryna corrected. Then, unable to help herself, "I decided not to wait for you."

He laughed. It irked her. "What's the lucky man's name?"

"She changed it to Phoenix when she joined the troupe."

It took him aback, but he recovered quickly. "Lucky lady! Say, it's been ten years or so. Why don't you let me take you out to a little Thai place I know—I seem to remember you liking spicy food."

"Sure," she said, though she didn't know why. She never had been able to tell him no—had rarely wanted to. *Maybe I could gloat at how perfect my life has turned out without him,* she rationalized, even as she marveled that he remembered what sort of food she liked.

"Perfect! I leave tomorrow for a business trip, but I'll be back for Labor Day Weekend. How about I find you then and we can make more specific plans?"

"Works for me—I have to get down to Sherwood for a show."

His eyes lit like twin stars. "I haven't heard you play in ages. Mind if I join you?"

How to squirm out of it? "No, of course."

"I have to find some lunch and a drink—I'll be down as soon as I can." He swept her an elegant bow and pressed his lips to her knuckles, then turned and swaggered off.

He still had that cute little bounce to his walk.

Ryna wasn't sure what she wanted to kick more—his ass or her own.

"Who was that?" Niki asked, tucking a bit of ice down her cleavage as she and Tanek neared.

"Joshua."

She turned, peered into the crowd. "*That* was Joshua?"

"That was Joshua."

Tanek whistled lowly. "What did he want?"

Ryna shrugged with elaborate nonchalance. "Checking in, I guess. He'll be at our next show."

Niki put a sisterly arm around Ryna's shoulders as they started toward Sherwood. "Well, I shall entice him, and ensnare him, and make him beg for my favors—and then I shall tell him where to shove it."

"Yeah, me too," Tanek agreed, draping his arm around her shoulders from the other side.

Ryna laughed despite herself. "You two are the best. You really are."

Niki gave her a squeeze. "Let's go prepare the others so they can appropriately torture him as well."

A fist of pride and love clenched Ryna's heart. Niki always did know the right things to say. She wrapped her arms around her friends' waists. Her life truly was perfect.

"Looks like more corporate party leftovers," Phoenix observed as she and Moiré neared Cottage, indicating the other O'Malley siblings crossing the front yard, arms laden with heavy trays.

"I hope it's something good," Moiré said. "I'm starved."

"What've you got?" an unfamiliar male voice called out.

Brigid grinned at someone under the shade of the tree near the sheep pen—and stumbled, the pie flying out of her hands.

Oh, please let that land right-side up, Phoenix thought with a wince and felt the wish pull from her with a bright tingle. The pastry did an improbable mid-air flip and landed with the tin solidly on the grass. It slid with the impact, slopping a quarter of itself onto grass.

Brigid swooped down, cheeks as red as the pie's contents, grabbed the tin, and bolted in the house.

"Brigid Shanahan Sorcha O'Malley, get back out there and WIPE YOUR FEET!" Ma bellowed. "'Tis bad enough with the village folk forgettin' t'bless the house; I WILLNA tolerate it from me own flesh an' blood!"

Phoenix's eyebrows hiked as Brigid scurried to the doorway, hastily wiped her feet, kissed her hand, planted it on the doorway with a few murmured words, and hurried back inside. The ritual was so ingrained in the O'Malleys that it usually took Danny months to quit blessing every building he entered. For Brigid to have forgotten in the middle of Pendragon's run… The Gypsy peered toward the tree where a group of youngsters rested in the shade. She couldn't tell which one had called to the lass.

"Brigid lost her cherry on the law-awn! Brigid lost her cherry on the law-awn!" Eryn singsonged from inside Cottage.

"You'll be wearing the rest of the pie on your *face* if you don't cut that out," Brigid snapped on her way to the kitchen as Moiré and Phoenix entered.

"Brigid, be nice to your sister," Moiré scolded. "Eryn, don't torment her."

Phoenix tried not to giggle. Motherhood truly *did* begin at conception.

"Guess what I found in the privy," the littlest O'Malley chirped as the household descended on the free food.

"Nothing *I'm* going to ask after," Patches said from the window.

Eryn gave him a weird look. "I found the box for a pregnancy test."

Moiré froze with her hand in the basket of sweet breads.

Aunt Molly reached the butter crock down from the green hutch. "Awful place to have to sit and wait for it."

"It was," Moiré said quietly. "I'm due in May."

All motion halted in the house; Eryn with a carrot in her mouth, Auntie Molly stretching across the too-wide table, Patches half-tuned in the window. Brigid poked her head from the kitchen, alarmed at the sudden silence.

"Oh, Angie," Daniel murmured, dropping character (and almost his wooden bowl), and pulled her into his embrace. She buried her face in his shoulder as he stroked her hair.

"Do you have someone to go to birthing classes with you?" Aunt Molly asked.

She shook her head.

"I will if you need someone," Molly offered, resting a hand on her stage-niece's shoulder.

"Thanks." Angie sniffed, pulling herself together as she pulled away from Daniel. She dabbed at her eyes with an embroidered handkerchief.

"If you need anything—a place to stay or whatever—you let me know, okay, Ang?" Dan insisted.

"Gotcha, little bro," she said with a brave smile. "It's kind of neat, though, even if it isn't the way I would've timed it. I mean—I love babies anyway, and I always wanted one of my own. And it's not as if single moms are so rare now anyway, right? And look—Phoenix helped me pick this out to commemorate the day."

"'Tis beautiful," Ma proclaimed over Moiré's pendant, a gold rendering of a woman cradling an infant. "And your child will be the luckiest baby in the world to have you as a mom."

"Does this mean I can be Auntie Eryn next year?"

"I guess so, lass," Moiré said with a smile, resuming her character. "Now, where's Da so I can tell him the good news?"

Phoenix stood back and watched with a smile, silently wishing for even a tenth of the grace the Irishwoman possessed.

Ryna watched with admiration as Phoenix and the elders merrily wrapped up the variety show. She wished she had even a quarter of her love's improv talent—the audience adored her.

Toby and Elda probably adored her too. Ryna hated doing nine shows a day; she could only imagine what agony twelve must be.

Hurried footsteps turned Ryna's attention to the path as the youngest Merry Maid skidded into Sherwood. "You look as if you have the entire Village Militia three steps behind you," Ryna quipped.

Mutch shook her head between gulps for air. "Alaina Dale sent me—jam—at the Mead Booth. 'Tis barely begun, but hardly feels right without Gypsies."

Ryna saw an anticipatory grin flash across her father's face. "I'll get the fiddles," she offered, and dodged inside Hollow Hill. The leather-covered cases nestled companionably on the shelves to her right; she reverently lifted both down, pulling the shoulder strap of her own over her head, though she carried her father's by the handle. As an afterthought she fished a few bills and a handful of change from her cleavage and deposited the money in the collection box before pushing out the door and back into sunshine. A quick visual sweep revealed her love disappointingly absent.

"She ran back to the vardo for more film," Tremayne said with a twitching smile.

Ryna tossed copper-red tendrils out of her eyes. "That obvious?"

He shrugged and kissed the crown of her head. "That natural."

The Gypsies neared the cottage-shaped Mead Booth as the applause waned from the previous song. Patrons overflowed the benches and small tables dotting the multi-tiered courtyard—the musicians must have caught the crowd departing from the joust, or maybe one of the Shakespearian events at Flying Buttress Stage nearby.

Ryna found a perch near the edge of the sprawling group of minstrels where she wouldn't put anyone's eye out with her bow—and felt her father's quiet presence settle behind her. A beanpole of a man with a dark-stained guitar and a green shirt winked in welcome. She winked back. He had teased her as a child, and she was glad to see him still around. She'd have to ask why he hadn't been at the BLUE after hours.

A "lad" of about Ryna's height stepped to the forefront, limbering her medium-finished mandolin. Two knotted ribbon garters—one with stripes of green and black, the other with blue and purple—hung from the scroll. It had the handiest instrument strap Ryna had ever seen; the part that rested over her back had been worked into a sheath for her dagger. Her tights and shapeless tunic were faded from many years of wear, and a floppy green elf hat covered most of her cropped, sweat-matted, bright blue hair. After a glance to gather her fellow musicians she launched into the jiving notes and zippy tempo of one of her signature songs:

"Are you going to Scarborough Faire?
(oom-bop, oom-bop, bop-bop)
Parsley, sage, rosemary, and thyme
(oom-bop, oom-bop, bop-bop)
Remember me to one who lives there
(oom-bop, oom-bop, bop-bop)
She once was a true love of mine!
(oom-bop, oom-bop, bop-bop)
(oom-bop, oom-bop, bop-bop)"

Several rennies in the flowerbeds behind the flagstoned courtyard began a hand-jive; Phoenix slipped in as the next verse started. It was a rollickingly fun song; after listening to the old traditionals for years, Ryna always loved hearing a new take on them—even if this particular take was far from new. It didn't matter. It was still quirky, upbeat, and scandalously unperiod.

The audience liked this taste of the forbidden as well; the applause and hoots at the song's close caused passers-by to edge closer. Joshua peered between a couple patrons in the back. *All the better,* Ryna thought with a smirk.

"'Devil Went Down to Georgia'!" someone hollered from the crowd, and another took up the cry.

"'Devil Went Down to Georgia'—'"

"'Devil Went Down to Georgia'!"

Uncertain looks shuffled through the musicians.

"Well, we've *got* two fiddles," a fellow pointed out—he had a light-stained bouzouki and a tennis-ball-yellow stripe in his kilt. Ryna thought his name was Marcus.

"Anyone know the lyrics?" Nora asked. "Peter was a big Charlie Daniels fan, but—"

"I do!" Alaina piped up, interrupting the uncomfortable reminder of their missing comrade. "Key of G?"

"Which one you want?" Tremayne whispered.

"Devil. I've got the hair for it."

None of them had done the song before, but countless jam sessions had honed their ability to punt. Alaina played a few bars of intro, and only a couple people looked nervous. One girl stepped subtly back from the group; Ryna mentally commended her for admitting the limits of her knowledge. The other minstrels quickly fell into their niches, respectfully playing backup until the first refrain. Then the music exploded—and Ryna's heart soared. *This* was why she was a rennie—*this* was her reason for being—this moment, as their energy pounded through the music in perfect accord and the patrons' jaws dropped.

Alaina stepped up for a few more lines of song, then motioned the devil's entrance. Ryna jumped from the group right on cue, hamming it up with her sprightly best. She had them despite themselves—she could feel it in the spontaneous cheer that erupted as she melted back into the band with a slight, cocky bow. Even Alaina was grinning as she made "Johnny"'s introduction.

Tremayne didn't need Ryna's flashy trills and slides; his skill shone in the playful, almost negligent way he toyed with his instrument. When he went all out, he was the Charlie Chaplin of the music world. Ryna grinned, remembering the awe she'd felt as a child—and realized that her appreciation had only grown since.

A few more lines of melody, then father and daughter leapt into song, playing with each other—against each other—point and counterpoint as sweat slicked their hands and faces.

The band cut with telepathic precision at the song's end, leaving the fiddlers staring each other down and breathing hard. Blood pounded against Ryna's veins as applause pounded her ears; she could still feel the echo of the strings' vibrations against her fingers. Tremayne leaned forward and roughly kissed Ryna's sweaty brow, ruffled her hair to let off a little of the high before he burst.

They were drunk on it, all of them... and they'd scarcely begun.

The jam had been... glorious. Phoenix grinned as she passed Bedside Manor on her way to the last variety show of the day. Her soul still thrilled from the music, from the way sunlight had filtered through oak leaves to glint off hair and jewelry, from the smiles on all those familiar faces. *Now,* the herbwoman thought, *if only we can keep that optimism going.*

"Yoo-hoo! Gypsy!"

Phoenix cringed, her buoyant mood deflating. Only one person on grounds—besides maybe the Fops—would hail someone with "yoo-hoo." Someone wearing pink.

Far, far too much pink.

Phoe turned. *Of course, she catches me on the way to a show. I'd rather be stopped by the Royal Court. Again.* She kept her tone politely civil, though—she was proud of that. "M'lady?"

Half-a-dozen youths trailed behind Perky Patty. Except for one girl decked out to be Patty's handmaiden, they all wore disturbingly clean peasant garb. Not one of them sported so much as a patch. Not even a fake patch. *Dear gods,* Phoenix thought. *Is that how I looked last year?*

Patty shook her pen scoldingly at Phoenix. "A little birdie told me that you won best apprentice entertainer last year—why didn't you tell me?"

"You didn't ask?" *Smile. Remember to smile. I'm supposed to sound like I'm joking back.*

Patty twittered as if it was the most amusing thing she'd ever heard.

The rookies shifted awkwardly. Phoe felt profoundly sorry for these kids, who had no idea that things could be better.

"Oh, that was so funny—I can see why you won. Anyhoo, these are some of our new apprentices."

"Indeed." Phoe tried not to look as wary as she felt. She wondered if she was supposed to be surprised at this declaration.

"I thought—given your reputation—you could be their mentor? Teach them how to roll around in the mud or something—you used to be a peasant, right? Wouldn't that be fun? And so kind of you—I simply don't have the time to train them in on top of everything else."

"Um, sure."

"Fabulous! Oh—I keep meaning to ask Basil, but I've been *so* busy, so maybe you can help me."

Phoenix wondered what on earth Patty was talking about… but thought it best not to admit confusion. "Um—I'll try?"

"Wonderful! That's the unity I'm looking for. Now, why aren't you and the other Gypsies wearing the super new outfits I told Basil to go and get yesterday morning?"

Crap. And I thought we'd dodged that bullet. Phoenix steeled herself, hoping Patty wouldn't do as Ryna predicted and punish the Gypsies for the Costume Director's brush-off. "*Phuro* Basil went right after Cast Call like you asked, but the Costume Director didn't have anything for him."

"Well." Patty frowned. "I'll just have to take care of that myself, then."

"Oh, you don't need to trouble yourself," Phoenix said, backing her words with every scrap of Charm Magick she possessed. "I know you're awfully busy. It's really not all that important compared to all the other things you have on your plate."

"That's very kind of you, but really, it is that important. Now, you have fun, peoples! Toodles!" Patty wiggled her fingers at them and flitted off, handmaiden trailing behind.

Phoenix spared a moment of pity for the girl before turning to her charges. They looked cut adrift—and somewhat relieved. "Hi. My name is Phoenix. Out here, I'm the local grouchy hedgewitch, dispensing cures and leaches and birthing babies and all that."

The youngsters—the eldest probably hadn't hit high school yet—introduced themselves. Their names went by in a muddle that Phoenix vowed to sort out later.

"I'm going to take a wild guess and say that Academy—sorry, Rehearsals—consisted mostly of counting games and other stuff that had nothing to do with actually performing out here."

That got a couple tentative smiles.

"We picked out names," said a girl with honey-brown streaks in her chestnut hair—she seemed to be the leader. "And we decided a little bit about our characters—we're a pack of orphans. The local orphanage burned down, and now we're out on the street. Patty had us make up things to pretend the guests were—like we're supposed to pretend some lady's our long-lost aunt—but mostly they look at us weird and won't play."

Phoenix mentally smacked herself on the forehead. "Well, I suppose what Patty taught you would be one way of doing it," she allowed, "but I'll show you a couple techniques that work a lot better for me. The most important thing is to have fun. If you're enjoying yourself, the patrons will too. You can ask the folks at Irish Cottage—I've seen crowds gather to watch them peel potatoes."

That earned outright laughter.

"All right—what else?" the girl asked.

Where to start? "Well, we have to do something about your clothes."

"Our clothes?" A little boy about Eryn's age stared with befuddlement at his pristinely white, perfectly hemmed shirtsleeves.

"'You need to go roll in the mud or something.'" Phoenix fluttered her hands and tried her best to look pink; the imitation brought stifled giggles. "Really, though. There are some peasants around—their costumes are a good example. You can probably find them at the peasant sing-along; they have it near the juggling booth over by the BLUE in about half an hour at five-thirty. I'd help you more, but I have to get to a show. Maybe if you find me next weekend?"

"The sing-along got canceled," said a previously silent five-year-old girl. She shared a strong resemblance to the older boy. "One of the people at Bakery Stage told us to go there yesterday, but when we got there, one of the people at the juggling booth said Patty told them they couldn't do that anymore. It wasn't entertaining enough, or something."

"Can we come to your show?" asked the little boy.

Phoenix stared at all the hopeful faces turned to her. Well, why not? If nothing else, she could introduce them to her family afterwards.

And it was never a bad thing for a rookie to be connected with the Gypsies.

* * *

"Can I have a sip?"

Phoenix looked up from her seat on the porch of her vardo, enjoying the lazy evening sunshine as her family puttered around their vardos and the weekenders packed their things and left the campground. "Sure." She handed her leather mug up to Toby.

The fire-eater screwed his face into a most interesting expression. "What's *in* that?"

"Dark fizzy and chocolate syrup."

Toby turned so the entire camp could hear his comment as he called, "Ryna, did you get Phoenix preggers? She's out here drinking cola with chocolate syrup in it!"

"She did ask me for that home test," Niki chirped from her vardo.

"Hey, it's good!" Phoe protested. "Ask *Baba* Luna!"

"It's true!" came the requested backing.

"And *that* makes it normal?" Toby scoffed as he retied his headscarf. "The woman eats chocolate chips in her cheese sandwiches!"

"It's not weird until she wants sauerkraut with it!" Tremayne's voice floated out.

"Once!" Kaya cried defensively. "Once, and it was with a freezypop! And I had PMS!"

"You want me to come and tie him down for you, Kaya?" Ryna called.

"No thank you, princess. I've gotten good at it over the years, and he's laughing too hard to struggle."

Phoenix's eyebrows inched up.

"You didn't think all those scarves were only for decoration, did you?" Toby asked with a sly wink as she took a drink—and jumped back barely in time to escape a spray of cola and chocolate syrup.

Ryna poked her head through her lace curtain. "You haven't done *that* for a while, Phoe. You all right?"

Phoenix nodded, struggling for breath through the last of her coughing fit. "Yeah. Once Mr. Suave over here stops trying to kill me."

"No killing my soulmate," the redhead scolded Toby as she sat beside Phoenix.

"Thank you," Phoe said, and kissed her—the contact lingering as the familiar brush of energy danced an intricate waltz.

"Ryna's right—no killing our herb lady!"

Phoe broke the contact, giggling, and stuck out her tongue at Tanek.

He graced her with a charming smile and a shrug. "Well, it *might've* put me next in line."

Niki stepped down from her vardo and playfully socked him in the arm.

He threw himself dramatically to the ground. "M'lady doth wound me!"

"You!" she cried, tickle-pouncing him.

"So Phoenix, how did you get hooked up with those kids?" *Phuro* asked over the sounds of battle as he stepped out from his vardo and sat on the porch with a boot—not his own—and his sewing awl.

"Well, I fell in love with Ryna—they came with the package," she quipped, gesturing to the combatants.

He laughed.

Phoe pretended innocence. "Oh, you mean the orphans?"

Ryna nearly choked on the sip she'd stolen from Phoenix's mug. "More orphans? Doesn't anyone out there have parents? Gods, Phoe, how do you drink this stuff?"

"Well if you don't like it, stop wasting it on your unappreciative self," Phoenix said primly, reclaiming her mug.

Toby gave Ryna a couple smacks on the back. "At least they're being creative and banding together."

"The local orphanage burned down," Phoe supplied.

"Hey, did you see the oldest boy's face when you two kissed?" Tanek asked with a grin. The fight had abated; he lounged against one of the bench-logs around the fire pit. "You'd think he'd never seen a lesbian before. I think you broke his heart, Phoenix."

"I don't think I'm his type," Phoenix protested uncomfortably as Tanek made eyebrow-wigglies at her.

Toby snorted. "He's fifteen. I don't think he's gay, and you've got boobs. Believe me, you're his type."

Ryna looked surprised. "Fifteen? I didn't think he'd hit high school."

"Me either," Phoe chimed in, happy for the subject change.

"He turns sixteen at the end of September—didn't you hear him and Jen talking cars?" *Phuro* Basil asked. His lopsided smile made him look especially wolfish. "She was trying to distract him before we all drowned in a puddle of his drool."

"Hey, I happen to think Jen is quite drool-worthy!"

"Oh, so do I, Niki," *Phuro* agreed, "but she didn't have as much on display."

"Complaining?" *Baba* Luna inquired, leaning out the vardo door to display her still-bodiced shelf.

Phuro grinned, plucked one of the dandelions near his porch, and tucked it neatly in her cleavage.

"Oh, *there* you all are!" oozed an ingratiating voice.

"Oh, gods," Ryna said on a soft groan, her head bowed. "Her again. We have *got* to increase the camp's shielding."

Puzzled, Phoenix looked up to see a stick of a woman in an enormous straw hat. She carried a basket of eggs that Phoenix could tell were fake from ten feet away.

"You found us," *Phuro* Basil admitted gamely, but Phoe read a studied patience in his gestures. "Is there something you require?"

"'Is there something you require,'" she repeated, tittering like a schoolgirl. It was an awful sound. She flapped a limp hand at Basil. "Such a gentleman!" Her tone turned conspiratorial. "We're offstage, though, Basil. You don't have to act. I know what you're *really* like."

Ryna bristled; Phoenix noticed several of the others scowling.

"Is that so?" *Baba* Luna asked flatly, death in her eyes.

The goose's titter sounded a touch nervous this time. "Oh, you know I'm only funning you."

"I fail to find the 'fun' in it. Perhaps you should state your business and leave." Energy crackled from the camp matriarch, making Phoenix suddenly very glad to be on *Baba* Luna's good side. She'd never seen the woman so formal before. It didn't bode well.

"Oh, you take everything so *seriously*." An elaborate sigh. "And here I'd come all the way down here to tell you how *sorry* I was they knocked down your wagon thingie."

"Thank you," Niki said, her voice tight.

"Well, I'll be gone, then—*some* of us have real jobs." She flapped her hand limply again. "Toodle—oh! I almost forgot! The oldest girl at Irish Cottage is pregnant! I was in the privies and—"

"Thank you; we've heard," *Phuro* Basil said firmly. "Phoenix was with her when she found out, though we appreciate your telling people so that they can be sensitive to her feelings."

"Well, you know, the poor girl, young and single and all that," the gossip sympathized, crestfallen when none of the Gypsies took her bait to continue the scandal. "Well, I'll be on my way. Toodles!"

"Man, she really doesn't know sarcasm when it bites her in the ass, does she?" Toby asked when she was out of sight.

Luna snorted. "She doesn't have enough ass to bite."

"Who *is* she?" Phoenix asked.

"She pretends she's an eggler, but she's really the village gossip—with a thing for older men," the matriarch said tersely, one of her scarves a bright blue wad in her hands.

"I think I can speak for all older men when I say that we don't want her 'thing,'" Basil assured her, and leaned back to kiss her calf. "On the list of things I'd bed, she ranks below Harvey the privy monster."

Luna smiled and tickled his nose with the scarf.

Toby rolled his eyes. "If she gets any at all, it's proof that beauty really is in the eyes of the beer holder."

"I thought we'd seen the last of her when Eric kicked her out for stalking him," Kaya said.

"I think she heard he was gone—Peyton said something about how she spent all summer kissing Patty's arse," Ryna replied. "I ran into her yesterday; I can't believe I forgot to warn the rest of you."

Phoenix caught a flash of the gossip's costuming crouched between two vardos and considered telling the others—but the conversation had already turned to other things… and increased in volume just enough that they probably realized she was there and were feeding her.

Still, Phoe had the nasty feeling that the gossip wouldn't be the only one to wind up bitten in the ass.

An entire day of useless viewings.

An entire day of weakness so profound that he could hardly focus.

An entire day of enduring the Shadow Fae's mocking.

That cat would pay.

Liam's foot impacted his pet's ribs with a satisfying jolt; it thumped against the sprawling, beautiful tree that stood where the Bear should have been and cowered there, whimpering. The Fae fed off of emotion—but he had learned long ago that two could play that game. Liam's lips twisted into a smile as the creature's fear flowed through his veins, replacing the energy he had lost. "Hold *still,*" he snarled as his pet scrabbled to escape.

And then he felt it, the panic rising along his spine as every sentient creature fled the animate darkness that roared down the Narrows, all-encompassing and unstoppable. Fire roiled around it, images of destruction and terror flickering in its depths. Death. Pain. Torture. Charred lumps of blackened flesh that had once been human, ruined faces hideous and contorted, their stench searing Liam's lungs... The remembered feel of skin blistering, of his face's skin crackling as he screamed...

He wanted to run away. Oh, God, he wanted to run away... but the primal, horrific force of the creature ensnared him. This Fae was one to which the Three answered... and there was a reason even *they* quailed before it.

Slowly, so slowly, he forced his gaze to meet the thing's char-black eyes, surprised that his own had not melted from the heat...

"So. You are to be my portal." The voice was an inferno. Liam choked on terror as he clutched at his head, willing the pain to stop. The Three had said he must pave the way for one of their masters... but he had not believed... not this... not this *thing* born of terror and death and pain and chaos...

He steeled himself. Everything came with a price—he would endure this as he had endured the others. For Bea. For Bea. For Bea. Stiffly he forced his mouth to form words, his voice to rasp, "I am."

Its laughter crackled against his ears like prairie grass burning. And then, in a swoop and roar, it was gone, leaving only the faint, acrid stench of charred flesh behind.

Although he had not eaten in months, Liam leaned against a tree and retched.

Ryna woke half an hour before her alarm sounded, butterflies dancing in her stomach. No matter how many CDs they'd made, she always felt a certain thrill at the prospect of recording. There was something so beautifully *tangible* about it all.

Phoenix stirred and mmmed. "What time is it?"

"Time for bards to return to slumberland."

Phoe hauled the alarm close to her nose and squinted. "Funny—this thing says it's seven-thirty."

"There's no reason for you to be up, Phoe." Ryna hesitated as she raided the fridge, glanced back at her love. "Unless you want to come along, of course. There's not going to be much for you to do."

The raven-haired Gypsy flopped on her back, still bleary. "Would it be all right if I brought Christine's veil to work on?"

Ryna blinked in surprise. "Sure, if you really want to come."

"I want to see how you make those wonderful CDs." Phoe pushed herself up, flipped her fuzzy braid over her shoulder. One of the star-white tendrils had worked free of its tightly woven confines and now curled delicately against her tanned cheek.

Amazing, how adorable she was right out of bed.

Ryna grinned. "In that case, I'll make breakfast for two, give your glasses a quick clean, and we can take a morning stroll while we're waiting for Tata to wake up."

◇ ◇ ◇

Phoenix had expected the recording studio to look like the ones on TV—a room with a microphone separated by a plate glass window from the sound engineer and enough control panels to land an airplane. Instead, she found herself in a small basement room with beige walls and carpet of an indeterminate brown. Dial-laden boards and a computer obscured an old folding table. Two microphones huddled nearby.

That was it.

The mood was, in some respects, more professional than she had anticipated. Ryna and Tremayne worked towards checking off each song on their list with a swift efficiency. Still, they teased and joked in between and with their recording engineer, a fellow called Flicker. He was one of Tremayne's high school buddies and showed no shortage of humor. He steered them back on track when they strayed too far, though, and he did not hesitate to make them re-record until it suited him. He even laid down a couple tracks himself, creating a virtual symphony with his state-of-the-art keyboard.

"You want a listen?" Flicker offered. "You'll have to come over here; the cord's shorter than Ryna."

Ryna blew him a razzberry.

"That would be wonderful, thank you." Phoe carefully put aside the pearl-strewn veil and scrambled to her feet. The headphones settled heavily against her hair, ear pieces engulfing her in foam.

Flicker pushed a couple buttons and swiveled a knob.

Then—music.

Phoenix's eyebrows shot up in surprise as the previously disjointed takes melted together. The familiar tunes had an electric bent much different from the Gypsies' previous recordings—and not at all her usual preference. Still, it sounded good. She could imagine driving between faires with this CD on constant loop, keeping her company as Ryna napped in the seat beside her and the stars scrolled across the sky like the miles on the truck's odometer. "I like it," she said when she finally removed the headset.

"Yeah?" Flicker quirked a paternal smile. "It has to be mixed yet. Maybe bring the zills out front in a couple places, hoop up the bass beat."

"We thought it would be fun to try something different," Ryna said, leaning casually against the wall. Phoe could tell the praise pleased her, though.

"Perhaps we might order a celebratory pizza," Tremayne suggested.

Flicker lit up like his equipment. "Anchovies?"

"Half anchovies," Ryna compromised, giving him an affectionate poke.

"Three-quarters," Phoenix bargained boldly.

Ryna stared at her with an expression that almost made Phoe giggle. She hadn't yet come out of the anchovy closet, so it was bound to be a bit of a shock.

The two men, on the other hand, were looking at her like their hero.

The red-haired fiddler shook her head fondly. "Fine—order the whole thing with fish. I'll pick mine off and throw them at you."

"C'mon, all," Flicker said, rounding them up with a gesture. "The phone's in the kitchen."

* * *

Ring.

Two.

Three.

C'mon, c'mon, Phoenix willed, swatting at a mosquito attracted by the lights behind C-gate. *Pick up, Danny.*

As if on cue, her brother's voice reached through the receiver. "Hello?"

"Danny-boy?"

A hesitant pause. "That would be me."

"Daniel?" shrilled a woman's voice in the background. "Daniel, who's so important that you're taking time away from your family?"

"Mother," Phoe said on a horrified breath. No wonder he hadn't greeted her as enthusiastically as usual. "Danny, I'm sorry. I didn't know. Should I call you back later?"

Another pause, but this time when he spoke his tone warmed. "No—no, that's silly. She can wait. What's up?"

"I just—I know it's late, but I thought maybe I'd stop by tonight. Maybe when she goes home..."

A snort.

Phoenix giggled, though it felt hollow. She could picture the look on his face...

The phone clicked, and her mother's voice pierced the receiver. "Daniel is getting *married* in less than a week. Whomever you are, you will have to call back later. He has *family* to attend to."

Phoe had the phone halfway to the cradle, ready to let her mother assume it a telemarketing call, when she stopped. The last time they had spoken, Phoe'd hung up on her mother to prove her independence. Wouldn't hanging up now prove she could still be intimidated?

She put the phone to her ear. "I *am* family, Mother."

A stifling pause. Not so much as a hello.

"My sister and I are talking, Mother," Daniel said.

"How nice that she calls you. I'm glad she still has respect for *someone* in this family."

"Mother."

A righteous sniff this time. "*Fine*, Daniel. Just *fine*." She hung up the phone.

"Danny, I'm sorry."

"Eh. If she tirades on about you, she might come off her rant about the flowers and our delayed honeymoon. And how Christine shouldn't be wearing white. And how even though she shouldn't be wearing white, she *certainly* shouldn't have tiny flecks of black in her shoes."

Phoenix knew she should be shocked at her mother's lack of class.

She wasn't.

"Listen, Phoe, I'm not going to have time for a visit for the rest of the week—*you understand*, don't you?"

Read: the parents will be hanging around too much and you're trying to protect me, she thought, but said only, "I understand."

"*Daniel*!"

"Take care, Danny—don't let her run off with your ruby slippers."

"Bucket of water at the ready—I hope it works."

"Me too."

"I love you, sis."

"I love you too, Danny."

"Have Ryna give you a hug for me."

"I will."

"Bye, now."

"Bye."

Phoenix clicked the phone into its cradle before she could hear the silence on the other end—and slumped, resigned, against the graying plywood wall. Stars shone overhead, distant and cold against the night sky; insects wheeled around the electric lights. Suddenly the whole world reeked of rotting wood and the water-damaged paper fliers that hung limply from their staples.

Shadows shifted, lengthening almost imperceptibly.

The Gypsy pushed away from the food booth's wall, shaking off her sudden unease. Her stomach was probably just in knots over the upcoming wedding rehearsal.

It couldn't possibly have anything to do with the twitching darkness and almost-heard voices that hurried her steps toward the Gypsies' vardos.

Not a thing.

◇ ◇ ◇

A hideous smile twisted Liam's expression as he watched his love trot down the Olympic Staircase, darting furtive glances to either side. The shadows he commanded licked at her heels, surging ever closer—but not attacking.

"Make haste to your Gypsy whore, my sugar-bird," he murmured, and her steps sped as if in response to his command. "Soon you'll be running to me."

◇ ◇ ◇

"Family problems?" Ryna hazarded as Phoenix closed the door behind herself and immediately began brewing tea.

Phoe glanced at her as she rummaged through the cupboard. "That obvious?"

"Well, you said you were going up to call Danny…"

"Yeah, I suppose."

Ryna let the silence stretch, hoping Phoenix would be the first to fill it.

Minutes passed. The microwave beeped.

Ryna realized she was not going to get her wish. "Are you all right?"

The raven-haired Gypsy glanced up from the honey jar. "I'm fine."

"You sure?"

Phoenix shrugged, intent on stirring her tea. "I guess."

Well, it was *something*. "You need to talk about it?"

"I dunno. What would I talk about? It's the same stuff as always." She tapped the water off the honey spoon and placed it in the sink.

"You know," Ryna ventured as Phoenix joined her on the bed, "we've been together almost a year. You've gotten to know my family—*our* family—but I hardly know anything about yours, other than Danny."

Phoenix tucked her knees up, the tea's steam gently curling around her face. How could she stand to drink anything hot with the weather so awful?

"They're well-off monetarily—maybe that's the biggest problem. If they were poor, maybe they wouldn't be so concerned about appearances."

"Big on the All-American Family thing, huh?"

"Yeah. Poor Daniel; he's Mom's only hope. He pretends it's no big deal, but I think it's really hard on him having to put up with her guilt trips."

There it was—the casual dismissal of the other half of Phoenix's parentage. Having done it a million times herself, Ryna could spot the omission a mile away. "And your father?"

"Dad's probably all—well, you know."

"No, I don't—you never really talk about him."

"Strict, and all that. Spare the—" Phoenix faltered a moment, made a dismissive gesture as she raised her mug. "I'll spare the details—does it really matter? I mean, it's over now."

"But it still bothers you."

"Of course it bothers me!"

"Why? Danny's wedding and the rehearsal are only going to be a couple days, a couple hours each. I know how I'd feel if it was my birth mom, but it's not something to tie yourself in knots over for weeks."

Phoe looked about to blurt something—but bowed her head, let the steam cover her glasses. "Can—can we talk about something else, please?"

There was a huge piece of the story missing—Ryna frowned, but she refused to violate her love's request. A quiet plea like that from Phoenix was like a shout from someone else. "Sure. Hey, Flicker really liked you—I don't think he thought he'd ever find a girl who likes anchovies."

Phoenix pounced on the change of topic like a rennie on free food. "Really? He's neat—and all that recording stuff is so… wow. Does he do that professionally?"

The fiddler babbled inanely about the production process, but her heart wasn't in it. Phoe was too enthusiastic—it meant the other problem still bothered her. And if she wouldn't talk about it…

Well, Ryna would just have to find someone who would.

* * *

By the time noon rolled around, Ryna felt thoroughly restless. She'd made a dozen calls to Daniel's various phone numbers and eventually given up and left messages on three of his voicemail machines—not that she had a number he could call back. Still, it was a start—and maybe if he got her messages, he'd be more likely to actually pick up the phone the next time she tried. She almost—almost—

wished she had an email address. Phoenix had one that she checked weekly at the local library, but Ryna had never had anyone to write to until now.

She sighed and leaned her head back against the copper birch tree behind Cottage. She'd settled down to compose a song for Phoenix's impending birthday, but the strangely beautiful weather and her concern for her love had foiled any attempt to concentrate.

One of Brigid and Eryn's missing table posters stared forlornly at the Gypsy from the kitchen door. If only she could do something about *that*... it would certainly bring some cheer to the O'Malleys, and probably Phoenix as well. And, as an added bonus, maybe it'd counteract some of the crap that'd been going around all year. *But where in the world could I look that the O'Malleys haven't?*

As if on cue, Niki's truck rumbled up the lane from down by *Lady Fortune* Stage, a cloud of dust billowing like smoke in its wake. Ryna stood and walked to the road with a wry smile at her friend's timing.

Niki slowed and leaned out the window. Fiddle music from one of the earlier Gypsy CDs floated from the stereo. "Hey! What's up?"

"Wondering if you could do me a favor."

"I can sure try, hon. What do you need?"

"Cottage's table disappeared sometime after Closing Weekend, and the O'Malleys can't get a straight answer out of anyone. I don't suppose you'd know what happened to it?"

"Phoenix asked me the same thing earlier, and I never had a chance to get back to her. There are a bunch of tables down at the Big Blue Barn—would you know it if you saw it?"

"There's no mistaking it."

Niki shrugged. "I never spent much time in Cottage, so I couldn't say. Hop in the truck, and we'll drive down."

Hop? Scramble, more like, Ryna grumbled mentally as she clambered into her friend's pickup; it had none of the conveniently placed hand- and foot-holds that had sold her on her own vehicle.

It did, however, have Niki's personality abundantly strewn about, from the massaging lower back cushions to the lace covers for the sun visors. Niki was a creature of comfort, convenience, and aesthetics, and Ryna marveled at how that leaked into every part of her life. Even her truck was a fairly new model with all the light-up buttons and fancy gadgets. Tanek had gotten her a great deal on it, but still. Ryna's truck, although in good repair, was more functional than showy. She loved Niki dearly, but she'd never understand her friend's attitude that good enough could always be improved.

At the same time, though, it fascinated her. She wondered if Phoenix would like one of those massaging cushions.

They rumbled past Track, took a right as they neared the games area, and exited through a gate in the picket fence. A few cars and RVs dotted the parking field; the Gypsies passed them and headed down the gravel road that led to the highway. Ryna idly watched the train out her window; its long, mournful whistle echoed into the quarry.

Another left jounced them down a hill and toward the Big Blue Barn. It looked nothing like Ryna'd last seen it: dim and filled with smoke, music, and bodies. Sunlight cut a patch of gold on the shadowed dirt. Plywood, two-by-fours, cans of paint, and other building supplies populated the interior. "If it's anywhere, it's here." Niki cut the engine, hopped out of her truck, and sauntered over to where tables half buried in hay bales lined part of one wall.

Ryna sneezed as she slammed the passenger-side door. They looked like the standard picnic tables in the food courts.

Except—

It was faint, but one section of hay bales gave off a slightly different energy. Welcoming. Homey. She pointed to the spot. "There."

The two Gypsies went after the bales, and soon a bit of familiar gray-brown wood appeared, its edges and corners rounded with use. In moments they had it unearthed—dusty and filthy… but undeniably Cottage's. Ryna lovingly traced the simple carving at one end and felt its energies nuzzle up to her like a puppy.

"I have no idea why it's here, hon," Niki said. "The Halloween show should've had enough tables without swiping this one, but at least it wasn't stolen like everything else. I'll find a couple buff males to load it."

Ryna almost didn't notice her friend's departure. "Don't worry," she told the table. "I'm taking you home now. You've been missed, you know that? You got wanted posters, an announcement at Cast Call, and everything. I wouldn't be surprised if the O'Malleys throw you a homecoming celebration. Lots of potatoes."

The table seemed to like that idea; the honor of supporting dinner had to be much more prestigious than its current predicament. Table and Gypsy stood in happy silence for a few moments, contemplating tubers and basking in each other's presence until a new voice echoed through the barn's interior.

"Really? Man. The Irish have had a full-fledged search party going, and here it was under our noses the whole time."

"Hey, shortie," Toby greeted jovially.

"Hey, dragon breath," she returned. "Come to be all manly?"

"Yup. Mike, this is Ryna. Ryna, Mike. He's come to be all manly, too."

"A pleasure," Mike said with a lantern-bright smile. He was tall, blond, muscular… and reminded Ryna a little of Pierre, the French Viking from Scheherazade Faire. "Niki, sweetheart, you want to drive your truck up?"

She gave him a sultry smile and an ass-grab as she passed; Ryna didn't miss the appreciative look he cast after her retreating form. Ryna wished she could look that cute in overalls. The one time she'd worn them had resulted in her getting carded at a cheap twenty-four-hour restaurant to be sure she was old enough to be out past curfew.

It had been her twenty-second birthday.

Niki pulled up next to them and hopped out to get the tailgate; Mike and Toby lifted their prize and carefully maneuvered it onto the cargo area.

"Figured we'd help unload, too, and save you the trouble," Mike said as he settled in beside the table.

"Figured he'd show off to Niki," Toby whispered in passing, and hopped up as well.

Ryna tried not to giggle. She welcomed the help, though; the thing would've fallen on her head if she'd tried to take one end. She clawed her way back into the truck wishing for Niki's height—or at the very least, her grace.

The exchange went smoothly, and five minutes later Ryna watched as Niki's truck jounced away with Toby, Mike, and the standard-issue picnic table in the back. *And good riddance*, the redhead thought, turning to admire her prize. Cottage hummed with pleasure at the return of its Prodigal. Ryna grinned, glad she could do this one small thing to repay all the kindness it had shown her over the years, and went to the kitchen to find some detergent.

◇ ◇ ◇

"Curses!"

Phoenix ducked, the action reflexive after a year of living with Ryna. Sure enough, something zinged through the air three feet to her left.

"That's my pen!" Ryna cried from beside her on the log bench near the fire pit.

Phoe swallowed her oatmeal before she could choke with laugher. "So *that's* where you get it!"

"More likely Kaya learned it from her." *Baba* Luna glanced up from her caddy of spare jewelry parts and gave Phoe a wink. They were the only three around, aside from Kaya on her vardo's porch.

"I suppose. I've never seen Kaya throw anything before." Phoenix turned to *Phuro* Basil as he strode into camp. "I don't suppose you could craft her something that wouldn't give out."

"Craft her something that wouldn't give out what?"

"She killed my pen," Ryna grumped.

The camp patriarch sighed. "I told her a quill would solve her troubles, but she won't listen. Common ailment, apparently."

"Meeting not go well?" Luna hazarded, putting aside her supplies.

He plopped onto one of the bench logs, but not before dropping an ominous cardboard box at his feet. It landed with a whoofling thump. "The bright side is that things with the vardo aren't any worse than when I left this morning—unless, of course, Patty finds out I went over her head."

"And the shadow side?" Kaya asked from her doorway.

Phuro briefly rested his head in his hands, then looked up. "I spent all day waiting in the General Manager's front room just so he could dangle an unreachable carrot in front of us. His opinion is that whether or not we agree with Chaos Kitten's decision, done is done, and the vardo's gone."

Ryna rolled her eyes. "No surprise there."

"I sense a 'but,'" *Baba* Luna observed.

"But if we really want it back," he went on, "he told me to submit a formal request complete with blueprints, estimated cost, a building permit, and a bulletproof argument as to why it's necessary when we're apparently surviving without it now."

Phoenix cocked her head, trying to understand his dour expression. "So we fill out the applications. *I'll* fill out the applications, if you want. If four years of college and an English degree taught me nothing else, it's surviving pointless triplicate and writing air-tight papers. How bad could it be?"

Basil graced her with a tired smile. "Would that we all shared your faith, Phoe. Don't ever lose it."

Phoe was sure he'd meant it kindly, but she suddenly felt about five years old.

Ryna tossed her hair. "The problem is, even if we fill out all the paperwork, we'll never get what we're after if Patty doesn't feel like giving it to us."

Phoenix frowned. "But if we write a good enough proposal..."

Kaya sat beside her, took her hand. "You could spend a month writing the perfect proposal, and all it would do is sit at the back of a file cabinet with a bunch of stuff that hasn't been touched in a decade."

"It's bureaucracy," Luna explained bluntly. "You can fight it, but you can't win."

"Oh," was the only response Phoenix could devise.

"It gets better," *Phuro* Basil continued. "Patty-Cakes caught me on my way out and gave me this." He kicked the box. "She thought I'd come looking for it."

Kaya made a face. "Dare I ask?"

"I haven't looked yet," he said heavily. "I figured ignorance was bliss."

Luna bravely stepped up to the box and unfolded the flaps. Horror descended over the Gypsies as she pulled out a pink, sequin-studded scarf.

Kaya threw down her notebook. "I. Am not. Wearing. *Anything*. That. Looks. Like. *That*."

"There's more." *Baba* Luna, holding the filmy scarf like a week-dead skunk, gazed into the box. "And it's worse."

Phoenix could feel their negativity choking the life out of her. "Um, excuse me. There's something I have to... I'll be back." Without waiting for a response, Phoe rose and hurried away. She wasn't sure where she was going, but neither did she care.

How could they all stand to be like that? How could they watch something they loved die and not cling to the hope that somehow it could be fixed? For the love of the gods, they'd bested the Shadow Fae! How could one little pink fluffbunny and a bunch of froofy scarves take them down?

Phoe paused. Was that how Patty got such an excess of cheerfulness—did she vampire it from Pendragon's cast? The Gypsy shuddered as she turned right at the Bear and headed towards Sherwood. What if she was allied with the Shadow Fae?

Oh, stop it, she scolded herself. *Just because someone scatters more misery than Johnny Appleseed scattered trees doesn't mean she's allied with Ultimate Evil. Some people are unpleasant without any outside interference.*

She ignored the obnoxiously floral Secret Garden sign as she slipped through the familiar grapevine gates and into the embrace of the trees' shade. Cicadas trilled with joy at the lingering heat as Phoe traipsed down the steep, winding path. Bits of motion flashed in her peripheral vision, but she knew better than to look. If the residents of this wood wished to be seen, they would ensure they were. If they did not, there was no use trying to find them. Still, the knowledge of their presence made her smile. The knots in her gut loosened.

The beings here were not the same sort that had saved her family last September. She couldn't explain how she knew without being able to see them, but they felt more like the Victorian idea of the Little People. Had they lived down here before the advent of the carefully natural paths? If so, had they changed to fit the surroundings, or had they made their presence felt in such a way that the surroundings molded to them?

And if not... if they had simply been attracted to the doll-like houses... what had they displaced?

Phoenix leaned against the low bridge's rough timber railing, let the tension ease from her shoulders. She felt the woods still and a couple small presences join her as the lowering sun painted the marsh grass gold, then auburn, and the first stars ventured into the darkening sky.

There she is.

"I can see that," Liam told his minion, eyes never leaving the raven-haired vision. Perhaps she was real this time. Perhaps she wasn't. Either way, he was content to stare in rapt attention, mesmerized.

She seemed so at peace, trusting, oblivious. Vulnerable. How could she lean there, counting the newborn stars without a shiver of fear for the nightmares that called the darkness their home?

Beautiful innocence. A touch of breeze toyed with her hair, stirred the white tendrils from her face. He imagined his fingers playing there, remembered feel of the silken strands against his hands as he braided it that morning on Cottage's steps, with the sun barely cresting the rise of the shops across the way. He remembered the feel of her lips, sweet and yielding against his... remembered her soft weight in his arms as he'd carried her to her brother's car... remembered the melting look in her eyes as he'd kissed her hand...

The light outlined her like an angel. Like a goddess. Golden, auburn, sweet bird silhouetted in the flame of a phoenix. A woman to protect, to cherish, to have. A woman worth dying for.

The minion smirked—Liam could feel it. It sent an image of itself crossing over, touching her...

"Don't," Liam said, his command soft, though if she heard him, it would be the whisper of leaves in the wind.

I could.

He pinned the imp to the shadow of a tree with a glare. "She is not for the likes of you."

It glared back, incredulous at his harsh tone. *Is that so?*

"It is." Liam let his eyes go cold; the imp subsided. Liam released its murky form from the prison of his stare.

And I suppose she's for the likes of you?

"She will be." Of all the girls he'd ever courted, Bea had been the toughest of all... but challenges always brought the greatest rewards—and there could be no reward greater than her pale flesh, the soft surrender of her sighs, the inky curtain of her hair veiling their love...

"She will be," he said again, tasting the promise in the words.

And smiled.

"Hey, Kaya, do you have a minute?"

The dancer looked up from her notebook with a warm smile. "Sure, princess. Come—sit—tell me what's on your mind."

Ryna pushed aside the lace curtain shielding the vardo's doorway and stepped inside. Only a single small fan whirred despite the growing afternoon heat; Phoe and

Ryna's vardo had the air conditioner on full blast. But then, the older Gypsy lived for summer. Ryna took a seat on the bed. "Can I ask you a really big favor?"

Kaya tucked her pen into the spiral of her notebook. "Of course."

"Could you keep Phoenix entertained tomorrow morning?"

Kaya looked at her quizzically. "That's a *strange* favor, but not really a *big* one. Any particular reason?"

Ryna fidgeted. "Her brother's wedding rehearsal is tomorrow afternoon. The whole thing has her really upset, but she always dodges the question when I ask her why. I mean, sure, she had a lousy home life, but it shouldn't get to her that bad."

"Have you considered that maybe she doesn't want to talk about it?"

"I kind of came to that conclusion, yeah. So I called her brother—he said he could get together with me tomorrow morning, but I really don't want to leave Phoe alone to dwell on it."

A small frown creased Kaya's brow. "Doesn't that strike you as a little—underhanded?"

"I need to know, Kaya. I can't help her unless I understand."

"What if it doesn't help?'

"It has to." Ryna gazed at the gathering clouds through the lace curtain. "It hurts to see her so unhappy. It's like something gnawing at my soul. And I don't know how to make it stop."

Kaya's voice held a quiet understanding. "I have a book reading scheduled at the library, but there's no reason she couldn't accompany me."

"Really? That would be perfect. Maybe it'd even give her some motivation to send her own stuff out—she's been sitting on some of it for a year, now, almost."

The frown returned. "Be kind, Ryna. It's not easy—and she's very sensitive. She's still learning about being accepted; she might not be ready to face that rejection yet."

The fiddler huffed out a frustrated breath. "But she has all these dreams, and they'll never come true unless she *does* something about them!"

"That's true," Kaya allowed, "but she needs to make that decision herself—and not because she feels pestered. You know how much *you* hate it when people tell you what to do."

It was a good point; Ryna bowed her head in acquiescence. "You'll watch over her, though?"

"I will keep her so thoroughly distracted that she won't even realize she's *being* distracted."

Ryna threw her arms around Kaya in a spontaneous hug. "I owe you big."

An affectionate squeeze in return. "You owe me nothing but your happiness, princess. Nothing at all."

◇ ◇ ◇

"Somebody tell me why I'm here again."

Phoenix glanced sideways at her love. Although she tried to keep an open mind, Phoe could see Ryna's point. It was miserably hot out—had been all day, with clouds of mosquitoes as thick as Patty's skull. They steered clear of the Gypsies, most of whom were socializing near Bedside Manor, but the other rennies gathered for Wednesday's mandatory Rehearsal swatted and cursed profusely.

On the other hand, it gave her a break from Christine's wedding dress. Every little pearl whispered that she would have to deal with her parents soon. She did not cherish the reminder.

"Anyone? Anyone?" Ryna asked.

"Because masochism never goes out of style?" Toby offered.

Phoenix cocked her head and nudged her glasses up her nose. "So that's why so many people attend college."

"I'm here, peoples!" Patty announced. She seemed happy about it.

No one else was.

"I hope she doesn't make us do that stupid counting game again," someone grumbled from Phoe's left.

"Where is she getting these—*My First Management Book*?"

"It's probably pink, with little pop-up pictures."

"And if two things pop up at the same time, you have to start over."

Phoenix snickered in spite of herself.

"I have a brand new unity-building game for you today, peoples, right from the Royal Shakespeare Company! It's called 'Yes, And.' It teaches you to support your fellow actors' mini-plays by only allowing positive words! Whatever they say, you must respond with the words 'yes, and' before adding on." She hugged her clipboard with glee. "Oh, I just know this is going to help our unity so much!"

"Mini-play. Is that what she's calling them instead of *bits*?" Phoenix asked.

"Yes," Toby agreed, "and I think it's even dumber than our old Entertainment Director not letting us call first-year entertainers *rookies*."

"Yes, and I'd never say *rookie* again if only we could have him back," Ryna added.

"Yes, and I bet she's never even read Shakespeare," Phoenix said with a righteous sniff.

"Huh." Toby folded his arms over his chest. "Our unity seems fine to me."

◇ ◇ ◇

"Well *that* was a big, pink waste of time."

Ryna eyed Phoenix with a mixture of satisfaction and remorse as her love flopped down on the bed. Phoe was finally opening her eyes… but Ryna had begun to depend on her positive outlook—irksome as it could sometimes be. *If I was Tanek, I'd say Phoe was starting to realize Patty's inner evil—or maybe giving in to her own.*

"Smile and nod; be good little rennies, now—where's my unity?" Phoe mimicked bitterly. "A whole evening of not being allowed a real opinion—not that Patty-Cakes had to agree with anything *we* said."

"Yeah." Ryna started some water for tea. Maybe Phoe's mood was backlash from the parent thing, and after the wedding she'd go back to normal?

"I couldn't believe how she kept telling Annie, who everyone *knows* is an improv actor, that everything is really scripted and there's no such thing as improv. What happened to listening to and respecting your fellow actors?"

"Patty isn't a fellow actor." Ryna leaned back against the fridge. It hummed gently as she watched the seconds count down on the microwave. "She's the Artistic Despot."

"She thinks she's God." Phoenix plucked irritably at the nearest pillow. "If something isn't the way she wants it, she'll simply think harder until reality bends to her vision."

"Not even a *bear* could get this jar open," Toby complained from outside. "It'd have to chew the cap right off!"

"Oh, give it here, you big baby," Ryna scolded, happy to escape into the deepening night.

Murmured conversation and household noises floated from the vardos. Elda called a taunt to her brother as he stepped down from their vardo; Niki's laughter rang from behind her lace curtain.

"Some of the jam must've gotten on the rim and stuck it shut," Toby groused.

Ryna held the offending jar for a moment, let a flash of energy flow through her hands. With barely a twist, the lid gave. "Here you are."

"Kitchen Magick saves the day again." He kissed the top of her head. "I guess it pays to be small and helpless—you have to get creative."

She scowled playfully at him. "See if I save *your* manly hide from the evil jam jar again."

"Just as long as—Ryna?"

"Shh," she hissed. There had been… something. A sound, a prickling. The world had gone too silent—like a forest before the storm breaks.

"What?" Toby glanced around furtively. "What is it?"

Something was coming—Ryna could feel it building like the urge to scream. The stars winked a cold, silent warning.

A calico missile bolted past, hissing.

Karma.

"What the—"

"In," she ordered, roughly shoving him towards his home. She heard him stumble, but had already turned, reaching to shut her father's door with a wisp of Magick.

It didn't budge.

Something chittered.

"Close them!" she tried to yell, but the words caught. She felt suffocated, like facing into the wind—but the night was still. She lunged for Kaya and Tremayne's door, yanked it closed.

Chitter, chitter.

Slam! Slam! Slam!

A curtain of ink crept across the sky, blocking the stars' light.

chitterchitter—

She raced for the elders' purple and gold vardo. *Phuro* Basil stood by the sink; *Baba* Luna brushed her hair on the bed as Ryna jerked their door shut—and whirled to see Toby doing the same for their family on the other side of camp.

Run!!! Ryna felt more than heard Phoenix's warning—and instinctively obeyed.

chitterchitterchitter—

Closer.

CHITTERCHITTERCHITTER—

Closer—

Something sharp grazed her arm; she pushed off the ground in one fluid motion—

—heard Toby's door bang shut—

—felt something claw the worn leather of her shoe—

—slammed her shin painfully on her porch and would have fallen if strong hands hadn't seized her, pulled her inside. "Get the—"

SLAM!

Something thumped against the hardwood surface, screeching.

Phoenix threw the deadbolt home; Ryna was already pulling curtains shut. Karma flattened herself against her person's legs, ears back, rowling.

Another something.

Ryna jumped as three candles flared to life, belatedly recognizing the surge of Phoe's Magick. She blasted extra energy into her home's defenses, felt the boost of her love's power as creatures pounded the vardo from all sides, turning it into a snare drum. The fiddler bowed her head, squeezing her eyes in concentration, willing the shields to hold.

"Are we going to make it?" Phoenix whispered, her words strangely clear against the cacophony.

"They're not strong," Ryna said.

...but *gods* there were a lot of them, pushing, poking, trying to get in...

And then it ceased.

The silence rang loud in their ears; for a moment the vardo-mates simply stood, breathing, waiting for the next shoe to drop.

Karma sat down and licked her fur back into place. Dirty, nasty creatures. Nothing she couldn't handle—she had only fled to give her people warning, of course—but still!

Ryna tentatively reached a tendril of awareness beyond her shields, found only clean night air. She let out a shaky breath, relieved to feel her family unharmed.

"You're bleeding."

"Am I?" Ryna looked down to find a thin red line along her right forearm. She frowned. "I really hope this isn't like our last souvenirs from the Shadow Fae."

Phoenix pulled the first aid kit from under the sink. "We'll clean it up, have Basil and Kaya look at it; it'll be all right." Her voice trembled, though.

"Ryna? Phoenix?" *Phuro* Basil called from outside.

Ryna clasped her love's hands to still their tremors. "Phoe, it's okay. Let's go check in with the others."

"And have your arm looked at."

"And have my arm looked at," she agreed, leading Phoe to the door.

The others had gathered in the common area, giving reassuring hugs and looking around. "Are you two all right?" Basil asked.

Ryna nodded. "Well enough. Everyone else?"

"Thanks to you and Toby," Niki said, rubbing her arms. Tanek had one arm across her shoulders and a scowl on his face.

Tremayne smiled faintly. "Indeed. Well done."

"Thank Ryna and her cat," Toby deferred.

"Ryna needs healing," Phoenix said. "Her arm—"

"It's not much," Ryna said, but willingly submitted to the immediate attention of Kaya and *Phuro* Basil.

"It's not… infected," Kaya observed, one hand hovering over the injury. Ryna felt the brush of her energy like a cool stream. "Not like your other ones were."

"Best get it tended anyhow," *Baba* Luna pointed out. "I'll get the kit."

Esmerelda huffed out a breath. "Well, it doesn't look like those things damaged anything, but it's hard to tell in this light."

"We need better shields," Tanek said. "For the whole encampment. They shouldn't have gotten that close."

"Agreed." *Phuro* Basil gave one last look around. "It's late, though, and we're all tired. What we have now should hold for the night; we can improve our defenses tomorrow when we're rested. In the meantime, Ryna—"

"Coming. Phoenix?"

"Right behind you."

Ryna gave her a tight smile—and hoped the excitement had ended for the night.

◇ ◇ ◇

"We have marked her."

Liam repressed a shudder as the sparrow-like creature sucked blood off one of its claws. Ryna's blood, but still. "Is that supposed to impress me?" he demanded imperiously. "You marked her last year. I've seen her back. It bears the scars of your kind."

Amazing what scorn could manifest in such a small, immobile face. "That was no mark. Those were tokens of battle," it said in its strange, whispering voice, and fluffed itself. "This will heal quickly. It will not pain her. By moon-dark she will likely forget it was there. We will not."

Liam folded his arms. "If it heals, what good has it done you?"

"The wound will heal; she will always carry the mark. We have touched her and will again. You limit your thoughts and are too quick to dismiss." It cocked its head, a gesture eerily reminiscent of his love. "Do you intend to catch this worm or not? You must wait for small victories to mature."

A skeptical eyebrow raised.

It chittered—its version of laughter. "Concern yourself with your own part. This world now knows her as its own."

◇ ◇ ◇

Phoenix looked up from her book with gritty eyes. She'd given up on sleep long ago; it had only visited in snatches chased with foul dreams… not that being awake proved much better. Even *War for the Oaks* couldn't distract her.

Ryna, on the other hand, had curled up, yawned once, and rested soundly. Phoenix envied her ability to take everything so nonchalantly.

"It's past dawn—I suppose we should go out," the redhead said with a bleary yawn. And, suiting her words, tumbled out of bed, stretched, and headed for the door.

Karma looked even less inclined to move than Phoenix felt. The cat had sprawled across one of Phoe's legs, only the twitch of her tail revealing her unease. Phoe scritched the feline behind her ears, wishing she could stay behind as well, and followed her love.

Everything looked the same, though the knowledge of what had passed made the early morning stillness foreboding. The other Gypsies were poking their noses out… Niki stepped down from Tanek's porch, a satin brocade robe clutched around herself. Evidently she hadn't wanted to spend the night alone—not that Phoe could blame her.

Three grasshoppers sprang into the air as her bare foot touched the ground; the dancer yelped in surprise and jumped back.

"Apparently last night's visitors left some company," *Baba* Luna observed with distaste.

Phoenix pressed herself against her vardo's door. Grasshoppers were as bad as moths… and the ground teemed with them.

Kaya scowled. "I don't like this."

Tremayne put an arm around her shoulders and squeezed. Phoe could tell by his set expression that he agreed.

"They're only grasshoppers," Esmerelda said firmly. Half a dozen of the beasties bounded away from her as she strode to the fire pit and lit it. "Toby, get me some green wood. We're going to smoke them out."

Tobaltio gazed dubiously at his sister. "Will that work?"

"It will when I'm through with it."

"I'll help," Tanek volunteered. "I know where there's a fallen tree with the leaves still on."

Phoenix sat down on the porch, feet tucked carefully under herself. If the others were still out, it couldn't be *too* dangerous, right?

Still, she wished she could run back in the vardo and slam the door without looking like an idiot.

Toby and Tanek returned shortly, arms loaded with leafy twigs. Esmerelda gestured for them to empty their cargo on the newly born fire.

Phuro Basil joined them, a pouch of dried sage in his hand. He tossed a generous amount onto the flames. "Ryna, Niki, Toby, if you could keep the smoke low…"

Energy rose around the Air elements and spread; the smoke bumped off an invisible barrier and roiled downward. Phoe didn't know if smoke or the scent of sage usually affected grasshoppers, but these did not like it at all. Hundreds careened around the campsite, desperate for escape… but not one touched the vardos. It did not make Phoenix feel any better about them.

"So, Phoenix," Kaya called from her porch, "I have to go to the library for an author appearance when all this is cleaned up. Would you like to join me in a trip out for breakfast beforehand?"

"I would love to," Phoe readily agreed.

After all, she had *no* intention of sticking around to see if the little monsters would return.

Ryna shifted impatiently on Daniel's front porch and knocked a second time. He was expecting her. What on earth was taking him so—?

Her brother-in-law opened the door, hair tousled and battered Irish cap askew.

The Gypsy bit back a grin. "I hope I'm not interrupting."

He chuckled. "If only. C'mon in."

"Thanks." She followed him to the kitchen, noting the house's tidy disarray: gifts stacked in one corner, little plastic bottles sprawled across the dining room table, four to-do lists posted on the wall with neat scratches through several of the items.

"I haven't gotten around to breakfast yet. You want anything?"

"I'm okay." Ryna swung a leg over one of the kitchen chairs and sat, resting her chin on the polished wooden back as Daniel fixed a bowl of brightly colored cereal. "Phoenix isn't, though. She's really stressed about dealing with your parents."

Dan gazed at her a moment as if waiting for the punch line. When none came, he leaned back against a counter. "Understandable."

Ryna tossed her hair over one shoulder impatiently. "I tried getting her to tell me what the big deal was, but she avoided the subject."

"She ran away from them, Ryna. Did you expect she'd *want* to talk about it?"

"I can't help her if I don't know what's wrong." She met his gaze, let the pleading show in her own. "Please, Daniel. I can't protect her unless I know the enemy."

Daniel sighed and stirred his cereal with his spoon. Ryna could tell he didn't really want to talk about it, either, but hopefully his love for his sister would be enough…

"Our parents had… very definite ideas about how we should grow up."

"Phoe said your mom guilted you guys into whatever she wanted."

Danny nodded, still not looking up from his cereal. "She did."

"She didn't say anything about your dad."

"She wouldn't." A pause. "Mom at least you could ignore—or once in a while outwit. Trying to fight Dad's beliefs only made things worse."

Ryna held her breath as Daniel looked up, met her gaze unflinchingly.

"One of those beliefs was 'spare the rod, spoil the child.'"

Pieces clicked into place in Ryna's head; for a moment she could only stare, temper rising.

"He never seriously injured us—nothing that would require a trip to the hospital. He just had a very—physical—way of getting his point across."

Ryna had to get up; she couldn't sit still. She clenched her hands into fists to keep them from shaking. "I'm going to kill him. I'm going to take his intestines and wrap them around his—"

"I see why she didn't tell you," Daniel observed with a strange little smile. "Phoenix doesn't like to be around angry people. She probably figured she'd escaped, so it didn't matter anymore."

The fiddler struggled to keep her voice level. "Do you believe that?"

He sighed and put aside his cereal, stared up at the ceiling as if searching for the answer. "Father also believes that sons grow up to be men—and daughters grow up to be wives." He turned his attention back to Ryna; she could read the answer in the sinking of her guts.

"And as far as he's concerned, she's not a wife yet," she said flatly.

Daniel nodded solemnly.

Ryna ran a hand through her hair, leaned heavily on the chair back. "What do I do?"

"Dad's a big one for public face." Dan recovered his bowl; he stabbed at the contents with his spoon. "As long as she's not alone with him—and not shaming him—she'll be okay. She knows the game. Just—keep an eye on her. Please."

"I will," she promised. "I will."

Sunshine flooded the library's spacious interior; Phoenix hardly recognized it as the same place in which she had spent countless hours while growing up. A fresh carpet in a shade of light gray had replaced its stained and threadbare reddish-brown predecessor. The checkout counters were new, too, sleek and streamlined. She missed the comforting, used look of the place... although, upon reflection, the updated atmosphere might encourage more parents to bring their children here.

Kaya's lecture had gone wonderfully. Her audience ranged from teenagers to ladies whose hair had not seen color in decades... and for the space of an hour, they were all simply women with dreams of how romance should be. They all had questions and comments; Kaya listened with patience and answered with wit, compassion, and grace. By the time the last person filed out, Phoenix knew exactly who she wanted to be when she grew up. How lucky Ryna was—and what Phoe would have given to be raised under Kaya's loving wing.

And if they'd really been mother and daughter, Danny's wedding rehearsal wouldn't be such a stomach-dropping prospect. Phoe sighed. At least she would be there to return to at the ordeal's end...

"Come here." Kaya beckoned to Phoenix. "I have something I want to show you."

Phoe pushed away thoughts of impending doom as she sidestepped a ten-year-old steadying her stack of books with her chin. A smile of kinship shaped the Gypsy's lips, replaced a moment later with one of delighted surprise as she entered the children's section. Colorful posters of cartoon characters with books decorated once-plain walls. An inviting array of puppets awaited young hands on a nearby rack. Bright mobiles hung from the ceiling; decals and construction-paper alphabets adorned the large windows. Bins of books stood at the perfect height for little people, as always, but they no longer looked chewed-on.

Kaya stopped in front of one, a bold sign marked ***~P~*** on its splashboard. She pushed aside half the books and looked up at the curious Phoenix. "This is your spot."

Phoenix cocked her head, confused. "My spot?"

"Where your books will go. When I first started writing romance novels, sometimes the only thing that kept me going was visiting my spot in libraries and bookstores." Kaya ran a finger along the bin's edge. "It made it more real, somehow."

The raven-haired Gypsy quirked a pleased smile. She could almost see her own artwork inviting her to pick up a beautifully bound hardcover and explore its contents. "My spot."

"And no one can fill it but you."

Phoe looked from Kaya, to the spot, to the young readers surrounding her, the weight of that statement settling over her. Children happily plowed through the bins or sat with towers of books, all in search of a story to become their favorite. None of them knew… none of them *would* know the stories in her heart unless she put them within reach of those curious minds.

Phoenix set her shoulders. "I will fill it."

"You will." Kaya gave her a quick squeeze. "I have faith in you."

"I know," Phoe said. "It means a lot."

She only wished she shared that faith.

◇ ◇ ◇

Ryna glanced with concern at her love as they meandered past the BLUE. Phoenix's steps slowed for more than deference to Ryna's shorter stride… and all because of her stupid, narrow-minded, hate-filled parents. Even the thought of her parents turned Phoe back into the stuttering rookie who couldn't express an opinion without six qualifiers. It made Ryna furious even as her heart ached for her sensitive soulmate. She slipped her tiny hand into Phoe's. A brilliant smile rewarded the simple contact.

"You are safe," Ryna ventured as they started across Shepherd's Green, not knowing what else to say. "You know that, right?"

"With you here? Always." And squeezed her hand as she squared her shoulders.

"Phoenix, Ryna," Christine greeted with a warm smile as they rounded the Chapel's corner.

Ryna's nape hairs prickled with the sure knowledge that someone was glaring at her. She turned to see a tall, solidly built fellow with a square jaw standing on the other end of the seating area, a woman of middling height at his side. The redhead crossed her arms, raised her eyebrows in challenge.

The man's bullying scowl deepened.

Ooo. Don't like strong-minded women, do you? Ryna tossed her hair—and pointedly turned her attention to Christine and the spry, middle-aged woman beside her.

"… meet my mother, Amelia," Christine was saying.

"Named after the pilot," the older woman added, taking first Phoenix's hand, then Ryna's in a strong grip. The sparkle in her eyes and the gray laced through her medium-brown hair put Ryna in mind of *Baba* Luna.

Ryna liked her immediately.

"Ah, I see you've met my mother-in-law," Daniel observed, striding over to the small gathering.

"It looks like Christine is getting the sour end of the deal," Phoenix quipped.

Ryna wished she could go kill something. She had her target picked.

Dan gave his sister a one-armed hug. "I tried giving them the wrong directions," he confided. "It didn't work."

Christine looked shocked. A little. Or like she was trying to be shocked, anyhow. It wasn't working.

"Don't you worry about them, kids." Amelia patted Daniel's arm. "I'll go see if I can slip something in their drinks."

"All ready to go?" Dan asked as his future in-law ambled towards his and Phoe's parents—who immediately put on their public faces.

"Ready," Phoenix agreed, fidgeting with her bond ring.

"Hey," Ryna said, taking both of Phoe's hands. "I'll be sitting right over there, okay?"

"All right." Phoe took a deep breath, girding herself for battle.

"And if they so much as say one wrong word to you, I'm going to fly them over Cottage's sheep pen and dump them in it, okay?"

A giggle. "Okay."

Ryna kissed her love's knuckles. "If we can face the hordes of darkness, we can deal with two crotchety parents, right?"

Phoenix nodded in a way that was probably supposed to be confident and hurried after her brother.

Ryna wished with all her heart that she could follow. "She'll be okay," she told herself as she plopped on one of the benches. She hoped it wouldn't come to actually zooming people through the air. Cockiness aside, Ryna wasn't sure she could lift anything that mundane. Even pens had more sparkle to work with.

Amelia was still chatting up the parents, their public smiles stretched and tight. Ryna hoped they were *really* uncomfortable.

A little boy walked up to her, looked her over, and scrunched his nose. "Are you really a witch?"

It shouldn't have caught the Gypsy as off-guard as it did. "What?"

"My momma says you're a witch," he elaborated happily, wiggling up onto the seat beside her and swinging his feet. "Daddy says so, too. But you're not green, and you don't have a pointy hat."

From the mouths of babes, Ryna thought with a wry grin. "Not all witches wear pointy hats. And they're only green when they get sick."

"Can you turn people into toads?"

"No, but I can make pencils fly. And my mom can make people feel better when they're sick or hurt."

"Then how come everyone says witches can turn people into toads if they can't?"

"That's a good question." Ryna put on an expression of careful consideration. "I think it's because people don't understand witches, so they're afraid of them, even though they don't need to be. And they make up stories to exp—"

"Ernest, don't bother the nice lady," scolded a perfectly manicured woman as she marched up like a well-drilled soldier.

"He's no bother," Ryna assured her. "We're having a fascinating conversation about prejudice and stereotypes."

"That's nice," an equally stiff man intervened, seizing the boy's hand. "Come along, Ernest. It's time to visit Aunt Claire."

"Momma, can I be a witch, too?"

"We'll discuss that later."

Ryna waved pleasantly as her young friend's parents carted him away.

Christine's mother took his place. "Well, that was unpleasant."

"Phoe and Danny's parents live up to their reputation?" Ryna asked.

"My daughter says they're less odious when they're in public, so I made sure they knew they were among strangers," she said with a conspiratorial smile. "I spent a while gushing over *both* their children and how proud they must be."

"And?"

She made a face. "They ooze righteous intolerance… but I think they'll behave themselves for today."

"I really appreciate that," Ryna said. "I'm sure Phoenix does, too."

"My pleasure. Now, would you like to meet some of Christine's relatives? It'd do those hatemongers good to see you and your partner being accepted by some decent folk."

Ryna considered it a moment, but shook her head. "I told Phoe I'd be right here. I don't want her to look up and find me gone."

"You're a good woman," Amelia said, warmth lighting her eyes. "Phoenix is lucky to have you. And, since you're being so noble, I'll just bring the relatives *here*."

A chuckle escaped the Gypsy as the older woman strode off purposefully. The day was shaping up to be an interesting one indeed.

If there truly were nine levels of Hell, Phoenix felt certain such things as rehearsal dinners were reserved for the twelfth. Thankfully her brother and Christine had hired caterers to do the dinner on Pendragon's grounds, but it didn't help her twitching desire to bolt for the safety of her vardo. Phoe tried to ignore the covert stares and furtive whispers of her relatives, the exaggerated politeness where there had once been warmth, the way her little cousins were pointedly kept away from her… and her parents, always watching, scowls on their faces.

She poked at a bland hunk of chicken that had cost her brother a sum inversely proportionate to its taste. *I wish Auntie Ily was here.*

At least Christine's family had been kind—especially her brother Justin, Daniel's best man, who teased Phoe with the playful camaraderie of an old friend. And she did have Ryna, mixed blessing that it was. She treated this whole thing like a game—make the normals react, maybe coax a laugh out of her soulmate. Phoe appreciated the thought, but Ryna didn't understand that she only made things worse.

"I'm going to start carrying a bottle of hot sauce around your family," Ryna teased, wrinkling her nose at her chicken. "Doesn't anyone in this state believe in seasoning?"

"Just pepper and salt," Phoe told her. "And even that would ignite half the people here."

"I'm surprised you didn't starve as a child."

"How you holding up, munchkin?" Daniel asked, sidling up to where the Gypsies stood.

Phoenix looked up at him. "Do I have 'leper' tattooed across my forehead?"

He brushed her hair back and peered at her. "Looks more like 'lesbian' to me."

Ryna rolled her eyes. "In this crowd, I think 'leper' might be safer."

"Maybe. Lepers don't resist being cured," Phoe said with a wan smile that quickly faded. She had the disconcerting sensation that she'd been caught doing something she shouldn't—and whirled to find her parents uncomfortably close.

Ryna and Daniel turned, too—Ryna plastered a huge smile across her face.

Phoenix tried not to cringe.

"Robert and Claire Saunders, I presume?"

"Hm. Yes." Claire Saunders brushed her off with a gesture reserved for servants and immigrants. "Beatrice."

"Mother. Father." Phoe concentrated on keeping her breathing even, her gaze steady. How much had they heard? "I'm glad to see you."

Her father stared down at her severely. "Are you?"

"Hello—my name is Ryna. I'm Phoenix's lifemate," the fiddler piped up as if neither had spoken. "I've heard so much about you."

Robert's countenance glazed over as his spine stiffened with righteous indignation. "The Lord hears our prayers and will free our Beatrice from both your heathen ways and the devil's name you have claimed her with."

"I chose it on my own, Father," Phoe protested, trying to break from his claw-like gaze.

Her mother sniffed, adding the weight of her stare to her husband's. "Beatrice *will* settle down with a nice young *man* and raise children as God intended."

"Hasn't happened so far," Ryna observed cheerily. "Maybe you're praying to the wrong god?"

Phoenix wanted to run screaming, but she couldn't move.

"I think this party is about over, don't you?" Danny piped up with gracious nervousness; their parents' attention turned to him. "Phoenix, Christine was hoping you'd help her with that veil tonight; would you like a ride?"

Released from the prison of their eyes, Phoe took a shuddering breath. "Yes. Please. I'll go get it from Elda."

"You do that. Mom, Dad, I'm sure you'll understand."

Before they had time to disagree, Phoe grabbed Ryna's hand and towed her towards C-gate.

And prayed to any kind deity listening that her parents wouldn't follow.

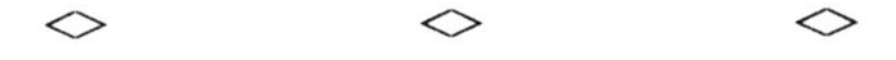

Ryna gazed with concern at her vardo-mate, busily shoving clothes into a backpack. She'd been utterly silent the entire walk back to the campground despite several attempts to distract her. "I noticed a new bumper sticker on Jen's truck this year," Ryna tried again. "It said, 'Sorry I missed church; I was busy practicing witchcraft and becoming a lesbian.' Maybe we could get matching T-shirts, wear them to your next family gathering."

Phoenix looked up, a weariness in her eyes that made Ryna's heart ache. "Could you stop? With the jokes? Please?" She looked away, finished packing. "It's bad enough having to deal with my family as it is."

Ryna stared at her for a moment, dumbfounded. "I was trying to help."

Phoe took a deep breath, blew it out. "I know. It's just—you don't know them. Throwing it in their faces like that will only make it worse next time."

"I'm sorry?" There really seemed nothing else she could say.

The raven-haired Gypsy huffed out another breath, tucked a star-white tendril behind her ear. "I'm sorry. I'm just—I hate dealing with them, and it has me on edge. And now I have to go to my brother's house and sit with Christine and that veil and a billion little pearls when all I really want to do is hide in a book."

Ryna nodded acceptance. "Take care of yourself, okay? Have that brother of yours buy you some chocolate or something."

That, at last, got a smile. "Thanks, Artemis."

And then, with a quick kiss and the slinging of her backpack over one shoulder, she left.

The fiddler stared at the door a moment after she'd gone. Why wouldn't she stand up to her parents? It wasn't like they could really *do* anything to her—not anymore. If she ran into her own birth-mother…

But then, I've always been more of a scrapper. That's not Phoenix's way, I guess, no matter how much good it would do her. Ryna plopped down on the bed, where her kitty had sprawled on her back, and administered a tummy rub. "Guess it's you and me tonight, Karma."

Karma blinked serenely at her person, unaffected by the vardo's sudden barrenness. And stretched, inviting a little attention to her underarm.

Ryna obliged, and a contented purring rumbled the air. The space was… nice.

When her kitty had gotten enough adoration for the time being, Ryna selected a drumming CD that Phoenix detested, popped it in the stereo, and went to see if Niki could be enticed into a few rounds of poker.

◇ ◇ ◇

The moon was nearing its final quarter.

Liam smiled grimly at it. He could feel the Shadow Fae's strength gaining. Discord ripened like a pomegranate, succulent and promising… he could feel that, too. He stood across the road from the Gypsies' trailers and drank of it; it fed his soul as it fed the Shadow Fae.

But… there was more. Greater. Deeper. It pulled him, and he followed—up the Olympic Staircase, past the BLUE, through Upson Downs. It might be folly—in all likelihood the dissonance he followed would lead him right for one of the many skirmishes between the Bright and Shadow Fae. It wouldn't be the first time he'd made that unhappy mistake…

Still, the more he knew of his predators—his prey—the easier he could use them for his own means. He hesitated at the section of picket fence to the right of Bakery Stage that swung open on faire days to release the Grand Parade. The path beyond it led to Fool's Knoll… one of the Bright Fae's strong spots. But if that was where his instincts led…

The fence stood partially open; cautiously Liam slipped around it. He turned down the path to the right that led behind crafters' shops—and stopped, horror choking him at the limp, outstretched hand on the ground twenty feet away. Its luminous skin shone starkly against the mass of Shadow Fae that obscured the rest of its body. "What passes here?" Liam demanded roughly.

The milling Shadows turned to him—some formless, some shaped like creatures that should never have existed. For a span of moments he walked a sword's edge. They did not like the interruption. Still, they had use for him—and some feared him.

Liam could see their victim better now—reed-like limbs akimbo, its light fading to a dull ash gray. A swift, sudden sadness pierced Liam's heart for the loss of its shining beauty.

"They are weakening," whispered a hulking Shadow, its voice harsh and rasping. "Soon it will be time..."

Liam smiled, dismissing foolish longing. There would always be sacrifices. It didn't matter. His plan was working perfectly.

◇ ◇ ◇

"You know what these remind me of?" Phoe asked as she tied a little parchment tag on a tiny plastic bottle of bubble solution. Sunlight streamed in the parlor's huge windows, making it hard to recall why she'd been in a bad mood last night.

"What do they remind you of?" Christine asked, squinting as she coaxed the miniscule strip of ribbon into a bow.

"Plague pouches."

Christine laughed. "Are you still giving them away?"

"Yup." Place the bottle in the pile, grab another. "Elda saves me her scraps, so I make a new batch whenever she finishes a sewing project."

"It must be so exciting, living on the road," the bride-to-be said with a wistful sigh. "You do know that no earthquake would disturb your brother until he's finished reading your latest letter."

"Really?"

"Of course!" Christine scowled at the little bottle. "Why is it that the women always get relegated to tasks like this one?"

"Because we want everything to be perfect and wouldn't trust anyone else to touch the things."

Christine giggled. "Oh, Phoenix, I do like you. I'm sorry you have to go through so much hassle with your family to be part of this."

"Me too—but it's worth it to be there for you and Danny." Bottle in the pile, grab another. "It's funny, though. I'd forgotten what cardboard cutouts my parents are."

"How so?"

"Well, it's like—they spend all their time trying to impress everyone with how much money they have, or what good children they have, or how incredibly Christian they are. I don't even know if they believe in God or if they just think they're supposed to and are trying to show off."

Christine paused, probably shocked at the bitterness in Phoe's voice. "I'm sure there's more to them than that."

A shrug. "Mother only ever said she liked something when it was already fashionable, and Father got all his opinions from religious radio and the intolerant parts of the *Bible*. I don't think they ever even asked me what my favorite color was. I don't know if either of *them* had a favorite *anything*. No wonder I fell in love with the life out at Faire. It's all so real."

"They got you a horse."

A snort this time. Christine was stretching, trying to find some good in people Phoenix was beginning to believe had none. "Every time they mentioned Pegasus it was to point out what generous parents they were and how well I did in the expensive riding lessons they sent me to."

"Maybe they were proud of you?"

Phoenix looked her sister-in-law-to-be straight in the eye. "They're not proud of me now."

Christine, bless her, simply removed Phoenix's latest bubble bottle and took her hands. "We are."

Phoe smiled, though her eyes had filled with tears.

"Bad day?" the fiddler asked hesitantly, putting down her instrument as her love stormed into the vardo. She had been about to head up to the BLUE, but this was more important.

"It was great right up until Mother called and I was stupid enough to pick up Danny's phone." Phoenix flopped despondently onto the bed.

Ryna sat gingerly beside her. "That bad?"

"I made the mistake of trying to get away by saying you were expecting me. She just said, 'Oh. Her. We'll discuss that later' and continued babbling on about how now that I'd taken my little vacation and seen the world, I really should find a nice boy and settle down."

"Youch."

"I am *not* looking forward to Sunday."

"At least you'll be on your home turf with all of us," Ryna offered, tucking the soft, star-white tendrils behind her love's ears. Then, realizing that it might not be the most comforting thought given the last encounter's outcome, she hurried to add, “I ran into one of the peasants—the one with the fox puppet. He set a booby trap for the jerk who’s been stealing power items—loaded up a crystal with energy and left it in his tent.”

Phoenix looked taken aback. Surely Phoe didn’t still think the Gypsies were the only ones who could do Magick? “Did he catch anything?”

Ryna shrugged. “Half a dozen dead flies right next to the crystal—and huge claw gouges in the dirt outside the tent. Probably just gave it one hell of a headache.”

Phoe shivered, probably remembering similar claws raking the flesh of her leg. “What do we do?”

“I don’t think there’s anything we *can* do,” Ryna admitted. “Aside from guarding our stuff better, anyhow. It’s annoying, but I doubt we’re in any danger.”

The raven-haired Gypsy frowned as if she wasn’t sure she believed it, but said only, “You going up to the BLUE tonight? I need some music to take my mind off things.”

“Well, then, my lady fair—grab your whistle and let’s away.”

◇ ◇ ◇

Shimmer.

Shim—

Liam frowned in concentration as he tried to force himself through the gargoyle atop the BLUE. He had seen the mortal world through the eyes of creatures he had possessed... but it wasn’t enough. He couldn’t trust that the Shadow Fae would carry out his errands. He needed the capability to make his presence *known*. It was proving to be damnably hard.

Shimmershimmershim—

Reality wavered like the view through a window in a rainstorm. Half-formed clips of music and conversation splattered against his ears. The marble squirmed in his fist, shifting, pulsing, sucking. Liam ignored his stomach, *forced* it to his will...

And then—

Two figures: one short, one taller, and Liam would have known them anywhere.

The taller one glanced toward him, and in a moment of rare clarity, he felt her peer more closely, felt her energy reach to see if anything was there.

Liam nearly dropped the stone in shock. *She’s gotten* good*!*

He smiled in pride. What a team they would make...

With determination, he renewed his task.

◇ ◇ ◇

"Ryna, did you see—?"
"See what, Phoenix?"
"You didn't… with the gargoyle?"
"No, nothing. Why?"
"Never mind. I'm crazy. Let's go inside."
Shimmer.
Shimmshim—!

Pendragon Renaissance Faire

Weekend Three: Unveiling the Mystery

~*~

The deepest secrets of the orient come alive and dwell in our village. Succumb to wonder as they steal away your senses and transport you to lands of magic and mystery. See exotic belly dancers performing the forbidden dances of their homelands. See caravans and Bedouin tents telling fortunes and permitting us small peeks into their foreign ways. Saddle up your camel, grab your scimitars, and ride towards adventure! (Theme sponsored by Shiek's Mediterranean Dining)

~*~

beep. beep. beep. be—

"Augh!" Ryna cried as an armload of garb descended upon her.

"Rise and shine!" Phoenix chirped.

"You're in a good mood this morning," the redhead observed, fighting through the unexpected garments.

"Yup! I thought since this is—you know—our anniversary, sort of—I thought maybe we could do something to celebrate." Phoe gave her a winning smile.

"You sound like you have a plan." Ryna retrieved Phoenix's spectacles and a bottle of cleaner from the shelf surrounding the bed. It always amazed her how dirty the things got; she couldn't imagine how her love could see out of them.

"It's—it's sort of a surprise. Well, not really a surprise because you'll probably guess what it is right away, but—"

Ryna cut her off with a kiss. "Show me."

Phoenix nodded, unable to gather wits enough for words.

A quirky smile twitched Ryna's lips. She handed Phoenix's glasses to their rightful owner and climbed into her clothes.

Once fed and dressed, the soulmates migrated through the just-stirring campground, up the Olympic Staircase, through C-gate, past the BLUE and Como Cottage, the Croft and Flying Buttress Stage. When they reached the ugly white tent, however, Phoenix tugged Ryna to the left, across Shepherd's Green and through the bright tents of the Celestial Pavilion, towards *Lady Fortune* Stage. Shopkeepers called comments back and forth as they set out merchandise and disassembled the plywood that covered their shops' fronts at night. One chimed in with a joke he'd heard over the past week, and laughter briefly filled the air. Phoe waved to one lady opening up a tent-shop covered in bright pennants—the vendor returned the wave and gave the dark-haired Gypsy a thumbs-up. Ryna let out a happy sigh at the comfortable, unhurried sense of purpose that filled the air. No matter how much changed…

"Here." Phoenix led her to a cluster of low wooden tables piled with round, white stones—the smallest twice the size of her fist. A colorful sign proclaimed them dragon eggs.

A fellow smiled warmly at Phoenix as he uncovered a modified guillotine. "I was hoping to see you today." He inclined his head to Ryna. "Good day."

Ryna returned the greeting with a smile and poked through a few of the "eggs." The white coating was almost powdery, and every stone sported a cluster of colored dots painted on it as the pricing guide.

"I was thinking," Phoenix said shyly, "that maybe we could pick one out together, and when he breaks it, we could each have half."

Ryna gave her hand a squeeze. "I think that's a wonderful idea."

Phoenix squeezed back, and they settled to the serious task of choosing their prize. It proved difficult. They all looked pretty much the same, though some energy-tingled brighter than others. Tanek or *Baba* Luna would've had a much easier time due to their Earth talents, but at last Phoenix and Ryna decided on a lumpy medium-sized one—the shop's owner nodded sagely and declared it a good choice. The women took a seat on a bench near the guillotine-esque contraption as he fussed with positioning their egg just right.

"Which one of you lovely ladies would like to pull the lever?" he inquired with a twinkle, dusting his hands on his britches.

"You go," Ryna offered. "It was your idea."

"If you're sure…"

"Positive."

Ryna watched her lover's studious efforts as the owner showed her where to kneel for the best leverage. She looked so beautiful—the inquisitive cock of her head, the way her glasses sat slightly off-kilter, the perfect curve of her lips as she cast a shy, eager smile at Ryna. Ryna gave her a wink, and the smile turned dazzling for a brief moment before Phoe ducked her head. A breeze tossed her raven-black hair against the pale sky as she pulled the lever, and Ryna knew she'd remember the moment forever.

CRUNCH!

With a merry look of anticipation, the fellow unlatched a couple clasps and dusted off the halves. A few booth workers had gathered; he displayed the treasure to them first, building suspense with every appreciative gasp and murmur.

Ryna felt Phoenix's large, firm hands clasp her shoulders from behind and tilted her head back. Phoe leaned down to kiss her nose.

At long last their treasure made its rounds and came back to them: a beautiful geode with black and white crystals like a miniature night sky. A ring nestled in the stone's hollow, star sapphire twinkling in the morning light.

Sudden tears sprang to Ryna's eyes as she watched her fingers reach for the gift.

"Everything happened so fast last year that I never had a chance to get you anything," Phoenix babbled. "I know you don't wear rings much, but I thought maybe you should have something—just to have; you don't have to wear it if you don't want. And since today is an anniversary of sorts—"

It was perfect, tiny; the silvery band fit her like a second skin. Ryna stood, whirled, and threw her arms around her love—which surprised Phoe enough that she quit talking and hugged back.

Their audience cheered.

I was right, Ryna thought through her tears. *I* will *remember this forever.*

* * *

"Ryna! Ryna, look, we got our table back!!"

The Gypsy abruptly found her hand seized by a pint-sized Irish dervish. She had little choice but to follow, laughing, as Eryn dragged her across Cottage's lawn and over the threshold with barely enough time to bless the house.

Da looked up from scrubbing down their Prodigal. "I see you've heard the news," he quipped.

"Ma's out trying to find out who found it for us." Brigid paused sweeping the floor and glanced lovingly at the table.

Ryna basked in the O'Malleys' joy, thankful she hadn't told anyone of her hand in the matter; it was far sweeter to simply see delight on a fellow rennie's face without needing to take credit for it. *Maybe that's why Phoenix left her gift-tips anonymous,* she thought with a flash of insight.

"Somebody got a sparkly," Torin observed pointedly.

Ryna gave him a wry look as Brigid and Eryn crowded 'round to see. "Twerp—who else knew?"

"Just me and Christine, I think."

"Wait, sparkly? Ryna has a pretty?" Patches unfolded himself from the corner where he'd been tuning his honey-colored guitar. "Let's see."

Gods, I feel like a lovestruck teenager, the Gypsy thought with wry humor as she displayed her bond-ring. "Phoe took me down to the dragon egg booth this morning—little did I know she only wanted the thing as a display box."

"Damn. You picked a lady with *taste*," Patches commented with a whistle.

"And I have none?" Ryna huffed.

"Not until last year you didn't. Now, if you'd had the sense to date *me*…"

"If I dated you, cents is *all* I'd have, you vagabond."

"Look who's talking, Gypsy!"

Brigid sighed. “It’s so romantic. Promise you two will give lessons to my boyfriend?”

“You do *not* want this rascal teaching your boy anything,” the fiddler bantered. “You’ll never get him out of the pub!”

“You know what to do with a flaming fiddle? Use it to light the bagpipes!”

“Oh, come on. The only reason the harpers take so long to tune is to make you guitarists feel good about something.”

“Uh—I meant you and Phoenix, Ryna,” Brigid cut in.

“Oh, I know.” Ryna shot her a rakish grin. “It was just a good excuse to antagonize him.”

Patches poked her in the ribs. “As if you Gypsies need an excuse for anything.”

“Not really. But sometimes it’s fun to have one anyway.”

Moiré, seated in the *seanchaí* chair, laughed as she dabbed at her eyes with a lace handkerchief. “Damn hormones. I keep crying at everything—I burned toast the other day and had to take five minutes to recover.”

Torin leaned over the to kiss the crown of her head... and tugged Brigid’s headscarf on his way to the kitchen.

“How are you doing?” Ryna asked. “Anything you need?”

The eldest O’Malley sister shrugged. “The morning sickness isn’t fun, but at least I have some of the more practical worries taken care of. The ladies at the nursery where I work are really supportive, and they don’t see how bringing the little one to work would be a problem.”

“Nice to not have to worry about where the money will come from,” Patches offered helpfully.

“It won’t be enough—it’s barely enough as it is.” She put on a determined smile. “But there’s time to figure it out. Perhaps I can get a side job selling cosmetics at home.”

“Hang in there,” Ryna said. “Maybe you should talk to Emily—she’ll know what you’re going through.”

“Moiré, can I braid your hair?” Eryn piped.

“No, you may not. But I could braid yours if you’d like.”

Moiré set to work on Eryn’s unruly flame-red tangle as Ryna climbed up in the window facing Tinker’s Tree. How many years had Tinker been gone now, added to the ranks of Pendragon’s memory-ghosts? Ryna wondered what—and who—else would move on before the Irishwoman’s child got a chance to know them.

Better to concentrate on Patches’ sprightly tavern song and the sticky roll Brigid handed her. Anything else was too depressing.

◇ ◇ ◇

"Phoenix, look! We're not clean anymore!"

The herbwoman turned to discover three of the grubbiest peasants she had ever seen... and she had witnessed some grubby peasants in her time. "Dear Goddess!"

"Yeah," the eight-year-old boy agreed with a grin. "We took our clothes down to the river in the rain and threw 'em in the mud and stomped on 'em for a while, then we had Kevin back over 'em in his mom's car—chariot—a couple times."

"It's Richard out here, doofus-brains."

"Rich's a stupid name for an orphan, spaghetti-nose."

Phoenix sensed a rivalry in progress. "Well, you certainly outdid yourselves," she cut in, hoping to end the squabble.

"Mom wasn't real happy with us," the streak-haired girl said, "especially when we ripped up our costumes a bunch. But I think she understood—after a couple comments about kids always needing to fit in with their friends."

"Don't let it get to you," Phoe advised. "Fitting in is what neckties, pantyhose, and business suits are all about. Parents just like to pretend they've outgrown conformity. C'mon. I'll introduce you to some more of the local peasantry."

She'd expected a lengthy search, but Phoe and her rookies only made it as far as Flying Buttress Stage when the peasants galloped past, baying like a pack of dogs and hot on the heels of a young maiden Phoenix did not recognize. The girl scurried up the boulders on the mound behind the stage. With one mighty leap she caught hold of the tree's lowest branch and, despite her skirt's hindrance, hauled herself to safety. The "hounds" circled, panting, whimpering in frustration as she cried for help.

"Back, back you scoundrels!" a nobleman shouted, wading into the fray with a few well-placed cuffs. He planted himself with his back to the tree and stood defiant, hand poised threateningly on his sword hilt.

The peasants cowered.

"Take my hand and descend, fair maiden; the danger has passed. There is no need to fear," he proclaimed—and covertly tossed a weighty pouch to Hayrold.

The brown-cloaked peasant caught it, sketched an unseen bow, and toddled over to Phoenix. "My lord over there pays us to be his virgin hunters," he explained, glee lacing his lower-class English accent.

The rookies stared, mouths agape.

"Who 'ave we 'ere?" Pratt asked, snuffling at Phoenix's entourage.

"You're supposed to scare the patrons with that, not the entertainers," Bryn admonished with a good-natured thwack.

"Oh, sorry—sorry. I get a mite carried away sometimes."

"These are some of the rookies," Phoenix said. "Patty left them woefully unprepared for life out here, so I'm teaching them what I can."

"Let me guess," the Leper hazarded with an eager grin, "we're the next lesson. Hi—I'm the Leper. Nice to meet you." He offered his hand for Rich to shake—and it came off. "Whoops... sorry about that."

"We're on our way to do a privy pack before it gets too hot—wanna play?" offered a teenage peasant Phoenix knew only as the Floppy Ribbon Queen, owing to the huge bow in her wavy red hair.

The rookies were still staring—but now they looked as if they couldn't decide whether they were being conned or not.

Phoenix grinned. They'd find out soon enough. She certainly had.

◇ ◇ ◇

Ryna pulled Hollow Hill's door closed with a shiver that had little to do with the interior's chill. She couldn't explain why, but soon after she'd left Irish Cottage an eerie atmosphere had rolled over Pendragon like a noxious fog. And to add to her unease, no one else seemed to notice.

Christine stood serenely in the room's center as Elda bustled around her, pins held tightly between her lips. Though they'd been a pain to sew on, Ryna had to admit that the pearls really made the outfit. "Last-minute alterations?" she queried, the words shrill to her own ears.

"Beautiful ring." Christine smiled warmly.

Elda's eyebrows quirked in surprise. She removed the fangs—pins, they were sewing pins—from her mouth. "Since when does Ryna wear rings?"

"Since my lovely soulmate sprung one on me this morning." She couldn't keep the beam from her voice as she displayed her bond-ring. It felt cool and real against her skin, a talisman that momentarily drove away disturbing thoughts.

Elda whistled. "Remind me to compliment Phoenix on her taste."

"Hey. No one else better know *anything* about Phoe's taste." The joke left Ryna's mouth dry as her unease returned.

"You rogue! Get over here and help me get her out of this dress before the dance show starts."

"You put enough lacing on this thing to tie *three* people up!"

"That's the point," Christine interjected. "One bridegroom and a very large four-poster bed."

Esmerelda laughed.

Ryna fumbled, closed her eyes, and took a deep breath. *Why can't I get a grip?! It's no worse than me teasing Kaya about her scarves last week.* She tried to keep her skin from crawling as she finished unlacing the back ties and Elda freed the sleeves. *Maybe it's just that I keep forgetting that under all the satin and lace, the nobles are rennies, too.*

The seamstress helped Christine shrug out of the bodice, Ryna unfastened the overskirt, forcing back her jitters as together they lifted the underskirt from the enormous hoops and over the bride-to-be's head. Ryna could see why Christine had joined Royal Court—she had far too much poise for a peasant.

"Do you need help?" Emily offered as she entered Hollow Hill with an armful of Morgan, preternaturally still in her mother's arms. Ryna nearly shrieked at the unannounced approach.

"If you could lace her into her regular garb, that'd be great," Elda said, carefully pulling garment bags over her creations. "Our dance show starts in a couple minutes."

"Of course." Emily placed her child in a picnic basket as Ryna grabbed her fiddle, called thanks over her shoulder, and nearly dashed out the door.

"Hey, you all right, kiddo?" Toby asked, a frown creasing his brow as she limbered her instrument.

"Stop calling me 'kiddo,'" she snapped. "I'm too old for that shit."

He backed off, eyes wide. "What's eating *your* harem pants?"

She sighed. "Sorry, Tob. It's just—something feels off, and it's making me edgy."

"Like you're trapped in a surrealist painting no one else sees? I thought maybe I'd been in the sun too long."

"More's the pity." Ryna tuned her A. "I'd rather be losing my mind than have to worry about the implications that I'm not. Still," she said, moving on to her E with a brave flippancy she almost felt, "it's probably nothing worse than we've already dealt with, right?"

"Right," her fellow Gypsy agreed.

"Right," Ryna repeated… and almost believed it.

"Damn," Liam swore softly as the Gypsies shimmered like a heat reflection on asphalt. "That complicates matters." He rubbed the painted sign's perspective from his eyes and rounded on his minion. "You. Why didn't you get rid of that thing before she put it on?"

The carrion sound of its laughter turned Liam's stomach nearly as much as the marble. It held up three taloned fingers.

"*They* put you at *my* command," Liam growled.

It gazed at him, its strange eyes blinking sideways. *Ignorant mortal,* it shot. *You have not even been told the items' purpose.*

Liam barked a laugh. "You think I need to be told? Obviously it is to weaken the Gypsies and their ties to one another, to make it easier for your superiors to drag Ryna here in my place. Or, it would, if you bothered to steal the *correct* items!"

The thing looked—infuriatingly—amused.

Liam leaned closer—a dangerous thing, like kissing the nose of a rabid dog. Only someone strong or stupid would risk such nearness. "We have less than a week. I want that bitch *defenseless*!"

It paused, consideration in its expression. Finally it sketched a bow—and scurried away in a swirl of silence, an air of purpose in its bearing.

Satisfied, Liam returned to mastering the stone.

◇ ◇ ◇

"Ugh," Ryna observed as she scooped ice into her mug from the large sack Mama Bernatelli held. The day had grown buggardly hot, though at least the pervading sense of wrongness had left the air

"Thank Goddess *that's* over," Niki agreed, stepping out of the way of the other sweating dancers.

"I wish," Mama said with a huffed breath. "My job's only half done. I'm beginning to see why our old ice lady wouldn't go volunteer."

Tanek ran his ice cube along the back of her neck. "You have our most heartfelt gratitude for your efforts."

The weariness on the Italian's face eased, probably as much in response to the burst of Magick behind the Gypsy's words as his way with a bit of ice. Normally Ryna would've frowned on his use of Charm—but she found it hard to disapprove of bringing a smile to someone who worked her butt off to ensure her fellow rennies didn't fall over from the heat.

"Don't forget to partake of some of that ice yourself." He gave her a devilish grin—and popped the cube's remains down the front of her bodice before sauntering off.

Phoenix pressed her own ice chunk to the hollow of her throat. "I think I'm shade-bound for a while."

Ryna kept her eyes casually on Phoe's face; the meltwater glistening attractively on her love's bosom was doing nothing to cool the redhead down. "Mind if I join you?"

"I was hoping you would."

They made for the sprawling oak near the Bear and Bedside Manor—mostly because it was close. A couple children, immune to the stifling heat, chased each other around the tree and its resident loungers, brandishing turkey drumsticks and quoting lines from the Royals Revolting show. They made Ryna tired just watching them.

"Well, there's one nice thing about working with fire," Toby declared with a grimace as he plopped down beside them. "Everything else seems cool in comparison."

"Ice?" Phoenix offered her mug without opening her eyes.

"I love you."

"How'd your show go?" Ryna asked, hoping he'd guess her real question.

"Calmer after a panicked and futile search for our torches."

Ryna's eyes flew wide. "*What*?"

Toby sighed. "Apparently they've gone the way of everything else out here—it made me glad my sister insists on keeping the second-best set in Hollow Hill for emergencies."

"I guess that proves the power item theory," Phoenix observed.

"I guess so," Toby agreed.

"Has Patty been by yet to notice we're not wearing her costume bits?" Ryna asked.

The expression that crossed Phoenix's face said she thought such rebellion suicidal.

"Nope!" Toby grinned. "And when she does, Basil has an argument ready for her. Hey, did I tell you? Some lordling caught up to me this morning asking about Emily."

Phoe fished in her mug for another cube. "Really?"

"Yeah. Wanted to know what kind of diapers she uses for Morgan. He looked pretty smitten."

Ryna felt a quirky smile bloom across her face. Oh, yes. The pall had definitely lifted. "Huh. Wonder what made him think we knew?"

Toby shrugged. "Probably because he—what in the *world* is that?"

Ryna followed his line of sight and gaped at the brown-cloaked peasant strolling casually past the Bear, an enormous burlap mallet over his shoulder.

Phoenix laughed. "Hayrold!"

"What?" He turned in frantic circles, obviously for entertainment's sake… and to get a pretty girl to call his name again. Phoe obliged; on the third call his face lit with childlike glee. "There you are!" He toddled toward them.

"What are you doing with that thing?" Toby asked. "It's almost as big as Ryna!"

"Hey!"

"I said *almost*!"

"It's for Bop-a-Peasant. Wanna play?"

The Gypsies glanced at each other. "We've got a little time before the dance show," Ryna said.

"Great!" Hayrold beamed. "We're playing in front of Bedside Manor. You each need a trash can frame—minus the bag."

Ryna wasn't sure which stunned her more—the request or Phoe's casual obedience. Toby looked at Ryna and shrugged, and the Gypsies relocated a few of the metal frames to the open area nearby. Toby took Ryna's in a display of teasing chivalry.

A few other peasants—Pratt and Bryn among them—already crouched in a semi-circle under their metal frames. Ryna recognized Marcus as well. They waved enthusiastically to the additions.

"So, how does this go?" Ryna asked as she and her fellow Gypsies completed the circle, nine trash frames all together.

"You ever play that game at the arcade with the gophers and the mallet?" asked the muddy peasant to Ryna's right; she didn't know his name.

"Yeah..."

"It's like that—only we're the gophers. Hey, it looks like Hayrold found our first customer!"

Ryna brought her jaw up with a click of teeth. *If I live to be a hundred,* she thought, *I will* never *understand where they come up with this stuff!*

Toby was still trying to squish into his container as Hayrold explained the rules to an awkward-looking twelve-year-old girl in a striped shirt. "... point for each peasant you bop, and in honor of Mid-East weekend, Gypsies are double points—"

"Um—I don't quite fit," Toby piped up; an arm, the attendant shoulder, and his head stuck outside the frame.

Hayrold giggled. "That's okay; there's always one that's broken." Then, to the patron, "He's the broken one; you lose points if you bop him."

Toby sighed. "I *knew* there was a reason no one ever hits on me."

"It has nothing to do with points," Ryna corrected with a teasing glint. "Your breath smells like lighter fluid."

"You need ten points to win a fabulous prize," Hayrold concluded. "And remember, this is *Bop*-a-Peasant, not *Maim*-a-Peasant, so please be gentle. And... go!"

The girl entered the ring of trash frames and turned in slow circles, bopping anyone who popped up as the peasants kept score.

Pratt added sound effects when he got hit; others began calling taunts. They took care to keep it light-hearted and fun; if they got anywhere near Vilification Tennis level, someone would wind up with a broken neck.

"Five..."

"Gypsy! Six-seven..."

"Bet you can't catch me—oop! Eight!"

"Nyah-nyah, over—nine!"

"Ten! Yay! She wins!"

Hayrold stepped forward. "Congratulations, m'lady! Well done! And as to your wonderful grand prize... are you ready? ...um, please put the mallet down. Thank you... and for your grand prize, you have a choice of any of these sticks!"

He presented the lass with an assortment of twine loops with sticks tied on them like medallions.

The girl pointed to one; her expression said she thought they were all weird.

Hayrold draped the twine around her neck as though it was a gold medal. "Something to remember us by," the peasant told her. "Wear it always."

"Who wants to be next?" Phoenix called. "Step right up and play Bop-A-Peasant!"

An older fellow went next, followed by a young boy. A lady in her thirties (and obviously in her cups as well) grabbed the mallet before the kid even got his prize—Hayrold had to declare her a winner on her third swing to keep her from clobbering any more of the rennies.

"Can anyone play, or is this for outlanders only?" came a suave voice from behind Ryna; she bit back a laugh as the peasants in the trash frames tried to genuflect.

Hayrold had an easier time; he threw himself face-first on the ground and held up the burlap mallet. "Of course you can play, Your Princeliness!"

"Father got a sword and a maiden rising from the lake," the suave voice said with a put-upon sigh. "I get a burlap mallet and peasant in the dirt."

"So sorry, Your Princeliness!" Hayrold groveled, almost unheard amidst the laughter.

A pair of fancy, custom-made boots strode into the circle. Due to her cramped position, Ryna's line of sight stopped at the man's waist—but that was enough. A firm ass showcased in black velvet tights confirmed the prince's identity; he was well-known for his retreating view. Not that she had been paying attention, of course.

Prince Gwydion planted himself in front of a peasant whose name Ryna didn't know. "You. Peasant. Pop up."

"But I don't really—"

"Pop up."

"Um, that's not the way—" Hayrold began to protest from the ground, but was shushed.

"He's the prince! He can play however he wants."

"Oh. Right. Wonderful job, m'lord!"

The set-upon peasant peeked out from the frame's top and immediately got bopped.

"One!"

A pause, though several others had popped up. The prince hadn't budged. "Again."

The peasant popped—and got bopped.

"Two!

Phoenix next. "Three-four!"

"Come on," Prince Gwydion chided. "Let's have some unity here. I want everyone to close your eyes when you count."

Laughter rippled through the ranks. Ryna popped up and saw that he had his eyes squeezed shut as he wavered in a circle, brandishing his mallet.

Everyone else had theirs open. This was too good to miss.

"I don't hear any counting, peoples! Where's my unity?"

"Five!" Ryna called, and he swung around to bop her.

"That's more like it. I need someone else to hit! Peasant! Say something so I can hit you again!"

Ryna began to suspect this particular peasant had angered the prince in a previous encounter.

"I've been framed," he whined.

Bop!

"Six!" yelled two people.

"Tsk, tsk, now we have to start over."

"One!"

"Ah, mocking the establishment," Toby commented with a blissful sigh from beside her. "Now there's a *real* sport!"

Ryna couldn't have agreed more.

◇ ◇ ◇

Woodland Stage, Sherwood Forest, Stocks, Front Gate—though it only stood one story tall. Bakery Stage, cut-off turret, *Lady Fortune*… Liam stalked his circuit of Pendragon's grounds. Trampled grass covered the area where Irish Cottage should have been—though rare, it wasn't the first time.

Games, Blue-Legged Unicorn, Bardstone.

Colorful ribbons fluttered around Maypole, mocking him.

Onward, restless, perturbed.

Globe. Twin Tree.

He grew tired of waiting for the Shadow Fae to decide the time was right. Tired of practicing small discords and having to trust others to accomplish their appointed tasks. Tired of rotting in this stinking hellhole…

Bear, and a petite redhead he had grown to loathe.

Liam paused, eyes narrowed. She just… stood there. Alone. Unarmed. Staring at the Bear's vacant stage… almost as if she was waiting for him to come along.

He drove the thought from his head. She didn't have the feel of one of the Shadow Fae… he'd fallen prey to their shapeshifting tricks often enough to recognize *that* game.

It must be a thinning of the veil, then. Fortuitous—although he hadn't the power to manifest on *their* side, he could certainly take advantage of it when bits of them slipped into *his*. Perhaps if he railed at her, he'd sully her precious bright energies enough to affect her mood. Giving her a bad day for reasons beyond her comprehension didn't even skirt the edge of revenge… but better that than nothing.

His hand twitched with the desire to strike her.

She turned, an evil grin on her face. "Go ahead and hit me. I won't stop you." She glanced around at the conspicuously empty streets. "Are you worried about someone seeing you?"

Her words sounded too familiar—Liam could feel time shifting, folding in on itself. His eyes widened in alarm. A trap—they had tricked him. He scrambled for a phrase—any phrase that would break the repetition, but could think of nothing.

"They're watching VilTen," she continued, gesturing at the empty lane, "and besides, you know they don't think real combat happens here. It'll be a nice bit of ambiance."

Liam scowled, fighting the tide of history. He had lost this battle last time…

"Oh, come on. You weren't this hesitant when it was just you and me, and you said *that* was a warning. I didn't take it—are you going to deliver on the real thing, now?" she goaded. "What will you do this time? Summon up some more of your goolies?"

"I… do not… summon," he gritted out, unable to halt the words. "Especially… not… goolies."

The echo of patrons' mirth wavered through the air, morphing subtly to the Shadow Fae's laughter.

"You just keep telling yourself that," Ryna said when the ruckus died down, giving him a patronizing pat on the arm. "And I'll just keep kicking the stuffing out of all the goolies you're not sending, and we'll all go on our merry way, how's that?" She smiled her most charming smile, turned—

Liam's hand shot out before he could stop it, caught her upper arm in an iron grip. The soft cotton of her rust-colored chemise shifted beneath his calluses. "Bea is mine," he hissed in her ear.

"Just like whoever gave you that ribbon around your arm is yours? I know it wasn't Bea. What did you tell her when she asked—did you say it was a favor accepted out of politeness from some lady you weren't intending to stay with? Or has your story changed since last year?"

"Bea is mine," he repeated, more forcefully, "and spreading stories about me to her won't change that. In the end, Ryna… And this will end." He spun her roughly around and forced a kiss on her—

—the same way she forced her knee to the most vulnerable spot it could reach: quickly, and with vicious precision.

Liam dropped to his knees, teeth gritted in anger and pain as the repetition of events past loosed its hold on him. It had been a trap, a test… another *fucking* test… but damn it all, he would *not* fail! Liam pulled dark tendrils of mist from the earth, gathered them in, and punched the trampled grass with all his might.

In the space of a thunderclap Ryna huddled on the ground, and he towered over her as she whimpered in pain—as if *she* had taken the blow. "That's more like it."

Ever defiant, Ryna glared up at him with a snarl—and faded away.

He had won. Against Ryna, against the Shadow Fae…

He had won.

"What *is* it with rain on Third Weekend?" Phoenix asked as she gazed past C-gate. She and Kaya had talked Toby and Elda into a quick walk around site during the Merry Maids' show—mostly to get them out of camp. They hadn't been able to stop anywhere, but the change of scenery seemed to brighten the fire-eaters' mood.

A brilliant flash of lightning punctuated the roiling gray sky.

"I can see the headlines now: lightning strikes Maypole, twelve dead," Tobaltio joked. "Thor came to collect the virgins."

"You're assuming they're virgins." Kaya pointed out.

"They're jail bait. I make it a point not to know these things first hand."

The sky rumbled ominously, lending weight to his statement.

Phoenix could feel the storm's restless energy building—feel its echoes in the other Gypsies. She squinted into the ever-more-frequent lightning. "I really hope this takes down the humidity."

"It looks like we're about to find out," Esmerelda observed. "Shall we head back to Sherwood? It's not much longer until the dance show."

"Let's take the long way," Kaya voted. "We've got the time."

"Do we?" asked Elda, rummaging for her watch as they meandered through the games area. A puff of wind tugged her saffron-yellow headscarf.

"We're *making* the time," Kaya said firmly.

"Won't find me arguing," Toby said. "Maybe if we're late, it'll give Prissy Patty a reality check."

"I bet her precious Secret Garden floods," Elda chimed in merrily.

"Hey, did you guys hear? Cottage got their table back," Phoenix piped up, hoping to steer the conversation from such a morbidly pink topic.

"Oh, I'm glad. The O'Malleys have always been so kind to Ryna, and that table was part of the original furniture," Kaya said. "Having it gone must've been like losing part of the family."

"Wonder where it was?" Toby asked.

Phoenix gave him a sideways look; his tone had been a little too casual. He *felt* a little too casual, and he *was* on site crew…

"Well, it's a good thing somebody was looking out for it," Elda said.

Toby flashed her a grin as they passed First Aid gate. "I'm sure it could look after itself—only needed a little time is all."

Phoe rubbed her thumb thoughtfully against the wood of her staff—and shook her head in amusement. *I guess I can understand not wanting credit for it... but getting that table back beats a whole* year *of my stealth poems hands down.*

"We're going to get rained on, aren't we?" Elda asked.

"We are," Kaya agreed. "Right... about... now."

As if to prove her words, the sky gave a gust of wind, a final grumble... and *poured.*

A collective shriek of surprise and dismay filled the air as patrons sprinted for shelter.

"Quick! Run! Get wet over there instead of over here!" Toby taunted.

Raindrops splatted on Phoenix's head and formed small rivers down her wire-rimmed glasses. Within moments her chemise's sleeves hung heavily from her arms. Toby's one perpetually errant curl of hair stuck to his cheek.

Esmerelda trilled in delight, her flame-colored garb rain-dark and plastered to her body. "Good thing the next fire show's not till four."

Kaya slicked her hair back from her face. "I think it's soaked through *all three* of my layers."

"Gypsy baths!" Tobaltio advertised as they passed Irish Cottage. "They're free!"

"We cannot have a bath without soap, brother!" Elda chided.

"Soap! Who has stolen the soap?" Kaya demanded of their captive audience, huddled under awnings and in crafters' shops.

"We are Gypsies. *We* are supposed to be stealing the soap!" Esmerelda complained.

"Soap! Soap!" Kaya cried. "Wet Gypsies without soap! Who has some soap we can steal?"

"It will keep away the plague! We need some soap!" Phoenix added.

"Free Gypsy baths!" Toby repeated his call, contributing to the rollicking, roving commotion. "Save money, take a free bath courtesy of the Gypsies! Bring your own soap!"

"You! Yes, you, hiding there under that awning! Do not tell me you were not sweating today!" Elda accused. "It was hot, you were sweating, yes? Come take a free bath!"

"Free Gypsy baths!"

"Who has the soap?"

"Keep the plague away!"

"Soap!"

"Soap!"

A thin woman with wet, rat-tail hair dashed out from her cover to offer up some hand-made soap she'd purchased from a tent near *Lady Fortune* Stage. She dragged her young son out, too, volunteering him for a bath… to which he squirmingly consented.

The Gypsies continued on… Toby jumped feet-first into a rapidly forming lake; his sister yelped at the tsunami and chased after him, scolding and threatening and laughing as Phoenix and Kaya continued their advertising campaign. They had almost reached Bakery Stage when Elda, breathless, finally gave up her pursuit.

"Has it occurred to anyone else that being covered in metal jingles makes us walking targets?" she inquired.

"Speak for yourself, Fire element," Kaya said with a grin. "I'm too short to be a lightning rod."

Phoenix glanced around the empty lanes. Musicians had understandably abandoned their grid spots (though a peasant madrigal group at Canopy Stage belted out an impressive rendition of "Rubber Ducky") and for once not a single noble blocked their path. "I think we need to arrange for a thunderstorm every time we need to get to a show!" she noted.

The rain tapered off as they neared the Bear, and by the time they reached Woodland Stage only an occasional drop still spattered the ground like the last stubborn efforts of a leaky faucet.

"Air dry!" Phoenix yelled as a breeze kicked up. She scrabbled atop a bench, peeled her sodden skirts apart, and held them out to take advantage of the wind.

The others followed suit.

"I wonder if I could get lift-off if I catch enough wind," Toby pondered, his voluminous yellow pants pulled to either side.

"Well, you're the Air. If anyone could do it, it would be you," Elda voted.

"Come see the humble start of the world's first flying Gypsy!" Phoenix bellowed.

"That one is dry!" Kaya complained, pointing to a passing patron.

"Some of us have enough sense to get out of the rain," he called back.

A few more witty repartees, several photographs, and countless group hugs later (no one protested a pack of beautiful Gypsies getting them wet), they hopped down from the benches and finished their journey to Sherwood.

"This ought to be interesting to dance in." Kaya plucked at her skirts. "I think my costume's heavier than *I* am."

"At least it looks like Basil put up the canopy so the stage'll be dry for you," Toby commented on his way backstage, then bellowed, "Come see the Gypsies' Renaissance Wet Chemise Contest!"

More than one patron paused.

Phoenix took up the cry as dancers and musicians readied for the show. "That's right! Step right up and watch Gypsies prance around in completely soaked clothing! You thought bodices were attractive; wait till you witness *wet* bodices! Two or three marginally dry benches left! They haven't invented Xerox machines yet, so we have to use wet butts and dry benches! Leave an impression in the Renaissance!"

The random, silly patter drew them in. Charm, the other Gypsies called it, though the normals called it charisma. Names weren't nearly as important as the fact that it *worked.* By the time Ryna and her father persuaded their instruments to stay in tune, patrons filled even the wettest benches.

Baba Luna began the beat, just loud enough to get the audience's attention; Esmerelda's tambourine emphasized the summons as Kaya sashayed between the curtains and onto Caravan Stage. Her cobalt-blue and gold outfit clung to her every curve, emphasizing her beauty even more than usual.

Ryna and Tremayne drew fiddle bows across strings in an eerie, low moan that slid up the scale as Niki and Tanek strutted through the curtains to stand a little behind Kaya.

The drum stopped.

The fiddles fell silent.

"Gypsy spin cycle!" Kaya announced. With the lead-in of three fast chimes of her zills, the instruments erupted in song as she twirled around and around, the other dancers joining her.

The audience roared with laughter and cheers.

"I think it should rain more often," Ryna declared as she waited in line for dinner.

"Me too," *Baba* Luna agreed as she advanced from curried rice to pickles. "That gave us some great material to work with."

"Speak for yourself," Kaya said from behind Ryna. "There's nothing quite like having your skirt cling to your legs when you're trying to look graceful and poised. I'm just glad we have a stage to dance on and don't have to worry about slipping in the mud."

"Dear, you'd look graceful and poised in curlers, a green mud mask, and a ratty bathrobe," Niki teased as she perched on Robyn's bridge. "I on the other hand nearly dumped myself on my butt during that second crossover." Niki's anklet chimed as she swung her perfect bare feet over the pool. Feet that were meant for sandals and a toe ring.

Ryna wished she had feet like that.

"Oh, both of you hush," Esmerelda chided, selecting a piece of flatbread. "At least neither of you flail when you're falling on your ass in the mud, like I did on my way to collect tips."

"There's a pond right over there with no waiting," Mutch suggested impishly from her seat among the audience benches.

"The slime layer's even diluted after the downpour," Little Jen put in.

Luckily for the Merry Maids, Esmerelda didn't believe in wasting food; she had a notoriously good aim. It probably came from growing up with a brother like Toby.

Baba Luna sat beside Jen. "So, Alaina, I want to hear this coffee poem that Marion's been telling me so much about."

Niki perked at the mention of her favored beverage. "Coffee? There's a poem about coffee and I haven't heard it? Alaina!"

The Maids' minstrel hastily swallowed her bite of food. "You want me to do it *now*?"

"You're here, we're here..." Toby pointed out. "Sing for your supper, bard!"

Alaina chuckled, putting her bowl to the side. "Very well, then—but I warn you, 'tis not my best." She cleared her throat, stood upon the bench, and began:

"O, caffeine, thou holy drink,
you clear my head and let me think.
When my brain has gone to pot,
you wake me up, yes, quite a lot!

"And when in class I start to drowse,
you kick me square between the brows.
You clear up every bit of fuzz;
behind my eyes you leave a buzz.
Hail, caffeine, hail!

"O, caffeine, thy sacred powers,
without which every student cowers...
Espresso, latté, or some Coke—a
blessing: cappuccino, mocha!

"A mug of you upon the table
makes the mornings tolerable.
Mountain Dew, and Jolt, and Surge,
weariness from me you purge!
Hail, caffeine, hail!

"I bow to thee, O coffee bean—
double, triple, sugared, steamed.
My eyes are wide, my hands do shake;
all this just to stay awake!

"Papers? Tests? I need not fear
just so a mug of you is near!
I'll dehydrate; liquids you plunder;
soon I'll have to piss like thunder!
Hail, caffeine, hail!"

Applause rocked Sherwood as Alaina Dale gave a theatrical bow and resumed her seat.

"I *said*, excuse me!"

The merriment hushed; all attention turned to a woman with a gem-encrusted Elizabethan gown. She was, of course, perfectly dry.

Ryna thought a dousing in the pond might do her a world of good.

"Can we help you, m'lady?" Tremayne inquired politely.

The woman made an imperious sweep with her fan. "Who is in charge of the costuming for this group?"

"I'm beginning to hate that question," Esmerelda muttered. Then, louder, "I am, as far as anyone."

"Are you, then." The noblewoman sneered. "I don't suppose you could've tried for at least a *little* historical accuracy?"

"The drenched-to-the-bone look is very authentic!" Toby protested.

Esmerelda bristled at the woman's comment, though her tone remained even and cool. "Anything particular you'd like to attack me about, lady?"

"Your use of color, for one," she said with a toss of her elaborately coiffured head. "True Romany never wore red." She pointed accusingly at the offending costumes—primarily Niki, Toby, and Elda herself. "And your cuts are completely wrong. Not to mention your fabrics. I don't know *where* you found your information, but you should destroy it immediately."

Phuro Basil stepped in before Elda decided to take one of the lady's hat pins and shove it through her neck. "Begging your pardon, m'lady, but the Artistic Director does not share your opinion. She criticized us for not fitting the public's preconceptions and gave us a box of accessories... which, admittedly, we are not wearing, but—"

"I don't care what Patty said," the lady cut in with a frosty smile. "*I* was hired to oversee costuming, not her. Besides which, Artistic Directors come and go. I will be here far, far longer. So try to clean yourselves up." With a final depreciating glance and a sniff, she whirled and stalked away.

A flash of power swept outward from Esmerelda; an acorn spontaneously fell from an oak to the puddle at the noblewoman's feet, creating a splash out of proportion to its size.

The woman shrieked as muddy water leapt onto her gown.

Phuro Basil frowned at Elda.

Esmerelda glared back. "Be grateful I didn't set her on fire."

"Who *was* that?" Phoenix peered after the cranky woman's retreating form.

Kaya rolled her eyes. "I heard rumblings that Patty got the old Costume Nazi fired—apparently this is her replacement."

"More like a power trip in a hoopskirt. Somebody needs to tell her that she's even easier to replace than Patty," Niki spat, coming to Elda's defense. "And for her information, Gypsies *did* wear *this* shade of red, so she can take her damn regulation book and shove it up her—"

"Love you Niki," Tanek piped in with a wide grin—and licked her nose.

True to her element, the distraction worked. Ryna was glad she didn't have that aspect of being an Air—it would've made practicing impossible.

Come down to it, she really didn't have many personality traits in common with Niki *or* Tobaltio. But then, Phoenix and Elda weren't much alike, so it *could* happen.

"Ryna, come sit by me," Phoenix called.

"Right there." Ryna finished scooping the curried rice, added a ladle of crock pickles and a slightly bruised peach, and went to sit with her love.

◇ ◇ ◇

"Dear Goddess!" Phoenix cried as the BLUE's door closed behind her. "I don't think even toy stores have this many teddies!"

She had never expected to feel overdressed in Niki's matching black leather pants and bodice. They certainly left little enough to the imagination… but skin seemed to be the order of the night. Even those who had gone beyond underwear hadn't gone there by much—though she did spot a few rennies in tattered bathrobes. Three nearly naked women were draped over her brother, and her future sister-in-law did not lack for attention, either. She was a shade of red only a blonde could achieve, but she appeared to be enjoying herself.

Tobaltio and Tanek ranked among her attendants. Phoenix was not surprised. *Only rennies,* she thought, *could pull off a combination bachelor/bachelorette party.*

The sprightly strain of an Irish jig wound through the general hubbub; Phoe headed toward the sound—and caught sight of Ryna dressed in a plaid bra-and-panty set, an unzipped biker jacket, and knee-high boots.

And nothing else.

PALIDYN 03

Phoenix collided with a table, sloshing foam from two of the drinks onto the scarred surface. The table's occupants laughed, clapped her on the back, and congratulated her on having such a beautiful wife.

"Yeah, um, that is, thank you," Phoe stammered, glaze-eyed. *I suppose I'm one of the boys now,* she marveled. *Funny, I think that fellow with the hat asked me to dance last year at the cast party.* It made her wonder which party she was supposed to be at—really, she belonged at neither.

Or, this being faire, perhaps she belonged at both.

Phoenix found a seat before she could run into anything else. It brought her some small comfort, though, that Ryna'd missed three notes when their eyes had met, and now her fellow bards were ribbing her behind the smokescreen of their music.

"Where's my maid of honor? Phoenix!"

"Coming!"

"Phoe... you've got to try some of this." Christine picked up a bottle of champaign and waved it around airily. "Where's your mug?"

"Right here." Phoenix relieved her fellow rennie of the bottle before she could spill it on herself. Phoe had never seen her brother's fiancée so toasted before. It was really kind of cute. She was all giggly and flushed.

Of course, the two attractive Gypsies purring in her ears probably didn't hurt, either.

"I've never had bubbles attack my nose before," she confided.

A swarthy man turned to her. "Good evening, m'lady," he said with a gallant bow. "My name is Bubbles." And proceeded to kiss and nibble her nose.

Phoe almost sprayed her champaign.

"Aren't they attacking your nose?" Christine asked once she'd finished giggling. "They should. You have such a cute nose. It deserves to be attacked by bubbles."

Bubbles gave her a questioning look.

Phoenix shook her head discreetly, took another cautious drink, and made a mental note to feed Christine lots of water before bed. Something tugged at her waist, followed by a muted *clunk*, a muttered oath, and a sudden lightening around her middle. She glanced down, puzzled, to find her leather belt and its accessories in a heap on the worn wood floor. Phoe bent down to retrieve it, muffling a yelp as a hiking boot kicked into her hand. She hastily straightened and reached around to refasten her belt.

Except... the clasp had not come undone; the belt had broken over her left hip. She frowned, puzzled, at the severed ends. They bore tiny teeth marks, as if something had gnawed through it. And if she'd bent down a moment later, that boot would've sent her stuff skittering across the floor. But why...?

My dagger, she realized with dawning horror... but now was not the time or place for a scene. She tried to make her voice light. "Looks like my belt broke. I'm... I'll just bring this stuff downstairs." She didn't wait for a response, simply pushed through the press of people and hurried for the campground before anything else could happen. Her vardo door closed behind her with a beautifully solid sense of security.

Phoenix gazed around her home, dagger clutched to her heart. She had to hide it somewhere out of the way, and there weren't many such places. Secreting it amongst their clothes or towels left too great of a chance that it would be lost on the way to the showers. Grocery-space was out of the question. *Definitely* not with their Gypsy garb... that would be the first place an intruder would look. That left... the broom closet?

Fitting place to hide a witch-blade, she thought as she wrapped the treasure in a scarf and tucked it in one of her extra shoes in the back. The cloaks and their few other hanging garments added an extra layer of concealment. No one would ever think to look there... *if they're looking at all. There's every chance that you're being paranoid.*

But paranoia was better than losing her most precious possession—or worse, having it fall into the wrong hands. She gave Karma a cursory scritch behind the ears and carefully locked the door on her way out.

Had the night been this dark before? The Gypsy shivered. It took considerable effort not to hunch her shoulders against invisible eyes. Suddenly the BLUE seemed a long way away.

Something small and hard smacked her forearm and stuck; Phoenix looked down slowly, unable to still the quickening of her heart.

A grasshopper gazed back, antennae waving, eyes dark and sentient.

She swatted it off with a yelp and bolted for the center of the road. How had a Shadow Fae gotten past their shields?

It couldn't, Phoenix told herself, taking a deep, steadying breath—and shaking her head in disbelief at her own skittishness. *It was a regular old grasshopper—you're scaring yourself for no good reason.*

Still, she couldn't help glancing at every shadow as she hurried down the center of the road... though she couldn't bring herself to peer too closely.

The sour smell wafting from the campground dumpster threatened to choke the life out of her as she neared it. The trees shifted oddly—was that a dark form crouched in their branches?

Her steps quickened further—though she paused at the Olympic Staircase's foot. The oasis of light halfway up granted little comfort, given all those trees with places for Shadows to lurk. Phoenix glanced nervously in the direction from which she'd come.

That *was* movement behind the dumpster—Phoenix watched, horrified, as something melted from the shadowy depths.

A slithering whisper to her right…

She ran.

Potholes and debris peppered the Olympic Staircase; Phoe stumbled twice before she even reached the light.

A gust of wind gave the leaves nervous, fretful voices. *Faster. Faster.*

Phoenix could feel the creature gaining on her, gliding up treacherous stairs. She didn't dare look back.

Hurry. Faster.

She labored up the last step and nearly fell with the ease of movement on relatively flat ground.

She could feel it not even three feet behind.

Voices, carefree and out of place, rang from the puddle of light surrounding C-gate.

Phoenix dropped into a sprint.

"Hey, what you running for? Afraid of getting wet?" called an exceedingly tall, burgundy-haired female dressed all in black and sporting a generous amount of dark eye makeup.

The Gypsy skidded to a halt before she plowed into the wall. When had the rain begun to fall? It was only a drizzle, but still… She made herself laugh. "Nope. Just running from the unholy minions of Hell."

The girl's two leather-and-piercings-bedecked companions laughed. "Oh, man," the male said. "I had a trip like that, once. Scared the shit outta me."

I only wish *I could blame it on drugs,* Phoenix thought as she gave the speaker a wan smile and darted through the snaking entrance to site. She could feel the Thing hovering on her periphery as she stood at the light's edge. Watching. Waiting.

Had the BLUE always been that far away?

"No time like the present," she murmured, took another deep breath, and dashed for the haven of the Blue-Legged Unicorn Eatery.

A musty puff of wind half a step behind her… Every cell of Phoe's being concentrated on this step, this panting breath—

These fingers reaching to capture her soul—

Hurry! Faster!

The doorway—

Safety.

A wall of sensation stopped her in her tracks: laughter and music, the smell of fire and alcohol and rennie sweat. Phoenix stood in the doorway, caught between light and dark, normalcy and something far, far older.

It was still back there—waiting.

Waiting, waiting.

Just outside the door, waiting.

Phoe skittered forward.

Half of the rennies waved toy ducks with condoms stuck over their heads as the band played a rousing rendition of "Rubber Ducky."

She couldn't tell them—not now. Not at her brother's party. Later, maybe, when it wouldn't disrupt the festivities.

Phoenix shoved aside her nagging fears and forced herself back into the swing of the party.

◇ ◇ ◇

"I have mosquito bites in interesting places," Ryna complained, scratching up a storm as the vardo door closed behind her. "My Magick bug repellant must've been on the fritz tonight."

"Well, you're the one who decided to go running around in your underwear," Phoenix pointed out as she stripped off her bodice with practiced ease… the pants gave her a bit more trouble, though. She sat on the bed's edge and made funny faces as she tugged at them.

Ryna laughed. "You didn't seem to mind my outfit—not that you have so many rocks to throw."

"I was covered. Sort of." A now-naked Phoenix scrambled under the patchwork quilt, much to Karma's delight. The kitty pounced on her hidden toes.

"You look like a blanket monster with hair."

"Oh yeah? Well, be careful or I'll turn you into caramel corn."

A skeptical eyebrow raised. "Carmel corn?"

"Sure. Some things turn people into stone or pillars of salt. I turn them into caramel corn." Phoenix shrugged. Ryna could tell because the blankets moved. "Salt's unhealthy, and a Ryna-sized boulder would break a hole through the vardo's floor. Caramel corn's much more interesting. And tasty. Besides which, it takes less effort, and I'm kind of tired right now."

"Tasty, huh?" The red-haired Gypsy put a hint of temptation in the question.

One eye peeked out from under the blanket. A very wide, innocent-looking eye.

"Pop, pop," Ryna teased.

The eye widened even further, if such a thing was possible.

"Pop-pop-pop!" This time she added a little bounce.

The other eye joined it.

"Poppity-poppity-pop-ooop!"

Weariness forgotten, Phoenix breached out from the covers with a playful battle cry, grabbed Ryna around the waist, and hauled her into the bed in a tangle of arms and legs and blankets.

Karma bolted to the entryway, well and safely away from the strange two-legged furlesses. She studiously bathed her face to show them what good manners looked like. It irked her to no end that they were too busy tussling to notice her pointed commentary.

"Wow," Ryna said when at last they lay spent and panting. "I never knew you had such a thing for caramel corn."

"Well, when it bounces like that..." Phoe gave her a sheepish grin and cuddled up close. "It was too cute not to have a quickie."

Ryna's eyes nearly fell out of her head. "A *quickie*?? Of all the things I never thought I'd hear you say—"

"That's *why* I never say stuff like that—ruins the shock value."

"You're such a goofball."

A pleasant silence settled over the vardo, massaged by occasional grumbles of thunder.

"If I hadn't come down to the gazebo, would we ever have kissed?"

"Of course. Fate would've kept tossing us together until we couldn't take it anymore. One more night like that one on top of Front Gate, and I know *I* would've cracked."

"Really? You wanted to—on top of Front Gate?"

Ryna waggled her eyebrows. "Poppity-pop."

Phoenix giggled; Ryna leaned over to kiss her, lingering a moment as she made the lights shut themselves off, the better to appreciate the storm.

"That was when I realized I loved you," Phoe said when they separated, her words almost lost in the pattering of rain against the roof. "Waking up the next morning, and you were still asleep, so peaceful and beautiful..."

Ryna paused, marveling. The clove orange had been such a surprise; she'd always wondered when Phoenix had decided she was interested. *I hadn't bet on quite that much forethought,* Ryna mused, *though maybe I should've known.* "I—I guess there wasn't really a particular moment for me. I didn't know you were interested, so I wasn't letting myself think about it," she admitted as she ran her fingers lightly along Phoe's side. "But I didn't have to think twice before I took the clove out with my teeth."

A hesitant pause gripped the air before Phoenix spoke again. "Do you think we'll find each other again next life?"

The redhead frowned at the shift in her lover's mood. "You planning on dying soon?"

"No, it's just... how do we know we haven't had twenty lives since the one with Rachelle and Emily, all trying to find each other but failing? What if I was born in Africa and you were born in China or something?"

"I suppose we *don't* know that," Ryna allowed. "But I don't think I was ever in China, even if I *am* short enough."

The raven-haired Gypsy propped herself on one elbow, not to be dissuaded by humor. "What if this life turned out to be one of those?"

Ryna ignored the way her insides twisted in reaction to her bedmate's anxiety and cupped her love's cheek in one tiny, warm hand. "We're bound, my Phoenix," she said softly, gazing into eyes darker than usual in the night. "It's older than Rachelle and Emily. You said it yourself—you've known me since forever. Bonds like that don't break. Not even in death, remember?"

The familiar promise made Phoenix smile at last. "Not even in death," she repeated, kissing Ryna on the nose before cuddling back down.

Ryna twitched her nose, but smiled.

"All the same," Phoenix said as she drifted off to sleep. "I'm glad it all worked out for this one. I can't imagine living without you."

"Or I without you," Ryna whispered. "Or I without you."

◇ ◇ ◇

"I think I'm going to miss Cast Call this morning," Phoenix declared as she stared at the mound of clothing on the bed. She grabbed the long chemise off the top and pulled it over her head, careful not to catch her glasses.

"Well, the wedding's not until nine-thirty," Ryna said. "Here, I'll tie you into that body armor."

"Thanks. I don't think I could get the back laces on my own." Phoenix grimaced at her corset. "Ugh. If I ever start looking like I want to go Court, wave this thing in my face."

Ryna waggled her eyebrows. "If you ever start looking like you want to go Court, that's not the only thing I'll be waving in your face."

Phoenix gave her a cheeky grin. "Promise?"

"Be good, or we'll never make it out of the vardo," Ryna scolded, giving the laces a tug.

The corset was—well, as comfortable as a corset could be. It felt like she couldn't get a deep breath or eat a decent meal, which Phoe supposed was the point. She couldn't bend at the waist, either, which was even more annoying. "I'm going to have to go outside for the rest, aren't I?"

"Yup," Ryna agreed gamely, the hoopskirt collapsed and over her shoulder. "Get your bloomered butt out there. This vardo's not built for nobility."

Phoenix did, shivering at the chill morning air and the wet kiss of dewed grass against her slippered feet. Ryna arranged the layers with competence and speed: hoop skirt, underskirt, overskirt, bodice, sleeves. Phoe almost giggled at the incongruity of her love helping her put her clothes *on*.

Awkwardness of the attire aside, Elda had done a fantastic job. The simple, elegant cut needed no decoration to show it off, though *Baba* Luna had reached into her vast jewelry coffers and produced a lapis necklace that matched the dress's rich hue. It looked quite nice, Phoenix thought, against her sun-darkened cleavage. Thankfully Esmerelda had styled the neckline the same as for her Gypsy bodice, otherwise there would've been some very strange tan lines going on.

"Your hairdresser has arrived," Elda announced. "Sit, sit. I've brought you a bench. It's even mostly dry."

Phoenix took a seat as gracefully as she could in the unaccustomed regalia.

"I think I'll leave some of this down," Esmerelda said as she tugged and braided and pinned. "You have such lovely long hair that it would be a shame to bundle it *all* up."

"Are the others—?" Phoe asked, fighting the urge to turn around.

"Busy draping the carriage with scarves and sparkles," Ryna assured her. "It was nice of Court to loan it to your brother and Christine, even if it does look like a reject from a Gypsy camp."

"Don't you need to get dressed, Ryna?" Elda's voice sounded stern and mother-like. Phoenix wondered if Toby and Tanek had been giving her a hard time or if the stress of making everything perfect had gotten to her.

"It's only garb." Phoe could hear the shrug in Ryna's voice.

"Go put it on, then."

"All right, all right." A sigh from behind her, and Phoenix could just imagine her vardo-mate sulking off like a petulant child with her lip all pouty and those big, olive-green eyes... For the hundredth time, Phoe wished she'd known the redhead as a kid.

"Eight-thirty," Ryna announced when she returned in her Gypsy best—which was, admittedly, not much different from her normal outfit. Her scarves were velvet and silk, though, and she'd left off her beaten leather belt pouch and mug. A leaf-shaped broach studded with faux emeralds lent a final, classy accent. "You ready?"

"In a—there." Esmerelda inserted a final white silk flower into the elaborate tapestry of braids. "And try to remember that it's bad form to outshine the bride."

"Too late for that." Ryna gave her a dazzling grin.

Phoenix blushed, tucking one of the star-white tendrils—still loose—behind her ear. "Thank you, Elda."

"You're welcome. Off with you now."

Phoenix rose from the bench, dipped her best curtsey to the seamstress, and made her way out of Gypsy camp, up the Olympic Staircase, and through C-gate.

Her bridesmaid's dress felt... strange. There was no familiar chime of coin belt, no swish of layered skirts... only weighty velvet outside a pocket of air and a lot of people staring. Phoenix fought the urge to thump fellow rennies with her nonexistent staff when they bowed to her. She doubted many of them even recognized her, and Ryna, grinning like the Cheshire cat, was the tip-off to those who did.

And then, barely on the other side of the games area, the peasants executed a flying dive grovel at her feet.

"Walk all over us!" cried Pratt of the mismatched boots. "We are not worthy!"

Phoenix hesitated, flustered.

"Truly we just want to see up your skirts, m'lady," the Leper whispered. And winked.

"Bloo-mers!" Dead chimed in happily. Puddle shushed him, looking embarrassed.

"Well, then, mustn't disappoint the loyal masses." As delicately as she could, Phoenix crossed the living carpet—to many delighted exclamations from the peasantry. Once she was on firm ground Phoenix thanked them for their kind service, quietly threatened to bludgeon them all later, and continued on her way.

Gods but it was annoying to have to act all genteel and gracious instead of slipping into her crotchety herbwoman personae. Annoying and... well... a little fun. With such a beautiful dress, she couldn't help but feel like a storybook princess decked out for a ball. And hadn't she dreamed about just that when she'd been little?

Well, that and running away with the Gypsies to escape her parents... Phoe quirked a mental smile. *Well, one out of two isn't bad.*

Ryna gave her a quick kiss before leaving her side at First Aid gate, and Phoenix (after flashing her pass) continued into the Summer Palace alone.

Christine sat primly on a wooden bench, head bowed slightly, as if someone had superimposed a Botticelli painting over a trailer park. Phoenix stood enraptured, certain that nothing so resplendent could be real. Crystals and pearls winked in sunlight that shimmered off golden trim, but even the pinnacle of Esmerelda's handiwork could not overshadow Christine's wedding-day glow. Princess Rose, shabby in comparison, put the final touches on the bride's hair.

"Ye gods my brother's got good taste," Phoenix blurted.

Christine looked up with a welcoming smile. "Thank you. You're quite the vision yourself."

"Shake," Princess Rose ordered, and Christine delicately shook her head. Everything stayed put, and the hairdresser nodded decisively. "How much time do we have?"

The cannon blasted, eclipsing Phoenix's words.

"Oh. Well, that was convenient," Christine observed. "We'll leave as soon as everyone returns from Front Gate. Sit and talk with me, both of you, before I start worrying about tripping on my own feet and stumbling down the aisle when I see Daniel in his outfit."

"Christine, you look more graceful falling on your ass than most of us do dancing," Princess Rose declared with a very unladylike snort.

The talk turned to small, inconsequential things, but did not prevent Phoenix's stomach from knotting. Even if she escaped right after the ceremony, her parents would corner her eventually. And what would come of that…

"Lady Carlotta, you are a vision!" Queen Guinevere exclaimed as she swept into the Summer Palace.

"Phoenix," Christine's brother Justin greeted, sketching a bow. Although his tights were black, his doublet matched Phoenix's dress. It suited him; his coloring was much closer to Phoe's than to his sister's. "You ready to fall on our faces together?"

A smile twitched Phoenix's lips as he offered his arm with awkward gallantry. It seemed odd, after all this time among rennies, that such a gesture wouldn't be the most natural thing in the world. She gave him a playful scowl. "Twinkie. Aren't you going to at least tell your sister how fantastic she looks?"

"Forgive me, dear lady." He bowed to his sister. "I thought such an understatement would be far too obvious."

"Smoooooooooth!" one of the other nobles razzed him. "We'll make a rennie out of you yet."

He laughed. "No thanks. I couldn't handle strutting around in this stuff fifteen days a year."

"Shall we, then?" King Arthur suggested with a dazzling smile.

With practiced ease the court lined up—heralds, then the king and queen, prince and princess. A whole array of other courtly people fell in, many bearing the royalty's triple-crown banners. Phoenix and Justin stood behind them, followed by Christine on the arm of Sir Lancelot. Phoenix wondered how many years it had taken for the marching order to become instinct.

A blast of trumpets, and the entourage swept through the picket fence in a bubble of splendor. Phoenix watched with amused sympathy as rennies bowed and curtseyed, trying not to twitch with impatience to hurry to their grid spots. Children stared in wonder—and for once, she was part of it. Children often laughed at Phoenix, or sometimes ducked their heads shyly, but they never gaped like that for a simple herbwoman. She could see why noble characters were so addictive.

A fanfare announced their arrival as the procession neared the Chapel. Phoe caught sight of the royal carriage waiting under a cluster of trees not far distant, layers upon layers of Gypsy decorations obscuring all but the occasional bit of garish paint. She sent mental kudos to her family as she caught Ryna's eye in the audience and grinned.

The Royal Strings, nestled discretely to one side of the Chapel, slid into a stately rendition of "Pachebel's Cannon" as the nobility melted into their places along the rows' ends. The morning sun danced around Daniel, the image of chivalry in his black doublet and hose and the rapier he'd borrowed from one of the Musketeers. Phoe heard Christine gasp softly and couldn't blame her one bit.

Two flower girls, adorable in their tiny hoopskirts, began tossing rose petals as they toddled down the aisle. With half the distance to go, the older of the two reached into her basket—and whirled, horror painted across her face. "I used them all up!" she wailed.

Titters rippled through the audience; Ma O'Malley leaned over from her aisle seat to assure the girl that it didn't matter—to keep walking. The younger flower girl stooped to retrieve yet another handful of the petals and deposit them in her own basket, oblivious to her companion's drama.

"You ready?" Justin asked quietly.

"As I'll ever be," Phoenix replied as their turn came to step, pause, step towards the Chapel and take their places to either side of the vine-covered arch. Phoe kept her eyes carefully ahead, tried to ignore her birth family, tried to think only of the rennies peppering the benches: minstrels, street characters, Royal Court, the entire O'Malley family… briefly she wondered who was watching Cottage.

The strings glided seamlessly into the bridal march, heralding Christine in all her radiant glory, an angel on King Arthur's arm. The audience turned to stare, and Phoenix thought for a moment she might have to pick her brother up off the ground.

Christine, despite earlier fears, only wavered slightly.

At last the strings fell silent and the priest cleared his throat.

"Dearly beloved, we are gathered here today…"

Phoenix listened with polite attention, sang the songs and pronounced the Latin with mindless precision. Strange—as a child this had been her dream wedding—only, of course, she'd been in a cathedral with a prince standing beside her.

Reality had been so much better.

She had been joined not only to her love, but to her heart-family—as it came, still in garb, dirty and sweaty from a day of entertaining. Her decorations had been the earth they stood on, the sky over their heads, and the fire burning bright and warm and Magick. She had been welcomed into a family with love and hugs and blessings instead of the vague approval of a distant God she couldn't touch.

Phoenix hoped her brother and Christine would have memories of their ceremony that were as fond as the ones Phoe held of her own. They really did deserve perfect happiness.

And then, all vows said in the established form, Daniel lifted Christine's veil, and the couple exchanging their first wedded kiss. They parted to much applause and swept down the aisle among sprays of bubbles, preceded by a frantic photographer who made them stop three times for the perfect picture. Phoenix and Justin followed them to the horse-drawn carriage to wave them off. Daniel gallantly helped Christine to her seat before taking his own, the driver clucked to the horses, and they rode away to the rumble of wheels, the flutter of scarves, and the chiming of Gypsy bells.

The carriage would make a circuit of the grounds—that, Daniel and Christine knew. They *didn't* know, however, that that every show they passed had a blessing for them. Phoenix grinned. She had to hand it to the rennies—hard as they were to organize, they all had a romantic streak a mile wide. Coordinating it all had been easier than she expected. *Must be how Danny and Ryna pulled off my birthday treasure hunt last year,* she mused.

"Well," Justin said as the newlyweds rounded Bedside Manor and disappeared. "On to the post-wedding snacks?"

Phoenix wrinkled her nose at him as they meandered towards the ugly white tent. "Speak for yourself. I'm not sure there's room in this corset for even *one* wedding mint."

Other guests trickled that direction as well; garbed workers stood patiently by, encouraging them in with smiles and polite words.

"Well. It's nice to see at least *one* of my children wed before I die," came a simpering voice. "And you, *finally* on the arm of a decent young man." Phoe's mother gave Justin a shrewd look. "They do say that one wedding begets another..."

"I'll meet you at the tent, Phoe," Justin said with an uncomfortable shift of his shoulders, and hurried off.

Phoe gazed after him longingly a moment, unable to conjure the words to call him back.

But really, what protection could he offer?

She turned to her parents, a guarded note in her voice. "Hello, Mother. Father. I'm sorry I didn't greet you earlier."

Her father frowned sternly at her. "Do not lie to your mother, Beatrice. I'll not bear your falsehoods on top of your betrayal."

"We're not stupid," her mother added. "We both know perfectly well you've been avoiding us."

"Oh, give it up," Phoenix said with a burst of exasperation. "Truth was a dead language in our household. You and Father were the only ones who could speak your minds, and you never even bothered to come up with opinions of your own."

Her mother's lips thinned; her father's brow formed a harsh, bushy V.

The stern reprimand had been her first warning; this discrete displeasure was her second. They expected her to cower now, to weep and repent. She'd played this game with them since childhood.

Stubborn, unexpected resolution welled in Phoe's chest. She wouldn't play it anymore. She'd faced hatred far more dangerous than this. She'd faced creatures her parents would call demons—and triumphed, with her family backing her every step. Even now, she could feel Ryna nearby, her help only a thought away—but waiting for that thought, trusting her ability to fight her own battles.

Willing to let her live her own life.

Beside that love, those people, these two were poor, pathetic mundanes who could not comprehend the beauties life offered. Phoenix met her parents stare for stare, guts roiling… but, strangely, her spine was straight.

"Why you can't be more like Christine, I just don't understand," her mother said, dabbing at her eyes. "She would never speak to her family this way!"

"Why you can't be more like Christine's family, *I* just don't understand," Phoenix countered. "They would never deserve it."

An ominous pause.

Her father dropped three words into the stillness, her final warning.

"Exodus 20:12."

Honor my father and mother? A grim smile shaped Phoe's lips. "Luke 6:31," she shot back, as she'd wished she'd had the courage to do a hundred times before. And now that the words were free, she could feel a thousand more clambering to be heard. "Does that mean I can shut *you* in a closet? Or what about when you locked the doors when Danny was out past curfew—in the middle of February? It's a good thing I was willing to brave your leather belt, or he would've frozen to death out there. Or when—"

Phoenix didn't flinch, not even when the stone-hard hand cracked across her cheek.

"Now see what you made your father do, Beatrice," her mother fussed. "You'll be all bruised for the pictures. How *will* you explain yourself?"

"He is not my father. That title belongs to Tremayne of the Gypsies. My mother is Kaya of the Gypsies. And your husband can explain it himself."

Claire choked on her rage; her face contorted briefly, and within an instant her tears and sniveling manner had vanished. "You are hereby written out of our will. You'll live the rest of your days as wretched, penniless filth, just like your perverted little Gypsy harlot!"

"If money makes you act like that, I'd rather be a pauper!" Phoe's hands were shaking. She could actually hear herself yelling.

Make them pay, a dark voice hissed in the back of her head; she could feel her Magicks gathering to strike out at them. *Show them there are more powerful things than fist and belt-strap…*

Phoenix fought the unexpected siren song, forced the energies within her to calm. That was not her way. No matter how much they deserved it…

Better to turn and walk away.

"*Beatrice Helen Saunders*!" The roar of Robert's words strangled her like a dog's training leash. She could feel it choking her, binding her to his will. "One more step and you are dead to us!"

She stopped, cast a glance over her shoulder at her childhood giants—now reduced to blustering fools. And they thought they could hold her. "Bea died a year ago. My name is Phoenix Tully, and I have more wealth than you can imagine."

And then the leash was gone. He could not use her name to call her; it would sound strange and stumbling on his lips.

A crowd had almost gathered. She strode through a hallway of stares, head high—and a sharp sting on her cheek.

◇ ◇ ◇

Da-amn! was the only thought Ryna's awe-struck mind could form. Every eye in the area followed her Phoenix, yet she was grace defined… and her parents stood spluttering in the mud.

Ryna waited until Phoe reached the Harvest Man—and made a respectful curtsey to it—before dashing after her. It'd taken all the redhead's willpower not to rush in as soon as she sensed trouble. She was more proud than she could say that she had not been needed.

"You rebel," she murmured. "Honoring Pagan idols in front of the Catholics."

"That's partly why I did it," Phoenix replied with the flash of an unsteady—yet defiant—grin.

"You want me to smooch you for effect?"

Wide, teary eyes blinked down at Ryna—her heart nearly stopped. "I hope that's not the only reason you'd do it."

"Never," Ryna said, and pulled her love down for a kiss—to great cheering from the masses.

"Thank you," Phoe whispered when at last they parted. "For being there, in case I needed you. And for trusting me to handle it myself."

"You did more than handle it, Phoe. You were wonderful." Ryna traced a thumb along her cheekbone, tucked a star-white tendril behind her ear. "You *are* wonderful."

"Telling them I took your last name wasn't too much?" she asked hesitantly as they started across the Green.

"Of course not! It hadn't even occurred to me; I never really thought of you with a last name at all. But if you like we could get it legally changed."

"I would. After all, I handfasted into your family. I have no desire to bear the mark of a people who consider me dead."

"Sounds good to me—I'll ask the others what we need to do."

Phoenix cast her a dubious look. "It couldn't be too hard. People do this sort of thing all the time."

"What, denounce a huge inheritance and proper religion to join a lesbian lover and her vagabond family in a never-ending battle against unspeakable evil as the chosen champions of the Bright Fae?"

To Ryna's delight, it made Phoenix giggle. "I *meant* change their names, silly!"

"Oh, well, I guess I thought I'd covered that somewhere in there."

Another giggle. Gods, Ryna loved the sound of her laughter. What a blessing that she'd be hearing it for the rest of her lives.

◇ ◇ ◇

Phoenix fidgeted with the folds of her lapis-blue gown, finding it increasingly difficult to affect ladylike serenity as she waited for her brother under Tinker's Tree. The horse-drawn carriage would bring him here at the tour's end… and then she'd have to tell him about the whole mess and hope it didn't ruin his day. She wished she could at least have her soulmate's steadying presence at her back, but Ryna'd left half an hour ago to do the dance show—and to take Phoe's place in the variety show after that.

"They're back, they're back!" Eryn cried, bolting out Cottage's door as the bridal carriage lumbered, jingling, across Shepherd's Green. "Torin! Torin! The Bernatellis brought *pie*!"

"Did they, now?" He bounded down from the carriage and swung her around in a circle before turning with utmost chivalry to help his lady disembark. Phoe hurried to assist her with the voluminous skirts of her jewel-spattered gown.

"Thank you," Christine murmured graciously as her white-slippered foot touched the ground.

"Hurry *up*! *We* can't have any until *you* do," the little redhead urged.

"Eryn Eileen Dimphne O'Malley!" Ma's voice bellowed from the window nearest Tinker's Tree.

Eryn stopped in her tracks. "Uh-oh."

"Get back inside and stop pesterin' the newlyweds!"

The youngest O'Malley scuttled off, followed by a laughing Christine.

Phoenix sidled up to her brother, hands clasped at her velvet waist. She stared hard at them, head bowed. Gods, she really didn't want to do this. Not today. "Um, Danny? We need to talk about something."

"What is it, Phoe-bea?" he asked gently, tipping her chin up—and paled in anger. "That's it. I've had enough of his bullying. I'm going to—"

"Wait, Danny. Don't." She grabbed his arm. "It doesn't matter—"

"It matters. I've put up with—"

"—hear me out. It's a small price for freedom. I needed to tell you now because you shouldn't hear this from someone else. I—" She took a deep breath. "I kind of got myself disowned. In front of everybody."

Daniel stilled a moment in shock before uttering a low whistle. "Are you—"

"Okay? Yeah, I guess." She gave him a shaky grin. "I curtseyed to the Harvest Man and kissed Ryna right in front of them, too."

That earned flat-out laughter. "You never do anything by halves, do you? Oh, Phoe-bea. I want a copy of your Declaration of Independence to hang on my wall."

It made the knot in her chest loosen. Things would be okay after all. She only had to survive the day, and it would all be over. "Thanks for being my brother, Danny—for understanding."

He waved it off. "Thanks for being born—it would've been awful growing up without you."

Phoenix wasn't sure which warmed her heart more—his words, the pride in his eyes...

...or the knowledge that she had earned it.

"Family before relatives," he said with a grin.

Phoenix nodded. "And you're my family. Always."

◇ ◇ ◇

"Have you seen my necklace?"

Ryna looked up from tuning her fiddle to find Emily hovering near the large blue vardo, her daughter in her arms. "I don't think so. What's it look like?"

"It's a Celtic cross set with moonstone—I got it last year at that booth sort of over by where the fortunetellers are. I've had it hanging off my belt so Morgan wouldn't grab it, and now I can't seem to find it. I know I put it on this morning..."

"Did you try the Information Booth?" Ryna suggested, though without real hope. "It won't get shipped to B-gate until the end of the day..."

"Nothing," Emily said, and sighed. "I suppose it was too much to hope that someone here had found it. I thought I'd ask, though, since I was down here to change the little one."

"I'll have the other Gypsies keep an eye out for it too," the fiddler told her, and Emily headed toward Hollow Hill as Kaya jingled across the stage, Toby behind her. "Emily's looking for her Celtic cross necklace."

Toby barked a short laugh as he hopped down onto the packed dirt. "Here? That's the one thing you can be sure this lot *hasn't* run off with."

Ryna tweaked one of her fine tuners and gave him a critical eye. "You sound almost as jaded as Tanek."

"He found out we didn't get a GEM for running around in the rain making a commotion," Kaya told her.

"But the Royals Revolting did," Toby added bitterly. "For putting on ponchos and making a joke about it."

Ryna snorted. "That gag's as old as their show."

"And it's not street theatre," Toby added.

"I keep telling you not to take it so personally," Kaya said. "Once you've been around long enough, I think management stops noticing when you're entertaining."

"I went up there and asked why we didn't get qualified, and Chaos Kitten told me it was because we weren't interactive enough."

"If you aim for recognition, you're going to be disappointed." Ryna convinced her E string to cooperate, then moved to the D. "Take Unicorn Awards, for example. You have to be here ten years and make a memorable contribution to Pendragon to get one. *Phuro* Basil and *Baba* Luna finally got theirs the year before last. Tata's been here even longer, done as much, and he doesn't have his yet. Neither do you, or me, or Elda—Kaya's up for her fifteen-year this year and she doesn't have hers, either—but some rennies get it as soon as they hit the decade mark. It's the way things are. Most times you get taken for granted and nobody thinks to regret you till you're—hello, what have we here?"

"What?" Kaya turned.

"That." Ryna nodded toward a nobleman and a dozen peasants gathered near Hollow Hill's gate. Each peasant carted a hefty burlap-covered box.

Toby quirked a smile. "That's the lordling who asked about Emily yesterday."

A few patrons stopped to see what was going on, then a few more. The Gypsies had all assembled for their show by the time Hollow Hill's door swung open to reveal a mightily startled Emily, Morgan in one arm.

"My lady," the nobleman proclaimed, sweeping off his hat as he went down on one knee. "Thou know'st me not, yet much hath I seen of thee. Thy courage, beauty, and bravery shine like a beacon in these darkened times. And so, humbly, do I beg the honor of pampering thee with this token of my affection."

The peasants swept off their boxes' coverings with a flourish, revealing cartons of diapers.

The lordling stood, then, and bowed over Emily's hand. He gallantly kissed her knuckles, gazing soulfully into her eyes, letting the contact of their fingers linger as he backed away. At the last instant he turned, replaced his hat, and strode off.

The peasants hastily deposited their burdens and followed.

The patrons cheered—quite a few laughed.

Emily stood there, flatfooted.

Tanek let out a whistle of appreciation. "Da-*amn*! He's *good*!"

"I wonder if he's got a brother who's willing to climb into a kilt?"

Ryna looked at Esmerelda and laughed.

◇ ◇ ◇

It was all Phoenix could do, standing patiently outside Bedside Manor, not to fidget. She tried to take an example from Christine, who waited with casual poise. Of course, Christine's ex-parents weren't fifteen feet away pointedly ignoring her… although, Phoe reminded herself, they could do worse than ignore her.

Tears stung the Gypsy's eyes. She longed for her regular garb and the reassuring weight of her coin belt. It was difficult enough to deal with everything without having to live up to fripperies, too. She touched her bond ring and reminded herself that Ryna was only a thought-hug away.

But gods, it seemed like a million miles.

"Wishing you could go roll in the mud?" a voice whispered in her ear, and Phoenix looked up to find Christine's brother standing beside her.

"How—"

"I've seen pictures of you in costume. All this get-up is probably as weird for you as it is for me," Justin said with a lovable smile. "Besides, you looked like you could use a friend."

"Thanks."

He leaned casually on the head of one of the little lion statues that flanked the staircase. "So, hey, what's coming up at this feast thing? Are we going to at least have forks?"

Phoenix gratefully accepted the diversion. "I haven't been to it yet, but I'm pretty sure we get something tastier than a turkey drumstick. And we get fruit—I only know because sometimes the leftovers wind up down in—"

Trumpets blared over the rest of Phoenix's words. Every eye turned to Sir Kay, standing with impressive splendor on the outthrust porch. The white streak in his short red beard gleamed in the sun. "Hear ye, hear ye! The Fantastical Feast in celebration of the nuptials of Lord Daniel and Lady Christine Saunders is about to commence!"

A few cheers from the crowd.

"There will be music! There will be wine! There will be beautiful, scantily clad women! No, none for you, lad. 'Tis too late for that," Kay admonished Daniel with a rueful smile, then turned back to the crowd. "The rest of us can enjoy them, though!"

A few more cheers. Robert and Claire looked scandalized. Not that Phoe was looking.

"I even have it on excellent authority that Their Majesties King Arthur and Queen Guinevere will be in attendance! And so, without further ado... are you ready for the Fantastical Feast?"

"Yea, verily, yea!" Phoenix shouted, along with a few other rennies.

"Oh, come now! Are you so faint with hunger that you can do no better than that? Let us try this again. *Are you ready for the Fantastical Feast*?"

"Yea, verily, yea!" This time the whole crowd joined in.

"This way, then, and let the merriment begin!"

More cheering, and the guests filed through the massive double doors. The wedding party hung back. Weddings, Phoe had begun to learn, were all about timing your entrances.

Sir Kay beamed at Christine, who beamed back. He gallantly kissed her hand.

Daniel looked proud enough to pop.

"We're next," Justin observed, offering his arm. "Shall we?"

Phoenix grinned. "You're getting good at that."

"It's the costume," he confided as they swept into Bedside Manor ahead of the bridal couple.

Phoe reeled a moment in the doorway, the spectacle enough to make her jaw drop. She had been inside Bedside Manor before, but it had either been darkened for the slide show or set up buffet-style for the morning-after-run breakfast. Now... a sea of people stared at her, each with an elegant place setting before them. Robert and Claire glared as if she was some repulsive strain of baby-killing bacteria. Phoe tried to let her gaze slide past them as if they were strangers.

She doubted they bought it.

Justin gave her an encouraging smile as they took their appointed positions to the right and left of the high-backed chairs that awaited their siblings.

"All rise in honor of Lord Daniel and Lady Christine!" Sir Kay called. "Hip-hip!"

"Huzzah!" Phoenix called, and one or two others along with her.

"Hip-hip!"

"Huzzah!" A few more, this time.

"Hip-hip!"

"Huzzah!" This time the cheer roared from the entire audience, followed by trumpets sounding the wedding march.

Christine and Daniel swept into the room to applause and clinking of glasses; Daniel kissed his bride before gallantly seating her in the high-backed chair nearest Phoenix.

Hardly had the newlyweds sat down—and the masses after them—than Robert Saunders rose again, goblet held high. "A toast," he proclaimed officiously.

"A toast," Phoenix murmured with the rest of the guests, raising her own goblet and hoping no one noticed the trembling of her hand. *His words can't touch me anymore. I am no longer his daughter,* she reminded herself… and wished it was quite that easy.

"To Daniel, a model son—and to Christine, the daughter we've always wanted, and a welcome addition to the family. May they carry on the family name with pride."

Phoenix tried to ignore the clench of her heart and the heat that suffused her face. Poor Christine looked mortally embarrassed, and Phoe could tell from the set of Daniel's jaw that her brother was about to do something very sweet and protective—and potentially disastrous. She replaced her goblet without drinking and reached over to where he was disentangling his hand from Christine's. She grasped it hard. "No. Danny. Please. It's not worth it."

"The hell it's not," he hissed back.

"It's not," she repeated firmly but quietly. "Today is your day—if you yell at them, you let them steal your thunder. Let them bluster. They're only hurting themselves."

Daniel frowned, but relented.

"A toast!" cried Christine's mother.

"A toast!" cried the masses.

"To my daughter, who has always brought joy to our family, and to my new children-in-law, who I look forward to loving for many years to come. You can do nothing *but* bring me pride."

Phoenix feared she might start crying right then and there.

The bride leaned over and gave her new sister-in-law a squeeze.

From across the room, Amelia gave her a wink.

Daniel's parents scowled.

Phoenix hoped whomever was in charge would hurry up and bring out the entertainment.

"So *you're* the one my namesake picked for herself."

Ryna spun from closing the door to Hollow Hill, having deposited the dance show's tips in the collection box. A petite woman with an elfin cast to her face met Ryna's gaze with bird-sharp intensity. Her curling blonde hair had gone more than a little gray. And she *glowed.*

Ryna liked her immediately. "If you mean Phoenix, yes, I am. My name is Ryna." She offered a hand.

"Charmed, I'm sure." She clasped the Gypsy's hand and—surprisingly—kissed the back of it. "I'm her Aunt Emily—Ily to the nieces and nephews who are allowed contact with me." She rolled her eyes. "And to my partner and various sundry others."

"You're Auntie Ily?!"

"Mmm." The older woman nudged Ryna's sleeve back from the hand she still held, exposing the tooled-copper bracelet that had been Ryna's first gift from Phoenix. "You'll want to be careful with that. It's very old." She gave Ryna a direct look. "And there are some who would rather you didn't have it."

Ryna started, knocked off her stride by Ily's words and her piercing, witch-hazel eyes. "What?"

"It's a thing of power. The original owner, Emily, was burned at the stake for witchcraft. Her brother gave it to his first daughter, named in her memory. If you believe the story, it's been passed on in our family like that for centuries, name and bracelet—until my brother broke the tradition."

The fiddler's mind reeled at the unexpected onslaught. She had guessed at its origins, but it had seemed too far-fetched to be real… and to hear this now, from a woman who seemed nearly mythical… "Do you?" she asked quietly, the words coming from a long way away. "Believe the story?"

"Ah, *Baba* Luna, you've caught a *lady*!" *Phuro* Basil called from Caravan Stage, jarring Ryna from impossible wonder.

"Alas, I do not have Tanek's charms—so I must use my own."

Ryna turned to find the camp elder striding toward the stage, a crystal ball in her upraised hand and Phoenix in her velvet finery trailing behind, looking bewitched.

Looking bewitching.

Aunt Ily cocked her head. "What do *you* think?"

The redhead grinned. "I think you should ask *her* that question. I have a feeling she'd tell you a story that'd knock your bloomers off."

"If only I had the time," Ily said wistfully. "If only I had time. Tell her I'll see her soon enough. Or she'll see me. It's all semantics." Then, with a wink, she turned and strolled into the crowd.

The Gypsy stared dumbstruck after her a moment, then down at her bracelet. How had Auntie Ily known about the disappearances this year? Or had she meant that Phoenix's birth-family would rather not see their heirloom on their daughter's lover?

Either way, she'd had a point. Bracelets could fall off, and she wouldn't lose this one for all the world. Though it pained her heart to do it, Ryna slipped it off and went to tuck it in her fiddle case.

◇ ◇ ◇

"Ear ye, ear ye, fresh corn on the cob, come and get it while it's—"

"Turkey drumsticks! Can't go home without your—"

"Lemonade! Fill the need with—"

"Priiiiiiiiiiime RIB! Get your prime rib sandwiches, right here—"

Phoenix watched quietly as the RFC kids hawked their wares in the row of booths near C-gate. Most entertainers held them in disdain. Maybe it was because they actually got paid. Maybe because they were locked into place and therefore couldn't do any "real" entertaining. Maybe because it had always been that way. But for whatever reason, in the feudal system of Renaissance faires, RFC workers were the serfs.

They quite possibly ranked even below the Royals Revolting in rennie public opinion.

But when Phoenix watched them, she just saw a bunch of teenagers, tired and footsore. The occasional patron who wandered past looked more interested in reaching the privies than stopping for a bite to eat, but the RFC kids gave it their all anyhow. A couple workers had resorted to shouting jokes at each other out of sheer boredom. Most of them involved Scotsmen and sheep. A couple were even ones Phoenix had not heard.

A tiny signal tugged the back of Phoe's consciousness; she turned to see her love trooping past the deserted Maypole from the direction of the Narrows, leather-covered instrument case slung over her shoulder. "Hey," Ryna greeted with a tired smile as she neared Phoenix's bench.

"Hey yourself. Free from the duties of leftover collection today?"

"Yup. Thought I'd head downstairs, put on some civvies, maybe dig out some marshmallows."

"Mmmmm." Phoenix smiled at the mental image of her partner waving around a flaming ball of sugar on the end of a stick. She wondered if she could come up with a new way to distract her long enough for it to catch; the game had become a sport among the Gypsies. "People talking about lighting up the fire pit tonight?"

"Hey, you! Gypsy!"

Both women's heads turned at the cry from the food booths. "Which one?" Ryna called back, forgetting Phoenix looked nothing like a Gypsy.

"You, with the fiddle!" The speaker was a gangly boy from the soup booth. "Play for us?"

Ryna hesitated. "Um, I dunno…"

"Oh, please, please," one fair-haired RFC kid begged, draping herself over the counter.

Phoenix could tell her lover was wavering. "C'mon, Artemis," she nudged. "They give us leftovers every day."

The fiddler nodded minutely and retrieved her baby from its case. A couple casual tweaks to the knob on the bow's end tightened the horsehair, and Ryna brought her beautifully detailed fiddle to her chin. The late afternoon light sparkled off the metallic tassel of coins, crystals, and charms that hung from the instrument's scroll; an errant bit of breeze fluttered the gold-embroidered ribbon tied beside it—the one Ryna said had been her token from the Bright Fae, found on a bracelet she'd thought lost. The busy sounds of Pendragon faded as everyone in the area paused, expectant. Four clear notes echoed into the stillness as Ryna checked her tuning: G, D, A, E.

She smiled.

Without warning, a sprightly Irish jig sprang from her instrument, bow flying over the strings with a speed that seemed almost inhuman. Hell, knowing Ryna, it probably was.

A young lady in the prime rib booth pounded out a complicated rhythm on the battered counter. Two stalls over at the juice and lemonade booth a fellow picked up a couple spoons and tapped against one of the metal iced tea kegs. The wondrous clangor echoed until the impromptu jam accompanied itself. As Ryna's jig slipped into a reel, Phoenix saw RFC kids peeking out from the back rooms. The fellow who had been hawking the foodstuffs from the street did a little dance over by the instant cash machine, and a jubilant whoop came from somewhere near the corn-on-the-cob booth.

Oh yes, Phoenix thought with a private smile. *She needed this. And look how they adore her.*

The reel slid into a minor key and morphed subtly into a Gypsy tune. Phoe could tell her lover was improvising by her euphoric smile and the way her Charm rose until she glowed.

BOOM!

The cannon's blast startled everyone from the beautiful world Ryna had created. The fiddler wound down with a graceful flourish, bowed, and turned to retrieve her things.

Phoenix was too busy gathering leftovers to watch her go, but the raven-haired Gypsy was willing to bet Ryna would never realize that her gift of five minutes of song had won her the love of every kid there.

* * *

"This is officially a really nice way to spend a Sunday evening," Niki purred.

Esmerelda laughed. "Glad you like. I had a craving to S'more-ify my graham crackers tonight."

Her brother rolled his eyes. "You and your graham crackers."

Phuro Basil chuckled. "It got you a fire, lad. Don't complain."

"I'm just complaining that she eats all the graham crackers."

"Oh, as if you even like the things," Niki jibed.

"I do when you stick chocolate and marshmallows on them!"

Phoenix smiled with utter contentment as she rotated her stick to evenly toast the marshmallow she was making for Ryna. Phoe loved the feel of Sunday evenings, the pleasant wind-down from an eventful weekend. Gradually the faire became theirs again as one by one the damn weekenders, who were only after the mythical drunken after-hours orgies, packed up their gear and left. The cool weekenders left, too, but that couldn't be helped.

"Ahhhhh." Ryna pulled the last of her bodice laces free and shrugged out of the garment. It landed with a muted *ching* as it hit her coin belt atop the pile of her outer Gypsy garb. She stretched luxuriously and scratched a couple previously inaccessible itches.

Ryna's chemise clung enticingly to her delicate, rounded frame—only a sharp warning from Tremayne saved Phoe's marshmallow from becoming a tiki torch.

"So," *Baba* Luna inquired, chin on her fist, "who wins the betting pool if *Phoenix* lights her marshmallow?"

"Betting pool!" Ryna cried.

"Why hasn't anyone brought out the Nutella?" Kaya scolded, artfully changing the subject as she rose from her log bench.

Tremayne's eyes glazed at the mention of the chocolate/hazelnut spread. *Like father, like daughter,* Phoenix thought wryly.

"Hey," an unfamiliar voice slurred as a man with unkempt blond hair and a battered T-shirt staggered into the flickering firelight of Gypsy camp.

Phoenix fought the sudden urge to run.

"Can we help you?" *Phuro* Basil inquired cordially, though Phoe noticed a tensing in his posture. It did nothing to reassure her. Neither did the way Kaya returned to the group before even reaching her vardo's porch.

He swayed, casually leaned against Tanek's vardo as he waved his cigarette prominently in the air. "Got a light?" His glassy eyes skipped around the circle until they landed on Ryna, almost as if he had been searching for her.

Phoenix choked on the warning that clambered to escape her throat.

"How 'bout you, pretty Gypsy? Bet you could give me a light."

"None of us smoke here," Tremayne said firmly.

"Jesus H. Christ!" He spread too-long arms wide. "Come on! Here I am in a camp full of people who blow fire and no one's got a fucking light?"

A mischievous smile played across Esmerelda's face; her eyes narrowed briefly as she stared at the man's cigarette. A wisp of smoke trailed upward an instant before the cigarette's end began to glow.

And then a three-inch flame leapt into being, scorching his fingers.

Panic blossomed in the man's expression. "Shit! Shit! Shit!" The message had gotten from his fingers to his brain and back; the cig dropped to the ground. "You guys are fucked up, man!"

"Funny, I was about to say the same," Toby muttered.

The man ground his cigarette into the dirt with the heel of his beat-up cowboy boot. "I ain't doin' nothin', kay? Just don't curse me or some shit, right?"

Tanek stood, eyes taking on an unholy glint as he backed the intruder against the nearest vardo. "Who sent you?"

"I ain't done nothin', okay?" The words tumbled over each other in the man's haste. "I ain't messin' with no witches. Jus' back off, an' let me go, an' I'll—"

Tanek braced one fist on either side of the man and leaned in until his nose almost touched the stranger's. "*Who sent you*?" he repeated, his voice low and intent. The Gypsy had somehow added a foot to his normal height.

"Just some… a voice, okay? Some weird joke or some shit—I dunno."

Tanek let the silence stretch. Staring. Not blinking.

Phoenix squirmed from the energies he radiated, and she wasn't even the one on whom they were focused.

"Listen, I was just walkin' along when my head, it goes all funny like. Like a bad trip or somethin'. I can't even remember what I came here for… shit, you ain't gonna blood sacrifice me or nothin', hey?"

Tanek's expression turned to utter disgust. "Just go." He stepped away, muttering.

The fellow stumbled, swearing, into the night, his crunching bootsteps fading in the tense silence.

"Well that was a little too weird," Niki said with strained cheerfulness.

Phoenix squeezed her love's shoulders in a one-armed hug—and wondered when she had put her arm there.

"Am I not the only one who thinks that was a little more than random?" Toby asked rhetorically.

Kaya wrinkled her pretty nose. "Considering he stank like Shadow Magick…" She glanced over to her stepdaughter. "You all right, princess?"

"I think I'm going to bed," Ryna declared unsteadily, arms folded tightly over her chest, and abruptly stood. She waved her vardo door open; it obliged and then politely shut itself behind her.

Phoenix cast a distraught glance around the fire's companions as she rose. Small nods urged her to follow her heart, not that she needed the encouragement.

Ryna sat on the bed inside, intently brushing Karma.

Karma purred loudly, every hair vibrating as she attempted to reassure her person. There was nothing to fear… not so long as Karma was there to watch over her.

"Hey," Phoenix greeted.

"Hey," Ryna returned, not looking up.

Phoenix perched beside her. "You all right?"

"Do I have a choice?" Ryna glanced up quickly, though the brush never stopped its gentle, firm strokes.

"You could go for spooked and unsettled. It's working for everyone else."

Ryna cracked the bare hint of a smile.

"Hey." Phoenix took her love's tiny, warm hands in her own. Karma seemed only mildly miffed that the attention ceased. "We're in this together. I'm your soulmate, remember?"

Ryna's smile softened. "I could never forget."

"Then talk to me. Please. Tell me what you're thinking."

The fiddler sighed elaborately. "Only how missing power items might be the sprites playing tricks… but random weekenders on dark errands is another thing entirely."

"Ryna, we knew we were singled out. The Bright Fae told us so after we defeated Liam." A flicker in Ryna's eyes stopped her short. "What, you think it's him?"

Ryna snorted. "I doubt the Shadow Fae left him the power for that sort of thing… if they left much of him at all. I'm betting he shook hands with oblivion last September."

The chill gripping Phoe's spine eased. After all, Ryna knew her stuff, and if she didn't think there was a threat, then there wasn't one. "They're probably just sore that we kicked their backsides last year."

"You're probably right. And if we beat them when they took us by surprise, we can certainly do it now that we're prepared." Ryna huffed out a breath and gave her love a warm hug. "Thanks, Phoe."

"Hey, what are friends for?"

Ryna leaned forward with the smile of a temptress. "Shall I demonstrate?"

"Oh my."

◇ ◇ ◇

"That was not what I meant."

Liam's minion blinked at him sideways. *It worked.*

"Hardly!" Liam shook the silver coin belt in the creature's face. It sounded a delicate, tinkling discordance. "This is not the ring!"

The creature looked nonplussed at the display. *The ring will come.*

"It better, after what you risked—sending a mortal—!"

You were sent.

"That's different. You picked some strung-out—"

Distraction. He kept their attention.

"And blew your cover," Liam seethed.

An infuriatingly amused twinkle entered the creature's eyes. It waved a taloned hand in dismissal.

Liam ground his teeth, wishing he dared lash out at the creature, drain its energy to fuel himself...

No. Not now. It still had its uses, flighty as it was, and it could not carry them out if it lacked the strength to move. Liam turned on his heel and stalked off as the sun sailed improbably toward the east and landmarks flickered and disappeared. The creature taunted him, but Liam ignored it. He would pay the thing back in kind soon enough.

And until then, there was always his pet.

The hem of Phoenix's embroidered chemise slapped frozenly at her ankles as she ran through the thin snow. It was gray with smoke—everything was gray with smoke. People babbled in the distance, a thousand recriminations, always behind the smoke. Her parents' faces formed in the dull swirls and eddies.

Still she ran, shivering. There was no moon, and somehow that frightened her worst of all.

Grumbling thunder turned to a horse's hooves, pounding nearer—suddenly she knew how Ichabod Crane must've felt.

Running, running, cold, confusion, running.

The smoke was alive. The voices were the Shadow Fae.

Her parents were the Shadow Fae.

Her hands glowed—but there was no moon.

A familiar cottage. She ran through the door, slammed it, bolted it.

Dark, and empty, except for the fire.

She shivered as the snow in her hair melted, staining dark tresses white.

Voices, outside, chanting,

"Hey, ho, anybody home?"

"Soul cakes, soul cakes—"

"Rose, rose—"

"Ah, poor bird—"

Firelight—but no smoke—no moon...

Phoenix woke screaming.

But no one heard.

Phoenix was not happy—that much Ryna had deduced, more from silence than words. It was one of the things that drove Ryna batty: when Phoenix felt sad, she got quiet. When she was cranky, she got quiet. When she was frustrated, or disappointed, or upset, or tired, or shy, or contemplative, or guilt-ridden... she got quiet. And it damn near took a decoder ring to figure out which sort of silence you were dealing with, to say nothing of the cause.

Usually she vacated the premises and gave Phoe some space to sort things out, but after an entire day's worth of space Phoenix was right where Ryna had left her—sitting on the bed making vicious strokes with her pen. Ryna didn't dare peek at the picture. Her goose was roasty enough already.

"I'm really, *really* sorry I was in the privy when you woke up last night," she offered for the twentieth time, though no less sincerely than the first.

"It's fine." The words came out with spikes. "Forget it."

"Really—"

"It's *fine*!" she snapped, though obviously it wasn't.

"Do you want me to leave?" Ryna asked in a small voice.

"It's your vardo."

"And yours. If you want me to—"

"No."

Ryna subsided. "Is it because the sex last night wasn't the greatest?"

The words hung in the air with humiliating frankness.

Phoe gave her a flat look and returned to her drawing.

Ryna colored. It was still a sore spot, even after a year of proving Liam wrong.

Then, almost inaudibly, "No." Phoenix seemed infinitely sad of a sudden. "It's not that simple."

The redhead perked. She hated when her Phoenix was sad, but at least she could deal with it. Phoe only needed a cuddle and something to distract her... Ryna crawled up on the bed, comfortingly close, yet not impinging on the privacy of her work. "I saw your Auntie Ily yesterday. She's a neat lady; I can see why you like her. A little on the strange side, but—"

"You saw Auntie Ily?" Phoenix took the verbal peace offering and threw it hard. "And you didn't *tell* me? Ryna, how could you? You know how much that would've meant to me, especially after everything with my parents!"

Ryna flailed mentally, surprised to see tears in her beloved Gypsy's eyes, and stuttered disjointedly. "I—I thought you knew—had already seen, or how would she—"

Phoe snapped shut her sketchpad, dumped it and her other supplies into a bag. "I'm going to Cottage."

"Now? Phoe—"

"Don't follow."

She slammed the door on her way out.

Ryna sat down hard. And wondered when she'd gotten to her feet. She pressed her face into her hands, then tipped her head back and ran them down her neck. Why did women have to be so difficult?

Well, hopefully she'd get up there, blow off some steam, and come back in a couple hours. Maybe then she'd be willing to talk rationally.

○ ○ ○

I should've let her leave when she offered, Phoenix thought bitterly as she stormed past the night-shrouded Track, pack slung over her shoulder and angry tears in her eyes. *It's not like she's ever here anyway. Me, me, me. It always has to be about her. She's so busy riding her drama-coaster that she can't even bother to tell me that my favorite aunt came to visit!*

She tried to tell herself that her mental rant wasn't fair, but the remonstration lacked punch. Ryna hadn't dropped the proverbial ball—oh, no! That would've required her to be holding the ball to begin with... and lately Ryna didn't even seem to recognize that there *was* a ball.

That hurt the worst, Phoenix realized as she let herself into Cottage and re-bolted the sagging green door. Surely if you loved somebody, you'd notice when they needed you?

Cottage certainly seemed to know. The quiet, soothing atmosphere embraced her, held her like a child. *You are safe,* it seemed to say. *Everything will be all right. You are home.*

Phoe carefully navigated the darkened interior—just enough of the light from behind First Aid gate filtered through the shutters to discern vague shapes. She knelt on the uneven hearthstones, trying not to think how she'd come here Final Weekend of last year, lonely and feeling unloved. Ryna's self-absorption then, too. What was it about Cottage that drew her when she needed comfort?

Old newspapers, twigs, and Magick—she was certainly angry enough—and firelight spread a warm orange glow into the room.

Surely it didn't take a genius to see how stressful Danny's wedding had been? Wonderful, yes—she gave thanks that her brother had found someone with whom to make a life. But dealing with the rest of her relatives...

Surely getting disowned should've been clue enough? She'd spent all day wishing for Ryna's presence, if nothing else, and the redhead hadn't so much as asked how she fared.

And then that thing with the creepy guy.

And the sex. Phoenix sighed. She wasn't naive enough to think it'd be fireworks every time. But last night... it had felt like Ryna was seducing her for her own reasons. The one or two other times it'd happened had made Phoe want to crawl out of her skin, too. It reminded her too much of Liam.

Usually she could shrug it off as Ryna feeling insecure... Goddess knew Phoe wasn't the only one with baggage. But last night, on top of everything else, and then waking from nightmares alone...

That part was unlucky timing, but still. Phoenix had needed her, and she hadn't been there. Again.

She sighed and stared moodily into the flames, wishing Ryna had followed her with a really big clue and an equally huge apology.

No such luck. Phoe scrubbed at her eyes, pulled the *seanchaí* chair closer, and settled in with her thoughts and the distant grumble of thunder.

◇ ◇ ◇

"Ah, love," Liam whispered, staring longingly through Cottage's window. These glimpses through the veil to the mortal realm could bring such mixed pain and beauty. He wished he could go to her, hold her, kiss away her tears. To see her so miserable and not be able to comfort her tore at his heart.

He knew it was all for the best. She had to break from Ryna's enchantment before Liam could claim her fully—damn that bitch for binding his sugar-bird with spells. Once she was free of them, though, she would come to him.

"Strange, that the connection still pulls you so strongly," whispered a voice nearby.

Liam glanced over to see the small, sparrow-like creature perched on the woodpile between Cottage's back step and the kitchen wall. "From my last life in England?"

It gazed at him a long while before speaking. "That was not your most recent. Merely the most relevant at the time it was revealed to you."

"You didn't answer my question."

"You look forward to taking her place," it mused, blithely ignoring him. "I wonder if you realize what that means."

"It means I can claim her. It means we can be happy, live our lives in peace—have children, raise a family."

It cocked its head… and chittered. "Your lineage is safe—have no worries there."

"And the rest?" Liam asked, unable to take his eyes from the vision in the window.

It chittered again. "The rest is for you to discover."

◇ ◇ ◇

"Nuh?" Ryna roused blearily; light filtered through the partially open curtains. She had a crook in her neck, and the waistband of her jeans dug uncomfortably into her side. *9:30 AM*, read the digital alarm—roughly twelve hours since the argument.

Ryna's heart fell into her toes. Phoenix hadn't come home.

Ryna tumbled out of bed and let inertia take her to the door, where she stuffed her feet in her loafers and let herself outside. Suffocating humidity weighed on her under the sun's glare, but she hardly noticed.

Surely Phoenix was okay; surely Ryna would've known if she wasn't. Still, if she was so mad that she hadn't come home…

It took every ounce of will not to let her brisk walk become a run as she reached the Olympic Staircase.

BLUE.

Games.

Track.

Cottage.

The back door stood open; Ryna hesitated a moment, Phoe's voice echoing in her head: *"I'm going to Cottage. Don't follow."*

Surely she'd waited long enough?

Ryna pussyfooted up the back steps, stood awkwardly in the doorway. Blocks of light painted the room from the open windows. Phoenix sat in the *seanchaí* chair, feet propped on the tinderbox, staring into the hearth's ashes and holding a tin mug beaded with condensation. She did not turn.

"I waited for you," Ryna offered.

"You shouldn't have."

The silence stretched until she could hear the small squeaking pops of the ice in Phoe's drink.

"I, um, left the door unlocked, too, because I think you forgot your key."

"That's nice." She sipped from the mug.

Ryna reached out with a tendril of energy, trying to read her love, and slammed into an icy wall. It hurt, though she didn't know why she'd expected else. "Well, nice talking to you," she said bitterly, and turned, hoping Phoenix would call her back.

She didn't.

By the time the redhead passed First Aid, she realized Phoe wasn't going to.

Ryna kicked viciously at a stray paperboard cup. It bounced and rolled unevenly into a nearby shop. Maybe she should find a job to keep her busy for the rest of the run. Surely some fast food place must be hiring temp workers—it would beat sticking around here.

Around noon Phoenix started to get bored. She wandered site for a while, but she was too restless to enjoy it.

What had Ryna expected, that she would come flying to her arms with tears of joy and repentance? The woman hadn't so much as apologized!

Still, maybe Phoe had been a little hard on her…

Distraction. She needed distraction.

She went looking for crafter friends to whom she could offer assistance, but people mostly were inclined toward idle chit-chat, and eventually she ran out of dawdles. She had to go home.

Gods, what she wouldn't give for Christine's veil and one more dumb little pearl…

Phoe placed her hand on the metal knob, chill in the muggy heat of the deepening night.

Maybe she could hang out at her brother's for a while?

Right after his wedding? I think Danny might want a little space, Phoebea. Giving herself a firm mental shake, Phoe opened the door. And stopped, breathless.

Candlelight, soft music, and the warm-chocolate smell of freshly baked brownies flooded the vardo.

Ryna never baked.

The fiddler looked up from filling delicate stemmed goblets with garnet-hued liquid. She nearly slopped it all over herself.

Phoe stared, wondering where she'd come up with the stemware—it was nice stuff, almost as expensive as the kind Daniel kept around for fancy cocktail parties. No road rennie would spend that much on something too fragile to survive the trek between faires.

Ryna looked like a first-day RFC worker at lunch hour. "I—I didn't think you'd be back for another hour, at least," she stuttered, hastily putting down the wine bottle. "I was pretty sure—I mean, I was hoping you'd be back for… but… dinner's not ready."

Blink, blink. "You made me dinner?"

"Marinated chicken with lime. And strawberries. And some sort of fancy rice thing with pine nuts."

Blink, blink, blink. Pine nuts? Marinade? When Ryna cooked, it was with everything in one pot.

And then Phoe noticed *Phuro* Basil's battered Special Occasions cookbook propped behind the sink.

"It doesn't even have ramen in it. And I found real plates and cloth napkins and everything. And there are brownies. I was going to make the strawberries into these neat little flowers, but—"

Ryna was *babbling*!

"Just—let's not be mad at each other anymore?"

The lost, pleading look on Ryna's face nearly broke Phoenix's heart—what could she do but take the redhead in her arms and hold her tight?

◇ ◇ ◇

"I feel like I'm on my way to be shot," Ryna said with a groan as the Gypsies slumped through C-gate towards another torturous Rehearsal.

"That would be far more humane," Tremayne disagreed.

"Hey, sis, I don't suppose you could sew up a little voodoo dolly of our beloved Amoebic Director?" Toby gave her hopeful puppy eyes. That and the tendrils of hair escaping his headscarf gave him a shy, little-boy charm.

As if Toby had ever been shy.

The seamstress shot her brother a darkling look. "I keep hoping a nice lightning bolt will strike her."

Toby quickly turned his attention to Ryna. "Lightning bolt? Please?"

"Don't I wish," she said, and meant it. "I can never seem to get them on command. Talk to Niki—she zapped one of those flying Shadow things with something that might've been a lightning bolt last year."

"Niki?"

"I'll do what I can, sweets," she said, "but that was the *only* time I've been able to do that. I'm pretty sure the Bright Fae were tossing in a little early help there."

"All right, peoples! Get in a circle, all in a circle, peoples!" the Pink Princess instructed as the Gypsies neared Bedside Manor. She waved her pen and clipboard like sacred rods of office. "No, no, not an oval, I want a—that's better. I wanted to start this Rehearsal with a special word for our minstrels."

Ryna didn't think she'd ever been so glad to be a backup musician, though she could easily pick out those who didn't share her fortune. Every last one of them cringed.

"I've seen far too many electric tuners out there. From now on, anyone tuning their instrument in view of the public must do so with those neat little metal forks. I saw a set at the local music store—they're the cutest little things..."

"How are we supposed to afford tuning forks?" asked a lady next to Patches. Ryna recognized her as the Celtic harpist Lord Marion had been chasing last year. "I know this is my second year, but I'm only making fifty cents an hour. It's not enough to cover gas, strings, *or* my costume, let alone tuning forks—and I'm sure there are other people out here making less."

Ryna grinned, suddenly understanding why Marion had developed such a crush on her. Not only did she have curly black hair—she had *spunk*.

Patty frowned a tiny little frown. "With your tip money, of course. And you *can* write it off on your taxes, you know."

Tremayne took one polite step forward when it looked like the harpist might try to take Patty's eyes out with her fingernails. "With respect," he said diffidently, "the ticket price went up this year. Your—ah—'guests'—assume that with a ticket price so high, we must be well-paid. They see no reason to put money in our hats."

"Besides which," the harpist said, taking Tremayne's example and attempting to control her temper, "it would take an entire show to get a harp in tune without a tuner—and they go out as soon as you move them, so I can't do it backstage. I do keep my tuner hidden."

"I'm sure you do," Patty said as she scribbled on her clipboard, "but the guests still know you're looking at it. Rennies are resourceful—I'm sure you'll all find a way around your problems."

"Voodoo doll," Toby whispered in Ryna's ear. She nodded sagely and tried not to giggle.

"One more thing. I have noticed," Patty expounded, "that no one plays 'Greensleeves.'"

Several pitiful whimpers. Ryna thought she might have created one of them.

"That's because we're tired of it," Patches piped up from a quarter of the way around the circle.

Patty rewarded him with a dazzlingly sweet smile.

Ryna pitied him.

"But the guests aren't, and that's what's important. The guests want to hear 'Greensleeves.'"

"The patrons like drinking songs." Patches was standing his ground—impressive. Potentially stupid, but impressive nonetheless.

The Artistic Director shook her head indulgently—but firmly. "We're trying to present a show that's suitable for all age groups. Drinking songs are not family friendly."

Esmerelda smiled wickedly. "And 'Greensleeves' is about a whore."

Patty's expression crumpled like a kid who'd been told there was no Santa Claus. "It's about a lady with green sleeves!"

Elda moved in for the kill. "She got them by rolling around in the grass with the song's composer. It's a commonly known fact that trollops were called 'greensleeves.'"

Truthfully, few people were aware of that tidbit, though none of the rennies saw a need to correct her.

"Well, the guests don't know it." Patty's glossy pink underlip poked out petulantly. "I want to hear more 'Greensleeves' out there this weekend, peoples, especially since the theme is Wine and Romance—emphasis on the romance!"

Several poorly concealed groans rippled around the circle.

Patty plowed on, ignorant of the rising price on her head. "All right, peoples, I think we should start out with 'yes, and' to get you out of your sour moods—foul tempers don't create good mini-plays for our guests! Count off by fives."

"Wonderful," Phoenix muttered from Ryna's left. "Thousands of gooey-eyed patrons who show up for the free alcohol. And we get to endure this—and now 'Greensleeves'—for *three* days! What else can go wrong?"

Ryna entertained the possibility of convincing the musicians to play nothing *but* "Greensleeves" and telling all the patrons it was by managerial request... but dismissed the notion. Hat-pass was bad enough already. She sighed—and wondered if Patty liked inflicting misery. She'd certainly raised it to an art.

◇ ◇ ◇

"'Greensleeves'," Phoenix fumed as she rummaged through the drawers. "I'll give her 'Greensleeves' all right."

"Yay! My poet's going for the paper—this ought to be good."

Phoe glanced up to see Ryna watching her from the bed, eyes alight with curiosity. She grinned back. "Do not anger bards, for our memory is long, and thy name scans well with 'Greensleeves.' Just about anything does, really," she added as she found one of their dwindling supply of pens. "Especially the words for old television themes."

"I wouldn't know," Ryna admitted. "I made a point not to watch when I was living with the woman who birthed me."

"Oh. Right. I forgot. Anyhow—they work quite well."

"And what are *you* going to make it scan to?"

"Not sure." Phoe plopped down on the bed.

Karma, seeing paper lying idle, did her feline duty and sprawled across it. She gave her two-legged furlesses her best cute look.

Phoenix let her have that sheet and started writing on a different one.

Ha. Kitty wins again. Karma licked her whiskers smugly—she had them so well trained.

A few minutes of scribbling later, Phoe presented the first verse:

Alas, Patty-Cakes, you've done us wrong
To put us through your stupidity
For we have worked here oh, so long
Without counting or 'yes, and' or 'unity.'

Karma batted at the words.

"Needs some work yet," Phoenix admitted.

Ryna shrugged. "First drafts are like that. We should do this for Talent Show."

"We could, but I'd been planning to run them through a copy machine and post them inside the privies down here. It's more fun listening to people gush and wonder and be the only one who knows."

"One of two," Ryna reminded.

"One of two," Phoenix repeated, and smiled.

Liam stood in the center of Hidden Valley's grove, ignoring the animate shadows that slunk against the treeline at the corners of his vision, darker patches in an already-dark night. Hidden Valley was part of their stomping grounds, just as the Bright Fae had claimed Fool's Knoll. He could hardly expect them *not* to be here—but it wasn't why he'd come.

He'd come because he'd always done his spells here. The energy and intent he had layered in this place would add power to his ritual.

One of the creatures chittered; a dark smile shaped Liam's lips. Oh, he would show them his mettle… and then they would regret ever toying with him.

But first, the Gypsies. And, more specifically, Ryna.

Her coin belt draped like the pelt of a silver dragon across the rock he used as an altar. It had not been his goal… but he was not sorry for its possession. The ring would come. His ritual would see to that.

Phoenix's staff sat beside the altar, scattered among other items his flunkies had taken from the Gypsies: two torches from the fire show, a piece of gaudy costume jewelry, a pen, an awl for leatherworking, a broken fiddle string twined around itself like a bracelet, a fancy veil, a boot knife. None were imbued with as much power as he would have liked, but the Gypsies' true power items were too well protected.

His minion had stolen other things, too: a leather mug, a staff, a hat, a necklace, a pickle sign of all the bizarre things… Lots of anonymous trinkets, seemingly chosen without reason. Liam shrugged as he laid them out around the others. He didn't understand their purpose—but that didn't mean they didn't have one. He doubted the Shadow Fae told him everything—just as he withheld information from them.

He placed the last item to his satisfaction and sat before his treasure trove, a smirk on his face. This would fix her, once and for all. "Break Ryna's ties," he murmured, his voice echoing strangely with the effort of will behind it. "Bring her to me."

The shadows shifted silently as he spoke, restless against the treeline.

Liam paused an instant. He had intended this as a simple enforcement of his will on the cosmos. But if the Shadow Fae decided to help…

"Break her ties," he repeated, this time louder. "Bring her to me."

The Shadow Fae's power built slowly, their whispers like the flutter of every frightened leaf.

"Break her ties. Bring her to me."

Darkness crawled his veins as voices resolved from the formless babble. And then—words.

His words, repeated by a hundred voices:

"ties to me break her tie her to bring ties break me her to her to me ties bring break—"

The noise buffeted him from all sides, turning his stomach, turning his soul as their energy poured in with his. Liam held himself stiffly, refusing to show weakness. "Break her ties!" he shouted. "Bring her to me!"

The voices yelled, too: "Ties me bring her break her to me bring her ties to me break her ties bring her to me break her ties—!"

Liam grinned in triumph as the voices slipped into unison, all that was unholy backing his cry with a final howl into the night:

"Break her ties! Bring her to me!"

Phoenix sat back and studied her sketch, a particularly charming portrait of Ryna that she'd been laboring over for the past day. She always had trouble making pictures of her love come out the way she wanted, but this time it looked like she would finally get it right. As she bent to put the last touches of highlighting in the drawing's copper-red hair, the vardo door slammed open.

"Gods," Ryna griped, kicking her beat-up loafers across the room. "If I was Christian, I'd give up bureaucracy for Lent."

Phoenix felt her heart fall. So much for the triumph of an artistic masterpiece. No way would Ryna want to see it until she'd finished her own tirade. And here Phoe had been so excited…

"What?" Ryna demanded flatly, evidently noting the change in Phoe's expression.

"Nothing." Phoenix looked away. She tried to inject a little interest in her voice when she turned back. "Tell me about your day—sounds like it was a bad one."

Ryna stared at her through narrowed eyes. "Don't change the subject. If you have something to say, say it."

"Really, it can—"

"Spit it out."

"It's just—Why can't you deal?" Phoenix finally blurted. "So things aren't the way they were when you were a kid. Things change. Some of us would like to have a pleasant day once in a while!"

The moment the words left her mouth, Phoe knew she'd gone too far. Her soulmate glared at her with rank fury. For an instant she looked as if she might say something—then she turned and stormed back the way she'd come, nearly ripping the lace curtain from its moorings.

Karma hopped off the bed and scrambled after her.

"Ryna—" Phoe called, but her love was gone.

"You okay?" Esmerelda queried, peeking gingerly around the curtain. "I was coming back from visiting Harvey, and Ryna nearly ran me down—"

Phoe looked away, vision swimming with tears.

"Had a fight?"

She nodded miserably.

"Mind if I come in?"

Another nod, and the slight shift of the vardo as it gained another occupant.

"Was it about her attitude?" Esmerelda asked as she perched on the bed.

Phoenix glanced up at her, startled. Had they been that loud?

Elda sighed and rubbed her forehead—a gesture reminiscent of her brother. "Ryna's very stubborn and very proud—she's been like that since I was making tiny little chemises for her. But she loves you more than she loves her pride. She'll be back."

"It's not like that. I mean, we've gotten into fights before—mostly when she was on an independent phase and felt like her space was being infringed on—but I never yelled back."

"I see." It almost got a chuckle out of the seamstress. "In that case, you probably just surprised her. Don't worry about it, Phoe, really. You know Ryna runs hot and cold. The atmosphere this year has everyone turning on each other."

"All the more reason I shouldn't have yelled."

"All the more reason you should've," Elda countered. "You're a member of this family. You have a right to your opinion. And she was getting obnoxious. Besides, you two are coming up on your first anniversary. People get weird around then. Even Tremayne and Kaya had problems."

"Yeah?"

"Definitely." Esmerelda stood. "I'm going to vacate the premises so you two can have some privacy when she gets back... but if you need a mediator, let me know, okay? Oh, hey, nice pictures."

"Thanks," Phoe returned, feeling better already.

How dare she! Ryna pounded up the Olympic Staircase. *I don't see her dealing with being scared out of her wits at someone criticizing her precious stories. The*

only time she gets a damn backbone is to tell me I shouldn't be upset over watching my home destroyed by visionless, banal—

Anger choked her; she tore off her bond-ring, unable to bear even that contact with Phoenix.

Throw it. The thought echoed in her head as she stomped toward the Narrows, and, unthinking, she flung the ring with all her might.

It arced delicately, a flash of silver in the moonless night.

And disappeared.

Ryna's stomach dropped to her knees as the reality of what she had done crept into her heart. She dashed to where that last glint of brilliance had shone and dropped to all fours in a desperate search, tears stinging her eyes. *I'm sorry; I'm sorry, oh, please, please...*

Wind brushed her ear, and in it a man's smug voice:

"Gotcha."

Her head snapped up, puzzlement giving her pause. *Gotcha?*

A Shadow Fae the size of a bulldog sauntered out of the night. Ryna scowled at its insolence as it locked eyes with her... and proceeded to squat three feet away, waiting.

The Gypsy spared not even a moment's thought before flattening it with a force of Air energies like a stack of encyclopedias.

Four eyes peered at her from a nearby oak; two small, chittering creatures dove for her head.

They exploded into black dust as Ryna envisioned a tennis racket knocking them from the air. Her scowl turned to a dark smile as she rose to her feet, Magick flashing in her eyes. *You want a fight? Bring it on.*

The night shifted and surged, responding to the silent challenge. In twos and threes and fours they came; Ryna unleashed her anger and frustration on them with a wild yell, destroying anything that dared stand against her. Let them come. Let them all come.

Fives and sixes and sevens—she stopped attacking individuals and started ripping apart whole groups... but a thin thread of fear vibrated in her soul. Something was not right. For every creature she defeated, three more melted from the night. A ring of the half-formed nightmare creatures surrounded her, shifting anxiously, as if awaiting the command for charge... or the end of a pre-meal prayer. This was no random encounter, no lone Shadow Fae easily conquered. This had been planned. She reached for the familiar ties she shared with the other Gypsies...

... and came up empty-handed.

A slouching creature of bulbous proportions lumbered toward her; Ryna forced herself to stand her ground despite the sudden speeding of her heart. She sent a blast of wind at it, but she was tiring. The air ruffled the thing's fur, but it did not budge.

"You'll have to do better than that," it taunted in a strange, guttural voice.

The words stiffened Ryna's spine even as her eyes widened at her Magick's negligible effect. She threw more energy into her attack.

With a disdainful sneer, the Shadow leapt at her.

The fiddler didn't have time to dodge; the creature plowed through her chest with mind-bending speed and emerged on the other side, laughing.

Ryna coughed, reeling with the dry-ice pain of its passage. She looked down, expecting blood or scorch marks... and saw instead the ground behind herself, dimmed only slightly by the translucency of her chest.

The Gypsy fought to stay calm, fought to drag enough air into her lungs for speech. This was not right—they shouldn't be able to hurt her, not this much, not through her shields... and *especially* not through her attack! "This is my world. You cannot defeat me. Get OUT!"

She sent a bolt of fire to punctuate her statement. It flew wide of its intended target.

The Shadows snickered.

"Are you so certain?" creaked an ancient voice.

And then they rushed in upon her, dozens of them, shouting, taunting, tearing away bits of her soul. Foot, ear, knee... She stumbled, choking on the raw agony that clawed her senses, unable to focus around the pain to answer the sharp questioning of her father's sendings: *Ryna! Ryna!*

She lurched toward the Maypole, seeking refuge; a raven-creature cut her off, claiming her left hand—her fingering hand—as it passed. And yet it was still there, she could still see it, see through it—

Tata!

Hold on! Coming!

A creature exploded in mid-leap, and then another—though not by her doing. Her father was coming. It would be all right...

Death-cold agony punched through the small of her back; her spine bowed as twin Shadow-badgers clawed through her stomach. Ryna doubled over, retching, coughing, weeping, hand clutched to her empty chest, vision nearly black with pain.

Neck, thigh, heart, elbow, wrist, bits of her essence torn away as she fought back blindly, stumbling away from her tormentors, until they came so fast she could no longer distinguish individual pain...

Her left foot touched seared earth, clearing her head with a sudden, swift bolt of panic.

No—NO!

A sucking void of black flame seeped through her toes—a cold fire that burned away sense with the power of its hatred. Voices babbled and roared. A fiddle wailed high and eerie—

TATA!!!

A horrible wrenching, deep in her gut; Ryna struggled to draw breath, to call out, fought with the animal's instinct that resists oblivion. A solid wall of Shadow Fae rolled over her. Her vision cavorted and twisted, dancing off into the distance. She watched it go as the cacophony burbled and blended to a liquid silence. For a moment she hung suspended in the middle of nowhere.

Dark. Silent. Empty.

Then she fell, fast and bright, like a star.

◇ ◇ ◇

Liam pitched to his knees, throat strained in a scream that would not sound. Sheets of ice rent his soul as the elemental horror ripped through his chest; his back bowed, skull touching his toes, though he dared not draw breath. His lungs had turned to dry ice; he could feel the slightest motion threatening to shatter them.

And then he collapsed, panting, trying to blink the tears from his eyes. The freezing pain had begun quickly to thaw—thank God for that, though the burning tingles that had replaced it were nearly as bad. He felt as if a winter night had stepped out of *him*.

It was summer, though, the night balmy. The stars overhead spun. Crickets sang. The train's whistle blew as it rumbled through the quarry. A tiny breeze tufted by, causing a blade of grass to tickle his ear. A warm breeze. A gentle breeze.

A knot of joy closed his throat. His plan had worked. It was real, all so very real.

"You should go," the Shadow Fae said, its voice sharp and cutting as a swirl of ice.

Liam looked up at it and quickly tore his gaze away, like ripping his tongue from a frozen flagpole. He forced his breathing to steady, stretched and shifted to prove it could not intimidate him.

He felt smaller; like his body wasn't quite the right shape—his hips too wide, a soft weight tugging at his chest. He raised one tiny, shaking hand before his eyes... gingerly reached up to touch his face. The calluses of his fingertips met with delicate cheekbones and a sharp, elfin chin. "Oh, God." He thought he might be sick. "What have you done? "

"You chose your sacrifice. You wished to take the place of the one they call Ryna." The Fae stared down at him with eyes like a winter storm... frozen, lethal—but Liam could not separate fear of it from the horror of his realization.

"In Bea's bed, not in her body! Dammit, how could you—"

"Foolish mortal, whose body did you think you would have?"

Liam staggered to his feet. He wavered unsteadily, but he could stand. The thick weight of Ryna's knee-length hair dragged at the back of his head. Everything looked so tall. This was wrong. This was all so wrong...

And they had intended this from the moment they offered him passage home.

"The veil is weak, still, and my brethren have not yet had time to fully claim your sacrifice," it said. "By dallying here, you risk this one's family undoing what we have wrought. They will be here soon. You must go."

"*Go where*?" Liam demanded, holding back hysterics, not caring what punishment such impertinence might bring. "I planned to stay with friends—none of them will recognize me like this!"

"They come."

It spoke truth; Liam heard a man's voice call her name. Ryna's name.

"You will pay for this," Liam hissed.

And turned.

And fled.

◇ ◇ ◇

The candle would not light.

Phoenix scowled at it. Sometimes it worked—more often it didn't, despite Esmerelda's patient coaching. Usually it lit when she was angry, or frightened, or even sometimes at an offhand thought... but rarely when she actually concentrated. Playing cat by pretending she was thinking of something else didn't do the trick. She could feel the energy inside herself—but it wouldn't hold steady.

She concentrated on that, tried to ignore thought. When Ryna came back, at least one of them would be calm. She would apologize. And if Ryna told her to leave...

Well, then. That was a worry for later. Right now, there was only the flame...

The desire for flame—

Her head snapped up at a sudden flare in the back of her mind; one of the Gypsies had grabbed at every scrap of power they could reach.

Tremayne bolted past the door, shining brighter than the sun on fresh snow.

Phoenix's heart lurched. There were only two people in the world who could make him run that fast. And one of them had her head out his vardo door, calling after him.

That meant...

Ryna.

Phoe scrambled from the bed, gravel biting her bare feet before she had time to realize she'd left the vardo... and had vaulted the campfire on her way out; her clothes still held the flames' brief heat.

Heavy footfalls sounded fast behind her; Phoe sent a wish that they would outdistance her since she couldn't make her own legs move faster.

Why hadn't she felt anything?

A sick wrenching drove her to her knees; it felt as if someone had caught her soul in a mixer and turned it on high.

"What's wrong?" Tanek clutched her shoulders, keeping her upright. The others cast them quick glances and hurried on.

"Fine," she said on a gasp. "Go—follow—"

"You're not—"

"GO!" she cried as a wave of dizziness hit her.

"Not until you can walk beside me. I'm not leaving you undefended."

Phoe closed her eyes, let the stabilizing beat of his Earth energies ground her. "I'm good," she said, though it was only half truth. "Thanks."

He gave her a brisk nod, but kept close as they pounded up the Olympic Staircase—and stopped dead right inside C-gate. A Shadow Fae half the size of the Maypole glared down at Tremayne with cold, glittering eyes, its form the utter black of midwinter night. The other Gypsies hovered near. Phoenix choked on the sudden image of abandoned campground cats freezing to death under the meager shelter of tent platforms. She whimpered—icy air sliced at her lungs.

"I will ask you again," Tremayne said, voice quiet and measured though Phoenix could feel him fighting panic. Could feel herself fighting panic. "Where is my daughter?"

The creature laughed; Phoenix clapped shaking hands over ears so cold she feared they'd shatter at the touch. The thing turned, strode toward Rowan Stage, and in the space between one step and the next, disappeared.

Tanek wrapped her in a tight embrace. He was warm. The night was warm. Why was she so cold?

Tremayne took a step to follow it; *Phuro* Basil restrained him.

Tremayne glared at him. "It has Ryna."

"We can't follow him—it," Esmerelda pointed out. "And even if we could, it doesn't mean it'd take us to Ryna. *If* it has her."

"It *has* her! She was under attack—she sent for me—I must have killed a dozen of the things off her before I even made it to the Olympic Staircase. And now she's not here."

"Maybe she fled," Toby theorized, rubbing his arms against residual cold. "She's a smart girl, and she's strong. Besides, conspiracy theories aside, Shadow Fae can't randomly kidnap Bright Ones to alternate dimensions. If they did, we all would've been in a world of trouble before now."

"She used to do this sort of thing all the time," Kaya put in, resting a hand on her husband's arm. "Drive off into the night and come rumbling back after dawn. She'll be fine. Give her time."

"Something happened. She should've sent the all-clear."

"*Something* had Phoe on her knees before we'd made it out of the campground," Tanek said. "I'm with Tremayne. Something's wrong."

Niki stepped forward with a compromise. "Why don't we take a tour of site? Together. If we don't find her—well…"

"Then there is nothing more we can do here." The fiddler bowed his head for a moment, then fixed them all with a stern look. "But I still do not like it. And we search Pendragon's grounds first."

◇ ◇ ◇

Liam hadn't remembered the dirt road out of Faire being quite so long.

His feet hurt. He felt like something was trying to disembowel him. Everything felt so hard… but at least his legs had stabilized halfway across the parking field. It was strange… he didn't remember the other world feeling less solid—aside from the occasionally shifting landmark.

Maybe *he* was more solid now?

He was someone else now.

Liam glanced down at his chest…

No, don't think about that. Keep moving, down the road that produced dust with every step, past strangely empty shadows. It made his shoulders twitch, not being able to feel the eyes. The thought almost brought him to insane laughter—or tears.

Headlights flared from the direction of Pendragon; Liam jumped back at the shadow that sprang from his feet—stark, and long, and unfamiliar.

Ryna's shadow.

Liam wanted to run off into the bushes and scream.

A panel van slowed as it pulled even with him; the window rolled down to reveal a comely blonde. "Need a lift?"

Liam peered into the driver's face, seeing only polite friendliness there. He shook himself, forcing down the thought that this might be some trick of the Shadow Fae. Things like that did not happen here.

"Um, thanks," he said, managing a smile. His voice sounded high and strange to his ears, but the lady just winked. Was she… *flirting* with him?

"Hop in, then."

Liam made an effort to look casual and ladylike as he walked up to the passenger side—and barely suppressed a surprised "oof" as he yanked at the door. Actually getting into the seat required an undignified amount of scrambling, hips and knees protesting his efforts to reach footholds that never would have been a problem before. Dragging the door *shut* proved even worse; only a last-second grab for the headrest saved him from falling gracelessly onto the dirt road. *When did Chrysler start crafting body panels out of lead?* he wondered peevishly as the door swung closed with a pathetic click.

On the other hand, it was better than being Back There.

The thought steadied him some. Whatever he had to put up with, at least he was home now. Everything else could be compensated for in time.

"Where are you going?" Liam asked as the driver shifted out of park.

"Dubliner—rennie band playing there tonight. Wanna come?"

A pub. God, could he use a drink. "Sounds like just the thing."

For a moment Ryna simply lay still, eyes shut, thankful for the solid ground beneath her. She felt as though she'd been ripped skin from bone—but at least she could still feel. A good sign, she supposed, though a mixed blessing. She gingerly flexed her hands; they hurt, but not unbearably so. She would still be able to play her fiddle—a relief so great it brought tears.

A Shadow passed overhead; her eyes snapped open.

Trees towered above her, obscuring all but patches of the moonless sky. A warning sounded in their leaves' rustling whisper.

I don't like this, Ryna thought, holding back panic as slowly, very slowly, she got to her feet. Her legs wobbled; she leaned heavily on a nearby tree. *Where am I??*

Hush, hush, she could feel the birch whisper. *You're not safe here. You're not safe.*

Ryna jerked back, breath coming in pants. Trees talked to *Baba* Luna. They talked to Tanek.

Trees did not talk to her.

Something rustled to her right; she leapt sideways, tumbling into the thin, sharp fingers of a waiting bush. Ryna struggled, thrashing, until it loosed its grip on hair and cloth. Her arms stung where it had clawed her.

But it did not stop rustling.

The Gypsy glanced around, fighting to remain calm. The others—where were the others? *Tata?* she called in her mind—and felt only emptiness.

"Okay," she whispered. "Okay. Okay. Okay. You're fine; you're fine." She knew they were only words, just something to say to release the tightly-coiled fear in her chest. But they provided a smokescreen, white noise that let her think.

She didn't know where she was. She didn't know how she'd gotten here, but she obviously couldn't wait for whatever had dropped her to come back. She had to move. A direction, any direction. But—not toward the bush. Maybe the tree. Trees weren't supposed to talk to her, but at least that one hadn't grabbed her. Yet.

Still, she could feel it humming like a struck tuning fork, as if it wanted to communicate but couldn't. Ryna tucked her hands under her arms and hurried past it, head bowed.

Another rustle; she could feel the spring of a branch above and to her right. *Chipmunk,* she told herself, though she knew even without extending her senses that it was nothing so mortal.

Another, this one nearly at her feet. *Squirrel! Rabbit! Mouse!*

Something tugged her T-shirt from behind.

Ryna bolted.

Four steps and the ground sucked at her foot; she wheeled and ran the other way, crashing through underbrush that parted before her as if by Magick, left her stumbling into the suddenly clear space of a dirt path. Ryna paused, gasping shallow lungfuls of air, gaze darting right and left, trying to divine which way to turn. The worn root of a tree hummed under her moccasin; she jumped aside, but not before the root whispered *Left!*

She followed without thought. The path curved slightly, and she did too—and came face-to-face with a small, ornately-detailed house.

The Secret Garden?? Ryna looked around, stomach settling even as her hackles rose.

A small, bright light hovered within the tiny flower garden. The Gypsy stared transfixed; after a moment it seemed to see her, for it rose and floated nearer.

And was swiftly, silently snapped up by an inky bat.

Ryna thought she heard a tiny, pained cry—abruptly silenced. Sympathetic light flickered in her soul and died. She thought she might be sick.

Camp, she thought desperately. *I have to get to camp. I have to find—*

She wouldn't let herself think that her family might already have been found. She dashed up the hill to the Secret Garden's entrance—and stopped, mind wheeling. The Secret Garden had been built over the last part of the back trails that lead from the campground. It would be quicker to take that way... she ran back the direction she'd come, hurtling the flowers that had been so carefully tended by that small, bright light.

A clump of trees blocked her path, humming—*faster, faster!* they whispered as their branches brushed her arms—and then she was on the much wider track of the back trails.

Darkness lurked behind the forgotten water trailer, squirrel-like creatures bounded from the tree growing through its trailer hitch. Ryna ran faster, sliding, almost falling, the memory of pain still sharp against her soul. Rocks skittered under her feet with an unnatural racket.

Or perhaps the night was unnaturally still.

Where were the crickets?

Shadows skittered from a rotting pop-up camper; she did not need the trees' urgings to speed her feet.

Faster, faster.

At last the path merged with the road that bordered Tent City; Ryna charged between trailers and travel busses, heedless of the Shadows between them.

Not a single light shone from a window.

Not a single dog barked.

Ryna ran harder, ran for the vardos—

—and collided with an invisible wall. The impact sent her reeling.

A chilling laugh from somewhere to her left.

A little of the gloom lifted from within the camp.

Her family stood around the campfire at their elemental points. Ryna stared, transfixed, at the silver light flaring through them. Were they always so beautiful when they did Magick?

They were tense, though—angry, frightened.

And dark. Everything was so dark.

"Phoenix, Tata!" She pounded against the shield. Pain surged through her soul at every contact. Her family's light flared.

"You are seeing your world," a crumbling voice whispered, brushing the back of Ryna's mind like a rotted feather. A Shadow flickered to her right. The fiddler recoiled from its touch, shot a bolt of pure Magick to drive it away.

It retaliated; darkness wicked up the thread of her energies. Ryna gasped and hacked at the connection until it broke, but not before it smudged against her, leaving a stain like a physical thing.

It shouldn't be that easy. They shouldn't be that strong. Frightened and angry, Ryna reached for the comforting tingle of elemental Magick.

Her senses whirled. Tiny fragments felt familiar, but not in a manner she could define. This Magick was wild, multifaceted; the energies she was used to directing were an overfed lapdog by comparison.

"Now you face us on *our* battlegrounds, little one," a rustling voice mocked, and Ryna knew it spoke truth. She had no clue how to harness this. She was as helpless as a mundane.

The Gypsy closed her eyes, forced herself to breathe. She focused on what was herself, crawled within that shining sphere and slowly, slowly pushed back the bog of Shadow Magick and the bright chaos of a thousand zipping energies.

Something slithered along her shield like a rank fog.

She ignored it, feigning calm, reached out to her family. She had made a mistake—a horrible mistake—but what was done could be undone. They would come get her, bring her back, and then she and Phoenix would have a long talk and everything would be all right.

The light faded; the Gypsies stepped apart. *Phuro* Basil rested a hand on her father's arm. "You know Ryna. She's a scrapper. She'll be back when she's ready," *Phuro* said, and the vision winked out.

Ryna stared in mute horror. Her family was gone. The campground was empty...

...except for the dark, grating laugher.

...except for the panther-like forms slowly closing in.

...except for the Shadow Fae.

Brown-black liquid had already begun to settle in the bottom of Liam's pint. He watched, mesmerized, as gradually it overtook the tan ripples that cascaded down the insides of his glass like a sand-art waterfall. The dark, alcoholic smell wafted thick and glorious to his nose as he wrapped his tiny hands around the cool, silky glass.

When only an inch of the fine tan foam rested motionless atop his Guinness, Liam raised his pint. It was not his first, but the wonder of the foam's soft pillow against his lip... the perfect way the drink's bitter thickness coated his insides with cool black velvet... it was a beauty he would never again take for granted.

For a moment, the sharp cigarette smoke, loud drunken laughter, and harsh neon lights mattered not at all. In all the world there was only him and his pint. Sublime. Perfect. Steadying.

And then some clumsy lout smacked against the tippy little table Liam had claimed, and beer foam spattered like bird droppings on the scarred wooden floor, and the world returned with annoying reality.

At least the rennies who had hailed him and bought him drinks on his arrival hadn't noticed when he'd meandered off to the bathroom and didn't return to their table. Several had offered him rides back to Faire, and the *last* thing he needed was somebody dropping him back on the Gypsies' doorstep.

It could've been worse, he told himself. *What if I'd picked the bitch's father, or one of the dancers? At least this body puts me in Bea's bed.*

He needed a safe place to regroup, though, first... somewhere to learn the quirks of this new body and practice his Ryna impersonation until he could find a way out of this mess.

The trouble was finding a girl to take him home for the night. He'd watched people come and go for a couple hours, now, but all of them were in pairs or groups. Liam had begun to wonder if he might have to borrow money for bus fare and catch a ride to some gay coffee house.

Right as he was about to turn on the Charm and con somebody out of a couple bucks, a likely candidate *finally* walked through the door. She was roundercheeked than he generally liked them, but pretty in her own way—and she had that peasanty, Earth-mother thing going for her. A mop of short, brownish hair framed eyes nearly as dark as Phoenix's.

Liam gave her the sort of shy smile that passed for flirting between women. From what he'd heard and noticed, dykes couldn't be direct if their lives depended on it.

Sure enough, she returned it just as shyly, came over to hover beside the table. "Mind if I…?"

"I was hoping you would," Liam said with genuine relief. "I—I don't really know anyone here." He traced little doodles in the condensation ring on the table and looked up at her from under his lashes. "I'm sort of new in town."

Liam didn't miss the way she leaned forward a little at his words. "Can I buy you something? Another Guinness?"

"Yes, please." He broadened his smile a touch—and she hurried back with the drinks.

Hers was a soda.

So, she was the responsible, designated-driver sort? All he had to do, then, was get so drunk—or act so drunk—that she couldn't let him drive home and still have a clear conscience… and then "pass out" in the back of her car so she'd be forced to take him to her place. It was almost too easy—though he wasn't about to look a gift horse in the mouth. He was tired, pained, and just wanted somewhere he could sleep for a week or two.

It was a strange thought. He couldn't remember the last time he'd slept.

"Is it okay?" she asked.

He took a drink—and licked the foam off his upper lip like a cat savoring cream. "Perfect."

The woman's eyes darkened. "So—what's your name?"

"L—Ryna," he said, and cursed himself for fumbling.

She looked puzzled. "L'ryna? It's pretty; did you pick it out yourself?"

"Get a couple drinks in me and my tongue comes unglued," Liam said with a self-deprecating smile, thinking fast. Maybe better to go under a different name after all; it would be harder to track him once he disappeared on her. "Actually, it's Loreena, but I prefer Lyre." There. Lyre. That should be suitably Pagan-y to catch her fancy.

"Lyre. My name's Elise."

"Enchanted." Liam kissed her hand, gazing soulfully up into her eyes.

She melted at the touch.

Liam smiled in satisfaction, feeling some of his energy return.

Neon lights, Irish music, and women ripe for the wooing.

God, it was great to be back.

◇ ◇ ◇

Morning, when it came, was cold and gray. Phoenix hugged her knees and wondered how long she had been staring at the sky, waiting for it to get lighter, waiting for it to turn blue, waiting for Ryna to return.

It hadn't. *She* hadn't.

She was out there, somewhere. She could be injured, or unconscious... she wasn't dead—her thread was still there, but it was blank, cold; Phoe couldn't get any reading off it at all. It was like sticking her hand into fog.

And it was all her own fault. If she hadn't yelled, Ryna wouldn't have run off. Right or wrong, it hardly mattered; her love was gone, and the first thing Phoe would do when she returned was apologize.

She only hoped she'd have the chance.

Morning, when it came, was cold and gray. Ryna hugged her knees and wondered how long she had been staring at the sky. She wondered if days here were ever anything but gray, or mornings anything but cold. She wiped at the stiffened, dried tear-tracks on her cheeks. She had wept like a child, alone, frightened. She had tried to stop the tears, stop the emotions; she knew the Shadow Fae fed on such things.

It hadn't mattered.

She felt blank, now, sitting and rocking and staring into her family's camp. They used to only have shields over their vardos. Ryna wondered if the Shadow Fae had planned that, played her family so that they would block all things from this realm out of the entire camp.

Block her out.

She wondered how long they'd planned on dragging her here... how long they'd been waiting for the right time. Had Patty been part of the plan after all, so that the Morris Dancers wouldn't be there to bless the site? Or had that been sheer stupid luck?

They were distant thoughts. Distant, like fear, and hope, and the faint connective threads that still bound her to her family. She wondered if she would see them again, like last night.

It was quiet. Everything was quiet, and still. Not a breeze, not a squirrel, not a fly. Not a single Shadow Fae.

There was dew, here. It had settled around her, soaked into her clothes. Its presence surprised her. Who expects there to be dew in Hell? She wasn't sure she believed in Hell, really, but she had no other word for this place. Maybe Hell was a state of being, as some people said... in which case the term fit perfectly.

She wondered if that would last. The absence of Shadow Fae, not the dew. They had spent a few minutes, in the beginning, entertained with terrorizing her. Then they had realized she was frightened enough on her own and settled back to feast on her raw emotions—why work for something you could get free?

They were a little like rennies that way. She smiled sardonically at the thought.

They'll have to work damn hard for their food from now on, she vowed. *No more free rides.*

She wondered when they would be back.

She wondered what they would do to her when they returned.

She wondered if there was any way to go home.

◇ ◇ ◇

Morning, when it came, was cold and gray. Liam hugged the toilet's cool porcelain, leaned over, and retched. Pain lanced his head at the strain. When at last the spasm passed, he glanced miserably out the tiny window to the cloud-scudded sky beyond. *Thank God for small blessings,* he thought queasily. Sunlight might very well have killed him. He hadn't been this hung-over since… come to think of it, he had *never* been this hung-over.

He wondered how the little bitch was holding up. If he had to feel like this on his first morning of freedom, he hoped the Shadow Fae had her screaming so hard she couldn't think.

At least Elise had left for work. The last thing he wanted to deal with was some broad asking if he was okay. He vaguely remembered charming her into bringing him home, not that it had been hard. Something about a spilled drink down his front and needing dry clothes. Liam had only meant to feign sleep after she helped him into her truck, but the next thing he'd known he was being carried upstairs and tucked into bed.

And then waking and frantically opening every closet door in an attempt to find the bathroom.

It was an artfully decorated little room… very Renaissancian, though he found it hard to appreciate ambiance when it felt like someone was scraping out his innards with a spoon.

He put his forehead back against the toilet and groaned.

◇ ◇ ◇

"Phoenix, *front and center*!"

The raven-haired Gypsy flinched; unlike the others, *Baba* Luna didn't sound like she was in the mood to be told to go away. Phoe felt bad about brushing off her family, but it was hard to convince herself she was overreacting when she had to face the numb panic in Tremayne's eyes.

She put aside her book and padded to the vardo's door.

Baba Luna caught her eye the moment she stepped out. "You. Me. Garage sales. Now."

Grateful for the distraction, Phoenix grabbed her straw hat, her bota, her purse, and locked the door on her way out.

◇ ◇ ◇

"I can't do it," Ryna muttered, pushing herself up from the road outside her family's camp. "I can't just... sit here. There has to be a way... a portal, a hole, something... and I'm not finding it sitting here."

Besides, if the other Gypsies had been intending to come for her, they would have by now. The sun shone high overhead—had hung there unmoving for eons. They'd had plenty of time. They probably didn't even know she was here...

Brisk steps carried her out of the campground, glance darting right and left—she thought she caught a fleeting glimpse of a powder-blue pickup, gone almost as soon as she saw it... but the Shadow Fae were nowhere to be seen. In fact, they had not bothered her all day. She had the uncomfortable suspicion that they were taking her measure... waiting to see if the simple reality of her situation would break her.

If that's what they're after, they picked the wrong girl, she thought defiantly as she crested the Olympic Staircase. The words made her feel braver. She tried not to think about how misplaced that bravery might be.

They had bested her on her own turf... and now she was on theirs.

She strode through C-gate. Faire site looked disturbingly normal.

Their turf...

Still, there had to be a reason why they'd waited so long. Timing? They were in the middle of a new moon... but there'd been new moons before, and nothing had happened then. Even the Morris ritual, powerful as it was, shouldn't have made *that* much of a difference.

Thoughts spun uselessly through Ryna's mind. She wished she knew what she was looking for, wished her years of Magick had prepared her for this. She had no idea how to open a portal—even in her own world, where energy was familiar and easy to grasp...

Ryna shuddered, locking away the memory of the bright, scouring pain that Magick here caused. She wouldn't repeat that mistake—who knew what it might do to her next time?

But without it, she was as helpless as the normals...

Something small and metallic glinted near the barren spot outside of Maypole's ring, waylaying fears spiraling towards panic. Ryna edged closer, hardly daring to hope it might be her forsaken ring…

Closer, closer, the twinkle flaring intermittently as she neared—

—and ran into an invisible wall that sent electric pain coruscating through every fiber of her being. Ryna stumbled backwards, hands pressed to her face as Liam's image—anxious, triumphant—seared her mind.

And then, quickly as it had come, pain and image were gone. Ryna gingerly lowered her hands, trying to ignore the swell of hope that pressed her ribs. It had certainly hurt enough, though briefly. Maybe, maybe… *Please, please…*

No birdsongs, no squirrels.

Dark laughter rattled the air.

"As *Baba* Luna would say, 'well, crap then,'" Ryna declared. It had been foolish to hope, even though that spot had bridged the worlds twice…

But then, she hadn't *actually* touched it. Something had prevented her…

Shadow Fae, Ryna thought grimly. *And if they're trying to keep me out…*

But beating her head against it now would gain her nothing. Perhaps there would be something somewhere else, a key to get her in…

The thought, though nebulous, bolstered her courage.

Butterfly carousel, Rowan, Globe. She wondered what she was looking for and if she would know it when she saw it.

The twinkle again caught her eye as she came even with Twin Tree Stage. There, right in the center of the cobblestone octagon—there was no mistaking it.

Her ring.

Ryna pounced on it this time, braced for whatever punishment the Shadow Fae might mete out for its capture. The laughter mocked her again as she huddled, still and fearful… but this time she felt no pain. She opened one eye.

Nothing.

She opened her fist.

Nothing.

She looked down.

Nothing on the stage, either.

"Dragon piss," Ryna cursed, scrambling to her feet, and stomped onward. For a moment she thought she saw someone emerge from one of the shops—but man or woman, they were gone before she could gather her voice for a hail.

She cursed harder.

Bear.

Old Bedside Manor.

The Gypsy stopped short, staring, incredulous.

It'd been years since the feast hall's previous, more haphazard incarnation had graced the spot beside the Bear. Her child's recollection of it brought only vague images of broken clay mugs hanging against the walls inside and a darkness that made the adults' heads look like they were floating, disembodied. The warmth of her father's hand around hers, her mother's laughter. Singing—Cast Call used to be nearby…

And a book—there had been a book with a tooled black leather cover, and people had written their names in it—but not their real names. It had been some sort of sign-up, though she couldn't remember what for.

She cocked her head slightly. *It looks smaller,* she thought as she approached, stepped cautiously through the door into the interior.

Smaller—yes. And more period. She could feel the love with which it had been built. Before there had been the BLUE, there had been this.

Her footsteps, soft though they were, sounded loud on the wooden floor. The book was to the left of the door, just as she remembered. It lay open, the left page half-covered with the scratchy writing of a quill pen. Were her parents recorded in here? She wasn't sure what they'd called themselves, but maybe something would look familiar. Gingerly she reached out to touch it, to turn the pages backwards. The grainy, hand-pressed paper felt soft beneath her fingers, felt more real than any book she had ever touched.

The room shifted dizzyingly, brightening, broadening, stripping its dim, cozy familiarity. Love-worn furnishing morphed into vast tables of crudely polished wood and stools with ugly upholstery. Ryna let out a startled oath that echoed in the suddenly cavernous feast hall and clenched her hands to drive away the aching emptiness that had replaced the book.

And sat down on the varnished wood floor to think.

Liam glared at the plastic tube in his hand. You'd think, with as many times as he'd stuck himself in women, that shoving a tampon up his own hole wouldn't be such a problem… but apparently there was an entirely different angle of attack necessary for the task. The back of the box hadn't helped, and he was sore and bloody from trying to figure it out.

The whole thing made him want to gag. He tried not to think that if he didn't find a way to take a new body, he'd be spending a quarter of his life dealing with this mess. And the pain—that pumpkin-being-scraped-out-for-carving sensation hadn't been after-effects of Shadow Fae or a night drinking after all. Now he understood why his sisters scoffed at commercials that had women jogging while they were on the rag.

Forget running. He'd be happy to *walk.*

"Honey! I'm home!"

Liam cursed under his breath, braced himself, shoved the damn thing up there, and called it good enough.

"You all right?" Elise asked as Liam let himself out of the bathroom.

"I'm bleeding," he said, not having to fake the pained expression on his face... partially from cramps, and partially because he hadn't gotten the thing in quite right.

She set down her laptop case. "Poor Lyre," she sympathized, wrapping him in an embrace. "Did you find the drugs okay?"

Liam nodded. They hadn't helped.

"You know what cures cramps, don't you?" she whispered, brushing a hand lightly against the side of his breast.

Liam's eyes widened at the unexpected heat in his center. So *that* was how it felt? No wonder women melted in his hands! He'd have to remember that for Bea—Phoenix. He had to learn to call her Phoenix, now.

Elise tipped his chin up, bent to claim his lips. As her mouth and hands grew bolder, Liam surrendered to the soft pressure... for the moment. Let her explore Ryna's body as he explored the sensations it created.

One of her hands ran over slender waist, to hip, to thigh, to...

An unexpected whimper escaped Liam's throat.

He had a feeling he would enjoy this lesson.

◇ ◇ ◇

The inviting light of torch, candle, and hearth spilled from the BLUE's windows into the night's humid warmth. *Ryna's probably already jamming it up with the musicians,* Phoenix told herself as she hovered inside C-gate, steeling herself. The *probably* was killing her, the not knowing... but she feared knowing even more. *Don't think. Walk one step after the other, head over to the Blue-Legged Unicorn, and open the door.*

Alcohol, and smoke, and sweat. And firelight. The babble of voices and laughter. Music.

But no Ryna.

Phoenix wove through the crowd as casually as possible, avoiding anyone who might recognize her, and took the stairs two at a time, trying not to cry.

The song ended. Applause sounded from downstairs, and casual banter between musicians.

Phoenix stared listlessly across the games area, and Track beyond, hardly visible in the moonless night. A restless wind tufted against her face.

"Phoenix? Hey, are you okay?"

Danny.

Thanking whatever fates had guided his steps to her side, the Gypsy turned and threw herself into her brother's arms.

"Hey—shhh, shhh—it's okay," he whispered, stroking her hair. "Don't cry, Phoe-bea, don't cry—what's wrong?"

A dangerous hitch caught at her breathing. "Ryna and I—we had a fight yesterday night, and she ran off, and she hasn't come home yet."

"I'm sure it's okay," Daniel promised. "I ran into Marcus, and he was saying how surprised he'd been that she was at the pub last night for his show—guess he bought her a Guinness. He said she looked really tired, but she seemed like she was having fun."

Phoenix tried to focus through the sharp stab of betrayal that pierced her heart. "The—the pub?" The entire Gypsy camp had spent the night worried out of their minds while Ryna was at the *pub*?

On the other hand, at least it meant she was safe…

And why on earth had he bought her a Guinness? Ryna *hated* Guinness. Unless she'd been serious about taking it up because Patty hated it…

"Maybe she needed some space, you know?" Daniel paused. "Is there anything I can do?"

"Make everything like it was," she begged piteously. "Take down the damn tents on site, and get rid of fluff-for-brains, and bring back all the people who're gone and the stuff that got stolen, and make it home again."

He gave her a last sympathetic squeeze, then released her. They stared over the darkened landscape. The music and babble of the BLUE seemed very far away.

"Have you tried leaving something out for the faeries?" he suggested. "A lot of folks here swear by it."

She shrugged. "It's worth a try," Phoenix allowed, and made a mental note to leave some milk on her porch. She doubted the Fae could fix the real problem and bring Ryna home…

But being on their good side was never a bad idea.

After all, who knew what they were capable of?

Ryna crouched stubbornly at the foot of the Maypole. Animate shadows prowled the perimeter of the beaten earth, restless. She glared defiantly at them. They would *not* make her afraid. She would not allow them that power. They could not reach her. Not here. In this circle, she was safe.

"Oh, Ryna…" The voice was little more than a sighed echo, but Ryna would know it anywhere.

"Phoenix?" she called, her voice trembling in hope, before she could stop herself.

Her love shimmered into view just beyond the circle, kneeling beside the barren patch of ground where the Shadow Fae had claimed Liam.

Had claimed her.

The image looked almost too clear, as if someone had put a pair of binoculars to her eyes.

"Phoe?" Tanek's voice this time; the dancer strode from empty air to crouch beside his fellow Gypsy. "Hey, hey."

Take care of her, Tanek, Ryna begged mentally. *Whatever our differences, please, please watch over her until I get back...*

"She left, Tanek," Phoenix whispered, her voice cracking on the words. "She *left*."

"Not by choice," Ryna whispered. "*Never* by choice..."

"She'll be back."

Phoe turned a hopeful, tear-stained gaze to him. "You really think so?"

"Absolutely," he promised, fingertips lightly caressing her cheek, stroking her hair. He leaned forward to seal the vow with a kiss.

Phoenix clung to him, desperate, needy. They lost balance, tipped sideways onto the grass, but did not break contact.

She's lonely, Ryna told herself firmly. *She's scared. It's not what it looks like. Goddess, oh, Goddess—*

The Shadows laughed.

But Ryna could not look away.

Pendragon Renaissance Faire

Weekend Four: Wine and Romance

~*~

Red is a rose, so is merlot; your true love bring here, your love for to show. The time for love and affection is ripe, olde worlde style. Watch knights of ancient tymes battle for the attentions of princesses and queens, sample the finest of wines at our free wine tasting gala, and don't miss the annual romantic wooing—who knows, maybe the Royals Revolting will make an appearance! (Theme sponsored by Photofilm inc. and Sweethearts' Chocolates)

~*~

Some of the milk was gone.

Phoenix stared down at the little bowl she'd left out for the Fae. Granted, she had no way of knowing whether the Fair Ones or some random cat that had taken advantage of her offering… but maybe it was the thought that counted?

She shrugged. No sense in leaving it out to curdle in the hot sun. "Wee folk beware," she warned before tossing the milk onto the trampled grass. She put the bowl in her vardo, then locked the door and made her way up to site… trying to ignore the enthusiastic cries from the loud sex tent.

A large, painted-wooden sign reading "The Secret" hung above the one marked "Blue-Legged Unicorn Eatery."

"Patty's going to have a fit," Phoenix observed with no little satisfaction.

Cloth likewise marked had been appended to the nearby "Privies" banner, and as Phoe strolled toward Sherwood, she discovered The Secret Track, The Secret Flying Buttress Stage, The Secret Bedside Manor, The Secret Bear, The Secret Travelers' Shoppe, and The Secret Woodland Stage.

"Site crew's been dispatched to take them all down," Niki informed her, a mug of fragrant coffee in hand, as Phoenix stared up at The Secret Sherwood sign.

"I can imagine," Phoe replied.

"Needless to say, it's low on our priority list," she confided. "There are several urgent things that have suddenly come up. And then, of course, we'll have to start with the less visible signs to be sure they aren't missed. I doubt we'll get the obvious ones until after Parade Cannon, at least."

If Phoenix hadn't known better, she would've suspected that Niki was actually *whistling* as she departed. But of course, this *was* Niki, and it *was* morning, and so that couldn't *possibly* be a spring in her step.

Still… it did lend hope to the day.

◇ ◇ ◇

Daylight nudged Liam to consciousness; he opened his eyes and stretched, enjoying the decadently soft bed and the warm, curvy woman wrapped around him.

She hmmed and snuggled closer. Liam smiled. This was why he'd come back. Wrong woman, true, and wrong body, but that would change. And until then, he had a partner to practice on while he got used to functioning with Ryna's equipment.

Speaking of equipment… Liam grimaced, reluctantly capitulating to the call of nature. When he returned, Elise was propped on an elbow, waiting. "What're your plans for the day?"

Liam climbed back in bed and gently pushed her onto her back. He caressed the soft mound of her hip as he bent to capture her lips. "Staying." Kiss. "Right here." Longer kiss. "With you."

Her eyes got that soft glow that came from a proper wooing. "Do you have any idea how hard it is to find a woman who'll say that kind of stuff?" she asked, tracing a thumb along his cheekbone. "Usually it takes an entire date before you even get to hand-holding."

Liam slid his hand between her legs, grinned as her eyes darkened. He increased the pressure—just a little, just until her breath caught. "Doth the lady protest?"

She shook her bed-mussed head frantically, reached up to him.

"Ah-ah," he teased, and kissed her palm. "If thou wilt but lie still, I shall take thee to the height of pleasure and build thee a castle there."

Elise whimpered; he took a moment to drink her in with his eyes, letting the tension build until he could tell she was fighting not to squirm.

Yet she did not.

Liam grinned. She took instruction well. Those were always the most fun.

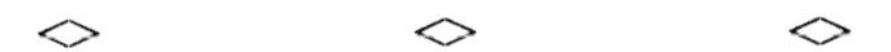

One of the simple luxuries of a hot day, Phoenix decided, was to sit under a shady tree with a mug of ice. Generally the Narrows were too crowded for lounging, but a couple fortunetellers had set up their garishly red vardos here, and the resultant parting of the crowds created a little oasis of calm… and even a couple tufts of untrampled grass. Though still early, the streets were uncommonly full. And one out of every six people seemed to think it their right to grab her backside. Jerks.

"Privy run! Privy run!"

"Coming through!"

"Make way!"

"Privy run!"

This could get interesting, Phoenix thought as two teams of peasants with ropes over their shoulders trampled past, pulling their trick Jiffy. She levered to her feet and trailed them into the privies near Globe, where two peasants were pushing back a plastic hut at the oval's far end.

"Phoenix! We were looking for you!" greeted the Leper.

"What's going on?" Phoe asked as Hayrold called instructions to the milling rennies.

"Chez Privy."

Phoenix nodded sagely and hung back until the privy revelers, with many satisfied giggles, declared themselves open for business. A pair of identical twins in their middle teens—Phoe didn't know the blond girls' names—ushered her through the trick priv's door.

Red carpet unfurled at her feet, leading to the real privy, sheltered in a small copse of trees five feet back. A passel of very pleased peasants stood to either side.

"We even have a purse-holding service," one of the twins said.

"And rosewater to wash their hands."

"And music—"

"Complimentary back massage—"

"And mints!"

"Wow." Even though the Gypsy knew what these folks were capable of pulling off, her mind *still* boggled. "Why were you looking for me? It looks like you've got everything pretty well covered."

"Gypsy escort service," declared a female peasant in an outfit made entirely of patches as they joined the others outside.

"We found our first customer!" Ilya crowed, proudly leading a little girl with pigtails to their creation. Piddle held the door for her with a flourish.

The little girl's eyes rounded. "Mommy, mommy, it's *big* in there!"

And the resulting parental laughter…

The sound filled them like a drug; peasants scurried in every direction attracting customers. Phoe watched helplessly as a fourth patron—a stringy fellow in a white shirt—was proudly escorted to the rapidly growing line.

"Shouldn't we get through the ones we have before dragging people over to wait?" she suggested for the third time, no longer feigning her character's grouchiness.

The others glanced to each other, unsure what to do if they weren't finding patrons. Phoe sighed in exasperation and went in search of ice. Maybe cooling her body would cool her temper, too.

Lines stretched from each beverage booth—scratch that option. Behind Globe Stage, though… Phoenix braced herself against the Royals Revolting's twenty-year-old routine and ducked through the fence's hidden door.

The area behind Globe was shaded—and empty; apparently not even the Royals Revolting had gotten a stage crew. A wave of I-shouldn't-be-here nearly turned her back before she realized it was the superiority vibes of the one act at Pendragon paid good money. Phoe squared her shoulders and went in search of ice—after all, it was there for whomever needed it...

She found her quarry in a stylish red cooler and picked a small piece to suck on, filled her leather mug, and stood a moment staring over the valley of trees beyond—a view similar to the gazebo's, though she couldn't see the swamp. Or the patrons filing through the Secret Garden.

The audience laughed uproariously.

Phoenix sighed and trekked back to the privies to distribute her treasure—to the delight of the peasants attending the patrons. She made the trip twice more, loaded with the others' mugs. After returning the third time, she sat leaning against the backside of an out-of-the-way privy and waited for her next errand. There was nothing else for her to do, not even when the peasants got bored with their game and broke camp, hauling their Jiff away with cheerful jubilance.

Phoenix listened to them go. For all their good intentions, she didn't belong with them—not anymore. Neither did she quite fit with the Gypsies and their friends. *Ryna hauled me out of my world and into hers, and now I don't belong anywhere,* she thought despairingly. *I'll always be an outsider and a rookie, even when I'm eighty-three.*

The privy providing her backrest shuddered as its door banged shut. The sound of someone taking a very long, very loud piss echoed from within.

Phoenix rested her forehead on her knees and cried.

◇ ◇ ◇

"Penny for your thoughts... though it's extortion at that."

Ryna whirled at the unexpectedly human voice. Liam leaned casually against the Bear, a smug smile on his face.

He was alive.

She was going to kill him. "You. *You* did this. How—"

"You're playing with her," he said, the words oddly out of keeping with her accusation... and yet, they struck an eerie chord in her memory.

Laughter rippled the air. *"Point!"* called a wind-thin voice.

Ryna's eyes widened. Vilification Tennis, last year... it must've been, what, Sixth Weekend? Her eyes narrowed. This wasn't Liam, then. It was some new Shadow trick...

But still—she'd won, last year. Perhaps if she played along, things would go as they should?

"Hardly," the Gypsy countered, hoping it was the right response. "I'm quite serious."

"About Vilification Tennis?" He gave Ryna one of the oddest looks she had ever received, but a glint behind his eyes warned her that things were not as they should be.

"She's my partner," the fiddler said, defiantly, a little too loud.

"I told you to stay away from her." He pushed off the Bear and loomed over her, every move precise to her memory. Did it matter what she said? His responses were the same.

Did she dare chance it?

"I'm not yours to command," she said quietly, intently, feeling echoes stir through her soul.

His hand twitched.

"Go ahead and hit me," she taunted. "There's no one here to see you."

He flickered, strangely. She had stepped away from the script—her heart dropped to her stomach.

"Bea is mine," he hissed, grabbing her arm with a taloned grip. She struggled as his other arm snaked around and grabbed her hair, yanked her head back so he could force his kiss on her. Darkness swirled around them.

She forced her knee to the tenderest spot it could reach with vicious precision.

The haze lessened—slightly.

He held her a moment longer to prove he could, then stepped back with a feral smile. "Physical violence, Ryna? Isn't that beneath us?"

Pain erupted in the knee with which she had tried to cripple him. Fire. Hot. Branding, lancing pain—

She fought it. It wasn't real. It couldn't be... She clenched her jaw against the cry that tried to work its way between her teeth.

The agony faded as Liam took another step back, his expression now of wry amusement. He shook his head at her. Then, as though she was harmless, he turned his back and walked away chuckling.

The wind gusted emptily through the trees. Her world was barren once more.

Phoenix's feet dragged as she passed the Bear. The dance show would be nearly over, now, and that meant facing Ryna. Facing the things she'd yelled at her love. Facing the distance that would be between them. Facing the possibility that Ryna might tell her to leave.

Ryna would never leave you, she chided herself weakly. *Not even in death, remember?*

But then, Ryna had never stayed away this long before, either.

Woodland Stage.

What if it wasn't by choice? What if the soul-wrenching pain that had driven her to her knees the night Ryna disappeared had some deeper, more sinister meaning? What if Tremayne was right and she was in trouble, and—

No. Marcus had seen her at the pub—therefore she *had* to be okay.

Petting Zoo.

The dance show was wrapping up; she could tell by the familiar music of doumbeks and zills and fiddle.

One fiddle.

Tremayne's.

Phoenix closed her eyes tight against the pain and sudden fear in her heart. Ryna never missed a show. *She's all right. She was at the pub. She has to be all right; there's some logical explanation...*

She felt *Phuro* Basil approach; he rested a gentle hand on her shoulder. He'd probably been watching for her, dear man that he was.

"She's not back," Phoenix said, wishing she could make it a question.

He squeezed her shoulder. "She'll *be* back."

"She will." Phoe lifted her glasses, rubbed hard to take the tears from her eyes, and sniffed. It was too much to contemplate, too many possibilities and little proof for any of them. "She will. And right now we have to collect tips and do the variety show."

Phuro nodded, backed off a step.

Phoenix took a deep breath, plastered a smile across her face, and headed for Caravan Stage.

Liam sighed, highlighted the text he'd written, and hit the delete key. Clattering pots, Elise's singing, and the warm, homey smell of spaghetti wafted into the living room. At least she seemed unlikely to interrupt his work... he was having enough trouble formulating this damn letter without her peering over his shoulder.

He'd come up with something of a plan, in between bouts of passion. He had to make contact with his love—that much was obvious—but he couldn't waltz into Gypsy camp and expect there to be no questions asked. This had to be done gradually, in a way that wouldn't arouse suspicions... and preferably in a way that gave him a chance to bind Bea—Phoenix—to him.

Women liked mystery. And so he would string her along a bit... write a letter, somehow get it to her tomorrow, and then figure out a way to manage a short visit at the end of Labor Day.

He'd have to make sure she didn't tell the other Gypsies...

A task—he would set her a task. If she was part of something that only she could do, it would make her less likely to go running to them for help… and it would draw her loyalties away from them and to him if she had to keep his secrets. It didn't much matter what the task was—getting some items for him, maybe.

I need you to bring my Magick supplies, he wrote experimentally. He had no idea what kind of components Ryna would use, so it got him out of deciding on specifics… and it implied trust in Bea's ability to figure it out on her own. She'd probably like to think that Ryna considered her competent enough to know what that meant.

He'd have to explain his absence, of course, but that was the easy part. He'd say the Shadow Fae were after them—and him in particular. It was true enough, and she could draw her own conclusions. Then, when he returned, he could pass any strange behavior off on his experiences… which, of course, he would never elaborate on. Too traumatic.

The keys clattered under his fingers as he fleshed out the idea. Brief—brief was best. It would be better if he wrote this by hand, but he didn't have anything of Ryna's to help him forge her script… not even a driver's license. *If I have to, I'll tell her I was worried that too much of my energy would be on it if it was handwritten, and that the Shadow Fae might be able to track it to her,* he reasoned.

Of course, there was the problem of getting down to Pendragon two days in a row. Maybe he could convince Elise to lend him her truck to pick up some clothes from his place…

Hell, while he was down there, it wouldn't be a bad idea to do just that.

Liam frowned in annoyance as the phone shrilled, breaking his concentration. Elise picked it up in the kitchen; he could hear her voice, though not her words. After a moment she stuck her head around the corner, a contrite expression on her face.

"I'm *really* sorry about this, Lyre…"

"I cannot imagine a single thing for which you would need to apologize, dear lady," he effused, turning to her with a huge smile as he punched the power button on the monitor. The screen emitted a small, fuzzy *poonk* and went dark.

"I hope you still feel that way after I've told you what it is." She sat at his feet, took his hands in hers. "My aunt has a shop at the Renaissance faire, and one of her workers had to leave town for a family emergency. She needs me to help her for a couple weekends, starting tomorrow. I'm *so* sorry; I promise I'll make it up to you somehow…"

Liam's smile turned genuine. "Would it be possible for me to join you? I've always wanted to see one of those faires, and I would hate to have to spend an entire weekend apart."

Her eyes lit. "Really? You wouldn't mind? I didn't want to ask—I'm going to be stuck in the booth most of the day…"

Liam raised her hand to his lips, a triumphant glint in his eyes. "My dear Elise, it would be no trouble. Trust me."

◆ ◆ ◆

"Tell me it's almost over," Niki pleaded, plunging her mug into Mama Bernatelli's sack of ice.

"It's almost over," Phoenix repeated dutifully.

"Parade Jam just ended. We have five hours left, and two more days after this."

Niki shot Tanek a dirty look. "Brat."

He shrugged. "Better that than delusional."

"Delusional? What's that supposed to mean?"

Phoenix turned from the rapidly developing argument—now migrating toward Sherwood—and took the long way around: past food booths, toward the Front Gate, and down the lane past the Stocks. How could they fight now, of all times, with Ryna missing and Phoe's world falling apart?

"Did it hurt when you fell from heaven?"

Phoenix, taken aback, stared at the voice's owner—a dark-haired guy in a business suit with a cell phone on his hip. From the fermented smell of his breath, he had come from the beer booth nearby.

"Did it hurt when they ripped out your brain?" Phoe wished she could have come up with something more eloquent… though it probably would've been wasted on him.

The insult took a moment to navigate his pickled mind. He grabbed drunkenly for her—and missed, but got hold of her walking staff.

She glanced furtively around for one of the security people in their yellow tabards with the red crosses and the matching flags that towered high above the crowd. Maybe this could end quietly. Maybe they could pry him loose from her staff and escort him off grounds.

No such luck.

The drunk leered at her.

Phoe loosed all her frustration in an expression of flat menace. "Let. Go."

He made another grab for her—and his hand stopped three inches from her breasts, wrist caught in an iron grip.

"You will apologize to the lady, yes?" Toby's blessedly familiar accent held a note of steel. "And you will give her back her staff."

The drunk had already released it, was using his free hand in an attempt to pry Tobaltio's fingers loose.

Toby squeezed harder; the man's face twisted in pain.

"All right, I'm sorry—I'm sorry!"

Tobaltio let go. He spat at the patron's feet. "These people in the fancy clothes. They are the worst for manners. Come, Phoenix." He put a protective arm around her shoulders.

"Hey, bitch! What's he got that I don't?"

"Blood in my alcohol stream," Toby told him implacably, steering Phoenix in a random direction that was Away.

It took them back toward Front Gate, but Phoenix wouldn't have cared if it led them to the heart of a midden heap. "Thank you."

"I'm sorry it couldn't have been with more flair, swooping in and kissing you silly—for example." He paused awkwardly—not half a year gone Ryna had done just that.

Phoe made herself laugh. It came out unsteady. This was all too new—the delicate dance between ignoring the issue completely and pretending everything was normal. "They let you out of Sherwood?" she asked, mostly to change the subject.

"Had to visit Harvey. Patty's precious *guests* will have to do without me for fifteen minutes." He punctuated the declaration with a swig from a round hip flask sporting two silver dragons.

A fellow with a stack of empty beer glasses and a gut to match staggered into Phoenix; she shoved him away and brandished her stick menacingly.

"Easy, easy, don't let him get to you, Phoe."

"I want to kill him," she rasped as Toby pulled her through a hidden door to the backstage area. It was almost quiet here despite RFC workers going about their business. "I want to impale his balls on little toothpicks and serve them to him like olives in a fancy martini glass."

Toby winced. "Ow. That was a visual I really didn't need."

"Why me?" Phoe turned pleading eyes up at her friend. "It's never been this bad. Why me, and why *now* of all times?"

"Ah, Phoenix, Phoenix," he said with great sympathy as he pulled her into a hug.

Phoe buried her face in his shirt, faded yet still unbelievably orange. He smelled like kerosene... a familiar, comforting sort of scent. The thought almost made her smile.

"You've got a lot going against you this weekend, Phoe. They're all drunk, they think it's the Second Coming of Valentine's Day, you look incredible in that outfit, and you're very obviously missing your partner. You might as well have a target painted on your ass."

"I might as well, for the number of times it's been grabbed."

He stroked her hair fondly. "It might not be so bad if you used some Glamour Magick and faded the red from your eyes. It's one of the first things people look for when targeting a sympathy screw."

"If only I knew how." Phoe sighed. How long did she have to be one of the Gypsies before she knew that people tried to get you into bed if you'd been crying? How long before Glamour Magick was an obvious solution? Before she even knew how to *do* those sorts of things?

"It'll be okay."

Phoenix knew he meant to be reassuring, but he sounded almost as lost as she felt. Her eyes brimmed with tears again, damn them. "I don't suppose it would help if I wore a box of antihistamine tablets on my cleavage and made a sign that says 'Allergic to Drunks'?"

Toby chuckled, his voice thick with tears. "That might work. Or you could try sneezing on them and claim it was the plague." He gave her a final squeeze, then backed up a step. A gentle breeze tufted away the worst of her heartache as he briefly cupped her face in his hands and ran his thumbs over her eyes—and kissed her nose for good measure. "Gypsy makeover—I'll show you how when we have more time."

"Promise?"

"Absolutely. Now c'mon, you. The prisoner must return to Sherwood for another show."

◇ ◇ ◇

Ryna rested her arms against the windowsill at the top of the tower in the Children's Realm. It was Ye Olde Climbing Tower in the real world, but the rock-like protrusions thankfully didn't exist in this reality.

By the light slanting through Sherwood's trees, the Gypsies and Maids should be gathering for dinner. It seemed like the sun had been in a rush for the horizon all afternoon, but that was probably because she found it so hard to tell time without the familiar schedule of shows.

Had anyone even thought it odd that she'd been absent? Had they thought to search for her yet?

Sherwood, eerily still, offered no answers—only a blessed moment of respite between mind-bending visions, a torturous waiting for the other shoe to drop…

No, a voice in the back of her head whispered. *Such thoughts mean they're winning. Treasure the gift. The rest will come soon enough.*

Ryna took a deep breath, turned her mind to other things. She wondered what her family was eating. Funny how she'd never paid particular attention before. Now it seemed so vital to know whether *Phuro* Basil had fixed chicken or pork, and what he'd put in the fried rice. Had he made crock pickles?

She wondered what food would taste like, here… and suddenly realized she wasn't hungry, though she hadn't eaten since before her fight with Phoenix.

Probably a good thing, she reflected, visions of Persephone and Hades and pomegranite seeds flashing though her mind's eye.

She wondered if she would ever taste food again.

Suddenly even the half-charred turkey drumsticks sounded palatable.

Ryna shuddered—and fixed her thoughts on finding a way home. Her family seemed closer here. Maybe if the worlds thinned in just the right way, they would see her…?

Colors shifted, wavered; the sun glowed a little hotter, a little more yellow. For an instant she thought she could see her family below, huddled glumly over familiar wooden bowls.

Another shimmer, and they disappeared.

Ryna frowned, leaning further out the window in an effort to will it so.

Nothing.

Something shifted near the vardos; but when she turned her head to look, it was gone.

Something else—!

Turn—!

Gone.

Ryna sighed, biting her lip in thought… a habit from Phoenix. She smiled. And concentrated on *not* paying attention. *After all,* she reasoned, *what you want, you can be sure the Shadow Fae won't give. That much is obvious after chasing that damn ring-sparkle around all day.*

An uneasy twisting of her innards, a restless shifting among the trees—there!

Ryna frowned—the lighting belonged a couple weekends later in the year, and everyone was wearing cloaks…

She was wearing a cloak!

Ryna couldn't hear words, not all the way up here, but Phoe said something teasing—and leaned forward to kiss the other Ryna so thoroughly that she fell backwards off the bench.

Peaches, Ryna thought, the remembered taste of her sweetheart's lips lingering as the vision shimmered back to emptiness.

A moment later a whiff of vinegar and tomatoes and onion tickled her nose, contrasting harshly with the remembered sweetness; she knew instinctively it came from the present. *They're having tabouli.*

Ryna clutched the precious nugget of information to her heart with a pang of wonder—and debated whether it was better or worse, knowing.

The stream of patrons in the Narrows thinned as the sun sank lower in the sky. Phoenix shifted on her bench and impatiently rearranged the plastic containers concealed under her topmost skirt. She wished she could go shower and spend some time with her fellow rennies—and from the looks on the RFC kids' faces, she wasn't alone.

"I'm sorry, sir, but we're out of fried cheese curds," explained a haggard-looking teen. "We stopped making them an hour ago."

"That's what the last three booths said," the surly patron complained. "There are still people here. You should still be making food."

"I'm sorry, sir," she repeated. "It's not my choice to make. Management wants to cut down on the waste at the end of the day, so they told us to stop serving when our last batch ran out."

The patron gave the teen an evil look and stomped off, still grumbling. He wasn't the first.

"God, I can't wait until Cannon goes," the teen's co-worker complained.

"Hey, mister!" called a boy in the next booth over. "Do you have the hour?"

A man with a red wagon full of bags and two kids in tow checked his watch. "Seven-thirty-five."

"Seven-thirty-five?" Phoenix repeated, bewildered, as the patron and his children continued toward Front Gate.

"You haven't heard?" A peasant of her own years glanced sideways at her. She had long, straight, blond-brown hair held back by a blue-gray kerchief. Phoe thought she recognized her as one of the Dousing Well wenches. "They let too many patrons in, so now traffic's so backed up that fights are breaking out. Whoever's in charge decided to extend the day by an hour to keep them entertained."

Phoenix jerked, incredulous. "Too many—Aren't there codes?"

An elaborately expressive shrug. "Not if you quit counting—or so the rumors say."

Phoenix wanted to deny it, but looking around, she knew it must be true. "Let me guess, the beer keeps flowing until Cannon sounds."

"Ye-ah." The weary disgust in the peasant's eyes made it clear that Phoenix had not been the only one with harassment problems.

"As if the weekend wasn't long enough already," the Gypsy griped, but thanked her before slipping backstage. The contracted workday ended at seven, and Phoenix refused to give Patty a minute more.

Fencing Booth, Irish Cottage, *Lady Fortune* Stage. Ryna restlessly paced Pendragon's grounds. She would find no portal home by sitting still, though she hadn't yet found one by wandering, either.

At least she wasn't making herself a sitting target for the Shadow Fae. And she was moving while she could... soon enough she would be huddled in Maypole's circle and counting the minutes until dawn.

Falconer Stage, B-gate, the tree near Scribes' Hall. She stood a moment beneath its welcoming shade before moving on... best not to linger long or the Shadows would know she loved it and take it away.

Bakery, Front Gate, Stocks, and—

Ryna stopped cold at the row of Disney-esque food booths challenging her from where the familiar structures should've been. They had never existed—she *knew* they'd never existed. Cartwheel Cove had been the campground once, but not *this*.

Mounds of grass decorated with young trees and shrubs rose like a chain of islands down the middle of the too-wide lane... Ryna hurried down the hill, hugging herself despite the day's heat. It was one thing to catch sight of the ghosts of buildings she remembered, but this alien force in her home, strange copy though it was...

"I disbelieve," Ryna said staunchly.

The food booths were still too far back. The little cobblestone nook beside the sandwich booth was gone—and the booth's placard nowhere to be seen.

A few pathetic pieces of playground equipment spattered the Children's Realm in place of the elaborate system of tunnels and bridges she knew and loved, and a gray, open-air pub squatted opposite the chain mail booth.

"I disbelieve," she repeated.

Mocking laughter.

Ryna bristled. As icily as she could, the Gypsy turned her back on the abomination and slowly walked away, tried to quell the thumping of her heart. Maybe Maypole wouldn't be so bad after all...

She scowled. Two days here, and already they had her wanting to scream and run whenever she sensed their presence. If only she could depend on Magick...

Dark sentience lurked in the Bear's towering form. It had not moved, its eyes hadn't flickered, but she knew at any moment they would.

Do not waver. Do not let them know you fear, whispered a voice in the back of her head. Ryna felt reasonably certain it was not her own. She calmed her mind to a blank, blocking out possibility of visions or attack.

The Bear did not so much as creak as she walked past.

Up the hill, down the hill, past Twin Tree and Globe, and still nothing.

There had been laughter. Surely something evil was coming...

Past the last of the food and craft booths, out into the open.

So close to Maypole.

So close, so—

"Safe." Ryna spoke the word out loud—to defy the Shadows, to reassure herself. Even though they had nearly killed her at the Maypole once—in her own world, no less—she felt better once she crossed its pounded-earth circle.

At least Maypole was fairly stable—a small boon from the Bright Fae, or were the Shadows not strong enough to make it go away here? For that matter, why were things so fluid anyhow?

Does this place control the other realities? Is it a place where memories come to hibernate? A reflection of possibility? Or is it just another place, like a dream, where things don't have to be as static as in the mortal world?

Ryna tipped her head back, watched the stars prick through the dwindling twilight. She wondered if she would ever find out.

And as the visions started, she wondered if she really wanted to.

"Safe" was such a relative word...

Phoenix wrinkled her nose in distaste at the wad of purple satin she'd pulled from her stash of loungewear. Jammies weren't supposed to be for sleeping in. They were supposed to end up in puddles of cloth on the floor before going to bed.

The thought brought burning tears to her eyes; Phoe banished them with a hurried change into the shorts and cropped top with the ribbon-accented V-neck. The metallic threads in the woven trim had earned them the title of Gypsy Jammies when Ryna had first spotted them on the bargain rack.

Sigh. It was futile to try to keep her mind off her love in a place the redhead had built with her own hands. Maybe if she ate a couple of those jalapeños she'd picked up with the leftovers—maybe it'd banish everything but immediate sensation. Even if only for a moment...

As she reached for the fridge, though, a strange, shadowy sentience brushed the edge of Phoenix's awareness. She recoiled, backing against the counter. "Show yourself," she demanded thinly, though she suspected it might not be the wisest thing to do.

A moth appeared in mid-air, fluttering lazily towards her.

She ducked to the side.

It darted after. Following. Watching.

Stubbornness put steel in her spine. No dumb little fluttery Shadow Fae was going to chase her out of her own home. Phoe snatched up the flyswatter. Finally, she had a target.

The first couple swats only caught air, but they put her in a hunting mood.

The invader fluttered behind one of the curtains.

Ha. Got you, you little— Phoenix smacked ferociously at its hiding place.

A moment of stillness.

Two moths emerged.

It took Phoe aback, but only a second. She lunged as one darted under a pillow. Triumphant, she yanked away its cover.

Gone.

She tore at the bedclothes, swearing.

Karma hissed; Phoe whirled to find her batting at five of the creatures. A sixth brushed so close to the brunette's cheek that she squeaked, flailing. She saw the swatter connect, but three moths passed through the plastic. Half a dozen more crawled along the surface of each cupboard; a military line crept up through the drain. With each turn they multiplied until the vardo was thick with them.

One landed on her arm, inflicting tiny pain with each step, as if its feet tore away a bit of her flesh each time it lifted a spindly leg. She could feel the creaking of the thing's joints, the slight vibration of its being as *rip, rip, rip* it walked up her arm. She smacked it off, grabbed the cat, and bolted for the door, cringing at the fluttery feel of the things under her hand as she grasped the handle.

And then she was outside, slamming the door, shuddering. She could feel the beat of a million tiny wings against her flesh, as stomach-turning as Liam's caresses.

She wanted to bathe in scalding water.

"Hey."

A gentle hand on her arm; Phoenix nearly jumped a mile.

Just Niki, and Tanek beside her.

"Lock it," she demanded harshly.

Niki looked at her, puzzled, at the vardo, and back. "What?"

"Lock it!" Phoenix put Karma down and scrubbed at her arms to make the weird tingling go away. "There's a cloud of moths, and—Goddess, no, Tanek—!"

Too late. The door swung inward.

Phoenix cringed away, covering her face with her hands. She could feel the fuzzy warmth of Karma plastered to her ankles.

"There's nothing in there."

"I don't care, just—"

"Phoenix, just look, there's nothing in there!" Tanek repeated.

"I don't *care*—I'm not looking—just *lock* it!"

"Okay, okay, okay," Niki soothed, though she sounded baffled. Phoenix could feel the air shift slightly around them as the dancer concentrated—then let out a frustrated sigh. "Tanek, would you mind? I'm not real good at that whole telekinesis thing like Toby and—Toby is."

A skeptical silence, then the the slight squeak of the hinge on Tanek's vardo door, the weighted footfalls of him hopping down from his porch, then up to hers, and the *snick* of the lock sliding into place. "It's locked, Phoe. Mundane keys save the day."

"You want to stay with me tonight, hon?"Niki offered.

"What about Karma?" Phoe asked, her voice still thick with panic.

"Karma can stay, too."

"Okay." With her eyes still firmly clamped shut, Phoenix allowed herself to be led into Niki's vardo, kitty trailing close behind.

"That was unnecessary," Liam said, his words echoing slightly off the bathroom tile.

He did not expect an answer, but he would wager he had been heard. *They* heard everything—especially if it came from one still tied to their realm. Even just a little.

More than a little, he admitted. *At least, until the Gypsies are well and truly broken.*

He had only wanted to watch over her. Given that the stone had gone missing when he crossed into this world, he'd had to recruit one of the lesser Shadow Fae to be his eyes. He hadn't expected its kin in residence at Pendragon to up the ante...

On the other hand, it *did* get her away from Ryna's home... and no one else had seen his messengers. If the other Gypsies believed Bea had slipped over the deep end and he alone trusted her every word and offered comfort...

...and protection...

A smile prowled Liam's face as slowly he unclenched his fist.

The Fae moth struggled feebly.

A crushing squeeze, and it was gone.

"Hello? Um, Niki? Are you in there?"

Three pairs of eyes reluctantly dragged themselves open. Niki groaned, looking more uncharitable than Phoenix had ever seen her.

"Niki? It's Tiffany? Hello? My curlers fell out of their case, and Jerry rolled over on them, and-now-we're-out-of-propane-and-I'm-cold-and... Niki? Are you awake yet? I hope I'm not too early..."

Karma twitched her tail in irritation as the noise continued—and closed her eyes again. Really. How was she supposed to find her person in the otherwhere if the other two-legged furlesses kept interrupting?

"As if the rumor mill needed more fodder," Phoe groused.

"What? We didn't do anything." At least, that was what Niki probably meant. It sounded a lot closer to "Whawdindanthn."

Phoenix cast her an incredulous glance. "Does it matter? It's Romance Weekend."

"Urm. You're right, you're right." The dancer sat up, rubbing her eyes and trying to get her brains back in her head.

"You ran out of coffee, so I'm bringing you some?" Phoe offered.

"*Yes*." Niki looked relieved that she didn't have to think further.

"...and really, the curling iron should be enough, right? I mean, no one will notice after all the humidity today. Oh Niki, I can't thank you enough for letting me use your trailer, Jerry says I'm just not used to tenting yet, but my watch got soaked in a puddle in the corner, and the noise kept me up all night—this lady, she wouldn't stop fighting with her husband in the tent next to us..."

"Should I get the door?"

"*Yes*."

"Okay." Phoenix tugged her jammies to rights as she padded to the door, trying to insert enough alertness in her expression that it wouldn't look like she'd just crawled out of bed. "Hi! I was bringing Niki some coffee; she ran out."

Jerry's girlfriend stopped mid-sentence and blinked up at her with bright perplexity, one hand brandishing the most complex curling iron Phoe had ever seen. The other held a tiny cloth bag bulging at the seams. "You're making coffee?"

"Well, I brought it over—"

"Do you think Niki would mind me having some too?"

"Sure; knock yourself out," Niki offered, sprawled on her back.

Phoenix cringed at the thought of Tiffany ingesting something to make her *more* energetic.

"Hey, how did you know to bring her coffee if she's still asleep?"

"Magick," Niki said flatly.

Tiffany giggled as she stepped up to the vardo's interior. She unzipped her case, resuming her stream of chatter as she pulled out a jar of lotion, some brushes, a few manicuring tools, a handful of cosmetic pads, and two bottles of skin-toned liquid.

"Want me to make it?" Phoenix offered—and seconds after Niki's assent realized that she had no idea which cupboard to reach for.

Mascara tubes, eyeliner pencils, large glass perfume bottle complete with atomizer.

"Um, Niki? Where did I put that coffee I brought you?"

"Left—bodice laces hanging off handle."

Tiny gold-toothed comb, silver contraption resembling a torture device, pair of tweezers that... *plugged in*...?

"Thanks. Guess I must need some coffee, too," Phoe joked airily.

Three plastic compacts, lip liner, two lipstick tubes—

"Where in the world did you get a Bag of Holding?" Phoenix exclaimed.

"Huh?" Tiffany looked up, her hand back in the bag for another haul.

"Never mind." Phoe hurriedly started the coffeemaker, bid her fellow Gypsy a hasty farewell, and escaped—nearly stepping in the bowl of milk for the Fae on her way out.

Karma followed—mostly to escape the noise.

No moths crawled across the windows of Ryna's vardo. The walls did not vibrate; the curtains did not flutter. In fact, it looked almost... *normal.* Phoenix edged cautiously up the steps.

The door did not fly open to attack her.

She put her hand on the knob.

Nothing.

And twisted.

Nothing.

And pushed.

It didn't budge.

And then she remembered that her keys were inside, forgotten in the panic to escape.

Phoenix banged her head against the door twice, softly.

This was not shaping up to be her day.

* * *

"Ready for another exciting, fun-filled day of drunk, amorous letches?" Phoenix asked cheerily as she wiped her feet and planted her kissed hand on the rough, green-painted wood of Cottage's doorframe.

"Bite me," Moiré enunciated. "If one more patron tells me how beautiful and glowing I am, I'm going to toss him in the sheep pen."

"I second that," Brigid chimed in. "Except the glowing part."

"You suppose the traffic has cleared out from yesterday yet?" Torin inquired, his broom rasping the floorboards with every brisk stroke.

"Wouldn't bet my contract on it." Da dropped a load of split firewood noisily on the hearth.

"Neither would I," Patches agreed, glancing up from his guitar. "Oh, wait, I'm not getting paid. It wouldn't matter if I did."

Phoenix folded herself into a windowsill, thankful the aspirin had finally taken the edge off her moontime cramping—which had hit, with all its attendant hassle, bare minutes after she'd finally gotten into her vardo. She winced, knowing Ryna was probably curled up somewhere wishing for a sword to fall on—the redhead always got her cycles far worse than Phoe did. She hoped that wherever Ryna was, she was all right and had a nice big bottle of painkillers.

Had that been why they'd been so snappy at each other all week? They did tend to get on each others' nerves around that time…

And if she had bad cramps, it might explain why she hadn't made it to her shows yesterday…

"Bless this house and all within—and the outside be damned. It all seems to be anyway," Marcus declared as he scuffed his feet on the threshold. "Hoo—were any of you folks at Cast Call?"

"No," came the simultaneous chorus.

"Pity." He plopped down on the tinder box. "Patty-cakes tried to cancel Vilification Tennis—until the rennies nearly mutinied and she thought better of it. There are rumors that she was trying to get back at us for not working until eight yesterday."

Patches rolled his eyes. "Why is it that somehow I'm not surprised?"

"About VilTen or the rumors?" Da asked. "I don't think she's observant enough to realize it would be a punishment."

"True enough," Patches agreed. "She's probably just being prissy. Hey, Marcus, you got an extra pick?"

"Sure—let me dig one out. Evidently we're also offensive to our Artistic Detriment's nose," he continued. "Her Royal Pinkness hath decreed we all need to shower more frequently."

With one lightning motion, Brigid pitched her dishcloth at the far wall. It impacted with a sodden splat and fell to the floor. "I'm not going to bathe all *week*, just to piss her off."

"Pardon me?" ventured a hesitant voice at the door.

All attention turned to the newcomer—and, with surprised gasps and yips, everyone in Irish Cottage dropped to one knee. Phoenix mirrored them, restraining her peasant-influenced urge to throw herself to the floor.

Gypsies do not sprawl, Niki scolded in her memory. *At least, not without grace. And a lot of pillows. And whomever the pillows belong to.*

"Rise ye up, rise ye up," Prince Gwydion commanded gently. "Especially a maiden named Brigid O'Malley. Is she present?"

"Aye, and of marriageable age," Ma hollered down from the loft.

"That will be welcome news indeed to the one whose message I bear," he said with a smile that caused Phoe to understand why Niki had taken such a shine to him the previous year.

"You're… a *messenger*… Your Highness?" Brigid squeaked.

"Every man is a slave to love; I come from one who is my brother in that happy bondage." With a sweeping bow he presented a lit oil lamp in the shape of a rose.

"He bids me tell thee that his love burns brighter than this flame and shall bloom as eternally as this rose."

Brigid was too busy making fish faces to reply—or even ask her suitor's name.

Prince Gwydion, having achieved the desired response, gallantly kissed the maiden's hand, turned, and swept out the door.

"Still planning to wait a week for your next bath, lass?" Da teased.

Brigid giggled, staring at her gift.

Phoenix leaned on her staff, smiling, and made a mental note to see what information she could get out of Niki.

◇ ◇ ◇

Fool's Knoll looked normal… but then, so had a lot of other things.

Ryna stood at the top of the stairs near Bakery Stage and gazed warily over the expanse of grass and trees. She felt like a deer at the edge of a forest… which was silly. Fool's Knoll was no more dangerous than anywhere else.

Maybe she should go back to the Harvest Man?

No. Nothing with a face—she didn't want to know what might stare back.

She took a deep breath; she took the first step into the glaring sunshine. It felt… brighter… here, than on most of Pendragon's grounds.

Another step, and another.

A water-filled kiddie pool waited beside the battered lawn chairs to cool tired feet. A toy duck snapped into being, staring at her with painted eyes. Cautiously she bent to touch it, rubbery and hot in the sun for an instant before it snapped out of existence.

Ryna's stomach lurched; she jumped back and hurried away. Things had disappeared in front of her eyes before—but she found it no less disconcerting for all that. Had it been real, something from her world that had formed a temporary connection with this one? Was it somebody's wish manifested, a random mention of a rubber duck? Or maybe the memory of a duck, similar to the way the old Bedside Manor had briefly shown itself…

Could she somehow harness the queasy energy of the shifts to get home?

From the Knoll's precipice it looked as if the parking field stretched to forever, and Ryna had the disconcerting sensation that, like an ancient map, the world ended there. *Here there be dragons,* she thought without humor and wondered if she would fall into some dimensional black hole if she journeyed that far. Or would she keep walking forever, never reaching the train tracks? Or maybe—worse—she could reach them, and follow them to the highway, to the gas station on the corner and an empty world.

Could she walk to Troubadour Faire if Pendragon ended and she had not managed to return to her family?

Of course, if the tales of Faerie were correct, a hundred years might already have passed, and her family with them…

Don't think like that, she admonished herself sternly. *I'll get home… and when I do, I'm gonna open up the world's biggest can of whup-ass on the Shadow Fae for dragging me here.*

A tiny dream catcher and a few strands of faded Mardi Gras beads hung from the Faery Tree. Ryna picked her way down the brief, steep incline and pitched a couple beer cans over the edge. They clattered down the hill. A bit of tarnished gold winked from the grass at her feet.

Wasn't the sun a little closer to the east than when she'd started up the stairs?

No matter. She sat facing the sapling, closed her eyes, and concentrated on the sun on her face, on bright, happy thoughts… the hum of fiddle strings vibrating against her fingers, the roughness of Karma's tongue when she licked nose or chin in affection, the spiced smell of *Phuro* Basil's cooking, the light that shone from her love's face each time she discovered something new…

I need her, Ryna thought, feeling the Phoenix-shaped hole in her heart. *Oh, gods, I'll never look at another ramshackle building without loving it. I'm so sorry, Phoe—you were right; you're always right, and I'm too focused on my own drama to notice.* She counted her faults against the Mardi Gras beads like a rosary, giving in to the tears.

At long last she sniffled, and sighed, and felt a scoured calm. A tarnished gold medallion twisted in the breeze, its blue string tangled on the Faery Tree's branches. It winked in the sun like the star in the ring she had forsaken. *Please don't let the Shadow Fae use its connection against her. Let her find it—and—and don't let her guess what really happened. I deserve it, but she doesn't.*

Ryna could only gift the tree a kiss—she hoped it was enough. She stood, climbed the hill, looked back briefly. The beer cans were back—one crumpled now. The field shimmered through the brightly colored patchwork of cars before settling back to half-dead grass.

You're not what you think you are, a gentle voice whispered.

The Gypsy flinched, pushed away the sound, and made herself walk slowly back towards Bakery Stage. She would not give it the power to make her run.

But she did not look at the swimming pool.

Liam shrugged uncomfortably and adjusted his straw hat. There was something distinctly surreal about walking around Pendragon in street clothes during a show day. Out of costume, no one looked at him twice—and he kept having to restrain himself from playing with the patrons.

He missed the familiar confines of his doublet, custom-made boots, and the weight of a sword at his hip. The damn wrap skirt he had on felt like walking around naked under a blanket—but it was the only thing in Elise's closet that wouldn't swallow him whole. That and an embroidered peasant top—though at least its sleeves had the right feel.

He picked up his pace as he neared Flying Buttress Stage. Bea—Phoenix—had been Vilifying as he'd passed the Bear. By his calculations, he had a little over half an hour to get down to Ryna's trailer, loot it, drop his message, and get out.

The guard at C-gate didn't even look up as he passed.

It was an unexpected bit of luck. Liam put his sunglasses and straw hat back on, thankful he hadn't needed to prove his identity without a pass.

The three peasants climbing the Olympic Staircase paid him not so much as a hello. Liam frowned. People always greeted one another on the climb.

The yellow-shirted pirate coming out of the privies ignored him, too.

Liam doffed his hat and shades. "Hi," he said, doing his best Ryna impersonation.

The woman jumped a foot. "Ryna! Where'd you come from?"

"Just waiting for the Jiff," Liam said on his way in.

So that was why no one had spoken to him—they didn't see him! He smirked. And here he'd assumed the Shadow Fae's gift of stealth had vanished with his body. He should've known better.

Still… it did make some things easier…

When he had finished his business (damn messy plugs) Liam strode to where the Gypsies always camped. The door to Ryna's trailer was locked. He scowled. Why couldn't the bitch live in a tent like normal rennies—or at the very least keep a spare key hidden somewhere obvious?

But no—she had the other Gypsies for that. And, failing them, her cursed Magick talents. Blessing his friendship with Tommy Johnson in Boy Scout camp, Liam removed a couple bobby pins from his skirt's waistband and set to picking the lock. It yielded without much trouble.

Ryna's calico devil bristled the moment he stepped in the door.

Liam didn't have time for games. He stalked over to the little furball before it could get any ideas about attacking him, picked it up by the scruff of its neck, unceremoniously tossed it outside, and slammed the door.

Not to be deterred, the wretched beast set to yowling on the front porch.

Liam cursed as he ransacked the drawers, hoping no one would come to investigate the racket before he got out.

One cupboard revealed a row of spiral bindings—Liam paused. He *did* need to learn how to forge Ryna's handwriting. Maybe one of these… he lifted down the second volume from the right, flipped it open to the middle. Small, ornate script covered the sketch paper, interspersed with ink drawings and the occasional poem. Though he'd only seen it once, he recognized his love's penmanship immediately.

Bea's journal, he realized with stunned delight. He checked the dates: mid-January until half through July. Recent, then, but finished—with any luck, Bea wouldn't notice its absence.

The cat's angry rowl brought him back to himself; Liam snapped shut the cover and tossed it on the bed, went back to looking for the other things he needed.

Pens, paper—keys to the truck. Useless. He could be tracked too easily that way.

Underwear, socks—those went in the pile with the journal.

Dishes, food, more food, cat food, broom closet. He briefly debated an extra pair of shoes, but decided against it. Where *did* the little bitch keep her money?

Jeans—he'd need those. Shirts—fiddle?

Liam stared, still and unexplainably sad, at the familiar case. Hesitantly he caressed the worn, soft leather, letting his thumbs drift down to the silver latches. They yielded easily, *snap, snap,* and he raised the lid to expose the treasure inside. Exquisitely delicate fancywork edged the honey-brown wood; he traced it with his index finger, a little awed. Although he had lain with her, he had never been allowed to touch her fiddle. He lifted it with reverent care, heart speeding at his conquest.

The chinrest felt alien against his cheek. It did not nestle against him as it always seemed to for Ryna. He plucked one string.

The note rang flat and hollow. It seemed… lonely. He shook off the ridiculous thought. Why should he care if no one ever played the thing again? He put it back roughly; the fiddle *twong*ed a protest of its violation as he slammed shut the lid.

A pouch cleverly disguised as decor caught his eye as he rolled the drawer shut; he emptied the battered leather of its contents.

Still no wad of cash.

Fuck it. He was running out of time. He'd have to make do with the clothes and the journal.

Liam stuffed his plunder in a duffel bag, dropped his note on the floor near the door, and let himself out.

The damn cat clawed his leg on its way back in.

Liam didn't spare the breath to curse; his instincts wanted him gone. He very nearly ran.

No sooner had he crossed the road than a beloved voice floated back to him:

"Huh. I could've sworn I locked… Ryna? Are you home?"

Liam turned away from the hope in her words and hurried up the trail behind gamers' camp.

◇ ◇ ◇

Empty.

Phoenix sighed. It had been stupid to hope. If Ryna was going to be here today, she would've made it to her shows.

Karma mowled piteously as she twined around Phoe's ankles.

"I know, kitty. I miss her, too." As the Gypsy bent to gather her up, an envelope caught her eye—someone must've slipped it under the door. At once curious and trepidatious, she sat on the rag rug and wormed the flap open with a finger, removed the folded white paper within.

Phoenix —

I'm sorry I cannot ask this of you in person—that I must send someone to deliver this, even—but believe me when I say it is the very strength of my love that keeps me from your side. Those we battled last year have grown stronger. I am all right, but I need you to gather my Magick supplies. I'll try to meet you by Lady Fortune shortly after Closing Cannon tomorrow. Please don't bring any of the others, or tell them about this. They would charge blindly to my rescue, not knowing that doing so endangers us all more than if they had stayed their hands. Please trust me on this, as I trust you by setting you this task.

I love you. I miss you. Be careful.

Ryna

Phoenix frowned at the note, its computer-printed characters cold and stark despite the words' meaning. Ryna never used computers. Why hadn't she hand-written it? And what supplies was Phoe supposed to gather? Ryna didn't have any, aside from maybe her fiddle… but that was hardly a supply, and if she was on the run, Phoe couldn't imagine the redhead wanting to endanger her most precious possession.

Maybe she needed Phoenix to go *get* supplies? There were a few shops that specialized in essential oils and incense and a couple that carried stones. Phoe could ask the proprietors what would suit her purposes…

Even so, Ryna never really used *things*. Why now?

Phoenix brushed off the thought. Ryna was counting on her for this; she'd just have to figure something out.

◇ ◇ ◇

Bea's diary was... exquisite. Perfect little pictures, breathtaking poetry, turns of phrase that captured his imagination and gently nudged it toward a world of unimaginable wonder.

Liam wanted to toss it into the bog not far from the back trails where he'd settled to read it.

It was all about Ryna—Ryna, Ryna, Ryna. That he was reading it partly so he'd know how to act like her didn't make it easier.

Oh, there were mentions of the other Gypsies, of course, but Phoe wasn't bedding *them*. There were no steamy little romance novel scenes written out about *them*.

Liam forced himself through it. He needed this information, no matter how distasteful the acquisition... but he couldn't help the low growl that sent small woodland creatures scampering.

If there was any justice in the world, the Shadow Fae were keeping Ryna extra busy.

◇ ◇ ◇

"We need a story."

"A story?" Phoenix straightened from the ice chest in Hollow Hill's corner as Elda strode into the room.

Phuro Basil looked up from tabulating the dance show's tips. "Ah," was all he said, and suddenly Phoenix knew. Her stomach dropped at her friend's tight expression—she wished she could show them the note. *No. Ryna's counting on you. You can't betray her trust like that.*

"We can't put them off forever," Elda pointed out. "Everybody figured they'd missed her yesterday. Folks came looking for her at the dance show today. They didn't find her. If we don't find something to feed the rumor mill, things are going to get ugly."

Phuro Basil sighed. "I know—and if she doesn't show up tomorrow, I'm going to have to file a missing persons report."

The words tangled in Phoenix's ears. "A—a what? But—"

Basil ran a hand through his iron gray hair. "I know... there's nothing they can do that we can't, especially if Tremayne is right. But she's been gone far over twenty-four hours. She hasn't even come back for her shows. I can't not, Phoe."

Phoe stared into his clear blue eyes, caught. She couldn't betray her love—or compromise her mission by risking a police "rescue."

He must have caught a flicker of her thoughts; his expression shifted. His tone turned carefully non-accusatory. "Unless you know something you haven't told us..."

Phoenix looked away. Anything she said would sound like a lie—so the only option left was to tell the truth. "When I went down to my vardo after Vilification, someone'd been there. I think it was Ryna, but she'd obviously taken pains to avoid me."

The other Gypsies' consideration weighed on Phoe with almost physical force, but she would not look up. *Let them think I am ashamed she will not see me. Please, don't let them guess...*

When at last the camp elder spoke, his words were slow. "If pressed, tell people she was called away suddenly. Tell them there's an emergency in her family. Make it two separate sentences, and it's as close as we can get when we don't have any clue what's going on ourselves."

Elda lifted an eyebrow, but seemed cautiously pleased. "It'll do. I'll tell the others."

As the door banged closed behind the seamstress, Phoenix wondered if anyone in their right mind would believe a word of it.

* * *

"I beg your pardon, but do you know where I might find Ryna Tully?"

Phoenix stopped short. No one ever used Ryna's last name. She doubted most people knew she *had* one. But more than that... there was a power in this man's voice that called to her soul even as it froze her with terror. She turned from collecting the dance show's tips to face the stranger... tall, beautiful, and endowed with more Charm than Tanek would've known what to do with. "Who are you?" she asked, wary.

"Forgive me." He swept a gallant bow, doffing his plumed hat as he captured her hand. "My name is Joshua."

Stunned pause. "*You're* Joshua?"

He straightened, settling his hat with a grin. "You've heard of me, then. I'm afraid you have the advantage, fair lady."

She wanted to slug that dazzling smile off his face.

She wanted to run screaming.

She compromised by standing rooted to the spot. "My name is Phoenix," she told him, though she didn't want to.

His turn to look surprised. His smile turned wry. "She told me you were beautiful. The word 'understatement' comes to mind."

Gods, he was *insufferably* like Liam! Phoenix cocked her head, suddenly wishing she could meet Ryna's other ex-lovers, see if the pattern went beyond these two. She was sure it didn't include her... at least, she hoped not. But if not, and if that was what Ryna wanted in a mate...

"She's out of town," Phoenix said abruptly, tucking a star-white tendril behind her ear.

Puzzlement furrowed his brow. "Out of town? She didn't—"

"It was a last-minute thing."

Again, he looked startled. Phoe got the sneaking suspicion it was calculated… he certainly didn't *feel* startled—mostly annoyed, but there was something else.

"I was looking forward to seeing her again, catching up on old times." He paused for dramatic effect. Phoe's nape hairs prickled at the suave, predatory glint in his eyes. "Say, you're her partner. Perhaps you could come with me—I bought two tickets to the local dinner theatre thinking she'd be here to join me, but perhaps *you* could catch me up…"

A vivid mental image wrapped around Phoe's brain of herself and Ryna, rumpled and glowing—and draped all over a smug-looking Joshua. She took a hasty step backwards, desperately frightened that she would agree…

"*Josh*ua!" Niki enthused, sliding between him and Phoenix, to Phoe's eternal relief. "You *are* Joshua, aren't you? Please say yes. Ryna's told me so much about you, and I'd *die* of embarrassment if I was wrong."

"My dear lady, you are perfectly correct, as I am certain you always are." He swept her a practiced bow and kissed her hand.

Niki fluttered and giggled. "You are too much! I can see why Ryna was so fond of you."

"Indeed—though it seems I've missed her. We were supposed to enjoy dinner together this week—I even bought tickets to the Chanhassen—but now it seems she's indisposed."

Phoenix watched Niki coyly fidget with her hair and wondered if the dancer had gone completely mad. "That's too bad… now you're stuck with an extra ticket you can't use…"

Possibility dawned across his face with a sexy grin. "Only if I find myself unable to convince a certain lovely Gypsy dancer to accompany me."

Niki's eyes widened. "Me? Oh, I'd love to! What time should I meet you there? I know right where it is…"

"The ushers seat at six o'clock—the tickets are for Thursday."

"I'll see you at quarter-to, then," Niki agreed. "I'd hate to miss even a minute of it."

"And I shall count the minutes until then, fair Gypsy." Another gallant bow, another kissed hand, and Joshua swept off.

Phoenix stared at Niki, incredulous. "What is *wrong* with you?" Phoe hissed, rattled. "Can't you see that's all Charm?"

"I know," she agreed, flightiness vanished. "I'm paying him back for what he did to Ryna."

Phoe's jaw dropped. Never had she seen this calm, vengeful side to her friend. She forced a laugh. "And saving my tail. Thank you."

"My pleasure." Niki wrapped one arm around Phoe's shoulders and gave her a squeeze. "Now, how about after your variety show you and me visit the pretty-smelling oils and stuff at the incense shop?"

The raven-haired Gypsy tried to mask her in surprise. It was almost too easy... who better to ask about the properties of scent than an Air element?

The way things were going, though, Phoenix would take all the easy she could get. "Count me in."

◇ ◇ ◇

Ryna could feel people around her. It was like closing your eyes in a still room and knowing you're not alone... except that opening her eyes didn't help. She'd taken to sitting with her back against the outer wall of Cottage's kitchen so she'd stop feeling like someone was sneaking up on her.

It only helped a little.

Her location granted her a clear view of First Aid gate and the privies. Not the most picturesque scenery, but lounging in the shade with Cottage's familiar bulk at her back, Ryna could almost convince herself things were normal. For the first time in what felt like forever, she wasn't fighting off the creeping despondency that tried to mire her with hopelessness. *Must be Cottage,* she thought—and paused, frowning.

Or maybe the energy Cottage gave off?

Well, crap, then, Ryna thought, the echo of *Baba* Luna's favored phrase bringing a smile to her lips despite the sudden wash of embarrassment. *I can't believe I didn't think of that sooner. Spirits don't need physical food... but they need energy, same as at home. I'm so used to getting it from my music and from playing with my family and all the other Bright Ones... no wonder I've been in such a horrible mood.*

Well, she could solve that easily enough, at least. Cottage was full of Bright energy... same with Sherwood. If she took the time once in a while to rest, recharge...

A flash glimpsed from the corner of her eye caught her attention; she turned to see Court on a brisk promenade toward the Summer Palace encampment behind First Aid.

Except—

Except nothing. It was only Court... *her* Court... headed for a break, like they had a thousand times before. No trick of the Shadow Fae, this brief, blessed vision of home. Phoenix was even there, wondrous to behold in her lapis-blue bridesmaid's gown. A vision from last weekend, then, probably not long after her brother's wedding... so regal, so graceful on Justin's arm...

Except that Justin had never worn the uniform of the Militia.

"No!" Ryna cried, bolting to her feet and sprinting to the rescue. Three yards short of her goal she collided with an invisible wall, granting her a sudden and acute sympathy for the bugs splattered across her truck's windshield. "Phoenix!"

Her love turned, a puzzled look on her face. The rest of Court pranced through the yellow picket fence with the flash of sunshine off sword hilts and the cheery bob of hoopskirts. "Who calls me by that name?"

"A peasant," Liam said with scorn. "And one who has mistaken you for the lowly herbwife who has not visited this village in years."

"Go lick a privy, Liam," Ryna spat. "Phoe, it's me. Ryna."

Phoenix cocked her head to one side, peered closely at her, and shook her head. "You bear a passing resemblance to her, but Ryna is dead. She has been for half a decade or more."

"Beg pardon, my lady, but your son—"

The words hit Ryna in the gut as a plump woman bustled up, towing a little lad in a velvet doublet. Chocolate smeared his face, and he clutched a wooden sword in one hand.

Liam laughed. "Come here, my boy."

The child ran to his arms with a delighted squeal of "Daddy!!!!"

Phoenix removed a handkerchief from her bodice and attempted to clean the little one's face. "You're a mess, my darling prince," she said with a fond smile.

"I got to fight a dragon, Mommy!"

"Was it made of chocolate?"

Ryna could not take her eyes off her love, could not wrench her mind away from the realization that she was *not* wearing her bridesmaid's dress, despite the similar cut and color. This dress had been designed to accommodate the barely-showing roundness of her midsection...

Ryna knew she had to think fast, had to find a way to talk to Phoenix alone. It had to be a spell, some sort of horrible entrapment of will that Liam had used to snare Phoenix...

Like the one he believed you used on her? a nasty voice whispered in her mind.

No. It's not like that. Phoenix is mine. She loves me.

Liam thought the same thing.

The Gypsy squeezed her eyes shut against the voice's stinging irony, wishing that when she opened them again, that the world would be empty—or, better yet, that everything would be as it should.

The cruel little voice snickered at her. *Foolish, arrogant mortal. This* is *how things are. You are no longer remembered.*

"No," she whispered as Phoe leaned over her son's head to give Liam a kiss... and couldn't stop the tiny, sprouting doubt that wondered... just a little bit... if maybe the voice was right.

◇ ◇ ◇

"Is that the last of them?" Phoenix asked as Tremayne brought another stack of dishes to the little wagon.

He nodded shortly as she arranged them so the piles wouldn't tip in transport. The other Gypsies and a couple Merry Maids munched on fruit for dessert, talking banally of the day's events. Phoe couldn't blame her father-in-law for avoiding them; the whole thing seemed so forced.

"Right." Phoe dusted off her hands. "I'll get my mug and be off—you want to come?"

Another nod.

Phoenix went to retrieve her drinking vessel from the bench beside Mutch—and immediately wished she'd left it to her family's care and gotten out while the getting was good.

"A little birdie told me that you're short one Gypsy?" singsonged the Artistic Director's voice. "The little red-haired one with the fiddle?"

Baba Luna muttered something nasty under her breath. Phoenix caught enough to leave her no doubt that Luna had her own ideas as to the birdie's identity. Phoe sat down hard.

Phuro Basil stood up courteously and swept her a gallant bow. "You are indeed most perceptive, m'lady. We are, regrettably, missing a member of our troupe." He sighed theatrically. "But, the show must go on."

She graced him with a smile. For a scant few heartbeats, Phoenix believed they had escaped disaster.

And then Patty opened her mouth. "Indeed it must—I'm so glad you understand. After all, Pendragon can't afford to pay for a performer who can't be bothered to show up!"

Tanek looked stricken, though Phoe couldn't imagine he hadn't seen it coming. "Have pity, Lady!" he cried. "She was called away suddenly—there is an emergency in her family!"

"I'm sorry to hear that—please extend my condolences," she said, fluttering sympathetically. "Do tell her I won't terminate her contract for her absence, and she can resume her normal pay just as soon as she comes back."

Another charitable smile, and then Patty and her pink skirts flounced away. Her rookie handmaiden cast a brief, apologetic look towards the Gypsies before hurrying after.

The egg lady, hovering near the petting zoo, did not look nearly so contrite. Phoenix glared at her until she turned and hurried away.

No one spoke for a long time. The Gypsies stared at their hands, the ground, the patrons—anything except each other. The Merry Maids concentrated on their fruit. Silence stretched.

And then it snapped.

"How can you be so calm?" Phoenix cried, standing up so fast she overturned her bench.

"Phoenix—" Kaya reached for her, but she pulled away.

"Don't 'Phoenix' me. Ryna's gone, they're going to pull our funding, this whole *faire* is rushing off in a handbasket, and we sit around chewing our cud like *cows*! Big, stupid, placid *cows*!" She stared hard at her family—a few flinched back from her gaze. No one offered explanations. Maybe they knew she wasn't in a mood to listen.

She wanted to fight. Something, anything, so long as she could hang onto it and wrestle with it, beat it until she stopped feeling so helpless.

The thought made her want to cry. This was her *family*.

"I—I have to go," she choked out, whirled, grabbed the handle to the wagon, and hurried toward Bakery, serving platters and wooden bowls jostling behind. Maybe if she threw her anger into dishwashing she might start to feel more like herself.

After all, it worked for Brigid.

◇ ◇ ◇

"Are you sure you don't mind?"

Liam turned from flipping through bins full of art prints and gave Elise his most patient, devoted smile. "Why should I mind?"

She fidgeted with the trailing end of her bodice lace. "It's just—you don't really know anyone here, and I've hardly seen you all day, and—"

Liam put a soothing hand over hers. "Go. Spend time with your aunt. You got me a temporary pass; I'll wander around a bit and meet you back at your car at midnight."

"You're sure you're sure?" she fussed.

"Positive. I'd only be tagging along. Really."

"I'll make it up to you," she offered, guilt wreathing her expression.

She was already doing him a huge favor—but Liam saw no need to let that slip. He kissed the back of her hand—then began nibbling the inside of her wrist. "Promise?"

She swallowed hard, her breath coming in little pants.

Liam smiled. Most satisfactory.

◇ ◇ ◇

"Hey, Cinderella."

Phoenix glanced up to see Tanek leaning against the doorway to the Bernatellis' kitchen. The other two dancers hovered a little behind him.

"Hey yourself," she returned, brushing hair from her eyes. A clump of suds clung to her ear, making little popping noises.

"We came to lure you to Drum Jam," Kaya said. "Toby and Luna will get the wagon."

"I don't know," Phoenix hedged. "Big crowds really aren't my thing."

"Please," Niki begged, making the face that—whether she realized it or not—could get her nearly anything. "It would be good for you."

With a sigh, Phoe relented. She had learned long ago that when these folks decided something would be good for you, they usually got their way... and, more often than not, they were right. *Might as well try,* Phoenix thought. *If I hate it, I can always leave.*

"The chariot awaits," Toby said with a grin as he bounded up to the door. Quite a bit of his shaggy ebony hair had come free from his headscarf, giving him a charming, roguish look. He and the dancers grabbed armloads of dishes and carried them to where *Baba* Luna waited with the wagon.

"Thank you!" the Gypsies chorused as Phoenix brought down the last couple bowls.

"It's-a not a problem!" Mama yelled back with a wave as they started off toward Sherwood. "You-a come, bring-a your dishes whenever you-a want!"

"Oh, don't worry—we will!" *Baba* replied.

People milled in the open area near Bedside Manor, and for once only clothes marked the distinction between entertainer and entertained. They all shifted and bounced in anticipation. They all looked as if they belonged.

"What do we do?" Phoenix asked as Luna and Toby made a wide detour with the wagon.

"Join in," Tanek said, giving her a rakish grin. An edgy energy crackled around him. The whole area felt anxious, restless, waiting. A rough circle began to form; two men waddled from around the feast hall's corner with a huge kettle drum between them, and the crowd, with a little prodding, cleared a space to let them pass.

"Look who's here," greeted a tall fellow with long, black braid of hair—and no shirt. Phoe recognized him (and his knowing wink) from one of the stained glass booths in Cartwheel Cove. He released the hand of the patron on his right to make room for her.

"Thanks," Phoenix said softly, and snuck in between him and Kaya. For a moment the tiny hand felt painfully familiar—but the calluses were missing, the brush of energy different. She stared hard at the center of the beaten ground.

Kaya squeezed her hand in sympathy; the fellow gave her a quizzical look.

Ryna never comes to Drum Jam, Phoe reminded herself. *Of course it's Kaya. Stop being silly. At least you get to see her tomorrow.*

A lean fellow with long gray hair stood in the circle's center, glancing around, waiting. As the last hands clasped he ran to the east side of the gathering, then circled sunwise, toward the south, waving his drumsticks above his head. Wild cheers erupted in his wake; Phoenix felt a shiver of Magick ripple brightly through her as he rushed by, gathering the offered energy. The patrons clearly felt the effects as well, some primal part of them acknowledging him as the High Priest of this rite. Phoe wondered how many knew the significance of the seemingly showy actions.

"Welcome to Drum Jam," the leader intoned when the circle had been closed and he once again stood in the center.

Uproarious whooping. He waited for it to fade.

"There are two rules," he called. "If you don't dance—"

"You drum!" the audience cried.

"If you don't drum—"

"You dance!"

And then, leader and followers: "*This is not a spectator sport*!"

A drum roll blended with the cheers as people bounced on their toes like children held back from a mound of birthday presents. Phoenix had never been part of something so large, and even though most of these people were untrained, the noise and energy made her lightheaded. Then the circle imploded and the drums settled into a beat that rumbled through her bones:

da-DOUM da-DOUM DOUM! da-DOUM da-DOUM DOUM!

Phoenix reeled among the moving bodies and swirling emotions, disoriented. She focused on the nearby members of her family, narrowing her world to familiar figures until she could think again.

And then she didn't need to think. She was only one small part of this huge, thundering rhythm, older than life itself, a giant heart that swept her up in the ebb and flow of its storm. There was no need for thought here, or worry... She let her body move as it wanted, beating the ground with her feet, dancing with her family, dancing with whomever came near, dancing with the drums, dancing with the earth itself.

Phoenix cried out to the cloudy sky and hoped she would never have to be still again.

*   *   *

"Oh, hell. We're going to get pissed on again."

Baba Luna's voice floated into Phoenix's vardo on a moist breeze that made the lace curtain shift. Thunder grumbled overhead. Phoenix breathed deeply, savoring the scent of rain on the wind, the twitchy feeling of being on the edge of something, about to fall over. It made her heart speed in anticipation. Wherever Ryna was, Phoe hoped her love was enjoying it, too.

"You think they'll still have Sacrifice Sunday?" That was Tanek.

A scoffing noise. "It would take a flood to put that fire out. You saw it last year." *Phuro* Basil. He could feel the coming storm, too.

They all could. Phoenix could sense it in them. It made Kaya want to dance. It made Luna want to sing. From Tremayne she got the image of staring out a window, waiting, watching. The others were too jumbled to pick out—though it took no skill to determine that the inhabitants of one particularly renowned tent had found a use for the wild energy.

"I'm just hoping the lot of them manage to carry off Patty," Esmerelda snarked.

"Hey, did you hear about the Scotsman who got blacklisted for bathing in Bardstone Welly's fountain today? He just dropped kilt and hopped in."

"You've gotta be kidding, Niki," Toby cried, laughing. "Gods, I wish I'd thought of that."

"*I'm* glad you didn't," Elda retorted. "I'd rather not have to do that show on my own."

They were all in their vardos, windows and doors open to let in the restless air. She knew because she could not see them in the common area. She wondered if they had changed yet.

Phoenix hadn't. She lay spread-eagled on the bed in her boots and chemise, Karma keeping a distracted watch. Her feet hurt. She had danced until the cannon's blast heralded Drum Jam's end. She wondered what would have happened if Closing Cannon *hadn't* sounded? Would the drummers have pounded out the beat until their hands bled? Would the dancers have gone on until their shoes wore through and they collapsed from exhaustion, like in the old tales?

A disturbingly loud *foomp!* sounded from the gamers' camp across the road, followed by ragged cheers that transformed into chanting: "Throw away the fucking water; let the goddamn fire burn—"

Phoenix shook her head to chase the echoes from her ears, twiddled with the bit of ribbon Liam had tied in her hair all those months ago. She'd tucked it into her journal—and completely forgotten about it until she'd been dancing today and a quiet, bright voice had reminded her. Had he done something to it, something to enchant her? Had her disregard for it been some deeply buried defense mechanism? If Ryna had given it to her, she would've carried it in her pocket for weeks...

Ashes to ashes...

She remembered those awful red arm bands he'd worn. If she closed her eyes, she could still see the charred cloth trying vainly to flutter, could still feel it crumbling to powder in her hand.

Dust to dust...

"Burn, burn, burn, burn, let the goddamn fire burn—"

Ribbons, ribbons...

"Hey, you comin' to Sacrifice Sunday, hon?" Niki called from right outside the door.

"I'm coming," Phoe said softly. She didn't especially want to join, but she knew what she had to do. The bright voice had told her.

Niki took the words as invitation and stepped up into the vardo. "C'mon, slowpoke," she teased, forcedly chipper. "Time's a-wastin'!"

Phoe levered up, followed Niki across the road to the assembled mob. She almost recoiled from the heat, and the crowd, and the memories, but Niki held her firm. That in itself made her want to run shrieking. *What is* wrong *with me today?!*

"This is for the prof who gave me an 'F' on the project I worked my ass off on all quarter!" cried a college-age male as, with great ceremony, he hurled a fistful of papers into the inferno. The flames scrambled over the sacrifice, devouring it eagerly. The onlookers cheered.

"Throw away the fucking water—"

An older man stepped to the fore. "My wedding ring—I'm finally free of that bitch!"

"Let the goddamn fire burn—"

A woman this time. "Here's a dozen dried roses because that relationship is OVER!"

"Burn, burn, burn, burn—"

"Go on," Niki prodded, nudging her forward.

Phoe almost bolted. It took every ounce of control she possessed to take one step, then another, until the heat blasted her face. The brittle smell of charred cloth mingled with the dusky wood smoke and sharp-scented lighter fluid. The hand that raised the scrap of ribbon trembled.

People quieted, waiting to hear what she would say.

She dropped the ribbon.

Flames leapt to engulf it, turning it to floating bits of char before it had even reached the woodpile.

Phoenix turned on shaking legs and hurried away, chemise still hot from the fire, echoes scorching her ears—

"Ashes to BURNburnburnburn!"

She began to run.

"Whoa, hey!" Tremayne caught her by the shoulders at the foot of the Olympic Staircase. "Are you all right?"

Phoenix forced herself to breathe, forced the terrifying visions to fade. *Old memories. Not even this life,* she reminded herself. "Got a little… a little too hot for me, I guess."

Tremayne didn't say a word.

She shifted uncomfortably. "And a little too familiar. With the mob and the flames and all, you know?"

He raised one eyebrow, more in surprise than rebuke. "It never bothered you before."

"Yeah, well." She didn't have a good answer for that. And she was beginning to feel defensive and cornered.

He must've sensed the shift, for he put a comforting arm around her shoulders. "Come listen to some music. I was on my way to fetch you."

Tremayne's voice and word choice didn't sound at all normal. The expression on his face looked strange, maternal. Phoe almost skittered back in alarm, but she could still hear the chanting behind her. Could she spend a whole night across from that?

And really, the changes in Tremayne weren't *bad,* merely *strange*. And, somehow, familiar…

Phoenix took a deep breath. "I would like that."

"Burn, burn, burn," Liam whispered, eyes vague as he leaned against a refurbished bus beyond the fire's light. The flames burned strange and sinister, just as they had a year ago when they'd leapt to devour Ryna's bodice lace, broken that first time they'd lain together. He'd been trying to get her out of his system that night in Cottage, though he would've admitted it to no one—hardly to himself. She'd had far too much of a hold on him since the first time he laid eyes on her.

So had Bea, but she had been quiet, submissive, pliable.

Ryna liked to be in control. She didn't need anybody, and she made sure everyone knew it. The only way to win against her was to be the first to leave. The little bitch must've put binding Magick in her sex to make him love her so—and then she had taken Bea with the same trick, purely to unman him further.

Well, he'd had the last word, last life, and soon he would have it in this one, too. Liam smirked, an echoing flame in his eyes. "Let the goddamn fire burn…"

"Nurg," Phoenix complained blearily, swatting her alarm clock until it surrendered and pervasive silence engulfed the room.

Karma toddled over to knead her person's tummy.

The Gypsy scratched behind the calico's ears and reveled in the resultant purring for a moment before dragging herself out of bed and into her garb.

Karma looked briefly affronted, but curled up and closed her eyes. It was light now; she could go hunting for her person again. Hopefully this time the nasty Shadow creatures wouldn't find her so quickly...

Phoenix tossed some dry cereal in her leather mug and gave Karma a final pet before heading out.

Tremayne hailed her as she closed and locked her vardo door after taking care of the Faerie bowl.

"Hey," she returned, falling in step with him as the dew soaked her shoes. The morning light and the wet, soft smell in the air lent a spring-like feeling to the day. Phoenix hoped it would wait at least a few hours before becoming blisteringly hot.

"How are you holding up?"

Phoenix shrugged, avoiding the question as she tried to block out the sounds of passion from the loud sex tent. "As well as can be expected after being hit with the falling piano that is Labor Day."

It made him smile. Phoenix was glad. They could all use more smiles, especially Tremayne.

"It's your birthday tomorrow," he observed. "Is there—"

"Not until she comes home."

Tremayne winced and nodded, but kept silent.

Phoenix bit her tongue. She felt like such a traitor, walking beside him, knowing his daughter was safe—well, as safe as could be expected—and not saying anything to soothe his fears. *Please, Ryna, come home soon,* she begged silently. *I know you think it's for their own good, but don't put them through this. Not Tremayne. Not your father.*

With any luck, she'd be able to convince her love to do just that...

No. Focus on something else. Anything else. Much more of that and they'll pick up on your thoughts...

"Tremayne, can I ask you something?"

He turned his attention to her, waiting, quietly, patiently.

"Is it possible for one of the Fae to get someone pregnant?"

His eyebrows rose a fraction, the corner of his mouth quirked. "I don't think my daughter is going to be able give you a child, no matter what lengths she goes to."

Phoe blushed. "I wasn't thinking like that. I mean, it's not me. It's someone I know, and I'm not sure she'd believe, but her story—"

"Mmm. Is it that pretty blonde from Irish Cottage?"

To her credit, Phoenix remembered to close her mouth.

He flashed her an amused smile. "She didn't sparkle like that before. And she looks as if she's eaten Faerie fruit." A direct look. "As it were."

Phoenix did a double-take. She'd heard tales about the dangers of eating the food of Faerie; not once had she guessed it to be an allegory for… something else. They displayed their passes to the C-gate guard and continued on. "So it is possible?"

"Stories like 'Tam Lin' must exist for a reason."

"But the Fae I've seen aren't anything you can mistake for human!"

Tremayne looked at her with an expression that reminded Phoenix achingly of her absent love. "Did you think that was all that was out there, little owl?"

Phoenix could only stammer that it was all she'd ever seen. The words didn't even sound convincing to her own ears.

"Perhaps you need to look harder."

Phoenix hardly thought that was the case—they seemed to be finding her easily enough—but resolved to open her eyes a bit more anyhow.

"Saved you a spot," Patches greeted cheerily when they arrived at Cast Call.

"Thanks."

"All right, peoples, peoples!" Patty called from Bakery Stage, waving about her pen and clipboard. "Now, that's better! Isn't this wonderful, a third day in a row of Pendragon Faire! I know I'm looking forward to it."

A few mutters. Nobody wanted to give her ammunition—not after Saturday.

"Anyway. To start everyone's day on a happy note, I would like to announce that the privies have been cleaned!"

A round of cheers.

They were the first popular words the Artistic Director had spoken.

◇ ◇ ◇

Day four—at least, as far as she could tell.

Ryna shifted in her soggy shoes and stared at the tally mark low on the picket fence that separated Fool's Knoll from the Front Gate area. She wished she had something more permanent than a bit of burned wood with which to write. She wished she could even be sure it was the fourth day away from home—as her family counted things, anyhow. She had no real way of knowing… and far too much time to worry about it.

Still, she had to do what she could…

At least the rain that had drenched Pendragon during the night had only lightened the marks slightly. It seemed so stupid—if she felt no hunger, needed no sleep, then she should feel no cold, no wet…

On the other hand, the elements were living things. Maybe it wasn't real rain. Maybe it was spirit rain. But, being in a similar state, she felt it as if she and it were both physical. At least, she assumed she had to be in spirit form. Physical bodies needed rest, needed nourishment—

A chilling thought struck her. If she was a spirit, then where was the rest of her? Would she even be *able* to return?

No. Don't think that. There's a way home; all you have to do is find it, she told herself as she pocketed the charred wood and straightened.

A flash of color on a nearby shrub caught her eye.

Niki's lucky veil.

It hadn't been there the moment before, she was almost certain. Ryna reached for it, surprised when her fingers touched the sheer, silky fabric.

It wasn't an illusion, then.

Cold rage built inside the fiddler as she freed the cloth from the shrub's branches. This was part of it, somehow. The Shadow Fae were behind the missing power items—they must have needed them to get her here.

Perhaps even keep her here?

Not if I can help it.

But still, what to do with it now that she had it? Hiding things wouldn't help—for all she knew, the Shadow Fae could track them down.

Unless…

A grim expression settled across her face as she turned her steps to the campground. If *she* couldn't get into her family's camp, neither could the Shadow Fae.

Ryna reached her destination surprisingly unchallenged, pressed her hand against the solid, invisible barrier. What if it was solid to *everything* here? *One way to find out,* she thought bravely, wadded the fabric into a ball, and tossed it hard.

It floated effortlessly through the barrier and landed three feet away.

Ryna released the breath she'd been holding, sent up a prayer to the Bright Fae to return the veil to its owner, and headed back towards site, determination in her stride.

"Ow," Marcus announced as he joined the pack of peasants beneath the tree near the Bear and Bedside Manor.

"Ow?" Bryn repeated.

"Ow," he confirmed. "This headache came out of nowhere and nailed me as I was passing by that shop at the tip of the island by C-gate. Shade—I love shade."

"I got one over there, too," Piddle seconded. "I thought maybe I'd had too much fun last night."

"Yeah—you and that bottle of Jeremiah Weed," Marcus teased, recruiting Bryn's lap for a pillow.

"Uncle Jerry!" Puddle exclaimed brightly.

Piddle snerked. "Uncle Jerry kicked my ass."

"Think something's going on?" Hayrold inquired.

Phoenix's eyes nearly fell out of her head.

"Whatever it is, it's not good," Bryn put in, resting a hand over Marcus' aching head.

The tingle of Magick brushed Phoe's skin, and her jaw nearly joined her eyes. She knew more people than just her family could do Magick… but the peasants? It didn't feel the same as the Gypsies' brand of energies, true… but there was no mistaking the power there.

Not that she begrudged them the ability—it just… surprised her, was all.

"Something's been up all year," Marcus said. "Power items stolen, weirder patrons than usual—"

"Weirder management than usual," Piddle added. "Maybe somebody should do a reading on the area?"

"Maybe—I keep feeling like something's watching me," Bryn said as the tingling subsided. "Better?"

"Much. Hayrold, have you checked with Hippie Slayer? See if she's noticed anything stirred up in Colorado?"

"No, but I should."

"Hippie Slayer?" Phoenix spluttered.

"Long story," Bryn said. "See—"

"More fun news," the Leper announced as he joined the group, grunting as he plopped down.

"Funky Formal next weekend isn't going to be in the Big Blue Barn," Pratt finished for him as he took a seat in the last scrap of shade. "They're moving it to the big white monstrosity."

"Oh, *that'll* be fun. Should we all wear our pink 'I Work For Stupid' T-shirts? Dim-witted bint."

"Hayrold!" Bryn scolded, playfully cuffing him.

"Sorry—getting into Vil mode."

"All right, folks," the judge announced as he strode up to the pile of bodies. "The Artistic Whatever has some changes she wants us to make in our show, and I've been told to go over them with everyone before we get up there. Who's in?"

A chorus of voices spoke up.

A pause.

"Phoenix?"

She plucked at the grass as she tried to convince her voice not to break. "Not today," she whispered, and felt the silence stretch around her.

"Okay, then. Briefly, no cussing—even mild cussing—no pop culture references, no jokes of a sexual nature—"

"So basically she's looking for all the ducky and bunny insults," Marcus surmised.

"What about teddy bears?" Piddle asked.

"NO!" the Vilifiers cried; several covered their ears in horrified anticipation.

Phoenix let it flow by her—she had no idea what they were talking about, and by the looks on their faces, she didn't want to. She sighed—and tried not to wonder if anything would ever return to normal.

◇ ◇ ◇

Liam sighed as he arranged the garish silk flowers for the eighth time. How did boothies endure standing in the same three walls with only the passing patrons for entertainment? He'd only been at this a day, and already the pull to the dusty streets made him itch.

"Hello, beautiful," Elise greeted as she ducked into the back room. "Tired of flowers yet?"

Liam put on a courtly smile and kissed her hand. "You are one flower of which I would never tire, fair damsel."

Elise blushed most satisfactorily.

He swept her a bow. "What service might I lend my beauteous princess?"

"Actually, um, my aunt asked if we could maybe paint the windows upstairs—from the inside, of course. She has everything outlined and a diagram of what colors to use where. If you don't mind."

Actually, he did—but it was better than the flowers, and he'd already refused to hang about the front part of the store for fear that the Shadow Fae's gift of stealth wouldn't hold up to the forced interaction of playing salesperson. "After thee, fair maid."

The shop's second floor reminded him of his Gramma Flynn's attic—rafters, wood, and a dusty smell. Plastic storage bins lined one wall; a small fleet of paint buckets huddled against its opposite. Clothesline strung along a third sagged under the weight of spare costuming.

The windows were simple paned glass, high enough that Liam knew he would have to stand on something if he wanted to paint further up than the first two rows of panels. He'd assumed Elise's aunt would've recreated one of her masterpieces on them rather than the uninspiring coats of arms she had outlined, but there really was no accounting for some people's taste. Liam dutifully went to shake one of the paint pails—and grunted in surprise at its unexpected weight.

Elise kissed the top of his head. "My great, strong warrior," she teased. "Why don't you get the stir sticks and the brushes?"

Liam complied, scowling. By the time he'd located everything, Elise had the lids pried off and a painting smock on.

Liam could only keep a scrap of concentration on his task. Mostly he watched the passers-by far below. Ghosts of conversation drifted up through the stairwell, as well as the echoes of the Royals' Revolting's show only a short distance down the lane. A group of Gypsies passed by, bangles and belts bright in the sun. He could tell by the sudden tightening of his heart that his love walked with them.

"Phoenix..." he whispered.

She looked up, shielding her eyes against the sun, but did not see him.

She would never see him.

No one knew who he was—or ever would again. To the world, he would always be Ryna. He would spend the rest of his life answering to a name he hated.

"Lyre?"

Liam turned to the woman who had shared his bed for the past few days.

She recoiled, then reached out. "Honey, are you okay?"

Liam looked away. Beyond the glass, Phoenix had moved on. He shoved his brush in a paint bucket. "Perfect. Completely. Perfect."

"Phoe? Honey, you all right?"

Phoenix shook herself, rubbed her arms against a sudden chill despite the day's soggy heat. "I'm... fine, Niki. It's—I could've sworn I heard my name."

Kaya glanced around. "If someone really wants your attention, they'll trill."

"Yeah, I suppose." Phoe forced lightness into her voice, unable to explain the darkness that had brushed the back of her neck like a caress.

Like Liam's fingers through her hair...

I'm going insane, she thought dully, scratching the back of her neck to take the feel off. "I'm—I'm going down to the Highly Publicized Garden. I'll be back in time to collect tips for the dance show and do the variety thing." She pretended not to see their looks of concern as she hurried off, first toward the Bear, then right and past Woodland Stage, through the grapevine gate...

The trails proved blessedly empty; most patrons were still at Post-Parade or eating a late lunch. Phoenix dawdled past the cute little houses, ignoring the poorly rhymed poetry placards nailed to the trees.

Poor trees...

Sunlight bathed the tiered pools near the hobbit hole. Someone had strewn rose petals in the water, a fragrant contrast to their murky depths. Phoe climbed to the top of the embankment, where she could sit in grass and shade.

A couple of ten-year-old girls meandered past in dresses more suited to the American prairie than the European Renaissance.

"Hey, neat!" exclaimed the one in the blue dress. "I bet the pixies ride down the waterfall on the little petals!"

"Hey, yeah!" agreed her friend in lavender. "Hey, race you to the top of the hill!"

"No fair, you've got a head start!" protested Little Miss Blue, tearing off after her companion.

"Cute kids."

Phoenix smiled bemusedly down at Mutch, leaning over the footbridge's railing. "Yeah."

The young Merry Maid shook her cropped hair. "You okay?"

Phoe's defenses snapped to attention. "Why do you ask?"

"Ryna's not around. You guys told Patty something about being called away and an emergency in the family, but I thought you were her family. Wouldn't Tremayne be called away, too?" Then, with a sheepish smile, "Besides which, Robyn said not to ask."

That last made the Gypsy laugh. "She did, did she?"

"The peasants are worried about you, too. You know you can tell us the truth and we won't spread it around, right?"

The look of veiled pleading in her eyes tugged Phoe's heart. *Poor kid,* she thought. Anyone with sense would notice Mutch's crush on Ryna—it had to be tearing her up, too, to know something was wrong but not know what. "Promise you won't tell."

"Cross my heart. Not the peasants, not the Maids."

Phoenix sighed. "We don't know what's wrong. Ryna took off last Thursday night."

"Marcus said she showed up at his gig."

"So he told me—she never came back, though. Or, rather, she came back to get some stuff, but nobody saw her. We don't know why she left or even where to start looking."

Mutch huffed out a breath. "Man. No one would believe me if I *did* tell. That has got to be the lamest cover story in the world."

"It's true!"

"That's part of what really stinks."

They paused as a couple wandered by, too wrapped up in each other to notice their surroundings.

"You could report her missing," Mutch suggested. "Make an announcement at Cast Call or something."

Phoenix stared past Mutch to the still grasses of the swamp. They could, indeed… except that wherever she was, she obviously didn't want to be found. What was the point in keeping *Phuro* Basil from calling her in to the police if they broadcast it to the entire faire instead? Besides, he'd already started spreading their cover story…

What a mess.

"She'll be back before we have to make any announcements," Phoe said, trying to calm her own fears. After all, Ryna could take care of herself. Phoenix only had to gather her supplies… and wait.

◇ ◇ ◇

Ryna had begun to wonder how much the prickles at the back of her neck had to do with something actually coming. Something always did, sooner or later. Perhaps, by now, it was a perpetual state of fear.

It felt different this time, though—a tug, a straining of her ears, as if she'd heard her name in a crowded room and now couldn't tell who'd said it or why. It was driving her crazy—making her restless. She couldn't stop pacing site, looking for power items as she went—around Cartwheel Cove, up the Narrows, past the Maypole (for a moment the familiar measures of "Road to Lisdoonvarna" teased the wind), past Flying Buttress Stage and around Track, past Cottage, toward the Harvest Man—

"—up in everything exploding around them—I don't think they've—"

The voice clipped off, like someone turning through a radio channel. It belonged to one of the peasants, though Ryna couldn't say which. She backed up a bit, head cocked, hoping to catch another snatch.

"—ou?"

Too far—nothing.

Forward half a step.

"—mit, Ryna disappearing at the same time everyone with any Magick ability at all started getting headaches around the Maypole…"

Ryna stood still as the earth, reaching with all her heart for more words…

"You don't think she had anything to do with it, do you? Ryna?"

"I don't think she did it." A slow pause; for a moment Ryna feared she'd lost them again. "But I think it has something to do with why she's been gone since that night she was at the pub. It must be bigger than all of them. I mean, come on. She's as much a part of this place as the Bear."

"Do you think it has anything to do with Patty?"

"Not unless she's Evil incarnate."

A pause.

Don't go away, don't go away, Ryna pleaded.

Giggles—haunting how real they sounded compared to those of the Shadow Fae.

"I mean in a serious way. She's too stupid to conjure anything but a pain in our collective asses."

"Sometimes the stupid ones have more luck."

"You don't suppose maybe they know and they're not saying?"

"Doubt it. I talked to Phoenix, and she didn't seem like she was hiding anything huge."

"Do you think we should tell them?"

"Do you think they'd listen? The Gypsies are kind of their own little group."

"Maybe if we went through Phoenix, dropped a couple hints…"

"It's worth a shot, anyway. Whatever's going on, whether or not the Gypsies are involved, it's really bothering her."

"Anyone know when…"

"No," Ryna whispered as the voices faded and vanished. "No, no, not yet, not yet—" She moved a step in one direction, then another… but whatever it was—however it had been achieved—it was gone now.

Ryna plopped down hard at the foot of the Harvest Man. Location. It had to have something to do with location. Location, and…

She plucked the grass idly, racking her brains.

Timing, which seemed redundant.

Location, timing, and… there had to be something else.

So…

So, so, so, so…

She was never looking for something specific. It always just—happened.

So don't concentrate—fat lot of good that does, Ryna thought.

And it was while she was not concentrating that the answer hit her brain like a two-by-four. *Focus.*

She couldn't be focusing—but the other people had to be. The conversation had faded when they changed their focus from her to Phoenix.

So she simply had to plant more seeds of herself around, think less, and wander more.

She sighed. So much easier said than done.

But—it was something. And she intended to make it count.

The weather turned surreally beautiful as Closing Cannon neared. The temperature dropped with the sun that painted long shadows across the thinning grass and lent an angelic, golden hue to all it touched. Even a bit of breeze picked up—just enough to keep the bugs off.

Phoenix hmmed contentedly from her perch on one of the sun-warmed boulders that separated Cottage's lawn from the Green. She would see Ryna soon. Anything else... well, it simply didn't matter.

Da strode past her from the direction of Cottage, a stout stick over one shoulder. Phoe perked from her after-dinner lethargy as Torin followed him with a sack of potatoes and they set themselves up on what remained of the Green. Her brother removed a prime specimen of spudliness from the bag and sent it flying at high velocity towards Da—who missed his swing completely. The tuber bounced twice and nestled against a hay bale.

By bits and pieces others joined—at first taking turns pitching and batting, but soon they recruited hay bales for bases and teams emerged. A group of Scotsmen (Phoe had seen them around, though they didn't belong to the Bagpipe Brigade) banded together due to their uniform-like kilts and were quickly dubbed the Sheep Shaggers. The remaining players—O'Malleys and a couple musicians—became the Pratie Mashers.

It was like no kind of baseball she'd ever seen; spudball combined the joyful lawlessness of Fondle Football (minus the fondling), the verbal combat of Vilification Tennis, and the challenge of hitting a potato that no one could throw straight.

"I don't know whether to be amused that they've centered a game around a spud—or offended on behalf of the Great Naked Potato that they're trying to pulverize it," Bryn commented as she, Ilya, Marcus, Hayrold, and Puddle sat on the hay bales and remaining boulders.

"Well, they haven't hit it yet," Ilya pointed out

"What is this whole Naked Potato thing, anyhow?" Phoe asked, turning briefly from the game. "There were all these little potatoes with 'Hail Spud' tags in the privies last year, and somebody said to get the explanation from you peasants, but I never had a chance to ask."

The peasants grinned. Apparently this was a favored subject.

"It all started with a sign," Hayrold began in his best storytelling voice. "The Potato Prophet was walking down the lane one day and saw a sign that read 'Naked Potato.' 'Naked Potato?!' quoth he. 'What the hell does that mean?!' For the sun was bright from behind the sign, and although he did not know its meaning, the sign had nonetheless been delivered unto him, and he felt the need to spread the word. He began preaching the word of the Spud to passersby. And lo, within the heat of his sermon, he came to look upon the sign again, but the sun had moved, and he realized his error—the sign read '*Baked* Potato.' 'Oh,' quoth he, 'Never mind, then.' And continued on his way."

"The damage had been done, though," Bryn took up the tale. "After a couple days of random spud-related blessings, a certain person who shall remain nameless—"

"Jack," Puddle muttered.

"Hey!" Hayrold protested.

Phoenix blinked. Hayrold's real name was Jack? She never would've guessed…

"—spelled out 'You Will Believe' in French fries on the hood of the Prophet's powder-blue VW Bug. Twelve rennies were seen to gather around the 'miracle' the next morning. The prophet was amused at how many of them there were, and chaos ensued."

"There were the ten commandments—" Marcus added.

"'Thou shalt not slice; thou shalt not dice; thou shalt not julienne fry,'" Ilya quoted dutifully.

"Except that Jack and I figured the Spud actually kind of *liked* being julienne fried, so we became the co-clerics of the Julienites," Puddle put in. "The Red Russets showed up then, too, but they've been gone a long time."

"The Julienites defeated them in the first holy war," Jack told her. "It was a happy holy war. Because everything born of the Spud has to be done with a spirit of fun—even our wars. And they *had* to go… heretics."

"They twice-baked and insta-flaked them," Marcus added. "It's like tarring and feathering, but it's all potatoes."

Phoe glanced to the playing field as Moiré took the bat, cheeks glowing as she readied for the pitch. She wiggled her bum adorably as she dug her toes into the ground.

The first potato sailed right by her, but she swung at the second and connected with a solid *crack!*

The potato exploded.

"I hit it!" she cried, and sprinted for the first hay bale.

Half the outfield dove for the ground, searching for a piece of the "ball."

Moiré pranced to second base, skirts lifted primly before her. Phoenix cocked her head, wondering if Moiré had always been that cute—and if so, why in the world she hadn't noticed.

"I got it! I got a piece!" cried one of the Sheep Shaggers—a fellow of middling years with a scruffy beard and a black wool bonnet that boasted an extremely long pheasant feather.

"What else?" Phoenix asked the peasants, half an eye still on the mad scrambling.

"Next came our proof that we were a real religion," Jack said with a gleam in his eye. "Opposition, in the form of the Anti-Spud and the AuGratin One, risen from the ranks of the original twelve."

"So of course there were the Forty Lashes, and later the Crucifixion," Ilya said with authority. "And then the resurrection about forty minutes later, because that's how long it takes for a really good baked potato."

"We had the nativity of the Sacred Tater Tot born from the Virgin—"

"Yeah, right," several peasants coughed.

"—Betty Crocker and her faithful—yet unconsummated—husband Duncan Hines. The three wise guys showed up with mold, frankfurters, and mirth in the form of a really bad Scotsman joke." Jack shook his head. "You'll have to ask Piddle about the joke. I'm not repeating it."

"There's even a neat picture by the sheep pen—the camel's in it and everything," Marcus added.

"There was the Bullshit on the Knoll—which could be heard all the way down to the campground," Puddle declared gleefully.

"With our communion of Vodka and the Holy Chaser Fresca—and Pringles for the offering, because those little host things aren't *actually* the body of Christ, and everyone knows that Pringles aren't *actually* potatoes," Jack said. "Thus was born our Frescan Monks—"

"That's me!" Marcus piped up.

"We've yet to decide if the Holy Chasers chase holy people or are holy people who chase things… or both. There are a bunch of other sects, now, too, but it's getting hard to keep up with them all," Bryn confided. "Even for us Condimentarians. We're the lore-keepers; we study how different people dress the Spud."

"And Laine here's going to be our First Knight of the Spud." Jack put a proud hand on Bryn's shoulder.

"As soon as you get around to figuring out what my ceremony is." She gave the hooded peasant a poke. "I've already completed the trials."

"We're working on it," he and Puddle chorused defensively.

"What are you *doing*, Moiré?" came Da's voice.

She looked up with an endearing smile. "Stealing third base. What does it look like?"

"Hey! I'm *on* third base!" a Scott of around Phoe's age complained, running after the hay bale she was rapidly dragging out of his reach. He had a mop of dark curls and looked like he might be the son of the one with the black bonnet.

"Throw a piece of potato over here so I can tag him!"

"It doesn't count unless it was the last potato!"

"How could you tell the difference?"

"So, interested in joining the ranks of the Most Holy Naked Potato?" Bryn—Laine—queried.

Phoenix quirked a smile as a ruckus erupted on the Green, resulting in Eryn making a dive for a bit of potato and skidding right through a Scotsman's legs—which made him jump and clutch his kilt to his bum.

"Sure," she decided. "Sounds like fun."

◇ ◇ ◇

Bea was… beautiful, there, in the slanting sunlight of early evening. Liam watched quietly from near the King of the Log game, concealed by clumps of children wanting one last chance to bludgeon their siblings with the soft bags. She talked with the peasants, laughed at their jokes, but Liam knew she was counting the minutes until she could see him.

See Ryna.

Liam caught himself drumming his fingers against his leg—and balled them into a fist to make them stop. He wished he could do something about his knotted guts. *Relax. She expects everything to be normal. All you have to do is play along.*

He tossed his hair. There. That was something Ryna did. It gave him a little more confidence.

His love's brother—Daniel was his name—tackled second base, scrambled to his feet, and made a show of picking straw bits off himself.

One of the children behind Liam let out a howl of outrage as his sister toppled him from the log; half the outfield glanced over to see the cause of the fuss.

Daniel's gaze lingered, turned puzzling.

Liam's eyes widened. Had he…?

No point in taking chances. As casually as he could, Liam meandered toward the broken turret of the Hand Maid Sweets booth, took a roundabout route to *Lady Fortune*. He had just tucked himself into an inconspicuous corner when Closing Cannon sounded.

Liam smiled in anticipation. *It's time.*

◇ ◇ ◇

"Run! Run! Runrunrunrunrunyeah!!"

Phoenix cheered at the Pratie Mashers' triumphant whoop as her brother slid into home bale.

Daniel picked himself up off the ground with his usual aplomb and removed the worst of the straw that stuck to everything at Pendragon.

Hayrold leaned musingly on his staff. "It's amazing—back when Puddle and I worked the Hay Roll, I thought I'd never get rid of the stuff."

"And then you find a piece in January and suddenly it's more precious than gold," Puddle added. "Ah, those were the days."

"Hey, sis?" Dan called as he jogged over. "Can I get your help with something in the kitchen?"

Phoenix rose slowly from the boulder on which she'd been perched. Something in his tone was… not right. "Sure, Danny."

"I'll help!" Eryn piped up.

"Requires a tall person, squirt," he said, affectionately tousling her hair.

Phoe followed him into the house—dutifully blessing it first—and then into the kitchen. Aunt Molly was the only one in the main room, but Danny still double checked before letting the green burlap curtain fall closed. It woke small tremors in Phoe's soul. "What's wrong, Danny?"

"I think I saw her, Phoe-bea," he said in a hushed voice. "Ryna. Over by the King of the Log. She left as soon as she realized I saw her. She was in civvies, but I could've sworn—"

"I know, Danny; I—"

"You *know*? And you didn't go to her?" Daniel took her by the shoulders. "Phoe, what's going *on*?"

"I don't know," she admitted, and quickly added, "but no one's supposed to know she's here, not even the other Gypsies. Please, Danny, please promise me you won't tell *anyone*. Not even Christine. Not yet."

He hesitated a moment, his expression wary. "You have my word—*if* you promise you'll come to me if you need help."

"Danny, I—"

"No buts." He shook her gently. "*You come to me*. I promise to believe anything you say, no matter how weird or far out you think it is—but I'm not leaving you alone to face it. Understood?"

She bowed her head—frustrated and grateful. If *Ryna* was having trouble facing it, what chance did Daniel have? And yet—he wasn't stupid. He *must* have realized that. What strength of love, that it didn't stop him…

BOOM!

Phoenix jumped at the cannonblast, even though she'd been waiting for it for what seemed like forever. She glanced at the kitchen door, bats flopping in her stomach. It was time…

"Understood." She met his eyes. "I promise to come to you—or send someone if I cannot."

He released her. "Your secret is safe. Now—go meet up with her. I can't imagine you two don't have some secret rendezvous worked out."

"You know me too well," Phoe said, wrapping him in a hug.

"It's my job."

She smiled into his sweaty shirt, taking comfort from his steady presence before darting out the kitchen door and down the lane toward *Lady Fortune*.

Ryna had been near, watching her… waiting to be seen? It was comforting, somehow, like a guardian angel, even as it disturbed her that she hadn't sensed her love's presence. How long had she been watching? Had she been here all day?

Catherine gave a friendly wave as Phoenix passed; the Gypsy waved back, the normalcy of the action bringing her calm. She had love—and protection. Things would be all right.

They would.

They would.

They—

"Phoenix."

She started as Ryna appeared three yards ahead and to her left, next to *Lady Fortune*'s sign. She looked strangely alien in the familiar T-shirt and ragged jeans… and so, so tired. The way she carried herself, with the sort of forced confidence that meant she was at the end of her resources…

And even here, even so close, Phoenix could not feel her. She held back tears. "Are you all right?"

A short nod, a brave toss of her hair. "They haven't bested me yet—and they won't. It's just… taking a little longer than I anticipated."

A thousand questions tangled at the back of Phoenix's throat. When will you be home? Where are you staying? Why won't you tell me what's going on? Instead, she dug absorbedly in her pouch. "I—I got your supplies. I know you're in a hurry, so I did the best I—"

The gentle, cold hand against her cheek nearly undid her carefully held resolve. "I've missed you," Ryna said quietly.

Phoenix closed her eyes, fought not to cry. Ryna needed her strong. Ryna needed her strong…

"I know this isn't normal, and I know you're worried, but it's the only way I can keep you safe. You know I wouldn't do this if it wasn't absolutely necessary, don't you?"

Phoe nodded—though she managed to meet her love's eyes. Same color… but so tired, so distant… "I know—I know." She sniffed—and cursed herself for it. "I trust you."

"I'm sorry I must place this burden on you, but I can trust no other."

"It's not a burden," Phoenix countered fiercely. "Even seeing you, that you're not… I only wish the others…"

"Soon. I promise."

Phoe nodded again, took a deep breath. This couldn't be easy for Ryna, either; her family was her life. "I wasn't sure what exactly you wanted, but I brought what I could—sage for protection, some stones for focus, a couple kinds of incense and essential oils. You never really use this stuff, but I thought maybe—"

"It sounds perfect—I mean, it should be enough, thank you," Ryna said as Phoenix handed her the small drawstring bag. "Almost as though you read my mind."

How could I when I can't even read your heart? Phoe wanted to wail, but bit her tongue. "If you need anything else, anything I forgot—"

"I'll ask. I promise."

Silence stretched a moment as around them the world continued on—crafters packing up, a couple noblewomen sauntering past with their hoops collapsed over their shoulders.

"When—"

"As soon as I can. In a couple days, no sooner. I'm sorry I have to miss your birthday, but I'll make it up to you later, I promise."

"Okay." Phoenix wished there was anything else she could say. "Okay."

"Listen—I don't want to, but—"

"I know. Just… be careful. Come home safe. I love you."

"I love you, too." The tiny hand came up, tucked a wayward tendril of star-white hair behind Phoe's ear. "Be safe."

Phoenix nodded again, not trusting her voice. She had to bow her head to keep her tears from showing.

A shifting of the air nearby, a soft crunch of gravel—and when Phoe looked up again, Ryna was gone.

"Damn it, damn it, damn it!" Liam swore under his breath as he ducked behind *Lady Fortune*—and punched the picket fence with all his might.

It rattled at the impact.

He shook his hand and cursed again, leaned forward and rested his head against the rough wood. It wasn't fair. *Ryna* was supposed to be the one hurting, not Phoenix. Not his love. Never his love…

And now he was stuck in this cursed body, forced to carry on this stupid charade until he could get his own body—or, at least, a *male* body—back… or until the bitch was beyond help and he could prove to Phoenix that she really loved *him* and he could reveal himself.

He sighed, flexing his wounded hand. It hurt, though not nearly so badly as his heart.

"Hey, are you all right?"

Liam started at the voice, turned to see a wiry fellow toting a large wooden box on one shoulder. His red headscarf made him look like a pirate, though for some reason Liam thought he'd look more natural in fur trader clothes. "Fine," Liam said. "I'm fine."

"You sure?"

"I'm fine," Liam repeated, and turned away, started trudging toward B-gate. Elise probably wondered where he was, and the last thing he wanted was to raise her suspicions. He was in a foul enough mood without having to deal with endless questioning.

◇ ◇ ◇

"Damn it, damn it, damn it," Phoenix swore softly as she snaked through C-gate. She wished she knew what she was cursing—herself, the situation, Ryna—

No. Never Ryna. Her love had enough trouble on her hands. And Phoe had just added more by getting all teary for the one chance they had to be together…

The litany made her feel better, though—a release of frustration for which she had no other outlet. "Damn it, damn it." She timed the words to her footfalls as she started down the Olympic Staircase. "Damn it, damn it, damn it."

"Hey, are you all right, hon?"

Phoe looked up to see Niki ascending the stairs, still in garb, her beautiful face creased in concern. "Fine—I'm fine."

The dancer stopped as they came even with each other. "You sure?"

A sigh. "I… I miss Ryna, is all." Her voice wavered with the truth of that pain; she cursed herself as the tears returned.

"Oh, hon," Niki said, reaching out to embrace her. "It'll be all right. She'll come back."

"I know." The raven-haired Gypsy huffed out a breath as they parted. "I just… had a moment, you know?"

"I know all about moments. You need some ice cream?"

It made Phoe laugh. Unsteadily, but still. "No. Thanks, though." She scrubbed at her cheeks, took a deep breath. *Ryna's counting on you,* she reminded herself. It granted her a little courage. "Hey, isn't that your lucky veil?"

"It is," Niki said, accepting the change of subject gracefully. "I found it on my porch when I went down to change—and Nora's mug was right next to it. At least, I'm pretty sure it's hers. Same design, anyway. Thought I'd see if I could catch her on site before she left—otherwise I'll hold onto it until next weekend."

Phoenix cocked her head. "I wonder how they got there?"

Niki shrugged. "Maybe somebody found it and didn't have time to take it upstairs. They probably figured leaving it with us was the next best thing, if they were in a hurry."

"Yeah, maybe," Phoe agreed, but something still didn't add up. Why would two missing treasures show up in the same place at the same time? And hadn't Nora said hers was stolen off her belt?

Well, maybe it'd fallen off when she wasn't looking. Not that it really mattered; at least they'd returned.

She only hoped others would follow.

◇ ◇ ◇

The sun was setting.

Ryna watched the beautiful, rosy hues fade with bridled panic. Another night, and the visions were getting worse—gods, how long did it take for someone to go mad?

Longer than it'll take for me to get home, she told herself firmly as she bowed her head and hurried through the Narrows, toward Maypole. If she didn't see the twinkle of her lost ring, she wouldn't be tempted to chase it, in case this time it was real…

Twin Tree, Globe, *Lady Fortune*, Hand Maid Sweets tower…

Her head snapped up. Wait, this wasn't right…

She dismissed the thought. She must not've been paying attention, and anyway, it didn't matter. She had enough time, if she hurried…

King of the Log, Irish Cottage, Track, Hay Roll, Stocks—

"Mermaid snot," Ryna cursed under her breath, fear rising in her heart. There was no way she could've overshot twice in a row…

She began to run.

Children's Realm, cut through to Woodland, up to Bear, left to Twin Tree, Falconer's Stage—!

This time she caught the queasy shift as her surroundings fuzzed and darkling laughter rattled her ears.

The sun was too low… and sinking impossibly fast. Even sprinting, she wouldn't make it.

They knew her destination. They weren't going to *let* her make it.

She didn't care. She had to try.

Scribe's Hall! Bakery! Chapel!

The sight stopped her, mind whirring. Ryna tipped her head back, stared up at the open-faced building in all its dimly yellow stucco glory. The huge stained glass window stared back like the eye of a god she had never specifically believed in. The burlap covering the two doorways in the back wall hung too still, as if playing opossum until she came closer.

Still, it *was* holy ground. The Christians *did* celebrate Mass here every week.

She could feel nebulous forms of the Shadow Fae lengthening.

Did she dare take the chance?

Longer… Closer…

Did she dare *not*?

Ryna marched up the dirt aisle, under metal arches not quite grown over with vines, up the little stone path, and onto the flagstones of Chapel's floor.

There were shadows here, from the altar table and from the gloom. But no Shadows.

They were outside. They lurked, waiting, but did not—could not—enter.

She was safe—at least for now. A smile played across her lips. She could feel their frustration. For tonight—for this moment—she had won.

Ryna gazed a moment at the stained-glass window, dim in the fading light. "I promise I will never, ever, *ever* make fun of Christians again."

◇ ◇ ◇

Bleak, gray light greeted Phoenix when she convinced her eyes to open. She might've happily slept forever, but for the nightmares... though she couldn't actually recall the visions that had jarred her awake, sweating, more than once.

Karma draped sympathetically over Phoe's foot. Poor two-legged furless—Karma had done her best, but she had only been able to ward off the worst dreams. There had been too many to get them all.

Kool-Aid. Kool-Aid will help, Phoenix thought, stumbling to the fridge, which proved annoyingly bare of anything except plain water. With a sigh she went after a new packet—

—and found a little round truffle instead.

Phoenix slid to the floor with tear-misted eyes, staring sightlessly at her only birthday present... and tried not to wonder if it was the last gift she'd ever have from her love.

A knock at the door. "Phoenix, honey?"

"Welcome, Niki." She scrambled to her feet and replaced the chocolate as Niki let herself in. Ryna had put it there, and there it would remain until she came home.

"Hey." The dancer nervously toyed with her bracelets. Very brightly colored bracelets that clashed with her vibrant clothes. What was up with that? "Some of us are—you know—going out. Thrift stores, or garage sales, or... something."

Phoenix dithered, wondering how Niki had landed the duty of inviting her. Short straw, perhaps, or a few unlucky rounds of rock-paper-scissors.

"C'mon, Phoe. Could be fun?"

She should probably get out. After all, Ryna had said she wouldn't be back for a couple days, at least... "Okay. But—give me a minute, okay? My hair's all ratty, and I need to find clothes and stuff."

A wink and a smile. "Got it. Pick something bright—the rule of the day is that nothing can match."

In spite of herself, Phoenix giggled. This might be fun after all.

◇ ◇ ◇

"Happy birthday, my love
Happy birthday, my love
Happy birthday, dear Phoenix
Happy birthday, my love."

Ryna had not stopped singing her mantra since the sun's rising. With any luck, Phoenix would catch a snatch—or even the intent—and know that she was loved.

And not forgotten. Gods, what must her family think by now?

She tried not to dwell on that. Such thoughts would not win her passage home. Recovering the lost power items might, though she had not found another since Niki's veil—well, aside from Nora's mug. It worried her. How many remained?

Hell, for all she knew, the whole lot of them were in the swamp behind the Highly Publicized Garden… still, she refused to give up. Failing all else, it gave her something with which to ward away despair.

Another circuit of Pendragon's site—wandering, peering in nooks and behind posts. Nothing, nothing, nothing… and then, ironically, the glimmer of Magick against Falconer Stage, as unhidden as could be. She rushed towards it, hoping it wasn't another illusion, and found two walking staffs propped up against the gray stucco. One, knobbly and dark with age, belonged to Mother Goosed… and the other, to Phoenix.

Ryna reached out gingerly to the second, surprised at the smooth, solid surface under her touch. She closed her eyes, imagined her soulmate's large, cool hand curling over the worn wood with casual strength… and stood rooted a moment, unable to focus through the pain in her heart. Gods, she missed her love's touch…

Gradually determination pushed aside the agony. If she couldn't be there for Phoe's birthday, at least she could send a present… and while she was at it, return Mother Goosed's stick as well. Footsteps firm, Phoe's staff thumping awkwardly beside her and the other tucked under one arm, Ryna set out for the vardos.

She got as far as Irish Cottage before the hairs along her arms prickled uncomfortably. Too wise by now to ignore the warning, the redhead melted against the ivy-covered chimney.

A bipedal Shadow Fae stalked past, fading in and out of sight. It would have been Ryna's height if not for its hunched shoulders, but the glint of ebon fangs convinced her it was far from powerless. "I can smell you," it whispered. "I can smell your fear."

Don't move, Ryna told herself, trying not to tremble. *It's bluffing.*

"I know where you are."

It's getting closer…

"Come out and play, little mortal."

Forgive me, Ryna begged the absent Mother Goosed, hid Phoenix's staff among the vines, and charged.

She was quick—but it was expecting her. The creature lunged, catching the makeshift weapon in its mouth. Acrid smoke rose in tendrils where its teeth contacted the wood; Ryna let out a yell and yanked, but the creature would not budge.

The tendrils became plumes; the staff blackened, charred, and snapped in half.

Ryna staggered backwards.

The thing pounced.

"Yah!" the Gypsy cried, swinging the remaining portion of the stick like a club.

It slowed but did not stop the Fae, though the stick broke a second time.

With her last, fleeting thought, the Gypsy sent up a prayer that Phoenix would find her staff before the Shadows did.

"Danny?" Phoenix pushed the heavy door shut. The house smelled warmly of soup and fresh-baked bread. "Christine, you home?"

"Hey, sis! Perfect timing—we're in here!"

Phoe kicked off her shoes and lined them neatly by the door, then padded after his voice. She paused in the kitchen's doorway; Christine was putting bread on the cooling rack, and Daniel had a knife in his hand and a mound of vegetables around him. He turned and playfully pegged his wife with an end-piece of carrot.

Phoenix smiled. "Your kids are going to have the happiest memories in the world—you know that, right?"

Daniel waggled his eyebrows suggestively.

Christine blushed an angelic shade of rose.

Phoenix laughed. "Should I be giving you two a moment?"

"Nah—I think we're caught up for the next hour or two," Danny teased. "Dinner's late for a reason."

"Daniel!" Christine cried. And chucked a potholder at him.

"Oh, as if Phoe and Ryna never have similar delays," he protested.

Christine shot her husband a quick, warning look, and hastily suggested Phoe give the soup a stir.

"Oh, Phoe, I'm sorry," Daniel said, suddenly chagrined, and hugged her from behind. "I didn't think."

"That's okay," Phoe said with an uncomfortable shrug. "She's—she has some things she has to take care of."

Daniel raised his eyebrows at her, questioning.

"She's okay, though," she added hastily. "We all are—I just didn't feel like going home to an empty vardo quite yet."

"Our fortune," Christine said firmly. "It means we get to have you join us for your birthday dinner."

"Thanks." Phoe shook off her funk. "You want me to set the table?"

"Go for it, sis. We got some new soup bowls as wedding gifts—they're in the cupboard with the plates."

The bowls were a lovely shade of dark blue and would hold enough soup to stuff even the heartiest eater. They were also from Pendragon—Phoe recognized the potter's stamp on the bottom. She wondered with a wry grin if they had been last-minute purchases. She set them down on the dining room table and had begun to dole out napkins when the doorbell chimed.

Christine emerged from the kitchen dusting her hands on her apron, a puzzled frown creasing her brow. "Now who could that be?"

She disappeared into the parlor and around the corner—Phoe heard the door unlatch, followed by Claire Saunders' fussing voice: "Who on earth owns that *awful* truck in your driveway?"

"Save yourself, kiddo," Daniel said under his breath as he headed to his bride's rescue. "It's too late for me."

"Daniel and I have company," Christine said politely, "so I'm afraid we won't be able to talk with you long."

"Well, we just came by to drop some things off."

Despite herself, Phoe hoped for a dessert… maybe even the one with the little chocolate curls on the top…

"Cardboard boxes?" Phoe could hear the raised eyebrows in her brother's voice. Their parents—*his* parents—*never* used cardboard boxes. They were far too peasant.

"Some of my sister's things," Robert said, his voice flat. "Emily willed them to you and your… children."

Phoe's tanned skin made a strange contrast against the crumpled white napkin in her fist. *Willed?*

Christine's voice: "Oh, Danny, Aunt Ily… I'm so sorry."

"Her… 'partner'… called us last Monday." There was a sneer to Claire's words. "She died two days before your wedding."

Two days before? Then how had Ryna—

"When is the funeral?" Christine asked softly.

"They already had it."

Phoenix clutched the napkin harder, felt the sharp stab of fingernails against her palm.

"And you didn't tell us? *Jesus*, Mom!"

The sharp crack of flesh on flesh, Robert's implacable words. "Thou shalt not take the Lord's name in vain. She lived a life of sin. She brought it on herself."

"God damn it, Dad, she was your *sister*! How can you—"

Another sharp crack.

Sullen silence.

"Get. Out."

Two tears beaded on the table. Phoenix squeezed her eyes shut, wishing she could close her ears to the shrill voice of the woman who had been her mother.

"You see what happened to your aunt, and still you encourage your sister's perversion? You're signing her death warrant yourself, Daniel Michael Saunders!"

"Out!"

The door slammed.

Phoenix stood, trembling, trying to remember to breathe. She bit her lip against the hitch that had developed somewhere around her heart.

"Hey, hey, hey."

Instinctively Phoenix turned, buried her face in her brother's shirt, felt his strong arms surround her.

"I'm sorry you had to hear that, Phoenix," Christine said gently. Phoe could feel her delicate hand stroking her hair. "I'm sorry you had to grow up with that."

"But it doesn't make sense!" Phoe choked on a hiccup. "Ryna said she saw her, but I never did, and I yelled at her, and—"

"Shh, shh." Daniel squeezed her extra tight. "Ryna loves you, and she knows *you* love *her*. That's all that matters. Everything else will fix itself."

Phoe nodded miserably and sniffled.

And wished she could believe him like she had when she was a child.

◇ ◇ ◇

"You've been quiet all night."

Liam wrenched himself away from Phoe's journal to meet Elise's eyes. An oversized T-shirt draped over her generous curves as she leaned against the doorway. She probably thought it a casually enticing pose. To be fair, her attire *did* reveal a decent amount of leg, but Liam wasn't in the mood to humor her hormones.

She pushed away from the wall, padded towards him. "What are you reading?"

"Something one of my friends wrote." He shrugged, shifted a little in the papasan. One good thing about being short—it sure made curling up with a good book easier.

"From home?"

"Yeah."

Elise perched next to him, ran fingers through his hair. "You miss her?"

"It's hard not to miss close friends," Liam said, carefully closing the book. She didn't deserve to see Phoe's writing, not even a glance—it was too private, and Elise could never appreciate the beauty of the soul transposed onto the spiral-bound paper he held.

To his surprise, though, Elise nodded and rose, compassion in her eyes. "I'll leave you to it, then… come to bed whenever you're ready."

Liam grasped her hand, looked up at her with a gratitude he truly felt.

She squeezed his hand a moment before releasing it, then padded toward the bedroom. She paused in the doorway. "Lyre?"

"Yes?"

"Why don't you drop me off at work tomorrow—that way you can take the truck, explore a little. Maybe if you got to know the area you wouldn't feel so homesick."

Liam blinked. He'd been planning to ask for the keys in another day or so, but if she was feeling generous… "Thanks. I think that would help a lot."

She nodded again, and disappeared… leaving Liam in the small pool of light from the reading lamp. He waited a moment, then carefully opened Phoe's journal to the spot his finger held.

It had grown easier to read as he'd immersed himself in his love's world. Something to look forward to more than resent. True, she and Ryna had shared good times—and some bad—but those times were over. Soon she'd be writing beautiful, loving words about him… and, having read what he would bet Ryna had not, he could be everything Phoenix wanted…

…and he would do it better than Ryna *ever* had.

◇ ◇ ◇

Phoenix woke from dreams of Shadows and terror to find an angel hovering over her.

"Shhh, shhh. Only a dream," the red-haired vision soothed.

"Ryna?" Phoe squinted in the dim morning light. Her voice refused to work right, and the world was a shifting mass of fuzzy blobs without her glasses. She scrubbed at her face and sat up. Where was Karma?

"It's me." The Ryna-blob gingerly sat on the edge of the bed. "Are you all right?"

"Uck. Dreams. Need glasses."

"Here." The Ryna-blob retrieved them from the ledge surrounding the bed.

Phoenix clumsily put them on. They were all spotty, but at least it was an improvement. "What time is it?"

"A little after seven—Listen, Phoe, I can't stay long…"

"*Seven*? How did you get here at seven in the morning?"

"That's not important. I told you I'd come, and I did."

"You did." A tiny smile spread across Phoe's face. The world began to clear a little, though it still felt like a happy dream to have Ryna near. "You came. Will you be at Rehearsals tonight?"

Regret fluttered across the tiny elfin face. "You know I can't, Phoe."

"Why not?"

"I can't."

"Patty's suspending your pay until you return." The moment the words fled her lips, Phoenix wished she could take them back. Ryna didn't need this, not now. She had enough to deal with already... stupid, *stupid* out-of-bed grogginess that made her say the first thing that came to mind...

The redhead looked pained. "Believe me, Phoenix, if there was something I could do, I would... but this is the only way."

"There's always another way," Phoenix countered stoutly. "All we have to do is think of it. We're a team, Ryna... you and me, our family..."

"We *are* a team—I need you to be my other half, here."

Phoe frowned groggily. Why did Ryna have to be so *stubborn*? "If this was going to work your way, it would have already. Please—let's give something else a chance... trust *us* the way you want *us* to trust *you*..."

"I do trust you... but I think freshly out of bed might not be the best time to discuss this." Ryna's expression softened. "It's early; you're tired..."

Phoe had to admit, she *was* having trouble keeping her eyes open. Her head nodded once, against her will.

"Poor love," Ryna crooned, delicately removing Phoenix's glasses and setting them aside. "I'm sorry I woke you..."

"No... no... Glad you did..." Phoe's protest came out all bleary as she snuggled down, dreams already dragging hard at her consciousness. "Wanted (yawn!) to see... you..."

"And now you've seen me," she said as covers snugged over Phoe's shoulders. "And now you can go back to sleep."

"Okay..." Phoe yawned again, fading. "Love you..."

"I love you too."

Soft lips pressed against Phoe's—and she knew no more.

Liam rose from the bed and stood over Phoenix a moment, fingers pressed to his lips, holding the precious feel of his love to them.

It had been a mistake to come so early and wake her—so recent from sleep, she wasn't as easily swayed to his thinking. He'd have to remember that in the future.

Still, it had been the only way... any later in the day and he would've risked running into the other Gypsies—plus, he'd needed to return Phoe's journal without her seeing it, and that required her to be either gone or unconscious. Thank God he'd learned that sleep trick to lull his sisters after nightmares... with any luck, she'd remember that he'd been here, and a soft warmth of love, and a longing to see him again—but no more.

Her chest rose and fell gently under the blankets. Liam's hands itched to reach out, touch her...

He curbed the desire. Much as he longed to feel her skin under his hands, it would be cheap without the soft look of need in her eyes... and he would not get that now. Better to walk away.

A quick peek out the trailer door revealed the Gypsies' camp empty—Ryna's hell-cat familiar hissed from under the vardo's tire where he'd kicked the beast. Liam ignored it as he snuck out of the place his love called home and headed up the trail to the parking field.

◇ ◇ ◇

"It figures that Patty would double the price of the showers," Tanek groused. "As if a quarter for a minute and a half of water wasn't bad enough."

How can they be so concerned over the price of a stinking shower when Ryna's still gone? Phoenix brooded as they tromped past Flying Buttress Stage on the way to Rehearsals. She'd been in a foul mood ever since waking to find herself alone... and it'd been that much worse for the vague knowledge that Ryna had been there and she'd been too groggy to appreciate it.

Tremayne remained silent, his gaze distant. *He* would've been able to stay awake. In fact, he would probably give his fingering hand for even a moment with his daughter... and here Phoe'd had the opportunity he desperately wished for and had blown it. *Stupid, stupid, stupid,* she cursed herself.

"Group hug!" someone trumpeted as the Gypsies neared Bedside Manor, and Phoenix abruptly found herself amidst a mass of peasants in jeans and T-shirts.

The unexpectedness of it jolted her from her self-deprecation. "Save yourselves," she stage-whispered, though immeasurably grateful to see her friends. "There's no reason for us all to suffer. Escape while you can!"

"Too late," said Marcus. "The pink pestilence has spotted us." He sounded awfully cheery about it.

"And me without my plague pouch," griped Mutch.

The youngest rookie giggled.

"*Pee*-poles! Get in a *cir*cle!"

"Shall we go make an amoeba?"

Phoenix grinned at the fellow who played Puddle—she almost didn't recognize him clean and articulate. He grinned back, gray-blue eyes sparkling. And nose-tagged her.

"Gah!" Phoenix swiped at her nose as the group gamely formed an oval. The Gypsies stuck together, as always, but Phoe noticed that the peasants tidily flanked her family.

It was, she reflected, a much nicer thing to shield her than thoughts of extra quarters for a shower.

* * *

"We think there's a connection between Ryna and the nasty black spot by the Maypole that gives everybody headaches."

Phoenix's mind lurched to a halt.

Mutch snorted. "Subtle, Ilya."

The street urchin shrugged. "Just sayin'."

Phoe gazed at the others seated around the table in Jack's trailer: Marcus, Jack, and Laine. They looked more dismayed at Ilya's bluntness than shocked at her announcement. To her credit, Phoe remembered to pick her jaw up off the table before attempting to use it for speech. "I think I need to go out that door and come in again, just to be sure this isn't the Twilight Zone."

"Sit." Marcus had a hand on her leg before she could so much as rise.

An expectant pause reigned; finally the Gypsy gathered wits enough to form a reply—though she couldn't keep the wary note from her voice. "Why would you think that?"

Jack sighed—apparently this wasn't at all how he had planned things as going. "A string of coincidences, really."

"I don't know if anyone else has noticed," Laine added.

Phoenix was bloody glad they hadn't. The last thing the Gypsies needed was people connecting Liam and the burned patch with—

She caught herself mid-thought. They hadn't mentioned Liam at all. So why in the world…? "What coincidences?" she asked.

Marcus ticked the points off on his fingers. "Everyone's stuff disappears—then Ryna's nowhere to be found, and suddenly that black patch starts giving Bright Ones headaches. And people's stuff starts coming back—although, as a warning, the village gossip is hinting that you Gypsies took it, since Niki was the one to find Nora's mug."

"WHAT?!"

"Not that anyone's really listening," Ilya pointed out. "But still."

Phoe put her head in her hands. The other last thing they needed…

Still, the peasants had a point—she'd been so wrapped up in worry for her love that she hadn't made the connections. The question was—what did it mean?

"And we… *felt around*… a little last Sunday," Laine said. "We didn't get any huge answers or anything—mostly pieces of a puzzle with no idea what the picture's supposed to look like—but we wanted to talk with you before we tried the other Gypsies."

Phoenix weighed her options. The peasants were sharp—they'd put together clues her entire family hadn't even seen. They were obviously just worried about what was going on and wanted to help.

Could they, though? If Ryna didn't want the other Gypsies involved, Phoe couldn't imagine she'd want people *outside* her family getting into this… but then, the peasants might go to the Gypsies after talking to her if she didn't convince them not to—and that could open up a whole new can of worms.

"You're right," Phoe admitted reluctantly. "Something's up, although I'm not sure how your observations fit into it. Ryna ran into some… unpleasant business, and she's off taking care of it."

"Unpleasant in a Magick sort of way?" Marcus hazarded.

A hesitant nod.

"Why didn't you tell me last Monday?" Mutch demanded, hurt.

Phoe gave her an odd look. "Because I feel like a nutcase saying it in my own head? Besides, the others are trying to keep it under wraps… it's not the sort of thing you really want as general knowledge, you know?"

Jack nodded. "Fair enough."

"You know we'll help, though, right?" Ilya said.

The Gypsy gave her a fond smile. "Thanks." She looked around the table, feeling suddenly blessed. These people, these friends, were laying their swords at her feet… and she hardly even knew them.

She wondered if they knew what they were getting into. Had she, last year, when she'd told Ryna that her place was at the Gypsy's side?

Perhaps she had, in some corner of her heart… after all, this wasn't the first life she'd faced darkness. *It's the same way for the peasants,* she realized with quiet certainty. They were all tied, though she didn't understand how or why… but these swords they offered wore the scars of many lifetimes' battles.

Even if the Gypsies didn't know it… even if Ryna didn't know it… Phoenix did.

She bowed her head briefly, then raised it. When she spoke, the words rang strangely.

"I accept your offer of aid, and pledge mine to you as well. If you need me, I am there. If you call, I will come."

◇ ◇ ◇

"It sleeps…"

"Shall we wake it…?"

"No, no, give it our message in fear and dreams…"

Liam's eyes flew wide. Beside him, Elise hmmed and shifted in the dark. For a moment he dared not move—simply breathed, simply tried not to draw the attention of the small, roach-like Fae that skittered from shadow to shadow, dancing attendance on the Three.

The Three.

His heart turned to ice. He could feel their attention on him—cold, calculating. He glared up at the ceiling, tried to make his voice hard and peevish. "What in God's name are you doing here?"

"Nothing in *God's* name..." they chorused, voices dissonant.

Liam scowled harder. He was not in the mood for smartass comments. "State your business and be gone. This is not your place."

"We bring news..."

"Of the one they call Phoenix..."

"She has gained allies..."

Elise whimpered in her sleep. Liam could feel the creature that belonged to the first voice focus on her hungrily.

"Should this concern me? Who besides the Gypsies could possibly pose a threat?"

Pain lanced his eyes as a vision flashed before him... familiar faces, though unfamiliar clothes. They were gathered with Phoenix in a trailer with light cabinetry and brown-and-avocado upholstery. He recognized the youngest Merry Maid, though he couldn't place the others.

The visions shifted; snippets of days at Pendragon careened through his mind. He snorted, incredulous. *Those* were Phoenix's allies? *They* were what had brought the Three to his bedside in the dark of night?

The... *peasants*?!

Liam choked back laughter. "You woke me to tell me *that*? Off with you. And don't come back without news worth hearing."

Their scorn fouled the air—and then they were gone.

Elise woke with a small cry.

Liam hushed her with a kiss.

"I had the most—"

"I know. It's gone now."

"Eyagh. What is that smell?"

"Garbage truck. We must have left a window open. Sleep now, fair princess."

With a few mumbled incoherencies, she nuzzled into her pillow and obeyed.

Liam stared at the ceiling until the gray of dawn snuck through the thin curtains. Only then did he trust his soul to sleep.

And dreams.

◇ ◇ ◇

Phoenix had a camcorder.

She frowned at it, startled. Her parents owned one, but she'd never been allowed to touch it, and the batteries on Danny's were perpetually out of juice. Nonetheless, it seemed like the most normal thing in the world to have nestled against her palm as she ran around Pendragon. It was late afternoon, cloudy and blustery, the kind of day she adored most. Flakes of snow shot down, sending Phoenix scurrying around before she ran out of tape and decent lighting. She ran and ran, but she never grew tired.

Phoe looked up from the LED screen to find herself outside a little waddle-and-dab hut, its roof the top half of a striped wedge tent. The clanking of hammer and anvil rang through the air. Patrons and rennies swarmed around her. "Where am I?" she asked a man in green tights.

"Why, thou'rt where thou stand'st, m'lady…"

"Oh. Of course. Thank you." As she neared the hut, she suddenly found herself inside a canvas tent. Confused, she ducked through the open flap to a view of Track and the pony rides. The people had disappeared. Odd.

Running on…

Irish Cottage looked fresh and new, though it didn't have the sheep pen. The ugly tent obstructing part of the Green was gone, thank the gods, though a turkey drumstick booth stood near Bedside Manor where the Greek food vendor should've been. She rounded the feast hall's corner… and stopped, awestruck.

A majestic tree stood in the Bear's place. It was not oak, or ash, or willow, or poplar, or spruce, or any other of the hundreds of varieties native to the area. In fact, it wasn't any sort of tree Phoenix had *ever* seen. Its branches sprawled like an oak or maple, but as she walked nearer, entranced, she saw that its leaves were not right for either—they grew in clumps of three with three lobes each. She threw her arms around the soaring trunk in a spontaneous hug—it would've taken at least two more of her to complete the circle.

You are young, so young, it hummed—though it seemed pleased at her presence. Then, *You must hurry. There is much to see and do, and your time runs short…*

Phoenix nodded, sad to let the giant go though she knew it spoke true, and hurried on.

She stumbled on an errant rock in the Narrows; a three-year-old dashed past, making a beeline for the little Hobbit Hole on her left. She followed the child, intrigued. His mother captured him, but Phoe continued on, gingerly opened the little door to reveal a cozy interior. A round stained-glass window faced south, and there was a little fireplace, too—

—and then it disappeared, leaving her facing the familiar line of crafters' booths near Globe Stage.

She stared up at the sky. The snow melted on her face, but it never touched the ground. Grass still grew in patches, but trampled, like at the end of the run. A thought hit her: *Is anyone left in the campground?* Then, *Am I staying with Ryna or Danny, now?*

"Phoenix? It's three in the afternoon. You awake?"

Phoe giggled at Jack's question. Of course she wasn't awake! No real world would act like this...

With that thought her surroundings dissolved, stranding her in a gray mist for a moment before her eyes slid open. "Welcome," she called groggily.

The door handle rattled. "Um, it's locked?"

The Gypsy wasted a moment wishing she had Ryna's telekinesis—even limited as it was. She tumbled out of bed and nearly tripped over the sleeping cat on her way to the door.

Karma glared at her, affronted. Some thanks for sleeping all night on the cold floor to protect her from bad dreams and whatever might come through the door. She indignantly licked her fur back into place.

Phoenix had the grace to apologize and give Karma a quick scratch behind the ears.

Karma rolled over on her back and stretched, hoping for a belly rub, or perhaps even a little scratch under the armpits. No such luck.

"You okay?" the peasant asked, shutting the door behind himself.

"Weird dream," she said, scrubbing at her face with her hands. "I was here, but it kept changing, and sometimes people were there, and sometimes they weren't. The whole thing feels like it'd be important if I could just figure out why. Anyhow. Hi."

"Hi," he returned, plopping down on the bed and giving her back a light scritching. "You up for some mischief?"

Phoe stretched and purred. "Mmmwhat kind of mischief?"

"Weeelll, I talked to some of the peasants, and Moiré, and we were thinking of heading down to the Sprawl of America to catch a movie and a bite to eat and generally cause some mayhem."

The Gypsy cocked her head. Peasants. In a four-story, ninety-seven-acre mall. Rampaging freely.

Phoenix was pretty sure she'd found the recipe for chaos.

"Count me in."

*　　　*　　　*

"I'm telling you, it wasn't a cutlass; it was a *scimitar*! You can't go around calling any old sword a cutlass when it's not!"

Phoenix giggled at the fervency of the bouzouki player's tone. "I believe you, Marcus, but I still say you're going to have to take it up with the toy company."

Laine gave an elaborate sigh. "Mislabeling plastic swords. What *are* these people teaching today's children?"

"Damn right! It's—you're mocking me, aren't you."

The peasantry laughed; the sound echoing through the empty halls.

The Gypsy slurped on the chai that Laine had insisted on purchasing for her and sighed contentedly. Her tummy was full of chocolate-peanut butter ice cream and the most sinfully delicious stuffed mushrooms she'd ever experienced. The movie had been awful, but the cinema had been empty, so she, Jack, Marcus, Laine, the Leper, and Moiré had amused themselves with making smartass comments at the screen.

"Oh, neat!" Jack exclaimed, motioning his comrades to the nearest plate glass window. The security grates had been lowered over the storefronts by the time the movie ended, but the mall was still open and no one particularly wanted to head home.

"Ooooh, I want," Laine said, staring covetously at a swanky denim coat with Renaissance-esque tailoring and the perfect amount of flare at the hips.

"Don't you love it when your tastes come into fashion?" Moiré asked conspiratorially. "I wonder how we missed this before?"

"Amazing how many stores pop out of the woodwork when there isn't anybody to block the view," the Leper marveled.

Phoenix made mental notes of the styling. Ryna needed a decent coat for wearing during shows when the weather grew chill. Cloaks didn't cut it when playing fiddle—even if you were your own space heater. If she liked it, perhaps Elda could make something similar…

But Ryna wouldn't be there to ask when she got home.

The thought hit so hard and so suddenly that Phoe couldn't breathe. It amazed her that she hadn't had more moments like that, given that her last trip to the Sprawl had been during those first blushes of not-yet-admitting-to-love.

"Shall we hit the fourth floor and make fun of the drunk people?" Marcus asked cheerily—and a little louder than strictly necessary.

"As long as we don't actually go into the nightclubs," Laine spoke up. "I had enough drunks grabbing at my tits last weekend to last me a lifetime."

"Here here," Phoe seconded, pushing aside memory. "I had a couple guys all over me like cold, dried oatmeal. And after that food fight last year, I know what that's like."

"Hey, whatever happened to the Bake Off?" Jack asked. "Don't the O'Malleys and the Bernatellis usually do that around Labor Day?"

"Usually," Moiré agreed. "Except this year Patty decided food fights were a bad example for the little patron kids—and without a food fight, there really wasn't much point in doing it."

Laine rolled her eyes. "Lovely."

When they reached the fourth floor, Phoe gaped at the number of men in tight jeans and women in little bits of not much making the rounds. Didn't any of them have to get up for work the next morning? Though really, she supposed, it was none of her business.

"Why, hello, there," a voice called over the throbbing backbeat that spilled into the halls.

Phoenix turned slowly, stomach hardening with dread at the inflection so like Liam's. Joshua smiled down at her, teeth flashing brilliantly white, his arm possessively around Niki. "Hello," Phoe returned guardedly, trying not to feel like a rabbit staring at a fox.

"Came to join us, did you?" Josh enthused.

Phoe felt the sudden need to bathe. It gave her some comfort that the peasants edged closer.

Niki's laughter sounded forced, though her date didn't seem to notice. "Oh, Josh, you're so funny! I'm sure Phoenix has other things to do tonight."

"I'm with the peasants," she said, nudging her glasses up and looking him square in the eye. "We're having fun."

He shrugged broadly, obviously baffled at why someone would prefer their company over his. "Suit yourself."

"Will you be out late tonight, hon?" Niki asked, inviting Phoe closer for a hug.

"I don't know. I'll be home before the sun's up." Then, softly, under cover of their embrace, "Be careful. Watch your drink, and don't go anywhere alone with him."

"I'm dumping my drink down his shorts the first chance I get."

Phoenix tried not to giggle as they parted. "Enjoy yourself."

Niki grinned outright. "Oh, I will, sweetie. C'mon, Josh. I hear a tequila calling my name."

"A call not to be denied..."

"I can't believe she's dating him," Marcus finally said when the pair had gone beyond earshot. He wore a look of stunned disgust.

"She's settling a score," Phoenix assured him. "He took advantage of one of her friends."

"Remind me not to piss off a Gypsy!" the Leper said with a grin.

"Let's head for the casino buffet," Moiré suggested. "By the time we get down there, it should be open—and I could eat their tables bare."

◇ ◇ ◇

Phuro Basil's favorite awl taunted her, displayed precicely in the center of Chapel's walkway—and too far out to allow a safe retrieval.

They knew what she was up to, then. They probably even knew about the small stash of power items hidden under the altar—she'd given up trying to run to the campground with each find.

Was it even a real awl?

Would they know they'd broken her if she stayed inside?

Ryna's pride warred with the hope that if they thought her broken they would revert to simpler tortures...

The metal gleamed in the waxing moonlight. If she didn't try now, would she get another chance? Would they let her have it if she *did* grab it?

She shuddered, remembering the dark teeth that had destroyed Mother Goosed's staff—and then torn at her soul. She'd gone back for Phoenix's staff, but it hadn't been there. The Shadow Fae didn't have it either, though, or they would've flaunted it by now. Doubtless they were waiting to pounce the second she stepped beyond her haven's bounds...

Unless she didn't have to step out...

It was madness. She could no more use Magick effectively here than a mundane could in her own world. It swirled and burst within her every time she tried.

Surely so simple a trick, though? One she had performed for years?

A flutter passed through her soul; she grabbed it and sent it toward the awl like a lasso.

The tool flew at Ryna; with a startled yelp she threw herself to one side. The awl imbedded itself in the wall where she had leaned a second before. Ryna reached out hesitantly to touch it. *I guess it makes sense. Magick must be purer here, so a little goes a long way... and I'm used to using a lot at once.*

When the awl did not move, she boldly wrapped a tiny hand around the worn wooden handle, gave a tug. It freed easily.

The night beyond fell silent—stunned.

Ryna brandished her prize in triumph.

◇ ◇ ◇

"'Allo, Gypsies!"

The familiar, boisterous voice brought a grin to Phoenix's lips. She tossed aside her journal and bounded to the vardo door.

Sure enough, Pierre stood near the fire pit—blond, tan, massive-shouldered, and six-and-a-half feet tall. To prove his sense of humor about the irony of his name, he had settled on a Viking with a corny French accent for his Faire personae.

No one who met him ever forgot his trademark "oh-ho-ho! I shall pill-age your vill-age!"

"Well, hello there, tweety!" he greeted, wrapping her in a bear hug and sweeping her off her vardo porch.

"Flap, flap, sizzle," Phoenix joked as he set her gently to her feet. "What brings you up from the oven of Arizona?"

"Figured I should conquer something besides Scheherazade Faire. And being as this is where my favorite Gypsies stop this time of year…"

Phoe quirked a grin. Given the number of times he'd emerged smiling from Niki's vardo last spring, she bet he had a particular Gypsy in mind. "Niki works grounds crew, but it's about time for her lunch break. I can take you to their headquarters—I'm sure she'd love to see you."

"Am I that obvious?"

"Everyone is around Niki. C'mon, the truck's up top."

"So," Pierre said as they huffed up the trail behind the gamers' camp, "where's your lifemate?"

The Gypsy stumbled—and hoped her companion thought some errant rock had caused it. "She's—she had to take off for a while. Hopefully she'll be back this weekend."

He gave her a shrewd look as they emerged into the parking field. "In other words, if I want details I should ask Niki."

"That'd be best," Phoe said quietly as she unlocked Ryna's truck.

They drove in silence until the dirt road turned to blacktop.

"How goes the writing?"

Phoenix flinched.

"It'll get there." Pierre gave her a sympathetic pat on the arm. "Should I go for strike three?"

It almost made her giggle; she turned left and headed down the bumpy road to the grounds crew's shack. "Here we are," she said as she put the truck in park; Pierre jumped out and dashed around to open her door and offer a hand down. She took it though she didn't need the help. He kissed it gallantly.

Phoenix fought back tears as she hurried to the shack. "Niki?" she called through the screen door.

"Right here, hon," the dancer said, rising from her seat at the scarred Formica table.

"I brought a present for you," Phoe singsonged with forced cheeriness.

"Oh?" Niki let the screen door squeal and slam behind herself—and flew into her visitor's arms with a delighted laugh. "Pierre!"

"Miss me, Gypsy?"

Phoenix ducked her head and snuck off, thankful they were too wrapped up in each other to notice her… even when she started the truck and drove away.

*　　　*　　　*

Night had fallen by the time Phoenix stepped outside her vardo again. The taste of wet earth, wet metal, and wet wood hung heavy in the humid air. Drawing breath felt like drowning, and even the mosquitoes had decided to stay put for the night.

The distant vending machines gave the mist fogging her glasses a surreal, dreamy glow. It was all so eerie and beautiful… a siren's song that called her from her vardo's porch. Up the Olympic Staircase she followed it, between the Maypole and Bardstone, and through the Narrows… past the disembodied echo of swordplay from Globe Stage, past eyes that blinked from darkened shops, up the hill and down, nearing the Bear's bulk.

Even hazy as her mind had become, the sight made Phoenix shiver from more than the damp chill. Every second it seemed nearer the verge of turning and staring at her, until she had veered to the right and followed the ethereal summons towards Sherwood.

Still, she could feel the Bear's wooden eyes on her back, dark and eternal. Perhaps it wasn't such a wise idea to wander a bewitched fairesite alone?

Little difference it makes now, something whispered reasonably in the back of Phoenix's consciousness. *If it wants you, it already has you.*

She knew she should be frightened that the voice didn't worry her—but like everything else, the thought felt misty and distant.

Down, down, past vacant picnic tables and trees that rustled in the still night. Past Woodland, under the Sherwood sign, toward the Secret Garden with its impenetrable darkness and steep, winding paths. Phoenix touched the grapevine gate—and shied away. Something wasn't right…

"You won't fall…" a voice coaxed, shadowy hands like rotted velvet entwining their fingers with hers, pulling her forward.

"Only a little stroll…"

"What could it hurt…"

The gate opened of its own accord, beckoning her onward. Something was *not right…*

Shadows melted from the darkness…

The memory of panther-sharp claws, of warm blood trickling…

"NO!" Phoenix cried, yanking free from the intangible grasp, the almost solid compulsion that strangled her will. And ran.

Down the bottom loop of Gypsy cove she pelted, veering hard to the left and panting up the hill past the Stocks and toward Front Gate. Then left again… she slowed, gasping for air, as she hugged the shops to the right, letting her steps carry her toward the safety of Cottage.

Though it was a Friday night, no orange glow flickered through the windows; no music filled the little thatch-roofed house. Phoenix cursed roundly with what little breath she'd gained and set out at a brisk walk, following Track's fence to the games area.

The BLUE squatted large and dark in her path. As she neared it, she felt only the faint threads of sleep within. How long had she been gone?!

Reality folded; Phoe whipped around as a huge white dog galloped past and disappeared halfway between the BLUE and C-gate. She picked up her pace, thankful for the temporary oasis of light that spilled over the participant-only entrance.

"Hey, Phoenix."

In the seconds it took for her heart to resume beating, Phoe recognized the voice—it belonged to eldest female rookie. "Aubry. Hi."

"Didn't mean to scare you," she apologized.

"Didn't expect another human," Phoenix returned. "Everyone else is asleep."

"We were headed that way ourselves," Kevin told her. "Mom had something else to do tomorrow morning and couldn't get us here on time, so we told her we had friends who could put us up for the night and she drove us down."

Phoe raised an eyebrow. "And do you?"

"Once we got here, yeah. Several times over." Aubry grinned as they started down the Olympic staircase. "It's amazing how many people have extra blankets and space and stuff. I'd figured the place would be packed."

A flicker of pride lifted the vet's heart.

"The little ones are already asleep; a pretty dark-haired girl with bright green eyes and lots of freckles adopted them. Said she always beds down around ten anyway, and—yow!" Kevin cried as he stumbled and went skidding down the length of two stairs.

"Kevin!" Aubry cried.

Phoenix rushed to kneel at his side. "Can you move?" she asked, ignoring the dark chuckle at her back. Every instinct urged flight, but she couldn't leave the rookies undefended.

"Give me a sec," he said, and with a great oomph pushed to his feet. A swath of dirt covered his front, but he seemed otherwise hale.

"Everything moves okay?" Phoe persisted.

He winced, but all limbs responded. "Bloodied the hell out of my hand," he said with a scowl. "Musta caught it on something."

Phoe examined it gently; it was filthy and badly scraped, but didn't appear to need stitches. "I can fix you up at my place."

"I'll meet you at Gillian's tent?" Aubry suggested.

Things skittered behind her. "You okay to get there on your own?" Phoe asked anxiously.

"Oh, yeah—it's only down the row. Thanks for fixing him up."

"Of course," the Gypsy murmured.

The things did not follow the rookie.

"So where is your place?" Kevin asked.

"This way," Phoe said, and almost laughed at his expression as they crossed the road. She remembered her own first venture into the land of the Trailer Gods. Even the smallest of the campers loomed over you, so much larger and more solid than a tent. Surely their inhabitants must be another species of rennie entirely!

And now, after a year on the road, it was simply home. She wondered if her rookie friend would be so impressed if he knew what it was like to live a year without indoor plumbing or consistent electricity. She wondered if it was strange that having this innocent rookie at her side made her feel safe. *He* certainly couldn't protect her from the Shadow Fae… but he *was* another living being. Maybe the Shadow Fae wouldn't attack when somebody who didn't know about them was near?

Something sparkled against the dark wood of her vardo's door, right below the handle. Puzzled, Phoenix reached out. A ring, suspended from a bit of thread…

No. Not *a* ring. Ryna's bond-ring.

Phoe's stomach lurched. How in the world had it gotten here? Had Ryna left it? Had something taken it from her? Why not keep it, then?

How? Why? How? Why?

"Phoenix?"

She shook herself back to reality. "Sorry—what?"

Kevin peered at her in the darkness. "You okay?"

"I'm fine," she said, squeezing the ring so hard the band bit into her skin. "Just—fine." She yanked hard; the thread snapped. The ring found a new home in her pocket. "C'mon in and we'll get you bandaged up."

"Nice," the rookie offered as he stepped inside behind her. "It looks all old and stuff. And hey—you have a cat!"

"Ryna built the vardo a long time ago, so the credit's all hers." Phoenix pulled open the cupboard below the sink and retrieved the First Aid box, the motions giving her precious moments to recover her composure. "And I think the cat has me—her name is Karma."

Karma hopped from the bed to investigate the previously inaccessible cavern.

"Grab the drinking water from the fridge and come into the light, here."

Kevin gamely obeyed, holding out his hand for inspection. "How long have you two—you and Ryna, I mean—been… you know… together?"

Good question, Phoe thought, but decided not to confuse the poor boy with talk of centuries. "We were handfasted last September, after Closing Weekend."

"Handfasted—that's like married, right?"

"That's right."

Karma completed her exploration of the cupboard and sniffed at her guest. He seemed far too busy to shower her with affection—useless two-legged furless. She hopped onto the bed and went back to her nap.

Kevin jerked as the cool liquid hit his wound, but otherwise held admirably still. “When did you know it was going to be forever?”

Phoenix handed him a clean towel and went for the antibacterial spray. “As soon as I saw her. It took us both a bit to realize we were in love, but the first time I laid eyes on her, it seemed important to know her better.”

“Like you’d finally run into someone you were waiting for?”

She looked up from wiping the last bits of the foaming spray from his hand, met his eyes for a moment. “Exactly like that. It felt as if I’d always known her, and figuring out her name was only a formality.”

His eyes held hers, his gaze intense and solemn, and for an instant she could’ve sworn he was far, far older than his years. “What did you do?”

A tiny smile twitched Phoe’s lips as she wound some gauze around his hand. “I stuttered, and stammered, and blushed, and cornered her backstage, and kissed her until she couldn’t think.”

Kevin chuckled. “Apparently it worked.”

“It did at that. There.” Phoenix tucked the last corner into the wrappings and gave it a pat for good measure. “Go up to First Aid and have them change the dressing for you tomorrow, and the costume shop ought to have some scraps of cloth you can use to disguise it. Normally I’d say not to worry about it, but it’s awfully dirty out here.”

“Okay.” He ducked his head a moment to hide a bashful smile. “Thanks—for fixing me up, and the advice, and stuff.”

“My pleasure. Now go and get some sleep; Cast Call comes too early for any being—sane or not.”

“Yes, Herbwoman Phoenix.” A flashed smile, the quiet thump of the door shutting behind him, and he was gone.

And Phoenix was alone with her thoughts.

And her cat.

And the ring.

“You let her get away.”

The voice whispered through Liam’s mind like the wind in the trees near Elise’s tent. He knew the words were not for him, but still they made him uneasy.

“You let the ring get away,” retaliated another voice, this one like stone grinding on stone.

More words followed. Liam did not understand them. Nor, from their harsh sounds, was he certain he wished to.

All at once the discussion stopped.

"It listens," whispered a voice, and Liam felt their attention turn to him. He wanted to curl up to protect himself from the intensity of those invisible eyes, but forced himself to remain still and silent on the air mattress he shared with Elise.

Calmly.

Heart pounding.

"There is always the tool."

"The instrument."

"Yes, the pawn."

With a sickening thud, Liam realized that returning to his own world had not changed one important thing…

He was still food.

And they were hungry.

Pendragon Renaissance Faire

Weekend Five: Plaid to the Bone

~*~

From Bay-Knock-Bairn to Ab-eer-deen, they've all came oot tae toss a caber. Kilts and bagpipes are the order of the day, as the Scots invade. See the famous Highland Games competition, where Scottish strongmen ruck up their kilts and roll up their sleeves to prove their mettle. Stout Tasting and Fyne Scottish Dance, Haggis and Bagpipes. Ale and "Och du Caber" (Theme sponsored by The Royal Ale Brewing Company)

~*~

"Is Ryna back?"

"Is Ryna here?"

"How's Ryna doing?"

"Where's Ryna?"

"Is Ryna still gone?"

"When's Ryna planning to return?"

The barrage nearly made Phoenix wistful for the corny Scotsman jokes that usually flew on Celtic weekend. *Phuro* Basil, beside her, answered their fellow rennies with courtesy and a regretful smile: no, no, as well as can be expected, she's not here this weekend, yes, hopefully soon.

Phoe marveled grumpily at his patience as she wrapped the gray morning sky around herself like the cloak she'd forgotten back at the vardo and willed herself invisible in the shelter of his comforting presence. She was tired of pretending it was all no big deal, tired of half-truths and polite evasions. She'd come to Cast Call hoping that "Swing Low" would make her feel part of something despite the leaden weight of Ryna's bond-ring nestled against her heart... but now she wondered if it was worth dealing with the masses.

"Hello? Hello, *pee*-poles!"

Although, really, the masses had nothing on Patty.

Attention reluctantly shifted to the stage.

"I just wanted to start off by saying that whomever gave me this lovely card—Ray Kiffer?—I don't know who you are, and it really *is* a wonderful card, but I can't accept it. You see, my name is spelled P-a-t-t-*y*, not P-a-t-*i-e*. Two *t*'s and a *y*, peoples. And Kate is with a *k*, not a *c*. So you see, the card isn't addressed to me at all!" She tittered like an annoying cartoon.

"Who's Ray Kiffer?" Phoenix whispered.

Phuro Basil shrugged. "Either a kiss-arse or the latest failed attempt at satire."

"Okay, now, before we go to the announcements, I just want to remind you all to put on sunscreen even though it's cloudy—the guests don't pay to see little lobsters running around in costume! And such *won*derful costumes, too… so many of you wearing kilts in honor of the weekend! Isn't it just so much more fun when you get into the spirit of things?"

"Phoe—can I talk to you a sec?"

The Gypsy looked up at Marcus, stomach twisting at his apprehensive expression. "Sure." She exchanged quick glances with the rest of her family before following him to where there were fewer ears. "What's wrong?"

"Last night a pile of the missing stuff turned up in the Chapel," he said. "Couple of folks in the Militia found it under the altar, I guess. They'll be announcing it up there pretty soon… but I wanted to warn you that the egg lady is putting it around that she saw Ryna dump the stuff there."

"What?! But—that's impossible!" Phoenix spluttered. "Besides, if she saw it, why wasn't *she* the one to find the stuff?"

The musician sighed. "Hopefully everyone else will wonder that, too—we're doing our best on damage control, but I wanted to make sure you were prepared."

"Thanks for the warning."

Marcus gave her an encouraging smile and returned to where the peasants always sat in middle of the left section of benches.

Phoe sighed. Whatever virtues "Swing Low" held, they couldn't possibly outweigh sitting through another moment of this crap. As Perky Patty tittered on, Phoenix trudged off toward Sherwood, her scowl matching the grim rumbling of thunder overhead.

"Some morning, huh?"

Phoenix glanced over to a well-dressed gentleman of her own years. His short, sandy-blond hair ruffled with the wind. "Yeah."

"Here. I hate to see a pretty lady cold and miserable," he said, wrapping his brown corduroy cloak around her shoulders.

Phoenix snuggled guiltily into the cocoon of warmth. "What about you?"

He waved her off. "I'm with the Magistrate's Entourage—our trailers are over this direction, and I've got a spare I can grab."

"Thank you," she said, insufficiently, as they passed under the Sherwood sign.

"My pleasure, dear Gypsy." A gallant bow, a kiss of her hand, and he hurried off, cutting a stunning picture in his dark brown brocade doublet and black hose.

"If you don't want him, can I have him?" Niki called.

Phoe joined her on Caravan Stage, holding the cloak up so it wouldn't drag in the dirt. "He'd probably be happier with you."

"Pish, hon."

"It's true. No one ever handed over their cloak when I was a peasant."

Niki grinned through the steam rising from her mug. "I keep telling you, dear, cleavage attracts chivalry."

"And free coffee," Phoe teased.

"And free coffee," Niki repeated. "*Always* free coffee."

Liam huddled, scowling, in the wooded area behind the shop Elise tended. He felt like someone had taken sandpaper to his eyes, and his stomach roiled with every sip of the herby tea Elise had made him promise to drink. He *hated* tea. And he hated the damned outfit she'd stuffed him in, cooing over how she'd make a rennie of him yet. The shirt's sleeves were awful and straight and bunched under his ill-fitting bodice, the muffin cap kept falling over his eyes, and the skirt…! He'd never witnessed a more hideous shade of brown. He looked like one of the damn kids that worked the RFC booths, and if he had to put up with any more of that woman fussing over his case of the "faire crud" he would send her to the Shadow Realms personally and let them snack on *her* for a while.

What in God's name had he ever seen in her, aside from free lodging? She was like all the others… fun for a roll in the sack, but bloody annoying beyond that. He moodily flicked a caterpillar off the table beside him. Stupid bint.

The quiet scraping of the back door announced Elise's arrival. "How's my patient?"

Liam checked his temper. There was only one way to put a stop to all this. He slid his hand up the inside of her skirt, looked up at her with carefully designed heat. "Well enough to play doctor."

She giggled at first, playfully protesting that someone would find them… but her protests didn't last long.

Liam smiled. They never did.

"Bless this house and all within, and may none of them get hit with the telephone poles they're throwing around out there." Kiss. Scuff-scuff. Hand-plant.

"*Dia dhuit*, Phoenix," Auntie Molly greeted from the *seanchaí* chair.

Phoe nodded in return. The house was unusually bare—just Molly and Eryn. "Good day to you as well. No visitors, and most of your kin gone… you haven't been hit with the plague, I hope?"

"Nope! But Brigid got dumped last week," the youngest O'Malley piped up tactlessly.

"I see." Phoenix said sagely. "I'd best see to her, then… a broken heart is a terrible ailment."

"Bless you," Molly said as Phoe headed for the kitchen.

True to form, Brigid stood by the sink, her scrubbie rasping against one of Cottage's brass platters as she polished it to a dull shine. "He made me pick between him and Faire," she announced without preamble—and then the floodgates opened. "I told him it's only fifteen days out of the whole year, and that I've been coming out here with Auntie Molly since before I can remember. Ma even offered to get him a guest pass—but it had to be his way or nothing. He said if I really loved him, I'd quit." She sniffled. "Self-centered egotist pig."

The Gypsy propped her staff against the wall and wrapped her arms around the young Irishwoman from behind. "I know it feels like the end of the world right now… but you *will* find somebody who won't try to manipulate you like that," she said softly. "I'm proud of you for standing up to him—it only would've gotten worse."

"I know." The vigorous scrubbing paused as Brigid leaned back with a weary sigh. "If *he'd* really loved *me*, he would've at least tried coming here—even for a day. And now I've got to spend the rest of the quarter staring at the back of his head in English class."

Phoe frowned as a sudden thought smacked her upside the head. "But if he's never been out here… who sent Prince Gwydion with that rose?"

Brigid whipped around, eyes huge.

"Your turn to get courted this year, sweetheart," Phoe said, squashing the lump that rose in her throat. "And may this one be far more worthy than the last."

"You mean—you think—I never would've—oh, thank-you-thank-you-thank-you!" the O'Malley lass cried, squeezing Phoenix hard. "Oh, oh, I've got to find the prince and have him carry a message for me!" She pulled away, fumbled with the hook-and-eye latch to the kitchen door, and bolted outside—nearly bowling over three patrons on her way to First Aid gate.

Things would be okay… they always were in the end, no matter the heartbreak in the between-times.

With a small smile, Phoe carefully closed the door.

Three elephants stood between Track and Cottage.

Ryna, caught mid-step on Shepherd's Green, stared stupidly at the pachyderms: big, gray, lumbering, dusty, and seemingly unconcerned with the fact that—as Peyton would've said—they weren't in Kansas anymore.

The Gypsy narrowed her eyes. *Three* elephants, even though the baby had gone off to star on the silver screen half a decade ago. It meant this was probably another echo… like with Liam at the Bear or the long-gone landmarks that popped up. Just Pendragon's grounds remembering days past. It made Ryna smile, though. She wondered if it had been an especially happy moment for the elephants? Maybe someone had given them some extra hay, or a slurp of their lemonade, or whatever it was that elephants considered a treat…

A terrier's shrill yapping sliced her musings. *Oh. No. Not—*

Ryna dropped into a sprint, stomach twisting with dread for what she knew she could not stop.

Yap! Yapyapyap—

"Lady, I told you, get your dog away from—"

"No!" she cried, reflexively lashing out with Magick to halt the terrier's impending doom. Her world reeled, but the image flickered—

—and the elephant became one of the Shadow Fae, hulking and ugly. It snatched a bundle of calico fury with one overlong arm, slammed it hard against the ground, and tossed it.

The Magicks snapped back on Ryna, sending her sprawling.

A woman screamed.

A limp Yorkie landed with a sick *thud* at Ryna's feet.

The Gypsy choked back a cry as she fell to her knees beside the tiny, broken body, Juniper's mournful howl echoing in her memory.

Karma looked up at her, pleading, bloody, pained, from where the little dog had been.

Ryna let out a wail—it really *was* Karma. Perhaps not physically, but her beloved fuzzy had come looking for her, and now the Shadow Fae… The Gypsy gathered her cat into her arms and curled into a ball, rocking, rocking as Karma faded away and the sun hurtled toward the west…

"No," she whispered. "No… no… no…"

"My thanks," Liam told the vendor, accepting the small plate of chocolate-covered strawberries. They numbered among the things he'd missed over the last hellish months as he walked past the booth time after time, remembering the taste but unable to satisfy his craving.

Perhaps he would share some with Elise; he found her remarkably less annoying after their little interlude replaced the energy the Shadow Fae had stolen from him. She was too tired now to do much fussing—and that meant *he* got to take care of *her*.

Every woman he'd bedded had been like that. He'd learned the trick in high school: start small—feed the lady flattery and bits of energy like strawberries until she acquired a taste for it. Then move on to chocolate—a kiss, a caress. They protested—but what woman, when pressed, would forgo chocolate? They only required a little Magick, a little directed will slipped into the delivery to make it harder to resist, harder to live without.

Liam drank of the power in every sigh, every whimper, every twitch drank deeply, let it fill him, plied them with dipped strawberries until they gave just a little more. Hazed with pleasure and Magick, they soon surrendered control. And the power that came of that…

Liam licked the melted chocolate from his fingers.

Let the Shadow Fae come.

◇ ◇ ◇

"There are never any peasants around when you need them," Phoenix groused as she neared the games area. To be fair, at this hour most of them were on Peasant Parade, but Phoe didn't know the route well enough to track them down, and she wasn't in the mood for Closing Gate Show, where they would roost afterwards.

She had almost given up hope when she spotted Hayrold in the open area by the BLUE, finger held out temptingly and a sign around his neck that clearly read "DON'T PULL MY FINGER."

Despite this warning, a blond teenage boy grabbed the outstretched digit.

"I wouldn't do that," Hayrold cautioned.

"Why not?" the patron demanded, still holding Hayrold's finger.

"Sign says not to."

"Pull it, Brandon—pull it!" one of the teen's friends dared.

Brandon did.

Hayrold squeezed a great stream of water from the bota between his legs; it hit Brandon square in the chest, causing laughter from his posse and cussing from the teen himself.

The group moved on, and Phoenix started to approach her friend when a man and woman, having seen the show, retrieved their daughter from the quarter rock bin and pushed her forward. The seven-year-old laboriously read Hayrold's sign and turned back to her parents.

"Go on, sweetie," the father urged.

"But his sign says not to," the girl protested.

"It's okay, Caroline. Really. He wants you to."

"I won't be held responsible for the consequences," Hayrold told them.

"I don't think—"

"It's okay. Really. I promise."

With a shrug and a sigh, Caroline reached out and pulled the peasant's finger.

Hayrold unceremoniously sprayed her parents.

The woman shrieked.

The man spluttered.

Carolinc grinned.

"This is outrageous!" The man glared at Hayrold. "You can be sure management will hear of this!"

"Hey, I warned you! You made her do your dirty work. Shame-shame!" The peasant winked at Caroline, turned, and toddled away.

Phoenix fell in step with him as he neared the Hay Roll. "I hope you don't get in trouble for that."

"What's Patty gonna do, dock my pay?" Hayrold cast her a wry grin. "It was only water."

"Point," she admitted.

"So, what's up?"

"Mostly wondered if the peasants have anything planned for tomorrow—you've been quiet this year."

"Hard to get enthusiastic over bits with *that* in charge," he said, making a rude gesture in the direction of the Bedside Manor offices. "It's always nice to know that the elephant is more entertaining than the entertainers."

"*What*?!"

"Oh, you didn't hear about that? Patty gave out *one* GEM last Sunday—to the elephant for doing a kilt check during Parade."

"What about Chez Privy? Wasn't that last Saturday?"

"Yes."

"Did she say *why* we didn't get one?"

"She said we were only entertaining ourselves—I made a guest book so we can prove her wrong. We're thinking about doing it tomorrow." The peasant untangled his bota from between his legs and raised it to take a swig—and frowned, giving it a shake before settling it at his side. "Let's detour to the iced lemonade booth before Drum Jam—I need a refill."

So *that* was how Hayrold could stand to wear his cloak and hood on hot days—a bota full of iced lemonade between his legs! It beat the hell out of a bodice cooler, but… "Doesn't iced lemonade make your bota all sticky and gross?"

"Yeah…"

"Well, how do you clean it out?"

Hayrold grinned at her. "Whiskey."

* * *

"Tea anyone?" Phoenix offered, poking her head out her vardo's lace curtain. Tremayne, Esmerelda, and *Phuro* Basil turned to her, firelight flickering across their features. Phoenix smiled. This, at least, was beautifully familiar.

"Do you have any apricot?" Tremayne requested.

PALIDYN 03

"As good as done." Phoenix ducked back in her vardo, dug around in the back of the tea cupboard, and emerged with a battered tin. She prepared a cup for herself as well—its slightly sweet, mellow taste suited the night.

Karma yowed weakly from the bed.

Phoenix frowned, concerned. The calico's energy felt… broken. "You okay, kitty?"

Karma yowed again to get her point across. She was hurt, frustrated, hurt, despairing, hurt, worried, hurt… and if this two-legged furless couldn't bring Karma's person back, the least she could do was provide some snuggles.

Thankfully Phoenix got the hint, left one of the mugs of tea on the counter, and carried Karma outside with her.

"Thank you," Tremayne said as Phoe handed him the remaining mug.

"Karma didn't want to be alone," Phoe explained as she took a seat on a log near the fire. Heat radiated gently against her skin, welcome in the night's growing chill.

"Hey Phoe, you coming to Funky Formal?"

She turned to stare incredulously at Tanek, decked out in spandex, leather, and… well… *gear*… was the only polite way Phoenix could think to put it.

He gave a charmingly sheepish smile and spread his hands wide. "A Gypsy must try, yes?"

"I am *not* going to ask which superhero you're going as."

"Wise choice," Niki complimented as she emerged from her vardo in a Catwoman suit. The lovely purr that underscored her voice added volumes to the illusion.

Elda smirked. "You won't get ten feet if Pierre sees you in that."

The dancer flashed her a dazzling smile. "That's the point."

"I thought this was supposed to be a super*hero* party," Tanek complained.

Niki shrugged eloquently. "I'm sure she's someone's hero."

"Besides, Niki looks too good in that outfit to *not* wear it," Kaya said from the doorway of her vardo.

Every eye rounded. She still wore her form-fitting chemise, the artistically torn bottom half revealing an admirable amount of gold leggings. They glimmered faintly in the firelight, as did the sparkling makeup she'd applied to all exposed skin. A biker jacket with chains of Gypsy coins gave the final touch.

"Hot stuff," Esmerelda complimented. "Who are you supposed to be?"

"Short-Chicks-Kick-Ass Woman. You almost ready in there, Toby?"

"Hey, you try arranging all these—dear gods!" Tobaltio spluttered to a stop in his doorway. "I might *ask* you to kick my ass if you do it in *that*."

Tremayne sipped his tea and smiled. "You'll have to get in line."

Kaya laughed. It sounded like faeries dancing. She kissed her husband affectionately on the top of the head. "You're first on my list."

Toby recovered enough to strike a pose. His flame-colored spandex sported random bits of tinfoil, pipe cleaners, and other oddities. "I am—Too-Weird-For-Words Man!"

"No argument here." Tanek poked him.

Tobaltio poked back.

"Ah, enter Grandma Garage Sale!" *Phuro* Basil greeted, standing, and for the first time Phoenix noticed that he had heavily accessorized with strings of garlic.

"Grandpa Garlic," *Baba* Luna returned, hugging him as best she could around her layers of junk. Phoenix had never seen more strange hats, jewelry, and handbags on one person—and yet Luna looked more colorful than gaudy. *Must be an old lady thing,* Phoenix reflected. Some of those prints had *never* been intended for simultaneous usage… *especially* not with that sombrero.

"You sure you won't come?" Niki asked, turning to Phoenix.

Phoe shook her head, but smiled. "I hate that tent enough when it's *not* flooded with annoying lights, loud music, and drunk rennies. I might hop up later to see the costumes, though."

"Okay," Niki agreed reluctantly as the other revelers bid their farewells and disappeared into the night. She was the last to leave, glancing twice over her shoulder.

The campground felt strangely hollow with them gone—the world reduced to a little island of flickering light against the eternity of the night sky. Phoenix stroked Karma, hearing a memory echo quietly through time…

The crackle-snap of the fire, the warmth on her face and the cold night all around as wind tufted at her ears. The night so ripe with possibility, and yet, so still. And no one in the world but two people in love, wrapped in a cloak.

"And Bea?"

"Yeah?"

"I love you."

The truth in those beautiful green eyes—for an instant almost brown in the darkness. And the only thing she could think to say was, "Oh, good."

"I guess we're all that's left," Esmerelda observed as the smoke fluttered against the stars.

"I guess so," Phoenix agreed.

Tremayne merely stared into the flames.

◇ ◇ ◇

Faire looks so much darker here, Ryna reflected from her perch on one of the boulders that marked Cottage's front lawn. She had grown braver, to venture abroad after dark. Or maybe, a little, had quit caring.

Perhaps this was a new game. Perhaps they wished to make her feel comfortable, and then they would start again. Maybe with visions, or maybe with creeping, enveloping blackness, like the smothering embrace of oblivion…

She tried to reckon how much time had passed, but the days had blended, and the fence bore far more marks than she had etched there. A week, maybe, if she could depend on the moon—pale, distant, and barely past its first quarter. But then, if the sun didn't behave as it should, why would the moon?

Something felt different tonight, though, vibrating slightly below the surface. Maybe there was a corporate party in the tent? Except… the restless, barely concealed energy felt more like a large group of rennies. Like an itch that you couldn't pinpoint, but it was something new. Different. Fascinating.

It fascinated the Shadow Fae, too… she could feel it in them. For good or ill, she did not know, but for now it kept their attention from her.

And that was a blessing indeed.

◇ ◇ ◇

The party was… okay. The costumes were neat, and often outrageous, and that was worth it. Sort of. Maybe.

Phoenix hovered at Cottage's door. Pendragon felt stark and garish with all those strangely dressed people, and the strange music, and the strange lights. The laughter sounded wrong. Even Cottage felt uneasy, brass plates rattling on the hutch with each thump from the tent's bass speakers.

It looked like a carnival of things not precisely friendly. She wondered if the other Gypsies felt it, but they were dancing amidst the crowd. At least, she assumed they were. She didn't dare open her senses to locate them. There was too much out there.

Brigid let out a hearty sigh from the hearth's stone apron. "I hate management," she declared, tossing another peanut shell into the flames.

"I hear you," Da agreed from the *seanchaí* chair. He was balding on top. Phoenix had never noticed it before.

"Weiner?" Daniel offered, reaching behind him.

"No thanks." Brigid sounded angry and despondent.

"I want a s'more," Eryn piped up. Phoenix couldn't see her. She was probably sitting at Da's feet.

"One s'more coming up, nipperkin," Daniel said.

"I'll get the graham crackers," Moiré volunteered, and went to the kitchen.

Ma had gone home. Auntie Molly was out there. The remaining O'Malleys seemed to be trying to hold off the invasion with the sheer force of their normality. It had the uneasy feeling of a tableau about to be shattered—the scene where the homicidal maniac bursts through window, slavering and laughing in his strange costume.

All those strange costumes...

Phoenix did not want to see the next scene... but she wanted to go out there even less. She leaned against the beat-up doorframe, stared warily into the night. Things low and prowling flickered out there... and someone watching from atop the boulder. The things did not see the watcher—or did not care. Only Phoenix knew, catching darkling glimpses of someone melting into and out of the night, all in utter stillness.

Phoenix had the disturbing sensation that it was waiting for her... and it would know if she used the back door.

Perhaps she should go to the watcher?

Two steps onto the lawn, Phoenix froze. What in the world was she doing? The Shadow Fae were not to be trifled with. She had the scars to prove it. And yet she took another step, the ground lumpy and uneven under her feet.

The figure did not move. Phoe couldn't tell if it watched her or the party.

Another step.

The world faded, stilled, hushed, but it was too late to panic. The Gypsy reached out a hand.

The watcher ceased to be.

Laughter swirled under cover of the pounding music as a vision blazed in her mind's eye: Ryna's face, blackened, changed, her hair brittle.

The Shadow Fae crept closer.

With a sharp bleat of fear, Phoenix vaulted the boulder and dashed for the tent.

Light. Color. Movement. Bodies in vivid spandex gyrated like a horde of strange demons. The Shadows were here, too—or people the Shadows had claimed. It didn't matter. They rushed closer, closer—

Dark!

Phoenix slammed her eyes shut as the music cut out. Voices babbled around her, punctuated by startled yelps—she could feel the Shadows pressing in, smothering her, pressing at her mind—

Light!

Music blasted; lights flashed color among the crowd. "Sorry, folks—someone must've hit a power cord," the MC apologized as the dancing resumed.

Phoenix's heart pounded in her throat. People jostled her with no word of apology. She could feel the Shadow Fae sitting back on their heels, waiting for—

Dark!

No, no, no! Phoenix shoved thorough the crowd, fighting panic with movement. She could feel them bounding after her, pressing, pressing—!

Light!

A moment of milling confusion, then gradually the gyrations resumed, chaotic colors and noises and impending death—and everyone else thought this was normal.

The Shadow weren't even sitting back this time. She could feel them licking their chops. The first two had been for sport. There were too many—this was too much. Where were the Gypsies?

Dark!

Fire!

The flame flickered pitifully over Phoenix's hand, born of panic and a desperate desire for self. Phoe almost laughed, incredulous, frightened. She cupped it carefully, breathing hard, staring, staring. As long as she filled her eyes with light, the darkness could not claim her.

She was safe.

Safe…

And then the flame died.

◇ ◇ ◇

Liam stood beneath Tinker's Tree, watching Ryna with grim satisfaction. She was only a hazy, dark blob atop the boulder, barely distinguishable as humanoid… but there was an… intensity… about her. And a longing. And who else would sit there, watching a party she probably couldn't even see?

Shadow Fae roamed this night, oh yes. They lurked at the edges of the tent's artificial light, feeding off the discontent bubbling right below the surface.

Feeding the discontent.

They were ignoring Ryna for now. He wondered if she thought herself safe. She was stupid if she did. You were never safe from the Shadows, not in their home. Not unless they had a purpose for you—and then you were the least safe of all.

He doubted she was cunning enough to turn their game back on them, manipulate them into thinking they pulled the strings. No, she was probably running like a scared little rabbit.

"How does it feel, bitch?" he whispered.

Phoenix hovered in Cottage's doorway. She felt the Shadows' presence, too. He could see it in the uncertain set of her shoulders, in the way she crossed her arms protectively over her perfect breasts. God, even in a floppy old pullover she was exquisite. The way her hair pulled free from its loose braid to frame her face… His hands ached at the memory of her smooth, perfect skin.

She stepped from the doorway, walked slowly across the lawn.

Towards Ryna.

Liam's heart seized with jealousy. Even disembodied, even stranded in Hell and cloaked in its darkness, that bitch still drew Phoenix to her. He could feel their connection like a live thing, thrumming, so strong that it blinded them both to the gathering Shadow Fae.

"You belong to the past," he whispered, inviting the night into his blood, gathering it like a storm.

Phoenix reached out—

—and Liam blasted Ryna with all the power he possessed.

She vanished.

The Shadows descended.

Phoenix ran.

Instinct drove Liam forward, cursing Ryna's shortened stride. With each step they gained on Phoenix, he fell farther behind. A dozen feet still separated him from the tent when the unholy creatures swarmed and the light went out.

Startled yelps and epithets greeted the sudden darkness. The Shadows fed off them—but cursorily. They had a larger prey in mind—and they were toying with her.

She's mine, damn you!

Light!

Chaos, bodies shifting like a pit of vipers. Liam blinked, blinded.

"Come and get her then," a rotting voice challenged; Liam looked up sharply to see a weasel-like Shadow on the support directly above him, sparks spitting from the long claw it ran along one of the colored lights.

This time when the power cut, Liam did not wait, shoving spandex-clad bodies aside as he pushed into the morass.

"Having trouble?" a voice rustled in his ear.

"Fuck you," he shot, knowing they'd already found her.

"We'll make it more sporting," the voice's twin whispered in his other ear, and the light returned.

The crowd parted as if by Magick, granting a clear view of his love.

Liam ran.

Halfway to his goal, darkness swallowed the tent and all within.

A tiny flame blossomed in the cradle of Phoenix's hands; its eldritch light flickered and danced eerily across her face.

An ape-like shadow locked eyes with Liam as it swung from one of the tent supports. With deliberate nonchalance, it blew out the light.

Liam dove to his love's rescue as he sent out a blast of banishing Magick—and toppled, landing scarcely a foot from where Phoenix huddled on the ground, arms clasped protectively over her head. Light and music returned. He scrabbled over and pulled her into his arms. She struggled briefly, but calmed at his hushing noises.

God, it felt so right to hold her. To protect her.

With the last breath in his body, he would protect her.

She raised her head; their eyes met, and the hope that dawned across her face broke his heart. How long had he dreamed of seeing love in her gaze? Now he had it, along with the bitter knowledge of her ignorance.

But in that moment, his world landed solidly, honorably, on its feet.

He would never tell her. It wasn't her fault she'd fallen in love with that bitch. Let her live in ignorance, if it kept her from pain. She would be loving him. Even if *she* never knew it, *he* would, and that was all that mattered.

Light, and sound, and color… a lot of dirty rennie boots, and Ryna kneeling beside her.

Ryna.

A cry caught in Phoenix's throat as she reached up to press her palm against her love's cheek. "You came," she whispered. "You came…"

A shadow passed through gold-flecked eyes. Something was not right.

Phoe pushed the thought away. Ryna was here. Nothing else mattered.

"Let's get you away from here," Ryna said, helping her to stand.

Dazed, Phoenix allowed herself to be led through the press of bodies and into the beautifully crisp night. "Where are we going?"

"Fool's Knoll. It's safe there."

Phoenix bit her lip as she followed Ryna up the steps beside Bakery. The tiny hand in hers felt so chill… *everything* about Ryna felt chill, and strange, and distant…

"Are you all right?" Ryna's words, at least, sounded real, as she and Phoenix settled beneath the trees and old-growth shrubs that lined the right rim of the Knoll. "They were never supposed to find you."

"But they did—now can't you come back?" Phoenix pleaded. "Can't we fight them together? Please? It—hurts, to have you so far away. Even when you're here, you feel like you're not. There's this… wall… where our souls used to touch. Nothing is worse than that. Not Shadow Fae, not anything."

"I never meant to hurt you," the redhead whispered, lips so close that the women shared breath. "I'll do anything to repair the damage I've caused."

Thought leaked from Phoenix's mind, leaving her floating in a strange, empty space. "Anything?"

"I swear it." And leaned forward to seal the vow with a kiss.

The small lips felt odd against Phoe's. She clung to them anyway, lonely, seeking warmth though she found only heat. A tiny hand slid under her shirt, sending tingling shivers in waves across her skin as it traveled up her side and brushed the curve of her breast.

One by one the bulky pullover and its attendant shirts came off, baring her pale skin to the night's chill as Ryna eased her to the ground, lips dancing where hands had so recently been; hands migrating lower... Phoenix whimpered as the button on her jeans released and a light touch eased below the elastic of her panties...

"I've missed you..." Ryna whispered. "The... *feel*... of you..."

Phoe barely kept from crying out, eyes squeezed shut in pleasure at the exquisite, expert touch... pushing... pushing...

Doesn't this feel good? a shadowy voice whispered in her mind. *Don't you wish it would go on forever?*

Sudden panic clawed Phoe's gut—she wanted to scream at Ryna to stop, stop, something wasn't right, but the words tangled and caught. She tried to struggle, but another will smothered her, held her still and submissive...

"*Look* at me... *Look* at me..."

The words dragged Phoenix's focus to the darkened eyes staring down at her, intent, greedy.

Ryna's eyes...

But not Ryna's soul.

The touch... the Magick... the soul that wanted to own her...

"Phoenix?" Tanek called from the stairs, punctuating it with the trill that would find any Gypsy in a crowd.

"Shhhh," Liam whispered, unnecessarily. Phoe couldn't have cried out if she'd wanted to.

Kaya this time: "Phoenix?"

And oh, she wanted to...

A small, questing tendril of energy knocked politely against the shields Liam had erected around her. Phoenix ripped free of his control, and though she still could not speak, she threw herself against the barrier, pressing against it like a small child against a plate-glass window. She could sense her family's nearness; she just couldn't reach them. *Tanek... Kaya... help...* she begged mentally, hoping her desperation and fear would leak through. *I'm over here...*

Hush, hush... Phoenix could almost hear the words, gently scolding but firm, as Liam muffled her in woolen thoughts and pulled her away from the shields, back towards compliance...

A tidal wave of Kaya's energy slammed down over Phoenix, shattering the barrier and leaving her clear-headed and dizzy. Liam protested hotly as Tanek pulled him off her; Phoe scrambled to cover herself, almost weeping. Oh, Goddess, it couldn't be. It couldn't be. Ryna had said he was gone for good...

Kaya: "Phoe, are you—"

"Ryna?!"

And if that was Liam…

"Can't this wait, Tanek? My lady and I are in the middle of something." Ryna's voice—Liam's inflections. Why didn't they know? Why hadn't *she* known???

"I'm all right," Phoe said, her words breaking as she pulled her clothes on haphazard, trying to quell panic, trying to quell her instinct to run. "I'm all right. I'm all right."

"First you run out on her, then you force yourself on her?" Tanek had Liam by the shoulders; he shook his captive hard. "What is *wrong* with you?"

Liam pulled free; his—her?—full-armed slap cracked like a whip in the night air.

"I'm all right. I'm all right." Phoe couldn't stop saying it, not even in the face of those horrid, alien eyes in Ryna's face…

Liam's soul…

Oh Goddess… Oh, Goddess…

The thing that had been her love turned and plowed down the overgrown side of the Knoll.

Tanek met Phoe's eyes briefly, a troubled look in his own as he turned to Kaya. "Get her back to the vardos."

"I'm all right," Phoe said as Tanek plunged down the hill and Kaya led her away, murmuring soothing words. "I'm all right. I'm all right…"

◇ ◇ ◇

"Oh, gods. Oh, gods, oh *gods*, oh gods…" Ryna's voice rose and fell with her anguished litany as she watched her love descend the stairs near Bakery, Kaya's protective arm around her waist. It had been real. This time, it had been real. And it had been… her—but not her—but…

Liam. It had been Liam. She couldn't explain the thunderbolt realization… except that, somehow, the pieces had been there all along…

That vision of Liam, triumphant, on that burned patch by the Maypole…

They'd traded places. Somehow, that night—he'd done something, or the Shadow Fae had, or he and the Shadow had, and now he had her body, and he had used it to…

"I'm all right. I'm all right," Phoenix's broken mantra would not leave her ears.

Liam had…

It had been real, and Liam had…

"Oh, gods, oh, gods, oh, gods…"

◇ ◇ ◇

Wild growth and ancient pop cans littered the slope of Fool's Knoll; Liam barely kept his feet as he crashed downwards, arms before him to warn of obstacles, ears trained on Tanek's curses and blundering progress through the brush behind him.

Liam cursed himself for running. They didn't know. They couldn't know. He should turn around right now…

But s*he* knew. He had seen it in her eyes.

Maybe he could convince the others their darling rookie had flipped?

It would never work. They would humor Phoenix, if only to prove her wrong, and Liam knew he stood no chance against a few well-chosen personal questions.

The ground leveled; Liam stumbled, nearly careened into the picket fence that separated the Knoll from the Front Gate area.

Left or right, left or right—

Right went back toward the shops near the entrance. Places to hide—

—easier to be cornered.

Left.

Heavy footsteps pounded in pursuit as he flew along the road that circuited Knoll, breath coming in stabbing gasps. If he could get to the rennie parking lot beyond B-gate…

A grunt—exquisite pain as Tanek caught a clump of hair and yanked him backwards; without thought, Liam lashed out in a powerful kick.

The Gypsy cursed, but he let go.

B-gate's lost-and-found shack loomed closer.

The footsteps behind him beat a threatening cadence.

Liam dodged for a bench directly outside the shack, risked a leap that nearly caught his toe, and hit the ground running. As he darted through the gate, Liam heard the bench crash.

A dog barked.

Ten feet—

Five—

Three—

Safe!

Liam cornered sharply at the second row of cars, sprinted down three vehicles, doubled back, and crouched in the lee of a rusty panel van. He strained to control his ragged panting, but he needn't have worried. The Gypsy thundered past like a herd of patrons at Beer Cannon.

A few moments to recover, then right, left, right, quietly—stealth more important now than speed. He forced himself to stop gasping for air, to listen for his pursuer's position over the frantic, painful beating of his heart. The Gypsy was closer, now, closer than he should have been. He was good at this, almost as if he could feel Liam's presence. Only someone with darkness in their soul could find him this well...

Still, it hardly mattered. He hesitated at shadows, though he didn't have nearly the reason to fear them that Liam did. And still Liam crept from one to another, nestling into their depths. They folded concealment over him like a mother carefully binding her child's nose and mouth against breath—or screams...

Campground. No one would search there.

He aimed for the back trails, sprinting from the last row of vehicles to the shelter of trees. Empty tents hulked in clearings scarcely big enough for the pallets on which they stood.

A length of rope grabbed at his neck.

Liam cried out and clawed at it—and after a moment realized it hadn't fought him. He stumbled backward, peering warily in his attacker's direction.

Clothesline.

Liam cursed and yanked the cord from its moorings to relieve the knife's-edge tension in his chest, sure he heard a shadowy chuckle to his right. A scowl settled over his features; he stalked down the remainder of the path, determined not to give them further entertainment.

He emerged across the road from the Gypsies' vardos. Firelight played along their sides; voices rose and fell in a soothing murmur. Someone was crying.

He should keep moving. Lingering anywhere near the Gypsies was insane—yet his feet carried him closer, closer, until he could see the gathering area. His love stood with her back to him, her face buried in Tremayne's shirt. Toby, beside him, stroked Phoe's hair, murmuring soothing nothings.

She shook her head adamantly, pulled away. "It wasn't like that. Ask Tanek. Ask Kaya."

"It looked enough like Ryna," he heard Kaya agree hesitantly. "But I think Phoenix is right. I don't think it was."

Esmerelda rested a concerned hand on Phoenix's arm. "But how would it be possible for—"

Phoe pressed a hand to her heart, her voice wavery and thick. "Even before I had any idea who she was, I knew Ryna was a part of me. That—thing—was *not* my soulmate. I'd give up road and move back in with the people who disowned me before I'd live with *that.*"

Tremayne drew her back into his embrace. "There's an explanation. We'll find it. We'll fix it. We won't lose either of you so easily."

Toby nodded. "I'll find the others."

Common sense slapped Liam upside the head, and he backed gingerly away from the gathering, numb with horror. It had to be a trick of the Shadow Fae—some cruel vision. It had to—

His heel caught something that yowled, then attacked in a dervish of teeth and claws. Liam flailed, caught his assailant's scruff. Ryna's familiar.

It hissed at him, fangs bared.

Liam hissed back and threw the calico devil-cat against the nearest vardo; it fell to the ground, limp.

"Who's there!" Esmerelda demanded.

Footsteps approaching.

Liam whirled and ran.

A dozen steps down the gravel road he dodged to the right, willed the shadow of a boulder to enfold him, keep him from sight.

Footsteps crunching past.

Liam eased to the side, watching with hawk eyes as the fire girl peered around. This close, she'd hear any sound he'd made. *Give up, prude,* he willed her. *Give up and turn back.*

She stepped closer to the tents.

He let the darkness surface, felt it gather behind his eyes. *We are many and you are one. Turn back.*

Her posture stiffened; she glanced behind herself and rubbed her arms.

Turn back.

A retreating step, a last, furtive look to the tents.

TURN BACK.

Reluctantly she did, though with a briskness in her steps as she returned to the trailers.

Liam released a quiet breath. The bits of Shadow that had taken residence in his soul whispered of revenge, of marching down to Hidden Valley and wresting what he wanted from the hands of Fate itself.

He hadn't the heart for it.

Instead, he wandered listlessly to the trail that butted up to where the Secret Garden now stood, to the last place he had seen his love happy, innocent and gilded in the fading golden sunlight of early evening.

A tree branch caught his hair, snapping his head back with tear-wrenching pain. In a fit of frustration he fumbled for Ryna's pocket knife, flipped it open, and hacked at the tendrils until they gave way. He wadded up the remaining locks to stuff them down the back of his shirt—and paused. There was still a chance—however slim—that the Gypsies would discover how to bring the little bitch back…

… and Ryna'd been so *proud* of her knee-length hair…

With a deliberate grin, Liam hacked at the tightly held clump of hair. Globs came loose in his hand. Bit by bit he released them, let them slide to the ground like boneless snakes as his love's words looped through his mind's ear…

"That—thing—"

"I'd give up road…"

"That—thing—was not my soulmate."

"Not my soulmate..."

Liam sank to the ground amidst the beautiful, chill, copper-red hair.

And wept.

◇ ◇ ◇

The hour crept towards four in the morning as the Gypsies trudged up the never-ending Olympic Staircase. It had taken interminably long for the other rennies to stagger to their bedrolls, and for what the Gypsies needed to accomplish, they dared not risk an audience.

Phoenix had told them, once they had all gathered in camp. She wasn't sure all of them believed her entirely... but she didn't blame them. They hadn't seen his soul. They hadn't felt his touch... and she hadn't told them about it. She couldn't. There weren't words through all the shame of it...

She hadn't confessed to speaking with him, either—let alone how many times.

All those times, and she hadn't realized... Phoe bit her lip hard, holding back the tears that bound her throat. She *had* known something was wrong, though—that was the worst of it. If only she'd questioned, if only she'd followed her intuition instead of stuffing it in a box and sitting on the lid...

If only, if only...

"Don't you think there should at least be some maniacal cackling?" Toby asked as the Gypsies paused inside C-gate, gazing around trepidatiously.

"I was thinking more of a shroud of black fog," Tanek admitted.

"Or a howling wind, at least," Niki said. Her voice shook. Phoenix wondered if it was from fear or checked tears. Or maybe cold. It was so cold, tonight. Funny that she'd only now noticed it.

"There are too many stars." Tremayne's voice was introspective.

Phoenix gazed up at the sky, at the waxing half-moon.

Half a moon, half a soul...

And he was right... far too many stars.

"All right, kids. Time to make with the Magick," *Baba* Luna said, rubbing her hands together. Phoenix wondered if she felt dirty, too. The *night* felt dirty.

"That way's north," *Phuro* Basil offered.

With silent nods the Gypsies shuffled to the beaten circle around the Maypole and took their positions. Tremayne walked the perimeter, then stood in the center.

Right where Ryna had stood...

A match flared in Niki's hands, lighting the brief torch of Toby's incense stick. He blew the flame to an ember as she whispered, "Those who dance with the dawn, be with us now."

A gentle hint of myrrh drifted on the night's breeze, and the stirrings of Magick echoed in Phoe's soul.

The candle Esmerelda held flickered to life, filling Phoe's vision as Magick flared through her, hot and fierce. "Blessed be the fire of the ages. May you protect us now, as always," Phoenix said—and heard a voice in the back of her mind whisper, *We hear. We come.*

"Spirits of Water, Guardians of the West, we welcome you. Be present and witness to our circle," *Phuro* Basil requested as Kaya scooped water from her bowl and scattered it to the ground. The offered droplets eagerly burrowed into the earth, gifting a power as strong and vast as the ocean, steady and fierce as its currents.

A flash of color blazed Phoe's mind as *Baba* Luna's words sounded to the earth-beat of Tanek's energy: "From the Earth and from the North, come to us."

Phoenix felt the earth supporting her, old and comforting as the circle closed around them, glowing faintly, part of them all… and part of something far greater and older than mere mortals.

Over the quiet, musical hum, Tremayne called out, "Fair Folk, Nunnehi, Good Neighbors: we beg your assistance and wisdom. Please, hear our call and answer."

"Hear our call and answer," Phoenix heard herself repeat, heard the voices of the other Gypsies repeat, as the night flashed brilliantly and the candle's flame jumped three inches.

"Hear our call and answer!"

Phoenix gasped and had to keep a tight hold on her spirit to prevent it from flying off to romp among all that beautiful energy. Only later did she realize that more voices than those that belonged to the Gypsies had called the last invocation.

It rained light. Phoenix closed her eyes and tilted her face to the vast sky, watched the streaking warm glow behind her eyelids, let horror and heartbreak fade for a moment in its beauty. The Bright Fae were here. Everything would be okay.

"Poor children."

Phoenix slowly turned and opened her eyes at the voice's familiar lilt. Two of the Bright Fae flanked Tremayne. She knew them, though she had never been able to draw them: child-sized and perfect, delicate features formed of gold and silver light. Their beauty brought a swift, longing ache to Phoe's heart… and yet it seemed as if some cosmic movie projector cast them there—cut out, disjointed, apart from the world instead of springing from it. More transparent than Phoenix remembered.

It was the female Bright Fae who had spoken—the one who had gifted Phoenix her ring. Phoe absently rubbed it with her thumb. It resonated with the Bright Fae's presence, faintly tingling and warm, as if the ring itself lived.

"Ryna's gone," Tanek said inadequately. He had seemed uncomfortable around the Old Ones last year, too. Phoenix wondered fleetingly if it was because they had more Charm than he did.

"She is," said the lady Fae, her delicate features forlorn. "And the aid we can give is at your disposal. Ask what questions you may have."

"How do we get her back?" Tremayne did not leave room for the possibility that they couldn't.

Both Bright Fae peered at him as if they could see into his soul.

The fiddler stood proud under the scrutiny.

Seemingly satisfied, they then turned their appraisal to the remaining Gypsies.

Kaya clasped her hands hard in an attempt to not fidget. Tanek *did* fidget. Niki stood rapt. Tobaltio and Esmerelda looked to be concentrating hard on willing a favorable answer; the elders stood patient. Phoenix's heart did not even dare beat.

At last the male Fae answered Tremayne, though he seemed to fade slightly as he did. "You must bring her to her body—and bring her body to her. The places where she is and will be must converge. It will not be easy. Not all of you are what you believe yourselves to be—that will make things difficult."

Tremayne bent his head, and not even the wind drew breath. His daughter. His decision of what to ask. He of the quiet wisdom… Phoenix could almost see the weight of it pressing him down. He of the few words, and they would be the Gypsies' only hope. If folk tales held truth, he would have to be precise—Fae could be capricious, and they might not fill in the blanks. At length he raised his head, looked unflinching at the immortals. "Where do we find her?"

"She is both nearer than you think," the lady said, "and farther than you imagine."

Phoenix rubbed at her eyes… it wasn't a trick of her vision. The Fae really were dimming, thinning with each question until they'd become almost transparent.

"When must we do this?"

The male Fae seemed to consider this answer carefully, and for a horrible moment Phoenix wondered if he and his companion would disappear before he answered. "One cannot survive divided longer than one lunar cycle, but the ritual is strongest at Brightmoon."

And then, without flash or flare, the Fae were gone, leaving the night cold, and dark, and mundane.

"If you cannot succeed then, you will not save her," the lady Fae's voice whispered from empty air, its echo hanging a moment in their ears before dissolving into the night.

The candle flickered and died; the thin, remaining wisp of smoke tickled Phoe's nose.

"That's Friday," came Esmerelda's voice from beside her, and a quiet horror settled over them all.

Friday. Not even a week...

"Well, crap then," *Baba* Luna declared.

Phoenix thought that pretty much summed it up.

◇ ◇ ◇

The fog lured her from the Maypole's protective circle. It seemed so normal, all misty and gray; Pendragon almost looked like it always had. Ryna wandered, pleasantly hazy, past landmarks that had been gone for years. The tree house, the sculpture of the three-headed dragon, the Front Gate that stood only one story high. She hummed absently, not thinking too hard, simply enjoying the literal stroll down memory lane. She wished she could show this to Phoenix, wished she could point out the familiar landmarks to her father, or Toby and Esmerelda, or the elders. They, too, remembered when site had looked so, better than she herself did.

Gray air thickened as she descended the hill toward the Stocks. Surprisingly, Cartwheel Cove hadn't reverted to its campground origins—though that was before her recollection. Never mind—maybe some of it had—she couldn't see much. The fog hung so dense here, like a living thing.

A breathy laugh clung to the tree on her left; Ryna spun, head clearing as a formless blob twice her height billowed out from behind the oak. It advanced menacingly, though slowly. It had all the time in the world.

She grabbed for Air Magicks, wove them and threw them—whirling, dissipating—

The creature billowed, engulfed her attack, and grew.

Threads of panic spun in Ryna's soul. Air—it was made of Air. She could not use its essence against it, not here in its own home. Desperate, she reached out blindly—

Crystal pain whirled through her, a million facets reflecting shards of energy that sent her reeling, fumbling, trying desperately to halt the chaos. Helpless without her Magick, Ryna ran, stumbled. A stench like the smoke from burning flesh loomed over her. Emily screamed—or was that only in her memory?

Frantic, she pushed onward, careening around the Children's Realm towards the relative safety of her home turf in Sherwood. Tendrils of the... *thing*... reached for her, smothering her with its odor and the memories it invoked. "Run, run, little Gypsy," its thin voice whispered.

Ryna could feel the visions coming, but could not stop them through the swirling confusion she had invoked.

"I'm all right; I'm all right; I'm all right..."

Caravan Stage melted from the fog, and Robyn's bridge, and Hollow Hill—the places where she had taken her first baby steps.

Just a little more…

Ryna only made it to the wind chime tent before hot smoke wrapped around her ankles. She pitched forward, landing hard.

"I'm all right; I'm all right…"

Emily's shrieks.

The smoke, wicking up her legs, burning…

Ryna struggled—

Rachelle struggled—

Over her hips, sizzling, searing—

"No!"

"Keep thy bloody hands from her! She be innocent, damn you all, she—!"

Her arms wrenched behind her back, bound by smoke—

Bound by rope—

Dirty smoke forced itself into her mouth—

A dirty rag, forced into her mouth—

Gagging on the stench—

Emily, hauled outside, her embroidered chemise torn, stained, her hands bound—

Phoenix, haphazardly pulling cloth over her alabaster skin…

Tasting ashes…

Becoming ashes…

Screams…

"Phoenix!!!!!!"

◇ ◇ ◇

Phoenix floated in the sweet oblivion of half-sleep, rocked by the normalcy of a violin tuning. A sharp, A a-little-less-sharp, A flat, A a-little-less-flat, A. And then E, then D, then G. Check E and A, a few fine adjustments, check them all together. A couple more adjustments, tweaking here, nudging there, a set of scales. There. Perfect. Her eyes drifted open as a minor scale tickled her ears. She smiled.

The vardo was empty.

The music was gone.

She hadn't the tears to cry.

Karma mewed piteously when Phoe moved to get up. Phoenix gathered the little bundle of calico fur in her arms and crooned to her for a while. She seemed so… thin, now—not only of body, but of spirit. "We'll get her back," the Gypsy promised, her heart sick for the both of them.

Karma mewed again, too weak to do anything else. They were losing her person by bits, and none of the two-legged furlesses understood…

Phoe sighed and put the kitty down, filled Karma's food bowl, and mechanically threw on her garb. She had no appetite for breakfast. Cast Call would not be for another hour, but Phoenix couldn't stand the thought of waiting until quarter to eight in a place so full of Ryna—and yet so empty.

She stepped into the chill morning to see *Phuro* Basil seated on one of the logs, already in garb, his contemplative attention in the depths of his earthenware mug. "You couldn't sleep either?" he asked.

"The sleeping wasn't so bad as the waking—though I wouldn't have done either without *Baba*'s help." She took care of the Faerie milk, slipped the bowl inside, and locked her door. Ryna would have done it with a thought, but Phoe had to use the battered key she'd been gifted—Fifth Weekend had it been? Yes, Fifth. A year and a day ago…

"Would m'lady like to wander site?" He stood, placed his mug on the porch of his vardo. *Baba* Luna would take it in when she emerged. Phoe might've left a mug like that, once, but with Ryna gone it would sit, and gather ants, and—

Stop it, she commanded herself. *Don't. Think.* She couldn't make her voice work, but Basil looked on her with sympathy when she nodded fervently and accepted his proffered arm. They walked in silence through the empty campgrounds and up the Olympic Staircase. Even the loud sex tent was strangely silent.

"Doesn't feel very safe anymore, does it?" he commented as they passed through C-gate. Wraithlike fog wisped thinly around them.

Phoe nodded, glad for his presence as the Narrows' booth fronts watched them walk past: popovers, shish-ka-bobs, wine, funnel cakes… A pipe skillfully carved into a turbaned sheik's head emerged from Basil's pocket. Use had yellowed the bowl from its once-white stone; Phoenix couldn't imagine how long he must've had it for it to acquire that color. The Gypsy elder only carried it when especially worried. And it took a great deal, Phoenix had learned, to phase a Water element.

She found it strangely comforting to see him rattled—and yet, at the same time, she wanted him calm, collected, and casual. She closed her eyes briefly, stretched to find the connection she held with Ryna. It felt like yelling into smog so thick she couldn't even see herself, and the effort granted her only the vague comfort that Ryna was out there… somewhere. Not how she fared, if she was hurt or even conscious—only that she was there.

When Phoe opened her eyes, they had reached Bedside Manor and the Bear. *Phuro* Basil clutched the pipe between his teeth as he plundered a small tin for tobacco—then removed the pipe and tamped the leaves expertly into the little bowl. This took a bit of fussing, and Phoenix quietly watched the process. It was surreal, walking through patchy mist with an old man dressed up like a Gypsy, who looked perfectly natural with both his outfit and his absorbed ministrations to his pipe. She could almost forget it was a fidget toy, that anything other than time passed around them.

Woodland Stage, Sherwood… the animals in the petting zoo were quiet; they had the sense to sleep in before a day full of commotion.

"Phoe, give us a light, would you, luv?"

Phoenix stared. Basil's voice—his words—were not his own. And yet he looked as if he'd said the most normal thing in the world. She paused outside the gate to Hollow Hill, gathered flickers of Fire to set spark to his pipe. The warmth flowed obligingly into her soul—

—and was sucked from her so fast and hard it left her reeling.

A discordant clangor sounded across the lane; both Gypsies whirled to see a mass of wind chimes collapsed lifelessly on the ground.

Phoenix leaned back heavily on the fence, legs none too steady. *Phuro* Basil, after ascertaining that she would be all right, cautiously advanced on the vendor's tent. It seemed a lot further away than it really was. He knelt by the fallen chimes. "Burned through," he called back.

No, Phoe thought. *I didn't—I* didn't! *It wasn't me!* She teetered over to where he knelt, steadied herself on his shoulder as she examined the rope he held. Synthetic—and melted at the end.

A sudden wind created music over their heads.

Phoenix felt strangely calm—and suddenly as if she might be ill. "Let's go wait for Cast Call… please?"

Phuro Basil did not argue.

◇ ◇ ◇

Ryna crouched, shaking, on Robyn's bridge. Her attacker was gone, though its stench clung to her like a death shroud. She'd defeated it. There had been… a spark…

She didn't understand it, but suddenly there was something *there*, right before her, and ready to be used. She'd grabbed it blindly, gathered it like a child's scattered jacks, wrenched her arms free, pounded her fists hard on the bare earth—and shot lines of flame from the impact in all directions. It had obliterated her attacker—and raced on to familiar shops and food booths. The wind chimes had fallen, stirring her to her senses in time to escape the structure before it fell.

Cartwheel Cove was burning.

She stared around in horror.

Cartwheel Cove was *burning*.

And it was all her fault.

◇ ◇ ◇

"You two're late," Toby observed with an arched eyebrow as *Baba* Luna and Tanek slid into the press of people assembled for "Swing Low."

"We had a bit of shopping to do," she replied cryptically. As the assembled rennies burst into song, she passed each Gypsy a small black velvet bag embroidered with what looked like an upside-down peace sign, but without the circle.

Phoenix recognized the rune. Algis—protection. A peek inside the bag brought forth the herby scents of sage and mugwort, the glossy sheen of several polished stones. She tucked it away and joined the song, already mid-way through the second verse:

"—low—"
"—Swing low, sweet—"
"—Chariot,
Comin' for to carry me hoooooommmmmmmme..."

"Swi. i. ing. Low."

A couple giggles; the rennies repeated as best they could.

"Swee. eet. cha. ri. ot.
Co. min. for. to. car. ry. me. home.
Swi. ing. low. sweet. char. ri. ot.
COOOOMMMMMMIIIIIIIN. for. to. car. ry. me.
HoooooooooooOOOOOOOOoooooooooome!"

Patty bustled up the aisle in a flurry of pink and clambered onto a bench. She teetered a moment, though the grin never fell from her face. "Peoples, peoples! I have an idea! How about, to start off this be-*yew*-tee-ful weekend..." she paused to build suspense, which only made those assembled sick with dread "... we have a great big 'Praise God!'"

Utter.

Silence.

A bird ruffled its feathers, shaking a tree branch, but the rennies could only stare in shock as Perky Patty smiled cheerily at the masses, certain they were stunned by her brilliance. "Come on, come on, peoples, let's hear it," she encouraged.

Only half the voices sounded, and half of those added an "ess" at the end.

The troops wandered away, grumbling.

The Artistic Director blinked, the picture of pink puzzlement.

Phoenix didn't want to be around when Patty got over her confusion and started being angry—the Gypsy felt sure that somehow, Patty would figure a way to take it out of their collective hides.

*   *   *

"Here."

Phoenix looked up from listlessly watching Robyn and Jen's show from a shady spot in front of Hollow Hill. She amazed herself by catching the grapefruit Tremayne tossed her. "Wow. I haven't had one of these in ages," Phoe said, thankful for the distraction. "Mother banned them from our house after a week on that grapefruit diet fad." She turned it over in her hands, at a loss. How on earth did one eat these things without a grapefruit spoon?

Tremayne removed his boot knife and made an incision along the fruit's tough rind, then dug his fingers in and pried until it gave way with a soft ripping sound.

Oh. Like an orange. Phoenix felt silly. She hastily removed her pocket knife—her special dagger was still tucked safely in the broom closet.

At first the peel didn't want to come off—and then it left a thick layer of white, icky stuff. Tremayne was already working at his—evidently you peeled this part off, too. Phoenix caught at the little stringy bits and pulled.

The fruit looked naked without its pithy coating. Phoenix unwrapped it gently, gingerly—it seemed too full for the thin skin that surrounded it, too bursting for the white veins that webbed it.

Still, the skin did not break.

Tremayne sliced carefully at one of the seams between the segments, used his knife as a wedge to coax it into halves. Phoenix did likewise. It squirted her twice before finally conceding. Then, following her father-in-law's lead, she tugged a little at the membrane to create a pocket of air and used her knife to remove it from one segment.

The tiny, juicy bulbs huddled in impossibly fragile colonies. Tremayne started in with his fingers. Phoenix did too, amazed when the clusters didn't break as she pried them from their skin. *This is the best way in the world to eat a grapefruit,* she decided as the tangy sweetness exploded in her mouth. When she had finished with the first bit, she removed the spent segment's casing from the next, sticky to the wrists from the juice as she turned the corners inside out to suck at the last little bits before going on to the next piece.

Unbelievably personal, this moment in the morning sun… it seemed strange to share it with Tremayne. With Niki, perhaps, but this sensuous way of eating a grapefruit, this delicate, precise work of wresting the sweet treasure from its coverings… from Tremayne?

His eyes met hers. "Tougher than it first appears."

Phoenix nodded, nose wrinkled briefly as another arc of juice spattered her glasses.

"She'll be okay," he said, as if assuring her that the ocean would be there if she drove far enough west.

Phoenix looked at the feisty little grapefruit. Leave it to Tremayne...

She smiled.

◇ ◇ ◇

Liam stared bleakly at the gray and maroon nylon of the tent's ceiling. He'd snapped at Elise's advances until she'd finally slunk off to her aunt's shop, leaving a slick of guilt behind her—not that he cared. Only one person in the world mattered—and he'd lost her.

Liam rolled over and stared at the tent's wall, trying to ignore the sounds of passion from two rows down, trying not to think of how he would never have the chance to make Phoenix cry out like that. He felt like a ghost. What was the point, if not for his love? All the planning, all the Magick...

His eyes hardened. Magick.

Liam raked his shortened hair from his eyes and tossed the blankets aside. The clueless bint had to have a candle around here somewhere; she was fairly addicted to the things. Especially the awful, floral-scented ones, though for once that might be to his advantage.

He found them under the altar she'd made of a plastic bin, a velvet scarf, and the various trinkets that girls of her sort found necessary for any ritual. At least she'd had the sense to wrap each pillar in paper and seal them in plastic bags to keep the scents separate. Liam selected a pink one—rose, for love—and reconstructed the altar.

It was too foofy for his taste, but it would work. He lit the candle, grabbed a little dirt from the perpetual supply that dwelt on every tent floor, and filled the chalice with water from the cooler. It would be simple, this time. No offerings. No invocation. Only the power of his desire as he whispered the words that came to his mind:

"As the air surrounds me,
As the earth supports me,
As the water cleans me,
As the fire warms me,
Grant me the honor to kneel at her feet.
Grant me the honor to kneel at her feet.
Grant me the honor to kneel at her feet.

"As the air surrounds her,
As the earth supports her,

As the water cleanses her,
As the fire warms her,
Grant her the pleasure that only I can give.
Grant her the pleasure that only I can give.
Grant her the pleasure that only I can give.

"Let the air surround us,
And the earth support us.
May the water cleanse us,
And the fire warm us.
Grant us the chance to right past wrongs.
Grant us the chance to right past wrongs.
Grant us the chance to right past wrongs."

Liam remained silent a moment, allowing the echo of his words to fade, allowing his Magick to seep into the weave of reality.

And then he blew the candle out.

Phoenix sighed as she stared over Pendragon's grounds from the cradle of her favorite tree's roots. Ryna had introduced her to this quiet, sheltering giant near the Scribes' Hall and B-gate. She welcomed its company as she awaited the peasants' arrival… though they'd refused to tell her the purpose of the rendezvous.

Normally she wouldn't have minded. The weather teetered in perfect balance between too warm and needing a cloak, and a light breeze stretched horse-tail clouds across the sky as the leaves rustled overhead. It was a great day to sit back and provide a little ambiance… except that Phoenix couldn't get her thoughts to shut up.

The Bright Fae had said they needed to have Ryna and her body in the same place, and unless the others had started keeping secrets, no one had a clue about Liam's location. Tanek seemed certain that he'd be back to try and see her… mixed blessing that *that* thought was.

And as if that wasn't enough, the Bright Fae had also said they were not all what they thought they were… and Phoenix quailed at the thought that—supposing they *did* find Liam—her Magickal inexperience might wreck their one chance at saving her love.

Or what if it was Tanek—what if Tanek only *said* he cared—or only cared until things got difficult?

Or if Kaya didn't *really* love Ryna as much as a blood child? What if she resented that the ones she'd conceived had all miscarried within the first four months, no matter what anyone tried? At least, according to Ryna; no one else would speak of it, and Ryna only behind closed doors. Maybe this was some psychological way to miscarry Ryna, too; maybe she thought she didn't deserve to be a mother to anyone?

Or maybe it was—

No. Stop thinking like that. If Liam can mess things up, it should be simple enough for nine Gypsies to put them to rights. Tremayne seemed confident enough this morning...

"Gang way! Coming through—move it or lose it! Get your butts out of the path—these peasants have no brakes!"

Grateful for the distraction, Phoenix nearly leapt to her feet, peering in the direction of Bryn's yells. Gradually the sparse crowd made way, and Phoe caught sight of the peasants.

At first she thought they were doing the land ski bit again. It had the same setup: pairs of peasants on the lead ropes like huskies. But then she noticed that the skis had been modified to a sled and the balance rope the skiing peasant usually held had been turned into a huge tether. And on the sled, secured by the tether, sat a boulder half Phoenix's height.

"What in the *world* are you doing?" she cried as they crossed the road and powered up the hill to where she stood—and stopped.

Hayrold cleared his throat.

"Roses come—and roses go," he proclaimed. "But rocks are forever."

And with that, the peasants grunted and groaned—and rolled the boulder onto the ground with a resounding *thud*.

Pratt swept her a bow. "For you, m'lady."

Phoe stared at him in bewildered disbelief—then at the rock—then back up at her friends. They were dirty and sweaty and panting—and grinning, every last one.

Phoenix began to giggle... and then it turned to a laugh. She threw her arms around the boulder in a giant hug. "It's perfect," she told them. "The best rock in the world."

The peasants grinned even wider—and resumed their posts with a flourish, this time with Bryn on the sled as they sped off.

The Gypsy climbed up on top of her rock—it had a nice flat spot perfect for sitting—and watched patrons scramble out of the peasants' way as they rumbled down the lane toward *Lady Fortune* Stage. She would never understand where they came up with ideas like this...

But, really, that was part of the beauty.

◇ ◇ ◇

It was a wonderful tree, a quiet and sheltering tree… it was the tree that grew between the Scribes' Hall and B-gate, the one she'd shown Phoenix last year.

And it had a boulder not even a bodylength from its trunk.

Ryna puzzled wearily at the flat-topped boulder; it was the reddish-ochre of the bedrock below Pendragon. An interesting little hole slightly above her waist probably made some little chipmunk very happy. It felt like a nice rock, and even though Ryna was very much not in the mood for anything to be out of the ordinary… she still liked it.

She'd come here for the shelter and calm of her favorite tree… but the tree hummed softly, and much as she loved it, she wasn't sure she wanted it talking to her at the moment. Ryna plopped down next to the stone and leaned back against its rough surface.

A clear plastic bag of sugary, marshmallow-accented cereal appeared beside her. Ryna stared at it, wondering how long it'd been since she'd last eaten.

"Must be Faery food," a familiar voice murmured; Ryna looked up slowly to see Phoenix perched atop the rock, studying it, her staff resting against the crook of her arm.

Her *new* staff. That meant either she hadn't found her old one or she'd given it up. Ryna wished she knew which it was, wished she could ask her love, but she dared not speak, dared not break the spell of this precious, blessed vision.

"I had something like that for breakfast." It was a little blond-haired girl, nine or ten years old by the looks of her, who spoke this time.

Phoenix's attention turned from the cereal. She beamed a delighted smile at the newcomer. "You must be Fae, then!"

A moment of thought, and then a grin lit the child's face. "Yeah, I am!"

Phoenix furrowed her brow, thumped her stick as she climbed down from the rock to circle her playmate. "You don't have wings!"

"Um… they don't come out until after noon."

Phoe gave her a doubtful look. Ryna almost giggled. "Don't they rip your clothes?"

"Nah. They're Magick, see? Magick just works like that."

"Ah. I see," Phoenix agreed, nudging her glasses up—Ryna's heart tightened at the gesture. "I don't suppose you could make me one, too? I need to go find my friend. It's all very complicated."

She knows. She must know, if she thinks she needs to be Fae to reach me… oh, Phoe, I'm so sorry…

"Sure—I could do that!"

"Really? Oh, thank you!" She turned her expression comically intent. "What do I have to do?"

The girl looked taken aback by her audience's seriousness. "Well, um… Faeries dance. So you've got to dance. In a circle."

Phoenix obediently did a little skipping step. "Like that?"

"You have to bounce around more. Here, like this." She hopped and capered in demonstration.

"Oh." Phoenix imitated the Faery, who giggled and linked elbows with her. Phoenix giggled, too.

"Sara! What are you *doing*?!" demanded a boy's voice.

The girl stopped dancing and disengaged from Phoe. "I'm teaching her to be a Faery."

Phoenix cocked her head at the new arrival, who shared a passing resemblance to her companion. She nudged up her glasses again. "Who's he?"

"He's my brother," Sara said, making a face.

"Oh. Is he a Faery, too?"

The boy made large, embarrassed negating motions with his hands. "I am *not* a fairy. No way. Nuh-uh."

"You could be," Phoe offered, deadpan. "All you have to do is dance in a circle with her."

"No thanks!" He gave Phoenix a weird look. "C'mon, Sara. Mom's looking for you."

Sara let out an elaborate, put-upon sigh. "Oh, all *right*. I'm *coming*." She rolled her eyes as her brother grabbed her hand and dragged her off.

"Fare thee well!" Phoe called.

"Good luck finding your friend! Remember, your wings won't show up until noon!"

Ryna couldn't help a wistful smile. If only wings were all she needed to set things right…

Phoenix climbed back up on her rock.

Ryna simply sat, still and silent, gazing up at her until her image faded and Ryna was left alone, the bag of cereal her only company.

Even so, she was grateful.

Phoenix sat in the window by the hearth, diddling with her pennywhistle as brawny men in kilts and T-shirts set up the next round of Highland Games and shepherded the last of the Post-Parade crowd from the Green. The rookies had made a good showing, earning uproarious laughter from the audience. Phoe couldn't help a certain swelling of maternal pride—her little hatchlings were learning to fly.

"The kids're getting a reputation," Patches observed from his perch on the tinderbox.

"Getting to be true rennies, too," Daniel said as he wiped down the table. "I went to my tent for my sunscreen and they were down there dawdling about getting into costume—one of them made some comment about nothing ever happening before noon on a Sunday."

Ma barked a laugh. "Fast learners, they are."

Phoe smiled, though with a twinge of sadness. Not even vets, and already they'd lost the urgency that made them not want to miss a second of faire.

Listen to you, old woman, she thought with wry self-knowledge. *One year with the Gypsies and you act like you've been here for twenty.*

It felt like she had, though, listening to all of Ryna's stories…

Thump!

Phoenix looked up sharply; Brigid stood mid-motion between the green hutch and the table's corner, hands poised as if they should still be holding the water pitcher, now on the ground. It was the gray one with the midnight-blue rabbit and no handle. Recently filled, too, from the amount of water soaking the floor.

"Oh!" Brigid said, abruptly coming back to herself, and crouched, trying vainly to mop up the excess with her apron.

Phoe glanced over to where she had been staring; a tranced-looking Kevin shook himself, knelt before Brigid. "Here, let me—"

"Oh, thank you; I—"

"No trouble; it—"

"Could you—"

"It would be—"

They reached out to right the still-leaking pitcher at exactly the same instant, and by the purest of coincidences—they touched. Brigid stared for a long instant at their clasped hands, her gaze creeping up by inches until their eyes met. Ever so softly, Kevin reached up to brush her cheek. Brigid leaned into the contact, eyes closed—

And then, in the space between one heartbeat and the next, their lips met and the pitcher tipped over again, emptying the remainder of its contents.

Eryn's impish singsong dropped into the stunned silence: "Brigid's got a *boy*friend! Brigid's got a *boy*friend!"

The teens pulled apart, beet red, and proceeded to do a lot of avoiding eye contact and scrambling to their feet and making sentence fragments.

Brigid began to giggle. "It's empty again."

"I'm so sorry; I—"

"No, no, 'tisn't—I need to—it's empty again," she explained, and hurried into the kitchen, still giggling.

Kevin just stood there with a goofy, shy, befuddled smile.

Ma raised her eyebrows and made a small gesture to the effect of "well, what are you waiting for?"

The rookie ducked his head, tugged his forelock, and scuttled through the green burlap curtain.

A *sploosh* as the pitcher fell into the powder-blue plastic rinse tub. Every last O'Malley bit their cheeks to keep from laughing.

"I would slam him up against a wall and ask what his intentions are towards my sister," Torin remarked dryly, "but it seems like a moot point."

Ma shook her head fondly. "I'm glad she didna have hold of our *good* pitcher."

Phoenix grinned. And hopped the rest of Kevin's rookie year went as well as her own had.

* * *

"Come play, come play!"

Phoenix looked up in surprise from collecting the variety show's tips and saw a pack of peasants ready to ambush her. "What are we doing?"

"Chez Privy again," Hayrold said. "We thought maybe you could help us out with some live music since Marcus is busy."

"Want me to take your tips in?" Tremayne offered on his way past.

The raven-haired Gypsy grinned with sudden inspiration. "The peasants need a fiddler for their privy."

The declaration earned her the most perplexed expression she had ever witnessed. "Pardon?"

Phoe bit back laughter—and explained.

The tiniest of smiles crept onto Tremayne's face; it brightened Phoenix's world to see it. "And where is... Chez Privy?"

"Over by the BLUE," Mutch informed him.

Tremayne shook his head in amusement and went to retrieve his instrument.

The peasants cheered. Within the minute, the ragtag entourage was underway.

"What sort of music do you wish?" he asked.

"Something soothing—preferably classical," Pratt put in.

"So not the '1812 Overture,'" Tremayne deadpanned.

"Not unless there have been a lot of beans involved," the Leper said as Phoenix stepped through the door of the trick privy and into the most enormous wedge tent she'd ever seen. A couple people with giant woven-reed fans had joined the cause, along with a table boasting a candelabra.

"Holy crap," Phoe observed.

"Only if we've had Mother Superior in here," Bryn corrected.

"See! See!" offered Puddle as Dead seized Phoenix's hand and led her to the true privy.

Phoenix opened the door. Decorative scarves hung from the walls, and a magazine rack had been added under the privy paper holder. There was even one of those obnoxious fuzzy toilet lid covers—and an air freshener in the shape of a little pine tree. *Only the peasants...*

"Where do you want me?" Tremayne asked after peering in behind her. He sounded impressed.

"Right next to the door," Ilya told him.

Tremayne nodded and unpacked his fiddle; he'd barely finished tuning when Mutch escorted the first guest in, playing "butler" as she showed the gentleman the many wonders of the realm's only four-star privy.

They came in a steady stream after that—some shy and unsure, some swaggering, and several with beer mugs. Phoenix wound up with the duty of taking care of any items that needed held... and wondered if anyone else noticed the irony of having a Gypsy in charge of the coat check.

They all left with smiles, though—and little maps to Bedside Manor with an accompanying picture of Patty so that they could personally inform management of their experience.

Nearly half an hour passed before Mutch ran off to the Merry Maids' next show, and the remaining privy revelers locked the outside door to give themselves a rest. Hayrold set immediately to counting the guest book entries and crowed over their enormous popularity.

Tremayne stood apart, smiling quietly but wordless. A couple of the peasants looked awkward. They were growing accustomed to Ryna joining their antics, but Tremayne rarely went out to play... and he'd been around so long that many rennies had lifted him to the level of an unreachable god.

That would never do, Phoenix decided. They all needed a little fun. She gestured to his fiddle and raised her eyebrows a hitch.

Tremayne looked hesitant, but settled to a spirited reel. Phoenix dug out her zills to prove anyone could join—though the peasants took very little provocation. Soon a bodhran came out, and then another, and several sets of wooden "bones" added a fast-paced clacking. For a moment they all forgot Perky Patty and their missing friends. For a moment they were simply a bunch of rennies having a good old-fashioned jam session in the privies.

For a moment, it was glorious.

Liam backed carefully away from Caravan Stage. He'd been watching her since he'd caught wind of fiddle music in the privies over an hour ago. She had been smiling—and laughing. She had been happy. Without Ryna.

It really would be all right. Liam's heart soared as the spring in his step took him out of Cartwheel Cove, past the Bear, and toward C-gate. Another week, two at the outskirts, and he would be home free.

Of course, there would be Elise to deal with, but he'd handled clingy females before. Hopefully in the space of ten months she'd find someone else to barnacle to—or, failing that, he could always pretend he'd never seen her before.

Bardstone Hall rang with one of Erin go Braless' rowdy tunes something highly suggestive about a blacksmith and a forge. Liam paused to catch the song's end and was about to move on when a tall brunette ducked up to the stage and dropped a tip in their basket.

Erica???

He shook his head to clear it. It couldn't be. Plenty of teens were big on trendy clothes, and neither of his sisters had displayed any interest at all in the Renaissance faire… still, he had to know. He hailed her as she emerged from Bardstone's shade. "My pardon, m'lady, but is your name Erica?"

Puzzlement crept across her brow. Dear God, she'd gotten tall… "It is," she admitted, fidgeting with one of her dime-store rings in a familiar gesture that tugged Liam's heart.

And suddenly he remembered that he was a stranger to her. How could he ask how she'd been? Or her sister? Or their parents? The child whose hair he'd braided would never believe his tale—and with an unexpected bolt of shame, he realized he wasn't certain he wished her to know it.

There had to be a way to ask, though, to give some reassurance, to let them know he thought of them…

"*Zere* you are!"

Liam turned at the cheesy French accent, though he found it hard to reconcile the voice with the leather- and fur-clad barbarian lumbering his way.

A *familiar* barbarian—though Liam knew he'd never seen the man at Pendragon. That left… one of Phoenix's sketches. Yes—a French barbarian. Named… named… *Damn,* Liam cursed mentally. He remembered laughing when he'd read it, but…

"Ah, you 'ave cut your hair—*oui*? But you cannot 'ide from me, my leetle bundle of red-'eaded trouble!" the barbarian scolded.

"I have no idea what you're talking about," Liam said loudly. "But I will have the Village Militia on your head if you so much as touch me!"

"Ze Gypsies, zey 'ave been worried *sick* about you," he expounded, nonplussed, grabbed Liam about the waist, and unceremoniously flung him over one broad shoulder.

It took Liam so completely by surprise that for a moment it didn't even occur to him to struggle. "Put me down!" he shrieked belatedly, beating the armored back with small fists.

A meaty arm clamped over his legs, keeping him from kicking. The leather of his armor creaked at the motion. "Zey say ze Gypsies, zey steal things—*oui*? Non, non—I, Pierre ze French Viking, *I* shall steal ze *Gypsy*!"

Erica was laughing at the spectacle—all the patrons were.

Liam thought he might be sick. He wondered if it occurred to anybody as odd that Pierre called him a Gypsy when he hadn't so much as a coin belt.

"I am *not* a Gypsy!" Liam hollered as Pierre lumbered off, away from Erica—away from his only hope of ever contacting his family. *The Gypsies can't possibly know,* he told himself, taking a firm hold of his fears. *You'll have another chance.*

"Ah, but you are in ze disguise—*oui*? You cannot fool Pierre!"

Liam sneezed as a patch of rabbit fur tickled his nose; he tipped his head back. Dirt, woodchips, and bits of trash passed below him. "Put me down, you hairy, smelly oaf!"

Pierre chortled—and continued his rambling monologue.

Liam made a vow to send the Shadow Fae after him and his next six generations. And gathered his wits for the confrontation ahead.

"This man, now, *he* has no worries about catching the plague. He could never keep up!" Phoenix declared, gesturing to a fellow staggering up the aisle with three enormous shopping bags.

The audience roared with laughter. They'd loved the entire show, though Phoe could tell from *Phuro* Basil and *Baba* Luna's routine gags that the Gypsy elders were feeling as sub-par as she did.

Baba Luna gestured elegantly, about to go into her "I can sell you a child to carry your burdens" bit from the looks of it, but the words died on her lips.

Phoenix turned the direction of her gaze and caught sight of Pierre striding purposefully down the hill, a shrieking redhead over his shoulder. *Phuro* Basil put a cautionary hand on Phoe's arm; she barely kept herself from reaching out—or shrinking back. Thankfully the entire audience had turned toward the commotion.

"Your woman, I 'ave come to return 'er to you!" the barbarian boasted at the top of his voice.

The audience tittered.

The other Gypsies drifted toward the stage. Phoenix noticed it only peripherally. *Oh, Goddess, her hair,* she thought with a mental wail—and almost laughed. It was the least of her worries... but at the same time, the only thing she could comprehend.

Pierre strode up the center aisle. The hollow steps to the stage echoed under his solid footfalls. He swung his cargo from his shoulder to under his arm, so he carried her like a football.

It wasn't Ryna. Phoenix couldn't believe, staring numbly into olive-green eyes that should've been familiar, that she'd thought otherwise.

Tremayne found his voice first. "You have brought my wayward daughter home. Come, bring her into Hollow Hill, and we shall discuss your payment."

The redhead started to protest, but Pierre upped his volume. "Ah, ze payment of a Gypsy, it is generous—*oui*? Perhaps Pierre, ze French Viking, shall 'ave a Gypsy of 'is own—*oh-ho-ho*!" Pierre bounced to the round door amidst gales of laughter, Tremayne several steps behind.

Phoenix wrestled her heart to the ground, tied it up, locked it in a box, and pitched it into the swamp. "Remind me never to run away," she joked dryly… and wondered how she would make it through the rest of the show.

"Thank you, Pierre," Ryna's father said quietly when Liam had been gently deposited on the ground.

The barbarian nodded, turned, and ducked his bulk out the tiny door.

Tremayne turned a somber gaze to Liam.

Liam tried to look helpless and confused. "What is it, Tata?"

"You can stop pretending, Liam."

The words hit his gut like a stone. Liam quelled the urge to run. It had to be a test.

"Pick your jaw off the ground," the Gypsy ordered sharply. "There is nothing of my daughter here. Did you honestly think you could take her form, and with it, her family? I've known you too many lifetimes not to recognize your soul when I see it, Liam—and I'm tired of your games."

Liam snapped his teeth together with a click. They really knew, then. He would get no second chance.

But, by God, he would take the Gypsies out with him. "She's dead."

"She's not. We *will* undo what you have done, with or without your assistance," Tremayne said conversationally. "But it would be in your best interests to start talking."

Liam snorted. "I've been to Hell and back. What do you people honestly think you can do to me?"

Ryna's father just smiled.

Phoenix cast a dark look at Hollow Hill's door. The last of the patrons had dispersed, and although Pierre had emerged while the variety show had still been in full swing, the other two were still inside. Only *Phuro* Basil dared enter—and he returned a few minutes later looking pinched and angry. The remaining Gypsies followed him to the gazebo.

"Phoenix was right," he said without preamble.

She'd known it—in her heart, in her soul, she'd known it, and yet to hear him say the words… Phoe sat down hard on one of the benches.

"Oh, Goddess," Kaya breathed.

The others looked ashen. *Baba* Luna cursed.

I will not throw up on Toby's boots, Phoe told herself sternly. *I will not, I will not.*

"We need somewhere to… store… him," *Phuro* Basil said, his tone brisk as he tamped some tobacco into his pipe. Distaste twisted his expression. "I suppose we could keep him in our vardos, but I hesitate to—"

"Danny," Phoenix said faintly.

Niki gave her a puzzled look. "What was that, honey?"

"My brother… he has this huge house." The words came out strange and halting. Phoe scarcely recognized them as her own. "Danny could… put him in the basement, or something."

A brief silence reigned. Esmerelda coughed. "Are you sure you want to involve him in this?"

"He made me promise to come to him if there was anything he could do." Phoenix said to her hands. "We can trust Danny."

"It's not a matter of trust," Kaya said gently. "Your brother is very devoted to you… but the potential danger…"

"We can take shifts," Tanek said. "One of us there at all times—except Phoenix."

She knew she should protest. She couldn't bring herself to do it. "Um—could you… excuse me…" Without waiting for a response, Phoenix rose and hurried up the hill. Someone else could tell her brother. She couldn't face the sympathy in his eyes, and if he hugged her, she knew she would fall apart and never be able to put herself back together again. She had to be strong. For Ryna, she had to be strong.

A few people hailed her on her way to C-gate, but Phoenix ignored them. There were some things more important right now than friends, or family, or entertaining Patty's precious *guests.*

Karma curled weakly beside Phoenix as the Gypsy fell upon her art supplies with a quiet desperation, drew the million tiny things that were her love. The campground outside grew busy, then quiet. As twilight dimmed the world around her, Phoenix reverently propped one perfect drawing on the ledge surrounding the bed and lit every candle in the vardo, then turned out the lights.

Immediately her home felt smaller, cozier. So had it looked the first night… Phoe uttered a tiny cry and blew out the pillar in the corner, the candlestick in the brass holder fashioned into a mouse reading a book, the votives in small decorative jars that speckled every flat surface. Even the darkness with its nameless fears was better than this softly lit reminder that half of her life was gone…

She hesitated over the last candle: a lumpy, dark blue mass in a cracked pottery bowl. Ryna had made it, and Phoe fed it the drippings from other candles to prolong its life. Its light brought her comfort out of proportion to its size. She felt her soul grow quiet, gratefully, and curled up on the opposite side of the bed to stare at it.

Only then did she realize the oasis of light encapsulated her drawing. The outline fuzzed in the candlelight; the copper-red of Ryna's hair became richer, the sparkle in her olive-green eyes brighter. The lighting in the picture itself shifted, creating shadows and highlights Phoenix had not drawn there. She quelled the disturbed squirming in her innards and stared hard at the image, drawing on it mentally, pulling, willing Ryna to walk through the vardo door. *I'll send my stories out tomorrow, I swear, just come home...*

◇ ◇ ◇

Tug.

Tug.

Tug.

It was a physical thing, like the beat of a heart. Ryna pulsed to it, following it, though she had no idea what it was or where it would lead.

Tug.

Up the hill, past Woodland Stage.

Tug.

Tug.

Left at the Bear, towards Twin Tree.

Tug.

Tug.

TUG.

Reality shifted around her; dizzy and disoriented, she grasped for the nearest tree.

TUG.

TUG.

The Gypsy looked up, following with her gaze the vortex that drew her spirit. The air shimmered between the two trees that flanked the cobblestone stage, and in that mirage, she saw—

Phoenix.

In that instant she knew beyond hope or reason that this was her one chance to go home. She released the tree, stepped into the distortion, and fell—

—bright—dizzy—heavy—

A knock at the door.

◇ ◇ ◇

The sound nearly put Phoenix through the window. Eyes rounded, breathing hard, she couldn't move her gaze from the door, hoping, fearing—

"Phoenix? You awake?"

Tanek. Only Tanek.

Phoenix didn't know whether to weep with relief or frustration—at herself for hoping, at Tanek for breaking the spell… "I'm awake," she called back, voice wavering only a bit, and tried to quell the sick, dizzy feeling in her soul.

"We've got a campfire going, Phoe… Kaya has Nutella," he tempted.

Phoenix looked at the drawing and sighed. Its mystery had faded, leaving a beautiful but ordinary rendering. She blew out the candle, cradled Karma in her arms, and fumbled to the door.

Almost, almost it felt as if Ryna walked behind her. She curled the feeling around her soul, snuggled in its embrace. It brought comfort, no matter how illusory.

There was indeed Nutella, and marshmallows, and even a few graham crackers that had escaped Esmerelda's cravings. The newcomer eased onto the ground with her back to her vardo, beside where *Phuro* Basil sat on one of the logs. He held out a fresh s'more and raised his eyebrows in invitation, but the thought of all that sugar made her ill. She shook her head, and he did not press the issue.

She let the conversation ebb and flow around her. Toby, Niki, and *Baba* Luna were absent—Niki sharing a bed-and-breakfast room with her barbarian, the others probably up at the BLUE. It felt quiet without them, but somehow more comfortable. The whole gang wasn't here. Phoenix wondered if they'd planned it, then wondered if she cared. At least no one was asking her to talk. All the words that came out of her mouth lately felt as if a strong gust of wind could blow them away.

If she pretended really hard, though, she could almost imagine Ryna was up on site with the others. Maybe she was on her way down right now, maybe she stood in the darkness beyond the protective semi-circle of vardos, and any moment now…

They could not see her.

The realization gave Ryna small tremors of fear. She was a ghost to her family, less tangible than the mists. Yet she could see them—and she could see the Shadow Fae, crouched, hungry, waiting beyond the encampment's protective shield.

She was of neither world, now, and both… or perhaps this patch of land simply held the worlds closer together. It would make sense. The Gypsies were the most cohesive Magickal group at Pendragon. If the worlds were going to cross anywhere, it would be in their camp.

She was safe, for the moment, at least. Hope tugged the corners of her mouth into a smile. She just had to make herself visible and her family would devise what needed to be done from their end...

Phoenix could tell, almost—Ryna could see it in her love's eyes. So could Karma—dear Karma; she looked sick, but she was alive, still. And her father... he kept cocking his head a little, as if listening for distant music.

Music it would be, then. Ryna let her soul play to their hearts, let the notes ring down the ties to her family, like tuning forks of the same key vibrating when one is struck...

◇ ◇ ◇

The air shimmered and coalesced on the other side of the campfire, behind Esmerelda. Phoenix shook her head to dispel the ghoulish vision, charred gray and the brown of used tobacco. And its eyes...! As bottomless as dark stars, and worse, they were *Ryna's*. Phoenix felt herself fall away in that regard, powerless to so much as twitch. Her stomach churned. She had called...

The Ryna-thing reached out, her smile the color of ash. "Phoenix."

At the shadow-soft utterance, Kaya whipped around. Fury bloomed on her face, and with a wordless cry of rage, a tidal wave of energy plowed into the shade. For an eternal instant Ryna looked surprised—even scared—before the image shattered under the impact and dissolved.

A cry ripped from Phoenix's throat; she dove forward, unseating Karma, and would have plunged headlong into the campfire if *Phuro* Basil hadn't caught her.

"Easy," he calmed her, "easy."

"No, you idiots!" she cried, struggling, though it would do no good now. "That was *Ryna*!"

A moment of stunned, horrified silence.

Kaya looked as if she might choke on death. "I didn't know," she whispered, her eyes pleading. "I—I didn't... I thought..."

Tremayne stared at her. His expression twisted for the barest of moments before he lurched to his feet and stumbled from the camp.

Basil's grip went slack; Phoenix slumped to the ground, staring blankly into the fire. *I love you,* she thought at the empty thread of her soulmate's connection, willing warmth and hope to her. *It was a mistake; don't give up, Ryna, please, we'll bring you back, we love you...*

Kaya's high, thin litany circled her thoughts like a countermelody:

"I didn't know, I didn't know, I didn't know..."

◇ ◇ ◇

Street lights glared off the faire dirt on the car's windows. Liam scowled at it, cranky and tired. The Gypsies had gotten no information from him—despite his best efforts, Ryna's father couldn't hold a candle to the Shadow Fae's tortures. Still, they *did* have the power to shuttle him around like a sack of grain, and that was annoying enough.

Liam would've scowled at the driver—Phoenix's brother—if he thought it would get him anywhere. The man was unflappable. Pissed off, but unflappable. Besides, a scowl was pretty pathetic when you were bound hand and foot, gagged, and shielded within an inch of your life.

A pretty blonde sat in the passenger's seat, but so far she had been silent.

He wished he at least knew *where* he was headed—but that information was on a need-to-know basis. And apparently they'd decided Liam didn't need to know.

After a time the car stopped in front of a huge, old-fashioned house with a sprawling front porch. It looked like the home to a hundred years of memories. He wondered whose they were.

"Out you come," Daniel ordered, reaching across Liam to unbuckle the seatbelt before lifting him in his arms. It was disturbing to be carried like a child—especially when it meant being this close to another man. Liam would've thrashed if he thought it would do any good.

The lady unlocked the front door and held it open, let the screen door slap shut behind him. A parlor—a dining room—a kitchen—an antique-looking door, and stairs descending into the darkness. Daniel's face remained calm as he navigated a labyrinth of subterranean rooms before nudging open a sturdy door. The harsh light of one swinging bulb illuminated a tiny room, its only furnishings a bucket and a sleeping bag.

Impact. The thin bedroll smelled sharply of animal urine. Liam couldn't believe Daniel hadn't thrown the thing out. No amount of washing would ever rid it of that stench… Liam was roughly rolled face-down; the knots that bound his wrists loosened. He didn't move. It seemed wisest.

The door slammed shut. A lock clicked into place.

Liam rolled to his back, tried to stand, but a burst of Magick left him sprawled and dizzy on the floor of his little cell. How had they…??

But no, it felt… reactionary. It hadn't been directed at him. And that meant…

Ryna.

He wasn't sure how he knew it with such certainty, but he blasted a question to whatever of the Shadow Fae would hear or answer. The familiar graven voice responded; it seemed almost to purr.

"Calm yourself, mortal."

Brilliantly dark pain exploded in the back of his head, and the visions came—first the Gypsies, the picture muddled with their emotions, but obviously in great disarray. Then Ryna's spirit, sprawled and senseless, almost obscured by the hordes of Shadow Fae surrounding her.

Liam sat up, unsettled. *Is that what I looked like at first?* he wondered—a gruesome thought. He shook it off, reminding himself that whether it had been or not, it wasn't now. And the little bitch deserved every inch of it, and then some.

He lounged against the wall and diddled smugly with a bit of straw that had adhered to his clothes from Pendragon. Why had he gotten so worked up? Now that he thought about it, he felt more a part of this world than he had since returning. More... attached. The little bitch's spirit was fading under the Shadow Fae's loving care—that was what came of weaklings who didn't know how to bargain to their advantage. Soon there would be nothing left but a wisp of memory, and then...

He had promised the Shadow Fae he would destroy the Gypsies.

As soon as Ryna was gone, his job was as good as done.

They had promised him Phoenix. And children.

Liam's face creased with a feral grin.

One way or another, he would get what he was promised.

◇ ◇ ◇

"Um, help?"

Phoenix peeked through the lace curtain to see Kaya inching carefully into camp, her arms so laden with cases of ramen that Phoe marveled she hadn't run into anything. Happy to escape writer's block and doubts that were getting her nowhere, Phoe hurried to relieve her friend of half the pile. "I know RFC leftovers have been slim, but I didn't think we were that much in danger of starvation! Here, put it—there."

Kaya gratefully deposited her load on Phoenix and Ryna's vardo floor and sighed. "It was on sale, and I know how fast this crew goes through it. Besides, I had to do *something* good after last night."

Phoe floundered. What comfort to offer? Kaya had ruined their chance to talk to Ryna, perhaps their last chance... *No. Don't think that.* "You didn't know," she offered awkwardly.

"I should have." The dancer plopped on the floor with an uncharacteristic lack of grace. "It just proves what I've been thinking since our meeting with the Bright Fae."

Phoenix sat, back braced against the cupboards, facing her friend. "Proves what?"

The golden eyes that met Phoe's were dark with despair. "That I'm not the mother I think I am."

"That's not true," Phoe countered, wishing she hadn't wondered it, too. "You're a wonderful mother. Ryna loves you."

Kaya shifted uncomfortably. "I didn't give birth to her, and I'm only ten years her elder, but I'm the only real mother she had, and I should've known my own daughter from some foul creature of the night." She hugged herself, hands tucked inside her sleeves so a floppy bit of fabric hung off the ends of her arms. "You were right. We were all idiots. *I* was an idiot."

Proud, confident, sassy Kaya. And now she looked so... lost. Phoenix's heart ached for her in spite of everything. "We're used to her feeling like the Ryna we know," she said in what she hoped was a convincing tone. "Even I have to admit she looked pretty creepy."

"If Liam has her body, she must be in... I don't know, wherever it is Shadow Fae come from. I should've realized she wouldn't look like our Ryna. If I was a real mother, it wouldn't matter."

"And if I was a real witch, I would've realized what was going on and stopped it. I suspected—but I wasn't smart enough or good enough to track it down." Unexpected rage choked Phoenix's heart. "Damn the Bright Fae," she spluttered. "Is this their idea of helping? Planting us all so full of doubts that we can hardly function? I see it in your eyes—I see it in everyone's eyes. We're all positive we're the weakest link—that or we don't want to believe it and we cast it on someone else."

"But we're right," Kaya cut in with devastating honesty. "If we don't face our own fears and shortcomings, how can we compensate for them?"

The raven-haired Gypsy leaned her head back against the cupboard, unspeakably weary. "What we need is confidence."

A small, hesitant pause. "Do you—do you think Tremayne will be cooled down enough to talk to me tonight? I don't want to spend another night apart from him, too."

Phoe met her friend's eyes, startled. "He didn't come home?"

Vigorous head shaking. "I spent the night at Niki's. Toby let me in—I didn't figure she'd mind, given everything. I didn't want him staying out there because he didn't want to see me. It's too dangerous; I didn't want him to end up like—"

"Then it was your choice, right?" Phoenix interrupted. "He was probably calm enough last night—he just needed to take a walk to collect himself."

"But she's his daughter—"

"And you're his soulmate. Kaya, he loves you. He *needs* you. Talk to him."

A hesitant smile crept across the tiny, elfin face as she picked at a loose thread on her sweater. "Okay."

"Good." Phoenix heaved a mental sigh of relief.

Now, if only she and Ryna could be reunited so easily.

◇ ◇ ◇

The first solid thing to gather Ryna's attention was sunlight, sharp and bright. She moaned and pushed herself upright. Every fiber of her being felt bruised. Thoughts danced around her head like lightning among clouds, none of them pleasant. Hopefully they weren't all real.

One she could not escape, though. She had tried to see her family—and it had worked…

… until Kaya had blown her through the safety of her family's shields.

Her cry echoed in Ryna's mind as the feeling of her wrath, hatred, and disgust flashed through her soul. Curling up in a little ball wouldn't save her from it. She tried to convince herself that her stepmother hadn't recognized her, hadn't done it to keep her away from her father. Tried to convince herself that thoughts so ugly must be Shadow-spawned.

Phoenix had known… but she hadn't done anything to stop Kaya…

"Shadow thoughts," she told herself firmly. "Phoenix loves me. We're soulmates. She gave me my ring."

"You threw it away," a cruel whisper taunted. "Why should she stay faithful?"

"Because—!" Ryna retorted, and with a flash of clarity she realized that the Shadow Fae had been the ones to egg her so far that she'd taken it off and thrown it. The Shadow Fae and Liam…

…and Phoenix would never know.

Ryna flopped back to the ground in despair.

◇ ◇ ◇

Phoenix wearily slammed the truck's door with her hip and picked her way through the darkened brush of the trails that led to the campground. Her arms ached under a sampling of the books that had surrounded her all day. It seemed like everyone who had ever written a book had also written one about how to *publish* a book, and her brain hurt from sifting the wheat from the chaff. And then, of course, there were the directories of publishers and agents, each offering wonders for "that one special book"—and acceptance-to-rejection ratios that made her heart plummet.

Still, she had the beginning of a list. She was proud of her list—and thankful that it had given her something concrete on which to focus. Though she knew it wasn't logical, Phoenix couldn't help but think that if she got this one part of her life moving forward, everything else would fall into place.

Things had gone well enough with her brother, at least—she'd stopped by his place to tell him she was okay, and he'd taken her out to dinner. She'd never thought she'd be happy to spend hours discussing childhood memories… but at least it was better than her current problems. And he *had* liked at her rendition of "Pinksleeves"…

Lights shone from Kaya and Tremayne's windows, but the others were dark and the fire pit cold. Where was everyone?

"Mer-row?" called a tentative feline voice as she fumbled her key into the lock.

"Hello, Karma-kitty," Phoe greeted. She shouldered the door open, nudged the light switch on, and surrendered her load of books to the bed.

Karma picked a thick tome and sprawled across it.

Phoe gave her a gentle scratch behind the ears, promised to return soon, and headed off to visit Harvey in the Jiffs near the blue dumpster. Last she'd checked, they were the least fly-infested of her options.

Strange, how night noises sounded so much louder when you were trapped inside a dark plastic hut. The shiver of wind through the leaves… the crunch of a passing footstep on the road… the splash of the human-made waterfall descending into the blue lake below…

Whispers blended with the rustling of tarps in the breeze, slipped in through the ventilation screens near the privy's roof. Phoenix shivered, trying to ignore them. *Paranoid. I'm just paranoid…*

The gust of air swirled around her… swirled before her.

Phoenix grabbed for the privy paper, eager to be gone.

Light and shadow twisted against the brown plastic not two feet from her face, coalescing as the rustling whispers surrounded her, tried to encase her, seeking entrance to her mind, her soul…

Phoenix yanked up her jeans, forced herself to reach through the thing to flip the lock, and *ran*—

—right into a trash frame.

The ground rose to meet her, slamming air and sense from her body as a bolt of energy brushed her back.

The thing cried out.

Something grabbed hold of her; she fought blindly.

"Phoenix! Hey! Phoe! It's okay!"

Sudden familiarity. Calming energy wrapped around her like a stream embracing a stone. Kaya. She was safe.

"You all right?" the dancer asked, holding Phoe at arms' length.

Phoenix nodded, accepted a hand up—wincing as several bruises made themselves known—and let Kaya herd her to where Tremayne stood outlined in the light of his vardo's doorway.

"It came out of the door," she explained as he stood aside to let her pass. Kaya shut the door, though she was still outside—but surely Kaya could take care of herself… "I can't even go to the *privy* without them coming for me! There was whispering, and this wind, and I could feel it getting closer, and I ran—Ryna never would've run; when Ryna was here she made them go away, she—" Phoenix could hear her voice rising hysterically.

Tremayne placed strong hands on her shoulders. The touch calmed her. "Even if Ryna was right here, Phoenix, you still need to learn to do this on your own," he told her, though kindly. "The same way Ryna has to do it without you."

"I'm Fire; she's Air," Phoenix protested, near to weeping. "Without fire, air might be a little cold, but without air, fire is *nothing.*"

"Neither of you is what you think you are," he said quietly. "Ryna believes what she wants to believe—but all the believing in the world is not going to make her other than she is. Ryna is Fire. She always has been."

"But—then what am I?"

Tremayne merely raised his eyebrows. And waited.

He was treating her like a rational adult, damn him, when Phoenix wanted to curl up on somebody's lap and have them make it all better. What right had she with her miniscule experience in Magick to think she could stand in the ranks of the Gypsies? To stand against creatures that could steal your soul into another dimension? *It's not fair*, she thought petulantly, wiping her cheeks with her sleeve. "I start fires, light candles. It's the only elemental Magick I have any talent for at all…"

"People forget, sometimes, that there are *five* elements," Tremayne said gently. "When you work with the other four, there are simple, outside results. You have to look within to see Spirit."

Spirit? Maybe… "I have strange dreams, sometimes," Phoenix hazarded, reaching.

"And when you wish for something?"

"It usually comes true, though maybe not how I intended."

"Dream Magick, Wish Magick. Charm?"

"*Tanek* has Charm!" Phoenix protested. "I'm nowhere near his talents!"

"Which is why audiences are riveted on your every word? Why you play so well with everyone that you earned the Cracked Cup last year?"

Phoenix stood silent. The words crept into her soul like water into a rock's crevices.

"Ever feel like your soul has floated up and away, trying to get somewhere else?"

"Sometimes, when I look at the stars, everything sort of collapses in on itself," Phoenix admitted. "I used to think that if I really *was* a changeling, perhaps that was how I got here."

"Spirit Travel. Convinced yet?"

He was right… part of her knew it, but Phoenix hesitated, remembering a plume of warm, orange fire blossoming away from her—and the quiet, still, certain voice within: *I am Fire*. "But I *knew* I was Fire. I *knew* it."

"We are all every element to some degree, but one tends to guide and shape us more than the others. Given your link with my daughter, it would only be natural for you to channel what she repressed—or perhaps that was simply your need at the time."

Phoenix sighed. It changed everything.

And yet, it changed nothing.

"So—I'm Spirit." She took a deep breath, squared her shoulders, and met her father-in-law's eyes bravely. "Now what?"

"Now, I attempt to teach you everything I know," Tremayne said with a proud smile. "Because in four days, you and I are going to be the ones who go out there and bring our Ryna home."

*　　　*　　　*

"Relax. Start again."

Phoenix sighed, closed her eyes, and pushed away her building frustration. The sun slanted through Irish Cottage's windows, washing gently against the worn wood and faded whitewash of its interior. Phoenix could feel time slipping through her fingers. And they hadn't had so very much to begin with.

Their task was easy enough—they only needed to follow Ryna's thread in spirit form, find her, and bring her back. It would necessitate thinning the veil, but Tremayne made it sound like that wouldn't be terribly hard if done correctly. Once they had Ryna, Phoenix would hold her in their world while Tremayne forced Liam from her body… and they would simply guide her soul to its rightful place.

An elegantly simple plan… and yet just learning to travel proved difficult enough that Phoenix wanted to beat the floor with frustration.

That would accomplish nothing, though. She took a deep breath. "I'm ready."

"All right." Tremayne's voice, warm and soothing, gave her a foothold on patience. "Shields up."

Phoenix smiled, the protective barriers snapping up with the barest thought. Shielding had been her first lesson from Ryna, given in her huge truck on that cloud-scudded October morning as they drove toward Troubadour Faire, leaving Pendragon miles behind.

"You are part of this world. Your physical self will remain as your spirit wanders. Feel your physical body grow roots that reach deep, deep into the ground. This is your anchor. This will ground you."

Phoenix let his words ride through her, let her body fuse with the earth, synchronize with the ancient, eternal beat in its depths. If she'd been a cat she would've stretched and purred; here, there was no nagging urgency. Only the sense that all was well. All would always be well. Whatever happened, life would go on.

"Center yourself there. Balance yourself there. Balance yourself, ready to spring. Ready to fly."

She crouched on the balls of her soul's feet, coiled the energy inside herself, and leapt.

A second of euphoric freedom.

A second of cloudlike white light.

A guttural roar; a Shadow descending.

Phoenix screamed and dove.

Arms circled her; a hand stroked her hair. Tremayne's fortress-thick shields slammed closed around her. Gradually her breathing slowed.

"All right?"

Phoenix nodded, opening her eyes, and pushed herself up from his lap. Her head whirled.

"I'll get you some water."

She tried not to groan as he headed for the kitchen. "I'm not sure that's a good idea. I haven't felt so dizzy since Amy Frantz gave me a ride on the tire swing in fourth grade." She could hear the stream from the ancient, yellow water cooler.

"Trust me. It'll help," Tremayne said, materializing at her side with a battered tin mug.

She managed only a sip, but it cleared her head some. "I'm never going to get this right."

"You will. Last night you could barely focus long enough to ground, and this morning you could hardly get out."

"And now I'm getting attacked."

"They wouldn't bother if we weren't a threat. And we're both tiring. They can sense that. We'll try again in the morning."

She shook her head. "No time."

He could feel it, too. She could see it in his eyes—the desperation thinly cloaked with patience. The set of his face remained firm, though. "We won't be able to do anything for her if we wear ourselves out before we get there."

"I suppose," Phoenix agreed. It made sense, though she wished it didn't.

Tremayne gave her an encouraging smile. "Even mages need to eat. Come. Basil said he'd have something special for dinner tonight, and then we need to get away for a couple hours to keep from going mad. Kaya suggested the dollar cinema—*Princess Bride* is playing. It's her favorite."

Phoenix smiled at the light in his eyes when he mentioned his wife's name, thankful that one thing, at least, was as it should be.

◇ ◇ ◇

Strange, the things you missed.

Her fiddle. Her cat. Her family. Her vardo—her truck. Those were obvious. But there were little things, too—the way Kaya's hair fell when she tucked a pen behind her ear. The hinges on Tanek's vardo door squeaking. They'd only been doing it for a couple days—for all she knew, *Phuro* Basil had oiled them already. Laughter—real laughter—and the harmless crackle of a campfire. Boots scuffing the dirt roads. Musicians tuning. The familiar embrace of a bodice. The smell of *Phuro* Basil's cooking, or Phoe's hair after a shower. The dry, hot-cotton scent of clothes seconds out of the dryer. Such piddly, dumb things, but they were home.

Ryna stared forlornly at her family's vardos from the Throne in gamers' camp, realizing for the first time how much of the defiant strength she had always claimed rested solidly on the fact that her family was there to love her and back her up.

And now she was too far to reach them.

Ryna hated feeling vulnerable.

She was tired, so tired... she knew she should go back to Cottage, or the tree by Scribe's Hall, or maybe Caravan Stage. She knew she should replenish her waning energy... but somehow, even that seemed like far too much work.

Something rustled behind her.

The Gypsy froze, praying to every deity she knew that the creature would pass her by.

◇ ◇ ◇

Wood smoke and myrrh. Warmth—more warmth than anyone that size should exude. The way she drank tea only holding onto the bottom of the mug. The cute little wrinkle to her nose that time she'd accidentally grabbed the wrong leather mug at a music jam and gotten a swig of Guinness instead of the lemonade she'd expected. The gentle touch of her tiny hands, the musician's calluses on her left fingertips, the way her bow sailed jubilantly over her fiddle's strings. Her sparkle. Those beautiful olive-green eyes with the gold flecks, and that far-off expression she got sometimes that reminded Phoenix, always, that Ryna wasn't quite human.

Phoe stared up at the vardo's darkened ceiling, hands folded across her stomach as she mentally recited the litany of All Things Ryna. She wondered if Karma was doing the same, huddled in a miserable ball in the crook of her arm. The other Gypsies slept; the sharp edge of alertness had faded from their energy signatures long ago. No surprise, really; Phoe teetered on the brink of exhaustion herself, but she couldn't relax enough for dreams to take her.

With a sigh, Phoenix levered out of bed (disturbing a woeful-looking Karma) and pulled on a pair of jeans and a turtleneck. She knew it courted disaster to wander alone on site after dark. Liam had accomplished his goal and gotten over to this side, but the Shadow Fae might have some other nasty up their collective sleeves.

She couldn't bring herself to care. Numb and a little reckless, Phoenix swung her cloak over her shoulders, tugged the hood up, and crept out the door, surprised at how her breath plumed whitely before her.

Dark vardos lined their communal fire pit, and beyond that, other hunched and silent trailers, their occupants absent or slumbering. Phoe threaded between them, then onto the dirt road. Tiny rocks crunched loudly beneath her loafers as she tromped up the Olympic Staircase.

Phoe hovered for a moment in the oasis of light near C-gate. What lurked out there? And who was she to think she could handle it when Ryna could not? Even the familiar hulk of the BLUE crouched ominously in the dark. Perhaps it would be wiser to return to the vardo and stare at the ceiling...

No. That thought was even worse than imagined phantoms that could steal her away. *Oh, for better night vision.* More bravely than she felt, Phoenix nudged up her glasses and stepped away from the light.

No burst of flames engulfed her; no band of Shadows leapt out to stuff her in a sack and carry her away. She took another step. She would not let them win. After all, Pendragon's grounds were no different now than any other time she had gone wandering... or so she told herself, trying hard to ignore the nagging voice in the back of her head that told her Ryna had probably thought much the same thing, that last time.

Still, nothing. She almost felt a little disappointed.

One step bred another, and soon the games area surrounded her. She kept her eyes down. Perhaps if she did not see anything, she would be safe.

Foolish, foolish, she chided herself, but could not summon the courage to raise her eyes.

A whinny floated across the breeze. Images flitted through her mind, of ghostly knights re-enacting the jousts that cost their lives. She wasn't sure if she'd rather believe her own imaginings or pass it off as horses tethered beyond the high picket fence. What if explaining everything away made her Magick disappear, too?

Still, she dared not look, not even when she passed between Cottage and the elephant rides. Remembered music haunted this place, and the image of a raven-haired peasant and a redheaded Gypsy doing an Irish swing across the lawn. Unable to bear the memory, Phoe took off at a sprint, careening headlong across Shepherd's Green, her cloak streaming like a banner behind her. She heard her feet hit the crunching gravel of the road past the Harvest Man and turned right to follow it.

"Phoenix..."

The Gypsy stopped short, though part of her wanted to run faster. Her cloak settled heavily around her. She held her breath, listening, reaching out with her other senses despite her better judgment.

Only eerie silence answered. It felt as if the otherworldly creatures that called this place home had left on a collective privy break. But why?

She didn't like it. At least when they stalked her, she knew where they were. A desperate urge to scream at them to show themselves seized Phoenix, but she thought wiser of it.

"Phoenix..."

There, again, that tug on her soul as her name rode a breath of wind. Phoe pulled her hood back up. *I'm hallucinating,* she told herself resolutely—and started walking again.

The next time it came, the voice sounded like a cry.

"Phoenix!"

An uncertain glance over her shoulder—Chapel watched her patiently, its dark mass outlined against a starry sky. "I'm coming," Phoe whispered as her feet carried her toward the seating area—and distantly wondered when she'd made that decision. The center aisle was hard and grassless under her worn loafers.

Chapel's interior gaped before her. Phoenix hesitated under a topiary arch, suddenly uncertain—though strangely unafraid. The burlap curtains on the back wall shifted restlessly in the wind, revealing twin glimpses of Shepherd's Green. She took a step forward.

"Phoe..."

Another step. Even reaching back, she could no longer touch the arch. She let her arms fall to her sides.

The curtains reached for her, entreating. Her cloak hung still. She nudged back her hood. It fell gently against her shoulder blades.

Another step, and her foot touched the flagstone floor.

An altar sat two-thirds of the way back, odd shapes lying helter-skelter across its fringed tablecloth like wide-mawed dragons. There was something familiar and a little disturbing about them.

Her heart hammered in her chest. She tried to remember to breathe. Another step.

The hushed roar of a swirling updraft surrounded Phoenix as she reached the Chapel's center. The world tunneled. So far away, the dragons turned their heads and blinked midnight eyes at her.

"You came..."

Phoenix nearly fell to her knees as solid reality exploded from the pitifully thin thread that connected her to her soulmate. It wrapped tightly around her, clinging for dear life. Phoenix struggled not to retch at the slithering Shadow-energy that coated it. She closed her eyes, breathing hard, and stilled the instinct to push it away. "Ryna," she whispered with all the pain and longing that bound her heart. She didn't dare disbelieve.

"I'm sorry..."

"Oh, love, no one blames you. It'll be all right." Phoenix was surprised she didn't choke on the words... but she had to sound as if she believed. She had to be strong. "Just hold on until we can bring you back—because we *will* bring you back."

"I love you..."

"Ryna, wait—" The world shifted and wavered—and the blessed, fowling embrace left her soul. "I love you too..." she whispered, but it was too late. The Chapel stood still and silent again; Phoe stared at the overturned candlestick holders on the table. Maybe it had been a trick of light and shadow, or of the wind, or of her desperate need to believe.

Maybe it had been—but somehow Phoenix really doubted it.

And for once in her life, doubt made her smile.

Ryna whimpered, fighting the urge to weep as she slowly lowered her forehead to the floor where she crouched in the Chapel's center. The rough stone scraped against the skin of hands and brow, but she hardly noticed. She felt as if she had been struck by lightning. Repeatedly. And then spent a couple hours relaxing on the rack.

But oh... Phoenix...

Phoenix *there*, their souls embracing across worlds, and those beautiful, whispered words...

Phoenix loved her still. Phoenix said they would bring her home.

Cruel hope... But to feel love surrounding her, driving back Shadows and fear, granting a small measure of self—if only for a bit...

Ryna would stand in a rainstorm with a claymore if that was what such pain earned.

"If I get kidnapped by the Shadow Fae, can I skip Rehearsal too?"

Niki glared at Tanek as the Gypsies puffed up the Olympic Staircase. "Don't even joke about that."

Phuro Basil looked like he was trying to muster his patience. "Remember, we're trying not to make waves. It's bad enough Patty noticed Ryna's gone."

Baba Luna snorted. "Bets on who let that juicy bit of gossip slip?"

"We can't prove anything," Kaya reminded, though her tone lacked conviction. "And at least she hasn't kept pestering us about our clothes."

"Wonder why that is?" Niki asked, easily diverted.

Speculation bounced among the Gypsies, but Phoenix couldn't bring herself to care. Her mind was limp with the exhaustion of a day of training with Tremayne. She'd told him about her encounter in the Chapel, though she had not mentioned it to the others. She didn't want them to start expecting miracles from her. She wasn't sure she had them to give.

Tremayne only nodded and smiled—as if he had expected no less.

"Hey, stranger," Bryn—Laine—greeted as they neared Bedside Manor. "We've been looking for you for the past week! Where have you been?"

"Around," she answered vaguely. "I had some things I had to take care of."

They did not believe her, but the Artistic Director called them to the traditional amoeba, forestalling further questions.

The evening's festivities ran the usual course, but Phoe was numb to the agony of it. She simply followed orders... and breathed a sigh of relief when the pink demon released them and she could return to the comfort of her vardo. Or Jack's trailer. It made little enough difference... although she'd hardly introduced her butt to the avocado bench cushion when Marcus plopped down next to her with a strange look in his eyes.

"Alright Phoe, what's wrong? You've been doing some pretty hardcore Magick. We can see it in your eyes—you're hardly here at all."

Phoenix's attention skittered to the trailer's other occupants: Laine, Jack, Puddle, and Mutch—she still didn't know the last two's real names. Their undivided attention had fixed on her.

"What's really going on?" Mutch asked.

Phoe tried not to shift uneasily. She really didn't have the energy for this. Not now. "You wouldn't believe me if I told you."

Jack raised both eyebrows. "Try us."

The Gypsy studied her friends' earnest faces. They truly believed that whatever she said, they could take it. Phoenix envied them. She wasn't sure *she* could take it—and she was wrapped up in the middle of it.

Well, what the hell... it couldn't hurt to tell them the truth. They'd probably believe she was making up stories, and then she could laugh it off, say she thought she had a touch of the faire crud, and call it done. "You know how Liam disappeared last year? That was us."

The expressions were skeptical—but not disbelieving. Not yet, anyway.

"He was into some Magick—dark stuff—to try and get Ryna and me apart." Phoe took a deep breath and plowed ahead before she could lose her nerve. "We made sure the things he was dealing with called in their payment."

Puddle this time. "Oooookaaaaayyyyy..."

"We thought that was the end of it—but somehow he managed to kidnap Ryna's soul to wherever it was he got sent and take over her body. And now the Bright Fae say that if we can't bring her back on the full moon, her soul will die and we'll lose her forever."

Stunned.

Silence.

Phoenix mentally reviewed her words, impressed at the calm of her voice. Her hands only trembled a little where they rested on her knees. Somehow, saying it made it so much less real. Now they could call her bluff. Honestly, who would to believe such a thing?

"Well, it makes the puzzle pieces we have look a *lot* more like a picture," Laine observed after a time. "What can we do to help?"

Phoe stared at her in disbelief. "Aren't you going to tell me I'm crazy?"

A wry grin shaped her lips. "Phoenix, I am the *last* person who would have any right to sling that word around. Besides, I'd believe anything that happened out here."

"The place is Fae enough," Marcus seconded. "And there are a disturbing number of not-quite-humans among the rennies."

A quirky smile tugged Phoe's lips as she leaned back. Their casual acceptance of the bizarre made it that much more surreal. Perhaps if she played along long enough, she'd eventually wake up. "You do realize no one else can know of this."

Puddle shrugged. "We can keep secrets."

"We can even start false rumors, if you like," Jack suggested with an impish grin.

"When are you bringing her back?" asked Marcus.

"Friday, late. After everyone's in bed."

"What do you want us to do?" asked Mutch.

"Do?" The concept both baffled and flattered her. She had no *idea* what these people could do. Not that long ago she hadn't even known they could do anything!

"Will you need protection? Extra energy? Diversion? Fire power?" Puddle offered.

"We may not know what you're doing or how you do your work, but you'll find we have our own ways," Jack added. "And at the very least, we make really effective batteries."

"Moral support, maybe," she answered after a moment of thought, still half expecting somebody to shout "gotcha." "The Gypsies are a pretty tight group—with something as delicate as this, I'm not sure they'll want strange energies in the middle of things, you know? But... if you could keep people away from the Maypole area, that would be great. The last thing we need is some random person wandering through."

The peasants glanced at each other and nodded, as if that decided it.

"Consider it done," Jack said. "You tell us where and when, and we'll be there."

One day until the full moon.

Liam could feel it as strongly as he ever had in the other world. The Bright Fae were coming into their prime, and the Shadow Fae were slinking back, biding their time. He wondered, idly, if he would've succeeded last year, had the moon been dark when Pendragon ended. Attacking when the Shadow Fae were at their weakest had been an unfortunate necessity… though he hadn't really believed, then, in anything as golden and beautiful as the Bright Fae.

They would help the Gypsies tomorrow, of course. He wondered how much that should concern him.

Dark laughter skittered across the edges of his mind.

Foolish mortal, worrying about flickers of light. Ryna is ours. The voice sounded so clear, it could almost have been his own thoughts… except that his own thoughts were never accompanied by that rotting darkness. Oddly comforting, that.

Let them feast on Ryna. Soon he would consume her family.

And then, at last, he would be free.

It started with a trip to China. It was a field trip… or something… Phoenix only knew that she should have been packed by now—her ride was here, honking the horn of a wedding-mint-green old gas guzzler out on the boulevard—but she had of necessity spent the day entertaining a guest, and now she was not ready.

China, of all places. She had never really wanted to see China, but she knew she needed to go. She had too many bags, and nothing fit in them quite right, but she had to hurry, and so she tossed everything in haphazardly: deodorant, a bottle of maple syrup, and a ceramic figurine of an owl in case she got hungry. But the owl grabbed her finger in its sharp beak and pulled her into the suitcase, and she could hear the annoyed *beep-beep* of the car's horn outside. *Now I will be late for sure,* Phoenix thought as the light from her room at Daniel's house grew more distant.

And then she was on a cruise ship—or an airplane—or maybe both. A brick fireplace housed a quiet fire burning with perfect flames. People milled around, the murmur of intelligent discussion covering topics of literature and groceries, and someone with a harp sat in one corner playing something from *Hamlet*. Strange, the harpist looked nothing like how Phoenix pictured Ophelia, except for her garlands: soggy and limp and coming to pieces. She was too short. Her darkly red hair dripped on the orange-brown carpet.

"*How should I your true love know from another one*?" she sang. Her voice sounded wet, too, but no one was listening.

A tall, dark-haired man stared into the distance. *Perhaps he should have been Ophelia,* Phoenix thought as he pulled a silk cloth tight over a metal charm as long as his hand.

"Out," he said, "it is time for you to leave."

And they all did, murmuring still about peaches and Jane Austen and thyme—

"Are you going to Pendragon Faire?
Parsley, sage, rosemary, and thyme
Remember me to one who lives there
For she once was a true love of mine."

"Pendragon?" Phoenix asked, but Ophelia was gone, her song fading from the place next to the beige filing cabinets where she had crouched damply with her harp.

Three people remained... the tall fellow, Phoenix, and one other she had never seen before, though she thought that she should know him. The tall fellow—Tremayne—stood directly in front of the fireplace. Strange. Tremayne's hair didn't look at all like that, or his face.

"This is not right," said the one whose appearance kept shifting by increments. His hair got a shade lighter, his eyes a shade darker, and then they would trade. He knelt on Tremayne's left. "This is not right."

Phoenix felt his unease, though she knew he was wrong. This *was* right... or, at the very least, had to be done. She did not comment as she knelt at Tremayne's right—a silent counterpoint to the fellow on the other side, still shaking his head and muttering.

Tremayne muttered something, too. It sounded like Latin. He threw something onto the fire—white cloth, or maybe a tissue. It landed on the wood but did not burn, rose a little in the air and simply floated.

As one, Phoenix and her counterpart added their offerings. Hers was a white silk scarf with some sort of pattern in blue. She had made it, though she had never seen it before. His offering—a scarf in red and black—rested on the logs, not burning, though an invisible hand plucked hers upwards, folding it into delicate shapes like the cloth napkins at the restaurants she had visited with her parents as a child. It fluttered toward her, strangely unsinged, though threadbare in patches. It occurred to Phoenix that maybe she shouldn't be able to notice the threadbare bits so distinctly from such a distance, though the thought only puzzled her momentarily. It landed in her cupped hands, seemed to settle in with a sigh of relief. *Oh,* she thought, stroking it. *It's like a little wounded bird.*

"It came back to you," observed the fellow she knew but did not. He seemed surprised, or perhaps impressed. It was Tanek. She wondered why she had not known that before.

"It has started again," said Tremayne at her back, and it made some sort of intrinsic sense, although she could not have said what had started, or how he knew, only that of course he would be right. Phoenix glanced over her shoulder, the scarf still nestled in her hand, and saw him staring into the distance while his hands tightly wrapped a scrap of sky-blue silk around the heavy metal cross Rachelle had worn to protect her from superstitious village folk.

There were clouds on that scrap of sky…

"Phoenix? What was that about the sky?"

"Sky?" Phoenix returned to her own eyes, the stark light and shadows of the campground, the trees across the road reflecting the warm russet light of the fire in gamers' camp. Niki's vardo door gave a quiet *snick* as she locked it and removed the key.

"You said something about the sky; I didn't catch it all. Are you feeling all right?"

What a stupid question. Ryna was gone, and the memory of a wounded bird made from scarves wrapped bands of grief around her chest. She feared she might be losing her mind. "I'm fine," she lied. It was blatant.

Niki pretended not to notice. That was blatant, too. "Get some rest if you won't come to the concert with us." A pause. "You're sure you won't come? A couple hours of music, of not thinking about all this would be good for you, honey, especially considering tomorrow."

"I'm sure," Phoenix said. That, at least, was the truth.

Niki sighed; Phoenix went into her vardo to hide until everyone left. Then she opened the fridge and removed an Asian pear, round like an apple and as cold as the moon. She stepped outside, leaving her door wide. The lace curtain fluttered fitfully as she stood near the dormant fire pit and stared up at the sky. Lightning laced the clouds, illuminating their shapes with an incandescent glow as they grumbled resentment.

Phoenix took a bite of her pear, crisp and a little sharp against her gums, but cool, so she didn't much notice.

The moon hung so near to full, always framed with the now-bright-now-dark clouds.

Artemis, Ryna, the Gypsy called silently to the night, and everything in her caught in a lump behind those words. *Tomorrow. We're coming. I love you.*

A tatter of mist floated across the sphere and dissolved.

"You will be my Phoenix," a familiar voice whispered; familiar eyes gazed down at her. Pale. Serene.

Phoenix smiled and licked sweet, chill juice from the warm skin of her hand. A gentle breeze tufted her hair. She watched for a long time in the silence of the wind, her head tipped back as far as it would go.

No matter how hard they tried, the clouds could not eclipse the moon.

◇ ◇ ◇

Ryna leaned against the Maypole's ragged surface. Almost full, almost full. She could feel the Shadows crouching, uncomfortable, exposed in this harsh light. They tried to cover it with clouds, but she would not let them. Staring, simply staring, she would keep the moon in sight by simply believing it could not be covered.

They would come. Soon. She had to trust in that. For if they did not…

The Shadows crouched outside the Maypole's circle, waiting for the light to die.

◇ ◇ ◇

"How you doing?"

Tanek's question shattered Phoenix's pointedly mindless contemplation of the gazebo's scenic overlook. She'd been standing there since dawn.

"I'm so nervous I think I'm going to throw up," she answered with all her heart—and nearly all her stomach. She wondered if she looked green. She certainly felt it.

He leaned against the railing to her left, and they stood in silence for a while, listening to the wind rustle the leaves. The air brushed coolly against face and hands.

Phoenix wondered why Tanek had come. Private seductions and large parties were his specialties, not random personal discussions. Unless someone had sent him…

"I wonder why they didn't take this thing down," the dancer reflected. "The whole purpose behind the gazebo is hiding from patrons."

"Maybe Patty hasn't figured out it's back here," Phoenix said quietly. A nearby crafter had an old Gypsy CD in their stereo—it went surprisingly well with the wind chimes that hung from the gazebo's center. She smiled. Ryna would be back soon.

"A lot of times, Ryna and I don't get along," Tanek said, "but I really miss her when she's not here."

"Me too." The weathered old wood felt rough under her hands. "Sometimes I stand here and imagine I can feel her here, too."

"Makes sense, with all the time she spent here."

Phoenix said nothing. She couldn't explain it, but she knew that wasn't the reason.

He shifted.

Phoenix waited. It was something she'd learned from Tremayne. People talked more if you didn't say anything. He was a wise man—her true father.

Tanek cast her a sidelong glance, took a deep breath. "Will you be staying—even if Ryna doesn't come back?"

So *that* was why he'd come. Phoenix bristled. "Don't even think that," she spat. "Ryna *will* come back. What kind of friend are you if you're giving up on her before you've even tried?"

"But I was—"

"But nothing." She turned, stared him down, saw him cower, and took a cold satisfaction in it. "Get your priorities straight, or get out of the circle. Because if your half-assed attitude gets Ryna stuck there, and Liam gets to stay here in her place, the Shadow Fae are going to look like fluffy little bunnies compared to me."

Fear spiked down the thread of connection they shared. Phoenix deliberately walked past him, crashed through the brush on her way up the hill, and struck aside the black burlap curtain. She held herself tightly and walked fast, hoping it would make her shaking cease. Threatening Tanek—a member of her chosen family… Phoe scowled, disgusted with herself and even more disgusted with him. She hoped he pulled it together. The thought of throwing him into the quarry gave her no joy.

Liam watched the door handle idly as it turned. It was too early for Daniel to be home yet. That meant one of the Gypsies, come to make empty threats of what dire things would befall him if he did not tell them how he'd accomplished switching places with Ryna—as if any of them could frighten him after the Shadow Fae. He settled down on his thin bedroll and smirked, looking forward to the afternoon's entertainment.

Sure enough, Tanek stepped through the door and closed it, an iron glint in his eyes. Disconcerted, Liam watched the intruder like a hare regards a fox. Tanek had never been so cool before, and there was something far too casual about the way he leaned back against the door, pointedly barring the only means of escape.

"I've known Ryna since we were in high school," the Gypsy remarked conversationally, fiddling with a dagger he drew from his belt. "She and Phoenix are like sisters to me—and you hurt them. So far you've gotten away with it."

"Your scare tactics don't work, little boy. Go back to your tutu and your zills."

Tanek ignored the comment. "It seems the other Gypsies are too noble for this," he said lightly, testing the blade's edge with his thumb—then turned to stare at Liam, eyes boring through the back of his head. "I'm not."

And in that gaze, Liam saw his plans.

There was a moment for shock, for disgust, for disbelief and inevitability.

The dagger disappeared with a shining flash.

Tanek slunk forward, knelt over him. Tendrils of Magick curled around Liam's will, telling him to be still as his captor reached out to twiddle with one of his shirt buttons. Slowly, so slowly, taking care to brush slightly against his breasts...

And then the button slipped free.

And the next...

Liam quashed the electric shivers that chased his spine. Rallying his wits, he swatted Tanek's hand and shoved him away. "I can't believe you're doing this to Ryna's body," he spat as he clambered to his feet, revulsion twisting his face. "What happened to the sister thing?"

"I'm not doing it to Ryna's body." Lightning-fast, Tanek slammed him up against the wall. Liam heard a distinct crack as his head rebounded off the hard stone. "I'm doing it to your soul." Then, while Liam was still blinking spots from his eyes, Tanek seized both of his wrists in one large hand and pinned them over his head. The captive struggled briefly, but granite may as well have grown over him for all the effect his efforts had. A swift bolt of terror shot through him. Never had he felt so small—so vulnerable...

But not helpless. Not while he drew breath. Liam stared defiantly into the Gypsy's blue-green eyes, forced his breathing to remain even as Tanek's other hand—strong, assured—slipped under Liam's shirt, expertly found the most sensitive spots, and plied their trade. *It's only a body,* Liam reminded himself firmly, ignoring the tingles dancing across his skin.

"This is what you do to the girls, isn't it?" Tanek asked darkly. "Make them submit, make them want you..."

God, this wasn't supposed to happen. He didn't want this—why did the fire coil inside him? *Only a woman's body, responding to a man's touch. It has nothing to do with me.*

"Force their silence if you don't force them outright..."

He battled the will that snaked around his own, fought the need that pulled at parts he wasn't even supposed to have. "I see how this is," Liam said on a gasp.

"You knew I'd kick your ass if I had my Magick. You had Tremayne shield me so you could rape his daughter's body while his precious little girl was out."

"Rape?" Tanek asked, feigning wide-eyed innocence, and leaned close, his free hand plucking at the buttons on Liam's shirt. "But your body says you like it."

The warm breath in his ear made Liam tremble. He wanted to strike, claw, hit, bite—but could only squirm in pleasure as his captor rubbed methodically against him.

He thought he might be sick.

It's only a body, it's only a body...

Dammit, it's MY *body!*

Tanek's grip loosened as he fumbled with his jeans, his concentration slipping a hair. Liam seized the ounce of free will the distraction granted him and fought with a surge of primal fear, kicking and yelling.

Two weeks had taught Liam to compensate for the worst of his height's handicaps—but not in a situation like this. Tanek laughed deep in his throat as he pinned Liam hard to he floor, seemingly without effort. "Oh, you want it rough? All right, then—remember you asked for it."

Liam coughed from his impact with unforgiving cement as his jeans and panties ripped away, exposing his privates to cold air and probing fingers. "No!" he cried, unthinking.

"No?" A pause—and then Tanek's touch turned gentle... teasing, pulling, drawing on all the places that Liam had learned to tend when he wished to show a woman how much he could please her.

He whimpered in fear—in pleasure.

"Atta girl," Tanek crooned, his will smothering Liam as touch and Magick distracted him, swamped him in immediate sensation, kept him from remembering to fight back. "Relax. Doesn't that feel good? I won't hurt you—shhhh... shhhh... good girl..."

Liam bit the inside of his lip until it bled and prayed for the end.

◇ ◇ ◇

"I've done it. I am the friend I say I am."

Tanek's voice—angry, cold, and challenging—dropped into the stillness as Ryna passed the Harvest Man. She stopped short, glancing nervously around. She couldn't see him, but...

"I've proven myself to you damn Bright Fae."

A leather gauntlet slammed to the ground at the idol's feet. For a moment she could almost see him, staring defiantly up at the carved wooden face.

"Now bring her back!"

And then he disappeared, leaving Ryna with nothing but the empty air once more.

But the gauntlet remained. Ryna snatched it from the grass—quick, quick, before the Shadow Fae could take it. It smelled of worn leather and Tanek's sweat—and a hint of patchouli. A faint warmth lingered where he'd held it.

"They're coming," Ryna whispered, clinging to the odd, unexpected bit of home. She had no idea what he'd meant by his words, but… "They're coming. They're coming."

◇ ◇ ◇

Liam could not blink. His eyes ached from tears and from too long staring at the wall, but he could not make himself blink. If he did, he would see those eyes staring beyond Ryna's exterior and into the deepest depths of him. For the moment he did not hear the memory of his own muffled cries, though he did not think he could ever erase the memory of the Gypsy's touch…

A man's touch…

He had nothing against gay men. He had gay friends. But he was not, himself, gay, and he wanted nothing to do with a man's part in any orifices he may have.

Especially ones he wasn't supposed to have…

The prisoner shuddered, gasped softly, and held his breath, trying not to cry. Trying not to see anything but the wall. Trying not to remember how, all unwilling, his body had responded to the touch.

"*That feels good, doesn't it? See how much you want it?*"

Tanek's words echoed in Liam's memory, far too close to words he himself had spoken with more than one woman. If it felt good, she must like it; if she responded, she wanted more. If she said otherwise, it meant she thought she couldn't admit her desire. Keep going, show her a good time.

He tried to believe it had been different when he was on the other end, that they really *had* wanted it from him, but the belief was small and shriveled in the emptiness that filled his soul.

How many women had lain like this because of him? They had cried out and sighed in pleasure; he had thought—

God, what if Phoenix had been telling the truth the whole time, and he hadn't been listening? What if he had done this to the one woman he loved so truly he was willing to do anything to have her?

Had she wept, with no part of her body that was hers alone?

God.

It was too much—bad enough, all those other women, but his Phoenix… his pure, innocent, beautiful sugar-bird…

"You tried to rape me in the Croft..." her words echoed in his soul, backed by the faint, broken thread she'd spoken on the Knoll: *"I'm all right, I'm all right, I'm all right—"*

Liam closed his eyes, courted the horrid memories of the last eternity, alone and helpless with his tormentor. He deserved it, every second.

He hoped Tanek would return. That thought, at least, he could bear.

◇ ◇ ◇

Phoenix sighed and put down her pencil. She didn't know why she bothered. She couldn't keep her mind on her art—she'd only produced a couple doodles of Ryna playing with Karma... and one, oddly enough, of an elephant. Mostly, though, she kept getting lured back to her journals from the past year.

Maybe it was for the best. After all, what better way to prepare than to remember the person they were trying to reclaim?

The Gypsies had planned a little over the past week. If the peasants' observations were true, Liam must have crossed over on the burned spot... and so that was where they would do their ritual. She'd told them of the peasants' desire to help. There had been a few protests, but the other Gypsies had finally conceded that an outer ring of defense would be wise.

"Hello? Hello, Gypsies? Is—um—is anyone at home?"

Thankful for the distraction, Phoenix opened the door and stepped outside. Emily stood near the fire pit, Morgan's sleeping form limp in her arms. "You're here early," Phoe greeted cordially.

"I was wondering—I hate to ask it of you, but—would you mind watching her for a couple of hours? Geoff called me up and asked if I could go out to dinner with him, and he did say I could bring Morgan, but I thought it would be nice—just for an hour or two—"

"It would be an honor. Go, have fun; moms need a social life, too."

Emily blushed and indicated a picnic hamper at her feet. "Everything she might need is in there—spare diapers, change of clothes, wipes, extra Nuk, a bottle of breast milk in case she gets hungry before I—oh, hi Ryna!"

Ryna?

Phoenix turned slowly, her guts a block of ice. Daniel and *Baba* Luna stood there—Phoe hadn't even heard them pull up—with Liam between them. All three were stock still, identical looks of horror on their faces... Liam's for a completely different reason than the others', Phoenix felt certain. Emily chattered happily away, too ignorant of the situation and deliriously in the throes of new love to have any caution.

“I’d heard you might be back this weekend, but I’d also heard you’d been kidnapped by space aliens, and you know how the rumor mill is out here—you never know what to believe.”

“Sp space aliens?” Daniel stuttered.

“Isn’t it amazing what some people will say? Where do they come up with this stuff, anyhow? Here, Ryna, could you hold Morgan a second?”

“Sure,” Liam said, face ashen as he slowly accepted the child.

Phoe wondered if she looked much better. She wanted to turn in disgust from this—this *thing*—masquerading as her soulmate. She wondered if he was mentally tallying up the months—and hoped, cruelly, that he had figured everything out.

“You’ll probably want to put the bottle in the fridge right away, but it’s going to need heating up—you have a microwave, right? Don’t forget to test it against your wrist first, to make sure it’s not too hot, and… I’m fussing, aren’t I? I’m fussing. I’m sorry. It’s just that I’m so *nervous…*”

“Of course you’re nervous,” Phoenix said, breaking her paralysis, and hugged her friend. “But you don’t need to be. Geoffrey is crazy over you, and you’ll have a fantastic time, and we get to fuss over a baby for a couple hours. Now off with you.”

Emily giggled, and blushed, and kissed her sleeping child before flitting off.

“Geoffrey?” Liam repeated, dazed—whether from Luna’s Magicks or Emily’s revelation, Phoe couldn’t tell.

“Give me her,” Daniel snapped, snatching the child from Liam’s arms. Morgan whimpered, but Danny comforted her in a way so natural it was almost offhand. Phoenix wondered if he had done so with her as a child. She picked up the basket. She didn’t know what else to do.

“I’m sorry, kiddo,” *Baba* Luna apologized. “We tried to get here earlier, but—”

“It’s okay. I guess something like this was bound to happen, and it’s not like it matters much now.”

Baba nodded. “Daniel, help me get him into my vardo—then you and your sister can wander site with Morgan.”

He nodded, and Phoenix watched as they steered the increasingly drugged-looking Liam into the elders’ vardo. All they had to do was make it another ten or so hours, and they’d be home free.

Liam rested his head wearily against the fridge, not at all grateful that his thoughts had cleared once Phoe’s brother had bound him hand and foot and the witch-woman’s enchantments were no longer needed to keep him too addled to attempt escape.

A *baby*.

His? Someone else's? But Emily'd been a virgin when...

God, Emily too?

He wondered if he would ever stop feeling sick. What if that little girl with the thatch of dark hair... what if that sweet little girl, so precious and innocent, had been conceived from that night?

No—impossible. Sure she'd been a virgin, but for all Liam knew she'd slept with every other man on site after that. He'd never been sure about her affections. She'd been so flighty—so *blond*—and he'd seen her tittering at any number of other men's advances. It didn't seem to matter to her, as long as the guy was tall and would melt when she batted her eyes. After all, look at this Geoff character. Who knew how long he'd been up her skirts. It was probably his kid.

God, what if—what if *he*...no. it had only been the one time. They said a woman just *knew*, but he wasn't really a woman...

Had Tanek used a condom? He couldn't remember... God. The thought alone was enough to make him sick. Liam shuddered. He had nothing but time, now, to worry about it.

And to remember...

◇ ◇ ◇

Gods, what a torturous night. Time had never crept so slowly—not even the day before they'd gone to get her horse Pegasus when Phoe was a child, and that day had seemed like an eternity.

But there had only been joyous anticipation then, and somehow fear dragged things out more. Fear, and the maddening knowledge that of all the people in the BLUE, only Daniel, a couple Gypsies, and a handful of peasants understood. She'd spent the entire night diddling with the wax of their table's candle and trying not to check her watch.

And now it read four-thirty in the morning, and they were all exhausted and wired and nervous... but her family stood near the Maypole, as ready as they would ever be. If Phoe looked closely, she could make out the peasants' person-shaped blobs forming a casual, wide circle around The Spot. Energy hummed from them. Laine had said it was to make people steer clear without realizing it... and Phoenix was more grateful for their presence than she could say.

"Um, Phoenix?"

Tanek's voice jolted her into an entirely different sort of nerves—a sort for which she really didn't have the patience. "What."

He took her hand, folded it around something small and hard before she could pull away. "Jasper, jade, and carnelian." He gave her a tiny, hopeful smile. "I'd get you your own, but you won't need them after tonight."

Phoenix looked down at the polished stones, dark against her pale skin. They shone dully in the clear, sharp light from above. *Truce.* "Thank you."

He nodded, retreated to his place beside *Baba* Luna.

Phoenix dropped the stones down her shirt; they nestled in the little space of her bra over her heart. They tingled slightly. "What next?"

"Stand beside me." Tremayne led her to the center of the circle her family had formed. Liam stood on the sere patch of ground—bound, gagged, blindfolded... and addle-witted as well, thanks to Luna's Magicks. Phoenix did her best not to shy away.

Tremayne sat, cross-legged; Phoenix mirrored him, joined hands with her mentor. Phoe took a deep breath as he had taught her, closed her eyes, and let tension flow away as she released it. Distantly she heard the other Gypsies calling the corners.

Ground. Center.

For a brief instant she gave thanks that it was so similar to the trick of joining with the stars that she had done since childhood—and then there was no thought, only light, and the familiar feel of Tremayne's energy holding to her.

No direction. No time.

Phoe pushed down panic. She had to trust. Had to do this. For Ryna.

The thought carried her beyond fear to determination, to the heart-thread that drew her like destiny.

The light faded.

Pendragon.

Attack.

Phoenix lashed out reflexively as a misshapen Shadow Fae lunged for her. Fire engulfed the creature, but Phoe scarcely noticed it as chaos spun through her soul, darkness among the shards of bright-sharp Magick that burrowed into her essence. Phoenix shrieked as she tried to block it, offense forgotten.

Other cries echoed hers—strange, inhuman, and pained.

And then all was still.

"Are you all right?" Tremayne asked.

Phoenix drew a shaky breath. It still felt as if she'd inhaled ground glass, but the world had steadied. She nodded, glanced around. "Did we—?"

"The Shadow Fae expected an easy kill. They know our measure now. We must find Ryna quickly. Come." And, so saying, started down the Narrows.

"The Magick—it backfired, when I tried," Phoe said as she followed. "It was like it attacked me..."

"It's... more pure, here. Feel."

The younger Gypsy did, reaching out tendrils of awareness. Things felt mistier here. Motes of Magick swirled around her, strange and fractured. Things didn't feel quite… attached, somehow. *She* didn't feel quite attached, couldn't feel the ground beneath her feet. She looked down.

The ground *was* beneath her feet… about three inches beneath them.

"Hey, neat! I can fly!"

Tremayne gave her a quirky grin. "Found your happy thought?"

"I will as soon as we bring her home." She rubbed her arms. "The sooner we get out of here, the better."

Tremayne nodded. "Do not attack with Fire next time. You will fare better if—"

"What's that?" Phoe cut him off, pointing to a small, huddled mound on Twin Tree's octagonal stage.

The mound raised its head, olive-green eyes bright in the stage's shadows. Phoe's breath caught as it stood, tottering, and reached out a tiny, pale hand. "Phoenix?"

"Careful…" Tremayne warned.

"I know." But truly, Phoe didn't care. Trap or no trap, she had to go to her love, had to hold her, keep her safe, bring her home… Phoenix dashed forward, pulling Ryna into her arms—

—and cried out in horror as she met not the resistance of flesh, but the crumbling of a long, cold log made entirely of ash.

Tremayne grabbed her arms, pulled her away from the ghastly sight of her soulmate turning to powder on the ground. "It's not real—Phoenix, it's not real!"

Phoe yanked her brain to his words, forced it to comprehend them. "I know," she said after a moment. She took a deep breath, pulled herself together as she wiped the dust from hands and clothes. "I know. I just… I wasn't expecting it, is all."

"It's not going to get easier," he warned.

Phoenix squared her shoulders, wished she could erase the sensation of her love crumbling against her… "I'm okay. I'm ready for it."

Tremayne released her, nodded, and continued on toward the Bear.

They had barely crested the hill when a flickering orange glow brought Phoe up short. "The gyros booth," she whispered in horror. "It' s burning."

"Burned," Tremayne corrected, dismissing it as he angled his steps down the hill and toward the path that led to Sherwood. "A long time ago. It was a turkey drumstick booth, then. Strange—that happened before they tore down Bedside Manor and replaced it with the feast hall."

Phoe's mind reeled as she trotted alongside Tremayne. Creatures that looked like her love but weren't, replayed events that happened decades ago—it was like falling down a rabbit hole, only worse. How could Tremayne take this all so calmly? How could he ignore the half-seen glimpses of movement in the food booths and shops, the distorted laughter that rippled from Woodland Stage?

"We have her."

A humanoid creature dragged Ryna by her wrist to the shadow of the tree that bore the Sherwood sign.

The image of Ryna crumbling to dust in her arms flashed through Phoe's mind as Tremayne grabbed her arm hard. *Trickery,* he sent to her in thought, but said to the thing, "What do you wish?"

"We tire of feeding on this one. The one with you is fresh..."

Ryna struggled vainly. "Tata! Phoenix!"

"I propose a trade," it burbled.

Phoenix stood, frozen in horror, as darkly glistening fangs showed where the thing's stomach should have been. *It isn't her. It isn't real. It—*

The thing paused, apparently confused at their lack of action. "You would ignore the pleas of your only child?"

Still Tremayne did not move. "I have no proof that she is who you say."

"You will not bargain," observed the creature's twin, stepping from the Children's Realm, its voice like thick oil glorping over rocks.

"We shall have you all, then," said a third as a dozen of the things emerged from the shadows of trees and shops.

The first pulled Ryna's hand closer to the gaping, misplaced mouth, a smile broadening as it anticipated its meal. "There is still some use to her, yet..."

A bolt of blindingly white light shot from Tremayne's hand, engulfing the creature that held Ryna captive. It spasmed—and disappeared.

The others vanished as well—as did Ryna.

The Gypsies stood alone.

"You well?" Tremayne asked, looking far from it himself.

Phoenix nodded tersely.

"Search quickly. Stay close."

She nodded again, nerves on a blade's edge as she threw back the curtains to Caravan Stage, yanked open the doors to the dressing vardo and the smaller, shingled vardo. If she made noise, Ryna would hear her. If she made sudden movements, she would frighten the Shadows instead of the other way around. Still, no matter where she looked, only emptiness greeted her.

"She's not here," Tremayne announced as he returned from Hollow Hill. "Knoll?"

"Or Front Gate."

He nodded briskly. "One by way of the other. Quickly."

Phoenix hurried after him as he skirted the Children's Realm and climbed the hill past the glassblower, past the privies, past the stocks, toward the Drench-a-Wench booth—and stopped, swaying with disorientation as she surveyed her surroundings. BLUE, games area, Drench-a-Wench—hadn't they been in Cartwheel Cove? "What—"

Tremayne stopped, too, looked around. "It... shifted." He shook it off. "The fastest way to Knoll from here is past Cottage."

True enough—and Phoe had no desire to dwell on how or why. She wanted to leave before this place got any stranger. "Let's check Cottage first."

Eerie silence pressed around the Gypsies as they quickened their steps through the games area, past the pony ride, the Fencing Booth, towards the... Mead Booth?

Tremayne grabbed Phoe's arm, pulling her to a stop. "That's twice, now," he said quietly. "This is not random."

Phoe's heart sped uncomfortably. "They're trying to keep us away from Knoll—or Cottage."

"She's there. Mind your surroundings."

He didn't need to tell her to hurry. As one they aimed directly for Cottage, clambering over the Track's yellow fences and soft sand, vaulting the hay bale seats and cutting across the trampled grass of the elephant rides. Phoenix very nearly bounced on her toes as Tremayne fiddled with the bolt on the familiar green door.

The O'Malleys' home embraced them with love and protection, but the place's very stillness told Phoenix that it sheltered no one else. "Knoll," she said, and Tremayne nodded. They stepped back onto the lawn... and stood there, gaping at the sheer number of Shadow Fae that roiled across the moon-drenched expanse of Shepherd's Green. "I think they've given up on parlor tricks."

"Kill them," Tremayne ordered.

Any number of incredulous questions sprung to Phoenix's lips, but she swallowed them. He trusted her to watch his back... trusted her as an equal when she felt like little more than a child. The knowledge that everything rested on her made her want to curl up in a gibbering ball... but they had no time for that—not now. Gathering her courage and every scrap of talent she possessed, Phoenix fought for her life.

Fought for Ryna.

◇ ◇ ◇

Battle. On the Green.

Ryna crept stealthily along Chapel's back wall to the burlap-curtained doorway on the left. She inched aside the cloth to peek outside.

Shadow Fae. They were thinner than normal under the moon's radiance... but they made up for their relative weakness with numbers. And they were attacking her family.

Tears formed at this cruelest of all deceptions. And yet—Phoe had said they would come for her. The moon was full. The time was right. What if this was the real thing?

What if it wasn't?

What's the worst they can do to me? Ryna thought with a weary sigh as she took three steps, leapt from the Chapel's raised area, and plunged into bedlam. *Tata! Phoenix! I'm coming!*

They looked up sharply, recognition and shock flickering on their faces.

Behind! her father warned, granting just enough time for Ryna to turn before the Shadows bore her to the ground.

◇ ◇ ◇

"*That* was Ryna."

"It was," Phoe agreed, fending off something frighteningly akin to a manticore. This was ridiculous—there were too many of them. They could fight and fight and fight, and still they would never reach Ryna's side. In a fit of frustration, Phoenix pulled bits of Spirit around her soul like a waterproof cloak, willed the inky filth of the Shadow Magick to bead up and roll off her like rain. It formed black puddles at her feet, writhing with sentience. The next Shadow Fae that attacked met a swift, painful end courtesy of a bolt of lightning that lanced from the shield.

Tremayne flashed her an appreciative grin. "Nice work."

Phoenix smiled triumphantly and extended the shield to Tremayne, and together they carved a swath to Ryna's rescue.

They would never have seen her under the mound of Shadow Fae had they not known to look. Phoenix set upon Ryna's predators with an angry shout, kicking and clawing until only a dog-sized lizard stood between her and her soulmate. She booted it hard; the Shadow flew three yards and landed with a yelp she scarcely heard. "Ryna," she whispered, gingerly brushing back a wisp of long, copper-red hair. Her love lay quiet and still.

"Can you get her?" Tremayne asked uncertainly as he kept the Shadows at bay.

"If I can fly, I ought to be able to run with her," Phoenix said, scooping Ryna's unconscious form from the ground. "Besides, I have to hold on to her, remember?"

"I remember. Let's hurry—I think they figured out your shield's too strong. I want to get her home before they regroup."

"I'm with you." Phoenix stood, settling Ryna's weight more comfortably. "Let's go."

◇ ◇ ◇

Moving. She was moving—and rapidly. Warm arms and love enfolded her. Ryna mmmed slightly and opened her eyes to see the familiar booths of Upson Downs rushing past. Her head hurt awfully.

"Phoe? Tata?" she murmured groggily.

"Shhh," Phoe said, never slowing her pace. "We're taking you home, Artemis. Just hold on."

Ryna did, clinging to her soulmate with unearthly strength.

Mead Booth, Como Cottage, Juggling Booth.

Maypole, just ahead, just ahead…

Her father's sudden cry: "Phoenix, watch—!"

The ground rushed up far too fast as Phoenix pitched forward; Ryna braced herself for the impact. Phoe dropped her at the last second to free her arms and barely avoided squashing her flat. For a moment the redhead did not move, curled under the protection of Phoe's body.

"Up! Up!" Tremayne ordered, hauling Phoenix to her feet. The raven-haired Gypsy grabbed Ryna's hand on her way up, was running toward the seared spot before Ryna had even caught her balance.

Ten feet.

Seven.

Five.

Two—

A fountain of flame burst from the earth, engulfing Phoenix; Ryna jumped back with a terrified shriek, pulling free of her love's grasp.

"No! Ry—" Phoenix cried as the fire snapped out of existence.

They were gone—they were gone…

The full moon shone overhead—clear, serene, and mocking.

◇ ◇ ◇

"Phoenix! Phoenix! Come *on*, dammit! *Phoenix!*"

The voices sounded far away. Idly she wondered how they expected her to go somewhere when she had no sense of direction. She floated peacefully. How silly for the voices to sound panicked.

She could feel Tremayne's presence nearby. He was floating, too. He felt… worried and sad. Phoenix wondered why the voices didn't sound panicked about him. He floated closer. Warm light and his calming sense of presence embraced her, cradled her like a child—

Phoenix blinked up at a circle of pale, drawn faces. Niki supported her with one arm, offered a glass of water—the sacred water—with her free hand. Tears ran down Toby's cheeks, though the others looked too stunned to cry. Phoe hurled herself back at the dark floating place, but it was gone. Her soul landed with a thump of reality as Tremayne said softly, "She didn't make it back."

The words echoed in the void of her mind. "Not... back? No. No, you don't understand. We do the ritual, she comes back. That's how it works. The Bright Fae said so. We did the ritual. She has to be here. She has to."

"I'm not sure what happened," Tremayne said. "The veil, maybe... maybe we had to have Liam out first."

"Then we do it again," Phoenix replied stoutly. "Now. You. Me. Ground and center; we'll go back and—"

"We can't—Phoenix, we can't." He clasped her hands firmly, his gaze holding hers, silencing her. "Not now. There are too many of them, and they're expecting us now. They know we're coming. We'll never beat them on their territory. I love her too, but I can't risk losing you both."

She knew he was right, damn him. She tore her gaze from his, looked away—to Liam, olive eyes distant and pained. All this, and he had the nerve to look sorry—! With an incoherent cry she lunged at the horrible parody of her love, tackled him to the ground, and pummeled him mercilessly.

"Phoenix!" she heard someone call from somewhere beyond the red fog that smothered her world. Gentle, firm hands pried her off, and then she was held fast in *Phuro* Basil's arms as he tried to calm her. She couldn't make out his words over her hiccupping sobs. *Ryna!* her soul screamed.

A faint, weeping echo reached to her across worlds. Ryna was there—hurt, and frightened, and alone. She had no family to hold and comfort her. Phoenix pulled herself together, gathered what tattered strength remained to her, and sent reassurance and love along that impossibly thin thread. Ryna must know they had not given up on her. Must know there was hope.

"I'm okay," Phoenix murmured at length and drew away, embarrassed at her outburst. How selfish. She was not the only one to love Ryna.

Indeed, Kaya wept softly against Tremayne's chest nearby; his tears glistened in the moonlight as he stared into the distance. Tanek, Toby, *Baba* Luna, and Niki bent over the prisoner, and the energy radiating from them made Phoe shudder.

Phoe had a duty to this family, too. "This isn't finished. We'll try again. We have to. Ryna is counting on us. Equinox is coming up, right? That's a powerful day, things hanging in the balance, should be ideal, right? We'll figure out what we did wrong, and next time we'll do it better. We'll bring her back then."

"Of course we will," *Phuro* Basil agreed.

"Good." Phoenix nodded decisively. She scrubbed away tears with her sleeve and wondered when she had started to shake so badly. *Shock,* she realized, and glanced over at Tremayne again. He looked, she objectively noted, like hell.

They all did. It was, in some unfathomable way, comforting.

Phoenix went to where Tanek and Toby had wrestled their captor upright. She felt the wary eyes of the entire troupe on her as she stood so close that she could feel the heat radiating from the small body.

Not nearly as much heat as should be there…

Liam stared dumbly at her, sluggish traces of fear in his stance. He'd won this round, and he didn't even have the balls to look proud of himself.

Never in her life had Phoenix felt such perfect hate.

She spat on his tiny, elfin face. And walked away with furious tears burning her eyes.

"Hey," Niki called, double-stepping to catch up.

The raven-haired Gypsy could not bring herself to face her friend. "I'm sorry I've been so needy."

"Sweetheart, it's natural. No one begrudges you being taken care of."

"What about Tremayne?" Phoenix replied evenly as they strode through C-gate. "He's her father. Kaya's her mother in every way that counts. The rest of you are her chosen family. You're bonded to her, too. Don't you need to be taken care of?"

"We all take care of each other. Which is why you're going to stay with me tonight."

"I'm all right."

"Really? I'm not. And sometimes the best way to be taken care of is to focus on someone else."

Phoenix was quiet for a moment, mulling that over. When they reached the base of the Olympic Staircase, she said, "So shall we take care of each other, then?"

Niki grinned, albeit a little shakily. "That's what sisters are for."

Meghan Brunner

Pendragon Renaissance Faire

Weekend Six: Sherwood Hate To Miss Yew Ale

~*~

Join Robin Hood and his Merry Men as they grace our village with Friar Tuck's Ale and Little John's tales. The village is alive with the days of old. The whims of fancy and fantasy collide with our hamlet and lead us into a world full of pub crawls and archery tournaments. Join Robin as he challenges the Sheriff to the first annual archery contest. Follow Friar Tuck through his Parade Pub Crawl. Ready your Lincoln Greens and your stout Yew Longbow. We're off to Sherwood! (Theme sponsored by Classy Legs Hosiery)

"Phoenix? Oh, holy shit, Phoe, honey, wake up..."

The hand shaking her, more than the urgency in Niki's voice, finally persuaded Phoenix to peel her eyelids open. Even then, she could only murmur a rather unintelligent "Unrh?"

"Phoenix, you need to get up. Now."

"Hacom," Phoe demanded blearily, scrubbing the sleep from her eyes. It didn't help, though vaguely she noted that it couldn't possibly be morning yet. All the light in Niki's vardo had the gently orange glow of incandescent bulbs, made fuzzier by her lack of spectacles. In the back of her consciousness, she could feel the other Gypsies' alarm. *Wow,* Phoenix mused. *This must be serious.*

"How come?" Niki cried. "Can't you hear the wind out there?"

Phoenix tuned in to her surroundings a bit more and caught the harsh buffeting of air against the vardo. Niki must've turned on her radio; a soft male voice reported quietly, "—CCO weather update. The day's looking to be beautifully mild: temperatures in the low seventies with gusts of wind around eight to ten miles per—"

The world tilted as the vardo rocked onto two wheels; candles and jewelry slid to the floor. Niki threw herself to the airborne side to provide extra ballast. A little voice in the back of Phoenix's head began shrieking, but the rest of her just curled up and contemplated going back to sleep.

A vigorous pounding at the door prevented her.

"Tanek! Thank the goddess!" Curtains, scarves, and papers trembled uneasily in the suddenly noisy wind as Niki flung wide the door.

Tanek stepped in, pushed the door shut to block out the howling.

"What's going on out there?" Niki demanded.

"Near as we can tell, backlash from trying to get Ryna back."

"Can't someone fix it?"

"You and Toby are the Airs. If anyone—"

"I can't! I mean, I tried, but it got worse, and the weather guy says nothing's wrong, but the vardo went up on two wheels, and—" She teetered on the edge of hysteria, Phoenix noted with interest. She had never seen Niki so close to losing it.

"Shhhh." Tanek clasped her hands in his, and for a moment Phoenix could feel the pulsating earth-beat that surrounded them. The worst of the hair-trigger tension melted from Niki's posture, though she still looked poised to bolt. The earth-beat faded. "Better?"

"Thanks." Niki sounded much more in control now. Phoenix would've believed her calm if she hadn't caught the sharp jolts of edginess spiking down their connection.

"My pleasure. We're all gathering outside to see what we can do; even if we can't stop it, maybe we can minimize the damage. You ready, Phoe?"

Phoenix blinked at him. She understood the question, but the answer seemed far away.

Tanek shot a concerned glance at his fellow Gypsy, who shrugged. "She's been like that since I woke her up. Must be left over from that sleep thing."

Sleep thing… Vaguely Phoenix remembered *Baba* Luna insisting on sleep and a kaleidoscope of colors luring her into darkness. She wasn't sure whether to be grateful or miffed, especially since there was a crisis afoot and she couldn't bring herself to care.

"Shit. Well, at least *somebody's* calm about this whole thing. Maybe she'll come up with a solution the rest of us haven't. C'mon, Phoe."

Obediently she slid from Niki's bed and toddled into the moonlit night.

Reality blasted her square in the face as the wind tore at her with primal fury. Dear gods, how could she have missed anything this all-present? This malicious? No wonder the others seemed half a step away from screaming!

Screaming.

Ryna's voice, screaming.

All gods, what have we done?!

Phuro Basil had one arm around her shoulders, steering her toward the cold fire pit. Ashes danced like snow in the maelstrom, caught in the hair and eyebrows of the Gypsies gathered there, clothes blown tight against their bodies. "I'm sorry," she whispered, though she doubted Ryna could hear. "I'm sorry. I'm sorry." She felt like a sacrificial virgin in her white nightdress—except she wasn't a virgin anymore. *No embroidery,* she thought strangely. *It should have embroidery... and blood...*

An empty five-gallon plastic water jug rolled by, thumping off obstacles. A rennie in his bathrobe moseyed to the nearest privy, apparently unconcerned that the wind slammed the door open and shut.

Still, Ryna screamed.

Phoenix wanted to scream, too, scream and scream into the suffocating wind. She closed her eyes against the flying debris and wished she'd had the presence of mind to grab her glasses. Too late now, standing amidst the ashes with Tremayne, in the fire pit's center instead of in their usual place beside it. The others stationed themselves at the cardinal points. She could feel hands clasping around the circle, energy gaining the virtues of each mage as it traced familiar paths. Air. Fire. Water. Earth. Spirit. Phoenix struggled to stay afloat, guide and befriend the tides of Magick. She gave thanks that she didn't have to spearhead this mission; as it was, she had to fight the urge to retch from exhaustion. Tremayne wavered on his feet. She held to his hands to steady him, though she had no idea what she would be able to do if he actually fell.

Thrash and flail until someone pulls him off me, I suppose. The thought made Phoenix giggle. She thought she might be going mad.

The steady, solid earth-beat started again as Tanek took the reins. In her mind's eye, Phoenix watched as great faceted amethysts grew over Gypsy camp, enclosing it in a protective sphere that sheltered it from the storm.

Fronds of hair settled limply against her face. She opened her eyes. Tree branches still lashed like whips, but it seemed distant and unreal. Everything felt so unreal...

A surge of Magick flashed through her family's circle, radiated out like shock waves. Phoenix could feel the storm dissipating, spreading out over the rest of the city, diluting its power.

The other Gypsies swayed where they stood as the energy between them faded. The too-full moon gasped between drowning clouds, emerging scarcely long enough to shine harsh light on exhausted faces. Phoenix wondered if she had smudges under her eyes. She hoped so. If she was going to feel this horrible, she wanted to look it, too.

"Let's all go back to bed." Kaya's voice sounded harsh with weariness.

"There's nothing more we can do tonight," *Baba* Luna agreed. "And Cannon is going to come way too fucking early."

Liam gazed blankly at the gray walls of his dungeon. *Jubilant,* he thought. *I should be jubilant. Even with all of them together, they couldn't bring her back. That bitch'll spend eternity in the hell she sent me to.*

Small comfort it was, wretched and alone, with only the wind's muffled wail for company. Even here he could hear it… and if he thought too hard, it sounded like a certain red-haired Gypsy screaming. Did anyone deserve that? Even Ryna?

Especially Ryna, he reminded himself, but could not forget the wet impact of spit against his face, the look of hate that pained him more than bruises or a bloody lip.

God, what had he done? How had he thought she would love him? Even if Ryna deserved this horror, did Phoenix? The woman he loved, the woman for whom he'd sacrificed his soul—literally… was all the torment of those months spent only to buy her pain?

"Better her than me," he whispered in an attempt to convince himself. "Better any of them—all of them—than me."

How they all loved that little bitch… and no one had missed him at all. He squeezed his eyes tight against the sickening thud of knowledge that descended into his soul.

Outside, the screams continued—edged with dark laughter.

Phoenix groaned, staring hopelessly up the seemingly endless Olympic Staircase.

"I hear you there," Niki agreed. "Come on, it's not going to get any shorter by standing here."

Phoe grunted, but followed as best she could. She wished she could curl up, go back to sleep, and ignore the world. But waking from nightmares covered in ashes and alone was a far worse prospect than waking from nightmares covered in ashes and clinging to Niki—even with the momentary horror of realizing that her anchor wasn't her beloved fiddler.

The guard at C-gate nodded them through without checking their passes; Phoenix bleakly wondered how much of that coincided with his especially warm smile at Niki. She didn't envy the woman all the ex-attachments running around. Phoe only had *one*, and look how much trouble *that* had earned her.

The Gypsies squinted against the dirt that flew in their eyes as the wind pushed them back a step. Patrons and rennies alike bowed their heads to the gale, faces half covered with a spare sleeve or a scrap of cloth. A little dirt had swirled on the campground's roads, but nothing like this. They should've suspected. After all, campground *was* in a hollow.

"Maybe Sherwood will be better?" Phoenix suggested as they plowed past Maypole girls struggling with ribbons that would rather be kites.

Niki nodded, blindly grabbing for Phoe's hand. Immeasurably thankful for her spectacles, Phoenix led her friend down the Narrows—past a windblown

Royals Revolting show on Globe Stage and a juggler struggling with his clubs at Twin Tree. Kilts blew in swirls of plaid as the Bagpipe Brigade did their valiant best to perform on the Bear's raised green; the poor bagpiper fought against the silencing gusts as the dancers squinted through the dirt that flew up from their feet. Woodland Stage boasted a couple clowns, their whiteface dulled and only a handful of spectators in the benches. Even the animals in the petting zoo cowered in groups, butts to the wind to evade flying debris. Phoenix led Niki through the gate and into an unexpectedly crowded Hollow Hill.

"You're kidding," *Phuro* Basil stated flatly.

Baba Luna snorted. "With that busybody, do you think she needs to?"

"What joy did we miss now?" Niki asked, detouring by the stand mirror as she removed one of her scarves and began tying it over her hair like a headband.

"Your godlike powers are responsible for the weather." Alaina Dale wrinkled her nose, apparently intent on her tuning. "The egg lady cornered me this morning. According to her, you lot were doing some Satanic ritual in the dark hours of the morning, over by the Maypole. Why anyone would try raising the minions of Hell in the full bright of the moon, or why they'd be stupid enough to do it in the open—and right next to a fertility symbol, no less—she wouldn't say." Her mandolin produced a sour note for emphasis. She shook her head and tweaked one of the tuning pegs. "Although she did make a huge deal about how she'd had to avoid the peasants' detection… I guess they were playing guard for you or something."

Scarlett Will snorted. "Wonder what *they* did to piss her off."

Phoenix glanced uneasily around the room. The Merry Maids looked irritated, but trepidation shadowed the faces of her fellow Gypsies. Who else had seen? How many would believe her? How long would it be before the news wound its way to Patty, if it hadn't already?

"You missed the fun at Cast Call," Mutch announced as she strode in, banging the door closed behind her.

"You mean aside from the all-male Robin Hood troop they hired for the special events?" Alex asked, disgust painting her face.

Toby looked up sharply from filling his hip flask—ignoring Elda's frown of disapproval. "They *what*?"

"Marketing didn't think Merry Maids sounded as saleable as Merry Men, and since they couldn't replace us in the middle of our five-year contract, Patty hired some actors from her old community theatre to host the ale crawl and the other stuff," Lord Marion complained bitterly. "And they're just as annoying as she is."

"Hard to believe," Niki said.

"Yeah. Especially after her lightbulb moment at Cast Call." Mutch affected a confused, petulant expression. "Sherwood hate to miss yew ale—oh! *Sure would* hate to miss *you all*! Yew, like a yew bow! Oh, that's so clever!" She tittered inanely.

Niki made an incredulous noise as she bobby-pinned the scarf in place and used the trailing end to make a veil. "*That's* our theme this weekend?"

Jen smirked. "I don't suppose anyone told her our bows aren't made out of yew."

"Shhhh!" Mutch flapped around, acting flustered. "You *pee*-poles!"

Gypsies and Merry Maids dissolved into giggles. Even Phoenix found herself chuckling—it felt strange.

She wondered how long the light mood would last.

Shift.

Ryna's head snapped up at the wrenching sensation; warily she rose to her feet, surveying the area around Rowan Stage where she had sheltered from the windblown dirt.

Only—the dirt was no longer blown by the wind. It had gathered, was headed for her—thick, purposeful. Sentient.

It woke small, frantic terrors in the pit of her soul. She had to find a more secure shelter. Fast.

But where?

Bedside Manor. It had glass windows—

Don't run.

Startled, Ryna looked swiftly around, but she was alone. Still, the bright voice in her mind had been so clear… and it made sense. They fed on fear. Running would hand it to them in a fancy gravy boat. How had she lost sight of that?

Saunter, then. She would saunter—quickly—toward Bedside Manor. And pretend not to notice the dust storms growing more dense behind her.

Before her.

Around her.

Butterfly Carousel.

Calm—remember to stay calm, she told herself to stem the panic that began to choke her.

… as the dust choked her…

Remember.

Maypole.

Remember.

Carefully she built a shield around herself, a little at a time. A trickle of Magick… no grabbing for it like she always had. In small bits, it didn't overwhelm her.

"Ashes to ashes," whispered a dark voice, reaching, hungry.

Mead Booth.

Ignore the voice.

Remember.

A little more, a little more… bit by bit her shield began to feel solid… began to feel safe.

"Dust to dust."

Dust.

Dust.

Flying Buttress Stage.

Remember.

"Ryyyyynaaaaa…"

She turned sharply; the sand that covered the Track billowed and resolved into a man on horseback, coalesced until Liam stared down at her with a smug smile. "She's mine now, Ryna. Your family lost. She's mine."

"You lie," Ryna said stolidly. "They'll try again. They won't give up on me."

"Ah, but will there be anything left to give up *on*?"

Ryna gathered herself, stared levelly at him, and was about to reply—when a flash of calico sped along Track's split-rail fence and launched itself at Liam with a yowling "Raaaow-ffffttttttt!"

"No—Karma, no!" Ignoring the pain and confusion it engendered, Ryna yanked the trickle of Magick until it became a rush and drove the winds in opposite directions, ordering them to disperse.

The calico dropped to the ground as the bulging, swarming mass of dirt that had engulfed her exploded like a firework.

"Karma!" The Gypsy rushed to her fallen friend, but pulled up short as the dirt snapped back, thicker than before… and charged.

Run, Karma, Ryna sent the silent cry as she tore off toward the safety of Bedside Manor. With any luck, it would forget the cat and follow her.

Faster, faster—

A quick glance back as she passed the chess booth made her grin—her plan had worked. Ryna's feet pounded the ground, faster, faster, as the looming, relentless mass towered ever nearer—

And then it descended upon her with a roar, the swirling dirt burning like flame as it pounded her skin. Ryna coughed rackingly, one hand clutching her chest, eyes squeezed tight against the pain as it filled her soul. She could feel it scrubbing away at her essence, erasing her, bit by bit…

How long before she was nothing but dirt as well?

Ashes to—

Dust to—

Remember…

◇ ◇ ◇

Dirt. And dirt. And more dirt.

Dirt turning white aprons reddish-brown, dirt dulling the glass in shop windows, dirt coating every leaf on trees and vines. Dirt under fingernails. Dirt whirling in miniature storms in the privy areas. Dirt invading eyes, and nose, and mouth. Dirt everywhere, getting into everything, and by the time Vilification Tennis ended, Phoenix had long since ceased trying to rid herself of it. *Three years from now I'll blow my nose, and it'll still come out black,* she thought glumly as she followed the other Vilifiers into the courtyard behind Bedside Manor. They hunkered up the steps to the break room, heads ducked and tip-collectors held close.

As she stepped into the dim interior, Phoenix wondered briefly if world had stopped; it felt so strange not to have the grit pounding her. A line formed at the water cooler as people rinsed the dust first from their mugs, then from their mouths.

"Okay, folks—listen up," the judge called. "I don't know how many of you noticed, but Patty was watching today."

"Kinda hard to miss anyone wearing that much pink—even with all the dirt," the taller of the Erin go Braless women sniped.

"If the official Pendragon colors are blue and gold, can we make pink our official anti-color?" the blue Ragamuffin asked.

"Hey, Hayrold!" someone called from across the room. "You ever squeeze out of her why Chez Priv didn't get a GEM?"

"Lots of dumbass little reasons. And I got a lecture about compromising security."

"She thought we were using it as a way to smuggle people in," Piddle added, causing derisive laughter.

"From the privies behind *Globe*?" Percival hooted.

"We did it a second time by the BLUE," Hayrold reminded him.

The green Ragamuffin rolled his eyes. "Still. It seems like an awful lot of trouble. Anybody who's been here a year knows twenty easier ways."

"Thank God she hasn't figured them out; we're in enough trouble as it is," the judge put in, swinging the discussion back on topic. "I'd hoped Patty would ignore us after her earlier scolding, but she hasn't."

"She's going to ruin us!" Chastity complained. "The last time we had a rain day, we drew a bigger crowd than the Royals Revolting! Nobody's going to come to hear us call each other poo-poo heads!"

"Be that as it may, she took particular issue with a few insults, and one of yours ranked at the top of the list, Hayrold." The judge flipped through his notes. "I quote: 'If it is true that success is ninety percent perspiration, then whoof! It's nice to meet you, Mr. Darnell.'"

"What?" Hayrold complained. "It was clean!"

"It was about the owner."

"It was a compliment!" he protested.

Sternly raised eyebrows from the judge.

"Sort of," Hayrold amended. "In a backhanded way. But it was still a compliment to the owner!"

"Compliment or not, if you use it again we'll be scratched from the grid."

Hayrold sighed and grumbled—but relented.

"What else?" Percival asked.

Phoenix listened, unable to care, as the judge listed their trespasses. After spotting the Artistic Deadweight among their spectators, Phoe had stuck to her tamest material. She'd heard worse from kids a third her age—though she suspected it didn't matter. Patty just wanted something on which to skewer them. And if she couldn't find it, she'd make it up.

"And to top it all off," the judge concluded, "Patty wants it known that her favorite pink velvet ribbon is missing. She also said to inform people that if it turns up at the office, she won't ask any embarrassing questions."

"Maybe she should talk to the Gypsies," suggested the scornful voice of the shorter Erin go Braless woman.

An uncomfortable silence smothered the room. Phoenix's jaw set in irritation. No one would meet her eyes—but none of them could look away, either. Hayrold scowled, a retort on the tip of his tongue when Phoenix cut him off.

"The least you could've done," she said, "was ask me plainly." She unceremoniously dumped the contents of her tip mug on the floor and stalked out of the room, banging the door shut on the protests behind her.

Curses pounded through her mind in time with her footfalls as she thundered down the stairs and plowed through the double-door gates that faced the trees that had once shaded Queen's Tea—and stopped cold, glaring at a burly patron with both arms braced against the wall of Bedside Manor. Waves of distress clutched Phoenix's chest. She doubted they were from the man.

"You!" she hollered, and spun him around by a meaty shoulder.

As she had suspected, a scantily clad teen young enough to be his daughter cowered against the wall.

"Why is it everybody thinks they have the right to touch girls whenever and wherever they want to?" Phoenix demanded, shoving the attacker hard. She could feel storm clouds gathering behind her eyes—and let them, let the rising Magick work through her, snake around him in malignant tendrils.

He stumbled backward, shock fumbling across his face.

"Only the most disgusting, lacking men have to molest women. You want to prove you've got a schlong? Get a date like a normal person!"

Fear crept into his eyes. He hadn't bargained for this raving madwoman who brandished her staff like she might use it somewhere extremely painful. Hadn't bargained for the emotions she forced on him—terror, degradation, shame, helplessness.

Phoenix stalked him, fury—and Magick—bristling her every hair. "You think it's manly and cute to fondle anybody with tits. Well, there's a person attached to those tits, and that person doesn't want your goddamn hands all over them. How would you like it if I grabbed your package and squeezed it like an overripe melon?"

He quivered, cowering.

Tear out his soul, a quiet, inky voice whispered in the back of her mind. *You have the power. Give him what he deserves...*

The Gypsy set her teeth, banishing temptation. *No. That is not my way.*

Still, she held him a little longer—made him wonder what she would do.

And then she released him.

The man turned and ran as if the Wild Hunt had marked him as their prey.

Applause exploded from all sides; Phoe realized to her shock that she'd gathered an audience. She glanced to where the man's victim stood—Chastity and the judge were calming her down. Piddle offered her a stick, pretending it was a flower. The teen laughed shakily. A man wearing the yellow and red Safety Services tabard hurried onto the scene. The girl would be okay, then—she was being taken care of. Phoenix was grateful for that.

The shorter Erin go Braless woman approached Phoe hesitantly.

Off balance and sick to her soul, Phoenix turned her back and walked away. She couldn't deal with her—or the other Vilifiers that had gathered. Not now. She needed somewhere safe, somewhere with laughter and music and love—and none of the horrors that permeated her world.

"Bless this house and all within; may they never be groped by—what in the world is that?"

"It's Pat," Eryn declared, a twinkle in her bright green eyes as she glanced up from wiping the table where Pat perched.

"Pat," Phoenix repeated, shock dispelling the last of her mood as the safety of Cottage enveloped her. She gave her feet a last scuff before entering. "Pat looks suspiciously like a rubber chicken in gold lamé tights and a feather boa."

"That's because he's a flaming chicken." Brigid made it sound like the most natural thing in the world.

"A flaming chicken. Has anyone brought this to the attention of the Fops?"

The two patrons—a middle-aged couple with an abundance of shopping bags—glanced at her with quirky smiles before going back to taking in the ambiance.

"Pat is our mascot for Death Awareness Weekend," Ma said as she straightened from poking the fire logs.

"Since the Irish canna seem to write love songs without killing someone off, it seemed important to educate everyone what hooked up on Wine and Romance

Weekend." Brigid looked singularly pleased with herself as she warmed to her topic. "You see, people used to leave their doors open—just like this. The chickens are so stupid that sometimes they wander right into the fire, and then they start flapping around and get caught under the baby's cradle—which catches fire, too. I guess it happened pretty often, because one of the leading causes of infant mortality was—"

"Flaming chickens," Phoenix concluded. Part of her wanted to declare it too outrageous to be true, but it was the sort of weird factoid a rennie would know. Besides, the corner of her mind that housed Emily's memories held a certain concern over keeping an eye on her baby brother's cradle...

"That settles it," Moiré declared from the loft. "We're eating all the chickens the day my bairn is born."

"But Moiré, we dunna have any chickens!" Eryn protested.

"Aye, we ate them all the day *you* were born, wee scamp," Ma said as she retrieved a couple logs from the stash beside the hearth.

"Maybe we could get a flaming chicken stomper to put them out—supposing we did have them?" Brigid suggested.

"Isn't that why Cottage is so close to the elephants?" Phoenix asked. "Elephants have flat feet to put out flaming chickens."

Erin meeped in horror.

Phoenix winked at her, then turned to the Cottage populace. "Is Torin about?"

"Ah! I forgot—he went looking for you, herbwoman," Moiré leaned over the loft's railing and offered up a sheepish smile. "You know how it goes—bun in the oven, brain out the window. I can't keep a thought in my head for three minutes."

"Did he say where he was headed?"

"Sherwood. He didna leave long ago."

"Those new peasants have been lookin' for ye as well," Ma added. "Said they havena seen hide nor hair of ye all day."

The rookies. Of course. Phoenix pushed her glasses up to rub at her eyes. She'd forgotten all about them—and only hoped Patty hadn't found out she'd skipped out on her duties. "I do have gridded shows. They must not've been looking very hard." She sighed and resettled her glasses. "All right. I'm going back to Sherwood—I'll probably be there the rest of the day if anyone needs me."

Actually getting back to Sherwood, however, put Phoenix in mind of salmon trying to swim upstream to spawn—and no few of the onrushing tide made it clear that they'd happily be her destination. Phoe ignored them, thankful for the safe harbor of the fence surrounding Hollow Hill. No patrons could reach her there.

Esmerelda and Toby were half through their fire show, Phoe noticed, latching the gate behind herself—and nearly yelped as someone touched her shoulder. She whirled to see Tremayne, his face set and grim. Where on earth had he come from?!

"Your brother's here," he said quietly, steering her toward the dugout's wooden door.

Phoenix wanted to protest—she didn't want to be involved in anything this solemn. But her voice betrayed her, and then she was inside.

Danny took one look at her and sighed. "There are times I really hate being the lesser of the evils."

"What now?" Phoe asked, almost flippant in her resignedness. "Liam escaped? Drowned himself in his breakfast cereal? The FBI has come to investigate a missing person? Somebody dragged the swamps and found where the Shadow Fae dumped the rest of him? Little green spacemen have come and—"

Her brother held out a plastic grocery bag. A strange bulge weighted the bottom.

The sight almost brought Phoenix to her knees. "Oh—gods, Danny… no… tell me that isn't Karma in there. Not Karma…"

"No—no, shhh." He dropped the bag, gathered her in his arms.

She clung to him, buried her face in his shirt. "Not her cat—I couldn't bear…"

"I'm sorry, Phoe-bea. That was really stupid of me. I should've thought… it's not Karma. I promise. I promise…"

He was still talking, but Phoe's mind had caught on his words, wrapped around them and refused to let go. "Not Karma?" She sniffed, wiped her nose on the cuff of her chemise—and looked down.

A single coil of copper-red hair snaked from the bag's confines.

"Oh." She pulled free from her brother, reached down to touch it—but drew back. It seemed wrong, somehow. Like petting roadkill. "Where—"

"The trails behind the campground… about halfway to the Secret Garden. Christine had never been back there, so I was showing her, and… I couldn't leave it there. I didn't want someone else to find it and start spreading stories. Or worse, from what I know of Magick, use it against her."

"Thank you," Phoe said quietly, gathering up the bag with its soft weight. *Not at all like a dead animal,* she tried to convince herself. Why hadn't any of the Gypsies thought of this? Nine of them, and no one had… she could feel Tremayne's presence at her back, silent, reassuring. Daniel looked wary, as if he expected her to start tearing at her own hair.

It almost made her giggle. They were so silly… there was no room left for tears. Not now. Maybe later, when she was alone. Maybe then… but for now she clutched the precious treasure, the last bit she had of her love…

Thank the gods it wasn't Karma…

"Thank you," she said again, rising. "Thank you. I need to—"

"Yes, of course," Danny said. "If you need—"

"I will," she assured him. "Thank you." She backed toward the door. "Thank you." Into the sunlight, not caring that she clutched an anachronistic plastic bag. "Thank you."

The door swung shut.

Phoenix snuck around to the dressing vardo with the rose painted on its side and let herself inside. It was cramped and dark—only a couple small windows illuminated the copious storage cabinets—but she could not risk the winds outside. As the final cheers went up for Elda and Toby's show, she lit two candles, plopped onto the worn wooden floor… and opened the bag.

The hair shimmered in the candlelight just as it did on Ryna's head. She hadn't expected that. She also hadn't expected the couple ants or the bits of straw.

Phoenix frowned. That would never do. She removed the intruders.

It felt just like her hair.

Lovingly she drew out the first clump, then the next, then the next, draping them in her left hand until the bag was empty and she had the bottom ends lined up. They curled a little, just as they did when freshly washed. She dug a couple binders from her phoenix-tooled pouch and fastened one a little ways down from the ragged, hacked-off ends. She knew she wasn't as good at this as Esmerelda, but it felt like something she should do herself. Humming softly, smoothing out tangles and foreign matter as she went, Phoenix began the meticulous task of braiding her love's hair. Not a single strand must be lost.

Tremayne's fiddle let out a plaintive wail…

Not a single strand.

◇ ◇ ◇

"London Bridge is falling down,
Falling down, falling down;
London Bridge is falling down,
My fair lady."

Ryna timed the absentminded song to her footfalls as she wandered toward C-gate, past the deserted lane of food booths and crafters' shops that comprised Upson Downs. She had been singing as she walked for a while. She didn't know why—besides that walking passed the time, and her own voice was better than the stillness in her ears, or what the Shadow Fae might put there. Such a silly song; she hadn't thought of it in—years, it had to be, but now she couldn't get it out of her head.

"Ryna's world is falling down,
Falling down, falling down;
Ryna's world is falling down,
My fair lady."

She giggled. She would've cried, but it was so *funny*! No, no, who needed the Shadow Fae to twist the words when she could do it herself?

As if in response to her thought, eerie voices buffeted her like windblown dirt:

"Build it up with screams and bones,
Blood and bones, screams and bones;
Build it up with screams and bones,
My fair lady."

Ryna shivered and walked faster, wishing she had a cloak to pull around herself for protection—wishing that, even if she *had* one, it would do any good.

◇ ◇ ◇

Phoe's cloak was real.

The world was not.

At least, that was how it began to feel as she wandered Pendragon's streets. Her cloak shielded her from the harsh wind and swirling dirt. The hood shielded her reddened eyes from questioning glances, protected her from the need to smile. People left you alone if you huddled in a cloak.

Perhaps every cloak granted invisibility… or perhaps Tremayne was right, and by Wishing things she made them so.

The trick privy stood proudly in the center of Bedside Manor's green, an enormous construct of tables and benches behind it. The peasants swarming the makeshift fortress had the pleasant feel of rennies busily entertaining themselves—a mirage, surely. Even so, Phoenix stopped to watch, hoping to forget the weight of the copper-red braid tucked safely in her leather pouch. Niki had given her a scarf to wrap it in, poor little braid.

"I found a mascot!" called a Gypsy-dressed woman with copious tassels adorning her garb—and an enormous plush camel balanced on her head. Phoenix recognized her from the Fantastical Feast show. The camel lady had the hand of a patron woman with a beautiful green dress and impressive white-feathered wings like an angel's.

"Wings!" Puddle warbled. He scampered off and returned with another patron—this one looking a little drunk in her chain mail bikini and tattered black-feathered wings.

As most of the peasantry worked to get their mascots ensconced, a couple of the guys marched around with sticks as the border guard. After several passes, they stopped, yelled "Changing of the guard!" and swapped a few clothing items before continuing.

Ragged laughter rippled through the gathering crowd.

The Leper spotted Phoenix and shambled over. "Come, join the insanity!"

"Um… okay," she agreed, following him through the Jiffy-gate into the fort.

"We're annexing the food court in the name of the Great Naked Potato," Bryn greeted cheerily. "We have it on good authority that we will shortly be laid siege to."

Phoe blinked. "By whom?"

"The Village Militia," supplied Ilya.

"Several of the Knights from Royal Court," added Marcus.

"And the pirates," someone else chimed in.

"The Musketeers—"

"The Scotsmen that do the pike drills—"

"I've got food!" Hayrold's voice rang out.

Cheers went up at the declaration—and the peasants predictably dropped their assorted tasks, swarmed out the privy, and mobbed him.

"Funnel cake!"

"Save some for the rest of us, Auntie Tassels!"

"I am, I am! But I must test it first to be certain it has not been poisoned."

"I'm not eating that if she licks the whole cake."

A chuckle from the youngest rookie. "I suppose I shouldn't tell you he dropped it in the dirt, then."

"Dirt's an essential seasoning! Besides, it's not like it would matter today," Piddle observed, his normally off-red shirt a muted rose-brown today.

"Gods, I hear you there." The remark came from a Gypsy with curling blond hair and a red, black, and silver outfit—she too hailed from the Feast show. "I took a baby wipe bath and I think I removed half my tan line!"

Puddle gave her a quizzical look. "Bath?"

Dead looked puzzled, too.

Can't imagine why, Phoenix thought with a wry grin and helped herself to a little of the cake. Things felt more solid here, among friends. It was a good feeling.

"Hey, when did we get a flag?" Kevin asked around a mouthful of food.

A timorous voice piped up before anyone could answer him. "Um, who's in charge here?"

Phoenix looked over to see Patty's rookie handmaiden staring around like a turkey drumstick in a room of hungry patrons. The fort's populace—the four or so of them that had noticed—glanced at each other, trying to grasp the concept of someone having authority over a horde of street entertainers.

At last Hayrold stepped forward. "I am—as much as anybody—I guess."

"Oh." The rookie didn't look comforted. "Because—um—you have to take this thing down."

"Take it down?" the Leper objected loudly. "But we just got here!"

Everyone was paying attention now—and most of them protesting.

Hayrold, so far, was being remarkably calm. "May I ask *why*?"

"Patty said so?" A quiver marred the handmaiden's voice.

"And I repeat—why?"

An uncomfortable shift. "She said that you're not being entertaining enough. That you're not contracted to play with yourselves."

"But—we're just getting started," Aubry said. "There are people coming to play with us—the Musketeers, the Scotsmen—"

"Patty says the guests won't get your little in-joke, and you have to put everything where you found it and go back to doing patron interaction stuff." She said it in a rush, as if reciting it. "I'm really sorry… but she sent me down here to tell you to break it up. And I wouldn't be surprised if she started pulling passes."

With that, she left her fellow rennies fuming and scurried away—though she had to push through a ring of patrons to do it.

*　　　*　　　*

"You look about as happy as a privy on Labor Day!"

"Thank you, *Baba* Luna, for that lovely mental image," Phoenix grouched as she stomped into Hollow Hill. She slammed the door behind her, shutting out the scouring dirt. Emily sat in the far corner with Morgan, and the camp's elders were tallying tips.

Well, *Phuro* Basil was tallying tips. *Baba* Luna was fishing around in her cleavage, presumably after an errant bit of currency. "Do I want to know?" she asked.

"The Artistic Dimwit made us take down one of our bits right in the middle of doing it."

Three jaws dropped.

The door opened, and Tremayne's lanky frame ducked inside. The scowl on his face matched his disgruntled mutterings.

"You too?" Phoenix asked ruefully.

"Damn nursery rhyme stuck in my head. You?"

"Thoughts of anarchy. A bunch of entertainers had this neat fort built out of benches and tables and those metal trash frames—oh, and the trick privy—and then Patty-cakes sent her pet rookie down to tell us to disassemble it. She said we weren't 'being entertaining enough. Guests won't get your little in-joke, and you have to go back to doing patron interaction stuff. You're not contracted to play with yourselves,'" Phoenix mimicked cruelly, slamming through one of the coolers.

"She—made you stop?" Tremayne spluttered. "Mid-bit?"

"I know." Phoe tossed some ice in her mug and used the remaining moisture on her hands to take off the worst of her cleavage's grime. "Right when we were about to be ambushed by half the groups at Pendragon. Somebody even had a cannon fuse shoved in a small barrel that they were going to roll at us with the fuse lit. And now most of the street entertainers have gone on strike—they all went down to the campground, and there's a lot of muttering about calling the press and doing an exposé on the kind of pay and treatment we get here, for all the good it would do. Some of the others are thinking about picketing outside Front Gate—again, for all the good it would do."

"And if street goes on strike—" Emily mused.

"Then the place really *has* gone to the dungheap," *Baba* Luna finished.

"Oh, Phoenix," Emily said, sympathy heavy in her voice. Morgan cradled in her left arm, she stood and gave the Gypsy a hug. "It'll be okay. I know this is only our second year, but I'm sure things will get better."

"I suppose you're right." Phoenix grabbed a paper towel to clean herself off—and only succeeded in smearing the dirt around. She gave up. "I'm just dirty and cranky and tired of dealing with all this."

"We all are," Emily confided. "But think, if Patty-cakes didn't do stupid stuff like this, what would we have to mock at Talent Show tonight? And someday when we've been here as long as the rest of your family, it'll make a great story to tell the rookies."

Phoe glanced at the other Gypsies. She wondered if they were having any better luck convincing themselves it would all be okay... but by their too-set expressions, she doubted it. It wasn't a heartening thought. She made herself fake confidence, but words would not come. Instead, she kissed Emily's fair brow, then little Morgan's tiny fist, and escaped gratefully into the pervasive dirt beyond Hollow Hill's concrete walls.

* * *

The world was restless, out there. Phoenix could feel it in the nervous energy that swirled around her vardo, like animals preparing for a storm.

But inside... inside it was so still. Tranquil. A bubble of peace where Phoenix could lie on her back, freshly scrubbed and in civvies, and pretend that time didn't exist. A hundred years could pass, and still the vardo would stand, the eye of a storm that had long since gone. Nothing could reach her. Not here.

Tremayne politely knocked on the door. "Phoenix? Will you be joining us?"

Except that. Phoe made a face at the ceiling, but she hefted up off the bed, gave Karma a few farewell scritches—the kitty didn't wake from her slumber—and stepped outside. Night had fallen. She supposed she should have noticed that.

"I'm glad you're coming," Niki whispered, giving her a tight hug.

Phoe mustered a smile. "Sitting at home sulking gains me nothing."

"And perhaps loses you quite a bit," *Phuro* Basil pointed out sagely.

There were times, Phoenix reflected, that she really didn't care to hear wise advice. But he only meant well, so she nodded agreeably.

They did not head for the Globe, though, where Talent Show had been scheduled since time out of mind. It had been moved to Flying Buttress, ostensibly because it might rain and there were worries over the lighting equipment, the attendance, and the instruments (probably in that order—Ryna would've been horrified). Popular opinion, however, held that it was one more way for management to break down time-honored traditions.

Phoenix wondered where they thought they'd fit all the people… though she needn't have worried. When they arrived, the show had scarcely begun, and there were plenty of front row seats left. Two frightened soloists, a rollicking farce on management and Faire life, a fellow reading his own poetry, and a spoof on the Royals Revolting's show later, a third of the benches remained empty… and didn't look as if they would gain occupants in the near future.

Was this what they were reduced to? How many of the people in the benches were scheduled to perform, too? How many had gone to Globe and, seeing it dark, figured there would *be* no Talent Show?

It was better to not think about it, and so Phoenix lost herself to the rhythm of the night: jokes at the expense of management, some lively acts, a few people who should never have been allowed on stage that long or that drunk… and Sir Lancelot's dull monotone stringing it all together. Everything was an honor to him, or a privilege, and Phoenix wondered if he even knew who any of the performers were. According to Ryna, two guys with funny hats used to be in charge—but they'd been gone for years. A pity—apparently they'd been really good.

The last act made up for Lancelot's monotony, though; a bunch of the old-timers quietly assumed the stage with guitar, cello, squeezebox, and lyric sheets and stepped into the most simple, beautiful song ever created. It was Pendragon distilled, all things bright and beautiful that kept them coming back despite the hardships. A song of memories—people past, places gone, inside jokes that made many of the rennies laugh through their tears. Phoenix listened, eyes misting in sympathy… understanding the sentiment though few of the references made sense to her.

Wavering voices joined the chorus; the Gypsies wept openly.

They knew. Ryna would've known.

Phoenix stood, softly excusing herself as she scrambled over people to the aisle and clomped ungracefully into the cold, lightless faire beyond. *All for one night when there were too many stars,* she thought. *Sometimes I think I'll never see them again.*

The song faded as she passed the Croft, replaced by the swelling noise of the BLUE. She clutched at the door handle, struggled with it until the portal yielded. Voices chattered just as loudly in the back of her head, underscoring the memory of Ryna's screams.

"Hey, are you all right?"

He was very solicitous—genera-rennie in his goatee and jeans and poet's shirt. She didn't know him. She didn't care. She pointed to his flask. "What's in there?"

"Vodka with citrus. Want—"

"Yes. Please." She accepted his offer, took a hearty swig… and nearly sprayed it in pure reflex. It tasted like she'd taken a gulp of kerosene and chased it with a lemon—but she bet anything that foul had to be strong, and… well… nothing else seemed to work. "I love you," she said with true feeling, handed back the flask, and headed toward a table with a few people she knew from street.

* * *

"You know what I think keepth away the plague? I think alcl… lalca… clelco…" Phoenix frowned in consternation. People were snickering at her, she knew it. She pointed at her mug. "Thith thtuff."

"Booze?" offered Puddle… what the hell was his real name, anyway?

"Yeah, I think booze keepth the plague away too." She took a swig. So far she'd sampled gin, tequila, bourbon, rum, brandy, and a couple kinds of whiskeys and scotches. The drink she'd settled down with, though—the one she had now—was special. Hayrold… Jack… his name was Jack… had made it for her. He said it was called a Gypsy Girl.

"I named it that because she warms you up and takes you straight to bed," he'd explained with a teasing wink. "I'm sure you could identify."

Phoenix surely could. It tasted like candy, and since she couldn't have one sort of Gypsy girl, she might as well go for the other. At the very least it made her ears warm, and tingly, and the world spin if she moved too fast. Especially her head. It was something like being in love, really, only with more coordination.

"I'm a kluth," she remarked as she bopped her glasses with her thumb. Again. "And I potht all my etheth. Where do they go? B-gate ith clothed. They'll jutht wander around, poor little etheth."

"Looks like some sidhe's drunk," Marcus commented with a crooked grin.

"I'm not drunk—and I'm not a Thee!" Phoenix paused, then beamed with realization. "I'm a brownie! Who wanth to eat me?"

Raucous laughter.

Phoe slapped her hand over her mouth, mortified. Where in the world had that come from? "I think I need thome air. Have ta go… thay hi to Harvey." Clumsily she rose from her bench.

"You need help?" Marcus offered.

"No… I can thay hi… jutht fine… by mythelf." That said, Phoenix staggered out the door. It proved harder than it should have been; the ground refused to obey the laws of physics.

Stupid ground.

After the third try she got a grip on the privy door handle. The rest of the task went fairly well—although the privy paper took a great deal more effort to remove than she remembered it requiring in the past.

Outside, lightning strobed, making Phoenix blink at the sudden-light, sudden-dark. The air felt tense, expectant. Without stopping much to think, the Gypsy toddled off towards Track.

She heard the steady sound of hoofbeats galloping past, but when she whirled—almost falling at the sudden movement—only the pennants stirred.

Flash.

Johnny smiled down at her from atop his ghost-gray mount. The horse pranced restively. Johnny held down his hand—Phoenix tripped over her own feet in her haste to back away, landed hard on her backside.

Flash.

Only pennants. She scrambled upright and cautiously picked her way forward. The sand must have been raked at the day's end; no hoofprints dimpled the ground.

But he had been so real…

Walk away. Walk away, and don't look back.

Besides, she could feel something pulling her onward…

She passed Bedside Manor and Canopy Stage, but when she came to Front Gate, she halted.

Oh. Front Gate. Of course. She pushed open the heavy, decorated-wood door of the building to the gate's left and crept into the dark passage beyond. It seemed terribly familiar in the way that reminds a person of something completely different. For a moment she caught a flash of dreary stone corridors, chill and a little damp. And then she was outside again. An enormous tarp awning had come loose from one of its poles; it thrashed and snapped in the gusting wind. For a split instant it looked like one of the Shadow raptors… Phoenix bolted through the swinging door and up the wooden stairs.

Streaks of lightning romped amidst vaguely seen shapes over the vast parking field. One particularly brilliant bolt connected with the earth, backlighting a herd of galloping horses.

Gunshots rang on the wind, though they sounded centuries old.

By the next flash the horses were gone.

Phoenix turned away and scrambled into the main tower, slipping twice as she fumbled up the ladder to the third story. Better to look over Pendragon's grounds; she wasn't sure she could ever stand to see the parking field again, with its aching loss of freedom.

The village spread before her as she stepped onto the balcony. Lines of triangle-shaped pennants were strung like bodice laces across the space inside Front Gate, below. So far below. Phoenix looked down, spread her arms wide, and with the rush of wind that battered her clothing, could almost imagine herself falling.

A few raindrops ventured down like advance scouts before the sky, in the space of a deep breath, released its burden. Phoenix heard a raw, heart-tearing scream... and then realized it was her own. Not piercing at all, it lost itself to the driving sheets of rain. Here she had stood more than a year ago, imagined stars falling like the hearts of the Fae, stood beside Ryna and wished for the impossible. A year ago this weekend, it had been granted. And now, and now...

Not even in death, echoed the words in so many different voices, so many languages, stretching back to infinity like a three-way mirror. Moon Lady and Phoenix, bound forever in spirit...

But one of the mirrors had shattered. Only the tiniest shards still held that eternity.

Please, Ryna, don't give up, she begged with eyes squeezed tight. *Don't leave me. I don't think I could survive with a hole the size of forever in my soul.*

Reality flickered, sliding sickeningly out of joint. The flag on the end of the gate shifted in and out of focus, stilled and started and stilled again like a slide show. The colors were backwards, and there were two towers, now, two flags, slightly overlapping.

I'm drunk, Phoenix told herself as she struggled to bring her visions into some semblance of order. *I'm drunk, and I'm seeing things.*

"But does that make the them any less real?" whispered a voice in Phoe's mind. *"Some things have to be believed to be seen..."*

Slowly, cautiously, she turned to face the ashen figure perched on the waist-high wall. "You look awful," Phoenix blurted.

Dark lips twitched on the cadaverously gray face. Eyes as vast as the sky regarded her solemnly through the veil of rain. The brighter bursts of light faded her almost to nonexistence. Like the horses.

"We won't give up," Phoe promised fervently, awkwardly. "We'll get you back—"

The smile warmed. A tiny, tiny hand reached out to cup Phoenix's cheek... but Ryna had begun to lose bits of herself; fingers and nose and arm and knee and ears blinking in and out.

This was not forever. It was not meant to be, but the raven-haired Gypsy clung to it. There was so much to say, and words were slippery, like rain—

Flicker.

The brave smile, words without movement of lips: *"I love you."*

Flicker flicker.

"Wait! Ryna, you're Fire!"

Flickerflickerflicker.

"Ryna!"

Gone.

Gone.

Gone.

The world grew stable again, and whole—but so empty. Phoenix sank to the plywood floor and stared at the space where her love had been, unable to blink for fear the afterimage would die.

◇ ◇ ◇

If she had actually eaten in the past two weeks, or if she had a stomach, Ryna would have leaned over the railing and been violently, violently ill.

Realities were not made to overlap like that. After her last few encounters, Ryna was more than willing to admit that fact. Wherever you were created, there you should stay. If you disrupted the natural order of things—whether by your own fault or not—the cosmos took it out of your hide. Crossing from one to the other proved bad enough, but trying to make two worlds meet with yourself as the focal point...

And yet—she'd had to try once more. To see her Phoenix, to tell her how very dearly she was loved. If they never saw each other again—she had to leave Phoenix with at least that.

Stop that, she commanded herself. *If the Gypsies are still trying, you owe it to them to hold on. Just a little longer, hold on.*

But Goddess, the price of that holding. The moon was fading. She could feel its protection withdrawing, and with its dying sphere the triumph of the Shadow. It would not be long before they beat down her shields and she wouldn't have the energy to rebuild them or fend off their corrupting darkness.

Ryna wondered what would happen then. A slow descent into madness? Utter oblivion? Conversion to their side?

It doesn't matter, she decided with all the confidence she could muster. *I'll be out before then. "Your fire," Phoe said. She's right. I have to remember my fire, remember to keep fighting. And if I lose... she knows she was loved. And... I know she loves me, too. We'll find each other again next life.*

The concept brought a strange peace. One way or another, things would be all right. She need not worry about it again.

It was then that the balcony vanished, the gate reverting to the one-story structure of a much earlier era. The impact from the drop should have been terrible... but Ryna hardly noticed it. Instead, she found herself walking peacefully away from Front Gate and back into the midst of Hell, her love's image still in her eyes—and a quiet confidence in her heart.

◇ ◇ ◇

"Phoenix!"

The Gypsy slowly turned her head. It felt as if she had never used her neck before. The woman who was Bryn during weekends and Laine the rest of the time stood in the frame of the balcony's door, looking surprised and alarmed.

"Do you know that I've been on thircuit for a year now, and I've never onth got drunk?" Phoenix had no idea where the words came from, but the voice that said them sounded a thousand years old.

"Well, I think you're making up for it now. Come on, up you go." Laine reached down to haul Phoenix upright. It nearly unbalanced her. "You can't stay here all wet and cold; I'm sure the Front Gate people don't want to have to clean up your carcass before the Magistrate comes up here for Opening Gate." She made her tone lightly bantering, but Phoenix could tell by the crease between her eyebrows that she was worried.

"They wouldn't have to," Phoe slurred. "Faerieth don't die."

"Maybe not—but brownies are much better when they're warm," Laine said as they staggered to the opening in the floor... and, with a small miracle, made it down the ladder in one piece. Phoenix's feet and hands didn't want to obey her will; they wandered aimlessly for a bit before latching on to the next rung. She missed the last step and nearly landed on her ass.

She wondered if the floor would've broken. It was only plywood, after all. Not even any sealant on it. But maybe the people who had built this thing hadn't expected anyone to drip water on it in the middle of a thunderstorm.

Stupid people.

"The rain'th running down my glatheth," Phoenix complained when they made it through the door.

"Think of it this way: they're getting a good wash. Come on—careful, the steps are slippery."

Phoenix glanced to her right, out toward the parking field where panther-like Shadows romped. But no horses. She looked quickly away. Maybe they hadn't seen her. More steps. Damn. She fell on her ass again. Laine might've said something, but it was hard to hear over the pounding rain.

And then Laine wanted to go through a squeaky door into a dark room so they could get back onto site. Hadn't she ever watched any scary movies? *Things* lived behind squeaky doors. Especially in the dark. Maybe if people oiled their hinges more often, they wouldn't have that problem. But Laine sparkled—not like Ryna sparkled, or the other Gypsies, but she sparkled some. And sparkly people *must* know those things. So if she wasn't scared, it must be okay.

And anyhow, it was too late, because the door slammed behind them and Laine was fumbling for the other handle. Phoenix wished she'd hurry. Thunder made the building rumble. Made the Things nervous, or hungry. They were all around, all around.

From ground level Pendragon looked like an abandoned set from an Alfred Hitchcock movie. Except, of course, that it wasn't abandoned. Phoenix would've insisted on returning to the balcony where it was safe, but that would mean going back through the squeaky door, and she didn't want to push her luck.

The rain drummed on her head. She couldn't hear things sneaking up on her.

Then again, maybe she was better off not knowing.

Lightning reflected off a million lakes and puddles. It would've been a minefield trying to circumvent them, but they just went through. Which was just as well. Phoenix had enough trouble without avoiding puddles. Damn, she didn't remember the ground being that hard to walk on before. Several times her companion's steadying grip on her hand kept Phoe from careening into the ground.

At least they'd made it as far as Bedside Manor, vacant and eerie. Laine veered left, but the Gypsy pulled her to a stop.

"Come on, not too much further," the peasant coaxed.

"I don't want to go that way."

"There are more trees that way. A little shelter, at least—"

"You don't want to know what'th that way, trutht me," Phoenix said flatly. She supposed it would've had more impact if she'd been able to get all the consonants in there, but it would have to do. The Bear and the lions were nothing she wanted to deal with at the moment. Not with everything else.

Stupid booze.

Laine obviously didn't understand, but apparently also didn't want to bother arguing in the sheeting rain. They started towards Upson Downs.

Movement flickered in the food booths. The Gypsy tried to catch it out of more than the corner of her eye, but moving her head too fast made her stumble—and after seeing a fanged, ape-like thing behind the counter, she decided she didn't want to know.

Flying Buttress Stage stood skeletal and imposing in the brief flashes of light. Phantoms leaned over the viewing box, ready to leap out and devour the two women. Phoenix gave thanks that she didn't have to convince Bryn to stay away from *that*, too. She didn't want to know what lurked among the benches.

The Mead Booth rose up on their right; they cut between it and Como Cottage. Things peered from the windows, and Scottish Croft was no better.

BLUE, BLUE… the BLUE would be safe, maybe, but it was empty, and dark, and Phoe *really* didn't want to know what had taken up residence there. Maypole… but Laine pulled her toward C-gate.

And light. Phoenix stood a moment in its blessed shelter, reveling in the relative safety from the night's gut-twisting terrors. Laine did not want to wait, though. They were still getting rained on, and so they had to keep moving.

The fear was making her sick.

Maybe it wasn't just the fear.

They made it to the top of the Olympic Staircase before Phoenix had to lean over, grab a tree for support, and puke. Laine held her hair off her face.

"I think I thaw my hot dog," Phoenix marveled. "But I'm not thure."

"Yeah, well, the small woodland animals can have your hot dog now. I'm sure the Gypsies will get you a new one. You done?"

"I think tho. Why are there tho many thtairth?"

"I have no idea why there are so many stairs," Laine said with a grunt as they started off again. "But at least we're not trying to go *up* them."

Phoenix didn't even want to *think* about that. Especially with how nasty and tricky they were being right now, tipping at strange angles when she wasn't expecting it. She wondered if she started expecting it if maybe they'd hold still. All the rocking was making her nauseous again.

Stupid stairs.

And there were red eyes peering at her from the woods, dark forms that slunk from shadow to shadow. Laine didn't seem worried, so everything had to be okay… which was good, because Phoenix had to barf again.

The potholes in the Olympic Staircase had filled with water. Phoe accidentally stuck her foot in one. It didn't make it any wetter than it had been already, but she cursed anyhow. It seemed the thing to do.

"Almost there," Laine said encouragingly. Phoenix didn't have the heart to tell her that the vardos were on the other side of the campground, and the small woodland creatures probably wouldn't get the hot dog before it got all soggy and washed away by the rain.

They followed the roads—Phoe couldn't understand why; the grass wouldn't have been any wetter—around past the big blue dumpster (the rain made tin splatting noises against it, and a Shadow Fae lurked behind it—she wondered if Shadow Fae could get wet) and past the privies, around past more tin-splatting trailers and RVs and nylon-splatting tents until finally they reached Gypsy camp.

Safe. Home. No nasty Shadow thingies here.

"That one'th mine," Phoenix said, guiding her companion around to the vardo's front. "Open thethamie!"

The door, to Phoenix's great annoyance, did not swing wide.

Stupid door.

"The door doethn't rethpect me," she complained, frowning petulantly. "It workth when Ryna doeth it."

"Hmm. Well, unfortunately, I need a good old-fashioned key to make it open. I don't suppose you have one of those on you? Or does one of the other Gypsies have a spare?" Laine tried hopefully.

"Don't wake them up. Ethpethaly Niki. The geth cranky without her coffee. I have one thomewhere..." Phoenix fumbled around. She was pretty sure she kept it on her pass. The question, of course, was where her pass had gone. It wasn't around her neck. She wondered why not. She should've put it there. Would've made it easier to find if she got drunk out of her mind, which she never did, but dammit, she should have thought ahead!

Stupid me.

"How about in your pockets?"

"Pocketh! Right!" She giggled. "What hath it goth in ith pocketheth?" That caused another giggle, and this one didn't stop. Laine had to go in her right front pocket for the key, but Phoenix didn't mind.

At last the door swung wide and Phoenix, still giggling and dripping, stumbled inside. Laine followed, closing the door.

Phoenix sobered a little. Or, at least, quit giggling. "Did you need a plath to thtay? I thtayed here onth, when my tent flooded."

"I'm fine, thanks," Laine answered from the depths of the refrigerator. "A bunch of us all stay in Jack's place."

Karma wobbled over and sniffed at her person's mate, then stared up at her in utter disdain. Here she'd been out all night trying to find her person when she herself could hardly Travel at all... and this moronic house-ape had to come home smelling like watered-down vomit. Rolling in dead mice was one thing, but... Karma went to sleep in the corner to show her displeasure. It irked her quite a bit that the two-legged furless did not seem to notice.

"What hath it goth in ith pocketheth?" Giggle, giggle. "Pocketheth, pocketheth, pockethethethethetheth."

"You need water," Laine declared. "Where are your glasses?"

"Water!" Phoenix looked down at her completely drenched clothes and fell over onto the bed in a gigglefit. "I have loth of water!"

"Yes, you have lots of water. Where are your glasses?"

"On my fath!" What a stupid question! "I'm not that drunk."

"How about the ones you drink out of?"

"Over there." She motioned vaguely. Laine looked exasperated. Phoenix couldn't imagine why. The glasses were right where Ryna kept them, the same place they'd always been.

The chestnut haired lass returned with a leather mug. It was Ryna's—the pixie playing the fiddle tooled into the side gave it away—but Phoenix didn't think her love would mind.

"Thit! I left my mug at the BLUE!" Phoe suddenly realized, and tried to stand up to go get it.

Tried to being the operative words. Laine was strong for her size. Like Ryna. "I'm sure someone will hold onto it for you."

"But my mug—"

"You can get it tomorrow. Drink."

The Gypsy drank obediently as her guest rummaged through the closet.

"Put these on. You're shivering."

Phoenix looked down. Her hands were shaking. She *was* shivering! Wow. That might explain why a good quarter of the water had gone down her front—not that she'd really noticed. She tried to get her buttons undone, but her fingers were clumsy, and numb besides.

Stupid fingers.

Laine took over the task of removing Phoenix's clothing with a businesslike competence that wasn't fun at all. Her hands were cold, not at all like Ryna's. Of course, her hair hung around her like spaghetti, and that might have had something to do with it.

"Fire thould be warm," Phoe said sagely. "I'm not warm, but I'm not Fire. Ryna'th alwayth warm."

"I'm sure she is," Laine agreed noncommittally. "There you go. Now sit so I can get your socks off."

Phoenix looked down, trying to remember when she had stood up—or when her pants had come off!—but she sat nonetheless. Laine peeled off her boot-orange socks. Phoenix's feet felt even colder without them, but new, soft, warm, *dry* socks made up for it.

"I have to go to bed," Laine said after tucking several blankets around Phoenix, "but I want you to drink some more water, okay?"

"Okay," the Gypsy nodded gamely.

Laine looked at her askance, but let herself out.

Phoenix flopped back on her bed. It was big and lonely, but it was dry. Beautifully dry in here, and safe, if not precisely stable. *I'll close my eyes for a minute,* she thought. *Just until the spinning stops.*

Stupid spinning.

* * *

Phoenix moaned as she lunged for her alarm clock and the room tilted. It took far too much skill to beat the damn thing into submission—it kept turning up a cheery blue glow at her. All at once, though, it stopped.

Wonderful, deafening silence. She put her head down on her arm and whimpered. And closed her eyes. It felt like rasping sandpaper over cement. "I'm ready to be done being drunk, now," she told anyone who cared to listen. "I don't want the room shifting anymore."

It occurred to her that she had all her consonants back—she thought she might puke, but at least she could pronounce "pockets" again.

"Gotta pee," she muttered, pinballing to the door—and fell off her front steps as the chill air and comparatively bright light hit her in the face like a lead tambourine.

Kaya stopped mid-way to Phoe's door. "How do you feel?"

"I think I puked on Bryn's shoe. I forgot to put out milk for the Fae. And I've gotta pee," she announced as she picked herself off the ground and tottered through the puddles to the nearest privies.

Kaya was waiting in Phoe's vardo when she returned. "Drink."

"That's what got me in trouble. And I don't have any pants on."

"Your pants are on the floor. Here, drink." Kaya gave her the leather mug and began rooting around in the fridge.

Ryna's mug again. "I forgot my lug—mug—at the BLUE. Laine—that's Bryn when she's not Bryn—said I needed to pick it up tomorrow. Today. Not last night."

"I'm sure someone grabbed it for you. Oh, good, it hasn't gone bad yet. Here, have some applesauce."

Phoenix felt herself turn green.

Kaya winced in sympathy. "Do what you can, Phoe. It'll only get worse otherwise."

Phoenix nodded meekly and accepted the mush. She would've felt more ashamed if she hadn't been busy trying not to puke on another set of someone else's shoes. "Who else knows?"

A far-too-casual shrug.

"That many?"

"Well, from what I heard, you *did* declare you were a brownie and that somebody should eat you. That's bound to stick in a few heads."

Phoenix let out a soul-emptying sigh and wondered how she'd ever go out in public again. "I am *never* drinking again."

*   *   *

"Brownie!" greeted a diabolically chipper voice as a crowd of peasants descended on her halfway to the BLUE.

Phoenix cringed. So much for hope. She had a feeling this one wasn't going to die any time soon. "Good morrow, Puddle. You look well."

"That's because I didn't get completely plastered last night," he teased brightly, shifting his dark cloak on his shoulders.

"I want to know why, if the Renaissance is the age of discovery, no one stumbled across sunglasses. I *know* they'd invented hangovers by then."

A flutter of sympathy crossed the Leper's face. "That bad?"

"I'd scream in agony, except I think the noise would kill me."

"You didn't drink enough water," Bryn chided, joining them.

"People keep saying that," Phoenix observed dryly. "Did anyone grab my mug?"

"Hayrold brought it up to Cast Call—he passed it off to one of the other Gypsies. Probably Niki." Bryn quirked a smile.

Phoenix wasn't surprised. Guys generally took whatever chance they could to exchange a few words with Niki. And Niki, being the sweet, gracious woman that she was, probably thought they were just being nice.

"Oh, this ought to cheer you up," the Leper said, pulling a sheet of paper from his pouch. After a little throat clearing, they all began to sing:

"Alas, Pink Patty, you've done us wrong
To put us through your stupidity,
For we have worked here oh, so long
Without 'mini-plays,' counting, or 'unity.'

"You sit in your tower all powdered and pink
With lackeys to kiss-ass like prideless whores;
You say we offend all your 'guests' with our stink,
Then make the showers a quarter more.

"Artistic Directors, they come and go;
Saying you rule doesn't make it so!
'Cause we're the cast, and we make the show;
We're always and ever a family.

"You cut our contracts, then make us pay
On whims for tuning forks just the same.
You drive away actors and lengthen the day;
You tear down our structures, then give us the blame

"Your sins are far too many to list,
But you've angered bards, and our mem'ries are long.
So threaten the ones who speak up when they're pissed,
Your cruelty only will make us strong.

"Artistic Directors, they come and go;
Saying you rule doesn't make it so!
'Cause we're the cast, and we make the show;
We're always and ever a family."

Phoenix felt her jaw drop to her toes. How—?!

"Torin gave us a copy at the BLUE last night after you left," the Leper expounded.

Danny. Of course—she'd shown it to him last week; she must've left her copy with him.

"We figure if we put them up every time we go to the privy, Management won't be able to take them all down," Bryn said.

"Yup!" Puddle agreed. "So we broke into the Bedside Manor offices and stole the use of their copier."

"*And* found out what Patty's been writing on that clipboard," the Leper added darkly. "Apparently she's been keeping a naughty-and-nice list."

"That's just what we need," the Gypsy griped. "A demented pink Santa Claus."

The others laughed.

"We should get a copy of that song to the minstrels, too." Phoe lifted her glasses and scrubbed a hand over her eyes, struggling to think through the oatmeal in her head. "Any guesses on who wrote it?"

A collective shrug. "Could be anyone," Piddle said. She had to look up to see him—thankfully the sky was gray. She squeezed her eyes shut in agony.

Bryn gave her a sympathetic smile and a burst of tingling energy as the first raindrops fell. "Go get your mug. We'll come find you after your show."

Phoenix gave her a grateful smile—as much for the bit of healing as for the shooing to Sherwood's refuge. If she was lucky, no patrons would come to any of the shows and they could all crawl back in bed where they belonged.

◇ ◇ ◇

The world was quiet and gray.

Ryna stared over the gazebo's familiar view, huddled in the cloak she'd rescued from Track's fence. It hung in soft folds around her—woolen, and warm, and the color of the sky. Her mind refused to focus, but she didn't mind. She let it drift, diddled with the pen she'd found nestled against one of the stocks. Kaya's favorite… she would be happy to have it home.

Kaya would know how to flatten her heart onto the flimsy, dirty, food booth napkin. Ryna didn't have the words… but she had to try. Had to tell her family she loved them. Had to trust that the words would come.

And in the meantime, if she was very lucky, one of the Gypsies might come down here, and she might see them… if only for a second.

She simply had to wait.

◇ ◇ ◇

There is nothing in the world as miserable as moccasin goosh, Phoenix thought woefully, trying not to put any weight on her feet as she picked her way along the marshy bits of land that edged newly formed lakes. The cold water saturating her insoles and socks slithered up between her toes with every step. The sleeves of her chemise clung like the embrace of a bog monster, and her harem pants slapped icily at her legs.

Niki trudged beside her, feet mud-caked and probably painfully cold in her sandals, but Phoenix envied her. At least she didn't have to deal with that nasty squishing, and her lush (though sodden) burgundy shawl kept the worst of the rain off.

"How are you holding up?" the dancer asked as they threaded through the sparse—and self-absorbed—crowd of patrons huddled in rain slickers and under umbrellas as they waited in line for food from the Upson Downs booths.

Phoenix couldn't find the energy to entertain them—or even pity them. She wished they'd go home. Stupid cattle standing in the rain. "I don't think I'll ever be warm again."

"Almost there."

Phoe didn't even look up when they finally stopped—simply huddled there, thankful that for the moment, at least, she could stand still. Drizzling rain pooled on the bottom rims of her glasses and dripped onto her nose. Her whole body ached… her eyeballs, under her fingernails, the pad of her smallest toe (either one). If this was the consequence for drinking, Phoenix couldn't understand why anyone touched the stuff.

"Here we go—this ought to help a little."

Phoenix blindly held out her hands for the steaming cup Niki offered, curled her fingers around the Styrofoam and willed the heat to seep into her flesh. The fragrant steam curled damply around her nose and fogged her glasses. She took a sip—it seared the tip of her tongue, but the pain felt good. Real. She welcomed the blackened feeling as she welcomed the chocolaty taste and potent caffeine kick.

Trust Niki to find the cure for a day like this in a cup of fancy coffee. "Thank you," she said, and took another sip.

"You wanting to go to VilTen?"

Phoe made a face, though she tried to muster some enthusiasm for her sister-friend's sake. "It'll probably be a good show. Adverse weather conditions make rennies silly and sarcastic."

"But you don't really want to," Niki concluded.

A sigh. "I guess. I don't know—I suppose we can be drenched there as easily as drenched here. I've already fallen on my butt once. It's not like it can get any muddier." The fall had been a great contributor to her saturated state—and the cold, clammy wedgie she couldn't rectify through all her layers. "But the coffee's really nice."

Niki purred in agreement, eyes half lidded as she enjoyed a moment of communion with her favored beverage. If there was a deity of coffee, Niki was its high priestess.

Phoenix knew better than to come between a woman and her religion. She patiently awaited her friend's return from her raptures and only wished there was something that could transport her away from the cold and the wet.

Aside from Ryna's kiss, and the warmth of her gaze…

Another drink of the scalding coffee. *Better to have loved and lost, my ass,* she thought bitterly. *Better to have loved and* kept, *thank you very much.*

"It serves her right, I say, after what she did to poor Liam—seducing him like she did and then dropping him like a hot potato. Why, I talked to him a week after Faire ended and she ran off with that little Gypsy slut; he was inconsolable. And now that little blond bitch claiming her brat is his when he isn't here to defend himself—it wouldn't surprise me if those Gypsies weren't behind that somehow, too."

The ingratiating voice nearly made Phoenix drop her coffee. "Hold this a moment," Phoenix instructed, handed Niki her cup, and pushed through the line of patrons to where the gossip in her enormous straw hat stood on the booth's other side.

The eggler had the nerve to give her a sickly sweet smile and the beginning of an overly friendly greeting.

Phoenix cut her short with all the strength she could put behind her arm. Her slap cracked across the bony cheek, creating a sudden silence around them. Phoe wished she could say she was sorry, or that she was surprised she'd done it. She wasn't, and the martyred look in the egg lady's eyes infuriated her more. "Next time," Phoenix said, strained, "get your facts straight before honking like a goose all over Pendragon."

While the scrawny gossip still spluttered indignantly, Phoe whirled and stomped away, heedless of cold and wet and the cough that pushed at her chest. Suddenly she felt very much like joining the VilTen match, and censors be damned.

◇ ◇ ◇

Ryna rolled the napkins carefully around Kaya's pen and fastened them with a bit of mud-caked ribbon. She didn't know if it was good enough, or said everything right, but hopefully the feeling behind it would suffice. All they had to do was know. She couldn't ask for more than that.

No one had come down to the gazebo. Maybe no one would. It had always been her place, mostly, anyhow.

Where to leave this, then… the vardo behind Caravan Stage, maybe? Someone from her family would find it—maybe even today. Providing any of the things she'd rescued had returned to their own world… Ryna drew her cloak closer around her and shuffled up the trail that led to the stage, climbed the steps that led to the vardo's dim interior.

A few coins from someone's belt spattered the floor. Ryna bent to pick one up, but it disappeared—and another appeared a little to the left.

They were like the ring, then—not really real. She straightened, looked around, gaze landing on the little bowed window that overlooked Robyn's pond. Yes—yes, there. Ryna gingerly placed her treasure on the window's shelf, stood for a moment with her hands pressed over the ribbon-bound package. *Go home,* she thought. *Please. Go to your owner. Take my message to her... to my family.*

It did not shimmer or disappear. Ryna hadn't really expected it to. She stepped between the faded orange curtains and left it alone, just in case it needed some privacy for its transition.

◇ ◇ ◇

Not even pink elephants get hangovers this bad, Phoenix thought woefully as she deposited the tips from the three o'clock variety show. Her headache had invited a sore throat to the party, and she felt as if someone had given her a forty-grit massage. She couldn't function beyond basic childhood responses, and all the instincts of her youth nudged her towards Cottage and a brother that could make it all better.

"Bless this house and all within, and may they never feel like this," she murmured, dutifully planting a kissed hand on the green wooden doorframe as she scuffed her boots a couple token times. Any more than that took too much effort, and her joints ached with the movement. She wondered if she really looked as bad as she felt. Probably, given the looks of startled worry on several O'Malley faces.

Torin excused himself from entertaining patrons near the fire. "Are you all right?" he asked quietly as he pulled her out of the doorway.

"I don't feel so good."

"You don't look so good," he returned, pressing a hand to her brow. "Do the Gypsies know you're sick?"

She shook her head, pulled her cloak closer around herself. At least her clothes were dry after changing a couple hours ago. "Didn't want them to worry. They've got enough to think about."

Several patrons were beginning to gossip by the warmth of the hearth—all murmured questioning and confusion, but hushed so the subject will not know he or she is being discussed.

Da broke the tension by teasing loudly, "Our village healer has the faire crud? Doesn't the irony kill you?"

"Oh, could it please?" she begged.

Sympathetic titters. Mystery solved. They went back to warming themselves.

"Poor Phoe-bea," Daniel soothed, gently stroking her hair. She closed her eyes at the familiar touch, feeling six years old again. It was nice. Life had been blissfully simple then.

"Here." Aunt Molly produced a few aspirin from her belt pouch.

Phoenix stared at them, marveling how something so wonderful could be so very small. With much gratitude she accepted a mug of water from Eryn and tossed them back.

"You should take a nap upstairs with Brigid," Molly fussed.

"I'll get her sick." It was a weak protest. A nap sounded awfully nice.

"She's already sick," Eryn chimed cheerily.

"Up you go." Daniel closed the argument by herding her towards the loft's stairs.

Phoenix climbed them. It didn't hurt any more than simply breathing did. Or, at least, not much. She tried not to cough as she crawled into the loft.

Brigid raised a bed-mussed head from her pillow of spare costuming. Her nose and eyes were all red, and a roll of privy paper stood guard by her side. A small wicker wastebasket kept it company. "You too?" she asked with a miserable grin, and sniffed.

"Scoot over, half-gill," Danny instructed, his head peeking through the floor.

The O'Malley lass lifted the covers in invitation; Phoenix nestled inside and promptly found herself cuddled. She wasn't about to complain.

Daniel knelt at their bedside, tucking covers and smoothing back hair. When he had everything to his satisfaction, each brow received a kiss, then he perched on a battle-scarred old chair. Woven ribbons had replaced its wicker seat long ago—and even they had begun to fade.

Phoenix closed her eyes as his voice floated softly over them, singing an Irish lullaby that seemed older than time itself.

⁂

The lilting song was a lullaby. She knew that much. For a moment she remembered it, remembered a room—her family's home—and the fire, and the moonlight. And the song. She had been ill, then. *Perhaps because her mother was Irish,* she thought. *Perhaps that is how the Irish sing.*

The air tasted crisp and fragrant, but not chill—one of those perfect autumn days where the sunlight matches the leaves and time seems to stop.

Except for the song. She glanced beside her to where a tangled head of light brown hair bowed over its work. An errant breeze tufted blond hair into Phoenix's face—the other woman's dirt-smudged fingers tucked it behind Phoe's ear. Regal brown eyes caught hers, and Phoenix lost herself to the soul behind them. It peered back at her through centuries.

"Rosemary," Rachelle told her. "Rosemary is very important."

Phoenix looked down at the plant beneath her hands. Rosemary. They were readying Rachelle's herb garden for winter. She knew that now. She wondered why she hadn't before. Her hands were not her own. They seemed too small. Or perhaps just right. Perhaps they had always been like this. They were her hands. Good hands.

For a moment Rachelle's hair caught the sun and flared a beautiful copper-red. She wondered why it wasn't like that always. *Perhaps someday it will be,* she decided, and thought no more on it.

"Tell me, Rach. Teach me. Why does your voice sound like eternity?"

"Perhaps that is how old I am," she replied lightly. She fingered the rosemary lovingly.

Rosemary. Very important. It's for—

"Moon Lady," Phoenix said affectionately—answer and question and gentle rebuke.

"Perhaps that is how long you have known me," Rachelle tried again. Her eyes looked green, reflected from the grass. But Rachelle's eyes were not green.

Or were they?

Beautiful slender hands, drawing music from the plants:

"How should I my true love know from another one?
By his cockle hat and staff, and his sandal shoon.
He is dead and gone, Lady, he is dead and gone,
At his head a grass green turf, at his heel a stone."

The autumn light faded. Time had started again. "But how? How do we find one another when we are separated?" Phoenix demanded. They were standing, the garden gone, though she did not know where she was. The plants still sang, even though they were gone.

How should I my true love know…

Rachelle looked at her, perplexed, her hands smaller now. *She* was smaller now. "We will. We did this time, did we not?"

It had not answered Phoenix's question. She wasn't entirely sure why. She brushed it off. "How will I bring you home to me? When we are separated, what must I do—"

Rachelle smiled, beatifically. She hardly looked like Rachelle anymore, but Phoenix knew. Even if the world was fading, loosening at the seams, she knew—

"Rosemary," said the lady bathed in moonlight and fire. "Very important."

It's for—

"Remembrance!" Phoenix gasped as her eyes flew wide. Beside her, Brigid murmured and shifted in her sleep. The sky beyond the loft's windows was cloud-drenched and cold. Below her, she could hear the Irish making final dinner preparations as Patches sang a woeful lament—

> *"Fortune my foe, why dost thou frown on me?*
> *And will thy favors never greater be?*
> *Wilt thou, I say, forever bring me pain?*
> *And wilt thou ne'er restore my joy again?"*

Patches was playing—the variety show would start soon. Phoe eased out of the makeshift bed and crept down the ladder to the main floor. Patrons crammed the Cottage, especially between her and the door. *Rosemary*, she thought, *is for remembrance.* Still half hazed, she clambered out the window and hurried for Sherwood, feet squishing, cloak flaring behind her. Illness didn't matter. Discomfort didn't matter.

She knew how to bring Ryna home.

Ryna shivered, missing her vanished cloak, wetter and more chilled than she could ever recall being. An amazing thing, considering how… thin… she felt. Stretched. Transparent.

Her earlier confidence felt stretched, too… maybe because the pen was gone. Bravery had been easy enough this morning, but she didn't want the napkin to hold her last words to her family. It took all her willpower to keep her terror locked up. The *last* thing she needed was for the Shadow Fae to get a whiff of that…

Even thinking about squelching it made the fear flare hot and bright. She could feel the Shadow Fae creeping closer to warm themselves by it.

Think safe thoughts—protected thoughts, shielded thoughts, thoughts of them unable to reach her. Remember happy times. Remember light. Remember love of family. Wrap it like a cloak around the soul—safe, protected. *Remember your fire. Remember your fire. Remember your fire.* She chanted the litany in her mind, huddled in the stage vardo's back corner.

She could hear them whispering outside, amidst the patter of renewed raindrops. They would wait. They had eternity.

◇ ◇ ◇

"I think I know the key to getting Ryna back."

If the Gypsies had used spoons and forks, surely they would've fallen to the ground. As it was, some rice dropped from Toby's fingers onto the wet leaves with a soft *plop*.

Phuro Basil looked around surreptitiously before resting his forearms on his knees and leaning forward, intent. "I believe we're all ears."

Phoe bowed her head a moment, thinking. Her instincts knew what it was about, but *conveying* that intuition… She peered up at her family, nudged her glasses. "Memories. I don't understand why, exactly, but I think that's the key. I had this dream—" She paused, sighed. This all sounded so ridiculous. She shouldn't have started.

Well, they were waiting. Keep talking. Maybe something brilliant would fall out.

"Not only memories from this life. It has to be older than that, deeper than that, if it's going to work. We've all been together in one grouping or another from the beginning of time, I'm sure, and it's going to take something that deep to override whatever the Shadow Fae did—I think maybe the reason I couldn't hold onto her was because… I don't know… maybe I don't have enough sense of who she is." She paused, looked around at her family, hanging on her every word. "Is this making any sense, or am I just blabbering?"

"A lot of sense," Basil said. "What do you intend to do?"

She gave him a wry grin. "Well, getting dead roaring drunk is out of the question. I tried that, and it didn't help at all."

An uneasy chuckle rustled across the group.

"Do you know how to remember?" Tremayne asked softly.

Phoenix shook her head. "Bits show up here and there, but it's not like I can bring them up at will, or—"

"I'll teach you," he promised.

"With three days until the Equinox?" Phoe didn't know whether she sounded more skeptical or despairing.

"You'll learn," Elda told her. "We're counting on you. Ryna's counting on you. It has to be enough time, because it's all you've got."

No pressure, Phoe thought glumly.

Tremayne squeezed her knee—Phoenix wished she could find the gesture reassuring. She felt so, so tired, and it all seemed so impossible…

"I don't think that's entirely it, though," Tanek disagreed. "Not all of it, anyway. I don't think that last ritual was *supposed* to work."

Niki frowned. "But the Bright Fae said…"

"The Bright Fae were awfully vague," Tanek pointed out. "And if what all the old tales say is true, probably out for themselves."

Baba Luna raised an eyebrow at him. "So you have a better idea?"

"I've done some… looking into things. Thinking. Why should thinning the veil be enough to bring her back? Wouldn't you need a little hole or something? Nothing big—but—"

"But the Bright Fae wouldn't want us making *any* hole in the veil," Elda mused. "I see your point."

"We'll have to shield it," Niki said. "Thinning the veil screwed with the weather bad enough. I don't want to know what putting a hole in it would do."

"It might create less of a problem," Kaya pointed out. "We were trying to pull her though something semi-solid, for lack of a better way to describe it. It rebounded like a trampoline when the tension released, but a hole…"

Toby flashed them all a grin. "I do believe we have a plan."

"It's something," *Phuro* Basil allowed.

"It will work." Tremayne's voice held a quiet confidence that Phoenix envied. "On Thursday night we bring Ryna home."

* * *

Drum Jam thundered nearer as Phoenix wandered up the lane out of Sherwood. Tremayne had ordered her downstairs to rest until after Cannon, when he would begin her lessons, but she was tired, achy, dispirited, and needed a distraction more than she needed rest and time to brood. She wished she had the energy to join the dance, but even *walking* seemed like an awful lot of trouble. She skirted the gathering with a weary sigh.

"It's in all the privies! Why would they do this to me?"

Phoe paused as Patty's words floated to her. She'd come even with the ugly vinyl tent that sprawled across the Green—and, unable to help herself, she peered inside. A soggy pink form, a sheet of paper clutched in one hand, faced off against their old Entertainment Director.

"You made changes," Eric said. "Did you stop to see if things were broken before you screwed with them?"

Patty's mouth worked for a moment, like a puzzled pink trout. "Why should I?" she finally asked. "I had good ideas."

"People liked things the way they were."

"But I explained why I did everything. I was friendly and cheerful! How can people not like me if I'm friendly and cheerful?" She sneezed delicately. Even sodden and smitten with the faire crud, Patty looked perky.

Phoe felt like a funnel cake left in a mud puddle.

Eric gave his replacement a look of disgust. "You're not one of them—and no rennie will play follow-the-leader with someone who's not already part of the game."

Her face puckered. She looked ready to cry. "What do I have to do?"

"Bring back their family. Rebuild the structures and traditions you tore down. Pay them decent wages. Trust them. They've been here long enough to learn what works and what doesn't the hard way—ask them… and listen. Most everyone will be happy to help make your job easier. I bet they even tried before you threw their efforts away. You have to stop patronizing them and care about them at least as much as your precious guests."

Storm clouds brewed in Perky Patty's expression. "Directors don't *ask*—they *direct*! That's *why* they're called *directors*! These people are a bunch of lawless anarchists who need to be taught some manners and some discipline! My father would've put me over his knee for half the stuff *any* of them have said to me!"

"And the whole of Pendragon will have you over a *barrel* for a *quarter* of what *you've* said. That song was only the seed. Soon—"

Phoenix backed slowly away, ashamed at having eavesdropped, and started through the Upson Downs. Maybe she *should* go down to her vardo…

A sharp Gypsy trill cut the air—Phoe instinctively rounded in the direction of the noise. Puddle, Hayrold, and Ilya waved at her from Flying Buttress's seating. She veered right to join them.

"Wet!" Puddle observed as she neared.

"Yeah," she agreed with a sigh. "Yeah, I am."

"Wanna play foxtail with us?" Hayrold offered. "It's fun. You'll feel better."

A smile twitched onto her face at his coaxing tone. "Sure."

The drums faded as the foursome cut behind Flying Buttress Stage and angled toward the open area near the BLUE. The crowds were rapidly thinning as people moseyed toward Front Gate. Hayrold, Puddle, Ilya, and Phoenix spread into a square, Puddle swinging the tail by its rough linen and leather streamers. It arced like a comet towards the brown-cloaked peasant; Hayrold lunged to the right and caught it by one leather lacing. He paused briefly to gather the other tails, idly swung it in a couple circles by his side, and tossed it to Ilya.

"Ready?" the young peasant called, then passed it to Phoenix.

The cloth-covered rock that made the comet's head smacked smartly against her thumb on the way to the ground, but Phoe just picked it out of the mud. "Incoming!" she warned Puddle, stifling a cough and letting it fly as it passed the bottom of its swing.

"Nice!" Hayrold called as it dropped into Puddle's hands.

Phoe tossed her braid over her shoulder. "Thanks!"

Throw, catch. Throw, catch. Throw, chase after it, pick it off the ground, throw. Wonderful, mindless rhythm—no questions, no worries. She could feel the tension fading from her being with every swing of the foxtail. Cannon sounded, but the game continued. Throw, catch. Throw, catch.

"Hey, look at that," Ilya called, pointing toward Rowan Stage.

"It's amazing how sucky Faire can be and still produce a sunset like that," Hayrold marveled. "Sort of makes surviving the day worth it."

Phoenix stared at the painted, just-clearing sky. How had they known she needed this so badly? The game, the sunset, the moment of normalcy and wordless support. Just now, the task before her seemed less daunting. She bit her lip against the tears of gratitude and love choking her. *These are my people,* she thought, holding them tight to her soul. *This—is—my—home.*

Ryna stared, transfixed, at the beautiful clouds, orange-red-pink-purple, as if a great bird of fire had molted across the sky. From the corner of her eyes, four forms shimmered momentarily through her vision. She knew better than to try and look at them directly, only stared until both phoenixes had faded into the night.

Grateful for their beauty, their presence, no matter how brief.

Reality faded in… and with it, the need to visit Harvey. Phoenix yawned, stretched, rubbed her eyes, and winced at the sore spot on her knee where it'd pressed against the *seanchaí* chair's arm. Mellow music and conversation surrounded her like the flickering fire- and candle-light. Warm. Comfortable. Safe. She rearranged herself in the chair and beckoned back the hazy, dreamless sleep that had cradled her…

No such luck. She still had to go.

Grumping under her breath, Phoenix levered up from the chair, shedding a cloak some kind soul had tucked around her. "Cold," she griped to no one in particular as she closed Cottage's back door behind herself. The world was fuzzy; she'd forgotten to put her glasses back on. She coughed and flapped her arms a little until she could tuck her hands up inside her sleeves. Wind tugged her chemise against her legs as she hunched her way to the privies, hugging herself under a cloud-scudded sky.

What time was it? Midnight? Two? Three? The lessons with Tremayne had taken hours before she'd finally burst into frustrated tears and he'd brought her up to Cottage. Not that she'd stayed awake long once she'd gotten there… but at least at Cottage she wasn't alone.

She picked the beige-colored wheelchair-accessible privy; maybe it would be harder for a Shadow to emerge from a light-colored surface. There was more room, so at the very least it would take longer for it to get to her. Theoretically.

She latched the door behind herself, crept over to the seat in the corner, and prepared to sit. If it didn't hear her… She coughed.

A white blob she had taken for a mound of privy paper sprang to life with a soul-tearing shriek and thundered against the wall beside her.

Phoenix bolted for the door with a frightened scream and lurched into the night, fighting the unholy force that tethered her ankles. It gave with a sickening rip and she kicked madly about, trying to loose the Shadow-thing from her remaining foot.

The wind pounded her thin chemise, trying to drive her backwards, but the only cold she felt was terror. The creature kept wrapping around her boot, clinging with sentient malevolence.

The thing pounded against the inside of the plastic hut behind her.

Oh please, dear Goddess, don't let me die in the privies, she begged as she freed herself with one final, mighty kick, and ran like mad—

—right into the solid, warm, secure form of her father-in-law. Half of the folks who had been in Cottage were asking her questions all at once, but she could only point to the Jiff from Hell and try not to cough. "Monster… privy…"

A fuzzy blob she was pretty sure belonged to Daniel advanced on it with deadly intent, two other blobs behind him. Tremayne held her close, whispered something soothing she couldn't hear over the frenzied beating of her own heart.

Daniel flung the door wide.

Startled yells—and then laughter.

"Harvey's a *chicken*?!"

"How the *hell* did it get *in* there?" exclaimed a woman whose name Phoenix hadn't caught. "It's a looooong way from the petting zoo."

"Chicken?" She coughed again; Tremayne held her tight. A gust of wind plastered her chemise against her ass, and suddenly she realized she was no longer wearing her panties. *That must've been…* she realized, nearly faint with relief and humiliation. "I nearly died of fright over a *chicken*?"

The feathered fiend squawked and fluttered from the Jiffy, one of the musicians behind it making shooing motions. It pecked righteously at the ground. Phoe hoped some kind god would prevent either the chicken or the rennies from finding her underwear.

"No more running about without your glasses on," Daniel scolded gently, placing a fond kiss on her brow. "Come back by the fire and I'll make you something warm to drink, okay?"

"All right," she agreed, thankful for the five-day stretch before the next weekend.

Maybe by then they'd all forget.

◇ ◇ ◇

"Dinner is served."

Liam raised his chin from his knees, brushed a clump of dirty, ragged, short red hair out of his face. He needed a shower. He didn't especially care anymore. He met the hate-filled eyes of Phoenix's brother with utter weariness, then broke the gaze. The hair fell back over his eyes. He left it this time.

Phoe's brother dropped a box of stale cereal on the floor.

Liam winced, wondering what would come next. He could feel the weight of Daniel's stare pressing him down, down, until it was a wonder he didn't become part of the house's foundation, a body to be found someday when the house came down. Stories would have to be invented, of course, but none of them would be as frightening as the truth.

Finally... *finally* Daniel turned away, paused at the doorway, looked back over his shoulder. "Oh, by the way—that baby you held? She's yours."

His...

A daughter.

His.

Morgan.

"The Gypsies didn't want me to say anything—I think they were reserving that right for themselves—but at the moment I don't care. I just want to see you suffer."

Liam blinked dumbly at the door as it slammed closed. He wanted to shout back that it couldn't be his, that Daniel had to be lying, but the arguments didn't even sound convincing to his own ears anymore. She *was* the right age. Emily had protested, and he'd shown her a good time anyway. And now he was a father.

Liam curled into a little ball, trying to collapse in on himself until he went supernova. Then there would be nothing but a huge, light-sucking hole.

He'd been that long enough.

A daughter.

And he would never again see her.

He could only stare at the wall, imagining lost tomorrows.

◇ ◇ ◇

Karma draped over Phoenix's left knee. The Gypsy took comfort from her feline presence—Karma had probably intended that. After all, *somebody* had to keep watch. Tremayne had given her the knowledge, but he had his own preparations. She had to fly on her own.

Breathe.

In.

Out.

Don't think.

Don't doubt.

Simply breathe.

A truck rattled by blaring Vivaldi.

Someone sneezed; four people shouted blessings.

The folks in the loud sex tent advertised their local pantheon.

"Don't you ever quit?" someone yelled.

"No-oh-oh-yes! Yes! Yes!"

Damn it was hard to concentrate. *Maybe if I wait until night… ?*

Phoenix dismissed the thought. There wasn't enough time to be choosy. She coughed. Her chest hurt from coughing.

Never mind that—try again.

Not enough time.

She hushed her mental voice.

Dear gods, but that stereo was loud.

Slowly, though, it faded as her world narrowed to her breath, her heartbeat.

This breath.

This heartbeat.

And then to something beyond that as awareness of even basic life functions dwindled.

A hallway like over-exposed film, so pastel it almost didn't exist.

A door. There were hundreds, all identical, but somehow she knew that *this* was The Door. At least, for now. Phoenix stood at The Door, a non-existent hand on the imagined knob. Her spirit trembled. *Not enough time.*

She steeled herself, turned the knob.

Bright light flooded out to meet her, bringing a rush of overwhelming sound and smell and taste and texture…

Then the voices came. She knew what they said, though she did not know the words.

By breath and life and fire.

It was a simple room. Earth, or dirt, or something, maybe clay—she couldn't tell. It was brown. Maybe a cave. She thought she should be able to see details—it was so plain—but somehow she could not. It was all a great confusion, like trees blowing twelve ways in a storm, and after all, the room was not so very important.

There were many people, all women, all agitated, and afraid, and bustling, and tired. She had been here a long time. They had tried unsuccessfully to make her leave. They had no hope, but they were trying anyhow. *She* had no hope, but she refused to give up.

She could not see the people, either—except one.

By breath and life and fire.

The woman spoke the words between great gulps of air. She was beautiful, with eyes the same brown as her skin. Black, sweat-matted hair clung to her face. Lines of pain etched her entire being. It would not be long now, but did not weep. Perhaps she was in too much pain.

Two voices, one litany. Not enough time—there could never be enough time. With this, maybe, maybe—

"By breath and life and fire," Phoenix whispered in time with the voices chanting in her head. "Breath and life and fire and life and breath and fire and—"

A woman's exhausted cry, a baby's shrill wail, and the glimmer of light fading from beloved dark eyes even as their hope—their salvation—was born. Her own despairing voice in a language it seemed she should know, fading, echoing—

A baby's shrill wail—

"Yaagh!" Phoe shouted, scrambling upright, and coughed. Her breath came in shallow pants rattling in her chest; somewhere in the campground an infant voiced its displeasure. She was standing on her bed. Ryna's bed. Their bed, she was standing on it, and a greatly disturbed Karma stared up at her with reproach—and a little awe.

Awe? she wondered blankly, but thoughts came and went without attaching to anything. The fading dark eyes filled her mind; she knew they belonged to Ryna, *knew* it, before she could even register the gentle touch of the other woman tucking a strand of hair behind Phoenix's ear.

When had that been? What had become of the child? Who had been the father? She tried to cling to the memories, decipher even one more clue, a meaning somewhere, but it was all fading, all except for the quiet chant, the vow that had bound them in yet another life.

Phoenix closed her eyes, calmed her breathing, and prepared to try again. She had to find an answer. Somewhere. She *had* to.

By breath—

And life—

And—

◇ ◇ ◇

"Fire," Ryna whispered as the phantom flames rippled over beloved oaks. They had no leaves—they hadn't had any when the fire started. She felt safe, almost content to sit on Robyn's bridge and watch her home burn. After all, it wasn't real. She knew that this time. Snow covered the ground. It made no sense. Why would the Shadow Fae send a vision that didn't frighten her?

A seed of panic cracked in her heart. How much had they done that this nightmare held no sway in her heart? What other calluses would her soul wear before this ended?

Dear gods, would she end up like Liam?

What had it done to Liam, who had been half consumed when he arrived? The arrogance of that idiot, to think he could do business with the Shadow Fae and wind up on the winning side...

"The arrogance of that mortal, to think she can fight the Shadow Fae alone and wind up on the winning side..."

The words lashed her soul like a cat-o-nine-tails, left her bleeding, stinging, and raw.

"I'm not like him!" Ryna yelled in frightened defiance.

The flames shimmered; she could see herself in them, and Kaya...

"Are you all right?" Kaya perched next to her stepdaughter. It was the middle of the week, on site, not far from the Off With Your Head game.

"Yeah, just lost in thought." Ryna sighed. "I've had this feeling like someone's watching me lately. Even in my dreams. And it's not the usual sort we all feel, either, like something's just watching out of curiosity. It's like it's watching me in particular and purposefully staying just far enough away that I can't find it. Or maybe it's trying to lure me out. I'm not sure."

Kaya frowned in thought. "Is it a bad sort of something?"

Ryna shrugged, but it had an uncomfortable edge to it. "I walked by the Bear in the full moonlight a few days back and it gave me the shivers, but for all that it might just be mischievous. And if it's skulking in shadows, it probably means it knows I could take it out."

Another shimmer—

Sunlight. People all around. The Bear. Herself. Liam.

"And you might do well to remember that when the Dark Ones come to claim your soul, this all could have been prevented if only you had heeded my advice!"

"I do not start these fights with you; I simply finish them. If you insist on playing games, then do not be surprised when someone else wins."

"Do not turn your back on me, Gypsy!"

Ryna yelped as Liam grabbed a fistful of her hair and jerked her head backwards. "Why, Liam? Are you going to threaten me some more? Summon another goolie?"

Liam smiled slowly down at her and drew the tip of his dagger across her throat.

The Gypsy's eyes widened. "You're insane! If you're planning to kill me, this is not the place to do it! We're surrounded by people!"

"Patrons."

"And a few rennies. Everyone out here knows I wouldn't play along with you. They're going to know that's not fake blood, Liam, and if they don't realize it, my dead body ought to confirm things for them. They'll still have seen it. They'll still be witnesses. Do you think that's going to win you Bea's affection?"

With a snarl, Liam released her hair and shoved her forward. Ryna stumbled, whirled—

—but he was gone. And though she had been watching from the outside this time, Ryna could not see where he'd disappeared to.

"Creepy bastard," she muttered, shaken, and hurried the rest of the way to her show.

"Hey," her father greeted her as she settled in with her fiddle. "Are you all right?"

"Yeah." Ryna brushed it off. "Just ran into Liam; he was doing the 'I'm so dark and spooky' routine. Here, I think I'm in tune..."

Shimmer.

Her vardo, dimly lit, Celtic lullabies playing softly from the stereo. Rain like people whispering. She could almost make the words out. It sounded like they were talking about her.

Karma stared out the window and hissed.

Ryna saw herself peer into the darkness as well. A set expression crossed her face as she firmly pulled closed the drapes, snuggled into her nest of blankets, and shut her eyes. Her thoughts were as loud as speech:

If they want to whisper, let them whisper. This is my space. If anything wants in, it's going to have to try a lot harder than that.

Shimmer.

Vilification Tennis—but Ryna and Phoenix had already finished their round. Ryna saw herself standing by the Bear, staring haughtily up at Liam.

"Oh, come on. You weren't this hesitant when it was just you and me, and you said that was a warning. I didn't take it—are you going to deliver on the real thing, now? What will you do this time? Summon up some more of your goolies?"

"I... do not... summon," he said in lethally even tones, his eyes as friendly as an ice pick. "Especially... not... goolies."

The crowd howled with mirth in reaction to an insult.

"You just keep telling yourself that," Ryna said when the ruckus died down, giving him a patronizing pat on the arm. "And I'll just keep kicking the stuffing out of all the goolies you're not sending, and we'll all go on our merry way, how's that?"

Ryna tried to tear her eyes away, but could not. The fire washed over her—though strangely she felt no pain from it—and suddenly she no longer watched the little dramas of the past.

She *lived* them.

Salt air, the roll of motion beneath her, the rough rope against her skin, the wind pounding her ragged striped shirt. Phoenix stared with surprise at the sun-dark, calloused hands that expertly checked the sails' knots, then down at her body.

She was a *man*!

It seemed strange that it should surprise her. What else would she be? Her body felt familiar and natural, easily adjusting to the wild pitching of the masts hundreds of feet above the deck, where even a tiny dip in the sea became a wild, careening ride. This had been her life since before she had been old enough to shave. Once, she had been a homeless street urchin. Then, a cabin boy. Then—a sailor. She belonged here as she had never belonged anywhere on land. Oh, yes, the food was horrible, but no worse than what she had scavenged from the refuse heap as a child. It was a dangerous life—but no more dangerous than the streets.

And sailing brought the adventure of exotic countries with strange music and stranger people, like the one they had just visited—tropical, its people bearing skin darker than the sun could make it. And their stories! She didn't understand their words, but she knew enough to realize that these were tales untouched since time began—tales of a world the Christians had never imagined. Sometimes the stories were even carved into gold—more the pity that the conquistadors had melted those down for the metal.

And then the holy men had burned the histories carved into wood...

Phoenix had saved a few, smuggled them away in her meager belongings. It was forbidden, of course, but it seemed important. Surely she could find someone in one of their ports of call that could puzzle out the messages of the strange symbols… or at least keep them safe. That, above all…

Focus. You're here for a reason.

Time flowed like great waves. Same journey, different day. Rain and wind drove them hard against the dark sky like the very breath of demons. Strange creatures seemed to creep from ocean and cloud, seen only at the corners of vision. Madness.

Ryna. Where was—

He. Ryna. Or he would be, one day. Phoenix could tell by the coiled determination in his stance, by the way their souls touched… Just as she could tell by his eyes that he saw the strange visions, too… knew they would claim this ship.

And the stories. The thought brought quick, stinging tears to Phoe's eyes. It gave little comfort to know that when the ship went down, at least she and Ryna would perish together, wrapped in the cold, deadly embrace of their mutual love:

The sea.

The world pitched under her, and Ryna tumbled across the deck, slammed into the rail. She clutched the worn wood in an agony of pain, and for a moment she could scarcely remember to breathe.

Shouting—cold water washed over her and receded, though she hardly noticed. She was soaked already. Her left wrist hurt like fire. Broken, surely. She felt a brief, wild panic that if it didn't set right she would never play her fiddle again—and laughed into the storm. She'd never live that long. None of them would. Things darker than the sea had boarded their boat. Demons right out of that priest's nightmares, and they were laughing.

Ryna stood, defiantly scrubbed the saltwater from her face with her good hand, and blinked the haze of pain from her eyes. She ran as best she could, balance instinctively shifting to match the lurch of the ship, clutching her wounded arm to her breast.

She had no breasts.

Not that it mattered now—or at all, really. What a silly thing to notice in the face of the storm, and death.

Someone rushing towards her—Phoenix! Or, Phoenix someday… right now she—*he* was… the name would not come. But the look of concern in his eyes… *that* she would know no matter the time or place. Ryna gave him a brave smile. They needed no words, curtained by the rain and the wind.

Shouts.

They turned.

The wall of water crashed down on them.

Not again, she thought incongruously.

Shimmer.

◇ ◇ ◇

The Shadow Fae had tried something. There had been… a shift. A surge. Liam could feel it.

His expression twisted in a grimace. He hated that. Hated how he had been there long enough for them to get inside him—at least enough that he could feel them like a part of his own body. A part he could not control, but could control him.

How many people would have control of him?

A shift… The Shadow Fae had gained some ground. What ground, he could not say, nor did he know how they had gained it. But another chink had been widened.

Darkness melted from light; the knowledge of their presence crawled along the inside of his skin—but he was used to that, and to the sound of rotting things that filled the air. He forced himself to sit still, forced himself not to twitch, forced himself not to think of what they could do to him—what they had done to him. He tried to imagine he was in control.

The first of the Three spoke, its words an anaconda squeezing at Liam's soul. "We thought you would be interested…"

The second, its tone charred parchment crumbling to oblivion, "We have information…"

And then the third's shriek, a train's brakes before the collision: "Things you might wish to see…"

Liam felt his eyes round against his will as images shimmered through his mind, raping it as Tanek had raped his body.

And the Shadow Fae laughed.

◇ ◇ ◇

Opulence—fountains, flowers, white marble, fruit-laden trays. It was to be expected here, in the house of a wealthy merchant, but it made Phoenix acutely aware of her plain robes and stuttering voice as she read strange symbols from a scroll. Poetry. She was a poet.

Phoenix glanced briefly up at the merchant's wife, lounged at her ease among servants. Phoe's voice cracked as it had not since she was a strapling lad—not that she was so much more now, but still. She flushed red as Aphrodite's lips.

The merchant's wife laughed, musical, chiming. She was tiny and beautiful. Phoenix tried not to notice, though the poem *was* about her… her husband had tossed Phoenix a couple coins on the street as commission, and Phoenix had picked one written ages ago—vague enough to fit any woman, yet specific enough that any woman would believe it spoke of her alone.

It was woefully inadequate.

The merchant's wife rose, pressed a few more coins into Phoenix's hand, and whispered words that nearly made Phoe drop them.

Employment?! She would be paid to sit in this glorious creature's presence and converse, and entertain, and compose? Truly the gods were generous!

Sunshine and surroundings blurred; time passed. And if the Elysian Fields were more wondrous than this, she could not imagine. She had all the scrolls she could ever desire, food the likes of which she had never dreamed to taste, and a beautiful woman hanging on her every word. And these rewards paled beside those the merchant's wife bestowed personally.

Surely she was all nine muses personified. Phoenix knew she could write to the end of her days and beyond and never run out of new ways to describe her love or the bond they shared.

All on behalf of her husband, of course.

Thankfully he was too full of himself to believe his wife would cast eyes on another. In truth, he thought he held Phoenix's affections as well—a lie she endured in those times that his wife was ill or in her courses. It was the price Phoenix paid to be near her, to watch her bloom with the fullness of a child she had ensured her husband would believe to be full-blooded kin to those she had already borne.

Phoenix knew better.

More time—another child. Phoenix watched with love, composing epics about little ones in whom she saw the sparks of those she recognized—Tremayne, Toby, Niki, Tanek, Daniel. Stories of times and places forgotten, but with a haunting ring of truth for something imaginary. Stories of things it seemed important not to forget.

And then, one night…

Shouting. Anger.

Children crying. Ryna screaming—

Phoenix scrambled to consciousness, unwilling to face an end that had happened over two thousand years ago.

And wept for children who had been reborn as her protectors.

<> <> <>

They will be your downfall.

The oracle's words echoed in Liam's ears as the light faded from the boy-twin's eyes. Liam pulled the dagger from the child's heart and threw him to the ground where the girl-twin and their younger brother lay staring and lifeless. To think, he had believed them his own.

"Imbrius! Diokles! Run!" his wife screamed as she kicked and clawed and bit at him.

Liam backhanded her savagely—she flew across the room, landed among the bodies of her bastards. "*My sons* have nothing to fear," he snarled as two of his men rushed into the room. He pinned them with a glare. "You—take my boys from here. You—bring me sacks. Three of them."

Pale with horror, the men saluted, then departed—one shepherding his sons, still sobbing in terror. His wife had her youngest whelp in her arms, weeping as she rocked it and smoothed back the hair from its vacant eyes.

"You betrayed me."

"They're only children! By the gods, they're only *babies*!"

Liam felt his eyes turn as cold and dark as the creatures that had revealed their parentage. "And for that reason alone I showed them mercy. You and your poet will have none."

◇ ◇ ◇

Dark night—starless. The ocean, its roar cold and final. Ryna trembled, struggled against the iron hand clamped around her arm. Her husband cursed and shook her hard, dragged her across sand that shifted under her faltering steps. His eyes were black with rage and all things unholy.

She could hear the soft weeping of her love—her gentle poet—behind her as two men dragged him through the night. Her tears had dried behind her eyes as her children's blood dried on her skin, from where she had clutched their broken, bleeding bodies close. Only the eldest two had been spared, and those she would never see again. The twins and her scarcely-toddling baby were in bloody sacks carried by other of her husband's men.

Thunder growled. It would storm before long. Eager Shadows shifted along the corners of her vision—they were hungry.

He shoved her roughly to the ground beside a boulder; her poet's captors treated him likewise as the three sacks landed at their feet. Ryna's stomach turned—she looked away, swallowing fast to keep from retching.

And then came the rope, binding them like Andromeda—but there would be no Perseus to the rescue.

Only the stern, set face of her husband as the tide came in.

Shimmer.

◇ ◇ ◇

Alone… dark, alone. Phoenix huddled against the rough clay wall, afraid to move too much. Maybe if she stayed very, very still they would not come. Time would stop. They would forget her. There would be no men. She would not scream in pain from the knives. She would not feel their determined hands holding her down, hear their scornful voices telling her she had brought this on herself.

Because she had dared to discover—what?

A great secret, one she was not supposed to know…

Yes, she had done wrong—they said she had done wrong—she had known it was wrong when she did it—but why? Why was it wrong? Why was it wrong to know?

She had asked. She had the bruises as proof. She would always have the scars—if she lived long enough to scar. She wondered if it was bad when you were too frightened to weep.

A scraping noise, a piercing slant of light as the door opened a crack.

Relief flooded her—inexplicably—even before she saw the silhouette of a familiar man's frame in the piercing light. "I told you I would come for you," he whispered in a language of strange words but familiar meaning. "I will always come for you."

The captive could feel the flash of his smile even though she could not see it.

"We must hurry now," her rescuer said—

Phoenix opened her eyes, the foreign words echoing in her head. The vardo looked strange. Too modern.

Gods, I'm going to be ill, she thought, and closed her eyes, leaning forward and pressing her forehead to the bed, trying to deconstruct nausea and the remembered fire of blade edge biting into flesh…

Fleeting impressions: dirt floor, bare feet, hurried steps, Phoenix's trembling hand in hers.

How he could have done this…

Shadows, frightened whispers.

Shadows whispering…

Need healing herbs.

Pause, listen.

No time.

Kindly servant. No, this way…

Almost out…

Trap!

Beautiful head rolling across the floor.
Anguished cry, heart-rending.
Heart-piercing.
So much blood.
Clutching dagger in hand.
Clutching dagger in chest.
Pain.
Falling.
Sound of his weeping.
So much pain.
So much blood.
Red.
White light.
Shimmer.

Her dark, beautiful eyes blinked at him once.

Liam's sword dropped from nerveless hands, landed in the spreading crimson of her life's blood. He fell to his knees beside the fair one's head. It had all happened so fast—she'd thrown her companion to the ground, taken the swing that was supposed to fell him…

"You!" Liam rounded on the one who should have fallen, bloody sword in hand—

—but the man was already on the ground, his own dagger in his chest, mouth open in a last gasp of pain, his blood mingling with the fair one's…

With a cry of rage Liam hefted his blade, brought it down—and again, and again, and again…

It was a relief when they finally came for her. Him. Phoenix was a him again. She had spent too many days watching people die from hunger, or grief, or hopelessness, or the million ways the Nazis contrived to make room for more unfortunate souls. People she loved, people she knew, people she'd never seen before—but someone, somewhere, loved them, and would miss them.

Providing they hadn't been killed too.

She fingered the triangle that was her death sentence. She had only been there a week. She didn't want to be there long enough to gain that blank stare so many wore before they did not wake in the morning.

A truck… she had been chosen for transport to a new compound. It didn't look much different than the old one. They made her strip bare, herded her into a room for "disinfection."

Phoenix tried not to weep for the sheer terror that surrounded her. She could feel it invading her mind, her soul. Something was not right. This was no shower room, whatever they said.

More people, more people. She was packed in next to a dark-skinned man with familiar eyes, and immediately she felt her world calm and center.

Despite everything, Phoenix smiled.

◇ ◇ ◇

Men. In uniforms. With guns. Their words harsh, guttural.

Hunger. Hopelessness. Despair. And rain.

Bleak buildings. Bleak sky. Barbed wire. Numbers branded into flesh.

Death for wandering, or worshiping, or loving.

Brotherhood through suffering.

A pale-skinned *gaje* stood beside Ryna. She knew him, and did not.

He seemed to feel the same by the look in his eyes. "Where are you from?" he asked.

"Everywhere. I am Rom. You?"

"Little town. A long way from here. You probably never heard of it."

"Maybe."

"This is the end, then, I suppose." Attempt at bravery.

"Maybe. But we face it together."

"We do." He seemed to take comfort in that.

Strangely, Ryna did too.

Shimmer.

Liam sneered as he shoved the last child into the gas chamber and bolted the door. Filthy, stinking, dirty Jews. Goddamn Gypsies. And the fags… perverted deviants, all of them.

Yet, as the screams and pounding started, Liam's hand strayed momentarily to the bolt…

He shook himself, banished ridiculous notions. They didn't deserve to live. He spat on the threshold. God, they weren't even human.

Still, he couldn't look away from the small glass-covered hole in the door, couldn't stop the strange feeling that part of himself was dying.

◇ ◇ ◇

Phoenix blinked, dazzled at the impossibly blue sky. Where was she now?

When was she now?

Who was she now?

Here. Now. Me, a voice in Phoe's head answered, brushing away the questions as irrelevant. There was no time for such foolishness.

No time...

Not enough time...

Bare feet against stone as she hurried past the beautiful white buildings. She could feel a tremor in the earth, in the air around her. *Not yet, not yet,* she thought, and knew it would not be now.

But soon.

"Take them," a woman of her own height commanded, breathless, piling bags into Phoenix's arms. The bags held knowledge. Their stories. Their history.

She tried to refuse.

"Take them." Gentler, this time. Phoenix felt a strand of hair brushed behind her ear. "Bring them to a safe place. You know this is the plan. It is important. He'll try to destroy them. You know this."

Phoenix did. It did not mean she liked it. She had a horrible, sinking feeling that this was the last time they would see one another in this life. Her heart squeezed at the thought. "You?"

"I will be right behind you."

"Swear it?"

Fond smile, gentle kiss on the brow. "I swear. Now go!"

"The knowledge is all," she chanted to herself as she ran, trying to breathe around the effort, around her tears. "The stories are all. She swore she would follow. She swore! She swore! She swore! "

Phoenix's eyes snapped open, her lips still shaping the words as a hard knot of grief clogged her throat.

Right behind hadn't been close enough.

◇ ◇ ◇

White walls, stone streets, clear air, and the treasure of her heart running, thinking speed would muffle her weeping. The suffocating clot of danger in the air.

A few more days. They had that much. Their history must be saved for future generations—and if she stayed, no one would think her Phoenix had gone. That was important—no one must know. Especially not him.

Shimmer—same when, different where.

A scribe's hall, or library of some sort. Dim. Safe here. Edginess. Frustration. Helplessness. Urgency. Tremayne was here. So was Kaya—only they were not themselves.

The tremor became a rumble.

Not now—kind fates, not—

She bolted to her feet, picked up the hem of her robes, and *ran.* There had to be—a day, at least; one more day, and she could leave…

People yelled after her. She plowed through three novices without pause and dashed to the wide front steps. It was as if a shadow had fallen over the city; she could feel the death all around her.

Yelling. Her name. Distant.

And then she saw it. Horror and certainty dropped through her like a stone.

Her last thought, before the rush of waters claimed her, was *I'm not going to make it after all.*

Shimmer.

"Too much!" Ryna screamed, flailing against the flames' attempt to draw her back to their reality. She no longer knew how much time had passed—how many lifetimes—she could feel herself unraveling at the edges. She had died too many times—felt herself dying…

…she could feel herself dying…

She ran.

It seemed so much simpler once she was on her feet—almost too easy, but Ryna didn't care. She had to get away, get to the safest place she knew.

Cottage—

No. Maypole. That was near where Phoenix and her father had been trying to take her. Ryna leapt across the tramped circle that surrounded the wooden pillar… and hoped she wasn't too late.

Elders dying, books burning, engravings melted for their base elements, obliterating something far more precious, though already by then the language could not be read… the images chased through Phoenix's head, fleeting and vivid and disconnected, memories from a thousand lives.

"And yet we create, re-create, crying out our small, eternal stories, a reflection of all that came before and all that will come after," she told Karma. "What would we know of ourselves, had bards ruled the earth?"

Karma gazed back, her eyes green and veiled. Through them Phoe could see the mysteries of the Orient and ancient Egypt, all the long-forgotten secrets and legends mortals no longer knew. She wondered what cats thought about, what they remembered, what stories they could tell.

Karma gazed bleakly up at her person's mate and wondered when some food would finally land in her dish. The grasshopper she'd had before settling in for the night hadn't even been worth the title of snack, and it had left a funny, fluttery feeling on her tongue. She should've stuck to mice. They, at least, were warm and soft. And she was tired and thin from another day spent tracking her person through the worlds. Two-legged furlesses got themselves into the most trouble…

A knock at the door. It was Tremayne—Phoe could tell with only a little effort. Thankfully it did not require *more* effort. She wasn't sure she had it to give. "Be welcome," she called, not rising from the bed.

Quiet opening and closing of the door. Phoenix smiled up at him—a tired smile.

He smiled back, worry in his eyes. "You are not well."

"I'll be all right. Help yourself to tea if you want some."

Tremayne reluctantly conceded, though he retrieved two mugs. She gave thanks that he wasn't going to be like *Phuro* Basil, trying to convince her to let him work healing Magick on her. He didn't understand—it would muddle her head. She couldn't afford to be muddled.

He'd finally resorted to pumping her full of garlic-ginger tea. Vile stuff, but Phoe supposed it was why she wasn't feeling any worse.

A few moments passed in companionable silence. Phoenix concentrated on keeping the room from spinning. Too badly.

"What have you learned?"

Phoenix thought about that, though she had been thinking about it every moment, waking or sleeping… and sometimes it was hard to tell the difference between the two. "I don't know," she concluded, the answer no different than before.

He raised an eyebrow, handed her a mug.

Phoenix felt as if she was back in college again. Or, worse, high school. "I think I knew it all already, though," she expanded. "I got to see a lot of lives that we were together. They weren't all of them, but I already knew we had been together nearly forever. Or—at least—part of me knew. We died a lot. Never from old age. Something dark was usually involved."

Tremayne leaned back with his tea.

Karma came over to claim lap rights and sniff at his mug.

The fiddler scratched her under her chin and deftly moved it out of range.

The cat pretended she had never been interested in the first place and sprawled, purring, across his lap. This two-legged furless was strong. He would bring her person back. And in the meantime, he was willingly replacing energy Karma had spent looking for her…

Memories whirled in Phoe's head. "In the lives I saw, there was—trouble. Someone didn't want us to be together."

"The same person?"

"I don't know... but there was something bigger than that, something we were fighting, or trying to protect..." Reality grew hazy again. She wondered where she would be when she opened her eyes this time. "I can feel all my lives calling to me, thousands of years of fighting to preserve, fighting the relentless onslaught of 'progress,' whatever flavor it happened to take that century."

"Ground," Tremayne commanded, pulling her back like a balloon on a string.

She tried to concentrate, tried to grow roots to hold her in this reality. It helped some—or else Tremayne did something.

"Identity, of people, place, and self—echoes of the thousands of voices with which we have spoken in a thousand lifetimes. She makes me feel like I could cloak myself in the sky and make myself a constellation to watch over her, for if I could see her, even if from so far away, it would still seem nearer than the absent distance between us now. Maybe Orion—Orion is important." Phoenix smiled dreamily. It almost made sense. She wasn't sure how, but it did. Ryna wasn't so very far away, if she could just project herself right. "Rosemary. It's for remembrance. Do you think I look like Ophelia?"

"What connects you?" Tremayne's voice came from a long way off, and she wasn't sure where she found the answer that came. Her own voice sounded strange.

"Love. A promise. Destiny. We didn't used to have to search for each other. We were born to the same time, the same village, and it was enough. But now there are too many villages. They've gotten too big, and we wander, lost, waiting for time to find us again. This place draws us with the echoes of fond memories, and we come, wishing for a time long gone. We're really looking for the people. The connections. This place is a lodestone that draws us all, gathers us for the battle. We're battle-bound—"

"What battle?"

"*The* battle," Phoenix replied peevishly, exasperated at his ignorance, though she could not have explained better. "Battle against darkness, battle against light—but you have to find out what is darkness, what is light. Breath and life and fire—she and I keep each other whole. She told me to run. I only listened to her once. In the Age of the Lion comes destruction. We cannot stop things from changing, but we can be sure they are remembered. Someone has to keep the stories."

"What stories?"

"It's all in the stories—in all the stories—but you have to puzzle it out. It's the only place to hide real truth. Ask Karma. Cats remember everything. She wasn't always a cat, but she remembers anyway."

"What stories?"

"We are the Bridge. We remember. There are others, but the secret is in us, in our stories. Rosemary is for remembrance, you see. They used to know things like that when Emily was alive."

"Phoenix!"

"Fire and blood and spirit, ashes and wings and a scream like snow… We are very old. We have seen it all before." It was all so… clear. Like the end of a dream, when the world fills out and expands like the last shot of a movie. She could see forever, and all the creatures that dwelled there. She could even see Ryna, huddled against the pillar of Maypole, her music so faint… *I will come for you, my love…*

Ryna looked up, and their bond rang like a struck harp, the spun wire string drawing them together… drawing worlds together…

"—nix!"

Something snared a corner of her soul, and with a snapping crash Phoenix fell back into her body at all the wrong angles. The vardo's interior was far too bright, and everything looked askew. She curled up around Karma, who purred comfortingly, and tried to pretend she didn't still feel like she was falling.

Tremayne ran hands gently over her tortured limbs; gradually the raven-hared Gypsy felt herself smooth back into place. She felt whole, and very… empty. A single tear dripped from the corner of her eye onto the fiddler's worn jeans; she wondered when his lap had become a pillow. For a long time only the sound of their breath—and Karma's purrs—stirred the air.

"She's so distant," Phoenix whispered. "And I don't know how to pull her back. All the knowledge…"

"Then we'll use something else," Tremayne said softly, stroking her hair—half to give comfort, half to gain it. "We'll find another tie."

"But what? All I have is memories and love, and it's not enough…"

"Her fiddle."

Phoenix sniffled and looked up. A wise, comforting smile met her gaze.

"The power items disappeared until she did—then they started coming back," Tremayne said. "We must need to use something physical—"

"—and nothing has more of her energy on it than her fiddle," Phoenix completed the thought. Still wobbly, she tumbled off the bed and pulled at the drawer that cradled her love's most cherished possession, lifted the leather-covered case reverently from its nest, and placed it on her mentor's lap.

Tremayne released the clasps, lifted the hinged lid, and plucked a single string.

It twonged discordantly.

Phoenix smiled. Tremayne would take care of that.

And then they'd bring Ryna home.

◇ ◇ ◇

Ryna scrubbed her eyes—and looked again. Surely that couldn't have been…

But how else to explain…?

I will come for you, my love… The thought echoed through her mind—though it was not her own.

She shuddered as the Shadow Fae brushed like cats along the edge of her safe zone. Bits of her consciousness tried to skitter away; she fumbled after them, latched onto them with mental fingers that had long since gone numb. She wondered how much had already slipped beyond her grasp, and if she could ever get it back. She had given up on reality… now she would simply settle for a sense of self.

Just enough to hold until she could leave this place and its crazy-making visions.

Just enough…

Just enough…

The Shadow Fae circled, waiting. One more day, and darkness would overtake the light.

The night wavered, and Tanek stared at her, hollow-eyed, blood dripping darkly down his arms. It glistened in the wan moonlight. A feral, sharp-toothed smile crept onto his face. He casually stalked across the border the others dared not cross.

She should have felt his presence, any presence… but there was nothing. Ryna curled up into a tighter ball as he loomed over her, bare inches away. He knelt, bringing his face so close to her ear that she should have felt his lips brush her skin.

Nothing.

When he spoke, it wasn't his voice—or his words. She knew this was not Tanek, knew that she should close this thing out of her mind, but she could not ignore the words…

"I have a surprise for you," he whispered, and when he stood again the blood smeared his face like ghoulish war paint, his hair streaked dark along the temples.

Dark turned white as the image shifted; Ryna snapped closed her eyes, though the vision invaded her mind, too. She couldn't escape—

One more day…

Phoenix stepped out into the mists of the morning, the sun still below the treeline and the clouds tinged pink and lavender with a dawn that hadn't yet gotten over itself.

She shivered as she hurried across the dirt road to the privy. "Colder than a patron's titty in a chain mail bikini on Seventh Weekend," Ryna's voice grumped in Phoe's head with amazing clarity. It felt like the first coherent thought she'd had in forever.

The reminder of her love made her smile. Ryna would be coming home today. Phoenix knew it with absolute certainty. How could she not? They had been together this long, and their destiny was not yet fulfilled. Besides, it was the Equinox. A Holy Day. Magick was afoot on days like today.

Emily and Rachelle had met on a day like today.

Ryna would come home. She had to; that was all.

She just had to.

The lock rattled.

Liam gazed balefully at it but did not rise. He was not certain he could, not after days of the Shadow Fae's entertainment. He had thought it had been bad, knowing about Rachelle and Emily. He wished now it was all he knew. Had he been born to a single life where he did not stain his hands with his love's blood?

He trembled as the lock rattled—couldn't check a sigh of relief as Daniel walked in. "Time to shake hands with oblivion."

Liam reached out, a grim smile on his face.

He only hoped it would be so easy.

Phoenix looked up into the night sky, cloudless and beautiful above the Knoll, and tried not to wonder if Ryna was doing the same. She tried not to think how her brother and Liam were already at the Maypole, waiting, tried not to think of the honor guard of peasants that had set themselves to ward away the curious, tried not to think about how much rested on their success.

Esmerelda fed the fledgling fire with kindling and Magick; it lapped at both, hungry for more, puffing smoke toward the half-moon as it illuminated the nearby trees in a hunting glow.

Firelight and moonlight.

Ryna's light.

Except the moon wasn't full…

Phoe coughed, tried to mask it. Tremayne paused in tuning Ryna's fiddle to raise a stern eyebrow, but thankfully everyone else was too preoccupied to notice. Phoe shrugged at her father-in-law. She could deal with being sick. Illness didn't matter. Ryna did.

She gave thanks that this had been a day of fasting; she wasn't sure she could keep anything down. She'd hardly eaten all week, really, though the others had brought her meals. Food seemed so... trivial... though she'd made special sure that the Fae got their offering every night. She would eat later, when Ryna came home. They'd have a feast to celebrate.

Baba Luna diddled with her drum, testing its tension until the experimentation resolved into a beat. Kaya melted from the shadows, shawl snugged around her shoulders, feet answering the siren call of the drums. Phoenix could feel it too, the thrum that began in the bones, carried by the blood. She stood as Kaya circled the fire, steps tracing an intricate pattern.

DOUM, agreed Toby's drum, adding a backbeat. *DOUM. DOUM.*

The fire's heat beat against Phoenix's skin in time to the drums. It warmed the cotton of sleeves and skirt; almost without thought she rolled up the bottom of her peasant top, twisted and knotted it against her ribcage.

Warmth caressed her belly's now-exposed flesh, invited the subtle motion of hips and waist. Wood smoke wove and curled, lacing with hair, joining the careful pattern of feet and arms. The flames licked against the night in a dance familiar for millennia, yet always new. Phoe gazed at them through lowered lashes, letting the warmth and earth-beat mate with her soul, letting the Magick flow through and around her, becoming the hundred-thousand women who had woven the steps over time, raising power for themselves, or a loved one, or the Goddess.

There was no time.

There was no Phoenix.

She was the fire, and the sky, and the soft earth beneath her feet.

Phuro Basil's strong, sure voice lifted in a chant:

"Earth my body,
Water my blood,
Wind my breath, and
Fire my spirit..."

Baba Luna layered her words with his, blending, melding, unifying...

"Air I am
Fire I am
Water, Earth
And Spirit, I am."

Other voices joined, too; across the fire another woman danced, Kaya but not Kaya, familiar from a hundred lives that had come before. They circled the blaze, souls connected, part of the eternal moment that cradled them.

Ryna's fiddle called softly into the night as Tremayne pulled its voice into the song, swirling among the elders' chant. *Ryna, we're coming. We're coming, Ryna, we're coming...*

The cadence changed; their steps changed. Now faster, now slower, but always in time with the fire. The joy of its conjuring filled her, strengthened her. *This* was real. *This* was the power that would set things right.

She was peripherally aware that the others had gotten to their feet, that the drums were moving, that one of the peasants had ghosted up the staircase to tend the fire. Phoenix followed her family toward the slope on Bakery's other side, eyes mostly closed, letting their thunder be her sight.

Trees closed overhead as Kaya took her hand to be sure she would not fall. Down, down, and the quiet squeak of hinges as the picket-fence gate swung open, releasing them onto Pendragon's grounds. Still Phoenix danced, felt the tiny, flickering heat of the candles her family carried with them, each lit from the sacred flame of their bonfire. She could hear the tiny fizzles of their wicks, feel each leaf in the trees as they shifted overhead.

The beating of the drums replaced her heart.

The singing of the fiddle replaced her soul.

Dancing, dancing, past the giant, ugly tent and into the lane of Upson Downs. Food booths guarded them to the left, familiar structures to the right—Flying Buttress Stage, Mead Booth, Como Cottage—but Phoenix barely saw them through the ancient memory of a sacred processional path. When had that been...? Ryna used to follow her; Ryna, pregnant with the child she had died giving life to in that tiny hut...

Trees whispered, shaking their leaves in time as the Gypsies passed beneath their shelter. The candles created holes of flame in the night; it felt odd to not cup the fire in her hands. But no—she was the protected, the guided, the one for whom this procession traveled.

She was the Goddess.

The hand of her partner, her God, guided her with music to the patch of seared ground and halted there as the drums and candles circled them sunwise: once, twice, thrice. Daniel stepped forward with Liam; the peasants took their places as guardians, but these were distant things. Phoenix felt Tremayne's energy wrap around her, preparing to guide her on her journey. She closed her eyes fully, saw his shape in her mind's eye, a headdress of antlers crowning his brow. The chant continued in the circle around them, layered with the invocation:

"Elements of Air, we beg thee from the East! Hear us, come to us, shelter and protect us!"

"Elements of Fire, we beg thee from the South! Hear us, come to us, shelter and protect us!"

"Elements of Water, we beg thee from the West! Hear us, come to us, shelter and protect us!"

"Elements of Earth, we beg thee from the North! Hear us, come to us, shelter and protect us!"

Phoenix lost her family's voices in the sudden upward rush of Magick as she and Tremayne chanted, "Elements of Spirit, we beg thee from above! Hear us, come to us, shelter and protect us!"

And still, like a whisper, the words rustled against her soul:

Earth my body—
Air I am.
Water my blood—
Fire I am.
Air my breath—
Water, Earth,
And fire my spirit—
And Spirit I am.

◇ ◇ ◇

I'm here. Take me home. I'm here. I'm waiting. Take me home.

They're not coming. You're here. You'll always be here. They're not coming. This is your home.

The thoughts circled each other in Ryna's mind until she feared she'd go mad… until she wondered if she already had. She pressed her back against the Maypole's solid reality, rested her forehead against her knees, tried to enforce silence.

It didn't work. It never did. The Shadow Fae won; they always won. She might escape for a while, but they would find her. They always did.

The air shifted, bent sickeningly. Ryna refused to look. If she did not look, she would not see.

Too much darkness. Too much pain.

Shifting, bending… tearing…

You are darkness. You are pain.

And then…a hole. To her home. Insane, impossible, but… Ryna could feel it like fresh air creeping under musty blankets. She raised her head a little, opened her eyes, just a little—

A whiff of apricot and lilac…

Phoenix.

Ryna slammed her eyes shut, slammed her forehead into her knees. *Oh, gods, Phoenix...* She couldn't look. She couldn't see Phoenix die. Not again. She died, and she died, and she died, and Ryna watched, or screamed, or wept, but it never stopped. She wouldn't look. She wouldn't. The Shadow Fae had made the breeze. It wasn't real.

A strain of fiddle music crept in on the breeze—*her* fiddle's music—she would know it anywhere. And her father's hand at the bow.

Ryna quivered, resolve slipping, and very nearly looked.

"Ryna... Ryna, we're here..."

No. NO! The Shadow Fae were clever, but she was wiser. They'd been trying all day, but she wouldn't look this time—she wouldn't!

The apricot and lilac grew stronger—the fiddlesong curled around her soul. Ryna's eyes sprang open with shock at the sudden warmth and love that cradled her. No Shadow could emulate that...

She raised her head. Phoenix and Tremayne stood near the seared patch of earth, Magick and beautiful. And there was no blood—no blood...

Yet.

Her father this time: "Ryna, hurry—I don't know how long we can hold this."

They were there... *really there*... wavering, thin, but there...

Or so we'd like you to believe...

She had to believe. She couldn't take the chance that it was real and she had passed her one chance. They had said they'd come...

"Artemis, please, *get up*—"

Shaking, Ryna obeyed, lurched toward salvation even as her mind howled in fear. There had to be a catch, a trap—

Flame erupted from the ground, nearly engulfing her as it fountained three times her height. Ryna recoiled in horror as the blasting heat pounded her skin, her clothes, drove her whimpering to the Maypole's solid bulk.

"RYNA!" Phoenix yelled, but the redhead hardly heard. She could smell the death lurking in the flames, taste it, rotting-sweet-sharp-charred and thick... death, and pain, and fear. They fed on it... drew it like blood through a syringe, pulled, and pulled, and drained, until you were dry and empty—

"Ryna!" her father cried as his fingers flew over the strings. "Ryna, you have to come *now*!"

"The fire will steal my soul," she whispered, sliding down the Maypole's rough wood until she huddled, rocking, against its base. "First they take your fear, and then your mind, and then your soul..."

"Make it protect you," Phoenix said softly—her clear tone shining through Ryna's terror like the moon across a lake. "Do not let it touch you. You of all people should not fear it. *You are Fire*."

Fire? *Her*? No, no, she had to be wrong... Ryna was *Air*, had always been Air—

You are not what you think you are, whispered a bright voice in Ryna's mind as images flickered across her memory, a thousand little times the flames had come to her unbidden.

"I have never lied to you," Tremayne said. "*You are Fire.*"

"I am fire," she repeated with quiet, distant wonder, her voice hardly her own. It was almost too simple. Too right. Too real.

"Now come home," he commanded, his voice ringing authority against the song she had written so long ago…

"I am FIRE!" Ryna cried, and with a burst of courage she could not explain, threw herself forward. The flames would not burn her. She *ordered* them not to burn her as she hurtled through—

Brilliant light, brilliant heat—

Blindly reaching, her hand closed around the familiar wood of her fiddle's scroll—

Almost safe—

A sickening twist of space and time—

The world spun and heaved as the music screeched to a halt.

An instant to realize she held her fiddle, an instant to realize that somehow she had wound up on the opposite side of the Maypole, an instant to register the twin expressions of stunned horror that echoed her own.

A brief rush of wind, like a door slammed in her face.

Her bow fell from the air, bouncing once on its tip before landing where her father and Phoenix had stood a heartbeat before.

Ryna dashed to the charred spot before the Shadows could claim the treasure. Fingers trembling, she drew it with a quiet sigh across her fiddle's strings, but lacked the strength to create song.

The Shadows circled closer, ever closer…

"I am Fire," Ryna said, repeating it like a mantra. "I am Fire. I am Fire. I am Fire."

◇ ◇ ◇

Darkness—

Pain—

Shrieking—

Falling—

Phoenix pried her eyes open, scrabbled to the nearest craft booth, and retched violently in the bushes. The force of it nearly lifted her clear of the ground. Only acid burned her throat, but her stomach would not stop convulsing, rebelling against food it hadn't seen in days until she feared she would turn inside-out and die of it…

...and then she feared she *wouldn't* die of it...

...and finally, mercifully, it stopped, leaving her weak, huddled, and shaking on the cold, trampled ground. She tried not to whimper. Somebody stroked her hair in silent comfort.

"I failed," Phoenix rasped. Her ribs ached from the force with which she'd been ill—every breath was agony. She coughed. That was even worse.

"Shush, shush, honey," Niki soothed. It was her gentle, loving hand. "Shush, shush." She was floundering. Phoenix could tell. Not that Phoe could blame her.

It all seemed so ridiculous. Phoe had no idea why, but she was laughing so hard she couldn't breathe. It hurt so badly... and that made her laugh harder. Phoenix struggled to her feet, waved vaguely that she only needed a minute, and staggered out C-gate. A stray pop can tripped her, and suddenly it was all too much. With a wild scream she rounded on the backside of a food booth and commenced to beat the shit out of its plywood wall.

A coughing fit racked her so hard that she abandoned her attack and simply pressed her forehead against the grimy booth, scarcely able to see the ground for her tears. Her feet and hands hurt abominably, though tentative flexing revealed that she had not broken anything. "Why?" she whispered, shaking, reaching out to all the world for an explanation.

"People die in wars, child. It is an unfortunate necessity."

Phoenix looked up, startled, to see two Bright Fae gazing on her with sympathy. The same two—Phoe wondered if they were emissaries or team captains or something. They looked ridiculous, all golden and silver and immortal against the shabby backstage of the food booths with pop cans and cigarette butts bent and broken on the ground. How could they be so golden when the stench of burned turkey drumsticks had seeped into the cheap plywood, when the harshness of incandescent lights beat down on them?

"Why necessity?" she demanded roughly. "It doesn't make sense. You're the Bright Fae. You could've done... *something.*"

"We helped as was fit. If you cannot see yourself through a trial such as this, how would you survive a more difficult task?"

"I thought we were your Chosen." She wished her voice didn't sound like a whimpering plea.

"You are." The Lady Fae frowned, perplexed. "Did you think yourselves the only ones?"

"Foolish mortal," her partner said, though fondly. "Even *we* are not the only ones. Do not fear. Others will step to the line where you have fallen."

"And what of Ryna?" Phoenix whispered. "Will you give up on her, then?"

"You knew—all of you—that being what you are comes with a price. Her sacrifice will not be forgotten, nor will yours. You are fortunate that so many of you live to remember."

"Fortunate." Phoenix couldn't look at the beautiful golden creatures who had betrayed her. Her elfin ring sparkled coldly. *Fickle Fae indeed.* She would not grace them with more words, would not watch them leave, only noticed as the night faded back to fake light and darkness. When she looked again, there was no trace of them, not even a token on the dirt where they had been.

No comfort, no hope.

One more pound against the wall, but she had tired, her outrage spent. What remained but to still her trembling and go on?

A deep breath and a sleeve wiped across her face steadied Phoenix considerably. With queenly reserve she walked back onto site.

Liam gazed at her with wide green eyes. Phoenix pretended not to see him—or the way he cringed away from Tanek's bruising grip. *Phuro* Basil had turned away, trying to keep composed, probably. Niki wept quietly into Toby's shirt. Toby looked like Niki was the only thing keeping him on his feet. He was making the silly "shush shush" noises, too. Esmerelda leaned against the Maypole, staring blankly into nowhere. The peasants had gathered near the BLUE, near enough to be at hand, yet far enough to not intrude. Tremayne wavered on his feet, hands painfully empty; he looked dazed and not at all aware of Kaya's fluttering attentions. Her voice rose and fell timorously in words that seemed alien, though Phoenix knew she should understand them. *Baba* Luna tried to calm her with equal success.

"It's gone," Tremayne was saying. "She yanked it out of my hand; I couldn't hold..."

"You break anything?" Esmerelda asked quietly when she reached Phoe's side.

Phoe ripped her attention from Ryna's father. "Dented a food booth."

"I was thinking about the bits attached to you."

"My heart, if that doesn't sound too maudlin." Then, more quietly, "I'm sorry. I let you all down, and I know sorry doesn't cover it, but I'm sorry. I'll leave—it seems a fitting sort of punishment, and I can't imagine you're going to want me around all the time to remind you of what I lost you and... and it was a good year, and all good things must come to an end, and..."

Esmerelda gazed at Phoe with unreadable eyes for a moment before firmly taking her by the shoulders. "Would you make us lose two of our family at once?"

Phoenix turned her gaze to the other Gypsies—then turned away, sealing her heart against the pain that swam in the air. If she was going to spend the rest of her life with them, she would have to get a damn sight better at shielding.

◇ ◇ ◇

There was no mercy of the cat-piss bedroll and that wretched bucket this time.

The Gypsies had decreed that Liam stay with Tanek… and Tanek was angry. Very angry. Liam did not want to think what that might mean for his own fate, wrists tied to his ankles behind his back, gagged and helpless. He could only flop around a little—not nearly enough to create a sufficient racket that some kind passer-by might come asking questions.

He tried to focus on his surroundings, but there wasn't much to look at. A tiny kitchen on the right wall, a few functional hooks studding the left. On the remaining short wall, the bed—set higher up, with three rows of drawers beneath. Utilitarian cupboards. Bare walls. Nothing save dirty laundry to soften the linoleum floor. Liam wrinkled his nose in disgust. If you wanted to seduce a fair maiden, the first thing you learned was to make the bedchamber plush. It reminded them of romance novels. How in the world had Tanek earned his reputation?

But that was hardly a pleasant thought, either.

"Revenge not as sweet as you thought it'd be?"

Liam met Tanek's glare, though he could not stop the tears. He wasn't sure if he wept more for the memory of his love's screams or for fear of what Tanek might do to him.

Did it matter? He deserved it—nothing he could endure came close to the pain he had visited on Phoenix.

From the look in the Gypsy's eyes, Tanek agreed.

It was like that first night. Cold. Huddled. Terrified. Despairing.

She could see into Niki's vardo. They were in bed together—Phoenix and Niki. Like she herself had wanted to be once—except Niki had never noticed her, not in that way.

The scene shifted to Senior Hall in the high school; Niki and Tanek striding toward her in all their shining glory. *Like Venus and Adonis.* The thought felt scripted, as if it was not hers at all—only what her teenage self thought she should be thinking. Ryna—the older Ryna—knew they were not gods. They were just Niki and Tanek, full of faults and laughter… and oh, so beloved.

She even missed Tanek's smelly socks all over the place and Niki's tendency to carelessly draw every eye to herself. And all the other dumb little things that drove her nuts—especially those things.

Ryna could feel bits of herself slipping away, like stitches picked out of a tapestry. Pick, pick, pick, a bird gone, leaving puncture wounds on the cloth and a bunch of thread, oddly curled from its time spent as a bird.

"It still wants to," Ryna whispered sagely. "It remembers how."

But even if you put the thread back in, it wouldn't be the same bird. The curls would be in all the wrong places, but she could not weep for it, could not even bring herself to play her fiddle, knowing she would never again see home.

Phoenix raised her head at a polite but insistent knocking. She extended her awareness beyond the door but detected no recognizable energy signature. *Strangers, then,* she thought, scrubbing at the tear smudges on her cheeks. Her eyes were puffy and her nose was red and she was all sniffly, but the attempt made her feel better.

A lady of middling years and a lad of about seven stood on the ground before her porch. They both looked solemn—and the boy a little bored. From the look of their tidy, precise, formal clothes, they were obviously not from around here.

"Can I help you?" Phoenix inquired.

The lady smiled and made a practiced gesture towards the boy. "My name is Ruth, and Noah and I are here today to tell you about the wonders of the Lord, in which all things are possible."

The Gypsy blinked at them for a moment—and started laughing.

Ruth's expression betrayed her fear for the soul of this madwoman.

Phoe made an effort to breathe. "I'm—I'm sorry," she gasped out. "But if you had any idea what happens in my life on a daily basis, you'd probably mess yourself."

"With prayer and the love of Christ, you might find pea—"

"Prayer? Lady, I've prayed to more gods and goddesses than you've ever heard of, and it hasn't fixed a damned thing."

"So you're not interested in finding Jesus." Her voice turned hard.

"I'm sorry; we weren't aware that he was lost." Tremayne stepped from nowhere and gently steered the proselytizers away. "Him being the Son of God and all. Have a nice day."

"My savior," Phoenix said, plopping down on the porch and wiping away tears of mirth. "I suppose I didn't leave a very good impression, huh?"

"Don't worry about it." Tremayne kissed her gently on the forehead. "At least your fever's down some."

"Thank Goddess for small blessings." She sighed. "At least the winds didn't kick up again this time."

"There is that. We must have shielded well enough."

"Must have." After an awkward moment he cleared his throat uncomfortably and handed her a slim CD case. "Flicker brought these by today."

Phoenix squeezed it until the plastic bit into her hands. She wanted nothing more than to throw it in the stereo and play it until it wore out… but she wasn't sure she could bear to listen. Not now.

"Have you given up hope?" she asked in a small voice. Only after a minute of choked silence did she dare look up, and the fiddler's expression tore at the remains of her heart.

"I—am her father," he finally said, as if each word was sharp and brittle as glass. "Even after I feel her spirit die, I will have hope."

Phoenix turned her gaze from the emptiness in his eyes—it was like looking into the mirror of her own soul. *Sometimes,* she reflected sickly, *the cruelest sentence is life.*

*　　　*　　　*

A jovial mood rocked the BLUE; apparently Patty had not shown up at Rehearsals. Phoe tried to put on a good face, but the noise made her stomach seize and drove her into the cold night air.

Gods, but there were a lot of stars up there. Orion gazed down at her, mocking, almost. And sad. There was something special about him… some reason why she had always believed as a child that he was her guardian angel… a story… but it eluded her.

Oh, he liked stories, though, and poetry. She could remember that. She wondered how many lifetimes she had spent composing words to the stars, even as she whispered lines born on that very breath…

"Would that darkness in my heart
Brought swift mortality
For I from this would gladly part
And Gypsy-like run free.

"My heart within me crumbles black
Like ashes, burned by hope;
All dreams are placed upon the rack
And wishes bound by rope.

"I call within this wind-swept shell;
No answer comes to me.
I hold to this, my sacred Hell,
And burn eternally.

"A toast to true love, though we rail,
It is our constant plight:
We try to reach it, ever fail,
Yet keep it in our sight."

"Couldn't stand the hypocrisy anymore?" Tanek asked, appearing at her side.

She should have startled. She hadn't heard him coming. Still, it hardly mattered. "Everyone's being so… nice. I'm tired of them looking at me like I'm broken."

"Aren't you?"

"Not in any way they can understand. Or want to. It's scary enough to realize you won't see someone you love until the afterlife." She gazed steadily at him. "Eternity is a very long time for someone to be gone, Tanek. I can feel it—and *I* don't want to understand it."

"Where did you find that poem?" he asked, shying away from the topic.

She let him. What else could you say about eternity, anyhow? "Wrote it just now."

"What I wouldn't give to have your way with words." He shoved his hands in the pockets of his jeans, leaned back against the solid wall of the BLUE.

Phoe shrugged. "Half sure they come from somewhere else. The stars, maybe." She gave her fellow Gypsy an appraising glance. "Does any of this ever feel weird to you?"

"What, battling unspeakable horrors to literally save the soul of a friend? Having conversations with mythological creatures? Yeah. Sometimes I'm sure I stepped out of the script for some really bad fantasy movie."

His deadpan delivery made Phoenix chuckle. "Actually, I meant—I'm a several-thousand-year-old mage, you know? What am I doing running around in sneakers and jeans? It's like some undercover mission went horribly wrong."

"I remember feeling a lot like that when I first fell in with Ryna," Tanek mused. "One day, I'm this ordinary high school kid, and the next—poof!—Magick powers."

"Poof?"

He gave her a wry grin. "Well, not so much poof. But meeting her was… she was the most beautiful person I'd ever seen. And the world finally made sense."

"We're all here because of her—one way or another." Phoenix tipped her head back, gazing into forever. Maybe it was safer to leave your heart up there, after all. "Her light is what binds us all, makes us a family, isn't it."

"Yes, Phoenix," he said, his voice infinitely sad. "Yes, it was."

Pendragon Renaissance Faire

Weekend Seven: A Knight to Remember

~*~

On this final weekend before our village fades into the mists of time for another year, Jousting Knights and the Favors of Ladies are the order of the day. The precepts of Charlemagne live on, and Honor is the last word as romantic wooing proves that love overcomes all. Don't miss the Queen's blessing over one of the six fully armored jousts. Enjoy Ale and victuals as you witness knights battle each other for the heart of a fair lady. May the best man win! (Theme sponsored by Olsen's Cutlery)

~*~

"It's eight o'clock in the morning. Do you know where *your* panties are?"

Phoenix stared with stunned horror as Percival from Vilification Tennis held aloft the plaid underwear Phoe had gotten during that first excursion with her love. And realized that after her scare in the privies, she'd forgotten to go back for them…

Niki must've caught her expression, for she leaned over and whispered, "Yours?"

Phoe felt herself pale. "There was this chicken…"

The dancer nodded decisively. Hoots and whistles trailed her as she sashayed up to the stage, dipped the Vilifier for a thorough kissing, and practically skipped back to her place. When attention had turned from her, Niki surreptitiously passed them to Phoenix.

"I love you," Phoe whispered, staring at the torn fabric. They had been one of Ryna's favorite pairs on her…

"I am in *so* much denial this morning," Alexis grumbled as she plopped down beside the Gypsies' honor guard of peasants, breath frosting the air as she tried to disappear in her cloak.

"Join the club, sister," *Baba* Luna seconded.

"At least Jen's not dumping *you* in that pond," the Merry Maids' leader pointed out.

"Notice anything missing?" Peyton inquired.

"Your trophy wife?" Niki teased.

"Patty's always early," Tremayne observed, his tone pensive. "She's not here."

"If today was tomorrow, I'd say she had too much fun last night," Toby offered.

"Suppose the Secret Deathtrap finally ate her?" Marcus posited.

"Oh, gods, look," Laine said in hope and wonder as a stunned hush fell over the crowd.

Eric stepped up onto the stage and smiled at them like the rennie who tricked the patron. Phoenix could almost hear the prayers.

"We have a new show this weekend," he announced, "a disappearing act starring our beloved Perky Patty!"

Wild cheering ripped through the rennies. Patty was gone. Pendragon would heal. Ryna's fondest wish had come true.

In the midst of the joy, Phoenix buried her face in her hands and cried.

* * *

"Knock knock," Patches greeted the Cottagers as he unslung his guitar and warmed his hands in front of the fire.

"Who's there?" Eryn called gamely.

"Patty."

"Patty who?"

Patches smiled with pure devilment. "That's Pendragon for ya."

The O'Malleys laughed with a lightness Phoenix hadn't heard all year. They were all so giddy. Everyone so flipping happy. Phoe coughed into her shoulder and tried not to pull too hard on the French braid she was weaving in Brigid's dark hair.

"I can't believe after all that time of her trying to make her mark on this place, she's finally gone," Moiré very nearly chirped.

"A dog can leave its mark on a tree," Aunt Molly said as she stepped up from the kitchen with a pitcher of water, "but a good garden hose will take care of that. Would you like some tea, Patches? Coffee?"

"Tea would be wonderful."

Phoenix sometimes wondered if there was anyone at faire that *didn't* drink the stuff.

"Ouch!"

"Oh! Sorry, lass." Phoe took a deep breath, forcing herself to focus. "I'm not as good at this as Esmerelda." She could feel the sudden, quickly masked looks of pity—or imagined she could. They were too polite to ask—though she wagered they were all about ready to die from curiosity. "I see the rabbit pitcher's been retired," she said to break the tension, a shade too loudly, and nodded to the top of the hutch where the much-abused pitcher had found a home.

They all looked at her strangely. The thing had probably been sitting there all last week, but they accepted the diversion gracefully.

"It developed a leak," Da informed her, a teasing eyebrow raised at Brigid. "Canna imagine how."

"Look what I found! Bless-this-house-and-all-within."

Phoe looked up as Ilya pit-stopped to wipe her feet, then entered with a staff that seemed huge and unwieldy for her diminutive stature. A staff that had followed Phoenix around the country for a year...

Unexplainably, it felt like the final insult.

"Where did you find that?" Phoe asked, tying a ribbon around Brigid's hair. It took an effort to keep her hands steady.

The blond urchin started, taken aback at the lack of joy in the Gypsy's voice. "It was sitting out there leaned up against the fireplace side of the house—it was hard to see with all the vines. I wonder how long it's been sitting there?"

Phoe wrapped a hand around the staff's smooth wood. It felt... strange. The energy it gave off was her own—discoveries, and travels, and love, and hope. It felt terribly young, somehow. The loss made her heart ache. "Thank you," she said softly. Then, not daring to take her eyes from the relic, "Did... did Mother Goosed ever find her staff?"

"She did," Da said, an angry note in his voice. "In three pieces. They were all chewed up. And one of them was half charred."

"I think—I think this one belongs with her, then. Excuse me."

Quickly, before she could change her mind, Phoenix hurried out the door. She wasn't sure if she had the courage to give it up... but she knew she couldn't live with it in her house.

◇ ◇ ◇

It felt strange, being back. After all those days in the dungeon, and then the panic of having Tanek around all the time... now he was simply locked in the vardo, bound and gagged. If he closed his eyes and ignored his restraints, it almost felt normal. The sound of privy doors, of people calling to each other—a dog barking. Someone tuning bagpipes. No lingering taint of the Shadow, for all he could feel them, still. But he was used to that, now.

All very normal.

Only he wasn't. Not anymore. And that made the noises so surreal...

He wondered if he would ever feel like himself again. Maybe if they let him go and he moved to—England, maybe—and started a new life where everything was strange and new, it would all become normal... he could forget the horrors he'd lived, the horrors he'd caused...

Liam sighed. England or the moon—it wouldn't matter. As long as his soul accompanied him, things would never be right.

◇ ◇ ◇

Phoenix pretended, for a while, that the other Gypsies weren't gathering on the backstage side of the burlap curtain. She stared out through the trees, over the marsh peeking beyond them, and tried not to wonder if a rotted clove orange nestled somewhere in the underbrush.

She should go up there. They only had each other, now. She was one of them. They needed her. She didn't understand how, but she understood why—even though seeing each other hurt as much as being alone. Every Gypsy was a reminder that their circle would never again be complete.

Phoenix trudged up the steep path and took her place among her family.

Tanek hunched on the vardo's steps, picking at one of his patches. He was the only one sitting. *Phuro* Basil and Niki made a place for her between them.

Maybe if they stood there long enough it wouldn't be real. Maybe Ryna would appear—*poof!*—in their midst, and it would all be right again.

The harsh clacks and smacks of quarterstaves and the bravado of mid-fight quips floated into their circle. Phoenix wanted to go push both Alex and Jen into the lake to shut them up, but she kept her stillness. All the Gypsies kept their stillness, staring at one another in a desperation of finality.

But what, really, can you say, with the first step of a horrible forever in front of you?

Tanek pushed up from the steps, defiantly. "She'd kick all our asses for this, and you know it. Ryna wouldn't want us to mope our way through the stuff that counts. The show goes on." With that, he turned his back and stomped up the side stairs to the stage's vardo.

The other Gypsies looked at each other, at a loss, but they knew he spoke truth. Ryna never let anything get in the way of a show, and they did her a dishonor to let it all fall apart now. They did what she would have done—pulled themselves together, pushed themselves on. Niki and Kaya followed Tanek into the concealment of the vardo; Tremayne, Elda, Toby, and *Baba* Luna filed through the curtain that Phoenix held for them, took up their usual places in the niche between the stage and the blue vardo.

It had been red once—she could see where bits of the blue paint had flaked away. Phoe wondered if Ryna remembered it being red. She sat mid-way back on the left section of benches. Perhaps they would be able to see her and take comfort. *Phuro* Basil sat beside her.

A moment, and two. Phoe felt Tremayne brace himself as *Baba* Luna began the beat, quiet and low and staccato, calling the audience to listen, to watch.

They did; Esmerelda's tambourine shimmered only a little jerkily as Kaya swayed from between the curtains and stepped onto the stage, charming and beautiful, the distilled essence of Gypsy. Phoenix doubted anyone in the audience noticed the effort it took to keep her breath even.

The low moan of horsehair across strings as Tremayne's fiddle climbed—alone—into a high, sustained whine. The remaining dancers strutted through the curtains, stood a little behind and to either side of Kaya, eyes bravely staring over the patrons' heads.

The drum stopped.

So did Tremayne's fiddle.

The audience almost fidgeted with the tension that held the Gypsies rigid. Phoenix could feel them concentrating so very hard on motions that had long ago become instinct.

Kaya, recovering herself, chimed out a rhythm on her zills.

Toby's drum echoed her perfectly—though a little later than it ever had.

Kaya and Tanek's zills in chorus, almost begging.

The drum. Forceful. Make it right.

Then three sets of zills, and both doumbeks, and a brief instant where Ryna should have come in, should have been back to start it, and Tremayne belatedly realized the duty fell to him.

They had written this song together; even if Phoenix had not known it, she felt it in the wild, barely controlled grief that poured through his music. She saw it in the firm set of his mouth, the frown that pulled his brows down, the slight jerkiness of his arm as he forced back habit and played notes that belonged to his daughter.

Phoenix tried to pry her eyes away, tried to breathe against the suffocating weight of wrongness that pressed her almost to the ground. Ryna was supposed to be home, and she wasn't home—they had messed up, something had gone wrong, and she wasn't home. It was all so hopeless; she should be here, but—

Snap!

The fiddle cut out; half the wood of Tremayne's bow dangled lifelessly from the horsehair. To their credit, Toby, Elda, and *Baba* Luna plunged onward, though Tremayne uttered a brief, vicious word that caused their eyes to pop. It made Phoenix oddly, intensely curious. She'd never heard Tremayne curse before.

No time to ask; the fiddler had pushed through the burlap curtain. The dance show's remnants fell into an admirable improvisation, but there were no more lead instruments. Before she could get too nervous, Phoenix whipped out her pennywhistle and launched into the familiar tune, tears in her eyes. The audience all turned to stare. Phoenix was not blind to them—nor did she miss the grateful expressions of her family. They were passing thoughts, though, as Phoe walked slowly to join the percussionists. She could hear the sweet notes of Ryna's fiddle in her mind as she played on. For a bare moment, Phoe swore she saw the shadow of a familiar form on the other side of Hollow Hill's fence, watching with sadness… and love.

◇ ◇ ◇

Ryna lowered her fiddle and swayed, transfixed, as Phoenix played.

"So pretty. Poor Tata. So sad."

They didn't see her. She wasn't playing with them, either. She didn't see herself.

Kaya danced across the stage and onto the bridge, the other two following the graceful Gypsy's lead.

"Come help?" Ryna pleaded.

"They've moved on," a small voice chittered as the Shadows circled Ryna, prowling. "See how the show goes on without you? Your love has taken your place."

It couldn't be real… couldn't be real…

But somehow, she knew it was. "No—Phoenix—please—help…"

"You're ours now."

"No," she whispered. "No, no, no…"

A few Shadow Fae broke from the group, flowed up onto Robyn's bridge…

"And now that we have you…"

…onto the stage…

"We'll take the others…"

…and over, surrounding dancers and musicians alike…

"Starting with—this one."

And Toby—wonderful, funny Toby—disappeared.

"No, no, no, no…" Ryna sank to the ground, whimpering.

His drum had been silenced.

Still Phoenix played…

◇ ◇ ◇

"Hey," Phoenix greeted insufficiently as she ducked backstage.

Phuro Basil and Tremayne looked up from where they sat on the ground, leaned up against the picket fence. *Phuro* nodded shortly to her and stood. He rested a hand briefly on Tremayne's shoulder, then strode away.

Phoe sat down abruptly. The world was spinning again. Hopefully no one would notice.

They stared toward the gazebo in silence, listening to the variety show go on without them. They both knew they should get up, play their parts…

Neither made a move to do so.

Tremayne diddled with the broken pieces of his bow. Phoenix wondered, in a moment of horrid clarity, if he would ever play again.

"Do you have a spare?" she asked hesitantly.

"I do."

More silence.

Toby made one of his usual dumb fire puns. The audience laughed.

The chime of zills—but no sweet, teasing strain of music.

Tremayne turned to Phoenix, his expression so familiar that for a moment her vision filled with the memory of a woman with cropped, light brown hair. She wore a ragged, stained chemise, a noose around her neck, and brave sorrow for the daughter she would leave behind.

The connection hit Phoenix like the strike of wood against a horse's flank. How had she not seen it before? *All gods,* her mind cried, though the words could not escape a throat tighter than the rope that had strained under the weight of Evelyn Wellington's lifeless body.

This time, the loss was forever.

* * *

"If you're not going to talk to any of the patrons, you might as well find something to entertain yourself."

Phoe looked down at Mutch—and Ilya beside her—and nudged her glasses up. "I'm talking to patrons," she protested, though she knew it for a lie half a second after she said it.

"We've been stalking you for an hour." A wry grin quirked Mutch's lips. "The only person you've talked to is yourself."

The Gypsy cocked her head—had she been talking to herself? She couldn't remember…

"Come play 'Patty Says' with us," Ilya begged. "It'll be fun!"

Patty Says? It sounded amusing… or, at the very least, distracting. "Lead on, then."

"To the Green!" Ilya trumpeted, grabbed one of Phoe's hands, and hauled her off.

In short order representatives from the O'Malleys, Bernatellis, and peasants had gathered on Shepherd's Green—along with a goodly number of patron children. They quickly elected Phoenix as high priestess of the game; she stood facing the mob, possibilities whirling through her head.

"Patty says—form a circle," she announced.

The other players scrambled into an amoeba-like shape.

It made Phoe giggle. "Close enough. Um… Patty says… doughnuts are bad. Face the guests."

The rennies dutifully inverted their circle.

"Patty says—touch your toes."

"Oh yeah—*this* is familiar!" Anabella Bernatelli muttered. Several giggles flashed around the amoeba.

"Take a break."

Moiré and Puddle sat down.

"Ah-ah-ah! Remember to wait until I say 'Patty says', okay peoples?" Phoenix chirped. "If you do, you'll get an extra special prize!"

More laughter—the two who had been disqualified moved a little apart to watch the rest of the game.

A few of the pirates joined in after while, and some more patron kids, and three of the Musketeers, and even a couple members of Court—though Phoe credited Christine with that. Even so, nearly half of the participants had been relegated to the sidelines by the time *Phuro* Basil excused himself into the amoeba and requested Phoe's attention for a moment.

"Have you seen Toby?" he asked after pulling her aside.

Phoe looked up at the camp elder—worry shadowed his blue eyes. She forced down the automatic panic that fluttered in her stomach. "No, I haven't. Why?"

"No one can seem to trace his energy lines, and… he missed the fire show."

The panic burst its restraints and throttled her heart. "He *what*?"

"And the dance show that must be half over by now."

Phoe's mind reeled—this couldn't be happening. The last person to miss a show had been Ryna, and… "Do you need help searching?"

He looked around at the frolicking rennies, then back at Phoenix—and huffed out a breath. "We don't know it's an emergency yet. He might have lost track of time. I don't want to take you away from something that makes you smile."

Truthfully, Phoenix was loathe to leave as well, but she could hear the unspoken "but" in her fellow Gypsy's words. She squared her shoulders. "It's not so important. I can come back later."

Basil looked simultaneously relieved and guilty, but he forced a smile. And kissed her hand.

Phoenix gave him a peck on the cheek. She returned to her playmates, racking her brain for a graceful exit. "Patty says—you *pee*-poles are mean to me! I'm leaving—Mutch is now the new Patty!"

Mutch gamely trotted forward to take the Gypsy's place—but her expression betrayed her worry. "Trouble?" she asked quietly.

"I hope not," Phoe said with a brave smile. "But—if you see Toby, send him back to camp, all right?"

"All right," the Merry Maid agreed uncertainly. "Are you sure—"

"Positive." Phoenix gave her a quick hug. "With any luck, I'll be back before the game's over."

◇ ◇ ◇

"He's not here," Ryna said.

Phoenix didn't hear her. Ryna'd been following her love and *Phuro* Basil for a while now as they searched for Toby. They thought something had happened to him. They thought the Shadow Fae had gotten him. Ryna thought the Shadow Fae had gotten him, too. She'd seen him disappear. They had taken him.

But *where*? He wasn't here. Were there other places to take him, too?

"Not here. Not here—keep looking. Not here."

A smell like rotting leaves plagued Ryna's nose.

The trees were humming again.

One by one, Shadows crept from the shadows, as if oblivious to Ryna. She knew they were watching her, though. They always watched her.

"Careful. Careful, they're coming."

They inched closer to *Phuro* Basil, circled him.

"No… no… no…"

And then he disappeared, and Phoenix walked alone.

"Not here, not here… not here…"

◇ ◇ ◇

"Um—Phoenix?"

"Yes?" She turned from collecting the variety show's tips to see an elfin-looking lass in a gray bodice, a lace scarf wrapped Gypsy-like over one hip. "Aria, right?"

She grinned, nodded vigorously, and presented a double handful of chain mail and coins. "I found this under a bunch of leaves and stuff when I was looking for firewood in Hidden Valley. I thought maybe it belonged to someone in your camp or something."

Ryna's signature tingle vibrated through Phoe's hands as she unfurled the familiar silver latticework of coins and rings. Clumps of dirt hung to it, but clean spots still flashed in the sun. A few of the coins were missing; Phoenix wondered if they had been there the last time her love had worn it.

"It looked like someone was trying to hide it, but you'd think they would've found a better spot," Aria was saying, a long way away, as she brushed her hands off on her dark blue skirt.

"It's Ryna's," Phoenix said, a wild, stupid hope blossoming in her heart. If *Phuro* Basil could fix it— "Thank you."

"No problem," said the peasant, and she skipped off.

Phoenix stared at the treasure a moment more in disbelief. When had it gone missing? Had Ryna even noticed? She'd been wearing it when she played for the RFC kids, but—

The quiet *ching* as a bodice landed on a pile of discarded garb at the fire…

…that creepy guy…

But the other Gypsies had scared him off empty-handed—had he just been a distraction?

Phoenix turned, tip-gathering forgotten, and was halfway to Hollow Hill when Esmerelda plowed down Sherwood's hill, hauling Toby behind by one arm, her voice thick with tears.

"And if I see you so much as *sniff* at anything that even *looks* alcoholic tonight, I swear on all things holy that when we pull out of this faire I'm leaving your sorry ass behind, do you hear me?"

"I didn't mean to worry—"

"You missed three shows! We've had half the camp searching for you! How could you do this to us, after—"

He put a soothing hand on her shoulder, started to say something.

She jerked back. "Don't you touch me with that stink on your breath."

"I'm not him."

All the patrons in the area were watching, now. The siblings didn't seem to notice.

"Then prove it," she spat. "Sober up. Act like a man."

A pause. He pulled free and glared at her with cold, accusatory eyes. "When you get rid of the doll you hid in your pincushion with that lock of Daddy's hair."

Stunned silence. The Gypsies stared at proud, invincible, collected Elda.

Who turned and bolted like a scared little girl.

Toby cast them all a guilty look, then scowled. "I'm tired of keeping her dirty little secret," he informed them, shoulders hunched, and slunk away.

Phuro Basil, standing beside Hollow Hill's door, sighed and ruffled a hand through his hair. "I'll go talk to her."

No one objected. No one could move.

Phoe let the belt slink down into her phoenix-tooled pouch. It made a quiet, slithering chime, alien and unnatural without its owner's confident gait. Ryna's belt, her connection to her family—

Phoenix snuck away with the gradually dispersing patrons while the others still stared at each other in disbelief. Her leather belt pulled to the left, the weighted reminder like a small, lost child curled up in her pocket. How much more of her family would fall apart before this ended?

Irish Cottage rang with music; Phoenix could feel it tugging her soul, promising the cheer and sense of normalcy she craved. "Bless this house and all within," she murmured as she scuffed her boots on the threshold, then pressed her lips to the rough doorframe and quietly stepped inside. Musicians crowded the available seats as the O'Malleys filed past their table, loading wooden bowls with praties and stew.

Her brother handed her his serving and went to fill a new one for himself.

"We're having dinner early today," Moiré said gently, one hand on her arm. "It's so cloudy, and the light dies faster now that Equinox has passed..."

Phoenix stared down at the stew and mush and stifled a cough. She couldn't recall the last time food had looked good, but smiled thanks and took it to the window facing the privies. She couldn't sit in the others—they were Ryna's windows. It would be wrong without her there.

A sense of freedom sang through the music; Phoenix listened for a long while, trying to enjoy it as she clapped out the rhythm with Eryn, who sat at her feet.

"Do you want me to get you some Faery Glow?" the titan-haired O'Malley offered, tilting her head back.

"If you like."

"Okay! I'll be right back."

She scampered off to the kitchen as Peter gave Phoe a wink and started up a new tune:

"The fiddlin' Gypsy came over the hill
And down to Pendragon so shady
She fiddled and sang till the oak trees rang
And she won the heart of a lady."

Phoenix's heart slammed into her boots. She swung her feet to the outside of the house and dropped to the ground, causing a protesting chime from her belt—and its muffled echo from her pouch. She was almost to the pony rides when Daniel caught up with her, still wiping his hands on his trousers.

"Phoe—Phoe, come back. He's been gone all year; he didn't know."

She stopped, gazed up at him an eternal moment. "None of them do," she said softly, reaching up to cup his cheek in her palm. "I'm sorry, Danny. I just can't stay." Phoe brushed away the tears that spilled from eyes that had shared her joy and pain through so many lifetimes. A small smile shaped her lips as she stood on tiptoe to kiss his brow.

And then she turned.

And walked away.

* * *

Familiar world, alien, strange. Phoenix wandered, disoriented, through misplaced shadows and the floodlights' harsh illumination. No one especially noticed her. She wondered if it was because she was wearing a shapeless sweater, a cloak, and a long, loose skirt instead of the previous year's black velvet cocktail napkin. On the other hand, maybe she wasn't really there at all... just a physical body wandering Cast Party, snitching bits of free food more from habit than desire.

She had been to the Awards Ceremony, had watched proudly as Eric presented each of her protégés with a Cracked Cup—it broke with tradition to give multiples, but it had seemed wrong to single out only one of the tight-knit group. The kids had dragged her on stage to present her with a dream catcher they'd made from groundscores. A Best Mentor award, they called it—she felt guilty over that; she hadn't really done much, but the gift seemed to give them joy.

None of it seemed real. Last year with the first blush of love and a storybook ending fast approaching—*that* had been real. This, with everyone running around drunk on relief if nothing else… it was a horrible joke.

Patty had apparently cancelled the music portion of the party without anyone's knowledge, and no disc jockeys had been available on such short notice—so this year the usual BLUE jam got tossed on Bakery Stage with some borrowed sound equipment. The musicians didn't seem to mind missing out on the dancing. They certainly weren't missing out on food or booze; rennies anxious to show their gratitude fulfilled requests immediately—and threefold.

Phoe stood on the edge of the crowd, watching. "You'd be proud," she whispered into the night as "Pinksleeves" ended with a flourish and the audience cheered.

"Phoenix, is that you over there on the edge of the shadows? It is! Come up here and give us a song," Nora called jovially and swigged from her leather mug.

"I don't think—" Phoe hedged, not wanting to infect the night with her mood.

"C'mon, c'mon," Jerry prodded, and the next thing the raven-haired Gypsy knew, she was being cheered and nudged onto the stage.

She blinked in the glaring lights, tried not to skitter back from an audience that shifted and surged like a horde of the Shadow Fae.

Were there Shadow Fae among them? There had been at Funky Formal…

A nervous glance to her left and right. The musicians, ghostly in the light, smiled and nodded encouragingly. Someone in the audience cheered, and soon a wall of sound buffeted her with welcome.

She closed her eyes. No, no Shadow Fae. Only a trick of the lights.

One loud "Shhh!" and another, and another, and for a moment the audience—her invisible friends—sounded like a pit of snakes.

And then the true hush descended.

Phoenix took a deep breath. She hadn't a pennywhistle, and she wouldn't ask for a loan, sick as she was. So she sang.

She didn't realize her choice until the pure, sweet, joyful, melancholy lyrics of "Gypsy's Year" floated over the assemblage. Blinding stage lights pounded her, but a different brilliance filled her soul. *Ah. This is what Ryna must feel,* she thought distractedly as warmth welled within her and spread through the night. Summoning, calling, loving, remembering. She could feel all the creatures that had never drawn breath in this realm creeping in around the edges. Silent. Watching. A tribute to she who had called them for years… and never would again.

The faint sigh and fall of a fiddle echoed against Phoenix's voice, looping around the periphery, lifting her with the breath of horsehair across haunted strings… and faded, ringing one last precious moment after Phoe's voice slid into silence.

A chill gust of wind swooped across the stage, carrying it away. The song's life had ended.

But not the memories. Never the memories.

Phoenix bowed her head briefly, let the wind tug hair and cloak. *I love you,* she thought, and turned, and descended the stage, and strode into the night.

She never heard if there were cheers.

"No," Ryna cried, but soft, pleading, as the vision slipped away—or perhaps she did. She held the afterimage close to her heart though her fiddle and bow now hung slackly from her hands. The stage was strange and bare… the seats around her were strange and bare… the world was strange and bare.

Had it been real? Phoenix rarely sang—and never alone before an audience. It couldn't be real… but she had been so beautiful, light spilling from her in waves of—glitter, almost. Bright, shining, more radiant than Ryna had ever seen her. She *had* to be real.

Glorious reality.

Torturous blessing—the cruelest thing the Shadow Fae had yet inflicted on her. The Gypsy knew with sickening surety that the song—gift, blessing, terrible beauty, and curse… it had been her requiem.

Come back, come back…

She raised fiddle to chin, bow to strings, and played, and played… hoping her music found an audience even though she couldn't see them. Dark laughter rattled against her song as Pendragon's buildings faded, becoming a gently rolling field dotted with trees—with one elder towering above the rest, beautiful and Magick, where the Bear should have been.

Warmth, quiet, and flickering firelight enveloped Phoenix as she carefully shut Irish Cottage's door and nodded greetings to Ma, and Brigid, and a fellow who seemed vaguely familiar, though she couldn't place him. They were at the table, immersed in a game with dice, glass counters, and a printed cloth playing board. A musician she did not know sat in the corner picking out a quiet melody, though the only words she could catch were *while I'm in Lacy's kitchen*. She snugged her cloak around herself and sat in the *seanchaí chair*, put her feet up on the short bench, and let the warm peace of the place seep into her soul.

People came and went occasionally as the need for low-key socialization took them. Phoe didn't speak with them, and they respected her silence.

She closed her eyes, let the world filter around her. Music, warmth, gentle conversation, comforting energies, safe. It felt old and familiar, like the smell of sage and wood smoke and the way her bodice had hugged her perfectly the first time she put it on. She let time flow around her. What was time, anyway? A silly invention of mortals to keep themselves from getting confused. It had no place here.

"*There are places I remember*," sang the musician, soft and slow, this melody different from the last.

No place, here.

Place?

Here.

Home.

* * *

Everywhere… nowhere. A warm, formless haze of security. Cedar smoke curled around her, though there was no fire.

Ryna was there. Priestess. Sailor. Mother. Wife. Savior. Gypsy. Eternal.

Others of her family drifted by, too, and some for whom she had no name, though her soul curled like a kitten around them. A steady thrum pulsed through her like the beating of a great, primordial heart. So each life had begun, cradled within the Goddess-embodiment who would be her mother.

There was no time. No past life, no future destiny. No confusion in this heart of the earth, where the great now encompassed all whens. What a beautiful comfort to not need to dwell in a specific present. So simple. All life should be so simple.

A song. A lullaby. A love song. She had sung it sometimes, though the words had been different, then. A fiddle's voice threaded through it, the bow pushing the notes in and out like a needle creating a bird in an old French tapestry. She hummed along without knowing the tune.

It was a waltz. She danced. Ryna danced with her, though she had no shape. Funny how their souls fit so perfectly, one and one becoming greater than simply two.

"This and every other," Phoenix whispered, resting her head against her love's breast as gentle, tiny fingers stroked her hair. Ryna's voice sounded like eternity.

Phoe hmmed in contentment, nuzzled closer, and let it filter into her soul like moonlight.

* * *

Shift.

It was a strange sensation, all of time passing in a heartbeat.

The silence caught Phoenix's attention first. Yes, she heard the quiet crackle-snap of flames slowly consuming wood and the quiet breath and shift of someone near. The silence encompassed more than a lack of sound... became more a lack of *feeling*.

A heaviness tucked around her. Someone must have covered her with a blanket, long ago before everyone left—except, of course, the other person. She opened her eyes half expecting to see Ryna, so vivid had been the dream.

Her brother sat, pensive, his profile lit orangely by the low fire in the hearth he tended. He must have sensed her waking, for after a moment he turned. "Dream well, Phoe-bea? You were smiling."

"Ryna was here," she said with utter certainty, though she knew of course that her soulmate was gone. Not so very far—the redhead's love warmed her heart.

Daniel gazed at her with an unfathomable sadness in his eyes. It seemed strange—she felt so peaceful.

"Pretty dreams," she said to comfort him. "Though they didn't feel much like dreams. I haven't slept without nightmares in forever."

He turned back to the hearth. "It's a good place for that. Some people have a cabin by the lake... I have Cottage. All the important bits of growing up I've done have been here. It's amazing how much of life can happen in fifteen days a year."

Phoe stared at him, silent for a time. He seemed strangely vulnerable—and lost. She spoke, though mostly because it seemed a moment that demanded the sharing of deep things. "Pendragon is the core of our hearts—but Cottage is the heart of Pendragon."

He smiled, a solemn half smile. "The first time I set foot in the door I felt like I'd come home. The only other time I've felt that strongly is when Mother let me hold you not even a day after you'd been born. You were so tiny and helpless and staring up at me with huge gray eyes like you already knew who I was. And I knew it was my job to keep you safe."

Phoenix turned to the flames as well. "Shelter, safety, haven, laughter and tears, but always love. And acceptance, for who and what I am. Priceless things in a world of chaos—I am truly blessed."

"Same here. Do you have any idea how much you've taught me about grace, and beauty, and light?" A pause. "I wish I could've done more."

"You did what you could." Another pause, weighty. "There's a bite to the air, now. The leaves are falling."

He sighed. "And in a couple days I'll help clean this place out, pack it up, tuck it in, and kiss it goodnight until next year."

"Mmm." Phoe pulled the blanket closer around her to ward off chill and melancholy. "Good night, sweet Faire."

◇ ◇ ◇

She had stopped screaming, ceased struggling, ceased caring. Liam felt it as a strange emptiness, a silence in the back of his head where he hadn't even really known there was sound.

Without her the Gypsies would soon break. The Shadow Fae would win.

The Shadow Fae had already won.

Did Phoenix know? Was it killing her by inches the way it killed him to be without her?

He shifted against his bonds, trying to gain a more comfortable position. He wondered what it would take to bring someone to the point Ryna had reached. He wondered how long it would be before the Shadow Fae turned again to him for their prey.

Liam closed his eyes and leaned against the cupboards. He could feel them outside. With stunning irony, Tanek's shields on the vardo kept him safe.

What would happen when he was cast from that cursed protection?

Liam doubted it would be long before he found out.

And the Shadow Fae would be there. Watching. Waiting.

After all, what was time, to them?

Phoenix picked up her spectacles, peered through them, and made a face. They were filthy and smudged; they'd give her a headache looking through them all day. She put them back on the shelf where they belonged, finished dressing, patted Karma reassuringly, and let herself outside.

At first she didn't notice much of a difference. The vardos, the fire pit—these things needed no sight. But as she navigated beyond her familiar bubble, the world grew strange, blotches of color that had once been privies, and tents, and trailers. Some blotches moved—these she thought must be people, though she could not be certain. Everything looked large and lumpy, like a child's puzzle. Vaguely she wondered if she had all the pieces—or if all the pieces were to the same picture.

She climbed the Olympic Staircase by rote, stumbling twice in potholes and stubbing her foot on one of the logs that kept the dirt from sliding away completely. It sent her arms windmilling for a moment before she caught her balance.

The folks in the loud sex tent were going at it. Again. "Popity-pop," Phoe said, wondering if they liked caramel corn—and giggled.

Drear blocks of color formed the world beyond C-gate—mostly gray with here and there a fuzzy streak of bright trim. Phoenix huddled in her cloak, imagined she could feel Ryna's heat, her lingering scent of wood smoke and myrrh embedded in the fibers. She shivered; her toes and nose and fingers ached with the chill. No one along the Narrows hailed her—they were all too wrapped up in their own cloaks and regrets. The Bear stood as an indistinct pillar, but even so—especially so—she avoided looking at it as she veered right and down the hill that would take her to Sherwood.

Shopkeepers readied their booths; her ears gaped at the achingly absent sound of the Gypsies opening up the vardo behind Hollow Hill. Her family milled around the concrete bunker's entrance. The patrons would come soon, though Phoe was too cold to care.

Conversation paused as she approached the gathering. She knew them even without sight: *Baba* Luna's bright colors; Tanek's strong, sullen earth-beat; Niki's quicksilver light sluggish pre-coffee; Kaya's liquid grace; Tobaltio flighty yet solemn. And Daniel. Where were Esmerelda, *Phuro* Basil, and Tremayne? They were together, wherever they were, she could feel…

"Phoe-bea? Where are your glasses?" Her brother, too gently, his hand on her arm.

"They were dirty." She gazed up at his unfocused face. "I couldn't wear them that dirty."

"Phoe, you're going to need to see…" This from Kaya, worry rippling her feel.

"But I see so many things," Phoenix protested, frowning. "So many things. It's like this there, sometimes, everything all melted together."

"Honey," Niki interjected from where she sat on the bridge, anguished, pleading, but Phoenix couldn't understand why.

"Maybe if I see things the way she does—"

Tobaltio simply gathered her in his arms, tucked her head under his chin—he must've been standing uphill—and made shushing noises at her, stroking her hair. He shook a little; Phoenix wondered if he had begun to cry or if he was coming down off the drink. He felt painfully sober. Niki left her perch on the bridge and ghosted away. Tanek scuffed the barren earth with the toe of his shoe. *Strange the things we notice without seeing them,* she thought as Opening Cannon sounded, its blast soft and blurred with distance.

* * *

A breeze brought the soft sound of weeping to Phoenix as she sat in the gazebo, humming quietly. She could see bits of color as people wandered through the Secret Garden's trails. At first she thought it belonged to one of them, or maybe it wasn't real at all, but a second tuft of chill air carried it again, and this time she rose.

It came from on site somewhere. Phoenix floated up the hill towards the familiar quips of the Merry Maids' show, underbrush tugging carelessly at her cloak, and peered in the side door of Caravan Stage. Kaya huddled in the far corner. Phoe ascended the steps and knelt beside her.

"What's wrong? What's wrong—don't cry."

Kaya glanced up... she looked so small, so lost. She pushed hair back from her tiny face. "I—I found this... in the window, up there." She gave a great sniff, nodded to the bowed, glassless window above her. "My—my pen, my favorite pen, the one that's been missing, and these were wrapped around it..."

Phoenix gingerly took the napkins; Kaya sniffed again and tucked herself into her cloak. They'd gotten wet at some point, and the ink had run a little, but they weren't too hard to read. *I love you. I love you. I love you. I love you,* they said, over and over, in Ryna's unmistakable penmanship.

It made no sense. Why would something so nice make Kaya cry? "You know she loves you," Phoe said. "You didn't need this to tell you that."

"But... this is the last thing we'll ever have of her. We failed her, Phoenix, and now I'll never get to tell her I love her too."

Phoenix stroked the dancer's hair gently. "Don't cry," she said. "Don't cry. She knows. Ryna knows. You don't have to cry."

But, strangely, that made her tears come harder.

◇ ◇ ◇

It was time for Vilification Tennis—Ryna could tell by all the rennies gathered around the Bear. Though VilTen regularly drew large crowds, only the famous Final "let's see if we can get fired" Vil drew one of *this* magnitude.

Phoenix and a blond Gypsy in a black, silver, and red outfit—Ryna thought she worked the Feast show—stood behind the judge, each holding a long wooden pole as they unfurled the huge banner attached to the tops.

VILIFICATION TENNIS
best
this may be our ~~last~~ show!

Ryna caught sight of Eric, their old Entertainment Director, on the front balcony of Bedside Manor. He was laughing. Hard.

Patty must be gone then—Eric would only be able to stand there if Patty was gone. Ryna smiled... Pendragon would be all right, then. Things would return to normal.

But Phoenix looked so sad. Silly Phoe—Patty was gone. She should be happy.

Vilification Tennis started... calling the net, tossing the peasant, and then the first match's opening insults.

One of the cat-like Shadow Fae twined around her ankles. "They're going on without you," it purred.

Ryna paid it no mind, simply continued to watch the game. She did not see any of the other Gypsies there... of course, the Shadow Fae had gotten them all already, including Kaya this morning as she'd read Ryna's note.

Was that why Phoenix was sad? Was she lonely?

The others weren't here, though. Ryna idly wondered where the Shadow Fae had taken them. Maybe she just hadn't seen them yet. Given Pendragon's size, it wasn't so hard to wander all day and not see somebody.

The second match started—*Pog mó Thoin* went up—and Eric climbed up after them, trying to hush the crowd. He finally succeeded.

"The Unicorn is our most prestigious award," he declared, "given to those who have made outstanding contributions to Pendragon for over a decade. It is my honor to present this Unicorn to Jack—known here as Hayrold—as a symbol of the realm's gratitude."

With that, Eric held out a mirror framed in wood that boasted a laser-carved unicorn.

Hayrold peed a great arcing stream that landed right at Eric's feet.

Ryna giggled. She knew the water came from the bota between his legs. Still, it looked funny. Even Phoenix laughed.

Someone made a comment about Hayrold being the first Unicorn recipient to ever wet himself.

Many of the old-timers gave him the Unicorn Salute—fist to forehead with the pinky raised. Hayrold returned it, beaming.

Ryna almost didn't notice the Shadow Fae creeping closer to Phoenix, surrounding her. Phoenix did not seem to see them.

And then... she was gone.

Everything was gone... patrons, Vilifiers, judge, the sign, everything. The Bear stared blankly over an empty faire.

Ryna frowned in consternation. She hadn't even gotten to see the whole game.

Oh, well, maybe she'd see it in flashes later.

◇ ◇ ◇

Phoenix munched contentedly on the last of her baked apple as she meandered across Shepherd's Green. Papa Bernatelli had given it to her after Post-Parade and the Years of Service awards, and it was wonderful… warm and sweet, with some spiced mixture containing oats and brown sugar where the core should have been. It tasted like autumn.

Phoenix couldn't remember the last time food had tasted so good.

Maybe she should find some spiced apple cider for Kaya to put in the etched-glass mug she'd received with her fifteen-year certificate. She could probably use something that tasted like autumn, too.

"Bless this house and all within," Phoe murmured, scuffing her feet on Irish Cottage's threshold. The doorframe felt rough against her lips as she planted a kiss on its weathered green surface. Moiré, in the *seanchaí* chair, told a story to an enraptured crowd of youngsters as Ma stirred the kettle over the fire. The warm, starchy smell of boiling potatoes filled the house, mixed with the rich scent of wood smoke and the metallic twinge of hot cast iron. Torin waved to Phoenix from the rafters. She waved back.

Brigid poked her head around the green burlap curtain; she beckoned Phoe closer.

"Could you grab me the coffee pot with the hot water in it?" she requested when the Gypsy had maneuvered over.

"Surely," Phoenix agreed, and went to the fire fetch it, carefully carrying it by the wire handle that looped over its top. Brigid kindly held the curtain for her; Phoenix set the pot on the counter, tested the water in the dish tub (numbingly cold) and grabbed the side handle.

Her hand hissed; reflexively the Gypsy pulled it back. She peered at it a moment, surprised—it must've still been wet; she'd never heard herself hiss before. Stupid, stupid, to carry the pot by the top-handle only to grab the one on the side that had been directly in the flames…

Brigid seized her hand, dragged her down to the rinse spigot, and thrust it under the running water.

Phoenix giggled as the room floated and spun. Distantly she heard Brigid yelling for Torin in a panicked sort of voice. A great thump and heavy footsteps from beyond the burlap curtain, and Torin—or Daniel—or Alfie—or whomever he was this time—charged into the kitchen.

"She burned her hand! I heard it sizzle, and she was just standing there, staring at it…"

"You did good, you did good," he said, gently removing her. "I'll take care of her. You go ask Da for some burn spray and some bandages, okay? We don't need to bother the people in First Aid for this."

Brigid bolted through the curtain.

Phoenix giggled again. All this fuss and she couldn't even really feel it.

"You okay, Phoe-bea?" Daniel crouched behind her, holding her hand in the water.

"I'm fine—I'm fine."

"Okay. Well, we'll keep that under the running water until Da gets here, all right? He's an EMT, and he's got all the good equipment in the loft."

"Okay." What a silly word—just two letters. O. K. Who ever thought of making a word out of two letters?

"Everything all right?"

Phoenix looked up at Da and his huge tackle box. "I'm fine—I'm fine."

"She burned her hand… thought you should take a look at it."

Da crouched down beside them—Daniel took Phoe's hand out from the water. Da dried it off with one of his sleeves, pulled the green burlap curtain aside to let in a little more light. "That doesn't look too bad. Probably hurts like hell, though."

"I'm fine."

Da gave her a quizzical look, but opened his tackle box and pulled out some ointment and bandages and applied them to her hand like a mitten. "Keep an eye on her, Torin—she looks a little shock-y."

"I'm fine."

"I will."

"No more dishes for you, lass," Da declared as he packed his stuff. "You take it easy for the rest of the day."

"Okay. I'm fine."

"Why don't we go watch the Torysteller, Phoe?" Danny suggested as Da pushed back through the burlap curtain. "Maybe catch a couple other shows?"

"Okay," she agreed as he led her through the kitchen door. "Okay."

* * *

Funny how little epiphanies crept up on you while you watched leaves and clouds.

Lying on her back behind Hollow Hill, Phoenix couldn't imagine why the past year had gotten her down so much. At least, the parts that didn't involve her soulmate being hauled off by creatures of unspeakable evil.

Patty was passing; Pendragon was forever. People might leave, but they could always come back. So beautifully simple. Why had she felt so lost? She was a rennie. This was her home. And that was all that mattered.

"Phoenix, come eat," Kaya coaxed.

"Eat?" Phoenix repeated blankly. Surely it wasn't time yet.

"Yes, honey, eat. We skipped the variety show." Her voice sounded strange, as if she didn't think Phoenix was quite all there.

Come to it, Phoenix wasn't sure if she was all there either. "Oh," she said, and climbed stiffly to her feet. How long had she been where the vardo once stood? She let the shorter woman lead her down the treacherous little stretch of hill and rocks that formed the path by the bridge. A stone shifted wrong; Kaya steadied Phoenix swiftly. In a detached sort of way, Phoe realized she should've tried to catch herself, flailed or something.

The other Gypsies avoided her eyes as they huddled on the decrepit benches with their bowls of food, trying to disappear into their cloaks. Where were the Merry Maids?

One bowl remained after hers, though the rest of the Gypsies had already claimed their dinner. Phoenix was glad. The day it became natural to only set out nine bowls would be the day Ryna truly died. She carelessly dished up fried rice and curried meat and licked some sauce from her fingers. She wondered if it tasted like ashes to everyone else, too. Tremayne nodded politely as she sat beside him. He'd barely touched his food.

The Gypsies' halfhearted chewing seemed loud.

"Who's in charge of the costuming here?"

The comment dropped into their silence like a hairball. Phoenix raised her eyes slowly and fastened them with dawning horror on the scrawny patron with a pen tucked behind his ear.

Esmerelda placed her bowl beside her on the bench with great precision, swallowed her mouthful of dinner, and stood. She smoothed her skirts, then stepped over the benches between herself and her target with regal grace. "I am," she declared, towering over him. "And I don't care who you are, who sent you, or what stupid little power-tripping, bureaucratic bullshit you're trying to pull. These costumes have served us through more years, faires, and Entertainment-Artistic-Whatevers than your puny little patron mind can comprehend. I'm not going to outfit us all in bikinis, or add veils, or re-dye every garment we own. So you can take your high-and-mighty opinion and shove it up your—"

"Um, actually, I'm from the press," he stammered, brandishing his press pass like a protective talisman. "I was hoping to get some pictures, maybe do an article? But if this is a bad time…"

The Gypsies stared at him, poleaxed. Elda sat down hard, almost missing the bench, and started to laugh.

"It's been a really long season," *Phuro* Basil finally explained.

"So it would seem," the journalist remarked, sandy-blond eyebrows nearly meeting with his hairline as he whipped out a pad of paper. "Anything you'd like to share?"

Esmerelda's laughter turned silent from lack of air, though she tried to get out a couple incomprehensible words.

Phuro began calmly—with the help of everyone save Elda—to explain about their working conditions over the past year.

Phoenix just wanted to crawl under a bench and hide.

◇ ◇ ◇

No vardo stood behind Hollow Hill at the moment. Ryna lay on the rectangle of dirt where it had been and stared at the canopy of dead leaves overhead. The red-orange slants of sunlight lengthened, as did the shadows, but somehow it seemed that no time passed at all… or maybe that it passed her by, that she was no longer part of it.

It was a strange, wispy feeling. *She* was wispy, her sense of self no more substantial than a cloud. A little water, a little dirt, a little air. Wasn't that what made people anyway?

Sometimes lightning—sometimes fire.

I am Fire, she thought, and closed her eyes. She could see the sunlight behind them. Strange that this place was so comforting—strange that it should not be. This was not a Shadow-land, to which she had been kidnapped. It was simply a place where the Shadow Fae sometimes were. Like her world, but… purer. Dark darker, light lighter. Strange that she should only now realize it, but the Bright Fae were here, too, had been all along. The tiny, bright voices in the back of her mind, the whispered encouragements. If only she'd thought to look for them.

Belief—or lack of it—could be blinding.

Oh, well. Why would she need them? This was the spirit of Pendragon, distilled Faire—which was the same as distilled Ryna, she realized with a smile. She had always been part of this—and now, soon, would always be, forever and ever. Reasonable enough. She had been born to this. She was a child of the faires. It was where she belonged.

Except…

Except?

Her brow furrowed in thought; something tugged on the edge of her soul, trying to contain her, anchor her. Had she been thinking something? It seemed important, but…

But?

But nothing. Her frown smoothed. Whatever it was, it couldn't matter much, not here with all this peace.

Just a little water, a little dirt, a little air.

<> <> <>

Strange, how quickly the light died on the last day of the run.

Phoenix remembered that from last year, dimly, the way she remembered much of anything. A few memories stood clear and sharp, but she skittered away from them.

It seemed all the entertainers were at the final Closing Gate; faire site stood empty save for a few crafters and RFC kids packing their wares and closing their booths. Soon trucks would rumble in, headlights glaring into the cadaverous darkness of the deceased faire season. *No respect for the dead,* she thought mournfully as she neared the end of the Narrows by C-gate.

And then she heard the singing.

It floated from Bardstone Hall, beautiful and unearthly, melody and words twining around each other:

"O, heavy tiding—
Here for me there is no biding.
Yet once—
Yet once again, yet once again
Ere that I part with thee, adieu
Adieu—adieu
Yet once again, adieu—"

A fellow tromped past, wheeling some boxes on a dolly; either he did not hear or did not care. *How sad,* Phoenix thought, swaying slightly in the deepening twilight, rooted to the spot. Tears sprang unbidden to her eyes; it felt as if Pendragon itself had found a voice to bid them all farewell. Stung to action, she tugged her cloak closer and hurried out C-gate, unable to listen longer, unwilling to hear it end.

What happens when the song ends?

Heavy skirts swirled around her legs as she plunged headlong down the Olympic Staircase, heedless of its craters. Several tent-sized patches of pale, dead grass glowed in stark contrast with the beaten paths. Within a day, their number would double. Within a week, not a single tent or trailer would remain.

Not even hers.

Phoenix closed the vardo's door behind herself and sat, still garbed, on the bed, letting her home's dark, quiet interior muffle the outside world. Karma crawled mewling into her lap, and Phoenix sat for a long while curled around her, singing softly to them both.

People came and went outside. She heard the Gypsies calling to one another, forcing cheerfulness, and Phoe sat quiet, crouched, and small until they left for the BLUE. Only then did she creep to the door, slowly turn the handle, and cautiously peer outside.

Dark. Empty.

She stepped onto her porch, closed the door, tiptoed to the fire pit. And simply breathed, letting memory take her. A year ago, a year ago… but the ashes were dead now, cold, and ghostly gray in the darkness. Everything was so still, timeless. She reached for the connection that bound her to Ryna; it wavered like the last, fading strain of a Gypsy lament, resonating against the thin thread of her own soul as it had for a thousand lifetimes. As it had that hot Saturday afternoon when she sat behind Caravan Stage, leaf-shadows playing across her face as old poetry found its music. Ringing together like tuning fork and fiddle string, point and counterpoint perfectly blended, like the music Ryna and her father played…

And suddenly, she *knew*.

"Oh," she whispered as the simplicity of her realization nearly doubled her over.

What happens when that last, echoing twin note dies?

"Oh, Goddess. No. No, no—Oh, Goddess."

Twin worlds…

Twin souls…

The note…

The song…

Staggering, trying to run, the lone Gypsy lurched through the campground. The ground swayed under her feet—Gods, how could they all have been so *blind?!*

The fiddle.

Tremayne met her halfway up the Olympic Staircase, caught at her shoulders. She was pretty sure he'd asked her something, but the rest of the Gypsies were catching up like the streamers of a kite, and Phoenix was laughing, thinking how they must have all leapt up from the BLUE to dash out here.

Breath and life and fire and I will never leave you... Phoenix would have staggered if Tremayne hadn't held her so firmly. "It's so simple," she murmured. She felt tears on her cheeks, wet and hot and cooling. She reached up to touch one, stared at it, wondering when she had begun to cry.

"What? Phoenix. What." Kaya's voice came from somewhere beyond Tremayne's face. The world was Tremayne's face, intent, already half-knowing.

"We're doing it all wrong." She felt still, so very still. She wanted to scream, or maybe throw up, but she couldn't feel her stomach… Gods, it was so simple. And… so awful. "'You must bring her to her body—and bring her body to her. The places where she is and will be must converge.'"

All the world stopped… except for that tiny spark that was Ryna, and the confused memories. The Gypsies' stunned, horrified expressions… those were forever. They had not thought. None of them had…

That note was so thin…

Did they know?

Did it matter?

"What do we have to do?" Tanek's voice was quiet, but strong. His face had gone so pale. They had all gone so pale—

Tremayne's expression was set and still, resigned yet hopeful. He knew. "Get Liam."

Tanek did not question. He just ran.

"What's the plan?" Toby asked as Tanek's footsteps left the gravel of the road for grass.

"We can't build a bridge and drag Ryna out like we've been trying," Phoenix said. "We must make the worlds a bridge in and of themselves. Make a space that is all and one."

"But how do we do that?" Esmerelda pressed.

"The fiddles," Tremayne said quietly. "She has her fiddle—I have its twin. They were made from the tree that became the Bear… the tree that was sacred to the Fae. If there's anywhere that our world and theirs can be joined…"

"But doesn't Ryna need to be playing hers?" Kaya ventured.

"It will call to her." Tremayne closed his eyes briefly. "It has to. There's very little of her left."

Phoe blinked in surprise. If he could feel it as keenly as she herself did—

"Go," *Phuro* Basil barked. "Get it. Now. There's no time left."

Tremayne rocketed up the Olympic Staircase as Tanek puffed toward them, Liam over his shoulder.

"Bear," *Baba* Luna told him.

"Right." He gave Phoe a wink on his way by, but did not slow.

The others dropped into stride beside him.

◇ ◇ ◇

Liam stared blankly at the world whizzing beneath him, tried to ignore Tanek's shoulder in his gut and the cotton cloth that silenced any cry he could've made. Excited fear crackled among the Gypsies. Tanek hadn't been forthcoming when he'd burst into the trailer and snatched Liam up, but it didn't take much to figure it out.

One last powerful jump, and Tanek dumped him onto the bare, packed earth of the Bear's stage. The Gypsies—except for Ryna's father—had fanned out to points around the circle. Phoenix stood beside him, though she pointedly ignored him. Liam hung his head, stung, though he knew he deserved it.

"I have it," Tremayne panted, brandishing his fiddle as he dashed into the circle. "I have it."

"And peasants, too," Esmerelda observed with a raised eyebrow, eyeing the half-garbed ranks that followed him up.

"You have our assistance," said the one with the dark beard. "We'll try not to trip you up."

The Gypsies glanced to one another. Liam wondered if they thought they had any more say in the peasants participating than he did in being there.

"We're not sure what's going to happen, but we know it's not going to be pretty," *Phuro* Basil warned. "You've been very helpful, but—"

"Whatever it is, we're not letting you do it alone," put in a blond urchin.

Another girl—Liam recognized her as the youngest Merry Maid—nodded. "Ilya's right. After all, we love Ryna too."

"They are my family, too," Phoenix said quietly. "They stay."

An expectant pause filled the air. Tremayne nodded briefly. "Earth. Fire. Water. Air," he noted, indicating his fellow Gypsies.

A handful of the peasantry drifted over and crouched or sat at the cardinal points. Several remained, though. "We're better warriors than batteries," one said.

"Fair enough," Tremayne allowed. "Shall we begin?"

Another expectant pause. And then, by bits, Liam began to feel it.

Magick.

It started slow, a low rumbling against his breastbone as the fiddle's song climbed into the sky, but gradually it grew, and grew, as peasants and Gypsies alike began to glow softly.

"Air to raise us—"

"Fire to drive us—"

"Water to cleanse us—"

"Earth to ground us—"

And then Phoenix's voice, quiet and echoing against the fiddle's cry:

"Spirit to bind us."

And bind it did—no sooner had the words been spoken than the stage pulled sickeningly against reality, its energy speeding as it strained against time and space, seeking itself in the other world.

Oh, God—they... oh, God, a horrified voice whispered in the back of Liam's mind. He had only thinned the barrier, parted it a little, when he had switched places with Ryna. This was too big. He could feel it tearing, crackling along the circle's boundaries. Insanity. The Gypsies wouldn't be foolish enough to...

And then, with a blast of pure energy, the veil shredded. The air felt raw, abrasive, wounded—Liam could taste it, dry and cracked against the back of his throat. Phoenix dropped to the ground beside him, coughing so hard she could scarcely draw breath.

"Hold it open! Hold it open!" someone yelled against the suddenly driving wind as energy spiked around him, sharp counterpoint to the fiddle's unceasing song...

And then the Shadow Fae descended.

◇ ◇ ◇

Music—*familiar* music.

It tugged something nearly dissolved within Ryna's soul; she raised her head until she could see down the Narrows. How had she gotten to Maypole?

Her father's music...

The image came to her mind's eye—her family gathered around him, calling, seeking. They were trying to find her.

The music was trying to find her.

I'm here. She raised her fiddle from its cradle on her lap, brought it to its home against her shoulder. The bow sighed across its strings. Around her, the world throbbed as she matched her song to the music of her father's hand. She could feel the lifebeat of the spirit of Pendragon's grounds slow, intensify and bend.

A spark, a connection of worlds.

Ryna trembled with the wrench of reality shifting, felt Shadow and Bright Fae rushing to the hole in droves. Wind shook the trees in protest.

Still she played, played, played as the Narrows telescoped and bent, played until the tear became a gash, a gaping wound, and the veil shredded. She staggered under the force of its backlash, and for a moment Ryna could feel herself vibrating through the strings, melting into notes she could almost see, joining the energy that her family poured into her father, that her father poured into the song.

There was nothing but the song.

And love.

◇ ◇ ◇

The clear strain of Ryna's connection sang pure and true from beyond the protective circle of Gypsies and peasants. It had worked. Ryna had her fiddle. She hadn't given up.

Phoenix would've shouted with joy had she been able to draw the breath for it. She huddled on all fours, forehead pressed to the throbbing earth of the Bear's stage as the wind buffeted her from all sides. She knew she had to get up, had to find Ryna, but could scarcely think beyond the burning, raw fire of drawing air into her lungs.

"Hold it open!" *Phuro* Basil yelled above the wind, above the joyous call of Tremayne's fiddle.

Magick spiked and flared through the circle and through Phoenix, but there was more... a great horde descending, Bright and Shadow fighting as the tide of them tumbled ever closer. *They're coming!* she sent to her family, hoped her mental voice wouldn't be lost in the pandemonium.

And then the horde broke upon them. Phoenix could feel the chaos of it rolling over her, though unable to touch her for the brightly colored shield thrown over her like a blanket. She'd have to thank *Baba* Luna for that later.

Cries of fear, triumph, pain, and battle filled her ears, filled her soul. She could feel them all, feel their struggles... bursts of Magick from Bright and Shadow and rennie so fast as to be nearly indistinguishable. Phoenix wrapped the blanket of protection closer, welcomed the tingle of healing she thought she recognized as Laine. Gradually, her coughing eased.

The tumult eased.

The wind eased.

Phoenix's hair settled limply around her face. She willed strength to her arms, pushed herself to her feet.

"They didn't attack us—why didn't they attack us?" Niki asked, her voice faint. Phoe wondered if the winds had calmed at her command.

"Worry about that later," Esmerelda said briskly. "We don't need to borrow trouble."

Phuro Basil nodded. "Luna, Toby, Elda—stay with me to protect Tremayne. Phoenix, you're our best chance of finding Ryna. The rest of you, take out the Shadows—and protect the innocents. We've opened up the floodgates of Hell on our heads. And be careful with Magick. I don't know what effects this rift will have on it, but according to Tremayne, working Magick on the other side is like drinking from a fire hose."

Phoe glanced uneasily at her mentor. He had so much more experience. He was the reason they'd survived their first trips. He should be the one—

"You can't take his place," Niki said, reading her discomfort. "And he can't take yours. Ryna's counting on you. Go to her."

Ryna.

Phoenix closed her eyes for the space of a breath. It didn't matter what horrors lurked out there. Nothing could be worse than a life without her soulmate.

"We'll come with you," Marcus said, gesturing to himself and Laine. "You'll need backup."

"Thanks," Phoe said, extraordinarily grateful—extraordinarily humbled. She barely knew them, in the grand scheme of things, and yet—

No time for that—for thoughts, for gratitude. It would never be enough. Better to act, to step beyond the circle—

And into the storm.

Magick howled around her, fierce and untamed—and in an instant she knew that her previous attempts with Tremayne had scarcely brushed this world. How had Ryna survived here for so many weeks? Phoe knew she would've gone mad in the redhead's place. She wasn't qualified to deal with this bedlam, energies swirling like a blizzard of salt and pepper…

"You can't take his place. And he can't take yours. Ryna is counting on you…"

Phoenix drew a deep breath, squared her shoulders. She might not be enough, but she was Ryna's one hope. She would have to *be* enough.

She glanced back at the Bear's stage as the Gypsies scattered, a peasant or two with each. She sent silent blessings to protect them, but they were on their own now.

So was she.

Marcus and Laine had disappeared. She could see Toby, Basil, Elda, Luna, and Tremayne holding the circle… but their images were faded, like headlights superimposed over the back seat seen in a rearview mirror at night. Puddle and Ilya stood clear and sharp on the opposite side of the stage, looking confused. They clambered back over the rocks, fading as they did… and Mutch appeared solid and bright from around the other side of the Bear.

Phoe scowled. She didn't have time for this. Backup or not, she had to go. Now.

"Don't worry," Mutch yelled, trying to push her hair out of her face as she joined Phoe. "I'll protect you."

Phoe gazed at her for a timeless instant as a sudden kinship bound them amidst the flying leaves and debris. Then she grabbed the Merry Maid's hand and dashed down the Narrows.

Liam stared blankly at the darkness beyond the stage. He couldn't see much, but he could feel the worlds… feel which was home, which belonged to the Fae.

Could the Gypsies?

He glanced around the circle at their tense bearings, watched as they took pot shots at passing Shadow Fae. None attacked the humans—why should they? The Gypsies held open a portal for them, gave them one of their fondest wishes on a silver platter.

All because of him.

Liam bowed his head, shamed to even draw breath. All those endless months of wishing to return home, to be free of the Three and the creatures they commanded—or served… and it came to this. He was a tool to them, had always been a tool. And now, in returning, he had insured the Shadow Fae would have their run of this world as well. His friends, his sisters, his Phoenix… all of them would fall prey to the Shadow Fae now.

All for a wish that had never been granted.

All because of him.

◇ ◇ ◇

Dear gods, she's not mortal!

The stunned words echoed though Phoenix's mind in a dozen languages as she stared through the tempest, awed.

Ryna stood, back braced against the Maypole, more pure and perfect than ever. A vague smile played across her lips—haunting, sad, and beautiful—as the song danced around her, and with it the energies of her family back at the Bear. Flames blossomed against the pad of each tiny finger on the fiddle's neck, winking out as they touched the strings, then springing back to life. Bright colors glittered around her like pixie dust. The very air had stilled near her, and the faint howl of a wolf sighed against the tune she played.

Mutch gaped.

Ryna, we're here, Phoenix sent to her love. *Come to me. Come home.*

For an agonizing moment, Ryna didn't move.

Then… the questioning uplift of song… and a step. And another. Though oblivious to her surroundings, some buried instinct guided her from her protected circle, towards Phoenix. The raven-haired Gypsy stood still, silent, as Ryna neared her rescuers… and passed them, following the music's compass towards the Bear.

Mutch looked about to form question, but Phoe hushed her with a gesture. Together they followed the fiddler slowly, so slowly, over the uneven ground of the Narrows.

It reminded Phoenix strangely of her first night at Pendragon, following the Morris Dancers' haunting tune as their processional made its way around grounds. The measured, sure steps… the siren-call of the fiddle… the feel of Magick in the air, of time and place fading away…

The world lurched; Phoenix stumbled, though Ryna did not. If the wind could not touch her, why should time or place? Mutch clutched the taller Gypsy's arm. "What the—?"

Phoe looked sharply around—and let out a curse when she recognized the BLUE on her left, the games booths on her right. "This place changes," Phoenix yelled over the driving wind.

"What do we do?"

"Turn around—and pay attention this time!"

Mutch nodded, her lips a tight line. Phoe could tell she was trying hard not to panic—not that she could blame the girl. Even if you were told, even if you knew... somehow this sort of thing was never real until it happened to you.

Phoenix would save her own breakdown for later.

Ryna turned, following the call of the music. Phoenix thought fast as she and Mutch fell in behind the fiddler. There were hidden doorways between the food booths. If she could find one, cut across the center island...

"Watch it!" the Merry Maid cried, dragging Ryna out of harm's way as the oak that stood guard against one corner of the BLUE's trellis crashed into the game booths across the way.

Dark laughter filled the air.

A quiet requiem for the ancient arbor crept into Ryna's tune, and Phoenix felt her heart bleed with it. *Not now,* Phoe bid her love. *Honor its passing by living.*

"Isn't there some way to get her to hurry up?" Mutch demanded, bouncing on the balls of her feet as they neared the Croft with indescribable slowness.

The air twisted again, the world curling in on itself, but Phoenix held fast to their surroundings, filling every scrap of her awareness with the buildings before her, the earth under her feet, until the gut-wrenching sensation eased. They had not shifted. Phoenix flashed Mutch a grin, received a jubilant thumbs-up in return... and felt her hackles raise barely in time to keep Ryna from walking headlong into the throng of Shadow Fae waiting for them near the Mead Booth.

Their predators shifted, restless, hungry, and began to advance, drawn to the music like rats to the piper of Hamlin.

Instinct took over—Phoenix grabbed tendrils of the spirit of the grounds around the Shadow and twisted... willing it to engulf the horde. The Shadow Fae fuzzed out of existence.

Mutch's jaw dropped. "Did you..."

A glow of pride warmed Phoenix. "I think I did. I'm not sure where I sent them, though, and I don't think they'll be happy that I used their trick against them."

"And they saw us headed this way."

Phoe nodded, sensing the possibility for an ambush. They'd gone blessedly unmolested so far—but she didn't want to push her luck. "Detour—over Track—Go!" she urged, steering her group onto their new course. Damn—the fence. Could she pick Ryna up and haul her over it? The fiddler certainly couldn't *climb* the thing, and skirting it would take too much time...

A blast of sand hit them, scouring the tender skin of face and hands, gritty against eyes and tongue. Impossible to breathe, to see, though Phoenix could feel a Shadow Fae nearby, solid and eternal as the earth, stirring the Track's sand even more than the storm already had.

Ryna's steps had slowed—Phoenix could feel in her music that she wanted to go back the way she'd come. This was the wrong direction—this would not take her to her family.

I know. I'm trying. Have patience, Phoenix sent to her as, eyes stinging, blinded by the sand, the taller Gypsy herded her charges away from the force of the thing's power, hoping against hope it wasn't herding her. Still, she couldn't fight what she couldn't see—nor could she protect Ryna or Mutch from it.

The wolf's howl that echoed with Ryna's fiddle heightened—a Shadow Fae leapt toward them from the sand-cloud and cried out in pain as a bright, snarling flash attacked it.

Phoe felt a relieved smile shape her lips. *Thanks, Basil.*

The sand finally quieted by the time the threesome had been driven back to the pony rides and the far lane by the Fencing Booth. Not a single grain touched Ryna, not a single leaf slapped pale cheek or hand. Phoenix suspected she'd be spitting the things out in Colorado, still.

"Past Cottage, then over?" Mutch suggested.

Phoe nodded shortly, glad the thing hadn't followed them. "We're running out of options."

The barrier between the worlds wavered, thinned—Tanek dove from behind a tree, three fast, scrabbling Shadows on his heels. Ilya and Niki stood over him, fighting to keep them at bay.

And then, with the brevity of a fire blow's plume, they were gone.

Fencing Booth.

Drink booths.

First Aid.

Jerky cart.

Mutch grabbed Phoe's arm, pointed to Cottage not far distant.

Phoenix peered into the darkness—the doors stood open, promising sanctuary. She nodded vigorously, gently steered Ryna towards the familiar haven. Her song gained a happy, Irish lilt as her feet connected with the wooden porch. Mutch followed her inside, scuffing her feet and kissing the green-painted doorframe. Phoe brought up the rear—and for a moment, the world fell blessedly still. Ryna's fiddlesong echoed comfortably in the homey space.

It'll be all right, the walls seemed to whisper. *Be strong. Be strong.*

Phoe straightened, energies renewed and centered. She followed her entourage back outside, into the whipping wind and down the uneven stone walkway.

Under the Irish Cottage sign.

Onto the Green.

A boulder pounded the ground three yards to the left with an earth-shaking THUMP. Phoe glanced back, horrified, to see one of the stones that bordered

Cottage's lawn missing… and the Earth Elemental that had caused them such trouble at the Track reaching down to grab the next one in line.

Ryna's song gained a note of alarm.

They were a quarter of the way across the Green. Could it throw that far?

Halfway.

Three-quarters.

"Incoming!" Mutch shouted. Phoe could feel the solid mass of it nearing, bearing down, and willed it not to hit them…

THUMP!

Two yards behind.

The veil wavered again, and Phoenix watched through the distorted lens of reality as one of Chapel's burlap curtains ripped free from its moorings and with sudden dark sentience dove, batlike, right for Ilya. Lightning crackled from Niki's fingertips, and the possessed burlap veered from its course and tangled around its attacker's neck. Tanek grabbed at it, the dagger in his free hand tearing it to shreds. Each shred gained life of its own, flocking, beating, pecking—and then exploded into a billion motes of black glitter.

Ilya grinned as she, Tanek, and Niki wavered and disappeared. The flare of vision had taken only seconds.

"Chapel! Watch it!" Mutch cried, pointing.

The building groaned, fighting a wind bent on its destruction. Phoenix had only a moment to stand, horrified, as its decorative vegetation thrashed and the remaining burlap curtain stretched eerily toward them, seeking salvation.

And then, with the splintering crash of a ship breaking over rocks… it fell.

The impact echoed across her being, nearly doubling her over as the Bright Magicks that surrounded it sundered and were crushed. Her head swam at the sudden vacuum it left, the ghastly chime of breaking stained glass filling her ears.

Ryna stumbled, her song faltering—she felt it too.

A small, bright voice flashed a warning in Phoe's head—she forced herself upright as a hunched, bipedal Shadow lunged for Ryna from the Chapel's wreckage. She had no time to warn her love before ebon fangs crunched into Ryna's fiddle with a sound like bones splintering. A disdainful toss of the thing's head ripped the beloved instrument from her hands as a streak of light drove the creature into and through the ground.

Ryna screamed—the first sound she'd uttered—as her connection to the Gypsies' song snapped and rebounded like a broken guitar string.

Phoenix's soul echoed the cry—in pain, in terror. The worlds had begun to separate—Phoe could feel it, like a drop of water between two fingers, slowly pulling apart.

She had to hold on. She had to bring Ryna back. Phoe reached out, arms aching as though she'd not used them for decades—her hands burned as they passed through her love.

She had no time for shock. Phoenix could feel the life fading from her bones, could see the brightening sparkle in the red eyes that surrounded them.

"Run—*run*!" Mutch screamed.

Ryna ran, Phoe two steps behind her, guarding her back.

The Shadow Fae descended in a swarm, some flying, some running, some flowing—but they were not the only ones. Something beside her imploded and sucked itself into oblivion. Other bolts of salvation shot around her—some eliminating foes, some simply delaying them, but every unhindered step brought Phoenix and Ryna closer to safety.

Closer to Liam.

Splintering, cracking, breaking, and a quiet, pained scream—one of the trees in the grove where the Queen used to have her tea crashed down, barely missing Ryna.

Bedside Manor.

Something next to her right ear burst like a demonic firework. Phoe would've yelped if she could've drawn enough breath. Knives of pain lanced her side—whether from the Shadow Fae or from too much running she couldn't tell, but it hardly mattered now.

Ryna mattered.

That was all.

Phoenix rounded the Manor's corner and caught sight of the Bear, still and stiff. She hadn't the energy to be angry *or* relieved.

Something three-quarters her size loped toward Ryna; Phoe willed extra speed to her legs… and knew she wouldn't make it.

Mutch rocketed from nowhere with an incoherent cry and tackled the thing as three blasts of Magick—one of them Phoenix's own—enveloped it.

She had no time to wonder about the Merry Maid's fate. Only the thinnest of echoes still held the worlds as one.

Ryna flew onto the Bear's stage, Phoe a bare step behind. All the world slowed as Liam raised his head.

I love you. Phoenix could read the words on his lips, though she could not hear them over the wind. *I'm sorry.*

Phoe's heart froze in its rhythm, though she scarcely had time to feel it. She coiled herself to fight with every scrap of her being, saw Toby, Elda, Basil, Luna, and Tremayne prepare to blast him from his residence.

All or nothing.

Good-bye… Phoenix. He smiled a beatific smile, and then simply was not there.

Ryna's body stood a moment—stiff, vacant—before her soul melted to its home—at the exact instant the Gypsies opened fire to send him back to whatever hell had spawned him.

Phoenix stood beside her in a heartbeat, the barrier she formed around them so solid that it took her aback. Her family's Magicks snapped off.

With a quiet roar, the worlds separated.

Time stood eerily silent, suspended.

"Is that—?" she heard Puddle ask.

"It is." Phoenix could feel the wide grin on her face, but could not take her eyes off the beautiful little elfin fiddler with the copper-red hair. *Everyone* stared at the wonderful sight, the familiar soul behind it, the warmth that sang down their ties and filled a place too long empty.

"Home," Ryna said, wonderingly, and then again, and again, as if it was the only word she knew.

"I am impressed."

They all turned at the male Bright Fae's voice. His lady stood at his side—as well as another Fae, so faint it was nearly invisible.

"Liam is no more," the third said, wonder in its wispy voice. "I had not thought it possible..."

Phoenix rounded on them. "Get. Out."

They looked taken aback—and angry. Phoenix didn't care.

"Not even a year gone, you were honored by our presence," said the lady.

Baba Luna's gaze was unflinching. "That was before your turf wars nearly got my granddaughter killed."

"We are not responsible for the actions of others," the male informed them haughtily. "We warned you of the price. Is this how you repay our kindnesses? The times we have heeded your request for aid?"

"You have repaid our kindnesses to you in a similar fashion," Tremayne said softly, his arms protectively around his child. "You have aided us when it suited you. You gave riddles when we needed clarity. You may not be responsible for the actions of others, but neither were you responsible for undoing the damage. We did not create the war you wage. We have paid enough. It is time you go."

"We may leave, but nothing will change," said the third, wispy voice. "Do you truly wish to face what comes without us?"

"We have faced it alone all year," Esmerelda said icily. "Leave."

The male bowed mockingly. "As the lady wishes."

And then, without fanfare... the Three were gone.

A strange, wet weight pulled at Phoe's finger—she glanced down as her Faerie ring shimmered and melted into the joy-tear that had formed it. The drop clung to her skin a last, cold moment... and fell to the windblown earth, where it perished.

Part of Phoenix's heart died with it.

"Bitch." Esmerelda spat at the ground where the Three had stood.

"Home," Ryna whispered.

Phoenix closed her eyes. Home. Ryna was home. She would concentrate on that.

And hope the Bright Fae were wrong.

~Epilogue~
Pendragon Renaissance Faire
Monday After Closing Weekend

It had been real… all of it, real, though Ryna felt as if she'd lived half of it in a dream. The Drench-a-Wench booth and the Children's Trilogy of Games lay in shattered ruin beneath the ancient oak that had so long stood at the BLUE's corner. She remembered playing from its branches, once or twice, when things had gotten a little drunk out, and very late, and someone had decided it might be fun for the band to climb the tree. She could still feel that music, a little, when she touched the thick trunk, though its humming had stopped.

Her chest seized with the pain of its passing. The last time a tree that beloved had fallen, the Bear had been built. And her fiddle.

Her fiddle…

Her father put a comforting hand on her shoulder. He knew. He had offered her his, once she'd regained enough sense to realize her music-child had gone beyond retrieving. She couldn't take it, couldn't cause him the pain she felt in her own heart.

"This wood would make good tippers," Kaya said. "Basil, do you think…?"

He coughed, clearing his throat. "You're right. Maybe a couple sets of bones, too. I'll pick some of the downed bits later today."

Ryna nodded, forcing back tears. "It would like that."

Phoenix squeezed her hand in silent comfort. Ryna didn't need to look to know there were tears in the raven-haired Gypsy's eyes.

They moved on, trying not to comment on the damage that littered Pendragon's grounds. Vardo-shaped souvenir booths tipped over, fortuneteller tents in heaps of cloth and broken poles, privy banners ripped from their moorings. Three of Cottage's boulders dotted the Green where they'd been thrown—Ryna wondered how the rennies would explain *that* one.

And the Chapel.

It lay in a mound of rubble, as if felled by the footstep of a careless giant. Ryna knelt by its weathered timbers and cracked stucco, bowed her head in respect. So many nights it had sheltered her, and now…

Had it been because she had come to love it?

Chunks of stained glass nestled amid the rubble; Ryna retrieved a few, vowed to make something pretty of them so that the Chapel's light might shine on, and followed her family to Bedside Manor.

"RYNA!!!!!"

The redhead's eyes rounded in horror; she barely refrained from bolting as the mass of rennies that had lined up for the yearly champaign breakfast charged across the Manor's green for a group hug.

A fraction of a second before they descended, Phoe wrapped Ryna in a tight embrace, shielding her from the hordes.

So many people... Ryna buried her face in her love's shirt, breathed the familiar scent of apricot and lilac and tried to block out the world. *They're real,* she told herself, fighting down panic. *They won't change. They won't hurt you. They're real.*

Questions assaulted her from all directions as the group finally broke up. She reeled, unable to process them all, unable to do much but sway a little. The Gypsies and a few peasants were laughingly—but firmly—telling everyone to give her some space, spouting rehearsed answers as Phoenix led her toward Bedside Manor, saying something about how Ryna hadn't slept in a very long time and wasn't feeling well and would it be okay if she grabbed some food so she could go sit for a while?

Oh, of course, of course...

It all blended in one big babble. So many people, and really no difference between them. She was part of them all, and they were part of her. And none of them realized it. She wanted to cry.

She thought longingly of that ignorance, of the time there had only been her soul in her body. And yet... it seemed a lonely thing to wish for. She followed Phoenix up the stairs and into the dim, spacious feast hall. No hearth, no book with names. And it didn't change—she couldn't help a twinge of disappointment. She'd wanted so badly to show her love...

The tables overflowed with food—food, food, food. All the food. She started to giggle; Phoenix looked at her strangely, but Ryna waved her off and got a plate. Phoe might try, but she couldn't understand.

There were noodle salads, fruit salads, lettuce salads, oranges, peaches, apples so perfect that they must be kin to the one that tempted Snow White. Sandwiches, pickles, eggs, stuffed mushrooms, hot dishes, cold dishes, olives... the tables stretched forever. Ryna took a little of everything, not sure she'd even be able to coax her roiling stomach to house it.

They sat in the shade of Tinker's tree, guarded by the solid comfort of Irish Cottage. Brigid looked at her a little strangely and brought out her own leather mug for Ryna to put her mimosa in, saying it wasn't right to drink out of plastic on site.

The food didn't taste strange, though she thought it should. The chicken noodle soup her family had forced her to eat last night had tasted normal, too. Somehow, there was something terribly *wrong* with that.

Her family and the peasants gathered 'round with their plates, forming a friendly barrier with their bodies and energies. They chatted and laughed, but it wasn't nearly so frightening and wild as the crowd in front of Bedside Manor had been. Others joined—a few musicians, Mutch and Little Jen and Alexis—but they had to sit beyond those she trusted most.

One of the peasants spit a watermelon seed at her.

Silence descended.

One of the other peasants elbowed him, an incredulous look on his face.

Ryna blinked at him in shock, looked down at the little brown thing in her lap.

Then she took a bite of her own watermelon and spit one back.

Relieved laughter. Ryna felt the tension in her shoulders ease… and wished her stomach would take their lead.

One of the musicians—Nora, she thought—passed a spiral-bound, one-subject notebook through her circle of guardians. It had a green cover. Ryna opened it, curious, to see page upon page of names she recognized, accompanied by addresses, telephone numbers, and encouraging comments.

Alexis said something about how if she needed to stay in the state after the other Gypsies had to move on, the people in the book had offered to put her up or help her out any way they could.

The book was very nearly full. Some of the names belonged to friends who hadn't worked Pendragon in five years or more.

"Thank you," she said, and tried not to shiver. Although it was warm in the sun, she could still feel the chill breath of winter in the shadows.

Winter… and death.

And no one else knew.

Glossary

Academy. Training for rookies, takes place for the six weeks prior to Pendragon. Current Artistic Director has replaced them with "Rehearsals"—which are the same thing, only less effective.

Artistic Director. The position formerly known as "Entertainment Director"—gotta love middle management.

B-gate. Participant entrance near Scribes' Hall and Royal Falconer Stage. Lost-and-found is located there, hence people who have lost something (their mug, their keys, their mind) are encouraged to go to B-gate.

Bakery Stage. The home of the Bernatelli family, who portray Italian bakers. Also home to the infamous Orgasmic Pecan Pie.

Bardstone Hall. Sheltered stage near C-gate and the BLUE. Occasionally called "Birdstone" thanks to the swallows that nest in the rafters and poop on the stage.

Bedside Manor. Large building containing the hall where the Fantastical Feast is held, located near the Bear.

Bear (the). Enormous chainsaw-carved sculpture that serves as a major landmark and the anchor spot for one end of the Narrows and one outlet of Cartwheel Cove's loop.

BLUE. Short for Blue-Legged Unicorn Eatery, formerly the Blue Unicorn Tap. Management decided that besides BUT being an unpleasant nickname, a Tap didn't have a family-friendly enough ring to it, and so changed the name. This same family-friendly logic, however, did not convince them to give up their weekends featuring free beer sampling or the numerous booths selling alcoholic beverages.

bodhran. (rhymes with moron) Irish traditional drum. Sometimes it seems like every musician can play one of these.

bota. A wineskin.

C-gate. Participant entrance beside Bardstone Hall, the closest exit leading to the campground.

cabriolet. A rickshaw people can hire to haul them around site. It takes two people—one pulling, one pushing—to keep it rolling. Smart people get out of their way. Stupid ones get run over.

cannon. The cannon on Fool's Knoll blasts several times to mark important events: Opening (at nine AM), Closing (at seven PM), and Parade (around one in the afternoon) Cannons sound each day. On Sundays, Beer Cannon is added at noon to tell alcohol booths they may now dispense their goods.

Canopy Stage. A raised wooden platform near the food booths by Bedside Manor. The only canopy in the area shades picnic tables, not the stage.

Caravan Stage. A large plywood platform in front of a three-sided vardo where the Gypsies perform their acts. Located in the part of Cartwheel Cove known as Sherwood.

Cartwheel Cove. The "loop" that branches off to the left of Front Gate (when Front Gate is at your back) and encompasses the Stocks, many food and craft booths, the Children's Realm, Sherwood, and Woodland Stage. The other end of the loop lets out at the Bear.

Cast Call. Pre-show (eight in the morning) meeting at Bakery Stage where announcements are made and the actors sing "Swing Low, Sweet Chariot."

circuit. The procession of faires a road rennie travels. Since some shows run at the same time, there are a number of different circuits possible. "She works (the) circuit."

civvies. Civilian (modern) clothing. In other words, anything that isn't garb.

Closing Gate Show. A variety show at the end of the day where rennies are encouraged to do short skits.

clove orange. A clove-studded orange given to someone in whom the orange's keeper has a romantic interest. The recipient removes a clove and eats it. If the removal is done by hand, the giver kisses the receiver on the hand. If the removal is done with the teeth, the giver kisses the receiver on the lips. More flexible people have used such appendages as toes, but unless you know you can get your toes to your mouth without causing injury, it's not a good idea to try. The clove orange is not supposed to be passed back to the one who gave it.

Como Cottage. The home base of the Royal Herpetological Society. The cottage itself is only accessible to those who work there; the herp folks show their snakes, turtles, and such from the fenced-off yard.

crafter. Someone who sells their handiwork at a faire. Most crafters own booths, though some own tents.

Croft. The Scottish version of Irish Cottage, located near Flying Buttress Stage.

doumbek. An hourglass-shaped drum. Hitting the head's center produces a low-pitched DOUM while hitting the head closer to the rim produces a higher-pitched *tek*.

Drum Jam. An event occurring from six-thirty until Closing Cannon, it involves many drummers and a mob of dancers, all making a joyful racket.

faire crud. Illness that circulates for the last half of the faire run, often due to changing temperatures, over-tired actors, and too many people sharing the same mugs.

faire-folk. See **rennie.**

Fae. Non-human beings, often called Faeries, Little People, Good Folk, Ageless Ones, and Fair Folk (not to be confused with faire-folk). These are good names to use when calling on the Bright Fae. When calling on the Shadow Fae... you're on your own.

Fantastical Feast. An elaborate dinner-and-a-show available to any faire-goer... for an additional fee, of course. Fantastical Feast is held in Bedside Manor.

Flying Buttress Stage. Sheltered stage between the Jousting Track and Upson Downs. It takes its name from the lavender-painted flying buttresses that accent the stage's second story (used for storage). Special events such as beer tastings and the wooing contest take place here.

food book. Given as an award for a GEM (and also available for purchase), they contain six dollars' worth of twenty-five-cent coupons redeemable for food on site.

Fool's Knoll. Backstage area located behind Bakery Stage, Fool's Knoll overlooks the parking lot and hosts the cannon.

Front Gate. The large, three-storied structure where the patrons enter.

gamer. Someone who works at a game attraction such as Jacob's Ladder, the Sliding Joust, and the Hay Roll.

garb. Costumes; what rennies wear during the show days.

GEM. Great Entertainment Moment—rennies get a food book if someone from management catches them doing good street theatre. GEMs are announced each day at Cast Call.

Globe Stage. Once upon a time it looked like a boxing ring and hosted the Human Chess Match, but a fancy two-story amphitheater-type construct has been built around it now. Rumor has it that this addition was written into the Royals Revolting's contract. The Shakespearean Players can also be found here.

grid. A spreadsheet available only to entertainers. It indicates which performers will be at which stage and when. Events on this schedule are said to be "gridded." Can also be a verb—"I hate it when they grid bagpipes next to the harper."

grounds. See **site.**

groundscore. Items found on the ground, presumably abandoned by their previous owners. Groundscore ranges from tattered ribbons and loose change to jewelry and cans of anchovy-stuffed olives. Kind people turn important-looking groundscores (like missing mugs and walking sticks) in to B-gate.

guest. What the current Artistic Director likes to call patrons.

Harvey. The monster said to live in privies. Sometimes used as a euphemism for needing to visit the privies—"I have to say hi to Harvey."

hat. A container (hat, basket, mug, bra, etc.) used to gather tip money. ("Passing the hat.") It can also refer to the money gained from tips—"How was your hat last Saturday?"

hawk. To verbally advertise a show, booth, or game. People who do this are "hawkers." This term can be especially appropriate when faire crud starts going around.

Hidden Valley. Wooded region of the campground located in a ravine behind the shower house.

Hollow Hill. A brick-faced concrete sphere covered with grass, located in Sherwood. A Tolkien-esque show used to be centered here, but now it serves as a break room and storage area for the Gypsies.

Irish Cottage. A cottage inhabited by the Irish—the O'Malley family to be precise.

***Lady Fortune* Stage.** A stage that looks like a huge, three-masted, land-bound ship.

Mead Booth. The cottage-shaped stand-alone booth located roughly between Flying Buttress Stage and Como Cottage. It sells, logically enough, mead.

Narrows. The aptly-named stretch of lane between the Bear and the Maypole.

Olympic Staircase. Tortuously steep stairs that lead down to the campground, made of dirt shored up with wood. They usually wash out after the first good rainstorm.

Opening Gate Show. Character interaction that entertains the patrons while they wait outside Front Gate for Opening Cannon. It sets the tone for the day's show by introducing various storylines (Sheriff vs. Robyn Hood/Gypsies, King Arthur and his Court visit the town, etc.)

ORT. Pronounced "ort" (like a seal barking), it stands for Official Renaissance Time, what everyone sets their watches to at Cast Call.

Parade. Known on hot days as the "Trail of Tears" or "Death March," this is what the one o'clock-ish Cannon heralds. It is theoretically mandatory for entertainers. The parade route starts on Fool's Knoll and progresses around the site, ending in front of Irish Cottage for the Post-Parade Show.

Parade Jam. Percussionists and dancers who do not wish to march in Grand Parade gather for the Parade Jam, usually held at the Bear, and improv for half an hour. When Parade comes by, the dancers line up and shimmy enticingly.

participant. Someone who works at a faire.

patron. Person who pays to get into the faire.

Peasant Parade. Peasants marching around the village singing songs in the afternoon. They make several stops to harass various stages and crafters with bad puns and end up at Front Gate for the Closing Gate Show. You'd think by that time of the day they wouldn't want to run around anymore.

period. Authentic, not "modern." Since King Arthur reigns over a faire containing Robyn Hood and the Three Musketeers, the time period is obviously open to a lot of interpretation. It is said that anything is period if wrapped in burlap.

plastic hut. A privy.

playtron. A patron who dresses in period clothes. Many times their playtron status is given away by an anachronism (tennis shoes, sunglasses) though many costumes are quite elaborate.

Post-Parade Show. Held in front of the Cottage with the premise of being a variety show for the visiting Court (it's really for the patrons' benefit).

POT. Peasant Official Time, generally several minutes slower than ORT. POT is always given in "ish"—"POT is ten-thirty-ish."

privies. The port-o-potty facilities themselves or a place where such facilities congregate. Also called plastic huts or Jiffys (Jiffs being the brand name of the port-o-potties at Pendragon). Home of Harvey the Privy Monster.

Privy Counselor. Newsletter published each weekend of the run.

Queen's Tea. Informal event formerly held near Bedside Manor wherein Queen Guinevere and her ladies had tea whilst being entertained by the locals. Seeing a potential for profit, management turned it into a scripted variety show, relocated it to a big vinyl tent, and now charge for admission.

rennie. A participant at a Renaissance faire.

RFC. Realm's Fynest Cooking. This is the highly inaccurate division name for the branch of Pendragon that owns most of the food booths. RFC booths generate high-priced foods such as turkey drumsticks, which are generally held in low regard among rennies. Some food booths are independently owned; they have considerably more respect (and better food).

road rennie. A rennie who makes his or her livelihood traveling from faire to faire.

rookie. A first-year participant.

Rowan Stage. Multi-tiered stage tucked in the corner beyond the Maypole. The backdrop is a quaint fairytale-looking hut.

Sacrifice Sunday. Bonfire held in the gamers' camp on Sunday night of Labor Day Weekend. Participating rennies throw in a sacrifice that symbolizes a part of their life they have gotten over or past.

***seanchaí* chair.** The best seat of the house, traditionally reserved for the wandering bards that kept Ireland's history and lore. At Irish Cottage, the tradition is that once you sit in it, you may not rise until you have shared a song, story, or joke. The modern English transliteration is "Shanachie."

Shepherd's Green. Large open area between Cottage and Bakery—now largely covered by an ugly vinyl tent that hosts Queen's Tea and corporate parties.

site. The patron-accessible areas of the faire.

Stocks Stage. A raised wooden platform with two sets of stocks, where patrons can have their friends and loved ones publicly humiliated for a modest fee.

street. Non-gridded entertainers who run around amusing patrons and themselves with often outrageous antics are said to either "be" or "work" street. The term can also be used like a stage name—"Did you see how much fun the peasants were having out on street today?"

Summer Palace. The Royal Court's answer to the campground, these trailers are found behind the First Aid building. In context, "I'm off to the Summer Palace" sounds much less anachronistic than "I need to go backstage; my corset/tights/etc. are killing me"

Track. The stretch of sand enclosed by a low yellow fence where jousting shows take place.

Twin Tree Stage. Small, unassuming cobblestone octagon in the Narrows. It derives its name from the trees growing on two of its sides (though there are many more nearby).

Upson Downs. Area of food and craft booths on the Flying Buttress Stage side of Track.

vardo. A Gypsy's wagon or trailer. Traditionally pulled by horses, now pulled by pickup trucks.

vet(eran). Someone who can now refer to someone else as a rookie without getting accused of being the pot to call the kettle black.

weekender. A rennie who doesn't live on site during the week. A "damn weekender" is a weekender whose main reason for being a rennie is to find drunken after-hours orgies.

Woodland Stage. Balcony-like stage with a backdrop of trees. Located between the Bear and Caravan Stage.

zaggarete. A Gypsy call made by placing a cupped hand over the mouth and doing a high-pitched, fast lililililililili sound.

zills. Finger cymbals.

Character Listing

Alaina Dale. Alaina is the resident minstrel for the Merry Maids. She travels with her lute, either singing songs about the Maids' exploits or composing more as the occasion warrants. Her hair resembles nothing so much as a bob of toffee, and her eyes are a bright candy-apple green. She is a weekender.

Alexis (Alex). Alex portrays Robyn Hood, leader of the Merry Maids. She has sharp, elfin features: slightly pointed ears, brown eyes, a mop of mahogany hair, and fine eyebrows. She and Jen are romantically involved. She is a weekender.

Anabella Bernatelli. Anabella is one of the older "children" of Bakery Stage. She is quite buxom, and her dark eyes captivating. She also has a fun sense of sisterhood to anyone who comes by Bakery Stage to visit. She is a weekender.

Antonio Bernatelli. Antonio is one of the older "children" of Bakery Stage. He has a mane of jet hair and a protective streak a mile wide. He is a weekender.

Arbryna (Ryna) Tully. Ryna is one of two fiddlers for the Gypsies' dancing show. She is short, has copper-red hair that falls to the backs of her knees (and the temper to match), olive-green eyes flecked with gold, and a certain elfin look about the ears and chin. She is soulmate to Phoenix; daughter of Tremayne; stepdaughter of Kaya. She is a road rennie and has grown up traveling the circuit. Her element is Air.

Aunt Molly. Molly is a denizen of Irish Cottage. Her character is Ma's never-wed sister who sees little reason to pick *one* man. She has red-brown hair and friendly eyes. She is a weekender.

***Baba* Luna.** Luna is a camp elder and does a fortune telling show for the Gypsies. She also plays doumbek for the dance show. She has twinkling brown eyes, dark brown hair streaked with gray, and jewelry that would look gaudy on anyone else. She is wife to *Phuro* Basil. She is a road rennie. Her element is Earth.

Brigid O'Malley. Brigid is the middle sister, age seventeen, of Irish Cottage. She is a sun-dark lass with chestnut hair, gray eyes, and a dimple when she smiles—of which she is horribly self-conscious. She has perpetual boy problems. She is a weekender.

Christine. Christine is an angelic vision of golden hair and blue eyes. She plays Lady Carlotta of the Royal Court. She is Daniel's fiancée. She is a weekender.

Bryn. Bryn is a street peasant perhaps most famous for her Bite Me boxer shorts. She is on the short side and always wears her long chestnut hair in two braids. She is a weekender.

Da O'Malley. Da is one of the driving forces in Irish Cottage. He is a beanpole of a man with curly brown hair. He is a weekender.

Daniel (Dan, Danny) Saunders. Daniel plays Torin O'Malley, the lone brother and second child of Irish Cottage. He has brown-green-blue eyes and curling chestnut hair. Although he is closer in appearance to Brigid, his blood-sister is Phoenix. He is the faithful defender of all his sisters, blood or adopted. He is son to Robert and Claire Saunders and Christine's fiancé. He is a weekender.

Emily. A second-year entertainer (noble) who works street. She has blond hair and blue eyes—and an infant daughter named Morgan by Liam.

Emily (Em) Sanders. Emily was a peasant woman in late sixteenth century Hertfordshire, England. She was short, with blond hair and sea-green eyes. She lived with her father, mother, and younger brother Alfie. She was the desired love of Johnny, though she turned him down to be with Rachelle and learn her witchy arts. She was one of Phoenix's previous incarnations.

Eryn O'Malley. Eryn is the darling youngest child of Irish Cottage. This nine-year-old imp has unruly, flame-red hair and an energy level that just won't stop. Her best friend is Ilya Bannister. She is a weekender (Ilya's parents look after her).

Esmerelda (Elda). Elda is half of the Gypsies' fire show. She also plays tambourine for the dance show. She has brown eyes and dark skin. Her ebony hair is held back with a headscarf. Her costume is all flame colors like her brother Toby's, but with an artfully sedate charm. She is a road rennie. Her element is Fire.

Evelyn Wellington. Evelyn was the primary midwife/herbwoman in late sixteenth century Hertfordshire, England—that is, before she was hanged for witchcraft after delivering a deformed baby to a mother who died. She had curling brown hair and a quiet grace. She was Rachelle's mother.

Harvey. Harvey is the privy monster. He lives in the privies. He is generally considered to be blue due to the colored water in the plastic huts. His only known relation is Gloria, his city cousin who inhabits all flush toilets. Not only is Harvey a road rennie, he's omnipresent.

Hayrold. Hayrold is a street peasant most easily identified by his brown cloak and hood. He is one half of the Vilification Tennis team *Pog mó Thoin.* He is a weekender.

Ilya Bannister. Ilya is a nine-year-old street entertainer with blond hair and blue eyes. Her best friend is Eryn from Cottage, and her parents are crafters. Ilya is a road rennie.

Jack. see **Hayrold.**

Jen. Jen portrays Little Jen of the Merry Maids. She is big-boned but not large of girth. Her truck is in a constant state of decay, though she refuses to give up on it. She and Alex are romantically involved. She is a weekender.

Johnny. Johnny was a son of the lord of the manor in late sixteenth century Hertfordshire, England. He was a sturdy man with coal-black eyes and short, dark hair. In the winter he wore a beard. His schemes to win Emily's heart resulted in the death of both her and Rachelle. He was one of Liam's previous incarnations.

Karma. Karma is a long-haired calico with an attitude. But then, she's a cat. She is Ryna's familiar.

Kaya Tully. Kaya is the Gypsies' lead dancer. She is short, has honey-brown hair and golden eyes, wears clothes that suggest more than they actually reveal, and is wonderfully graceful. She is wife to Tremayne and stepmother to Ryna. She is a road rennie. Her element is Water.

Laine. see **Bryn.**

Liam (William) Flynn. He has a dark goatee and slightly curling hair to his shoulder blades, usually pulled back in a tail. His eyes are blue. He is well-muscled and rakishly handsome. He's spent the last ten months disincarnate and plotting how to get Phoenix and revenge on the Gypsies. Unbeknownst to him, he is Morgan's father.

Lord Marion. Marion is the only male of the Merry Maids; he fills much the same position as Lady Marion does in the traditional tales of Sherwood, and pretends to be involved with Robyn during show days. He is a weekender.

Ma O'Malley. Ma is the quintessential Irish mother and one of the driving forces in Irish Cottage. She has gray-streaked auburn hair and is medium of height and well-padded all around. She is a weekender.

Mama Bernatelli. Mama is one of the driving forces of Bakery Stage. She is strong and looks like she would be good for hard labor. Her heart is boundlessly generous. Marco, Cicily, and Maria are her children. She is a weekender.

Marcus. Marcus is a musician who primarily plays bouzouki. He has long, curling blond hair. He is a weekender.

Moiré O'Malley. Moiré is the flaxen-haired, blue-eyed eldest child of Irish Cottage. She is quite concerned with appearances. She is a weekender.

Mutch. Mutch is the youngest member of the Merry Maids; she's still in junior high. Despite the confusion her name occasionally causes, she insists that since it was the name of the miller's son in the traditional tales of Sherwood, she's entitled to it. She has cropped, sandy hair, light brown eyes, and a raving crush on Ryna. She is a weekender.

Niki. Niki is one of the Gypsy dancers. She has golden eyes, wavy caramel-brown hair, and always sounds a bit like she's purring when she speaks. Although her coloring, if not her height, makes her look like she could be Kaya's child, she's not. She is a road rennie. Her element is Air.

Papa Bernatelli. Papa is one of the driving forces of Bakery Stage. He has white hair, a kindly smile, and lots of wrinkles. He is a fantastic cook. He goes home most evenings.

Patches. A charming rogue in patched clothes, Patches is his own band and frequently plays at Irish Cottage. His six-string guitar is honey-finished and has a small leather pouch hanging from between a couple of the tuning pegs. He is a weekender.

Patty Kate. A perpetually pink and perky nuisance, Patty is the current Artistic Director.

Peyton (Pey). Peyton is a street entertainer who plays a rebel Irishman named Young Ned of the Hill. He is tall, with long-fingered hands and tousled, sandy hair always a little in need of a trim. He is a weekender.

Phoenix. Phoe portrays a Gypsy hedgewitch/herbwife street character by the same name, who is in a perpetually bad temper. She has dark brown eyes and black hair with two white tendrils that frame her face. She wears glasses. She is soulmate to Ryna, sister to Daniel, and daughter to Robert and Claire Saunders. She is a road rennie. Her element is Fire.

***Phuro* Basil.** Basil is a camp elder, cook, and storyteller for the Gypsy troupe. He has clear blue eyes, bushy iron-gray eyebrows, matching hair, and a slight paunch though he is quite spry. He is husband to *Baba* Luna. He is a road-rennie. His element is Water.

Piddle. Piddle is a tall peasant with a pink shirt. He wears his semi-long light-colored hair in a distinctive topknot. He is one half of the Vilification Tennis team *Pog mó Thoin.* He is a weekender.

Pratt. Pratt the street peasant has softly curling shoulder-length black hair and garb that has seen many years of better days. A wooden bowl hangs from a length of twine around his neck. His boots are mismatched and on the wrong feet. He is a weekender.

Puddle. Puddle's heart is significantly larger than his vocabulary—and his apparent brain power. He is a street peasant who earned his name from doing laundry in the small lakes that form on site after rainstorms. His best friend and constant companion is a fox pelt puppet named—appropriately—Dead. He and Dead are both weekenders.

Rachelle (Rach) Wellington. Rachelle was a midwife/herbwoman in late sixteenth century Hertfordshire, England. She was tall, with light brown hair, thin eyebrows, slender hands, and a strong physique. She was Evelyn's daughter and Emily's beloved—that is, until Johnny killed all three of them. She was one of Ryna's previous incarnations.

Ryna. See **Arbryna.**

Scarlett Will. Scarlett is one of the Merry Maids, always in scarlet, like her namesake. She has quite a crush on Daniel (Torin of Cottage). She is a weekender.

Tanck. Tanck is the Gypsies' lone male dancer. He has a heavily-patched costume, sun-bleached hair, blue-green eyes, the powerful, almost arrogant gait of a dancer, and an aura of Charm that has made many-a-maiden's heart go pit-a-pat. He is a road rennie. His element is Earth.

Tobaltio (Toby). Toby half of the Gypsy fire show. He also plays doumbek for the dance show. He has brown eyes, dark skin, and mid-length black hair that is perpetually sneaking from under his red headscarf. His costume is all in gaudy flame colors. Esmerelda is his sister. He is a road rennie. His element is Air.

Tremayne Tully. Tremayne is one of two fiddlers for the Gypsies' dancing show. He is lanky, has brown-green eyes, acorn-brown hair, and a certain elfin look about the ears and chin. He is a man of few words, though those he uses are always well-chosen. He is father of Ryna and husband to Kaya. He is a road rennie. His element is Sprit.

Upcoming from Faire-Folk Books:

Coming next:

Return with Ryna and Phoenix to Pendragon Faire, where they discover that their experiences with Shadow and Bright Fae have only begun to lead them *Towards the Fates*...

After that...

Join Niki and Tanek in *Following the Desert Sun* to Scheherazade Faire in Arizona—and their adventures four months after the events of *Into the Storm.*

ABOUT THE AUTHOR

A veteran rennie, Meghan has been telling stories for as long as she's been able to talk and will continue doing so until there is no sky left to hear them. She has long experience at privy reveling and potato peeling and is a proud member of the coin belt brigade. As to everything else... including a certain strange delight in referring to herself in the third person... she pleads the fifth.

The author may be contacted through her website at:
http://www.faire-folk.com

photo by BJ Palashewski

Printed in the United States
18801LVS00001B/127-129